JACKEE

Frank J. Campanelli Jr.

LINUS
Learning

Published by Linus Learning.

Ronkonkoma, NY 11779

ISBN 10: 1-60797-981-0

ISBN 13: 978-1-60797-981-4

Printed in the United States of America.

This book is printed on acid-free paper.

Print Number   5   4   3   2   1

DEDICATION

"To every girl who has adream."

"To the greatest game ever invented."

A special thanks to my family especially my wife Patricia and our children, Gerard and Maria. And a special acknowledgement to my Grandson Jonathan for helping me edit the manuscript.

Table of Contents

Chapter Twenty Four:

Chapter Twenty Five:

Chapter Twenty Six:

Chapter Twenty Seven:

Chapter Twenty Eight:

Chapter Twenty Nine:

Chapter Thirty:

Chapter Thirty One:

CHAPTER ONE

Jackee and Her Family

*P*ing! Ping! Ping! The noise could be heard by all the neighborhood. Young Jacalyn, Jackee for short, was hitting baseballs in her backyard. This was an everyday occurance. Two hours a day she hit baseballs from the iron mike her father set up in the batting cage. It all started as a game, but now it was a serious part of her life. William, her father had three daughters and finally decided he was never to have a son. To him it seemed strange that for a man who loved baseball so much, that God would grant him one child who could play the game. The older daughters Rebecca 13 and Evelyn 10 were good athletes but they only liked basketball, field hockey, or cheerleading. Jackee, the last of his children, took an immediate liking to baseball. She started playing catch with him at age 6, and in less than a year she started throwing the ball back almost as hard as he was throwing to her. She had picked up a bat twice her size and tried to swing it, prompting William to finally buy her an aluminum pro set little league approved bat. Jackee from that day on, slept with it along with her favorite animal, Babe, a 3 year old stuffed bear dressed in a baseball uniform.

Jackee loved the attention her father gave her. Not that he didn't spoil the other two girls, however, it was easy to see that he treated Jackee a little bit better. It seemed Rebecca and Evelyn didn't mind because now their mother Carmela had more time for them. Neither one of them were interested in playing, hearing or seeing baseball. Jackee, on the other hand, took to baseball like a duck takes to water. Her throwing at first was awkward but after a few lessons she began throwing much like any 6 year old boy. Her swing, once she started using her new aluminum pro bat, was not bad for any 6 year old. William saw the change and realized that Jackee needed more upper body strength. He began having fun with her so that she would develop the strength needed to swing a bat properly. The monkey bars in the backyard were used for pullups, chin ups and hand over hand drills. Agility drills with a jump rope, situps, toe touches and wind sprints were now becoming an everyday routine. Proper diet in the Jenco household was not a problem since Carmela always provided a healthy diet for everyone. Little adjustments, like more milk, a little more red meat, chicken and more vitamins were made. It eventually came time for Jackee to choose a position that would compliment her skills. Since she had better than average speed and her arm strength was greatly improving, it was decided that the outfield or possibly second base would best suit her.

William had told Jackee stories of the great players he saw growing up. There was Mickey Mantle who, if he hadn't injured his knee in the 1951 World Series, would probably have been the greatest player who ever played the game. Many old timers said that Babe Ruth not only saved baseball after the Black Sox scandal in the 1919 world series, but he was also the greatest baseball player who ever played the game. Ruth was not only a great hitter, but he also was a stellar pitcher before becoming a full time outfielder. William never saw Ruth play since he only started watching baseball in the 1940's.

Joe Dimaggio and Ted Williams he did see, toward the end of their careers. Mickey Mantle he saw from the beginning and was amazed at his ability to hit for power from both sides of the plate. When Mantle first came up to the major leagues, he was considered by most scouts to be the fastest player in the majors. After his injury, he had to be heavily taped up to even walk on the field. With all this pain he still dominated both the National and American league and put up numbers that earned him a place in the Baseball Hall of Fame.

One other of his heroes he told Jackee about, was a player who had the courage to play major league baseball when there was no other player of color on the field. His name was Jackie Robinson. Robinson was hand picked by the Dodgers Branch Rickey to be the first to break the color barrier in major league baseball. In 1947 Robinson was the first of his race in the majors. He was ridiculed, spit on, threatened, had his family threatened and was called every vile name that bigots could dream up. He was almost never allowed to eat with his teammates and had to sleep in a segregated sleeping area. Even though he had all these adversities, he won rookie of the year in 1947. One other problem was that Robinson was 26 when he started in the majors. Just being the first of his race to play major league baseball would have earned him a spot in the hall of fame but he also was elected on the great nine years he played for the then Brooklyn Dodgers. This was a great story and Jackee loved all her father's stories but she was more concerned with her improvement and how her father saw it. Her work ethics seemed to please him and he continually encouraged her.

The Jenco's all ate dinner together. If one of the girls was delayed at school for any event the family waited for dinner. One exception was if William was to be late because of work. Since he was an accountant there were times when a client had a business or tax problem that required his professional skill. Carmela and the girls would eat dinner and a plate would be fixed and placed in the oven for William until he arrived home. Around the dinner table any and all problems were discussed. Anyone could bring up a problem no matter how small or how silly it seemed to be. No one was ever criticized or made fun of at the dinner table. It was a cardinal rule. Everyone was treated equally and no subject was off limits. Everyone had a chance to speak and if possible most problems were solved or a future solution presented. Jackee, now seven, heard that they were having tryouts for girls little league softball next Saturday. It was for 7 and 8 year olds. Jackee wanted to know if she could try out and what might be the best position. Her sisters thought that the older girls trying out would dominate getting picked first. William was very confident in Jackee's ability so he suggested the infield would be her strongest position. Finally, Carmela gave final approval for the tryout by telling her to give it her best effort and she would be praying for her. For the rest of the week Jackee worked hard on her throwing and hitting. Dad decided to throw her a few softballs to get her swing orientated to slow pitching. They practiced on Thursday and Friday. William had to stop pitching on Friday because once she adjusted her swing, she began hitting rockets back at him. Being so close to the batter left him little time to defend himself. He found his reflexes had slowed a little.

Saturday finally arrived. Jackee and the whole family were at the field exactly at 8:30am. Rebecca and Evelyn were so excited for her that they even offered to hold and clean her glove while she batted. All the players were told to go to their position of choice on the field. Jackee took the field between second and third base. Coaches would evaluate each candidate and move them according to their skills. Each young lady took their turn fielding ground balls and throwing to first base. Coaches would be able to judge arm strength and accuracy. Finally it was Jackee's turn. She fielded the ground ball smoothly and threw a perfect strike to first base. The player on first took the throw in the center of the glove and began to shake her hand as if she had some pain. The coaches did this 5 or 6 more times and the results were exactly the same with the exception of the player at first who seemed afraid to catch the ball. Coaches were in shock, and most of the parents were in awe of what they had just witnessed. Mr Summers, the head coach, thought to himself, " I just found myself an all star shortstop."

With the completion of fielding, the three coaches now were going to have hitting practice. As each player registered Saturday morning they were given numbers starting with number one. Nineteen girls registered to try out. Number one would be the first batter while number two and three would be the on deck hitters. As each hitter finished batting they would take a position in the field and the next number would be on deck. This would continue until batter number nineteen completed her swings. Coaches Hemus and Magger would take turns pitching while head coach Summers organized the hitters at home plate.

All the girls were told that they would make the team, and all would get a chance to bat and field. Sharpton league rules were, besides requiring that all tryout candidates make the team, provide that every player who shows up for a game must play at least two of the seven innings in the field and bat at least once in the game. Finally, number twelve was called by coach Hemus and Jackee jogged in to take her position in one of the two on deck circles. Jackee gave her glove to Evelyn, and took out her batting gloves. These were a Christmas gift from her parents, and her father explained how they should be worn and stored. Finally, Jackee came to the plate and drove the first pitch over the left fielder's head. Each pitch after that was hit hard in some place on the field. After the second pitch to Jackee coach Hemus asked coach Magger to get him a glove so he could protect himself. One father sitting in the stands was heard telling the father next to him that his twelve year old son doesn't hit a ball that hard. Practice ended and the coaches gathered all the parents and players in a group. The coach discussed the Rules for the coming season.

"First, all practices and games must be attended, unless excused by a coach. Each parent would get a phone chain containing the phone number of every coach and member of the team. Second, winning or losing will not be our main concern. We will try to install a winning attitude in the players and hope they strive for and have success. Our main objective is that they have fun and learn the fine elements of the game. Third, parental interference will not be tolerated at a game or practice. You can talk to any coach before or after a game but never during, unless it is an emergency. Fourth, all special needs for any player must be disclosed to the coaches before the season starts. All medical clearances from a family doctor must be filed before opening day. Fifth, our games are on Monday, Wednesday, Saturday, and we Practice at 6pm, Tuesday and Thursday at this field. Our games start at 6pm, and we meet and practice an hour before the game. If you can not make a practice, or a game remember to call a coach. A set of league rules, safety features and the phone numbers will be given to each parent or guardian."

After the introductory rules, the head coach went over some of the safety concerns. "There will be no contact with another player while running the bases. No one is allowed to slide into any base. Helmets must be worn when on deck or at bat and running the bases. Catchers must wear full protective gear while catching in the game or warming up a pitcher. Only league approved bats may be used in a game or practice. A player is never allowed to fight on or off the field during a game or practice. Arguing with an umpire is never allowed by a player, or parent, before, during, or after a game. Finding qualified people to umpire is a very difficult task and it is the league policy to avoid any confrontations. You can always cheer on your team but you must not direct remarks towards the opposing team. All games will last 7 innings, or two hours. No inning may start after the two hour limit is reached. A mercy rule of an eight run lead after five innings will be considered if both coaches agree. No game will be played in the rain or if there is a sign of lightning. The game will be suspended and rescheduled. Safety is our main concern and fun is our prime objective."

Every member of the Jenco family was excited about how well Jackee had played. William talked to her immediately after practice ended. He mentioned that she had to get a bit lower on ground balls and pitches on the outside of the plate should be hit toward right or right center field. He also said how proud he was of her actions in the field and at bat. Infact her hitting was much better than he expected. There also was no doubt in his mind that she was by far the best player on the field. Rebecca and Evelyn fully agreed and told her they heard parents talking about how good she was. Carmela didn't say a word but the look on her face said it all.

Practices were much the same every time, except now the team started to take shape. All the coaches work very hard to make every player feel welcome and to play the game to the best of their ability. At first some of the players had been afraid of the ball but the coaches quickly changed that fear into desire to play. Soon all 19 players knew their positions and how to hit a softball. Jackee hit third in the lineup and played shortstop. Coaches were amazed at how much ground she covered between second and third. Very few balls ever got by her, and the throws to first were always on target. On popups she covered most of the infield and a good part of the outfield.

Although most young girls have excellent agility, Jackee's was in a class by itself. Her hitting ability was beyond belief. The first ball she hit in a game was a line drive right at the opposing team's shortstop. When the player saw the ball coming, the eight year old just moved out of the way and the ball rolled to the left center field fence. Jackee came into third base with a stand up triple. Her second at bat was a line drive that hit the left field fence on one bounce. This brought cheers from the Dodger side of the field. (Jackee's team selected that name since coach Summers was a big LA Dodger fan). The other side of the field was not so happy. The Cubs was the name of the other team and some of their fans were angry. They were calling Jackee a ringer and others not so nice names. Players on the Dodgers had no idea what they were talking about or even why things were being said. They remembered that league rule number three said parents were not allowed to comment about opposing players. Even though Jackee was not always in the game, her presence was the talk of the league. Games against the Reds, Cardinals, Giants, and Yankees all had the same outcome. Parents never expected to see this kind of play from a seven year old. Finally the league decided that she had to move up a class to the nine and ten year olds. This was most difficult for Jackee to do. She knew no one on the team and since her sisters were older, no one on the team was known to them.

Jackee continued her daily routine of hitting, throwing and a bit of weight lifting. Very light weights with more reps was the key. She also ran for fun with her mother and sisters. Playing on a new team and at a new level meant some adjustments had to be made. The Blue Jays had a shortstop and the team resented that a younger player came in and moved that player out. However, there was no doubt which player was better. Jackee was far superior to the other player in all facets of the game. Her statistics were off the chart. She was batting over .800 and she was on base almost every time up. Fielding wise, she was even better than when she was with the Dodgers. She was the most graceful player on the field, much like a ballerina performing a solo dance, instinctively she moved like a professional. You could see her move as the batter started to swing. Parents were amazed at her skills and many could not believe what they were seeing.

The season continued much the same as the first game that was played. Jackee was voted onto the all star team and also won most valuable player in her age group. During the season and even after, she was asked to try other sports. Soccer, track, lacrosse, and even tennis, but she said that baseball was the only sport that interested her. There may have been another reason for her not being interested in other sports. Although there is no actual proof, other sports require different sets of muscles to be used. This may cause a strain on her baseball muscles or even a change in her basic baseball skills. This, of course, is not a proven theory but she saw no reason to take a chance.

Schedules often have to be adjusted but not Jackee's. Hitting, throwing, running and light weight lifting were done almost every day. She was starting to fill out much like her dad. She had his shoulders but the facial and physical qualities of the mother. William continued to supervise her progress. He relied on sports doctors, coaches, and some trainers to assist him. A hitting coach was brought in to analize her swing. He did make some small adjustments but found her natural swing to be near perfect. There was a discussion about the possibility of trying Jackee as a switch hitter. Later, a consensus was reached that this change may affect her natural swing. Also her reflexes were for a right hand hitter and the natural instincts may cause her to react differently on the inside pitch batting left handed.

A fielding coach was also hired. He found her to be a better than average fielder who covered a great deal of ground. Her arm strength surprised him, and he rated her at the top of her age group. Cut offs and field position on different game situations was discussed. His final recommendation was that she stay a middle infielder playing softball but if she switched to baseball he would recommend second base as a better option. Still later, a track coach talked to her about her running and how to improve her agility. He found her to be a good student and fine tuned her running and body control. Lastly a physical trainer raised the level of her workout schedule and even recommended a diet. All this came together as Jackee continued to grow and hone her baseball skills.

During years nine through twelve Jackee played in the twelve to thirteen year old league. Again the competition did very little to improve her skills. In reality her presence on the field raised the level of the other players. Parents could not believe how good she really was and why their child could not come close to her skills. They never realized how much work it took to reach that level of play. Some parents became very jealous and a few even wanted her barred from the league. They thought that this was someone who created a negative effect on their child instead of a positive one. There was also a vile rumor from some opposing parents that this player was really a boy and not a girl. If these parents could have seen Jackee off the field this stupid rumor would not exist.

Jackee was a young lady. She loved to dance, sing, help her mother cook and bake. She played with her sisters and even had some sleep overs with other young ladies. The life she led was very filling and she seemed to enjoy every minute of it. She was not allowed to do anything until her homework and studies were completed. Chores around the house were never left for someone else to do. There was always time for family activities. During the winter when it was hard to do outside activities, she went to the soda shop for a sundae or malted with her friends. There were even some movies or pizza parties with teammates and family.

Big changes came when Jackee entered middle school, a whole new world opened and her life would change. Middle school, seventh and eighth grades were totally different from elementary school. Here you change classes and teachers every period. Instead of having twenty five other students in class you now have over a hundred and many more in gym, lunch and library. Elementary school you had your same classmates from year to year. All the students came from the same section of the district so you knew most of the students in the school. Middle school took in the whole district and most of the faces were new ones.

Sharpton had four elementary schools, eventually going into a middle school and later to ninth grade junior high school. From there they entered the high school which housed tenth through twelve graders. Many of the athletes were lucky since they played or competed against players from their district, so the athletes were ahead of the game because they knew more students than the others. Jackee knew a great number of the females from school or her summer softball program. The summer travel softball team she played on was in the final stretch of the season. There was the local tournament, then the county and finally the state championship. Jackee was still far and above any other player they had played against. She won every top award in every playoff or championship she participated in. Her bedroom looked like the showcase of a school rather than a single player. Certificates, trophies, plaques and other awards filled most of her room. Add her dolls, stuffed animals, precious keepsakes and general bedroom items, there was little room for much else. William suggested that part of the den be turned into a showcase for all family awards. Everyone was delighted with this suggestion and it would make it easier to clean Jackee's room.

First days of school, especially a new one, are alway exciting. New friends, new teachers, new classes that change every 50 minutes and a cafeteria that actually served decent food. Science was her favorite subject although she was a straight A student in every subject. In her whole school career she never received less than an A in anything and never missed a day of school. This was a tribute to Carmela who made sure there was a well balanced supper most every night. She made sure the girls had plenty of rest even with their busy schedule.

As the days flew by, different sports were posted with tryout dates. There was no football in middle school. If a boy was mature enough he may try out for the junior high team. It was rare that a boy actually played but very often boys who showed promise were invited to practice with the team. This gave them a head start for next year. Track and field drew many students as did soccer. The school had both a girls and boys team. There was wrestling, cheerleading and basketball to round out available activities. In addition many clubs were also available. Jackee immediately joined the science club. One additional piece of information was that the high school wrestling team won the state championship last year for the first time ever. What interested Jackee was that a few years earlier they had a female wrestler on the team. She had given a good account of herself on the mat but only lasted one year when her father was transferred and the family moved. When the wrestling coach was hired, he insisted that a feeder program be set up. A parent club was started and they entered a wrestling program that ran almost year round. It had four different levels and the parent club had a team at each level. By the time a boy tried out for the junior high team he already had at least three to four years of experience. Even though it was prohibited for a coach to coach his kids out of season, the high school coach still oversaw the training of the wrestlers.

Cheerleading was a big deal at middle school. If a girl made the basketball cheerleaders, she was almost assured of being a cheerleader on the junior high and high school teams either in basketball or football. Many of Jackee's friends tried out and she cheered each of them from the stands. She had no interest in trying to be a cheerleader. When the ten girls were selected, seven were friends of Jackee and she was happy for them.

Winter seemed like a long one. Holidays like Thanksgiving and Christmas helped to break up the monotony. Christmas was a big event in the Jenco family. Every room in the house was decorated with Christmas decorations. Even the bathroom had Christmas towels, mats and candles. Christmas was a season that was not only religious, but also a season for gift giving and caring. Usually the days before Christmas the Jenco family visited both the Veterans home and the children's orphanage. William and Carmela started this when the older girls were little and continued it every year. This was a way of showing their children that beside the family, God and country were also very important. Small usable gifts were given to Vets who had very few family or friends visit them. St Mary's children orphanage had infants to 13 year olds. It was funded mostly by donations from local churches, merchants, businesses, and the community in general. This orphanage had a binding effect on the community. Everyone felt that they were a part of it.

The Vets were mostly local or nearby citizens. Everyone in town knew most of the Vets from church, neighborhood, relatives or associates. They were a very honored group and consisted of both male and female from World War 2 on up. The last World War 1 Veteran, who was over 100, passed away a few years ago. His real age was unknown since all his records were destroyed after his birth. The family, being very poor, failed to get a new birth certificate and eventually settled on December 25th as his birthday. A year never was specified and no one really cared. When he enlisted during world war 1 it didn't seem to matter, so they listed him as being born on December 25,1885. He won a few decorations and was a big hero in the community. When he entered the Vets home the community just adopted him.

St Mary's children's orphanage is an independent religious foundation. A few babies are cared for but most of them are adopted very quickly. Most of the children there are unwanted or abandoned. There are some handicap babies that eventually go to the rehab center. When they started the orphanage only female children were taken. Later, a place for abandoned boys had to be found so St.Mary just expanded its facilities. Nuns run the orphanage and most of them are trained nurses or teachers. Every year the orphanage is audited by the government and checked by the health department. It has never received anything but an A plus rating. The Sisters are very proud of their orphanage and volunteers seem to feel the same. Many students do volunteer work at the facility.

William and Carmela have always made this orphanage their most cherished charity. Rebecca, Evelyn and Jackee automatically followed their parents and now belong to the tradition. Of course the three girls favor the orphanage rather than the Vet's home. Young children are more interesting than adults. All the girls have received instructions on how the children are to be treated. Special instructions were given for the babies and handicap children. Some children are antagonistic and they need to be handled very carefully. There has never been a problem that the Jenco girls could not overcome or adjust to. This made them most qualified and trusted to work with any child.

One day an incident came up that really affected Jackee. A new little girl was brought to the orphanage by the police. She had been abandoned by her drug addicted mother and father. The police found she had been starved, battered and nearly killed by her parents. She was only eight and a total disaster. None of the Sisters could get the child to do anything. They were barely able to feed and bathe her. She would not relate to any adult and never mixed with the other children. Saying she was a loner was a gross understatement. Then dramatically a strange thing happened. Jackee and her sisters were giving out presents and cookies to the children and out of the blue, like a bolt of lightning, this little girl took Jackee's hand and would not let go. Everyone was amazed. There seems to be no probable reason for this to happen. No matter where Jackee went, little Rose was there holding her hand. When Jackee sat, so did Rose. Rose would eat if Jackee gave her food or other goodies. It became a ritual, Rose would wait for Jackee to come and then latch onto her. As time passed she let Jackee bathe and dress her. This seemed like a breakthrough except she still did not play with the other children or even give in to the Nuns. It appeared only Jackee had the charm to help Rose. A few couples tried to adopt her but they all failed to break through her protective shield.

One night at the dinner table Jackee asked her parents what they thought might be the problem with Rose. Neither parent spoke at first, then Carmela said, "she assumed all the abuse the child suffered damaged her ability to relate to others. Carmela continued by saying that there were probably other factors that played into it but she still thought that abuse was the main one. She could not fully explain the attachment Rose felt for Jackee but it was clear that Rose did not trust adults. If an answer could be found, it might lead to some break through that shield Rose kept around her. After that it might be possible to start to heal the wounds that she seems to have".

Suddenly out of nowhere Jackee asked if her parents could adopt Rose and make her their child. Rose would then become Jackee's sister and a part of a real family. William and Carmela were taken back. Neither said a word. Finally William said that a couple with God's help have children and take the responsibility to raise them but adoption should be decided by the whole family. Carmela offered that first such a decision be discussed between husband and wife. If they agree the rest of the family would be entitled to offer an opinion. Once everyone is on board a dialogue with the Nuns would have to occur. Rebecca and Evelyn were beside themselves, the thought of having a small sister again appealed to them. The parents had a long night, finally at 2 am they decided to get some sleep as William had to be up early for work.

At 7am, the alarm went off. William opened his eyes and saw the look on his wife's face. That look said discussion is over. There was nothing left but to ask the girls. When they came down for breakfast William and Carmela were about to ask their opinion when the girls started to explain how a new sleeping arrangement had already been worked out and it included Rose. William offered the following suggestion, Sunday we will go to Mass and ask God if this is the right thing to do. After church if everyone agrees we will go to St Mary's and ask the Mother Superior about the procedure for adoption.

After the 9am mass all agreed it was the right thing. They then proceeded to St Mary orphanage and spoke to Mother Superior. It turns out that the Nuns were ecstatic that Rose was to be adopted. They all had been praying that a family would come forth and Rose would accept them. The Jenco's were a perfect match. Since the first day Rose had grabbed Jackee's hand the Nuns felt that Rose had already adopted Jackee. It was a win, win formula. A great family gets to adopt a little girl and Rose gets to be with her best friend.

Legal adoption is usually long and tedious, but with the Nuns' help it was completed by late spring. A huge party was arranged just as if Carmela had given birth. All their friends and neighbors came with gifts not for a baby but for a young girl. Rose never had a party of any kind and much of the party she spent crying and thanking people.

Rose became the super star of the family. Unlike her previous self imposed isolation she quickly fit into the Jenco lifestyle. It was decided since her birthday on May 24 would be her 11th, she should start school as a fifth grader in September. Between now and September everyone in the family would help her get the education she missed by not going to school. This proved to be a great benefit for Rose. When September came she could read and she could write. Jackee was by far her best teacher and many nights they would be asleep in the same bed. When at any of Jackee's games, Rose would cheer the loudest and always held her glove and bat between innings. Rose followed Jackee around so much it seemed to her parents that Jackee had a second shadow.

September saw some major changes in the family. Rose entered fifth grade, Jackee started 8th grade, Rebecca, now in college, had a job for the local daily newspaper. Evelyn began her senior year. William was the new senior partner in the accounting firm where he worked. Carmela had the hardest of all the jobs. The others had their chores around the house but were otherwise occupied with their daily activities. Carmela had to coordinate all the meals, household activities and keep everyone else on schedule. It was a major task but since she loved her family it was always accomplished. With all that, she still found time for the church, school activities, some sick calls and finally a few moments to spend with God.

The year finishing middle school passed quickly with a great many surprises. Rebecca and Rocco Manelli talked about getting engaged. Evelyn completed her senior year, again with straight A's. Rose was the top student in 5th grade and even made a few friends. Carmela and William almost cried when Rose announced that she wanted to have a sleepover with a few girls from school. Jackee was still doing her softball thing, as well as maintaining top grades in her classes. Her softball year had been even better than her first year. She batted over .600 and had the most hits in the history of the school for a single season. If official records were kept it would have been a new record for an 8th grader in the state.

Jackee was scheduled to play for a very exclusive girls softball traveling team in the summer. This team played the best competition in the country at the 14 to 16 year old level. With most of the family attending, she played the whole schedule traveling to New York, California, Florida, Texas and finally Pennsylvania for the finals. In the final game for the national championship, Jackee drove in the tying and winning runs. In Fact she had 4 RBIs, scored 2 runs, played fantastic defense at shortstop and was declared M.V.P. for the tournament. During the tournament she batted over .500 when they let her hit, and drove in 16 runs in 8 games. She walked 12 times (a tournament record), had 13 hits (1 homer 2 triples 6 doubles 5 singles) played errorless defense and made an unassisted double play. Her coaches were happy to have her on the team, and to a man said, they had never had a player with her qualities and probably never will again.

Rose had been at the tournament, with the rest of the family, and now asked William if she could train with Jackee. She was so proud of her big sister and wanted to be just like her. Rose had just turned 13 in May and William said he would think about it and let her know. Since he is older now and has more responsibilities at work his time is limited. Jackee tapped Rose on the shoulder and said that she would be delighted to work with her. Rose had the biggest smile on her face when she told Jackee that she loved her. A new plan was now taking shape in the Jenco household. William and Jackee sat down and began planning a ninth grade strategy. William had checked the state handbook and it did not have a rule against girls playing on a boys team. Finally, since a female did wrestle on the boys team a precedent had been set and no new rule had been passed to prevent it from happening again. Only one other argument could be used against her. Wrestling did not have a girls team and that is the basis of how the girl got on the boys team. They may say that softball is the correct alternative for girls and therefore it represents a fair and equal sports program. Worst possible outcome may be that a court has to decide the issue. William felt that the effort could go as high as the state supreme court for a final decision. Both agreed that it was worth the effort.

Every coach who worked with Jackee agreed that she was as good or probably better than most 16 year old boys. They saw no reason why she should not be given at least a tryout. It was common knowledge that situations like this almost never go unchallenged. Training now became intense. There was no way they were going to leave anything to chance. Jackee's activities increased to a point where little else mattered. They had basically 6 months to get ready. Weight training was increased. Upperbody, leg and arm strength were the main concerns. One major problem had to be dealt with, Jackee had developed from a young child into a beautiful young woman. She was the very image of her mother when Carmela was a young girl. When the middle school had their moving up ceremony and dance, Jackee had three offers from boys to escort her to the dance. She was very popular with both male and females in middle school. Her face and figure had been the envy of a great many friends.

William had no way of knowing if this was a real problem. He decided to ask Carmela her opinion. As it turned out Carmela told him the only possible answer she could give, "Why don't you ask Jackee?" William had a stupefied look on his face when he said, "I never thought of that." A few days later when they were alone, William asked Jackee if she fully understood the dangers of trying out for the boys team. She thought that they would consider her to be a joke or maybe ignore her altogether. William said "It's going to be a lot worse." If you do well you are showing up the boys and their egos will be hurt. The supposedly dominant male is being shown up by a female. Also if you do make the team you will be replacing one of their friends or even them. If you become a starting player one of the boys they have played with will not play. All these things will happen at once and more importantly, it changes the dynamics of the locker room. Even though you dress in another room you have to be with them at meetings, on the bus going to away games. No matter who you play they probably will not have a female player on the team. Home games will not be as bad as away games. Home games are controlled by our staff and security. Away games we have no control over. Your teammates may suffer some verbal abuse, but the bulk will be directed at you. Insults like hey you need a girl to help you win. What happened, "you ran out of boys at your school?" "Did you guys lose a bet?" Now let's talk about what some of your team mates might say and this would be mild compared to the other team. What, "did someone steal your dolls?" "We don't need a dyke on this team." "How many steroids do you take a day?" Now the other team will have unlimited things to say. Like,"do you stand up to pee?" "How many times did you have to sleep with the coaches to make the team?" "Do you wear a cup or jock support?" "Do you cry more if you break a nail or make an error?" I am sure the other team will have a lot worse sayings. Here is the bad part, you can not fight back. Not a word or action can you take. You must be completely oblivious just as if you were deaf. Your only answer has to be with your bat and glove. If you do try to retaliate, in baseball terms, you have rabbit ears and are actually listening to their garbage. That will only bring on greater insults. You can not show any emotions whatsoever. "Do you believe you can handle this?"

Jackee asked her father if she could think about it and give him an answer tomorrow. Most of the problems she had before were usually taken care of by the umpires, coaches or other parents. It had never made her uncomfortable but this stuff that her dad said really cut into her. The next morning with everyone gathered at the table Jackee gave William her answer. "Dad, Mom, I am scared to try this but I am more scared not to. I have worked for the last ten years to develop my skills to be the best I can. It would be an insult to both God and my family if I did not give it my best shot." Everyone at the table congratulated her and voiced their support. Rebecca, who was late for work because she waited for Jackee's decision, told her that she agreed 100% with her and that the paper she worked for would back her decision because it is the American way. Evelyn said how proud she was to have a sister with the courage to fight discrimination and prove to the world that women have rights too.

Rose was cheering the moment Jackee gave her answer. She was proud of her sister and loved her. She said to Jackee "you are better than all of them and I know you will win." The mother and father were totally in agreement with her decision and they were prepared to back her no matter what happens. Yet in the back of their minds both of them feared what may lie ahead. Being the first to try anything new was dangerous but this was really uncharted waters.

CHAPTER TWO
Jackee Starts Baseball

*W*illiam had each of her personal coaches come in to see if there was any more they could do. Most just stressed and reinforced what they did before. Only the batting coach made some adjustments because as her body changed so did her swing. With a few minor tweaks over the next week her swing became the same sweet swing it was before. A logical first step is to approach the junior high principal. Mr Hustler was a first year principal at Cedwick junior high. William had only spoken to him once and found him not to be much of a leader. In Fact the only word he could think of to describe him was "nerd." William and Jackee had decided to confide in him her desire to try out for the school's baseball team. They figured that doing this before the school year started would allow it to settle down before the spring season began. This would eliminate a big distraction before tryouts. A meeting was scheduled for the Friday before school was to start. At 8am Jackee and her father were shown into Mr. Hustler's office. William started the meeting by explaining Jackee's past accomplishments. Eventually he dropped the big one, telling Mr Hustler that Jackee intended to not only try out for the boys baseball team but to make the squad.

For a long moment Mr. Hustler seemed to be in shock. Finally he spoke and stammered through the words. "I have no idea if this is allowable." William immediately told him that although there is a restriction for boys playing on the girls softball team, no such restriction exists on the state, county or local level for girls playing on the boys team. The principal did not have an answer but wisely said he'd contact the district athletic director and all coaches for baseball in the high school and junior high. He also promised a meeting will be held with all the interested parties.

Jackee began junior high and loved the school and her teachers. Her classes of earth science, American history, algebra, spanish, english, phys ed and health completely filled her schedule. Classes were much the same as the middle school except these classes had much more material to cover. She was pleased when she recognized so many of her fellow students. Surprisingly the students seemed to be very friendly and usually went out of their way to talk to her. Girls seemed to be much more chatty than the boys. The three boys who asked her to the middle school dance all stopped to say hello as did a few of their friends. The first part of the school year was going very well but the Jenco's had not heard from Mr Hustler about the meeting with the coaches. Finally, William called and was told by the secretary the meeting could not be held until after Thanksgiving. It seemed all three baseball coaches also were involved in coaching fall sports and would not be available until their fall season ended. William was not happy with this but there was little he could do. He considered going directly to the superintendent or even the board of education but decided against it. Going over the coaches heads might antagonize them at a future meeting. He reasoned that if he could get the coaches on his side, the superintendent and the board of education would be more likely to grant their request for Jackee to try out with the boys team. One other very important reason was that if a coach felt disrespected, when the time came for the tryout, he or she might hold a grudge against Jackee and not give her a fair tryout.

Jackee's days were filled with studies or some other activities. Most everyday she hit and trained. When her schedule permitted Rose spent her time with Jackee. She loaded the iron mike and after Jackee hit she would help find all the balls and load it up again. When Jackee finished hitting she would then do weight training, sprints, agility drills and distance running. Rose did each of these, but on a much lower level except the running. Rose loved to run and got better every day. She had long legs and unusual speed for such a young girl. It was obvious to the naked eye that Rose was throwing a ball much like a boy and she was gaining strength and agility. Agility for some strange reason, was easy for Rose as it is for most young girls. Their agility at an early age is far greater than the boys at that level. In fact, William had said many times that he could take a team of 8 and 9 year old girls, train them and go out and beat most similar boys teams. The key is the agility and hand eye coordination that is very strong among younger girls and very much lacking in younger boys. However, down the road as boys start to become more active and start gaining muscle and strength, things start to even out.

Most weekdays only Rose and Jackee workout. Weekends were a different story. William had some time to spend with them and his coaching and encouragement gave them additional drive to keep going. Holidays and vacation days gave them time to work out and also quality family time. Rebecca and Evelyn looked forward to these family activities and participated as much as their time allowed. Thanksgiving was coming up and everyone was looking forward to it. Jackee and William were even more excited since Mr. Hustler called to tell them a meeting was scheduled for the Monday after Thanksgiving at 3:30pm with all three coaches. A family meeting was held on Sunday. William once again listed all the possible handicaps and dangers Jackee might face. He also said that she had to be prepared for the unknown dangers and the possibility of being blindsided by someone or something.

After three hours of family discussion Carmela said, "Jackee this is your decision and no matter what it is, we as a family will stand with you no matter what you decide or what happens." Jackee made her decision. " I am going to do this. I've spent thousands of hours and thousands of days preparing my body and mind and I swear to God no matter what happens, with His help and guidance, I will never quit." A Vet at the home once told me that this country is great because "Americans don't quit, they win."

3:15 on Monday William met Jackee at Cedwick Junior High. As they entered the office they saw only Mrs Craft the secretary and the principal. Mr Hustler explained that all three coaches would be there by 3:30. A little later all three coaches walked into the office and sat down. After the introductions were completed, Mr Hustler opened the meeting by explaining why they were there. He also said the district athletic director would not get involved until after this meeting took place. William was a little taken back but he found out that Weeks, the athletic director, was not a strong character and hated confrontations. William spoke first explaining why Jackee wanted to play baseball and how hard she has worked to get to this level. He stressed all her softball achievements and awards even though they would not be considered by the baseball coaches as equal competition. When he was finished the two other coaches waited for the varsity coach, Mickey Begali, to state his opinion. The three coaches already knew that there was no written rule in the state or county sports handbooks. Lastly, the school district has no rule in its sports handbook barring females from participating in baseball or any other boys sports.

Besides the girl who wrestled on the boys team, a girl played on the golf team for three years. Since the school only had one team and it was a non-contact sport, they let her play. It was also stressed that she was not very competitive. These were the only two incidents when a girl played on a boys team.

Coach Begali said he did not want any type of distractions when he had tryouts and scrimmages in the spring. He voiced the opinion that this would turn into a cheap publicity stunt and do nothing more than hurt his team's preparation for the coming season. Having a female tryout would cause discontent among his ballplayers. It may also be a huge source of controversy in the school, school district, and in the schools we compete against.

William immediately countered this by saying all new ideas and changes cause some concern when they are first tried. "Yet, isn't it the American way to give an individual the opportunity to try? Don't you coaches look at some of the candidates and think, this boy is wasting my time, and his, but you still give him a chance to try out. How many times have you seen someone who you knew would never meet your standards but because of his drive or desire you kept him on the team? We are not asking for preferential treatment, all we are asking for in a fair and equal tryout. Her treatment should be the same as any other candidate on the field."

Begali had no ready answer since whatever he might say would put him in an awkward position. What he eventually said was it was up to Dan, if he wants to give her a junior high tryout. Passing the buck was a universal way of getting yourself out of a no win situation.

Dan Wangel, the junior high baseball coach, was a very highly respected teacher and coach at Cedwick. He was known as a fair and competent coach and teacher. He taught phys Ed. Most students really enjoyed his classes but some felt he was too much of a disciplinarian. For years students faked being sick or injured so that they did not have to take gym. Dan solved this problem very fast. If the student claimed an excuse for not taking a gym class the usual direction was for that student to sit in the bleachers and wait for the class to finish. Now under Dan's new directive, the student had to report to the library and do a written report on one of fifteen subjects that the librarian had available. Librarian Alice Howell, who was also single and about Dan's age, got along famously with Dan. Together they made a list of sport subjects and sport books available to these sickly students. To the amazement of the other Phy Ed teachers Dan's classes always seemed to be full. Anyone who missed one of Dan's classes was either in the nurse's office or was wearing a cast.

Coach Wangel was a very good athlete, he had played football, baseball and basketball in both high school and college. Though his college was a division 3 school the competition had been very good. Until he injured his knee he had done very well in all three sports. This injury stopped him from playing football and basketball in his senior year. Baseball, with a knee brace, could still be played at a high level. Even with the brace his speed was still above average

This thing with a girl trying out had been on his mind since he heard about it last September. Since junior high football ended he began to consider what may happen at the meeting he would be attending. He asked around about Jackee. Everything he heard about her was positive and at times unbelievable. Some people thought she was a fantastic athlete while others believed she must be on growth hormones. The teachers he spoke to all said the same thing, she is one of the top students in the school and they loved having her in class. One of her summer softball coaches praised her as a player and person. He had never heard a coach rave so highly about one player. Lastly, he talked to the high school softball coach. Brenda Gill said she intended to bring her up to the varsity in the spring because she was the best softball player she had ever seen. When Dan told her about the meeting and what the Jenco's had in mind, she became completely devastated. When she finally regained her composure she shouted that she can not play on a boys team, it's not fair. Dan told Brenda that there was no rule against it and from what I hear she really is a great athlete.

Dan made his statement directly to Jackee. "Unless there is some rule or district policy, anyone who comes out for the junior high baseball team will be given a fair and honest chance to make the team. I show no favorites, my job is to prepare the athletes so they can compete at the next level and bring honor to the team and school." The next question he asked was personal. "Jackee, will you be sincere and give me your best effort and not make some kind of a publicity stunt out of this." Jackee answered, "I will leave it all out on the field". Dan answered, " I will be proud to have her tryout for the junior high team. Just remember, you will be treated just like any other candidate. There will be no special treatment given to anyone."

Mr. Hustler said, "I believe we have laid the groundwork here, but we still need the athletic director, superintendent and the board of education approval before it is final. One final hurdle has to be cleared, section 6 athletic association must also approve before the decision is final. The recommendations of our coaches should go a long way toward having these groups' approval. Thank you all for coming and a copy of the minutes taken by Mrs Craft will be sent to all the parties involved, including section 6."

While driving home William and Jackee analyzed what had taken place at the meeting. William felt that it went better than expected. He was surprised at the junior high coach. From the way they all spoke he assumed that the varsity coach would make the decision. Jackee said she heard only good things about coach Wangel and she felt he would definitely give her a fair tryout. Another reason she felt good about him was that he directed his questions directly to her and not the father.

It was always amazing to Carmela that she barely finished cleaning up after Thanksgiving and then she was preparing for Christmas. All the Jenco girls finished school the Friday before Christmas. They had 4 days to get everything ready because the following Tuesday was Chriatmas Eve. A meal had to be planned, the house had to be decorated and all presents had to be bought, wrapped and hidden. Finally a day had to be set aside for the family visit to the Vets and St. Mary's. This would be Rose's first visit since Jenco's adopted her. She would never go back to the orphanage and the Jenco's would not force her for fear of her reliving what must have been a bad time. Jackee talked to her and said, "when you are ready, you can join us."

Rose was a little apprehensive since she did not have a good experience there. Carmela and William felt she was now old enough to understand what happened and they explained to her how grateful they were at having found her in the orphanage, and how much the Nuns helped them in the adoption process. Rose realized how much she owed the Nuns. A visit to the orphanage may be a good way to thank them. Every family member came and brought small but useful gifts to the children and Nuns. Staff members were so happy to see how well Rose had adjusted to the Jenco family. There was great fear that she would never fully adjust to a normal family life. When they saw her with the Jenco family members they realized it was like she had actually been born there.

Visiting the Vets home was even more successful. Usually various animals are brought in for them to pet and mingle with. The next best thing is children. Presents are an added treat but the visitors, especially the children, really light up their life. Carmela, with the participation of the whole family, made special treats and desserts. Usually unwrapped gifts or treats are not allowed. However, Carmela Jenco's treats are always allowed. She followed all the dietary rules to the letter and made sure everything was inspected before it was set out family style.

Christmas tradition for the Jenco family starts with attending 8am Mass at St. Mary's Roman Catholic Church. Father Nicholas always said the first mass on Christmas day. His Chriatmas mass is usually very unique. He makes every part of the mass seem more important on this day. Although sermons were supposed to be related to the readings and gospel, this day he made it more about the joyous event this day represented and how it affected the family. His Christmas sermons were usually short and to the point. He realized that families needed to get back home for many traditional activities but more important the children would be anxious to return home to either open gifts or continue to play with them. St Mary provided 56 families with gifts and food from the generosity of their parishioners. As pastor, he felt it was his duty to personally thank them for helping purchase, box, wrap, and finally, deliver the precious packages. Another group of parishioners would be preparing dinner in the church recreation center and meeting hall for the homeless and people who had no place else to go. Dinner will start immediately after the 11am mass and finish at 4pm.

Volunteers, mostly families including the Jenco's, would prepare the food, set up the tables, serve the food and finally clean up the hall. As was part of their tradition the Jenco's had breakfast immediately after mass then went over to the church hall. When the clean up was done they would return home for their buffet dinner at about 6pm. Carmela, and usually, Rebecca would leave the church hall about 3pm and prepare their meal so that everything was ready by 5:30, when the others should be returning home.

When they did get home, they found the house in order and the delicious aroma told them that food was ready. A carved turkey with all the trimmings, a sliced ham, home made bread and cakes, five different vegetables and two kinds of potatoes. A special treat for Rose was a macaroni and cheese dish. Assorted fruits, nuts and even roasted chestnuts were on one corner of the table. Everyone was starving since they had not eaten since breakfast.

After dinner was finished and the dishes were done, all the leftover food was put away, the family finished opening presents. Rose had opened most of her gifts but the family had one more for her. Her sisters had asked the parents if a special necklace could be bought for her. When Rose opened the package she found a platinum necklace with her name in diamonds. She was stunned and began to sob. She never received a gift from her biological parents. This was the first really personal gift in her life. It was so beautiful and now she fully realized what family and love was all about. She hugged and kissed each one but when she got to Jackee she lost it. Jackee held her and Rose hung on for dear life sobbing uncontrollably the whole time. Everyone, including William, had tears in their eyes. When things quieted down they spent the rest of Christmas listening to Christmas music and going over presents.

Once Christmas day ended William and Jackee decided to plan her training schedule for the next 3 plus months. Tryouts are usually the first week in April for the junior high. It was decided that the infield would be Jackee's strongest position. Hitting would be most important followed by arm strength. She was used to throwing a softball 60 to 90 feet. In baseball the distance between bases is 90 feet therefore her throws would have to be in the 100 to 130 feet range. Another change of distance would be the cutoff throws from the outfielders to the infielders. That might increase the infielders' throw home from about 150 to180 feet. This meant she would have to build up her arm strength to hit a target on one bounce at that distance.

When Saturday came, Jackee, William and Rose started a long toss program. It started at about 90 feet and after getting her arm loose added about 10 feet every couple days. Weather permitting, by January she should be throwing strong at 175 feet. In February they should be working on accuracy and strength. Hitting was only available when the outside conditions were bearable. William had rented time at an indoor baseball academy. A hitting coach who had previously worked with Jackee was a partner in the academy and blocked out time for her. Many local varsity baseball coaches used this facility to prepare for the coming season. Coaches are not allowed to coach their players out of season but this did not stop them from attending the sessions and making suggestions to the hitters.

As it turned out Jackee could hit on Monday, Wednesday, and Friday from 4 to 5pm. Most other desirable times had already been booked by other high school coaches. Some college and minor league players who lived or went to school locally usually got preferential treatment. Having them hit at the academy was a great publicity angle. Some of the higher level players used wooden bats but most everyone else used aluminum ones.

Weight training and running took a hit when Jackee came down with a bad cold during the winter break. It took 2 to 5 days before she was fully recovered. All hitting had to be stopped either because of the weather or the fact that she could not properly breath in the academy. Carmela took charge and had her back on her feet in 4 days. She lost about 5 pounds and now had to rebuild her body. By the end of February she was pretty much her old self. Strength, breathing and endurance came back as strong as ever. Feeling the sickness was behind her, she intensified the workout and found no ill effects.

William was pleased at what he saw on their weekend workouts. He felt that her progress was right on schedule for the April 1st tryouts. It did take most of March to bring her throws up to speed. Along with the academy hitting, their outdoor cage could also be used. Late February had fairly mild temperatures and it extended well into March. According to scouts the fastest junior high pitcher may reach 80mph, so the Iron Mike was set at 80 miles per hour. High school pitchers may be 5 to10 miles higher but they were rare. He felt comfortable with the 80 mph but would raise it a bit just before she started her season. Jackee was hitting every good pitch she saw both at home and at the academy.

A protective screen was purchased to protect William when he threw live batting practice to Jackee. This proved to be a great investment since Jackee was now hitting hard line drives back at him. One theory on hitting that William believed in was that when you first start, try to hit the ball hard up the middle of the field. Once you had that swing working the next step was to start hitting line drives to all fields. Since William did not have a great arm he had to move the protective net closer to the batter. As Jackee got better he was thankful he had invested in the net because it probably saved him many injuries. It is a well established fact that hitting off a live arm is better than off a machine. You can time a machine because it does the same thing over and over again. A pitcher may change every pitch. From a live arm you must follow the pitch from the pitcher's hand right until it hits the bat. Iron Mike is not very likely to hit you. A pitcher on the other hand is a whole different ball game. Weather conditions, moisture, and the pitcher's experience are all unknowns.

End of March had Jackee exactly where William wanted her to be. She seemed to be both mentally and physically prepared for whatever was to happen. They talked again about her approach on the field and what she might encounter. One last thing he told her, "remember, God is on your side and no one can make you feel inferior unless you let them." After a big hug he said, "no matter what happens we are very proud of you."

April 1st came and Jackee left for school armed with books, lunch and a gym bag. Her bat was strapped alongside her bag. The school day was much the same as any other day except for some strange looks she was getting from both some boys and girls. A few girls from the softball team stopped to wish her luck and say how they were disappointed that she was not playing softball on their team.

In the girls locker room a locker had been set aside for only her use. Quickly changing into her practice sweats she then headed toward the baseball field. Passing out of the locker room door she met the girls softball coach. Coach

Gill said how disappointed she was that Jackee had decided on baseball, still she wished her luck and mentioned how proud she was to see the old boys club challenged. Jackee had no idea what she had said but she thanked her anyway.

While approaching the field, she said a prayer and reminded herself that she would give this her best effort. Already on the field were a few boys and coach Wangel. One of the boys she knew saw her and immediately picked up a baseball and began playing catch with her. A few moments later all the boys trying out came onto the field. Coach Wangel gathered all the candidates in the middle of the diamond. Coach said that every candidate will get a fair chance to make the team, He then gave his rules:

"1. You must be here every day unless sick or excused. Remember if you are not in school or cut class you are not eligible to participate.

2. There will be no bullying, fighting or ranking on any candidate.

3. Safety is a major concern. Since I have no assistant I must rely on your good sense not to present a dangerous situation.

4. When you leave personal items in the locker room, be sure they are secured.

5. We have a limited budget and will not be given additional equipment, so take care of what we have. Baseballs are limited so we must save all we can for practice."

Coach Wangel now addressed the fact that a girl was trying out. He said, "we have a young lady trying out for the team. I am proud that she chose my team. There is no other sport like baseball. It does not have a clock. Each team is given the exact same opportunities and no one can change that. Each team is entitled to every inning, every out and every strike. You will never see someone holding the ball until time runs out. There are no ties, someone wins or loses no matter how long it takes. It is the constitutional right for any American to play the game. Miss Jenco is entitled to that right, therefore I am proud to welcome Jackee to our tryout and expect each of you to give her the same respect that you would give any other member of this team." Jackee was so grateful to Coach Wangel because right now she was totally relaxed and truly a member of this team.

Coach Wangel said batting practice would be first every day we get outdoors because April weather is so unpredictable. He had an alphabetical list and numbered it from one to twenty two. Number one was at bat and number two was on deck. After the batter finishes he or she will go to their desired position and the next number will move to the on deck position. Jackee positioned herself between second and third. No other candidate was near her. Four boys were between first and second, three boys were by third base. Being left all alone at shortstop provided Jackee a great opportunity to show her speed and ground cover. As balls were hit, she ranged far and wide fielding each ball and rolling it back to the pitcher. Pop ups were her specialty. William always made her practice pop ups on a windy day. He claimed if you can catch a ball when the wind is blowing, on a not so windy day it would be a snap. William remembered from his little league days how much trouble the players had with pop ups, especially on windy days. He made sure Jackee would never have that problem. He taught her to gauge where she thought the ball would drop and to immediately run to that spot and then pick up the flight of the ball. Doing this will put you under the ball or close to it. It will also give you more time instead of looking over your shoulder which slows you down, you are at a full sprint to the ball. This did happen in practice when a ball was hit down the left field line about 60 feet beyond third base. Jackee immediately sprinted to that spot and made a sliding catch. Everyone on the field and a few spectators were impressed by what they saw.

Coach Wangel shouted, "great catch!" and went back to supervising batting practice with a big smile on his face. Finally it was Jackee's turn to get on deck. Now would come the moment of truth. Everyone would be watching her performance and it would be the telling point and the talk of the school the next day. Coach was still pitching to the number 7 batter so it gave her a chance to relax and prepare herself. She took her bat from the side of the gym bag and found a note from William. It simply said "relax, enjoy the moment." She smiled and felt his presence close by. All the tips she received over the last 10 years were coming back to her, relax, stay back, watch the ball leave the hand, watch the ball hit the bat and hit the ball where it is pitched.

Coach Wangel called the next batter. With a little prayer on her lips she entered the batter's box and prepared to hit. First pitch was low and she hit a ground ball into left field. This first contact relaxed her and now she was ready to hit. Balls began flying all over the field. Of the next 9 pitches, 7 were line drives, three drives were hit to either right center or left center. One of the balls hit the fence in left center right near the 340 foot sign. Coach did not say a word except "next." When all the candidates had finished hitting, the coach divided up the team. Pitchers and catchers went to the two bullpens that were on the field. Outfielders went to center field and other players hit them fly balls. Infielders remained on the diamond, loosened up their arms, and went to the position of their choice. Two each went to the three bases and only Jackee was at shortstop.

Coach explained that their agility will be tested and depending on how they did a position would be given to them that will best help the team. A normal infield drill was used by the coach. Each fielder would field and throw 2 balls home, 2 to first and 2 to second. The second round would be exactly the same except after their initial throw they had to cover their base (a throw from the catcher and a return throw). No one in the infield had a stronger or more accurate arm than Jackee. Everyone of her throws was near perfect. Coach explained the final infield drill. 9 balls were placed in various positions around the infielder.

The fielder had to throw 3 balls to each base, home, second, first in that order. There was one little catch, the player had to do one at a time and after each throw returned to their starting position and repeated the process all over again. This was both an agility and conditioning drill. Coach wanted to see if their throws changed when they were under pressure and tired. In a game it was often the difference between an out or an error. Because most of the candidates had not yet really worked out, they became winded and tired. This drill greatly affected their throws. Jackee, although she was somewhat winded, still made every throw catchable. Pitchers were next. They worked off the mound doing fielding and covering first base. Balls were hit to the outfielders and pitchers had to back up home or third. Outfielders had one final drill. They had to throw to second, third, home and 2 relays. Lastly the catchers were drilled on balls hit around home plate and on foul pop ups.

Tryouts continued for the next two weeks. Coach Wangel selected his eighteen players and even kept the last 2 boys as a manager and scorekeeper. It was extremely difficult for a coach to tell a boy that he could not play America's greatest game. All the players came into a deserted boys locker room. Uniforms were piled in the coaches office and each player according to their number was issued a full uniform for games and a set of practice sweats. Hats were the last item issued. Players had to buy their own footwear and gloves. Catchers were given one new mitt and all the protective gear. If they had their own gear they were welcome to use it. The gear had to be equal to or better than required by section 6. Jackee was lucky enough to get number 7. This was her father's favorite because it belonged to Mickey Mantle.

CHAPTER THREE
Jackee Starts Competition

$\mathcal{C}$oach noticed a few extra fans watching practice each day but did not think of it as being unusual. However in the first scrimmage many more parents, students and faculty were present. He now knew that his new shortstop had a following. Actually, the increase in spectators excited the whole team, since only a few parents ever came to their games. Also he was surprised that when they visited other teams, their crowds seemed to be greater than usual as well. He started to see a trend that he felt would continue the whole season.

There were 6 teams in Cedwick's division and they each played a four game series for a total of 20 league games. Games were played on Monday, Tuesday, Thursday, and Friday. Rain dates were Wednesday and Saturday. Cedwick's first game was away against Howell junior high on April 16th. Coach Wangel had scheduled four preseason scrimmages. They were all played and he felt the team really began to come together after the fourth one.

As Cedwick worked out in their pre game practice, coach Wangel noticed more and more fans filing into the bleachers. There was one set of bleachers on each side of the field and both were now almost filled. Coach Hass from Howell and coach Wangel felt that there was at least 3 times the number of fans who usually attended their games. It now seemed certain that the presence of Jackee on the field was drawing many different onlookers. Their suspicions were confirmed when the local tv station sent a crew to the field. The only time a TV crew came to a baseball game was for the playoffs or a league championship game. A female reporter asked if she could interview Jackee. Coach Wangel asked if she could refrain from doing this until after the game. He knew how nervous Jackee may be and did not want to add a new distraction. The reporter said she understood and apologized for being so inconsiderate.

Upon completion of both teams infield practice, the umpires and coaches exchanged line up cards and discussed the field's ground rules. When that was done, Howell took the field and the umpire called play ball. As Cedwick prepared to bat coach Wangel told them to play their game and just have fun doing it. Cedwicks first hitter grounded out and the next one walked, and that brought Jackee up to bat. There was a buzz in the stands as she approached home plate.

She was nervous and a bit frightened but she remembered her father's words, "When you are in a slump or not sure what to expect, hit the ball up the middle. Keep your head down and your hands back and never take your eyes off the pitchers." Just as she had done many times before, she followed this advice and lined a single to center. Fans in the stands gave her a standing ovation.

Jackee's first official baseball game was a big success. Hitting a double, 2 singles, a walk, driving in two runs and also stealing a base was a good day's work. Her fielding was spectacular. She handled all the ground balls on both sides of second perfectly and in the fourth inning she raced toward left center field and with her back to home plate caught a pop up. Once again the crowd gave her a standing ovation. Final score Cedwick 6 Howell 0. Zac Webber, Cedwick's big left hander, gave up only 2 hits and one walk. Since Cedwick did not make an error Howell only had 3 baserunners.

Each game is alternated, so Tuesday Cedwick was the home team as they would be on Friday. The series against Howell was a big success. Cedwick won all four games and Jackee had 10 hits in 15 at bats. She also walked four times with no strikeouts and was errorless defensively.

Coach was very happy with the opening series. Winning was great and the team played well but he was most proud of the way they were handling the co-ed situation. He had warned the team that "reporters, cameras, and just plain curiosity types would be at their games until the newness wears off. However every new team we play the fan attendance will probably increase. You can also expect more bench jockeying from your opponents."

A strange thing happened at Howell's home games. When a few spectators started heckling Jackee the other fans told them to shut up. At home Cedwick had large crowds and the team only heard cheering.

Next team on the schedule was Bender junior high. This was the largest school, population wise, in the league. Their field was magnificent and they were always the best in the league. Cedwick had never won a series against them. Usually if Cedwick won one of the four games it was considered a successful season. The little league program that ran in Bender's district was considered to be one of the finest in the state. Each of their little league teams had at least four coaches. Players were expected to win and that attitude filtered up to the junior high and then the high school.

Against Bender Jackee had a great series. They had the best group of pitchers that Cedwick would face all year. Jackee had remembered what one of her batting coaches had told her. Usually a pitcher will do something different when he throws a curveball. This is true in lower level baseball. Most only throw a fastball or a curveball so any slight deviation means a different pitch is coming. She had studied the Howell pitchers and all six of the pitchers she saw, did tip off their curveball.

Bender pitchers were a little more careful and better prepared but she watched them warmup and pitch to batters, slight differences did appear. It had been drilled into her to always look for the fastball and adjust to the curve. She was always ready for the fastball but when she knew a certain pitch was coming, she added 150 points to her average.

Batting against Bender She was 9 for 14 and had 4 walks and no strike-outs. She was now 19 for 29 in league play. One of her hits had been a home run. One of Bender's pitchers had thrown a belt high fastball on the outer part of the plate and Jackee drove the ball 345 feet over the right center field fence. Every team mate was out of the dugout and cheering as she circled the bases. Coach Wangel asked the opposing coach if she could keep the baseball. He agreed and later the coach had the ball signed by the team with the date, score and opponent. Cedwick won 2 of the 4 games, winning both home games and losing the away ones. It was the first time Cedwick won two games against Bender. The crowd at Cedwick's first home game against Bender, was the largest ever at a junior high baseball game. No one could ever remember not only the stands being full but there were 100,s of others standing. Jackee seems to elevate the game when her family is there or when a crowd is present. She did not disappoint anyone in the first home game when in the bottom of the 7th inning the bases were loaded and her team behind by a run she hit a double down the left field line winning the game. Cedwick fans went ballistic and the celebration went on for a good 15 minutes. Final score; Cedwick 4 Bender 3.

The Jenco family was enjoying every minute with Carmela in tears and the girls jumping up and down and hugging everyone and William smiling like he just won the lottery. The celebration went from the field to the school. Later when the fans left and players began to leave, Jackee came out and gave the game winning ball to Rose. Rose slept with that ball every night. Carmela suggested they have dinner at their favorite restaurant and celebrate. Many times during the meal they were interrupted by people congratulating Jackee on the win over Bender.

Game 3, Bender scored runs in their last two at bats and won the game 6 to 4. In game 4 at home, Jackee drove in one run and had 3 hits. She also saved the team about 3 or 4 runs. In the 4th inning Bender had the bases loaded and 2 outs. The batter hit a pop up about 60 feet behind shortstop. Jackee with her back to the plate sprinted toward where she thought the ball would come down and finally dove and caught the ball. She laid motionless on the ground. She injured her elbow, knee, and had the wind knocked out of her but still clutching the ball. Fans were clapping and cheering until Jackee went into the dugout. This catch saved at least 2 runs and maybe a third one. In the top of the 6th Bender had runners on second and third with 2 outs, when their number 4 hitter hit a hard ground ball between third and short. Jackee sprinted to her right backhanded the ball and in one motion threw a strike to first base. Umpire called the runner out. Coach Wangel told Jackee that he had never seen two plays like that in the same game. Cedwick won the game 4 to 3 .

Next two series were played against Bristle and Meeker. They are the two smallest schools in the league. All of the 8 games were blowouts and Cedwick had a 9 game winning streak. Jackee added another 26 hits to bring her up to 55 for the season. Breaking it down she had 3 home runs, 3 triples, 16 doubles, 23 singles, 13 walks, and no strikeouts. Travis was the last school on the schedule before the playoff. They were the second largest school in the league, however they were not regarded as high as Bender, but were still very close. Their feeder program from little league, although not the size of Bender's, still provided a quality athlete for the baseball program at Travis.

Coaches at Travis had a motto, "Win at any cost." They encouraged their players to win any way you can, using any means possible. Most baseball coaches consider baseball to be a game and it should be a fun game at that. Travis considers baseball to be a war. Other coaches in the league did not particularly enjoy playing them. What they did enjoy was beating them, however Travis lost very few games in the season.

A few years ago section 6 decided to allow the two top teams to have a one game playoff. So you have a league champ and then a section champ. The top team being the league champ would host the championship game. Since inception Bender has won the league title every year. The district championship they won every year but one. Two years ago Travis beat them because they had a pitcher who was drafted by major league baseball right after the high school season ended. The pitcher threw a one hitter against Bender and beat them 1 to 0. This boy had 5 division one scholarships offered to him when he graduated high school.

Since Travis had beaten Bender in one of the four games they were in Third place one game behind Cedwick. Travis swept all the other teams so they had a 13 and 3 record. Cedwick only lost the two games to Bender. So now all they had to do is win 2 games from Travis to be in the championship game.

Game one at Travis was a total disaster. Jackee made her first error on a hard ground ball hit right at her. The short hop handcuffed her and she could not recover in time to throw the runner out. He later scored one of Travis's eight runs. Fielding for the rest of the game was good but hitting was a different ballgame. Although the pitcher was above average for the league, Jackee still felt she should have done better. Her 1 for 4, a single, had no impact on the game, in fact the whole team seemed to be intimidated by Travis.

Prior to game two, Coach Wangel talked to his team telling them, "Travis can only play nine players at a time. The large numbers they have on the bench are for show. They are only entitled to what we are entitled to. There is no team in this league that can beat us. We only beat ourselves because we do not play up to our ability. You go out there and give me your best and I guarantee you will beat them."

It did not take long for Travis to start the intimidation. In the previous game, off color and gender remarks were made at Jackee or at her teammates. A few did get a stare from the umpire. Some even got a chuckle from the Travis fans. When Jackee made the error a large number of comments followed, but nothing really serious happened. While batting in the bottom of the first inning a fastball was directed at Jackee's head. As Jackee was dusting herself off the home plate umpire called both coaches to home plate. He told them that if it happened again the player would be thrown out of the game and would be disqualified from playing any more games in the series. Travis' coach became very upset and said the ball just got away from the pitcher. Coach Wangel responded with "do you really think we buy that? If we did, we would also believe that brown cows give chocolate milk." The umpire smiled and said play ball.

This is something that William had anticipated. Early on he made Jackee do a drill that the old Brooklyn Dodgers used on their rookie players. While standing by home plate and in a normal batting stance a coach would throw tennis balls at the batter's head so he would develop the instinct to tuck his head in under his shoulder. Pulling your head down and into your chest protects your face and most of your head. Normally a batter instinctively tries to back away from the pitch and expose his face and part of his head. Even if you are wearing a helmet you can have real damage. But if you tuck your head only the top of the helmet is exposed. Little or no harm can come to you. William used this drill on Jackee many times until he was sure she reacted properly.

Back in the batter's box Jackee prepared herself for the fastball she knew was coming. On the knees and over the outside of the plate came the fastball and just as fast it went out toward right center field. It hit the fence on one bounce and when all the running and relays were over Jackee stood on third base with a stand up triple. While watching this pitcher warm up and how he pitched to the first two batters she realized he took a long time in his delivery to the plate. On the second pitch to the number 4 hitter she broke for home, startling the pitcher so much that he balked. This allowed Jackee to score the first run of the game.

When Cedwick took the field in the top of the second inning, they were a different team. They now had the lead and a new confidence. Jackee never considered herself a leader but here she was directing the infield and setting the outfield. Not only was she good at it but her teammates were following all her suggestions.

Varsity and JV coaches had completed their schedule last week so they were at this game. Both coaches Begali and Singer were very impressed by Jackee. She was by far the best player on the field for either team. A strong arm, excellent base runner, wide range of coverage in the field and above average hitter, and finally the leadership skills made her the best player. Though they hated to admit it, she was the best shortstop in their program. In fact she was the best shortstop they had seen all year. They even talked about the possibility of her playing for the varsity as a 10th grader. Seeing the great crowds that were attending games she played in, coach Begali thought how many more would come to see her play varsity games.

Game 2 ended with Cedwick winning 6 to 2. Jackee went 3 for 4 with one run scored and 2 RBI's. Her play in the field was nothing short of spectacular and the way she caught all the pop ups was truly amazing. The two high school coaches wanted to find out what the other team's fans thought of Jackee, so they switched sides after the third inning. What they heard only reinforced what they already suspected. One conversation was very interesting, one spectator asked a second one why didn't Travis have a female on their team? Was it because they were discriminated against or was it because no female had the courage to try. Both coaches decided to consider their next step for the following spring. Whether Jackee would play and at what position had already been decided by Jackee herself.

Games 4 proved to be a big disappointment. Once Cedwick won game 3, game 4 became meaningless. Both teams unloaded their benches and let everyone play. Cedwick won the game 16 to 14 with only backups playing in the game. To make herself useful Jackee coached First base the whole game. She absolutely loved all aspects of the game and even got into coaching some of the boys who hadn't played much during the season. Jackee had finished the season hitting over .600. However, the thing she was most proud of was the fact no one struck her out even once.

Both Bender and Cedwick finished with identical records 17 and 3. Since they split their series a coin flip would decide home field. Athletic director Sy Weeks met with the athletic director for Bender at section 6 office. Mr Weeks got to call and he called heads, winning the toss. He took home field and said that the game would be played at the high school field since it had much better facilities for the spectators. The game was to be played the next Saturday at 11am. Weeks also agreed to have maximum seating set up at the high school field. Both athletic directors knew that the first female player would draw a large crowd and probably some local or even state media. Neither one would mind a little more publicity for the district or more individual recognition for themselves.

Saturday proved to be a beautiful June day. Clear skies, temperature in the low 80's, with little wind. Ernie Banks, the hall of fame Chicago Cubs player used to say "let's play two." At the time he said this, the Cubs had no lights on their field so they always played day games. Since it appeared to be a perfect day and a great day to come out to see a ball game, the athletic directors had anticipated a big crowd. By 10:30 most of the stands were filled. Ropes were set up along the foul lines for any overflow. The varsity club at the high school set up a big refreshment stand but grossly underestimated the size of the crowd. The advisors were running around trying to get more refreshments and items to sell. Athletic director Weeks had instructed the ground crew to be extra attentive since the board of ed and all administrative people had been invited. Ambrose field, which had been named after the previous baseball coach of 32 years who had retired 3years ago, looked absolutely beautiful. Coach Begali was a little upset since the field never looked this good for any of his games including some playoffs.

Breakfast at the Jenco's was pretty much like any other Saturday. At 8am William had the pancakes, juice, coffee, rolls, bagels, milk and eggs ready on the table. Everyone ate their fill and cleaned up after themselves. Jackee ate very light and had to leave as she had to be at the school by 9am. Upon arrival she was directed to the nurses office where she was directed to change and store her clothes and secure her valuables.

While changing she thought back to breakfast. Her dad had asked if she was nervous. For some unexplained reason all she felt was great anticipation and a desire to start the game. Nerves were not a problem, she felt very confident in her ability and desire to play the game. The greater the challenge, the greater was her desire to play. William smiled at her and said, "You have reached the point where your passion and love of the game control your emotions." Then he hugged her really tight. Carmela and the girls hugged her and wished her good luck. Rose was the last and after hugging her said bring me home the game winning ball. Everyone had a big laugh and off Jackee went.

Around 9:30 Jackee went to the batting cage that the high school had in the back area of the ball field. Other teammates were there loosening up, putting balls in the iron mike or hitting off it. Jackee began with her stretching and loosening up drills. After running completely around the field she did 10, 20 yard wind sprints, and then did her bat drills. Before going into the batting cage and hitting she did her 20 purpose swings. These were the swings that before you swing, you assume a game situation and where you would hit a certain pitch. All iron mike's pitches are the same. No matter the make, size, shape, they all do the same thing, hurl a baseball type ball toward you. Most are fairly accurate but it is a good idea to wear your helmet and always be alert. Some new models threw curve balls as well.

Jackee hit 20 or so balls. Most were hard line drives. You can tell by the sound of the bat if the ball was hit hard. When she finished hitting she realized that many people beside her teammates were gathered around the cage. A young man with a portable microphone came up to her and started to ask a question. She cut him off and said she was preparing for a game and would be glad to speak with him after the game. He didn't like it but he soon found someone else to interview.

Cedwick took the field first as is the custom for the home team to do prior to a game. Bender followed and when they finished, the coaches brought their lineup cards to home plate. Umpires took the cards and then with the help of the high school varsity coach the ground rules were gone over. Ambrose field has a gate in left field. If the ball rolls under it or gets stuck in it, the ball is dead and the runners are allowed to proceed to the base ahead of them, If they have passed the prior base. No player can make a play on a dead ball, so once the ball touches this area the fielder should raise his arm and play should be halted. The umpires then decide where the runners should stop. The portable PA system then introduced the starting line-ups after which the Star Spangled Banner was played. Everyone on the field and in the stands stood and took off their hats and looked toward the scoreboard where the flagpole and the American flag stood.

Home plate umpire called play ball and Cedwick's team ran out onto the field. After 8 warm-up pitches and the customary throw by the catcher to second, the game was on. Zac Webber retired the first three Bender batters and came off the mound really pumped up. Cedwick's lead off hitter walked and was sacrificed to second on the next pitch. Jackee hitting next was intentionally walked. One of the section 6 rules is that if an opposing coach wishes to intentionally walk a batter he just has to notify the home plate umpire and the batter is awarded first base. No pitches have to be thrown. Cedwich fans were not happy since most everyone there came to see the game but also to see Jackee perform. As it turned out Cedwick scored two runs in the inning and now held a 2 to 0 lead. The game turned into a pitcher's duel as neither team scored again until Bender scored a run in the Fifth inning. Cedwick had opportunities to score more runs but had left 9 men on base so far in the game. Jackee had walked again in the 3rd inning and lined out to left field in the 5th. The ball was hit so hard that the left fielder never moved and the ball would have hit him in the chest if he hadn't caught it. Bender loaded the bases with one out in the top of the seventh. Next batter hit a hard ground ball between short and third, Jackee turned to her right sprinted two steps and dove head first toward the ball, fully extended she reached out with her glove hand and caught the ball in the webbing of her glove, she rolled onto her knees, and fired a strike to third base. The field umpire shouted "out" as the tying run scored. Most of the spectators were clapping and cheering the fantastic play they had just witnessed, Jackee was dusting herself off and trying to get her wind back. Bender still had runners on first and second with two outs. Zac was getting tired, but that play by Jackee gave him a second wind and he struck out the next hitter.

Cedwick, now batting in the bottom of the seventh, had the top of the order scheduled to hit. The lead off hitter once again got on base by hitting a single to center. Next batter laid down a perfect bunt and instead of the third baseman taking the sure out at first base, he tried to get the runner at second. His throw was wide of the base but it made no difference since the runner already had second. Bender's coach called for a new pitcher and told him to pitch carefully to Jackee. He also said he did not want to get beat by a girl so if the pitcher walked her it would be fine. Jackee got into the batter's box and squared around to bunt but the first pitch was outside. Bender's coach put his infield in a bunt defense to try and get the lead runner at third. Bender's pitcher threw the next pitch high and inside hoping Jackee would pop the bunt in the air. What neither the pitcher or Bender's coach knew was that Jackee liked the ball high and inside. There was a loud ping off the aluminum bat as the ball flew down the left field line and on one hop hit the fence. There was no doubt the runner on second would score and Jackee would be credited with a game winning RBI single. Rose would once again get the game winning ball.

A wild celebration broke out among Cedwick fans, this was the first ever junior high baseball championship. Jackee was mobbed by her teammates and later by friends and family. The senior umpire had retrieved the game ball and gave it to coach Wangel who in turn gave it to Jackee after the team signed it. Varsity coach Begali wanted to speak with William while J V coach Singer was congratulating team members.

Begali asked William if he thought Jackee could handle the pressure of being the varsity starting shortstop as a tenth grader. He also mentioned how each higher level would be more difficult then the last one. Pressure would be more so on her since she is a female and will have skipped the whole JV year.

William said, "you saw how she handled this season and the pressure of this final game. Look around and see the respect she has earned from the other coaches in the league. See the respect she gets from her teammates and how they interact with her. She also led this team in most offensive and defensive categories. I'll tell you now that she is the real thing, potentially a 5 tool player and above average in most of those tools. She could eventually break the gender barrier at any level she makes her mind up to try."

That was a lot to consider and coach Begali had to take the father's opinion as being somewhat biased. In the back of his mind he had a plan to contact as many coaches as he could and try to get an honest opinion from them. Yet if he believes his eyes Jackee will be his starting shortstop.

When all the celebrating was over the Jenco family headed for their favorite Italian restaurant for dinner. Again they were surprised at how many people stopped by to congratulate Jackee and even a few young girls wanted her autograph. She had no idea where to sign on a baseball. William had to explain the "sweet spot" on the ball. He also jokingly said that the ball one day might be very valuable. Everyone laughed but William seemed serious.

They arrived home to find many of Jackee's teammates waiting in front of the house. They said the booster club had put together a party and she was to be the guest of honor. So the whole family got back into the car and drove to Cedwick junior high. The cafeteria was packed and a big cheer went up as the Jenco family entered. There was plenty of food and soft drinks. Most of the school officials and even some board members were present. Later the principal gave a welcoming talk, and the athletic director and coach Wangel said a few words. Jackee was also asked to speak. She had never given a speech before and just spoke from her heart. She thanked everyone for being there and supporting her. She thanked coach Wangel for not only supporting her but alro defending her right to try. She reminded everyone that baseball was a team sport and that no one player wins a game without the support of the other eight. She also made the point of how her teammates took many insults and abuse because she played on the team, yet each of them supported her just as they would any other teammate. Finally she thanked her family who supported her every step of the way.

Next morning William, Carmela, and Jackee sat around the breakfast table and discussed the next step. William explained what his talk with coach Begali was about. If Jackee wanted to be the starting shortstop for the varsity, a complete summer and fall program had to be created. Was it possible to play in a summer baseball league? Softball was not an option. Only baseball opportunities would be investigated. William did know an individual who had played some pro baseball and now he coached a sponsored summer team. This team played in an independent league with many junior college and high school players. They played about 40 to 50 league games and then some kind of playoff. This could be an option. Since Jackee would be the only female, and only 16 a careful approach had to be taken. Finally it was agreed that in order for her to see quality competition, she had to take the risk. Jackee agreed that to improve her skills and awaken a higher competitiveness in her, she needed to compete at a higher level. Carmela was not so positive. Although she knew that this was the best option, she feared that her young, beautiful daughter would be changed forever. Because she wanted to show support for something she knew Jackee wanted, she kept these fears locked in her heart and gave 100 percent support to the summer league possibility.

William called Bats Howard, the summer coach he had spoken about at breakfast. Bats was a big man standing about 6'3" and about 200pounds of solid granite. He never went to college but he did serve 2 tours in the marines before playing some minor league baseball. If there was a picture in the dictionary to describe a disciplinarian it would be a picture of Bats. He did not make suggestions, instead he gave orders. There were only 2 ways he did things, his way or no way. Yet beneath this granite exterior was one of the most gentle, considerate men William had ever met. He had served one tour of duty with him and after he got over being scared to death in Bats presence, he realized what a great leader he was. If you had to go to war this was the leader you wanted to follow.

Little did William suspect that in his last year of service Bats and he became very close friends. Upon discharge William went to college under the GI bill and got his BBA in accounting. He stayed in contact with Bats even after his marriage to Carmela. Bats got out of the service and played minor league ball for three years. When he finally decided he would never make the show he found a job running the youth program for a local county government. Bats started and directed many sports activities for both girls and boys, and even was involved with the senior citizens. Baseball had been his first love, this is probably why the two of them were so close. Bats ran the summer program sponsored partly by the county. This was not enough to run a first class program so Bats had to get donations from the local business people. Once when talking about donation with Bats, William felt that if Bats asked for help or donations the donor would feel so intimidated he would give whatever Bats wanted.

At their meeting William told Bats about Jackee and gave him a complete history of her experiences to date. He also told him of the varsity coach's desire to start her as his varsity shortstop next season.

Bats shook his head and said "I don't have separate accommodations on our road trips. I also don't have any idea how my team or for that matter how the other teams would react to a female playing."

William looked him in the eye and said "Sargeant, if you tell them once how to treat a player on your team, I can not visualize anyone disrespecting your wishes." They both laughed and Bats said he would talk to Jackee and maybe give her a tryout.

Second Saturday in June, Bats arrived at the prearranged time he and William decided on. They all went to the high school field. Coach Begali, along with a few varsity players and coaches were there waiting for them. Coach had arranged for the field to be properly prepared by the ground crew. After all the introductions were completed, the players did all their pre game drills. Once everyone loosened up they did a few infield drills. Coach was even more interested than Bats because Jackee may be his core player for the next 3 years.

Bats directed the activities and designated certain coaches with certain responsibilities. Jackee was put through many drills and Bats really put the pressure on her. He hit balls to her left, right and made her charge them, then he hit pop flies all over the infield and short outfield. When he had her totally exhausted he hit more ground balls and made her throw to some base. She bobbled one ball but cleanly fielded all the rest. Every throw was right on the mark or catchable. He said to William, her skills are unbelievable and her ability to catch pop ups is uncanny.

He tested her speed by timing her to first and then around the bases. Her times were equal to some of the best players he ever had. Lastly, he wanted to see her hit. After she rested for a few moments Jackee picked up her bat and prepared to hit. Two of the high school pitches threw batting practice under Bats' direction. After a few pitches into the round Jackee began hitting line drives and deep fly balls, Bats noticed right away that she had a sweet swing and the ball jumped off her bat which meant she was getting her arms, wrists, legs and hips into every swing. He then signaled the pitches to throw some curveballs. Jackee followed each one and hit it where she saw the pitch. He then instructed the catcher to call for the pitches appling game situations to the pitch. Hit and run, she hit the ball about where the second baseman would play. Suicide squeeze she should bunt the ball anywhere except back to the pitcher. Jackee bunted the ball down the third base line. Bats called everyone in and they all gathered around home plate. Bats told Jackee she put on one of the best tryouts he had ever seen. She could definitely play on his team. He expected her to come to his city where he would make arrangements to secure her sleeping quarters. His team has started working out but they were still in pre season tryouts. Their first game was on July Fourth. Bats stated that the county does provide a nurse to travel with the team so Jackee could bunk with her on road trips.

CHAPTER FOUR

Jackee Plays Summer Baseball

*H*aving one of your children leave home for the first time is difficult for everyone. Carmela packed Jackee's clothes and William her baseball gear. Rose wanted to go with her since school was ending soon. William said that wasn't possible, but they were going to see many of her games, since the Dukes would play a few games near them. The family would also be able to drive to Dutch Hill where their home games were played. It was a four hour drive but on weekends it should not be a problem.

Dropping Jackee off in Dutch Hill was an emotional thing. Carmela and Rose cried most of the time on the drive home. In fact it took days before Rose stopped crying and could sleep through the night. William had reminded Jackee that at any time she felt uncomfortable he would come and get her. She had hugged and thanked him. One piece of good news brightened their day, Kim Stanton, the nurse who traveled with the team was a single girl and lived within walking distance of Baseball Paradise where the Dukes played all their home games. Kim bought the house from her parents after her grandmother passed away. It was a 3 bedroom 2 1/2 baths with a full basement on one acre of well groomed property. Kim's only stay over guests had all been immediate relatives. When Bats told her about Jackee she quickly offered to have her stay at the house. In fact she already had set up a room in case someone needed it during the season. People in the area thought that she had a little crush on Bats but the difference in their age made that seem unlikely. When the Jenco's appeared at the door Kim was excited to see Jackee and did not want to accept any money. William would not hear of it and told her that food and wear and tear as well as upkeep cost money. He thought that $1200.00 for the two months would be a fair price and if more was needed, she would just have to ask him. She was more than pleased since she would now have someone to talk with.

Kim and Jackee seemed to be very happy with each other and it had made Carmela feel better that a medically trained person was so close by. The Jenco's left and Jackee unpacked her bag in the spare room. When everything was put away the two women sat down and discussed the rules in the house and what Jackee could expect in the first week. A full detail of Kim's day was laid out and the schedule for Jackee had been programmed by Bats. Meals were discussed as well as a player diet for a young female ballplayer. Dietary meals for Dukes' players was established by the dietician for Crane County. Part of Kim's nurse training had a diet section in it and being very conscious about her weight, she took a great interest in what was served. She added to this by subscribing to the best medical journals on diets and needs for young adults. She drew up a special diet for Jackee using her favorite foods. It had been easy for Kim and Jackee to agree since Carmela always provided her with a balanced diet.

Early Monday Morning Jackee reported to Baseball Paradise with all her baseball gear. Most of the players were still in the locker room but a few were loosening up on the side lines. Eight AM sharp, Bats Howard appeared and announced that practice would begin at 8 sharp every day. He informed them that if they arrive after 7:55am they are late, and being late means you need additional conditioning. Something like a complete lap around the field and 50 pushups. " Do I make myself clear?" Everyone just nodded, he said "I can't hear you." Finally they all shouted " we hear you." He continued, "unless you can not tell the difference, there is a female player in your group. She is to be treated with the respect she deserves. The use of a four letter word beginning with an "F"is forbidden on this field. It is a disgusting and unnecessary word. In its place I recommend gosh,heck or darn. Offenders will be doing pushups until they learn to speak properly."

Bats had three helpers who were introduced to the group as well as the nurse. He mentioned that the nurse would provide some medical services, do all the taping, and provide each of them with a proper diet. "We strongly recommend you follow the diet when possible. There will be no smoking or drinking of unauthorized beverages on this team. If you are found drunk or arrested for drunkenness don't bother coming to the field, just pack up and go to wherever you came from. Caught smoking will get you a warning the first time, there will not be a second one."

"We will teach you how to really play this game. It is by far the hardest sport to play. Ted Williams said it best: "The most difficult thing to do in any sport is to hit a round ball with a round bat." "A fraction of an inch making contact on a bat could be the difference between a home run or a fly ball. A fraction of an inch can mean the difference between being safe or out. A ball or strike call or a fair or foul ball can be a matter of a fraction of an inch. You will learn to push your skills to their limit, and what you believe to be impossible will be easy later on. You can quit anytime you feel like it. No one will beg you to stay. We only want those players who will dedicate themselves to learning how to play. Notice I did not mention winning. Winning is not the most important thing here, playing to the best of your ability is. If you achieve that, you would have already won the game of life. Our winning percentage here is around 700. That means we usually win seven out of every ten games we play. It is done fairly, with teamwork and dedication to the greatest sport ever played."

Practice began and it seemed that 30 players were all working at once. Some were batting in the batting cage while others were batting off live pitching on the field. Infielders were getting ground balls, outfielders had fly balls hit to them and pitchers were doing drills off the mound. Since running and stretching had been done first, all the players were loose and only had to get their arms ready. Unless some of these players were here before, none of them had ever worked this hard or this long. Most of the baseball practices have players standing around and do nothing until it is their turn to hit or field. This was not the case here.

Jackee felt great because William always pushed her hard to strive for perfection. She fielded ground balls all over the infield. All the coaches were impressed by her work ethics and stamina. What impressed them most was her ability to make every throw a near perfect one and always with something on it. Two other shortstop candidates could not believe the large area she covered on ground balls or in the fact that every throw was where the first baseman could easily handle it. Never a wild throw or one in the dirt. This practice was also to see the first basemen dig bad throws out of the dirt, however with Jackee there were none to practice on.

Hitting became a practice stopper. Most of the players had been curious about how a girl would hit . Jackee hit hard line drives to all areas of the field and even hit one over the fence in right center field. None had expected that much power from a young girl. She finished off batting with a line drive just inside the left field foul line. Bats broke one of his own rules, he actually smiled as he watched Jackee bat. He now was sure that he selected her because he saw the great talent she had and not because she was the daughter of a close friend. He had a vision that her appearance in a game would add a great many more fans, especially female ones. Although they did not charge admission to their games they did ask the fans to donate whatever they could and to participate in the 50/50 drawing. This helped each team meet some of their expenses for the season. There was a notice posted at all the parks stating this fact. Much to their surprise, most fans attending were very generous.

This training went on for two weeks. At the end 25 players were left. 5 had packed up and gone home. The team carried 11 pitchers and 14 position players. There were 2 regular catchers and one of the other players could catch in an emergency. There were also many of the players who could pitch or play other positions if the need arose. Opening day for the Dukes was on the first Sunday in July, a double header against the Fargo Flashers. All the Jenco's were there from the night before, as well as an unusual number of local media. Bats had made it a point to let it slip out that for the first time ever a female would be starting for the Dukes. He rightly assumed that a much larger crowd than usually attended would be there. To his amazement the stands were almost filled. There was an excitement in the air that Bats had not felt in years. The Flashers had expected a larger crowd since it would be opening day but they didn't expect anything like this. Umpires took the opening day lineup cards, went over the ground rules and got ready for the opening ceremonies. When the players were announced the Flashers received a courtesy type of cheers. When the Dukes were announced they received much louder ones, all except Jackee who received rafter rocking cheers. After the National Anthem the home plate umpire shouted, "play ball." The Flashers went down in order and the first two hitters for the Dukes did also. Jackee batting in her usual position was the third hitter. Almost the whole stadium was on their feet cheering her. It took awhile for her to calm herself down but she kept telling herself stay within your game. On the second pitch which was on the inside, she hit a bullet right at the third baseman. He didn't have to move, only raise his glove to protect his face and catch the ball. When Jackee hit in the bottom of the third inning she got almost exactly the same pitch, this time she lined it down the left field line for an RBI stand up double. A few batters later, she scored the Duke's third run and now they led 3 to 1. When she batted in the bottom of the sixth the pitcher was pitching her on the outside of the plate. She waited on a curve and drilled a ball to right center that rolled all the way to the fence. With a pretty hook slide she had a triple. One batter later she scored the Duke's fourth run on a sac fly to center. Her last at bat in the bottom of the eighth she walked and later stole second but did not score. Final score of game one Dukes 4 Flashers 1.

League rules give the teams an option; they may play two 9 inning games or the first game a 9 inning and the second game a 7. Both coaches have to agree before the first game starts. The first game must be completed no matter how long it goes. The second game can end in a tie as long as it goes 5 innings and both coaches agree. Ties will count in the team's overall record. The Flashers won the second game 3 to 0. They out hit the Dukes 8 to 2. Jackee did get one of the two hits, a double.

As the season progressed 2 things became very clear,

1. Jackee was an exceptional baseball player and every game had many more fans because she was playing.

2. Jackee's presence on the field was not a stunt or gimmick like Charlie Finley would have staged. She not only played the game to a high degree but she raised the whole team's level. You could see imme-

diately that she was the team leader, although no one proclaimed it. Not by shouting or conjouling did she lead the team but by instinct and example. Her preparation and dedication to the game made everyone around her elevate their game. This would have been a great feat for a boy of any age, but to have a girl who turned 16 only last month, it was beyond anyone's imagination.

Game after game Jackee only got better. Bats has witnessed many players grow as they learned the game and developed their baseball skills. Jackee's skills developed beyond belief. Bats never had a player who knew instinctively where to be on every play. There had always been a problem with run downs. Players were never sure where to back up or where to cover. Immediately Jackee knew to shorten the rundown, chase the runner back to his previous base and then give the ball to the fastest fielder. Jackee was almost always the fastest player. Cut offs and backups were her specialty. Many opposing team runners were gunned down because she knew where to be and what base to throw to. Assists are not really a big statistic in baseball, not like homers, RBI's or batting average but many games are won or lost because a runner was thrown out or allowed to score. As their season rolled on, opposing players and coaches were afraid to test Jackee's arm. You will never see this in a box score, but it does relate to wins and losses.

Mid-season saw Jackee hitting .448 and with some power. She had 3 homers, 4 triples,13 doubles and only one strikeout. In Bats eyes she was the best two strike hitter he ever saw. He knew in 1941 Joe DiMaggio struck out only 13 times in 541 at bats. That is about 1 strike out every 42 at bats. Even Ted Williams who was the major league's last .400 hitter never came close to that. At this level Jackee showed signs of even getting better. She controlled her swing with a two strike count, but still hit with some power.

Second half of the season saw the Dukes really come together. Bats' discipline and training, along with Jackee's leadership had them playing like a well oiled machine. Their pitchers especially developed into a cohesive group. Great fielding behind them helped immensely. Every good play that you turn into an out means the other team has one out less and one base runner less to try and score. It also reduces the pitches that a pitcher throws in a game. How many times have you seen a fielder make an error and instead of having the third out the pitcher has to throw 10 or 20 additional pitches to complete the inning. That means he will not be as strong in the later innings. The more he throws, the sooner he will become tired.

The second half would determine who makes the playoffs. When the season ends the first four teams make the playoffs. Team one plays four and team two plays three. The team with the best record will always be the home team. All playoff games must be completed by the Sunday before labor day. Most of the players have to be back in school or college. Friday is a single game playoff. The winners will play 2 out of 3 with the first game on Saturday. On Sunday the game will start at 11am and if a third game is needed, it will start 20 minutes after the first game is finished. After the final game there will be a ceremony honoring the four teams but mostly for the winning team.

The second half of the season was a good one for the Dukes, they played really well and only lost 3 games the rest of the season. They were in first place when the season ended. Jackee's stats were a little better than the first half. She finished with 7 homers, 8 triples, 27 doubles, 39 RBI's and still only one strikeout. Her overall batting average was .451. Playoffs were to start next Friday and Bats had to decide on his pitch rotation. Since his team was to play the fourth place team, and since they won all four games against the Hawkes by hefty scores he decided to start his number two pitcher. There really was not much difference between his number 1 and 2. The second ranked team in the playoffs were the Flashers who he felt would defeat the Bay City Bandits in the other playoff game. His number one had beat the Flashers in both the series they played. Bats felt whoever wins the first game has a big advantage.

Just as Bats predicted the Flashers won big and would be the visiting team on Saturday for the finals. His number two pitcher threw a complete 9 inning three hitter against the Hawkes. Jackee was perfect in the first playoff game. She only had one hit but walked 3 times and was hit by a pitch. Her fielding made a strong showing in the game. She made 3 sparkling plays and each time was given a loud cheer for her efforts. One of these plays was on a hard ground ball that seemed to be headed for center field. At top speed Jackee reached down, caught the ball and in one motion stepped on second and threw a strike to first, completing the double play. The Jenco family, who had come down for the weekend, led the cheering section. After the 7 to 2 win, William and the family took Jackee and Kim out to dinner. While at dinner Carmela filled Jackee in on everything that has happened since she left. As they were eating dessert Carmela invited Kim to spend the Holidays with them if she had nothing better to do. Kim thanked her for the offer and said she would think about it and let her know. Game one of the finals was played on a gorgeous day in late August. As Bats had guessed, the Flashers used their number one pitcher and had to start number 2 and 3 against them. The Flashers coach knew he had been outfoxed by Bats. He did think about starting another pitcher but decided that if he lost there would be no need for his number one pitcher. His motto is "Go with your best whenever you can." He did decide on his own strategy, he would start his number 3 pitcher against Bats number 2. If he wins the game he will have his number 2 against Bats number 3 in game 2.

The first game started slow, neither team had a base runner in the first three innings. In fact the Dukes pitcher retired the first 12 Flasher hitters. In the last of the fourth the Duke's leadoff hitter singled to center. Instead of bunting him to second, Bats called for a hit and run. The batter hit a perfect ground ball exactly where the second baseman had been before he ran to cover second on the attempted steal. Dukes now had runners on first and third with no outs. Bats had remembered that each time there was a runner on second and Jackee was batting, the Flasher coach always walked her. As it stands now he would have to pitch to her or load the bases with nobody out and the fourth, fifth, and sixth hitters coming to the plate. Jackee knew her job was to at least score the runner from third. She was looking for a pitch she could drive out of the infield. With the count even at 1 and 1 she guessed a curve ball was coming, and she was right. It started over the plate then broke to the outside, Jackee waited on it then drove the ball to right center and it rolled all the way to the fence. When the ball finally was relayed back to the infield, two runners had scored and Jackee had a stand up triple. Before the inning ended, she scored on a sacrifice fly to center and at the end of four innings Dukes led 3 to 0. Game one turned into a blowout with the Dukes winning 9 to 0. Jackee had one more RBI hit and two more walks. She now had 3 hits in four at bats, 4 walks, and one hit batter. William and Carmela once again took the family and Kim to dinner and all were in excellent spirits.

Sunday was every bit as beautiful as Saturday. After church and breakfast, they dropped Kim and Jackee off at Kim's house and then went to the hotel to check out. Jackee finished packing what she intended to bring home and then changed into her uniform and headed for the field. Everything seemed to be ready for the game and the fans were starting to fill the stands. As She looked to see if her family had arrived she saw Coaches Wangel, Begali and Singer sitting in the stands. She was walking over to them just as her family arrived. She could not believe that the coaches had driven for at least 4 hours just to see a summer baseball game. Coach Wangel thought that Jackee was a little bigger and had grown over the summer. William smiled and said "in many more ways." Bats decided there was no need for a third game as his team was ready to end the season now. The league board has brought all the awards with them and they will be distributed as soon as a champion is decided.

Game two mirrored game one to some degree. Flashers went down in order for the first two innings. They did get a runner on in the third but failed to score him. Jackee got a double in the first inning but was left stranded on third. In the bottom of the fourth with a runner on first and no outs, Jackee was up. For some unknown reason the Flasher's coach decided to walk Jackee intentionally putting runners on first and second. This unprecedented decision by the opposing coach impressed Coach Begali. He saw her direct and lead the team from her shortstop position but now saw her as a complete and respected hitter. The number four hitter lined a ball down the left field line that scored both base runners but got thrown out trying for third on the throw home. After the Flashers scored a run in the top of the sixth, the Dukes exploded in the bottom of the inning. The leadoff hitter walked and stole second, and scored when the number two hitter singled to left. Jackee followed with a drive down the right field line, scoring the base runner and ending up on third. A few moments later she scored as the next four hitters all got hits and eventually scored. The score was now 9 to 1 at the end of six innings. Jackee hit one last time in the bottom of the seventh. Flashers had used four pitchers already and now a fifth one was waved into pitch. He threw a fastball right over the heart of the plate, Jackee turned on it and drove it over the center field fence. All her teammates were out of the dugout and waiting for her as she touched home plate. Coach Begali Said to no one in particular, "I got myself a shortstop and a team leader for the next 3 years."

Closing ceremonies were very quick after the 12 to 2 game ended. Trophies were distributed to all four teams by the league directors. The last two trophies were the league championship one to the Dukes and the MVP of the playoffs. Bats accepted the championship one and the other was awarded to Jackee. All four playoff coaches agreed that she had been not only the reason for the larger crowds but she was by far the most important player on the field. She not only took home the MVP award, but also gave Rose the game ball. Last thing the Flashers coach said to Bats "If she is back next year, I will protest unless she has a twin that will play on my team." Bats asked the coach, have you ever seen a ball player like her? Flash's coach said he never saw any player like her in amature baseball.

The day after driving home there was another Jenco meeting. Carmela, William and Jackee sat down to discuss the next step in Jackee's program. It was decided that since Jackee was starting high school that would be a big enough adjustment for her to make right now. They decided a month off or until she has her full schedule under control she would only do practice swings and some cardio activities. Going from a small close school to a big campus with many new programs and faces requires major adjustments.

Jackee fit right in the school program. She knew most of the leaders and most of the athletes. Since she was better than the average student, most all the academic teachers knew of her and were glad when she entered their class. All the coaches and phy ed teachers had known about her for over a year. Prior to the school year, a general Faculty meeting is always held. Here all the 9th graders enter the school as new 10th graders and are discussed at this faculty meeting. Advisors to the various clubs are always looking for new leaders. Recommendations from the junior high teachers go a long way in scheduling the new students in classes and activities.

In both sports and science Jackee's name received a great deal of interest. Sy Weeks, the athletic director said she could be more than a local legend. There is a potential for not only state but national recognition. Brenda Hill, varsity softball coach at Reagan high school was more direct when she said, "Jackee Jenco has the potential to be the best female athlete in the state." Since most of the faculty had not seen Jackee play, they were very skeptical. Faculty meetings are usually boring, but this one left the teachers looking forward to actually seeing these new students, especially Jackee Jenco.

Classes for Jackee were easy. A straight academic schedule heavy in science was prepared for her. Science always dominated her interest. In the back of her mind she was starting to formulate a possibility that sports medicine might be her true calling after baseball. Science came easy to Jackee and she loved the lab work. One of her past science teachers thought she would make a great doctor. This Idea sounded remote at first but now the thought kept coming back as a future possibility.

There was always a get acquainted day held at the high school for the new students. Classes begin on Wednesday for everyone but on Tuesday after Labor Day all the new 10th graders are invited to an orientation followed by a brunch. Everyone mingles together in the cafeteria, students and teachers alike. Once the welcoming address is finished and all the teachers wearing name tags are introduced. The students get their name tags and get ready for brunch. The whole cafeteria staff makes and serves the food. This had always been a tradition at Reagan high school and it served a good purpose. Students began to identify with the people in the school. Nurse, librarian, guidance counselor, custodian and of course the teachers. This also helped the teachers get to know some of the students. People who actually got the biggest benefit were the teachers who ran clubs or activities. Student council members were all over directing students or trying to enlist them in some activities. Mostly, this helps to break the apprehension some students may have. It also was a free meal for hungry teenagers.

Jackee was totally relaxed and looked forward to starting school. She did notice that more people talked to her and she liked that. When she met the head of the science department, Mr Rogers, he asked her to join the science club. She was going to do that anyway but she felt so honored that the head of the department had gone out of his way to invite her personally.

During dinner that night she told her parents all that had taken place. She was still excited by the invitation by Mr Rogers. William and Carmela both agreed that multiple vocations were a good goal. William mentioned that a former Yankee third baseman had become a highly respected specialist. His name was Bobby Brown. Jackee had heard a great deal about the Yankee teams of old. She heard how great the teams were and how they dominated baseball for many a year, however she never heard about a Dr. Brown. Jackee later looked up Bobby Brown. He played third base and shortstop for the Yankees. He was known as the golden boy and played in four world series. After his playing days were over he later became the president of the American league and finally a highly regarded cardiologist. He was now her idol and someone everyone should admire.

The first two weeks of school were the most enjoyable of her life. She pretty much settled into a routine that was very comfortable. Since the talk with her parents, her desire to learn was unbelievable. Rogers has given her special books to read and she finished all of them. Her new school schedule still left her plenty of time to train. Besides her 100 dry swings a day she ran with Rose. To her surprise Rose ran very well and really pushed her to run faster. She suggested to Rose that maybe she might consider running track.

After the month ended a new winter program was decided on. Light weights were to be used to strengthen arms and wrists. It was important to improve Jackee's left hand. She was totally right handed but in order to maintain good balance the left side of her body had to be developed. This would help her swing and coordination. The running and sprints did not change much because Jackee loved having Rose workout with her. They were very close and really enjoyed each other's company. Running became fun because they competed and challenged each other.

Halloween is an important day at the high school. Besides the dance at night, high school volunteers are divided into four groups and each group decorates the four elementary school gyms into a safe Halloween experience. A few years before a third grader was killed doing trick or treat on Halloween. When the services for the students were over the PTA, board members, administration and teachers held a meeting and came up with this plan. After the first one had been so successful it was put on the school calendar every year.

Most high school students have fantastic imaginations and their talents are unlimited. They are given the responsibility of creating the settings for each elementary school. As an additional incentive the high school has a committee that selects the school that had the best theme and decorations. Each high school student who participated in that group gets 5 points added to their next test. Generally each school is set up with the same haunted house and decorations. This work is done by the custodial staff. There are no gym classes at the school that day. The custodial staff has enough time to set up each elementary school before 1 pm when the high school volunteers arrive to do their thing.

When this began, local businesses and parents offered to help and it just mushroomed. Food, candy, drinks, prizes, decorations and even costumes are donated by local merchants and businesses. Fire and police departments are both participants as are every club or organization in the community. Every local church has someone assisting the schools. The four groups of high school students finished school at noon. This gives them a chance to eat lunch and be at the elementary school by 1pm. They have one hour to set up their booths and whatever else they decide on. Elementary students start coming in at 2pm and the whole activity ends at 4:30. The high school groups then clean up and have to get ready for their evening dance which starts at 7:30.

Jackee's group had a science theme. They set up 3 contest booths and 3 game area's. Candy and goodies stations were also set up. School aids, mothers, and even parents with younger children were invited to participate. With every elementary school offering this there really was no need for children to go from house to house trick or treating. Games and booths set up by the high school group was a big success. In fact the science booth with the volcano won the best prize award. If the elementary student performed the procedure properly the volcano would erupt with lights flashing and lava, actually foam, running down the mountain.

Preparations for the high school dance were almost identical to the preparations for the elementary schools. The custodial staff after completing their work at the four smaller schools now went to the high school to prepare that gym. Everyone from the PTA to local businesses met at the school and joined the staff in decorating the gym for halloween. Parents felt it was the right thing to do since these youngsters give so much of their time to the community. Since this program was started there has not been any child or for that matter an older child injured on halloween.

Carmela dropped Jackee off at the high school and told her to have fun and she would be back at 11 to pick her up. Jackee gave Carmela a kiss and began walking into the school. Other students, who recognized Jackee, were entering the school and asked if she wanted to join them. They entered the gym and saw how beautiful it had been decorated. A DJ was playing music. These were the songs the student council had selected from a questionnaire filled out by students. Jackee was a great dancer having learned from her older sisters. She kept in practice by teaching Rose to dance. There was no lack of dancing partners for her. A boy seemed to appear out of nowhere when she wasn't dancing. Many of the boys she knew from baseball or other sports. It also didn't hurt that Jackee was one of the prettiest girls in the room.

Close to 11 Jackee had her full of food, drink and above all dancing. As she was getting ready to go out and wait for her mom, Dan Silvio, a football player and fellow science class mate, asked if she would like to go to a movie one Saturday night. Jackee was stunned and did not know what to say. Finally She said, "I'll ask my parents if it would be ok and if they say yes it would be my pleasure to accept. Thank you for asking me and I'll let you know what they say."

Carmela was waiting outside the high school so when Jackee walked out of the gym she got right into the car. On the drive home Jackee told her all about the dance and that her group won best halloween presentation in the elementary contest. Finally she mentioned the offer of a date from Dan Silvio.

Carmela did not show any emotion or concern, saying only "we'll see what your dad has to say." Since it was after 11 the discussion will have to wait until breakfast.

Next morning they were sitting at the table but no one seemed to be saying anything. William finally asked how the dance went last night. Jackee said it was a lot of fun and I had a great time. She then looked at Carmela who only nodded toward her husband. Finally, Jackee said by the way a boy asked me out on a date. William started laughing and said "what took them so long?" Jackee felt the tension melt from her and she relaxed for the first time all morning. William also added he could not understand why the prettiest girl in the school had not been flooded by offers before now. All she really wanted to hear was that it was fine for her to accept the date. William told her that "if your mother agrees and a few simple rules are followed, I don't see why not."

"What rules are you talking about?" she asked.

"Well for one, he must come to the house to be introduced and to pick you up. We must know where you are going, what time he intends to have you home and finally what is his mode of transportation. Just a few things every parent should know about their 16 year old daughter's date."

None of these things seemed unfair to Jackee, in fact she was so happy her parents cared that much about her. When she told Dan about the rules he agreed that they were more than fair. Then they agreed to go to a movie next Saturday, later to the malt shop before heading home. Since Dan was seventeen, he could drive and had the use of his family's second car. Saturday at 6:30 Dan showed up driving a Mustang. After meeting the family and showing William his drivers license they were off to the seven o'clock movie. Dan told William, Jackee will be home by 12. This will give us time to go for an ice cream after the movie. The parents had agreed.

Both William and Carmela waited up for Jackee to return. Rose had waited up with them but had fallen asleep and was carried to bed by 10:00. Around 11:50 a car pulled into the driveway and both parents ran up to their bedroom before Jackee entered the house. After thanking Dan for a lovely evening, she said good night and waited for his car to leave. Then she locked the front door, shut off the lights and went upstairs. On passing her parents room she noticed the lights were on so she peeked in. They both seemed to be awake so she stopped in to thank them and let them know what a great time she had. A while later she happily went into bed and fell fast asleep. It seemed the school year was speeding by. Thanksgiving was here and gone. Food baskets were prepared and delivered. Visits to the orphanage and Veterans home were made before the Jenco's sat for their Thanksgiving dinner.

Christmas as always is a very special season for the Jenco's This one had two additional happy events. Kim notified the Jenco's that she would join them for the Christmas holidays and Rebecca told her family that Rocco Manelli after a year had proposed and they were finally getting engaged for Christmas. So besides the usual preparations an engagement party has to be planned. Carmela was an amazing woman. She not only prepared for Christmas, she also organized Rebecca's engagement party. Besides those two things, she prepared all the meals, set up the sleeping arrangements for Kim and kept the house immaculate. All clothes were washed, ironed, mended if needed, and properly put away. William's office staff wanted to know how he always came to work in a perfectly ironed shirt. He told them he has a woman who does his shirts, and if she does a good job, she gets to sleep with him.

Kim could not believe Jenco's Christmas schedule. First the day before when they visited the orphanage and the Vets home. Next came the Christmas morning excitement, breakfast, getting to church on time and then returning home for the present opening and later going to the church to set up the meal for the homeless and others. Then coming home for their meal. They sat down to dinner with two additional guests. Kim and Rocco just pretended that they did this every year. Rebbeca announced that it was decided the engagement party will be held on January sixth, at St Mary's Hall, which is adjacent to the church.

Kim left for home the day after Christmas saying she had a date for New Years and had to organize her programs for the winter sports. After she left the Jenco's sat down to plan Jackee's preparation for the coming season. Jackee felt last year's program served her well. William agreed but felt that a better conditioning program was needed to prevent injuries. William was in contact with a trainer that works with the US Olympic track athletes. He promised to send him a copy of their training schedule. A day later by special delivery the schedule arrived. Rose, who was now into track, was very excited about this new program. Rose wanted to know if she ever could be good enough to be an olympic athlete. Jackee told her that there are no limits as to what you can achieve. When they looked at the program both agreed it was a doable one. They found a time when both their schedules were in harmony and a plan was created.

CHAPTER FIVE
Jackee Starts High School and First Year of Baseball

*J*ackee had a great Christmas week. All the family activities were always fun but when Dan came over one day with a Christmas present, she was shocked. He just came unannounced and asked to speak with Jackee. Beside giving her the present he asked if she would like to attend a New Year's Eve party at his house. His parents had a "bring in the New Year celebration" every year and he will use this as an opportunity to introduce her to the family. Jackee immediately asked her parents for permission. They agreed with the condition that whoever drove Jackee home did not have a drink that evening. Dan readily agreed and said since he does not drink, he would be the one to drive her home. He also asked if it would be alright if he picked her up at 7:30 and had her home by 1:00 am. They agreed.

When Carmela and Jackee were alone one day. She asked what the rules are for kissing on a date. For some strange reason she never discussed dating with her older sisters, and since she never had a real date the subject never came up. Carmela wanted to laugh, and she would tonight when she told William about this, but she also did not want to hurt Jackee's feelings. She did tell Jackee that no real rules existed for kissing. It would mostly be up to the young lady and how she feels about her date. You know your moral and religious rules so let them be your guide. Later when she told William they both had a laugh but William said, "have we forgotten to properly prepare her for dating?" Carmela said, "nature would take care of this, it usually does."

It turned out easier than Jackee thought it would be. After meeting Dan's family and dancing most of the night,12:00 came and everyone kissed and wished each other a happy New Year. She must have kissed 20 people, some friends, some family and some complete strangers. The first and by far most exciting kiss was from Dan. All the ones after, for lack of a better word, were generic. As they were saying good night at her front door, she thanked him for a great evening and said she would be happy if he asked her out again. Then she kissed him with a real big hug and felt as if her heart skipped a beat. She passed her parents room when she went upstairs and it seemed to her that they were still awake. This time she went straight to her room and decided to save the highlights of this date for some other time.

Next morning, when Jackee finally came down for breakfast, she wished her parents and Rose a happy new year and kissed them. She said she missed spending New Year's Eve with her family. Later, she told them all about the party and how Dan's parents had welcomed her. One detail she purposely left out. Dan did get her home by 1:00 am and did not have a hard drink all night. Still there was no mention of a kiss. As Carmela and Jackee were cleaning the table, she casually asked if Jackee solved her kissing problem. Jackee smiled, blushed a little and said "I followed your advice and it was one of the happiest and best moments of my life."

William asked Carmela what Jackee had said about her kiss situation. He knew that she would ask. All Carmela said, "I am not sure what I told her but I never had a kiss that was the best moment of my life."

Winter is a long and dreary time. Daylight is short and usually cold. Running, weather permitting, every day helped make the time go by. Days with inclement weather were basically shut in ones. Only practice swings, weights and agility drills helped pass the time. School work was a priority on these days because more time could be set aside for it. Jackee had made arrangements with her teachers that they would give her the homework for the following week. This gave her the chance to plan and complete it before the end of the week. It worked very well and gave her plenty of time to do other things.

William did not have to rent time at the indoor batting arena. Coach Begali always had his team hit Monday, Wednesday, Friday from 4:00 to 6:00pm. He paid a flat fee for two months starting the first hitting day after New Year and ending the last Friday in February. The first Monday in March was his first day of tryouts. The Reagan high booster club paid the bulk of the fee but the players had to pay $25.00 each to hit at the baseball academy. Baseball academy added new iron mikes that threw curveballs. This was a novelty and of course everyone had to try them out. Players usually adjusted very quickly because the pitch was exactly the same every time. There was only a change when a defective ball was put into the machine.

Jackee hit both fastball and curve very well. However on the curveball machine she finally realized what William had said about the curve ball. He said, watch the pitcher's hand and when the ball is released see if you can pick up the spin. If you can identify the spin you will know if it is a fastball or something else. There is only a matter of a split second but the trained eye might be able to do it on some pitchers.

No coach, parent, or bystander tried to give advice or change Jackee's swing. Her swing was a very strong and compact stroke. With her bat control there was no wasted motion in bringing the bat into the hitting zone. Combined with her bat speed it produced a near perfect swing. This also explained how this 16 year old girl could generate the power she showed. Whenever Jackee hit, there were always people watching. Many parents brought their daughters to see the "Girl Wonder" hit. Occasionally a parent would ask her to speak, and or encourage their daughter. Jackee at first was very shy and a little afraid she would say the wrong thing. She did feel confident in saying, "It takes a lot of concentration and hard work, but the most important thing is that you must believe in yourself and in what you can achieve. Never let anyone tell you that you are not good enough or that you can't do something. You are made in God's image and with God nothing is impossible."

Dan and Jackee had one last date before tryouts. They went roller skating and then spent two hours talking at the malt shop. They agreed that there will be no dates during the upcoming season. Both were going out for spring sports. Dan was a lacrosse player as well as a football player. Jackee had seen him play in the fall and saw he was a very good athlete. She had known he was an honor student because he was in some of her advanced classes. His athletic ability was a complete surprise. They finally agreed that the first Saturday after their season ends will be a date night.

March 1st finally came, It had been a long and hard winter. The days were still cold but they were getting longer with more sun every day. Jackee had completed her full program and was in the best shape of her life. On the days that were kinder she hit off her iron mike. Rose loaded the iron mike and kept it well fed while Jackee hit. After the hitting was done, running and catching was next on the list. Jackee noticed that Rose's arm was getting stronger all the time , and then realized so was hers. She thought that her arm was now in mid season shape. She diffidently was bigger and stronger than ever before and felt very positive about the approaching season.

Sunday before tryouts she spoke with William about what she could expect in the coming season. He said to her, "what you encountered playing in the summer league would probably be much more than you will see in high school. Now you know some of the players on the team and the others probably have heard about you. There should be no surprises during tryouts. Scrimmages, non league games and league games will be different. Teams that you play in the league will be prepared for the fact that you will play and your ability will also be known to them. Expect trouble from Bender and Travis. Remember the higher level you go, the greater the bench jockeying will be. Some of it may be off-color and some will be vicious."

Tryouts started at 4:00 on Monday. Coach Begali and Singer had 50 candidates out on the field. The Varsity team will carry 16 players, JV will carry 18 to 20 players. It was a normal March day, sunny, but cold. A player never gets loose on days like this. You throw, run and do other things to warm up and then you stand around and wait to hit or field. By the time they are ready for you everything has cooled down. Although the infield had not yet been worked on by the grounds workers it still looked to be in fairly good shape. Jackee decided to start hitting ground balls. Without trying to be bossy, she organized the infielders as Bats had done in the summer program. Players trying out for the left side of the infield will hit a ground ball to the right side players. There would be hitters, feeders and retrievers. After the infielder fields a ground ball he throws it to the retriever, who then gives it to the feeder who in turn gives the next ball to the hitter. If the infielder missed the ball the players backing him up would get the ball and throw it to the retriever. Jackee had two separate groups working together. When each fielder had his 25 ground balls, he switched places with one of his backups. After all the right side players were finished they switched places with the hitting group. That group now received 25 ground balls. Just as the last infielder finished, Coach Begali called on them to hit.

Hitters were told that they had 10 swings off a live arm. If they took a pitch that the catcher called a strike, they lost one of their swings. This prevented a player from standing at the plate all day waiting for a perfect pitch. Jackee took her turn at bat and put 10 balls in play. There were a few line drives and one ball that hit the left field fence on one bounce. Even wearing batting gloves on these cold days does not stop the sting you feel after hitting a baseball. Her hands had become callous from all the hitting she did over the winter, yet some pitches still made the hands tingle. As in most tryouts it is easy to see players who had not prepared and surely would not make either team.

Coach Begali was talking to Coach Singer. "Did you see the way Miss Jenco organized the infield practice and that not one player complained. I do believe that she will be my captain in her junior year. She should be one now but I don't dare choose a 10th grader over a senior. If she failed to do well after the season started it would destroy the cohesiveness of the team."

Tryouts lasted two weeks and in that time 13 boys dropped out, leaving 37 to fill the two teams. Begali picked his 16 and one boy was let go because he was a senior and would not be allowed to take a spot on the JV team. Coach Singer was intending to keep 18 players anyway so when two more boys quit because they did not make varsity, his team roster was complete.

Practices became more organized with the smaller groups. Now there was more time for hitting and fielding, plus the fact that the days were getting longer and a bit warmer. Players were now getting to know one another and positions were being assigned. There is an old saying in baseball that to be a good team you must be strong up the middle. Shortstop, second base combination is the glue that holds that theory together. Turning a double play can break the back of any rally. Getting two outs on one play either ends the inning or reduces the opponent to only one out.

Sonny Swift was the second baseman and the team's leadoff hitter. He was a junior with good hands and a strong arm. As soon as Jackee appeared on the field in early March he introduced himself and said "I am your second baseman." This was followed up by, "because of your great range we should turn more double plays this year so let's work together as much as we can." If Jackee had any doubts about her standing on the team, they disappeared immediately.

The combination of Jackee and Sonny were a big hit right from the start. They knew where the other would be on every play. Sometimes they would just throw the ball to the base and know the other one would be there to catch it. Coach Begali was amazed how well they played together and told Singer they were the best double play combination he had ever seen in high school. In the four scrimmages they played prior to opening their league season, Jackee and Sonny turned four double plays and only played in parts of those games.

Jackee batting in her usual third place in the order hit over .500 and was on base over 65% of the time. Sonny hit over .375 and always seemed to be on base. Coach Begali selected an excellent second hitter. His unusual name was Jesse James. Jesse was a good hitting junior, who played the outfield, had average speed and just a fair arm. His biggest quality was that he always put the ball in play. His bat control was well above average and he was a great hit and run batter. Number four hitter was Jesse's brother, naturally, he was called Frank. Their parents must have had a great sense of humor. Frank was a senior with a deadly bat and a very strong arm. If the pitchers held the runners on first close to the bag, Frank would throw them out stealing. Even if they got a good jump he still found a way to get some of them. Last key piece to the strong up the middle theory was the center fielder named Scott Sanders. Scott was one of the fastest runners in the school. He had a strong arm and a very productive bat. The track coach begged Begali to let him run in track meets when not playing a game. With Scott, Frank, Sonny, and Jackee, the Reagan Rockets were the best up the middle team at least in their league.

Four scrimmages of the best opponents Coach Begali could get were played before the regular season started. He always tried to pick superior teams so that his players would see good competition and raise their game. It seemed to the coach that if you played poor teams you got over confident and didn't try your best. As a result the team played great baseball and won all the scrimmages easily. The team was now ready for league play.

All league games start in early April and Reagan's first series was against Bender. Reagan would be the visiting team on Monday and Thursday. Once again the crowds started building as the weather improved. Many more fans were attending and many of them were females. Coach Begali was not surprised when he saw the stands half full while his team was practicing before the game. When the game started 75% of the stands were occupied and fans were still coming in. Coach knew why most of them were there and it wasn't to see a high school baseball game. They came to see something new and they were not disappointed. Sonny reached first on an infield single and Jessie followed with a hit and run single to right. With runners on first and third Jackee stepped to the plate wearing her usual number seven. On the third pitch she saw, Jackee lined an outside curve down the right field line. When the ball got back to the infield Jackee had a stand up triple and two RBI's. The applause and cheering from the stands sent a chill up Jackee's spine, and she knew the crowd was on her side. From this point on it was downhill for Bender. Coach used every player in the 14 to 1 romp.

Game two at home was Jackee's debut in front of the home crowd. When she batted in the bottom of the first inning, she was given a standing ovation by the packed stands on both sides of the field. Once again she rose to the occasion by driving in Jessie from second after he hit a double. She lined a single to center. This game also was a blowout by a 12 to 2 score. Game three was the only close game and Reagan won that 7 to 3. Game four, played at home, was once again well attended and Jackee gave them something to cheer about. In the bottom of the sixth, with two outs and nobody on base, she hit her first varsity home run. A line drive down the leftfield line that was just fair and barely cleared the fence. Reagan completed the sweep by a 13 to 0 rout. Bender scored a total of 6 runs in four games. When they allowed her to hit, Jackee drove in 7 runs and scored 8 and went 7 for 9 with 7 walks.

Howell was the second league series. Although they were a bigger school than Reagan, there was nothing they could do to prevent a sweep. Once again the crowds at both fields surprised the Howell coach but not Coach Begali. He loved having his team in front of large crowds. Each of the Howell games had been a blowout and coach Begali was having fun. He felt he was getting even for all the times his team had been on the other side of the score.

Jackee had another great series but this time her fielding was dominant. Game three at home, Howell had 2 men on base with 2 outs and the score tied at 2 all in the top of the sixth . Howell's number 6 hitter, a lefty, blooped a ball down the leftfield line. Jessie had earlier moved toward left center and the third baseman was playing half way because this batter could bunt and had excellent speed. The batter had faked a bunt on the first pitch to bring the third baseman in so he could hit either by him or over his head. As it turned out he fell away from an outside fastball and hit this bloop off the end of the bat. Jackee, realizing that she was the only one able to make a play, sprinted full out to where she anticipated the ball would drop and at the last second spotted the ball and flat out dove for it.

She caught the ball in her glove but hit the ground hard, knocking the wind from her lungs and causing the ball to pop up. With a desperate lunge she recaught the ball in the webbing and just lay prone on the field. This almost was a replay of her catch against Bender the year before, except on that play she held the ball immediately. The umpire checked that she had the ball, he signaled and called "out." The stands erupted in a wild cheer, even the Howell fans were on their feet cheering. Coach Begali and everyone on the field ran to where Jackee laid. Jessie, Hoot, the third baseman were the first to get there but they did not touch her. Coach Begali turned her over and lifted her belt as she started to breathe. There were tears in her eyes as she said, did I hold the ball?" Coach said not only did you hold it but it is yours to keep. He slowly got her up and walked her back to the dugout. While they were walking the fans were still cheering. Her whole team was at the dugout waiting to greet her. Just before entering the dugout she looked up at Carmela in the stands and saw tears in her eyes. All Jackee could do is mouth the words "I am okay." Jackee hadn't realized that they were tears of joy and not sorrow.

More often than not in a ballgame, after making a great play the batter hits in the inning. Jackee did hit in the bottom of the sixth with the bases loaded. There was only one out and she was looking for a pitch she could drive to the outfield so that the go ahead run would score. Howell's coach had seen enough of her and told the pitcher not to give her anything good to hit. The pitcher followed orders and walked her on four pitches allowing the tie breaking run to score. Reagan still had the bases loaded and Frank coming to bat. He hit a fly ball over the centerfielder's head and all three runners scored on his double. Howell went down in order in the top of the seventh. Final score was 7 to 2. Game four was never in doubt and Howell quietly lost 8 to 0. This gave Reagan an 8 game winning streak.

The series against Bristle and Meeker were all Reagan. They never trailed in any game and every player was in almost all of the games. To everyone's surprise the team's fifth pitcher pitched a complete game shutout in game four against Meeker allowing only three hits and two walks. Sonny and Jackee turned two double plays bringing their total to eight for the year. Reagan now has a 16 game winning streak and never in the school's history has the baseball team ever gone undefeated. In fact outside of wrestling, no other team in the school had completed an undefeated season.

Last series of the season was against their arch rival Travis. Because of their attitude toward winning, they were not a likable team. Game one would be at Travis and it would be an important one. Travis had only one loss. At 15 and 1 they are guaranteed a berth in the playoffs. However, if they beat Reagan three out of four, they could not only win the league title but also have home field advantage in the whole Championship round. Game one produced a full house at Travis field. Jackee was still the main attraction as clearly many more women were present than usually attended. Coach Begali was glad because for some reason Jackee seemed to raise the level of her game when large numbers of fans were present. When she did raise her level it seems to spread to the other players. Defense dominated game one as the score remained tied at 1 since the second inning. Jackee doubled in the first inning and scored on Frank's base hit to right field. Travis scored in the second inning on a walk and two hits. Since then it was a pitchers duel. Travis' coach walked Jackee in the third inning with two outs and she stole second but Frank lined out to the third baseman to end the inning. Coach Begali had not wanted her to steal in the sixth inning after she drew another walk. He wanted Frank to hit and not be intentionally walked. This was really a good call since Frank hit a 2 and 1 pitch over the left field fence. Travis did load the bases in the bottom of the seventh with two outs but Reagan's pitcher struck out a pinch hitter for the final out.

Game two away was critical for Travis. If they lost, Reagan would win the league title and they would be second. This was their final chance. The coach tried giving a pep talk to the team but the Travis players knew that winning the next three games, and two being at Reagan, left them little hope. They did feel that they had a better chance in the championship round since they would only have to beat Reagan once.

This game resembled the first game except that Reagan left many runners on base. The score was 2 to 2 and Regan had seven men left on base in four innings. In the top of the seventh with the score still tied at two each, Travis scored a run. Scott Sanders tried to make a shoestring catch on a line drive to center with two outs. He missed the catch and the ball rolled to the fence. By the time Jesse could get to the ball and get it to the relay man, the Travis player had circled the bases and scored the tie breaking run. Travis now led 3 to 2. Scott came into the dugout and told the pitcher it was his fault, he should have played it safe and fielded the ball on one bounce.

Reagan batted in the last of the seventh. With one out and nobody on base Sonny singled to left. Jessie followed this by hitting a single to right on a hit and run. Reagan now had runners on first and third with Jackee coming to the plate. Coach went to the mound and told the pitcher, "she beat the JV last year by hitting a high inside pitch. I want you to pitch carefully and keep the ball down and away but not over the plate." After two pitches, Jackee was now sitting on a 2-0 pitch. The coach signaled the catcher to call a curveball. Most people figured he would throw a fastball so he doesn't fall behind 3-0. If possible you never want to put the winning run on second. Earlier in the game Jackee had picked up on the fact that when the pitcher threw a curve, he held his glove differently when he set his fingers for a curve ball. When he took his sign, she saw the glove indicate that a curve ball was coming. She could afford to guess wrong and take a pitch if she was wrong. She prepared herself for a curve ball and saw the ball breaking toward the outside. Hitting just under the curve she drilled the ball to right center field. When the ball hit the 340 foot sign in right center field, the game was over and Reagan was the new league champion. Jackee was credited with a double because that is the last base she touched. If she had walked to third she would have gotten a triple. Fans were on their feet as soon as the ball left the bat. Everyone converged onto the field. As Jackee was trotting in, her teammates grabbed her and carried her off the field. Reagan had their first league title in baseball and still had an undefeated season.

Jenco's family was leading the cheering and Rose was trying to find the game winning ball. Coach Begali took care of that. He got the ball from Travis right fielder and gave it to Jackee. Before Jackee went home he would have someone put the game score, teams and date on the ball and have every team member sign it. The booster club had prepared a small buffet in the school cafeteria and a caterer was preparing to deliver more goodies within the hour. It's good to have a player's parent, who has a catering business in town, and a parent who is a policeman, that can guarantee the food will arrive on time. Everyone who was still at the game was invited to attend. Without telling anyone, Sy Weeks had made arrangements for section 6 to present the trophy to the team tonight. Out of nowhere someone touched Jackee's shoulder and she turned to see Dan standing there. Without realizing what she was doing she threw her arms around him. He held her and said he had seen many of her games but never wanted her to know he was there. Nothing was harder than watching her get hurt when she made that spectacular catch to save the game against Howell. He had to call her teammates to find out if she was hurt and how bad. Jackee had trained herself not to look into or hear anything from the stands. This was a protective device against anyone trying to interfere with her game. Jackee and Dan went to the celebration in the school.

Wednesday was a fast practice since most everyone was still exhausted from the night before. Mostly stretching and hitting with the next pitchers preparing for the last two games. Coach Begali called an informal team meeting after the practice. He asked the players how they wanted to play the final two games. Do we go for the undefeated season or do we get everyone into the game and just get ready for the championship round. After a very short discussion they all agreed that an undefeated season would be the hallmark of a champion.

The next game at Travis had fewer Travis fans. In fact there were differently more Reagan fans in the stands. Begali's team just exploded and everyone in the lineup had one hit and many had multiple hits. The top four batters had 10 hits. Altogether Reagan had 19 hits and scored 15 runs. Getting blown out away is bad enough with a bus ride home but getting blown out at home in front of your fans is devastating. Coach Begali put all his backups and even used pitchers in the lineup.

Friday's game four was played on a beautiful spring day. It was a great day for baseball and the fans came out to cheer their team on to an undefeated season. Since almost no Travis fans showed up, Reagan fans filled both sides of the field. Once again the Travis coach tried to get his team up for the game. He told them, "let's break Reagan's winning streak." His team responded in a half hearted way. Their pitcher did retire Reagan in order for the first two innings but Travis also failed to score. Bottom of the third the seventh batter for Reagan led off the inning with a walk. The number eight batter laid down a perfect bunt and beat the throw to first. The ninth batter bunted both runners up a base and with one out Sonny was intentionally walked to load the bases. Jessie hit a long fly to center scoring Reagan's first run. Jackee now was up with two outs. She hit a drive to left field that the fielder let roll through his legs. Both runners scored and Jackee ended up on third. Frank finished the scoring in the inning by hitting the first pitch over the left field fence giving Reagan a 5 to 0 lead. Whatever life Travis may have had was now completely gone. They did manage a few hits and even scored a run but for all practical purposes the game was over. When the Reagan relief pitcher struck out the last Travis batter a huge cellabration started. As the Travis players were getting on their bus to leave, people from the stands, parking lot and school were pouring onto the field. The booster club and most clubs and teams were coming to congratulate the new undefeated team. This show of school spirit really gave the baseball team a big lift.

First game of the championship series was to start the following Friday. Number one seed Reagan was to play the number four seed Bender at home at 4:00pm. While the second seed Travis was to play the third seed Howell at home also at 4:00pm. Coach Begali had been thinking about his pitching rotation and about who they would play. His pitching was easy to figure since all his pitchers were unbeaten. Anyone of his first four pitchers could pitch any of the games. He knew what Bender had and unless his team just fell apart they should be able to win the game. Final game could be different. Everyone expected Travis to be the opponent but Begali was not so sure. He saw something in the final Travis game that only a coach might notice. Travis looked like they lost more than a game, it appeared to Begali that they really lost heart. Everyone figures to lose a game but you bounce back and fight to win the next game. When you lose heart, the desire, drive or whatever you want to call it, it's gone. Begali knew Howell had a good number one pitcher and was not a bad hitting team. He also knew if Howell took it to them early in the game, Travis would fold like a cheap suit.

Sure enough when Friday came Reagan defeated Bender by a near blowout and Howell rolled over Travis in a rump. These last two games played by Travis were shameful losses and that had never happened to them before. This might give hope to the other teams in the league that they can be competitive against the bigger schools.

Saturday, the day of the championship game, Jackee had her usual light breakfast with the family. She left for the game at 8:30 and arrived at the nurses office at 8:45. A nurse was always available when a sporting event took place at the high school. Coach Begali knew about this so he asked the nurse if Jackee could change in her office, the nurse readily agreed and said she would like to talk with her. After Jackee changed and was heading out to practice the nurse did start talking to her. She asked if Jackee had any problems with the boys. "Every boy on the team treats me like a sister. I treat them like I was their older sister, but don't tell them I said that." Jackee did ask one very personal question. She told the nurse about the catch she made in the Howell game.

The nurse said "I was at the game and saw the whole thing. It was an amazing play and I was worried that you were hurt."

Now, Jackee said "I did get hurt but I was afraid to tell anyone for fear that they would take me out and not play me for a while. I'll tell you but you have to promise not to say anything to anyone." The nurse agreed and Jackee told her she had hit her chest very hard and her breasts were very sore. After a careful examination the nurse gave her a clean bill of health but recommended she wear an athletic halter to protect her chest. Jackee thanked her and said she would look into it. She headed for the field and for the first time in three weeks felt normal again.

Howell arrived early and was doing their normal pre game drills. Reagan players were also getting ready since they would be taking infield first. Sonny and Jackee were playing catch and going over Howell's hitters. Since they had played them a four game series, not much had to be changed. One thing was changed, however. They decided to switch coverage on steals and hit and runs. Howell used more hit and run since it was very difficult to steal on Frank. So Sonny suggested keeping them guessing would disrupt their strategy. He suggested they use the open mouth method. When the situation may come up he would shield his face with his glove and if his mouth is open he would cover the base. If his mouth is closed, Jackee will cover. They told Frank their plan and Jackee suggested that before the first pitch is thrown to the next hitter, Frank is to look at her and if she is covering, she would reset her cap.

While Howell was taking infield practice, Coach Begali went over the signs for the game. Although he gave very few signs during a game he always wanted them to look for one. His philosophy of the game was to just let the players play. Good players seem to grow better if you let them just do what you taught them. Following Howell's time on the field opening ceremonies were held. Introduction of all players and coaches, exchange of lineup cards and the National Anthem. Lastly, the cry of "Play Ball."

First inning was very fast and quiet. Howell went down in order. After two were out Jackee walked, but Frank hit a long fly to right center and the center fielder made a nice running catch. Second and third innings had a few baserunners for each team but neither team scored. In the fourth inning Howell had a runner on first with one out. Sonny gave a closed mouth sign to Jackee and she in turn reset her cap looking at Frank. The runner broke for second and the batter hit a ground ball directly at Sonny, he fielded the grounder and flipped the ball to Jackee, who was already at second base and she fired a strike to first, completing a well executed double play. In the bottom of the fifth Jeese led off with a single and on a hit and run Jackee lined a ball into right center. The centerfielder raced over and did backhand the ball before it got by him and made a perfect throw to the cutoff man who in turn threw a strike home and the catcher put the tag on Jesse sliding into home plate. Jackee took second on the throw home. Frank was walked intentionally. Jackee knew she could get a good jump off second and proceeded to steal third on the first pitch to Scott. He later hit a 2 and 1 pitch to right field that the fielder caught but had no chance to throw Jackee out at the plate. After 5 innings Reagan led 1 to 0. Howell had a rally going in the sixth when the first two batters hit singles. With runners on first and third and no outs the next hitter hit the ball up the middle on the second base side. Sonny made a dive and backhanded the ball and flipped the ball over second base. While the ball was in the air Jackee at full speed caught the ball as she stepped on second and fired a strike to first barely gettin the hitter. Even though they got the double play, the tying run still scored.

Bottom of the seventh, the game was still tied at one each. After Jesse lined out to the second baseman, Jackee batted. She hit a line drive off the glove of the third baseman. By the time he recovered the ball she was on first. With the count 0 and 2 on Frank, the pitcher threw a curve ball in the dirt and it got away from the catcher allowing Jackee to take second. On the next pitch Frank hit a ball between the first and second baseman, and it looked to be a base hit. The first baseman backhanded the ball and made a perfect throw to the pitcher covering first. As soon as the pitcher took the throw he turned around and fired a strike to the catcher. Jackee had to hold third. The count on Scott went to 0 and 2. Jackee remembered that every time the pitcher had an 0 and 2 count on the hitter he threw a curve ball down trying to get the batter to go after a bad pitch. As soon as the pitcher split his hands, Jackee, who had a walking lead, broke for home. The pitcher realizing that this was a steal attempt tried to hurry up his wind up and just threw a fastball. This was not what the catcher had expected and he had trouble adjusting to the pitch. Jackee slid under the tag and was called safe by the home plate umpire. Most of the fans did not realize what had just happened and it took a while before the cheers started. Players, fans and family poured onto the field. Howell players were just stunned by what just happened. Very few if any had ever seen a steal of home plate. None of the coaches had ever seen one with two strikes on the batter.

Sometime later, after all the celebration was done and the championship trophy given to Reagan by section 6, Begali took Jackee aside and asked her about

the steal. She told him that they had discussed the possibility of such a play earlier in the season. "Everyone agreed that the best time would be when the other
team least expected it to happen. Two outs and two strikes seemed to be a perfect
time. The pitcher ahead on the count, probably would try and make the batter
go after a bad pitch. I gave the sign to Scott and hoped he remembered it. His
main job was to protect the plate and keep the catcher from blocking the plate.
If the catcher did, Scott just had to swing and his bat would be interfered with,
the umpire would call obstruction. This would create a dead ball situation and
Scott would be awarded first and I have to go back to third. See it was a win,win
situation and she laughed." Begali told her that he fully agreed with the section 6
committee when they awarded her the MVP trophy for the tournament, he just
wished it was bigger. He also retrieved the ball from Howell's catcher. It had been
signed by the team and all the necessary details added. Like so many others, this
ball ended up in the hands of Rose.

While the celebration was going on Dan had worked his way to Jackee
and once again touched her shoulder. She turned toward him and said I missed
you in the stands. Dan said he was in the parking lot watching the game but came
to the field in the sixth inning. He didn't want to make her nervous. While accepting congratulations from fans, teammates and family she held Dan's hand. She
reminded him that they had a date Saturday evening.

Saturday at 7:00 sharp Dan rang Jenco's doorbell. Rose opened the door
and escorted him into the living room. Rose said Jackee will be down in a few
minutes. She asked if he was coming to Jackee's 17th birthday party. Dan said he
hadn't been invited yet. Rose said "I'm inviting you and you better not disappoint
me." He smiled and said he would never refuse her invitation. William walked
into the room, welcomed Dan and invited him to Jackee's birthday party. Laughing, he told him Rose already invited him. Jackee came down and apologized for
keeping him waiting. He said Rose had made him feel at home. She walked over
to Rose and gave her a big hug and thanked her. As they were leaving Dan said
they had no real plans for the evening but he would have her home by midnight
if that was acceptable.

Starting the first Saturday in June, the recreation department has some
kind of entertainment at the local park. It was free and most times it is a dance
type of entertainment. Tonight there is a disc jockey playing music from every
generation. There are mostly young people here but some older couples usually
come to the dancing entertainment. They danced for a while then sat down to
catch up on what had happened since March 1st. Jackee started first by saying "I
don't know if I should say this but I missed you. I felt like one of my family was
missing."

Dan said he felt basically the same but he knew what she was trying to do
and he did not want to interfere in any way. He said he was so proud of her and

what she accomplished. "I never met anyone who had the drive and courage that you have." Jackee told him that she did not want him to hide in the background. She wanted him close by from now on. He agreed to be at as many of her games as he can. They danced and talked for the rest of the night. When the music ended they went to the malt shop for ice cream. What neither one of them suspected was how popular Jackee had become. Since this was a local shop in a small town everyone now knew her name and what she had done. They were offered all the ice cream they could eat for free. Most of the people in the store congratulated her or asked for an autograph. When things started to quiet down they finally had their ice cream and barely had time to make it home. When they got to the front door of Jackee's house, she hugged him and apologized for ruining their evening. He said "there will be many more like this because she is a one of a kind player. Don't ever feel bad about it. Just keep going and try to be the best. I'll try to help just like your family does." She had her arms around him and would not let go. Finally he kissed her and said she better get inside or he will be in trouble with William. She asked him if he would come to her house after church. He said he'd try.

CHAPTER SIX

Jackee Plays Second Year of Summer Baseball

*D*an arrived at about eleven. He joked about how he did not want to miss lunch. The family had just returned home from church so Carmela hadn't prepared anything yet. Most of the family headed for the living room. Rebecca and her fiance Rocco, Jackee and Dan, Evelyn and William, were just sitting down when the doorbell rang again. Rose, who was helping Carmela prepare lunch, ran to the door. She was startled at first by the size of the man but then she recognized him as Dad's friend. Bats came into the house and were shown directly into the living room. William greeted him and introduced him to Rocco and Dan. Carmela came in, said welcome, and asked if Bats would join them for lunch. Bats thanked her and said only if she had real Marine chow. William laughly told Bats, Carmela made the best s.o.s this side of Parris Island.

When everyone settled down William asked what Bats was doing here. Bats said "would you believe I was in the neighborhood and just decided to stop in?"

Shaking his head William said only if I believed in the Easter Bunny.

Bats said he came up to talk about what Jackee had in mind for the summer. "She told me last year that she would like to play one more summer with me. Through some of my friends locally I have kept current as to how she did this spring. I am aware of the great year and all that she accomplished. 1 minute after she slid home to win the championship I was called with the full description of the game." Looking directly at Jackee he asked "are you still interested in playing for me this summer?"

Jackee looked at William, and he just gave her a sign that this was her decision. She said to Bats, "I learned so much from being one summer with you and I truly believe there is so much more to learn. Will you let me play on your team and teach me more?"

· Bats laid out a whole new plan he had come up with. New teams, a new schedule and a complete campaign with Jackee as the center of attraction. Jackee immediately refused saying all the boys on the team would resent her being cast as the star of the team. Bats told her he knew this would go against her wishes but there are other considerations. "First and most important you are a one of a kind athlete. There have been many great women athletes, but none of them played baseball. Even if one did, they are nowhere as good as you are. If I did not know you and someone brought me your accomplishments and told me all about you, it would be my opinion that this is an athlete headed for great things. Jackee you can't hide what you do on the field any more than you can hide the fact that you are a beautiful girl. What I want to do is make you the main attraction rather than a sideshow. I realize that this may put a great amount of pressure directly on you. You showed me last season no matter how much pressure you had, you handled it without a problem. Without any publicity except word of mouth you caused our attendance to add 50% more fans. Even the other teams saw a dramatic increase in their fan base. If we put out a campaign letting people know who you are, it would double our fan base and at least double our contributions. One of our contributors is willing to supply all your cosmetic needs free of charge." Jackee immediately jumped in and said she can't accept these gifts for fear of losing her ameture standings. "Kim wants you to stay with her if you decide to play and she is more than happy to accept all these gifts. She also said Jackee has no need since she has natural beauty but I need all I can get."

A big smile crossed Jackee's face and she said "I would love to stay with Kim and she needs less than I do." William and Carmela agreed that the choice was for only Jackee to make since she is the one who has to live with it. Jackee did agree with the understanding she and Bats would address this to the team once it is formed.

During lunch Rebecca and Rocco announced that their wedding date had been set for the second Saturday in September. All the sisters would be brides-maids along with another of her friends. Rose would not be out of place because Rocco had a thirteen year old brother who is a perfect match for her. The three girls immediately offered to help any way she needed them to. Rebecca told Jack-ee that she has to concentrate on her summer program and mom and the other three girls would be plenty.

Later, Jackee and Dan went for a walk and she asked him if he had any thoughts on what Bats had said. He looked her in the eye and said, "your mom and dad made it very clear that only you can make the decision and only you are responsible for carrying it out. I'll miss you very much and I'll drive to some of your games or maybe come with your family. You know I have a summer Job and I need the money for college applications and such."

She squeezed his hand and said for the first time in her life she wished she didn't have to play baseball this summer. Dan grabbed her by the shoulders and said, "don't ever say that. You have worked so hard to get where you are and many people are behind you and support what you are doing. I never want to be the cause of you not trying or failing. No matter where you are I'll always be with you and no matter what you decide to do, I'll back the decision 100%."

June 13th and Jackee's 17th birthday was on a Friday, folklore suggests that this day is a day when weird things happen. This was not the case for Jackee. As usual on anyone's birthday Carmela prepared their favorite breakfast. When Jackee came downstairs she found blueberry pancakes, melted butter and maple syrup. Milk and juice completed the breakfast. A birthday card from the family was under her plate. All her birthday mornings since she could remember were with the whole family. Rose of course had been there since she was adopted. William announced that tonight Carmela would get the night off as they were headed for their favorite restaurant to celebrate. Jackee knew that next year Rebbeca would be married and probably not be able to be at her breakfast but she hoped she would make her 18th birthday dinner. Carmela made sure that Dan and Rocco were invited to the restaurant.

6:00 the Jenco's arrived at the restaurant and found Dan and Rocco waiting. Soon they were seated and all the food was ordered. What was now becoming a constant thing, people came up to their table to congratulate Jackee and get an autograph. Mostly the younger girls had her sign a special book or most often a baseball. She was blushing and kept apologizing to the family. Actually the family had this happen often but for Dan and Rocco it was a new experience. Dan had it happen to them at the malt shop, and at the time he thought it was a one shot deal. Now he realized just how popular Jackee was and how important it was for her to continue. He said out loud to the parents, "you must be so proud of her and what she has accomplished and the great potential for what she is capable of doing." Rocco had no idea what was going on. He thought it was rude for people to interfere with a person's night out.

Jackee reached out, took Dan's hand and whispered "thank you." When the meal was finished the lights were lowered and a beautiful birthday cake fully decorated with lighted candles came rolling out to Jenco's table. The cake had been ordered by William but unknown to him, was paid in part by the local girl scout troop. The bakery's owner had actually made the cake for free and only charged the girl scouts one dollar so they could claim credit for it. All his children graduated from Reagan high school, his son played baseball, and his two daughters softball.

After Jackee blew out the candles and cut the cake, pieces were first given to the Jenco family and their guests. Jackee asked if a piece of cake would be given to anyone in the restaurant who requested it. When all had been served a small piece remained, it was carefully wrapped and given to Jackee to take home. William tried to pay the bill but the owner told him his family coming here increased his business by 25%. A fifty dollar tip was left for the staff and the owner was thanked for a great evening. Dan drove Jackee home and they spent some time talking in the driveway. She thanked him for his words at the restaurant and hoped that he really meant them. He said they were his true feelings and how he felt about her would not change. After a good night kiss, she said "we have two more Saturdays before I leave. Then, if you're available, I'll see you tomorrow at 6:30."

"I'm not only available but I will be waiting." She got out of the car and Dan said, "see you" and drove away.

The next two Saturdays were almost exactly the same. They drove to the park, danced, had refreshments and talked. Only difference was that last Saturday they again went to the malt shop. Fewer people stopped to talk to Jackee but she was still popular among the younger girls. Dan commented on the fact that people are still congratulating you and seeking your autograph. Jackee told him how at first, it had frightened her, now she just just accepts it. She told him she was leaving Sunday for the summer baseball program and that she would really miss him. He said he felt the same and that he would try to attend as many of her games as possible. They kissed and with tears in her eyes she got out of the car and headed inside. Both parents were up. They had packed the SUV and prepared food for the trip. As Jackee came in they saw her crying and went to her. All she said was "I know I have to do this but it really hurts to leave Dan."

William told her "if it hurts you know it's real." She hugged her mom and dad before going to her room.

Driving down to Dutch Hill was very somber. After the 8:00am mass they had a quick breakfast and headed out by ten. Less than four hours later they were in front of Kim's house. Bats came out to meet them followed by Kim. She hugged Jackee and said how glad she was to have her favorite roommate back. They took in all the luggage and William gave Kim a check for thirteen hundred dollars. Kim started to refuse but William insisted that this was the only way Jackee could stay with her. She thanked him and asked them to have a snack she had prepared especially for them. When they finished eating and putting away all the clothes and gear, they said their goodbyes and Carmela, William and Rose headed home. After Bats left, Kim and Jackee settled in, getting reacquainted. Jackee told Kim about Dan and how happy she was to have found someone like him. Kim mentions she and Bats had a few dates and she found him to be the most gentle and kindest man she ever met.

"Gentle!" Jackee screamed, "are we talking about the same person?"

"I know how he is on the baseball field but with me he is like a soft teddy bear. I just melt in his arms and feel like this is where I want to be." laughed Kim.

"Well Kim, you see him in a totally different environment. We see a leader, the guardian of our team, you see a companion who probably adores you."

Jackee asked Kim if she knew anything about his plans for promoting her. Kim said she did and that "all the plans centered on promoting the fact that not only are you playing but you are one of the stars. He told me that he is trying to keep your wish in mind. Trying to promote the fact that a female is featured on the field but is also trying to portray you as one of the stars and not the star. Because he believes you are the star of the team, it's hard for him to not just say that. I think he believes you are being short changed by not getting full recognition for your talents. There is also fear that the pressure might be too much for a Seventeen year old to handle and that it will affect your game. He feels you need to be promoted but not destroyed. We both believe that the program he planned will protect you as well as promote you safely."

Monday morning at the first scheduled practice, Bats laid out his usual speech plus this year's new program. He introduced Jackee to the players by saying, "this young lady will be protected by you at all costs. Last year she was the MVP of our tournament, and I can tell you she has grown and improved since then. You will treat her as the team captain because she more than earned that title. Because of her you have new uniforms and equipment. Because of her each of you who make the team will receive a new pair of custom fitted shoes and a new glove. Because of her we will have better travel means and better sleeping arrangements when we have to stay overnight. All she gets out of this is the same as you plus all the abuse the other team can throw at her. I expect you to respect her on and off the field, just like you would another teammate. Also, to protect her from the other teams and fans. Jackee has been trained not to fight back, except with her glove and bat. I was trained to protect those who can not protect themselves. It is what America is all about and I want to see you carry that flag."

Bats then introduced his three assistants Coaches Reese, Morgan and Subert. Kim was introduced and she explained what her job entailed. Finally the 32 boys were told that nineteen would make his team and one or two may be on the taxi squad. This consisted of players who could be called upon to fill in for players hurt, quit or on emergency leave. "Now get out to the field and let's start building a championship team."

Practices seemed to be better organized and many new drills and exercises had been added. Since Jackee had kept up with her conditioning she found the new exercises to be very stimulating. It seemed that every boy was trying to keep up with her. She did not understand why this was happening but she thought it was good for the team. That night when she mentioned it to Kim she told her that it was ego. "They probably never had a girl beat them at anything and it was unthinkable that one could be a better athlete than they are. You hurt their pride and this will drive them to do better. Bats had expected and hoped this would happen and when they see what you can do they will respect you and you will never be questioned again." Jackee thought hard about what Kim had said and decided she was right and she would have to push herself harder to keep ahead of them and act like a team leader.

When the fielding part of tryouts came, Jackee was doing better than most. She did notice one player who had soft hands, a strong arm and very good range. Coach Reese, the infield coach, had called out a couple of " good jobs" in his direction. Jackee approached coach Reese and asked if it would be alright for her to start working a double play combination with that ballplayer. Realizing that Jackee was not only a good ballplayer but also had an eye for talent, he gave her approval to work with him. Early on the third day of practice she did her stretching next to him. She said "my name is Jackee and I would like to work with you on turning double plays."

He said "my name is Edward Thomas but my friends call me ET. I would really like to work with you because you are so talented. Just watching you helped me raise my game."

Immediately they started to practice. Someone hit ET 25 ground balls all over the second base area and he had to field them and throw a strike over second base. Jackee would have to be at the bag or running across it and catch each ball while stepping on the base. Then it was reversed and Jackee would field 25 ground balls and throw to ET over at second. When Coach Reese mentioned this to Bats, he nodded and said "I knew she would pick him because I already penciled him in as my second baseman. I only hope he can hit." They now had three iron mikes and cages set up at Baseball Paradise. This was part of the deal Bats made with the company. All Jackee had to do was take a picture standing next to the machine. Jackee was to receive nothing in return. The players hit off the iron mike and then off a live arm. Coaches provided the live arms until the pitches were ready to throw off the mound.

Five boys decided to leave and go home. One other was found drunk in his room. He was never seen again at tryouts. Practice was becoming more intense. New drills and longer practices were now part of the day. In the week that followed one boy was injured and decided to leave another boy just plain disappeared. One day he was there, the next day he was gone. All the coaches agreed that since two of the four who might be let go were pitchers they would be kept on the taxi squad as backups and batting practice pitchers.

There was a week before the first game. This year Bats booked many new and more competitive teams. Jackee did not know that she was the main reason why these teams decided to play the Dukes. They all charged admission and figured to advertise that a female ball player was coming to town. Bats had made it known that Jackee's appearance had increased spectator interest by at least 40%.

Jackee and ET were the talk of the camp. They did everything together but sleep. To seal this relationship, Bats found out that ET could really handle a bat and made him the number two hitter in front of Jackee. Number one hitter was Lightning, a fast contact hitter who played centerfield. The fourth hitter was Moose, a big, strong, power hitting catcher. Number 5 & 6 were Howie the first baseman and Stoney, a right fielder, who had a cannon for an arm. At 7 & 8 were Randy at third and Chuck in left. Bats had three players he could use for DH. These were players who could hit the ball but their defense was not as good as some others. Every starting player had a backup who could fill in if the need presented itself.

Opening day was against the Flashers. They were basically the same team that the Dukes beat in the finals last year. Since this was to be a double header on Sunday the Jenco's, with Dan in tow, came to the game. What they and the almost full house witnessed was a well trained team playing a very good one. There was very little competition on the field. With ET and Jackee leading the way, the Dukes won both games. Just as Bats had assumed many more women came to the game. As the announcer told the crowd before the game began, there is still no admission charge to attend the games but we do ask that you make a voluntary contribution to help defray some of the overhead. A fifty fifty and a few donated door prizes were given away each game. Bats told the county executor that they would take in more money doing this instead of charging admission. He was right. People were very generous after watching the game and also with the fifty fifty during the game.

The Dukes were to play 40 games in 8 weeks and the championship, the week before Labor Day. They played two games on Sunday, one each on Tuesday, Wednesday and Friday nights. Every team had lights and with three off days for makeup games and travel time the schedule seemed workable. In game after game, Jackee helped lead the team and 70% of the time, won the game. Half way through the season the Dukes were 14 and 6. Jackee was leading the team in hitting and runs scored, Moose was leading in home runs, and Lightning in stolen bases. Their pitching staff was better than any they had seen so far. If they continued at this pace they should be one of the teams in the tournament. Bats had already figured that if the tournament committee wanted to make money, his team would have to be in it. He also reasoned that Jackee would be the big fan draw. Everywhere they went so far the crowds had been much more then anyone had expected. Jackee was a gold mine with a bat and glove and they all knew it.

Although she was reluctant at first to grant interviews, she slowly adapted to the fact they helped make the team popular. Interviews were only given on days off, never before or after a game. Jackee had consulted with Kim and they came up with a fool proof plan for each interview. She would always thank the county and her coaches, especially Bats. Then she would praise her teammates and tell how great they were and how fantastic she was treated by them. Next, she would tell how great the fans were at every field she played in. This was not always true and in fact some teams really tried to intimidate and abuse her. In those games most times her teammates or even some of the fans in the stands came to her defense. Kim could not believe how many offers Jackee received to advertise different products. The list went from cereal to makeup and at least 20 other products. She could have made a small fortune. There was even a rumor that a car dealer offered her family a new car if she agreed to do one ad for them. Her best time when she was not playing was talking to young girls and boys. She talked about her family, especially Rose and how all her sisters were close to each other. School was important and how she hoped to become a doctor one day. The hard work it takes to be a success and how nothing and nobody should stand in your way. Signing autographs was never done before a game, it was done after the game. Signing would last until it was time to travel or they threw her off the field.

Second half of the season was even better, the Dukes were 16 and 4, giving them a 30 and 10 overall record. Their pitching really started to produce quality outings. The four games they lost had nothing to do with the pitching. In the four games the team scored only 4 runs and the pitchers gave up only 9 runs. They were in every game right to the end. Bats congratulated the team for playing so well under the circumstances they faced. To prove his point he told the players they had been selected as the number one seed in the tournament. The top four teams will be the home team in the first round. Round two, of the four remaining teams, the two highest seed will be the home team. Round three will be the best 2 out of 3. The highest seed left will be the home team. Games will start on Tuesday, travel day Wednesday, second round on Thursday, travel day Friday, finals on Saturday with game one at 11:00am. One big thing Bats told his team, we can have home field advantage in the finals by winning the first two games. There is one time we will not, that is when game two of the finals is played. Visiting team will be the home team in game two. This is usually done so that you do not have to travel to their field. "It means they will bat last but it still will be on our field. Advantage Dukes."

Game one started at baseball paradise field at 6:30 pm. There was a full house to see the Dukes play the Dante Devils. The Dukes had played them during the summer and had swept all five games. Once again Jackee raised the level of her game by going 3 for 3 with 2 doubles, a single, and a walk. She had 2 RBI's and scored 3 runs. ET had an RBI, and scored 3 runs. Moose was the big stick with a homer, double, and 4 RBI's. When the game finally ended the score was, Dukes 12 Devils 1. Games played under the tournament committee had to have an admission charge to help pay the expenses for the tournament. The price was two dollars for adults, one dollar for 12 to 18, under twelve free, and families were five dollars for the whole family. In most cases, the normal Dukes' fans paid less than they usually donated for regular games.

Next game on Thursday was against the Bayhaven Crushers. During the summer the Dukes beat them 4 out of 5. They are considered a good team but far from great, and their fielding execution was poor. Their coach concentrated on hitting and had defense as an afterthought. He figured they could out score their opponents. That may work well if the opponent has average or poor pitching. This was not the Dukes team. Their pitching was superior to most other teams. Once again Lightning, ET, and Jackee lead the team. The top four batters had nine hits and three walks. They took advantage of every poor throw and fielding lapse the Crushers made. The Dukes easily won the game 14 to 2. The baseball axium "good pitching stops good hitting" prevailed in game two.

Dutch Hill Dukes enter the finals having outscored the first two teams 26 to 3. Their opponent in the finals was the second seed, the Tricity Panthers. This team was in the other division and supposedly the best team. Bats only had limited information on them. He had heard that the coach was upset when his team did not get top seed. The Panthers coach felt they played in a tougher division with much better teams. He thought that a power rating should have been used rather than just records. Their record was not too shabby as they were 29 and 10 with one game that could not be played.

The Jenco family, with Dan included, arrived Friday evening. Everyone had left work early so they could have supper with Jackee. She was so happy to see Dan that she ran over and kissed him first. This had never happened before but it was soon forgotten as she made her way down the line hugging and kissing every one. William encouraged Kim to come with them, and she finally gave in and joined them for dinner. Over various Italian dishes, Jackee was filled in on what was happening at home. All the wedding plans have been completed and two more fittings for the bride and bridesmaids still have to be done. Guests were sent invitations and we are waiting on responses. Rose told Jackie about her first track meet and that she won first place and a gold medal. Jackee said how proud she was of her and how there will be many more medals to win and her trophy case will eventually be full. Dan told her about his summer job and how he almost made enough money to pay for all his college applications. He also told her about a few college coaches who talked to him about attending their school. Most were division three schools with very little aid. He figured if he had a good football season this fall and a good spring in lacrosse the offers might get better,

After dinner, Jackee said she had to get to bed because batting practice was at 8:00 am. She looked at her dad and reminded him what a penchant Bats had about being punctual. Sleep Rest Inn was only two blocks from Kim's house. When they dropped Jackee and Kim off, Dan got out with them. They sat on the porch and talked for only ten minutes as it was getting late and Jackee needed her sleep. She hugged and kissed Dan and thanked him for coming. He told her to have the game of her life and really enjoy it. She smiled, thanked him again, and went inside.

Saturday morning at 7:00 am Jackee was up. She said a few prayers, had a light breakfast, changed into her uniform and headed for the field. All the coaches were there at 7:00 and everything was prepared for hitting. Stretching and a quick run around the field preceded batting. They hit in the batting order posted on the dugout wall. Starting players hit first for as long as they want. DH's and backups hit until 9:30. Fans were starting to come into Baseball Paradise. Bats called for infield practice and the players took their positions. While Bats hit infield, Subert and Morgan hit to the outfielders and Reese worked with the pitchers. The Dukes had a standard infield practice designed by Bats. Each infielder starting with third got 3 ground balls to throw home. When that was completed, they got 3 more ground balls to throw to first, then 2 ground balls where they had to cover their base as the catcher got the throw from first and threw to them at the base, they returned the throw to the catcher. Lastly they got 2 ground balls to throw to second simulating the double play, again, when the catcher got the ball from first he fired the ball to the player covering his base. Not a word was ever spoken. Bats trained them to know what was being hit and what they should do with the ball. There were lots of pushups and laps around the field before everyone learned the drill. Outfield practice consisted of two throws to each base including home where they had to hit the cutoff man. Finally a relay to the right and left where the outfielder had to hit the cutoff man and then the catcher shouted what to do with the ball. Lastly the players were brought in by charging a ball and throwing home. Now everyone on the field talked and cheered for the player getting the ball. First the outfielders, then each infielder, and each player who finished was at home plate cheering on the next player. Bats then hit a popup over home plate and the catcher called for it and made the catch. This is how it ended if Bats hit the popup. This drill was completed in 15 minutes or less. The drill was a thing of beauty and the other team almost always watched and got psyched out.

The Panthers now took the field for their pregame practice drill. When they were done a meeting was held at home plate. Coaches and umpires were introduced, lineup cards were exchanged and ground rules were gone over. The announcer introduced all the players and coaches. Umpires are usually not recognized, but since the ground crew was still working on the field, they were introduced. These were the four highest rated umpires they could find. All had been trained at a professional umpiring school. They looked, dressed and acted like professionals. The ground crew had completed their work and the field looked like a major league diamond. Bats signaled for his team to take the field and just before they started to warm up the announcer called for everyone to please rise for the National Anthem which was sung by Sergeant Major Susan Brite, a special forces soldier from the local army post. When Sargeant Brite finished and was escorted off the field, the home plate umpire shouted one of our country's greatest sayings," PLAY BALL!"

The Panthers batted in the first and went down in order. Lightning bunted the first pitch and beat the throw by the pitcher. ET, on a hit and run, hit a ground ball that the first baseman backhanded and threw a strike to the pitcher covering first. Jackee came to the plate and did exactly what she was taught. If you're in doubt, hit the ball up the middle. She did just that, and grounded a single to center scoring Lightning. Moose followed with another single but Howie lined into a double play as the first baseman jumped up, caught it and beat Moose back to the base. Bottom of the third, Lightning led off with a walk and went to third on a hit and run by ET. Jackee followed by pushing a bunt toward second, the pitcher charged off the mound, fielded the ball and flipped to first. Umpire called Jackee out but the run score and ET moved to second. Moose was intentionally walked, Howie and Stony each flew out to end the inning. Duke's lead lasted until the seventh inning. The Panthers put together a rally where they scored two runs to tie the game but left the bases loaded. Bottom of the seventh, Chuck hit the left field fence and stopped at second. Lightning moved him to third with a bunt. ET and Jackee both walked, loading the bases and, after a change of pitchers, Moose followed with a grand slam home run. Losing by 6 to 2 in the top of the ninth, the Panthers put on a rally. They had one run in and runners on first and second with one out. Their number four hitter came to the plate and with everyone playing him deep hit a bloop to short left center. As soon as the ball was hit Jackee turned her back on home plate and sprinted after the ball. She peeked over her shoulder, spotted the ball and dove for it. After catching the ball, while lying flat on the ground, Jackee flipped the ball to Chuck who was running toward her and he fired the ball to second completing a double play to end game one. Since both base runners were running because they thought the ball was uncatchable the Dukes could have had a triple play if there had been none out.

All the fans were on their feet cheering the final play of the game. Bats looked at the Panthers coach and he was just shaking his head. Later when the coaches were talking about game two and possibly game three, the Panthers coach said "I had heard about your shortstop but it never dawned on me that she could be that good."

Bats told him she is the most electrifying player he ever had and probably ever would. "Her defense is near perfect and she handles a bat like she was born with it. You should have seen our attendance for the year, it was up over 50%. Just look at the crowd today, have you ever had a crowd like this?"

Duke's players were surrounded by family and friends. Jackee's family and Dan were worried that she might have been hurt on the last play. She told them only the wind was knocked out of her. Kim came over, pulled her to the side, and asked how she was. "I seem to be fine except that my you know what hurts a lot. Even with the halter when I hit the ground it was chest first." They decided that when Jackee showers later she will get a cream to rub on and that should ease the pain. Jenco's set up dinner plans inviting both Kim and Bats. The dinner conversation finally got around to Jackee's impact on the summer league.

Bats told them that the whole league was indebted to Jackee for playing. He said he was one of the few who knew how good she really was. "Most others thought that it was a gimmick to increase fan attendance. When these coaches saw for themselves the true talent and the level she played at, they knew a new dimension had been added to the game. I personally want to apologize to Jackee for what I put her through and the great pressure that she had to endure. There is no other player that could have put up with the pressure and still played their 'A' game. She not only played but even improved on last year's performance. We tried to make sure that her ameture standing was not compromised and that at all times, her dignity and self respect were protected."

William thanked Bats for his handling and protecting his daughter. He also said that this would help her with all the future problems she might face. Jackee thanked Bats for giving her the opportunity to compete in the game she loved and for all the new baseball skills she learned from him. "It is much more fun to play this game when you are shown how to do it right." Later that night, Dan and Jackee were talking on Kim's porch.

Dan had not said a word at dinner and Jackee wanted to hear his thoughts. He said it was not his place to question what happened or even what may happen in the future. "It's easy to see that you are someone who is on a mission. Your skills and determination are not even a question any more. I know this may sound crazy but it seemed to me that you were not trying to keep up with the other ball players but that they were trying to keep up with you. You are definitely a star, who desperately tries to avoid being called one. Jackee, please do not let me influence your future. Make all your decisions the same as you do now. Just remember that I will be there if and when you need someone to talk with, hug or have a sundae with." Jackee hugged him and they kissed. This was much more than a good night kiss, it seemed to be the bonding of two hearts that will now beat as one. When their kiss ended Dan told Jackee to get to sleep and to have the greatest game of her life tomorrow.

Kim was waiting and asked Jackee how she felt. She said emotionally she felt great but her chest was very sore. Kim set up a hot tub with a special salt added to relieve the pain. Jackee was in the tub for 20 minutes and found it very difficult to stay awake. Finally, Kim helped her out, wrapped a very large Turkish towel around her and put her to bed. In the morning Jackee got up and felt pretty good. As she prepared for church, Kim came in and asked how she slept. Jackee said like a baby and almost all the pain was gone and only a little soreness was there.

After church she had a quick breakfast with the family then headed to Kim's to change. By 10:30 she was at the field and started doing her pre game activities. There were some difficulties swinging a bat. She found a short stroke did not have the same level of pain as did the full swing. Also the long throws across the infield gave her some pain. Regular throws were bearable but cutoff throws hurt the worst. When the Dukes took the field for their pre game practice, Jackee did well until the cutoffs. She bullied her way through it and kind of laid back before the game started. While the Panthers were taking their pre game practice, Jackee noticed that they were going to have a full house and more. She also noticed that beside two different camera units a great many important people were present. Bats was all over the special seating area shaking hands and talking to many people. This was not his usual routine, he normally does not talk to anyone immediately before a game. She decided that since this was a special game, more glad handing was necessary to keep everyone happy.

Just before the Panthers took the field and after introductions, lineup cards were exchanged and the anthem was sung, Bats had the team gather around him. He told them, "this is the game you waited for all your life. Go out there and take what you worked so hard for this season. Show them that you're the best and leave no doubt in anyone's mind."

The home plate umpire called play ball and the game was on. Lightning and ET were on first and second when Jackee hit a hanging curve down the right field line. Jackee ended up on third with two RBI's. Moose followed that with a sacrifice fly and the Dukes led 3 to 0. They did not score any more runs in the inning but a message had been sent to the Panthers. Bats sent them out to an on your feet cheering crowd. With the stands rocking Jackee looked over at the Panthers and thought to herself, that's how the Christians must have looked before the Romans released the lions.

As they gathered around the pitcher the second baseman rubbed the ball and handed it to the pitcher. This had been their ritual every game, before going to their infield positions. This time, before leaving the mound, Jackee said to them, "let's make this one the last game, I got to get home and get ready for school." The whole infield laughed and went to their positions.

Panthers hit like they had no heart. The Duke's pitcher, a big strong lefty, completely dominated the hitters. In the third inning Jackee had an RBI double, and in the fifth, an RBI single. Leading off the seventh she walked and eventually scored on a double by Stony. She did not expect to bat again and was glad since she hurt herself by going into the hole between short and third, backhanding a ball and throwing a strike to first for the out. The Dukes had men on in the eighth inning so Jackee was due up in the top of the ninth. Bats told her to go for the cycle. This means she would have to hit a home run in this at bat. That last throw to first had hurt something awful. She had decided unless she got a perfect pitch she would take a walk. Her mind was made up, she was only going to swing once, make contact and take what comes. After three pitches, she had a 2-1 count. Guessing fastball, that is exactly what came toward the plate. It was belt high and right down the middle. Jackee put whatever she had left into the swing and regretted it immediately. A sharp pain went through her chest and she had to catch her breath. The baseball traveled toward the left center field fence. As she turned first she saw the ball hit off the top of the fence and land back on the field. Jogging into second she could hear the crowd moan. Although she should feel disappointed, she only felt the pain and was glad it was over. Bats stopped the game and sent in a pinch runner for her. As she shook hands with the runner and started back to the dugout she realized that everyone was on their feet and giving her a standing ovation. The whole Dukes team was in front of the dugout waiting for her, and she could not believe that the Panthers were out of their dugout cheering. She looked up into the stands and saw her parents hugging each other and her mother crying. Rose was jumping up and down screaming her name. Dan had a big smile and was cheering with Rose. After the game ended, and it was a blowout, 12 to 1, trophies and awards were given out. The last award is the MVP of the tournament. Judges had unanimously decided that Jackee was the winner. When she accepted the award, she said this was a team effort and not just about one player. She thanked Bats and the coaches, all the players from the teams they played, county officials, her parents and finally the fans all over who always made her feel welcome. Rose also got her game ball.

All the congratulations and goodbyes being over, the Jenco family headed for their car. Standing by the car were coaches Begali and Singer. They had just driven down for the game but had a flat tire and arrived as the game started. Since the stands were already filled they just watched standing behind the backstop. Coach Begali had a smile when he said he was also checking up on his middle linebacker who left practice early on Friday and missed practice on Saturday for personal family reasons. Dan said he was sorry but had to see Jackee play and he promised to be ready for their first game next Saturday. Jackee thanked them for coming and said she had to shower and change before leaving for home. William dropped Jackee off at Kims and went off to load the car for the trip home. The hotel had stored their luggage for them until after the game. Kim was waiting for Jackee and asked how she felt. Jackee said she was hurting in her chest area and the pain was greater than yesterday. After her shower and packing all her remaining clothes and gear, Kim gave her two special pills to ease the chest pains. She gave her a few extras to be taken before bedtime and in the morning after breakfast. Kim gave her a hug just as William pulled into the driveway. Dan and William loaded the car and just before starting for home, William thanked Kim for taking care of Jackee.

CHAPTER SEVEN

Jackee Looks for Answers and Prepares for a Wedding

$\mathscr{W}$hen they finally arrived home they dropped Dan off first and then drove home. Everyone helped unload the car. Rebecca and Evelyn had not come to the game as they were completing all the wedding plans. There was a meal on the table and when everything was put away the family sat down to eat. Both girls knew about the game because William called after each inning to update them. Rose stuck the baseball and MVP trophy in their face but both already knew about them. Rebecca looked at Jackee and told her "I am so proud of you and the great things you have accomplished and even greater things you will accomplish in the future."

Evelyn said how hard it was for them not to be at the game. "We wanted to be there to celebrate and to cheer for you. As sisters we have a strong bond and even though we weren't there you knew we were right beside you the whole time. Besides we sent Rose and I am sure she cheered loud enough for all of us. You, mom and Rose have a fitting on Labor day. That should be the last one unless some alteration has to be finished. Thursday has been set as the final fittings if needed. All plans for the wedding, reception and rehearsal dinner are completed. Limos, DJ, bakery and father Nicolas are ready."

Jackee said she was tired and had to get some rest. Rebecca walked her to her room and told her how beautiful she was going to look in her bridesmaid gown. Smiling, Jackee said "you know you are the most beautiful of all the sisters, and besides the bride is always the center of attraction at a wedding." She thanked Jackee and went down to talk with Carmela.

While Jackee was preparing for bed she noticed the bruises on her chest. She put some cream on that Kim provided and also took two of the pills she recommended. Next morning before the rest of the family came down Jackee asked if she and Carmela could talk. Carmela knew something was wrong but had been afraid to approach the subject with her. Jackee began by telling her about the injuries to her chest. She started out by saying that she always thought her mother had a great figure but she had not wanted to develop like her. "If I were built a little smaller than you, I would not hurt as much."

Carmela said, "that's pretty much how I felt growing up but I soon learned that the better your figure the more boys are interested. This also includes later in life when men start to notice you."

"Mom, tell me something about how you feel when you kissed a boy-friend?"

"All kisses should have some meaning to them. Some are more import-ant than others. There are always special ones from special people however there are a few that find a special place in your heart."

"Mom, the other night I kissed Dan and I hugged him tight and never wanted it to end. I was so happy at that moment and I wanted to be that happy all my life. If I kissed other boys would I get the same feeling or was it Dan and only him who can make me feel like that? I overheard girls talk about what they do with their boyfriends on dates. It seemed to me that they were being used by the boys and not really being respected by them. Later you hear that they no longer date and move on to someone else. What is the right and wrong thing to do? "

Jackee, "if I could answer that question I would be the richest person in the world. No one is capable of telling you that. Each person must make his or her decision on right and wrong. Remember what I told you before, your moral and religious upbringing should be your guide. Jackee, you are the most dedicat-ed person I have ever seen or heard about. I may be prejudiced because you are my daughter but your dad and I believe you are a rare breed. Talent like yours is a blessing from God so please do not waste it. We have seen you grow from a sick and awkward child, to a beautiful talented young woman." She hugged and thanked her mom and said, she would always try to make them proud of her.

Five Jenco females walked into the bridle shop, three of them needed a final fitting before the wedding. When Jackee came out of the dressing room the other four were astonished at how beautiful she looked. Evelyn and Rebecca never realized the athlete was only one part of this wonderful sister. Rebecca told Jackee she could not come to the wedding because "I'm supposed to be the center attraction."

While they were all laughing Rebecca said "I'm glad Rocco committed to me before he saw you." All the gowns were completed except Rose's, it seems she grew some since the last fitting, but they said it would be ready by Friday.

Tuesday when school started Jackee was in her one month relaxation period and made the most of it. While the new 10th graders were having their orientation at the high school she was finalizing her schedule and science club meetings. She checked in with the baseball coaches but they were all involved with their football responsibilities. There was a rumor that section 6 was now eligible for state competition in baseball. Word was that each section could send the league champion to the state tournament. This consisted of 8 teams playing three games the second weekend in June.

Wednesday, when school started, she was going through her classes when Mr. Rogers asked to speak to her after school. She met him in the science lab after 8th period and thought something had come up about the science club. To her surprise, he handed her a brochure from a college that offered selected students a six year science program with an automatic acceptance to medical school upon completion. He also mentioned that this college had a better than average baseball program. He thought her perfect grades in science and her abilities on the baseball field was a marriage made in heaven. "Since you would already be 18 in June you are eligible to complete your senior year by taking these college courses. You would be able to graduate with your class the following June." She asked if she could discuss this with her parents.

This family meeting was about defining her future goals not for a season or semester but for maybe life. Her parents read all the information and asked her what she thought about the program. Jackee said it was unique and met many of her possible goals. She said, "is it possible for a person to strive for two career opportunities at the same time without compromising one for the other?"

Carmela held Jackee's hand when she said "if it can be done I know in my heart that you can do it."

"Mr. Rogers had said it was a plus that I will be eighteen If I decide to apply. I guess starting school late just might be to my benefit." Finally, Jackee said she would sleep on it and would they be upset if she talked to Dan about this. Immediately, Carmela told her that it would be a good idea. William was quiet and did not say another word.

Later when they were alone William wanted to know what he had missed. With a little smile she said, "this is just between us girls."

Jackee called Dan and asked if he had some time to see her. He said he would make the time and be over in a half hour. Thirty minutes later he was ringing the bell and Jackee let him in. After saying hello to everyone Jackee told her parents they were going for a walk. They were walking toward the park on this gorgeous night when Jackee said "I am going to tell you something and I want an honest opinion." She told him about the program and the college involved. She then explained her possible goals for the future, and lastly how any of this would affect their relationship.

Dan was a bit taken back and did not know where to begin, so he cut to the chase, Jackee, "you are the most wonderful girl I have ever met or even heard of. When I asked you for a date I didn't think there was a chance you would accept. When you did I just thought how lucky I was. When I got to know you I could not believe what an incredible person you really were. It came as a shock when you agreed to another date. The more I see you and learn more about you I realize how fantastic you are. Jackee, I shouldn't be saying this to you but I want you to know that I would deem it an honor to spend the rest of my life taking care of you. Next year I will be away at some college and we will be apart. We must both find our true goals in life and I want to be part of your goals and life. I did not know about the doctor part but I can see the baseball part and I want to be there when you achieve that goal. Now that I know about the other goal, I want to be there when you get that medical degree."

Half smiling and half crying she put her arms around him and held him for dear life. She said softly that with her family and him behind her, she could achieve anything. "Please always be my friend and be there when I need someone to talk to." They walked a while longer then he walked her home, kissed her good night and said to sleep on it.

Next morning Jackee came down to find her parents having coffee and waiting for her. Both seemed a bit nervous. Carmela asked what she wanted for breakfast. Her reply was just juice for now. "I talked to Mr. Rogers, you, dad, and to Dan, and putting it all together I decided to commit to the program and take early graduation. This could be a financial burden to the family but Mr Rogers said my grades and baseball skills could be a bargaining point with the school. He in fact will be my sponsor as he knows some of the instructors at the college. One other small detail he mentioned was one of his fellow fraternity brothers is the dean of medicine at the school. Now that this is settled let's get ready for Rebecca's wedding."

Thursday at school she told Mr. Rogers what her intentions were and that any help he could give her would be greatly appreciated. He was thrilled because she is the perfect candidate for this program, and her success would open the door for many who follow. He thanked her because he knew what a gigantic impact this is going to have on her life. Next she had to tell coach Begali who would be upset. She was surprised at how calm the coach was when she told him. Later he said he and Mr. Rogers had talked about this at yesterday's faculty meeting. The coach told her that he would love to have her for the next two years but he knew that it was selfish on his part. As a baseball player you are far beyond high school baseball. I knew that when we saw you play in the championship game last week. Just you give me one more year like the last one and we could be in the running for the state champion title. Jackee told him she would give him everything she had and guaranteed it would always be 100%.

Saturday, after his scrimmage, Dan and Jackee went to the movie and the usual sundae. After that they sat on her porch swing and talked about the coming year. She told Dan about the rehearsal dinner and he was invited as her guest, and she knew he could not make the church service as he had an away game, but he would be there for the reception. "Barring some unexpected event I should be at the cocktail hour." They kissed goodnight and it seemed their kisses lasted a bit longer and with more passion. When he was leaving he said he would see her at the rehearsal dinner at 6:30 Friday. The following week seemed to fly by. All Jackee's classes were very good and she found out that she was tied for second place in the class standings. Actually only three fourths of a percent separated the first four students.

Friday night came and Dan walked in about 6:15 at the favorite family restaurant. They had a private room in the back and Rocco's family was the host. They decided on the food arrangement. The Manelli's also frequented this restaurant so they knew what to order. A full table of appetizers was prepared and a limited dinner menu was available for hungry guests. When Jackee went over to Dan and escorted him to the table, it seemed her usher partner for the wedding appeared to be dissapointed. Dan sat next to Jackee and there was no doubt who she was interested in. They had a great time eating, dancing and getting acquainted. About nine, Dan had to leave and get into bed. Before every football game, the booster club provided breakfast for the football players and coaches. It was supposed to be a bonding thing and had been a tradition for years. Jackee and Dan said their goodbyes at his car, and after he left Jackee came back into the restaurant and stayed with the girls.

Saturday, the day of the wedding, was hectic to say the least. Flowers arrived about 9am at the house, they also had to be delivered to the church and to the reception hall. The girls all showered and at 11am the beautician arrived to do the hair and at 1pm a makeup consultant arrived to assist with makeup. William just wandered around the house because all he had to do was shower, shave and put on his tuxedo. The limo would arrive at 3:30pm to take them to the church. About 3:20 the girls started coming downstairs. He could not believe his eyes, one was more beautiful than the other. Rose was in a class by herself since she looked like a giant doll. His wife looked almost exactly as she looked the day they were married. Evelyn was stunning and Jackee looked like a young image of Carmela 25 years ago. Rebecca looked magnificent in her wedding dress, as if it had been painted on. They all got into the two limos and headed for St. Mary's church. A couple minutes before 4:00 the limos arrived. Carmela was escorted to her seat by one of the ushers and the girls were lined up with their usher escorts. Rebecca and William were last to line up. Father Nicholas gave a signal and the organ started playing. Rose and her escort led off followed by Mandy, Rebecca's friend, Jackee, and the maid of honor Evelyn. When all the ushers and bridesmaids were settled at the altar the organ played here came the bride as William and Rebecca walked down the aisle. Just before starting William asked Rebecca if she had any doubts about getting married. She told him she waited all her life for the right person and Rocco was him. When they reached the altar he lifted her veil, kissed her and told her he hoped she would be as happy as her parents were. She teared up a little, but turned to Rocco as William put their hands together.

When the service was over and all the pictures were taken, the limos left for the reception. There had been pictures at both families' houses, and before going into the church and coming out. Now there were more pictures at the reception hall. A special room had been set up for the bridal party. Some food and drinks and just a place to hang out until all the pictures were taken, and it was time for the cocktail hour.

Guests started arriving at 6:00pm. The doors opened to six tables of assorted appetizers. People in the wedding party came down to mingle with the guest, only Rebecca stayed away so Carmela went to see her. She was fine and just needed to rest for a while. The girls kept coming and going so Carmela went to join William and the other guests. Dan arrived about 6:40 and Jackee, who was getting a little worried, went immediately to him. She hugged and kissed him and wanted him to know she missed him. He took her hand and asked how the wedding went. Jackee said "it went off perfectly and the bride looked lovely but how did your game go?" He said they won and the coach told him he played a great game. They went over to the food so he could get something to eat and just as he was starting, the bridal party was asked to go outside. Everyone had to leave this room and go to the main dining room.

When everyone was seated at their assigned table they were asked to rise and the bridal party was introduced. When Jackee appeared for her entrance, Dan now realized how beautiful she really was. He could not take his eyes off of her and wondered what she saw in him. Finally the new Mr & Mrs Rocco Manelli were introduced and had their first dance and later everyone with a partner joined them on the dance floor. Immediately after, Jackee joined Dan and asked him to dance with her. While they were dancing Dan told Jackee "I didn't realize how beautiful you are. You are by far the most beautiful woman at this wedding." She blushed and thanked him but she said Rebecca and even her mother were more beautiful. He told her they are both beautiful looking women but "no one can compare with you."

Wedding ended at 11:00pm but no one seemed to notice that Rebecca and Rocco had left early. It was decided that all the gifts would be left with the Jenco's until the couple returned from their one week honeymoon. Everyone pitched in and all gifts were loaded in one SUV. William drove that vehicle home while Carmela drove Rose and Evelyn in the other car. Dan drove Jackee home and they helped bring in the gifts. When all the gifts were in the house, Dan said his goodbyes and Jackee walked him to his car. They kissed for a long minute and she asked him to come over either for lunch or right after. His last words were I'll definitely see you some time on Sunday.

All three girls went upstairs to change. Carmela told Rose it was past her bedtime and she would be up to tuck her in. Rose wanted to stay up but she could barely keep her eyes open. Later, Carmela found her gown folded neatly on the chair and she was sound asleep. Evelyn and Jackee were in sweats and ready to help put things away. William said he had everything under control and told them to get some rest because he was going to bed right now. Next morning, Carmela was up and had juice and coffee ready at 8:15. She called out that they had to hurry if they intended to make the 9:00 mass. The Jenco's walked into St Mary's with two minutes to spare. After Mass they thanked Father Nicholas again for the great homily he gave at the wedding, and for the blessing at the reception. He said to them he was preparing three more for the rest of the girls. Rose said to him, "not for me weddings are boring."

"They get better as you get older," Father Nicholas said to her. This exchange brought a smile to everyone present and once again they thanked him and headed for home.

Taking off their Sunday go-to-meeting clothes, and changing into lay-around-on-Sunday duds, was accomplished very quickly. Jackee and Carmela started to prepare brunch. Carmela asked if Jackee had a good time at the wedding. She said, anytime I spend with Dan is a great time. She continued, "he is my best friend and I never want to lose him. Outside of my family I never felt like that about anyone."

"Does he know about your plans for the medical program?"

"He does and he said he would stand with me for whatever I wanted to do."

"Jackee, this is the first boy you ever dated and these feelings are new to you. How can you tell if they are real or just some infatuation?"

"It's true, I never felt this way before and Dan may find someone else when he goes to college next year. All I do know, I really care about him and hope he stays with me forever. I do not know what love is but it hurts to think of a future without him."

Carmela looked her in the eye and said, "I hope you never lose that hurt because that is how you know it is real. Jackee, you just defined love."

Everyone helped clear away brunch. Carmela approached William about dinner, and he said "let's order pizza and some other goodies." She immediately agreed. Dan arrived about 4:00.

He told Jackee he was sorry but he was exhausted from the game and the late night. She said "I don't care, as long as you're here now."

He told William that it was the best wedding he ever attended. "Just think you have three more daughters to go."

William said "from now on we'll give them a ladder and digital camera and recommend eloping."

Carmela asked if he heard anything about college and Dan said everything was on hold until football was over. "My head coach told me that a few schools had already asked about my grades and future goals. I can only hope that the school that makes the best offer is also the best to attend. I can't expect a lot of help from my parents but I know they will help as much as they can. In the long run it's not about the school, it's about the effort the student makes to achieve his goals."

Considering what Dan had just said, William thought this was an adult observation by this young man. He wondered how Jackee saw him and later asked Carmela what she thought. Carmela told him that she considered Dan to be the perfect match for Jackee. William walked away shaking his head and wondering what he had missed.

On the swing, Jackee and Dan were discussing the coming year. With football going until thanksgiving their time together would be limited. Jackee suggested that they see each other only on Saturday or Sunday. "I'll be at all your games unless I have some other obligation. We can limit our phone calls and we can talk in school. My classes are full and I have lunch in the science lab so we may only have a few minutes before you go to practice. Your final game is on thanksgiving day so let's make a formal date for the Saturday after."

He agreed and said we can spend from that day until the end of February dating. "Come March, we both go into the spring season and there will be no time except a few hours on the weekend."

Rose started the fall track season and was branching out into different events. Her coach had suggested that she try some of the field events since she seemed to be fairly strong. She picked up these new events like she has been doing them for years. William now had to consider what type of training would be best for her. He knew one thing for sure, he could not structure her training schedule. What do you do when in doubt? You go to the pro. The head track and field coach at the high school had assisted at the Olympic tryouts for track and field. Coach Flagon heard about Rose and told William he would be happy to speak to an Olympic coach about her. One Saturday William took Rose and Jackee to the high school to meet with Coach Flagon. They were surprised when a second person was present. He was introduced as the assistant Olympic track and field coach, Coach Thorpe. When coach Flagon contacted him about Rose he thought he had to meet her in person. The two coaches took Rose out to the field and put her through a few drills and exercises. All Coach Thorpe said was that Rose was the real thing and he saw her as a future Olympic star. He gave William a complete training and dieting program and told them to stay in touch. He personally would follow her career and may even recommend some different programs. Rose was so excited she told Jackee how great it was to have someone like Thorpe interested in her. She couldn't wait to get home and try the schedule he gave William.

Carmela looked over the diet and exchanged one vegetable for another but the increased pasta had to be dealt with. Different types of beans might be a good substitute. Training was basically the same as the schedule they followed last fall. There were some interesting additions that even Jackee wanted to try. The three of them sat down and worked out a schedule that fit their availability. Rose would have a few things she had to do on her own, but most would involve Jackee. Since her big sister would be with her most of the time, she was ready to start. No one told Rose that Jackee would not be here this time next year. She and Jackee were so close that they feared she might revert back to the withdrawal stage. Jackee had been working hard to boost her self confidence and to reduce Rose's dependence on her. It was made more difficult because Jackee depended on Rose some of the time.

Intense training began on October first. The first week took a toll on their bodies but next week it seems much easier even though they have increased the levels. By Thanksgiving day Jackee felt that her body was almost ready for the season. It also helped to know that after today's football game against Travis, their arch rivals, Dan would be free to see her. The whole Jenco family including Rocco attended the game. Usually Travis had a huge edge, but this being a homecoming game for Reagan seemed to fire up the team. Late in the fourth quarter Regan led 11 to 7 with less than two minutes left in the game. Reagan coaches had put in a special half back option that they used after they scored a touchdown and converted it into a two point conversion. So after they kicked a 26 yard field goal they now had a four point lead. Regan players were tired since most played both ways. This was called ironman football when athletes played both offense and defense. Travis seemed to always have a rested player waiting to go. This would be their last possession and they were driving toward the goal line. Dan broke through the line and blocked a pass. On the next play Dan faked a blitz and the defensive end broke through for a sack. The third play was a short pass with the receiver going out of bounds stopping the clock with 30 seconds left. Fourth down they had to throw the ball into the end zone and everyone knew it. What they didn't know was Dan and the linebacker both blitzed and sacked the quarterback for a loss. The whole stadium was cheering as the Reagan quarterback took a knee ending the game. As Dan was leaving the field he told Jackee that he would see her after dinner tonight.

Dan arrived at 6:30 just as the Jenco's finished their turkey dinner. They were setting the table for dessert. William congratulated him on the fine game he played and wondered if he had been hurt. He said he had a couple of stingers and an ankle twisted in a pile on. It is well known that Travis players live on the edge of dirty football. There was no proof but he thinks a player purposely twisted his ankle on the play. "We were all exhausted at the finish and glad there was no more time on the clock. Four players collapsed in the locker room and three others had to get a shot from the doctor. I was so proud of my teammates not because we won but because they never quit and left everything on the field. You do know that we were considered three touchdown underdogs? We used the old saying to ignite the team. It's not the size of the dog in the fight but the size of the fight in the dog that makes the difference. The big home field crowd also helped. In front of so many friends and relatives nobody wants to look bad."

Dessert was served and Carmela outdid herself. Pies, Cookies, puddings, special holiday cakes, and ice cream were put on the table. Carmela served everyone and when she asked Dan, he said he didn't have to watch his diet so he wanted to try it all, although he settled for a piece of homemade cheese cake with pineapple topping. When everyone had their dessert, William thanked Carmela for a great meal and then everyone dug in. Only Rose had seconds. The clean up took about 15 minutes and Jackee said they were going for a walk.

While walking Jackee asked if he was really ok. Dan said he had a few cuts and bruises but should be fine by the weekend. "We have three whole months before the next season. I decided not to play basketball but instead get ready for lacrosse. Since I am not a starter why take a spot that could be filled by a younger player. Besides, I want to get to know you better and try to plan the rest of the school year." Jackee agreed with everything he said, especially the part about getting to know each other. They walked for a while, then Dan said "I am really beat and need some rest. Is it alright with you if we see each other Saturday night?" Jackee said it was a date and she would be waiting for him at 7:00.

Jackee and Rose had a long workout on Friday, trying to work off the big dinner from the day before. Rose seemed to be going to a new level as it was getting harder and harder for Jackee to keep up with her. Since this was also increasing her stamina she never complained. She mentioned to William that she could not believe Rose's dedication. William said "she learned from the best so why are you surprised?" It never occurred to her that she was the reason Rose wanted to be so good. She then remembered how young girls had looked up to her at the indoor batting cage and at the games she played.

She asked Carmela what that meant, and Carmela told her, "whether you like it or not you are a role model for many young girls and as you go higher more and more women and girls will use you as a symbol of what women are capable of doing."

"Mom, I don't want to disappoint anyone and I certainly don't want to fail but what am I supposed to do?"

"Just keep doing the best you can and be who you are. Stay within yourself and never back down from a challenge."

"Mom, that is so hard and so much pressure put on me."

"You are 100% correct, but I have seen you do it and I believe with all my heart that you can and will change certain stereotypes."

Their Saturday night date was great as far as Jackee was concerned. They walked hand in hand and when they passed other girls Jackee felt that they were jealous of her taking Dan out of circulation. These dates also gave her more desire to work harder and prove to Dan that she was the best. It seemed strange to her that she never had to do this before but now all she really wanted to do is please Dan. His being there gave her a new drive to achieve her goals.

Christmas season seemed to start the day after Thanksgiving and really went into high gear the following week. The Jenco family started taking down Christmas decorations from the attic in the second week of December. Everyone helped out and even Rebecca and Rocco participated. Getting a real Christmas tree was also a family event. Sometimes everyone agreed immediately on a tree, other times it was hours before everyone was happy. Instead of William getting short tempered, he would just smile and think it's hard to get two women to agree on something, it's almost impossible to get four of them to agree. A funny thing he realized was whenever there was a huge disagreement as to the best tree it was usually decided that one of the first ones they looked at was the one picked. Whenever this happens William always kept what he thought was the best tree nearby. He would never pick the tree, but he would eventually lead everyone back to the one he put on the side.

Evelyn arrived home from college the week before Christmas. She had finished her exams early and headed home with additional news. It seems she accepted a fraternity pin from a senior at the college named Jon Zarrelli. "He is a pre med student who has already been accepted to John Hopkins. His Parents are both Doctors and will be away for the holidays. He will finish final lab exam on December 23. I invited him to spend Christmas week with us if that is acceptable with the family. I'm sorry I didn't let you know sooner but he only told me last night about his parents." Evelyn was on the verge of tears when Carmela put her arm around her and told her it would be a pleasure to have a friend of yours spend the holidays with us. Rose promptly said, we could fix up Rebecca's old room or I can bunk in with Jackee. Carmela told them Kim was not staying here this year as she and Bats have become engaged. They are coming for Christmas dinner but will stay at the motel. Evelyn, now crying, thanked her parents and told them no one has ever had better parents.

Visiting the orphanage and Vet's home used to have five people, but now there were nine. Dan`s mother had made a bunch of italian pastries and cannolis, plus some special cakes and cookies. Mrs. Silvio's American war veterans auxiliary made or bought gifts for both the orphanage and Vets home. Two cars had people, and one car had gifts when they pulled into the orphanage parking lot. Everyone carried as much as possible into the building. The Nuns had been forewarned and met them at the door. Rose led the way in and each Nun was aware of what she had accomplished in school and in track and field. After the presents and goodies had been distributed the Nuns had the choir sing some Christmas songs. Two hours later the Jenco parade headed for the Vets' home. Almost all the rich desserts had been left at the orphanage because most of the Vets were on a restricted diet. A great many of the Vets knew William, not only from his visits but he was veteran's representative to the American Legion, VA, and local VA hospital. Nursing home Vets were usually glad to see anyone. The only time most armed forces are needed is in times of war or national disaster. Old Vets are just set aside and not much attention is paid to them except by family or friends. Jencos have served in every major conflict and William always felt he owed these men and women something. Administrators and caregivers thanked them for coming. As they were walking toward the cars, William said he was treating everyone to ice cream at the malt shop.

Dan and Jackee drove back with Rocco and Rebecca. Jackee asked Rocco how he enjoyed the visits. Rocco said the first time he was involved, he could not believe how excited both the children and Vets had been and that the Jenco's had been doing this for over 25 years. He also said that his parents thought that William and Carmela were two of the finest people they ever met. "Never once did they disagree with anything my parents wanted for our wedding. My father wanted to pay for the extra guest that he had to invite, William would not hear of it and said all are welcome."

Jackee said she was tired and had to rest up for Chrismas Eve. Since everyone else was inside or gone she lingered with Dan for a few moments. Finally they kissed good night and it was a little longer and with a little more passion.

Christmas Eve is a very busy day. Presents had to be wrapped, labeled and put under the tree. Baking for Christmas dinner had to be completed and finally foods that can be cooked in advance had to be finished and put away. Jon had been introduced to the family less than 24 hours ago and he already felt like he had been here for years. Since he was an only child, nothing like this ever took place in his house. Some paid strangers decorated the house and tree, the cook prepared all the meals, and very few, if any, people came to the house. He never imagined a home could be this warm and filled with love for one another. He now realized what had attracted him to Evelyn. It was not only her outward beauty but her inner beauty that he didn't even know existed. For the first time in his life he felt like he belonged here and for the first time since his confirmation he would be going to Church with someone.

Carmela prepared a buffet dinner and the whole family including Bats and Kim sat around and had food and drink. Bats was trying to make people feel comfortable when he said, "most people found it strange that an almost 50 year old marine Vet could be engaged to a 30year old beauty. To tell you the truth, I let her take advantage of me and I know she is after my money and good looks."

Everyone laughed and Kim said "I was really after his G.I. insurance policy." Kim continued, "he is the kindest, most gentle person I have ever met." William told her she could get a few companies of marines who would never believe it.

Jackee chimed in, "I agree 100% with Kim, I have seen both sides of him many times and deep down he is a kind man." Bats thanked them and told Kim she was the piece of his life that he had been missing.

There was one thing William had always wanted to know, "you could not have been born with the name Bats, what is your real first name?" Bats looked around the room and told everyone there that they must swear never to tell anyone else. When they all agreed, he told them his name was Malcome with an e at the end. "I was named after my mother's grandfather who supposedly came from royal blood."

"Well," William said, "I'll take your orders but I will not bow to you."

"You mean you're not going to kiss my ring," Bats said.

"And not anything else," Willian countered.

Christmas day was a clear 40 degree day and all were up early for breakfast and church. As everyone was ready to leave Rebecca and Rocco drove up and right behind them was Bats and Kim. Carmela and William were thrilled to have everyone attend church with them. Bats said "I hope your chaplain lets me come in."

"Our Church is open to everyone and no one is refused or barred" Carmela said. Kim and Bats took Rebecca and Rocco in their car and followed William to church. After they parked the cars and were walking to the front door, standing there waiting for them was Dan.

Jackee ran and threw her arms around him. Without thinking where she was, she kissed him and said "Merry Christmas!" Father Nickolas must have been inspired because he gave one of his best sermons. Lastly, he thanked all present for coming to celebrate Jesus' birth with him and again wished them all a Merry Christmas and a safe and healthy New Year.

Back at the Jenco residence people were all over having something to eat, opening presents, drinking a traditional eggnog, or just plain relaxing. Jon had a gift for Evelyn that his mother recommended. It was a bracelet that she received but never wore. In fact it was still in the original box, all Jon did was wrap it and put Evelyn's name on. William had taken Evelyn out to the stationary store and recommended a good pen and pencil set. He reasoned that a doctor could always use a good pen. Dan gave Jackee a pair of earrings that his mother picked out. He could not tell his mother if Jackee had pierced ears or not. His mother thought he would have noticed if she wore clip-ons. Jackee gave Dan his gift and they opened them together. Dan was happy with his new equipment bag and Jackee said the earrings were beautiful. He asked her if she was happy with the gift and she said "I got everything I wanted when you were waiting for me at the church." She squeezed his hand and did not have to say another word. There were many other gifts under the tree, in fact, everyone had something including Bats and Kim. Kim received a house gift from the Jenco's and Bats had received a whip. He said he could now get rid of his cat -o- nine tails whip as it was getting old.

Once all the gifts had been opened and the wrappings all cleaned up, more drinks were handed out and the table had to be set for Christmas dinner. Everyone stayed for dinner but Dan. He had to open gifts and have dinner with his family but would return later. Jackee walked him to the door and he told her he would be back as soon as he could. She kissed him and told him she would be waiting to have dessert with him. When she came inside, she immediately helped prepare the dining room for dinner. All the women pitched in while the men sat around talking and watching some bowl game or March of the Wooden Soldiers. Christmas dinner was all the favorite foods and desserts. Carmela made sure that there was enough left over for Kim and Rebecca to take back home and that there was still something left for her family to nosh on. Clearing the table for desserts was always a problem so Carmela decided to have a separate table set up for only dessert items. This worked out very well as self service was better than asking and serving individuals. Dan walked in right on time and selected a dessert with Jackee. He told Carmela he thought her cheese cake was the best he ever had. Bats teased Carmela and said her food was almost as good as Marine chow.

Rocco and Rebecca had to leave and get to his parents' dinner. Bats and Kim said they had work the next day but more importantly they had to set their wedding plans. They decided to get married the Saturday after the Super Bowl. "Since that is a perfect time between seasons and gives us a good time for a honeymoon. It will be a small affair and we are looking forward to you and the family being there."

"Bats, you and Kim are family," Carmela told them. "What the two of you did for Jackee was the best ever. We will be honored to celebrate with you on your wedding date."

Kim said "I'll be sending you all the information." Jackee and Dan went for their usual walk. Dan told her he had a part time job until the spring season but they will be able to spend some time together. Jackee told him that she and Rose are into their training schedule and she would be hitting indoors starting in January. The weekends would be a good time. She thanked him again for coming to church and for the earrings. They kissed and she felt everything was perfect.

Now the workouts were more intensive because Rose was also running Indoor track. Rose wasn't a big fan of running inside because she had a hard time breathing during the meets. Her coach didn't care as she was the fastest runner in the school and her indoor times were still breaking the school records. The first indoor meet in January she ran the mile in 4:48 that not only broke the girls record but also the boys. Jackee had known Rose was getting quicker since now Rose was beating her in every distance run. Their work outs became very competitive and they both loved it. Because of the great strain it was on the legs William kept insisting that they both do more stretching. Rose sometimes cheated on that and he feared she would pull something. The track coach kept experimenting with Rose. He taught her how to throw the shot put and the first time she did it correctly she unofficially set a school record. He tried her in the high jump and pole vault and in both he got the same results. One time he kiddingly asked William if she is really the daughter of Jim Thorpe.

Life now became boring except when she was with Dan. Every day was workout, hit, run, lift weights, throw, study, go to a meeting, get up, go to bed, watch your diet and finally, go to meets. If it weren't for her dates with Dan she would be like a robot. One additional challenge she put on herself, she decided to go for the number two or one student in the class. Although it seemed impossible to catch the number one student, she decided to try and at least become the second highest. Her baseball skills by mid february were at least tryout level or better. Condition wise she was in the best shape ever. Mentally she was ready for the baseball season and prepared to enter that 6 year medical program. Rose in the meantime had won every event she entered.

Her dates with Dan had dropped to only one a week since he was working more and trying to keep up his grades. Rose had her invitational meet that is usually held for all the local high schools. Section 6 holds it at a college or some other big arena. This year it was to be held at the arena. More sections were invited and there would be much better competition. Jackee had finished hitting indoors and was getting ready for tryouts. She basically was getting Rose ready for the invitational meet. On the last Saturday in February the meet was held. Over 25 high schools were invited. This would be a whole day affair with the finals starting about 4:30pm. Rose qualified for the finals in all four of the events she entered. She placed second in the shot put when she threw it 46.2 feet. In the 800 meters she won with a time of 2.26.2. In the high jump she came in second with a 6.2 foot jump. In her last event, she ran the mile in 4.43 and was beaten by half a second. She was very disappointed but her coach was ecstatic and could not stop congratulating her. When they were giving out the awards and she received the silver metal she was given a standing ovation. In fact, except for the pentathlon winner who got the biggest ovation, Rose's was next. Driving home she told Jackee that she will never lose another race like that again. She thought that she had lost the mile run because she did not see or hear the runner until she passed her. Jackee told her "you were the youngest girl to compete and you did a fantastic job of staying in every race. Could you do better? Of course you can and for the next

3 years you are going to dominate this meet." Rose felt a little better but she still had a bad taste in her mouth.

Their Saturday night date started later than usual and Jackee asked permission to come in a little later. After she got permission, she and Dan headed out for the evening. They went for a sundae and after they finished he drove to a kind of a lover's lane and parked. While sitting close together they talked for a time and then began kissing. After a time their kisses became more passionate. Dan pulled away and told Jackee he had to stop but she did not understand why. He just said to her that he loved her and did not want to take advantage of the situation. She said "I love you so much that I want to be with you and kiss you the rest of my life."

"Jackee, I hope and pray that we have a thousand nights like this but tonight can not be one of them. Believe me when I tell you that I could kiss every inch of you and spend the whole night doing it but we must wait until the right time when just you and I matter."

She still did not understand and felt that she did something wrong. Dan drove her home, thanked her for a great evening and kissed her good night. She watched him drive off and went into the house. Immediately she went to her room and after putting on her pajamas said her prayers and laid in bed. Most of the night she just tossed and turned but slept very little.

Next morning she was waiting at the breakfast table when Carmela came down. Instinctively Carmela knew something was wrong. She sat next to her daughter and said "do you want to talk about it?" Jackee innocently explained what had happened the night before and wanted to know what she did wrong. Carmela told her she did nothing wrong and that it was her fault that this happened. "Mom, you weren't even there, how could it be your fault?"

"Jackee, we need to have a mother, daughter talk. Do you understand how babies are made?"

"Of course I do. We had that in our health class."

"Well, you enjoyed kissing Dan and felt an emotional bonding with him."

"Yes I did," Jackee answered.

"Well when men get that feeling it stirs a sexual drive in them that wants more. That more is the touching of your body and that causes you to want more and eventually it leads to sexual contact. It is a natural human reaction. Dan thinks so much of you that he was willing to suppress his desires and not take advantage of an inexperienced young girl. I always liked him but now he has my respect because he not only loves my daughter but also does not want to hurt her."

"What you are saying to me is that he did not want to continue kissing me but instead wanted to protect me."

"That is part of it, he knew that if you continued, you would have let him touch your body. Your desire level would have increased, and because you feel so much for him, it could have eventually led to sexual contact. Jackee, I want you to be honest with yourself and tell me, would you have stopped him if he touched your naked body?"

"I guess that you are right because I did not want him to stop kissing me and I hated it when he did stop. How can I be so smart and yet be so stupid in real life situations."

"This is not something you can learn from a book. Human behavior is different with every individual. You can have 5 boyfriends and each one will treat you differently, some good, some bad. You found yourself a great young man, you cherish him always because he is one in a million. Do you know if his friends heard about this they would think him to be stupid for not having sex with you."

CHAPTER EIGHT

Jackee Plays Second Year of School Baseball and New Program

$\mathcal{J}$ackee called Dan after church and asked if he could come over for a few moments later in the day. He agreed to see her after supper. Around 6:00 he rang the doorbell and Jackee went to the door. He came into the house, greeted all present and left with Jackee after she put on her coat. She called over her shoulder that they were going for a walk. She said, "I am so stupid and did not know how to act last night."

Dan said to her "it was not your fault, you did nothing wrong except being who you are. This is the reason I asked you out in the first place. I have no desire to change one thing about you. In my eyes you are perfect just as you are. No one has the right to change perfection."

"My mom told me that she thinks you are one in a million and that I should cherish you. She explained how you protected me even though I probably did not want you to. She explained how hard it is for a man to resist temptation and how easy it is for a girl to give in to it. You took control of the situation and protected me. Please Dan, always be there to protect me and I will be faithful to you all my life."

"The next four years" he said, "we will probably be apart most of the time, but I give you my word, you will always be with me and I will always protect you." He walked her home and told her he would see her around school and on Saturday nights.

First day of tryouts was the usual disorganized affair. Jackee was looking for Sonny. He finally came out late and immediately started working with Jackee.

She knew Frank had graduated so a new catcher had to be found. Scott was still here so three fourths of their up the middle strength was still there. Jackee organized the left side of the infield and Sonny did the same with the right side. Ten minutes later Sonny was hitting ground balls to shortstops and third baseman. Later it was reversed and Jackee was hitting balls and Sonny's group was fielding them. Scott started hitting balls to the outfielders. Carl Dolan, a returning pitcher, was working with the pitchers. Coach Begali was directing batting practice. The first three weeks flew by and finally the varsity and jv had the teams picked. Coach Begali kept 18 players of which 7 were pitchers. Their starting catcher had a good arm, not as good as Frank's, but good enough. He also appeared to be smarter in game situations and Jackee suspected he had some training from a professional.

Coach Singer took his JV team to the old varsity field and the varsity practiced on their home field. The two coaches discussed the players on the JV that may be able to help the varsity should a need arise. A backup catcher and a good defensive outfielder were the main priorities. Coach Begali scheduled four scrimmages against the best teams he could find. Since they won the championship last year, many teams wanted to schedule Reagan high school. These scrimmages produced many positive results. They found that the catcher, Bruce Davis, had a very good arm and he hit better than expected. Not as much power as Frank but he made good contact and got on base a lot. Carl Dolan was not the number one pitcher but he was a good number two or a great number three. Sandy Graham was without a doubt the number one. He grew three inches and gained 20 pounds of muscle. That was a very imposing pitcher standing on the mound. When they used the radar gun on him he hit a high of ninety and he had a good curve to go with the fast ball. Probably the next pitcher was Chuck Train, who threw a curve that fell off the table. Because of his curve, his fastball was even an effective pitch. The new third baseman Rocky Daniels was not only a great defensive player but his bat was deadly. Arnie Goldman was the right fielder because he had the best arm and proved he could track a ball down. His hitting was good but not consistent.

Coach had a team meeting and said, "this team has a twenty two game winning streak to defend. Our pitchers never lose a game, so all of them are number one. I intend to win 23 games this year. Which would mean we will win the State Championship. You new people should already know we have a young lady on this team. I want her treated with the respect she has earned. Without her we would never have won the league title or championship. That is why she is one of the two team captains. Sonny is also a team captain. I should not have to mention this but just to remind everyone there is no cursing on my field or in the locker room. Jackee, do you have anything to say?"

She said, "we are a team headed by a great coach, and we win or lose as a team. Never take your eyes off what we are doing here. We can beat last year's record by winning the last game of the season. That game will not only be our 23rd consecutive win but also the state championship."

Bender had a scheduling problem so their games against Reagan were moved to the next to last series of the season. This meant that Reagan had to play their toughest teams the last two weeks of the season. The first twelve games against Howell, Bristle and Meeker went according to plan. In some games they were competitive, in others they were not. Each school had tried their best to break Reagan's winning streak. Reagan's pitching really came together and each pitcher threw complete games except when it was a blowout and the coach wanted to get the others some game experience. With twelve straight wins and a streak of thirty four games, the series against Bender was up next.

Bender had beaten Travis three of the four games they played, which was the only game Bender had lost so far. First game of the series was at Reagan. Sonny and Jackee spoke to the team, before taking the field for practice, telling them that they were ready for Bender. "The coach will fill you in on a scouting report he received from a trusted friend. We want to tell you to raise the level of your game because Bender has to raise theirs to beat us. Remember how the teams we have played seemed to be trying very hard to break our streak. Bender has greater incentive, if they beat us they can win the league and go on to the state championship. Well we are not going to let them do that. We will go out and out hit them, out score them, out play them and sweep them in four games. Who's with us!" All the players jumped up shouting let's do it, before running to their practice positions.

After Bender took infield, lineup cards were exchanged, ground rules discussed and then the umpire said play ball. Sandy looked unhittable and retired the side in the top of the first. Sonny led off the inning with a walk and Jessie on a hit and run, grounded to first. With Sonny on second Jackee was Intentionally walked bringing Rocky Daniels to the plate. He was the new third baseman and hit very well in the scrimmages. The count was 2 and 0, when Sonny and Jackee took off on a pitch way outside. Rocky was intentionally walked and now Scott came to hit with the bases loaded. Scott walked on four unintentional pitches giving Reagan a lead. Next up is Bruce Davis the catcher. Bruce hit the first pitch he saw because he knew the pitcher had to throw a strike and it was going to be a fastball. As the ball was rolling to the fence in right center, three runners scored and Bruce was standing on second. The stands once again held a big crowd and they were loving every minute of this game. This early four run lead was a downer for Bender and Sandy kept them off the scoreboard, the game ended 9 to 0 and Sandy finished with a 2 hitter. Jackee had gone 2 for 2 with three walks. She was now hitting over .600.

Game two was at Bender and they had a full house. Bender's coach had saved his best pitcher for game two. Coach Begali had the scouting report on

Bender pitching and knew what he was up to. It really made very little difference since his first three pitchers were very close in talent. Coach told the team to "stay within your own ability and we will win." The crowd contained many young girls who just came to see Jackee play. She had promised to sign autographs after the game. Coach knew she did this and held the bus until she finished. Top of the first Reagan went down in order as Jackee flew out deep to left center field to end the inning. The score stayed 0 to 0 until the top of the third, when Jessie singled and Jackee came to bat. She had a 3 and 1 count when she signaled Jessie to run on the next pitch. This had been a situation Jackee had with Sonny and Jessie. whenever they were on first and Jackee had a 3-1 count they were to run on the next pitch. If it was a ball Jackee would take the walk, if it was around the plate she would hit it. The pitch was over the outside of the plate and she hit it down the right field line. When the ball got back to the infield Jackee was on third and Reagan led 1 to 0. Rocky drove her in with a fly ball to center. The score was still 2 to 0 in the bottom of the 6th. Bender had their first big rally going with runners on the corners and one out. Ther number four batter who looked like he was 25 years old hit a shot up the middle, Jackee ran and dove and cought the ball in the webbing of her glove, she rolled over and flipped the ball to Sonny on second who turned and threw out the batter easily at first base. Chuck finished it off with a perfect seventh inning. For the next 30 minutes, Jackee signed pads, baseballs, hats and even one bat. As she was leaving, a woman asked if she would speak at the girl scout Jamboree in late June. Jackee gave her the house phone number and told her to call with all the details. If she could make it she would be honored to speak. Coach heard all this and could not believe the impact she was having on women.

Game three at home with Carl pitching, was a disaster for Bender. The full stands and the fact the team was going for their 15th straight win of the season really pumped up the team. From the first inning on Reagan had runners on base all the time. They built up a very comfortable lead and never looked back. Carl had one of his best games and with the great defense behind him kept the scoreless streak going to 21 innings and Bender had yet to score a run. The Bender coach was glad when the game ended but was ashamed of the 14 to 0 score.

Game four at Bender was over before Bender took the field. The team was down and they only had a JV pitcher available to start the game. The coach could have started his number one pitcher, but he wanted to win the last four games against Meeker to give the team a little momentum for next year. Reagan had a sophomore pitcher who played for both JV and varsity. Coach wanted him to get some varsity experience so next year he would fit right in. Zack Webber had excellent stuff and he had a perfect 6 and 0 JV record for the year. He was very nervous and gave up a run in the second inning. Since Reagan scored 10 runs it made very little difference. They completed the sweep and their pitching gave up one run in 28 innings. Jackee spent another 20 minutes signing autographs.

Reagan now had 16 straight and was going for a perfect season with only Travis left on the schedule.

Game one was at Travis and the stands were packed. As had been the case all year, Jackee was the center of attraction. There were more women in the stands than men. Even Travis female athletes came to the game to see Wonder Woman. She was having her best season and although she was exhausted, was having the time of her life. Travis had decided to get even for last year. They still believed that if they could sweep Reagan they would win first place by one game. They had a 13 and 3 record, and a sweep would put them 1 game up on Reagan. First game would be critical and Travis decided on a scam to get Jackee thrown out of the game. They would try to get her in a fight so that both players would be thrown out and not be eligible for the next game. Top of the first inning with Sonny at second and Jackee batting instead of the usual walk, all the pitches were high and tight. The whole time she was at bat the Travis players were calling her names and hurling insults at her. None of this affected Jackee and when the pitcher made a mistake and threw one between the belt and chest inside, She lined it down the left field line for a double and an RBI. Again in the top of the third and 2 runners on they started again calling her names. People in the stands started screaming at the Travis players. The umpires stopped the game and told Travis dugout that if they continued the game would be forfeited to Reagan. He also warned the people he had the authority to clear the stands or call a forfeit. There was no further trouble and the Reagan players just destroyed the Travis team. Game one ended by the lopsided score of 15 to 0.

Game two at home was not even a contest. Reagan led all the way and Travis never got a runner to third base. Fourteen consecutive scoreless innings and eighteen straight wins. Fans filled the stands and cheered the whole time. Game three at Travis had a few parents but a large number of girls in the stands. Travis' coach brought up some JV players and more or less sat his seniors. This game ended in another shout out and now the Reagan pitchers had allowed one run in 7 games.

Last game of the regular season saw Reagan going for their 20th consecutive win for this year and forty two over two years. There was barely any room for the spectators to stand. The stands had been filled 30 minutes before the game was to start. There were TV cameras and special people all over the place. When Reagan took infield practice people cheered the whole time they were on the field. When it was Travis' turn to take the field there was nothing but the usual talk in the stands. When Jackee got a hit in the first inning the cheering was so loud that you would have thought Babe Ruth had hit a grand slam home run to win the game. Jackee tipped her hat to the crowd the way her father had taught her. When she scored Reagan's first run, she got more cheers. In her final at bat for Reagan she hit a double to left center, and with the score 12 to 0 the coach removed her from the game. He had seen Bats do it in summer ball. As Jackee jogged off the field everyone in the stands and sitting on the field stood and cheered. When she entered the dugout, they continued to cheer until she came out and tipped her hat and mouthed the words thank you. The game finally ended and Travis got on the bus to go home. Most people however stayed and continued to cheer for the team that has won 42 consecutive games over two years.

Rose got a game ball with the date, teams and score. All the players and coaches also signed it. Jackee was being interviewed by a local TV station where there were some magazine representatives, one of which was a leading sports monthly. The TV reporter had been promised that they would be first since they had a deadline to meet. Everyone else was directed to her parents or coaches. Mr Rogers met with the parents prior to the game, telling them that a coach and an administrator from the college Jackee was interested in were here to speak directly to her. A meeting will be held at the Jenco's home later that evening. Right now the celebration was still going strong. Once again the booster club prepared refreshments in the high school cafeteria. They never expected this size of a crowd so emergency calls went out to local businesses to prepare and bring more food and drinks. Within half an hour food was being delivered and the celebration continued.

William gathered his family and headed home to prepare for the college meeting. Jackee had to stay a while longer for pictures and more interviews. Dan had promised to drive her home as soon as she was finished. Around 7:30 Jackee asked if she could leave because she needs to shower and get something to eat. Taking control, Dan escorted her to his car, he had already loaded her school backpack and gym bag in his car. They now headed to Jackee's house. There were a few more cars than usual near the house. When they walked in the whole family was there and Mr Rogers with two men Jackee didn't recognise. She excused herself and ran upstairs to shower and change. Twenty minutes later she came down looking like she stepped out of a teen magazine. Mr. Rogers introduced the people from Olympus College. Mr Zimmer was the varsity baseball coach and Dean Grant was the dean of admission. Dean Grant told the Jenco's that the admission office had gone over Jackee's application and after our own investigation, had determined that she was the perfect person for the 6 year program. "We are also prepared to offer her a full academic scholarship plus free room and board. We can not force her to but we would like her to be a posted student for this program. It basically would include a few speaking engagements and her picture on our brochures. Some future interviews may also be part of it." William had two questions. How would this affect her ameture status and how about her study time and baseball activities. Coach Zimmer said this would have no effect on her ameture status and her schedule that has been prepared for her will leave plenty of time for workouts, practice and eventually games home and away. Jackee asked her parents if they could go see the school before making a decision. The last week in June "I should be free since baseball, my exams and the senior prom that Dan invited me to should all be over."

Coach Zimmer told Jackee that what he saw her do on the field, "I can almost guarantee that you will be my starting shortstop as a freshman." Jackee thanked coach Zimmer and Mr Rogers for all he had done and told the two college reps that she was very impressed with their presentation. They thanked the Jencos and left.

The state baseball finals were to be held in the triple A stadium as the team was on the road that weekend. A representative from each section met at the state office and selected one of eight cards. This was not to determine who was the best team but rather which teams would play each other. Rules for the tournament were very simple: "number one will play number eight, number two will play seven in game two, three would play six in game three and finally number four would play five in game four. Winners of the second round will play for the championship on Sunday starting at one pm. A coin toss will always determine the home team. All home plate umpires have been given a coin to be used."

Coach Begali called his team together after practice on Monday. "We are seeded seventh so we will play Armsted high school who is seated second the second game of the first round. Our game is scheduled to start at 2:30 on Friday. Teams were not seated by record or power rating. They were seated by a card draw, so there is no way to determine how strong or weak a team is. We have to assume that each team is strong since they won their section. Every team we face in this tournament will be a championship team." Early Friday morning Reagan left for Barkerville, where the stadium is located. When they arrived they were shown a locker room to change in and a special guard had a locker to store valuables. Jackee had her own private room. When everyone was ready, the team went to a designated area for practice. At exactly twelve noon game one started. Coach Wangel and Singer went to scout the teams. Between Jackee, Sonny and Scott, Coach Begali had enough help.

Game one was won by Montclair in a close 2 to 1 contest. The scout coaches came back and were very impressed by the quality of both teams. Just as Begali had expected, these all would be very competitive teams and since they were by far the smallest school, they were definitely the underdog. The second game between Reagan and Armsted began exactly at 2:30. Sandy was all pumped up for this game. It had been rumored that many college and major league scouts would be in the stands. Reagan was the visiting team and went down in order in the first. In fact the first three innings each team had nine up and nine down. Top of the fourth Sonny led off with a hit and Jessie followed with a perfect hit and run single. Jackee due up next, pushed a perfect bunt past the pitcher and made it to first without a throw. Sonny scored, giving Reagan the lead. Rocky followed with a single, scoring Jessie and sending Jackee to third. She scored when Scott hit into a double play. With a three run lead, Sandy just pitched his game. Although he did allow his first run in four games, he still finished with a three hitter along with 10 strikeouts. Reagan only had three more hits the rest of the game. Jackee walked her only other at bat.

All the coaches scouted games three and four. Since Reagan was scheduled to play the second game against the winner of game three, that game held their immediate interest. Clarksten won game three and met Reagan in the second game on Saturday. That game was scheduled for 1pm. According to the coaches they were a running team that made contact. Once again Singer and Wangle scouted game one, while the rest of the team practiced for their game. Jackee and Sonny called the team together and decided to show Clarksten what a real running team looked like. "Let's play a very aggressive game, take every extra base, steal bases, take big leads, make them throw to bases, and keep putting pressure on them. But be smart about it, remember the other teams are scouting us."

Reagan was again the visiting team and batted first. Sonny led off and after 10 pitches drew a walk. On the very next pitch he stole second without a throw. The pitcher was so upset with the walk he failed to hold him close. Now he was trying to hold Sonny close to second and threw twice to second base. He groved the next pitch to Jessie and he doubled down the left field line. Jackee pushed a bunt past the pitcher and the first baseman had to field it since the second baseman was trying to hold Jessie close to second. When the first baseman fielded the ball he flipped it to the pitcher trying to cover first. With her speed Jackee easily beat him to the bag and because he was running away from home plate, he was in no position to see Jessie, who never stopped running, and scored. With a big lead off first, Jackee forced him to throw over three times. Even though she had to dive back each time it was worth seeing the pitcher so frustrated. Just to rub it in, she stole second on the first pitch he actually threw Rocky. Clarksten's coach came out and brought in a new pitcher. When the top half of the inning was over Reagan had a four run lead before Clarksten ever batted. Chuck had his best curveball and all Clarksten could do was hit ground balls. Defense being one of the strongest qualities of Reagan, they made every play including two double plays by Sonny and Jackee. After seven innings, Clarksten went home and Reagan prepared for the final game at 1pm Sunday.

Sunday morning after church and a light breakfast with her family, Jackee was on her way back to the motel that housed her team. She asked William if he had any advice. William said, "Your way beyond anything I might know. I have never seen you play better than you are playing now. Just keep doing the best you can and remember to leave it all on the field."

"Dad, I want you and mom to be proud of me."

"Jackee, we have been proud of you all your life. Just look at what you passed on to Rose. Saturday, she won her three events and broke school records and one section record in these events. All she talks about is making you proud of her and when she can try out for the Olympics." They dropped her off at her motel and went back to their motel to pack. Rose had stayed at Dan's house after her track meet and now, she and Dan were driving up to the championship game.

They arrived just as infield practice was starting and William made sure two seats were waiting for them. Rebecca and Rocco were there as well as Evelyn and Jon. Jon could not get enough of the Jenco family. He once told them he loved watching the Brady Bunch because they were such a close family. "It was hard for me to believe that families existed like that except on television. When I came to your house for Christmas and saw your family dynamics, I realized what I had missed and how much I want what you already have. Evelyn is your whole family wrapped up in a beautiful package and I am never going to let her go." Jackee spotted Rose and Dan sitting with the rest of the family. To everyone's surprise, in walked Kim and Bats. Bats told them he would not miss this game for any amount of money. Reagan took infield last as they were the visiting team. Their infield drill was flawless and the crowd really started to get into the game. Carl Dolan was to start for Reagan. He also had three consecutive shutouts in his last three starts. After infield practice, Sonny and Jackee took the team into the dugout. Sonny began by saying "up to now our year has been perfect. Let's finish the season and give our school something to be proud of."

Jackee was next and told them "let's show the world what a small school can do. We were the smallest school in this tournament and we knocked off two giants. We have one more giant to go. Let's win this one for all the small schools, for the coach, our school, our loyal fans, our family but most important for ourselves. Win this game and no one can take away the fact that we were the best team in the state." Introductions followed the exchange of lineup cards and explanation of the ground rules. Before the umpire said play ball, coach Begali told his team that for most everyone here, "this will be the most important game of your life. Most will not experience a chance to win a championship again. So enjoy yourselves and show me and the world just how great you really are."

Hanover high school was one of the biggest in the state. They also defeated their opponents easily in the first two rounds. There was no scouting report on their pitcher but they knew he was one of their best. He was a tall righthander who threw hard but did not have a good second pitch. So look fastball was the word on the bench. Their team was a good hitting team and only fair on defense. Sonny, Jessie, and Jackee talked about how it was up to them to show the way. Sonny did just that. He made him throw 9 pitches and worked a walk. Jessie moved him to second on a hit and run by hitting a grounder between first and second that the first baseman picked up and threw to the pitcher covering. Jackee up next was looking for a fastball she could hit up the middle. On the fourth pitch she got her pitch and hit it over second and into centerfield. Sonny scored as Jackee took second on the throw to the plate. Rocky lined the next pitch off the second baseman's glove and Jackee could only go to third because she thought he might catch it. With runners on the corners Scott hit a ground ball to short, the shortstop flipped the ball to the second baseman as Rocky came sliding in. He could not complete the double play and Jackee scored the second run. Carl allowed a few base runners in the first and third innings but did not allow any to score. So after four innings the score was still 2 to 0 . Reagan batted in the top of the fifth, with one out the number nine hitter Burt Bradley, the right fielder, hit a double to left center. Sonny surprised everyone by bunting and beating the throw to first. Jessie up next drew a walk to load the bases. Now with the bases loaded, Jackee came to the plate. Looking for a high fastball she could drive to the outfield and score Burt, she got that exact pitch, high inside over the plate. She turned on it just like she had done 100 times in batting practice, she knew she got all of it and it would go deep. What she did not know was that the ball was hit perfectly and it not only cleared the left field fence but went well into the parking lot. The Reagan side of the field were on their feet screaming and cheering and started shouting, "Jackee, Jackee, Jackee." Rose was cheering so loud that Jackee thought she heard her. Now with the score 6 to 0, Hanover had the look of a defeated team. Coach told his team that there were nine more outs to get and many have lost games because they forgot to keep playing their game. "Just go out and play your game."

Carl had six runs to work with and intended that nothing unusual would happen. He told Bruce he was going to throw strikes and not walk anyone, "but if I get two strikes on anyone I'll go for the K". He threw 15 strikes in the bottom of the fifth and got three more outs. Reagan went down 1,2,3, in the top of the sixth. Hanover had their big hitters coming up. The first two batters hit singles and the number four batter lined a shot right at Rocky who caught it backhanded and could not get it out of his glove. The fifth hitter hit a short fly ball toward center field, Jackee ran as hard as she could to where she thought the ball would drop. She and the ball arrived at the same time, she lunged for the ball, caught it and before she fell flipped the ball to Scott who was charging in from center. As Scott got the ball from Jackee and was still running toward second base he threw a one hopper to first to get the runner before he could get back, completing the double play. Hanover was done and they pretty much showed it on the field. There was no hustle out to the field and you could tell they were just going through the motions. Jackee batted one last time in the top of the seventh and of course received an ovation from all the fans. She drew a four pitch walk and then Rocky flew deep to left center to end the inning. The bottom of the seventh, the first two batters made quick outs. Begali called time out and sent in someone to take Jackee's place. She jogged to the dugout and accepted and acknowledged the ovation she received. The next Hanover player popped out to Sonny to end the game. Reagan was the number one baseball school in the state.

Pandemonium broke out all over the field. Reagan supporters were pouring onto the field to congratulate the players and coaches. Rose was the first family member to reach Jackee and she jumped on her causing both of them to fall. When the rest of the family tried to reach Jackee it was impossible since she and Rose were completely surrounded by Reagan supporters. Bats recognized Coach Begali and said to him, "you and I have become part of history in baseball. We never knew it then but we sure as hell know it now."

Begali told him that she carried the team for two years and never once took any credit for the team's success. "She gave so much of herself to the team I don't know how she is still standing. If my players had half of her drive and dedication, I could win another 45 games straight." Kim, who was holding Bats arm, thought to herself, *there must be hundreds of girls like Jackee who never get the chance to reach their potential because no one will give them the chance.*

William and the rest of the family finally reached Jackee. Carmela was still crying and hugged her and told her how proud we are of you. She kissed her mother and told her, "you and Dad are the reason this happened. I never could have accomplished this without you. Without your support I would have never thought of doing something like this. I performed on the field, but you and Dad created the possibility."

Coach Zimmer from Olympus college had seen all three games and really could not believe that Jackee could be that good. He felt that they were lucky that she was leaving her junior year because if this were her senior year there would be 20 baseball coaches here. Coaches that were here probably knew she is a junior and not eligible to sign a letter of intent. Zimmer was not aware of the fact that 15 colleges, about half being division 1 schools, had already inquired about Jackee's intent. He then went down to the field and spoke with William about Jackee's visitation schedule. Before he left, he told William, "call me about any day your family is available and we will accommodate you."

Three more things had to happen before they could head home. First the championship state trophy had to be awarded to Reagan, and it was accepted by coach Begali. Second, the MVP award for the tournament had to be announced, and to no one's surprise Jackee won it by a unanimous vote. Third and most important, Rose received a game ball. It turned out to be the ball that Jackee hit for a grand slam. Begali directed Coach Wangel to go after the ball and pay whatever they want but get that ball. Wangel found the boy and offered him $10.00. The kid said he also wanted an autograph from the amazon who hit the ball. Wangel brought him to the side of the dugout and had Jackee sign a ball. She had no idea why she was signing a ball but just did it.

Jackee was interviewed by a TV crew, radio station and a few publications, this all took about an hour. After that she excused herself and said she had to change. One hour later they were headed home. What they did not know was the game had been broadcast back home. The booster club had it sent to the football field and anyone who wanted could come and listen to the game. They had about 450 supporters at the field. Local merchants supplied refreshments free of charge. As the game went on and it seemed that Reagan would win, the booster club went to plan B. A party was set up in the school cafeteria with un-limited food and drink. They knew they had about five hours before the bus and supporters would get home. Four and one half hours later the bus and just about everyone in the district was at the school. The reception committee waiting for the bus was enormous. As the bus approached the school people started cheer-ing. They could not get off the bus fast enough. No one in town had ever seen anything like this and as far as the players were concerned, they probably would never see it again. There were a few speeches congratulating the team. Coach Begali told the crowd this was the greatest team in the history of the school and probably always will be. Jackee was asked to speak, at first she said no but Sonny and Jessie insisted she speak for the team.

Jackee started by thanking everyone for coming out to celebrate with the team. "All the team players want to thank you for all the support you have given us. We could have never won without the support of the people, coaches, and especially the parents who gave us so much of their time and support. One last thing, I am giving this trophy to the school and dedicating it to every young girl who has a dream and refuses to let anything or anybody come between her and that dream." With an ovation that could be heard in the next town, Jackee gave her MVP trophy to Mr Steeler, who was now the principal of the high school.

CHAPTER NINE

Jackee Has a Farewell Party and Starts 6 Year Program

*H*er parents wanted Jackee's 18th birthday to be a special one. They had planned to make it a family and close friends party. Word spread through the community that Jackee was leaving Reagan and entering a special college program. The booster club and the community as a whole wanted to do something to show their gratitude for what she did for the district. William and Carmela agreed to a surprise party being held not at their favorite restaurant but at the high school cafeteria. Booster club said everything would be taken care of, all the family had to do was get her there at 7pm on June 13th. A cake had been ordered, but William was told that the bakery is donating a cake just made for Jackee. It wasn't hard to get Dan to become part of this plot. He readily agreed to pick Jackee up and get her to the school on time. This conspiracy went like this; Dan would pick Jackee up at 6:30. She would be told that he was driving her to the party at the restaurant, then he would tell her that "Coach Begali had a call from a college, and I had to pick up the forms to fill out and send immediately. Coach would meet me at the coaches office at seven that night to give me the forms. Jackee would not think it was unusual because I am still deciding on a college. She doesn't know that I committed to a college last week and was going to surprise her with the news on her birthday."

When Dan arrived at Jenco's house only Jackee and Evelyn were home. Supposedly the rest of the family was at the restaurant. Once they were ready, the three of them headed for the school. Dan explained to Jackee what he had to do and she said it would be fine. While Dan was telling Jackee, Evelyn called her parents to tell them they were on the way. As they approached the school, Jackee noticed a great many cars in the parking lot. Probably an emergency board meeting Dan said to her and they proceeded into the school. They had to walk past the cafeteria to get to the coaches office. Upon reaching the cafeteria Dan guided

Jackee toward a door, he opened it and helped her inside. The inside was tastefully decorated and over 500 people were shouting happy birthday. Jackee jumped back as if to run away, but Dan and Evelyn held her. She then started crying and could not believe that this was happening to her. Carmela and William led the family to her side. Rose threw her arms around her and started crying. She had learned only that day that Jackee would be leaving for college in August. Rose whispered to her, "what will I do without you?" and hugged her tighter.

Jackee said "we will talk about this later and I promise you it will be fine." Rebecca and Rocco congratulated her and then Jackee started mingling with the people.

Food, drinks, and all manner of goodies were now being served and a DJ was playing music. Bats and Kim were one of the first to wish her a happy birthday. Kim told her she had a surprise and would talk to her later. Jackee had only seen Kim at the state championship game for a few moments and had not really talked to her. Everyone had finished eating when the President of the booster club began speaking. Mr Booth thanked everyone for coming and hoped they had enjoyed the food. He thanked the merchants who donated food, drinks, and the fantastic cake for this celebration. He then talked about Jackee and her impact on the school, community and finally on sports. When he felt that enough had been said, he introduced Jackee and asked her to say a few words. She thanked everyone by saying that if she mentioned each individual she was bound to miss someone, so she made a general thank you. "This is by far the greatest birthday I ever had or ever will have. Your support and encouragement kept me going. People tell me I have been a great influence to many young girls. Well, if I helped one achieve success, all the pain and suffering was worth it. Thank You and God Bless You All."

When everything was done, the Jenco family packed all the presents and headed home. The whole family was at the house when her parents gave Jackee their parents. Jackee had wondered what happened that she did not get something from her parents. There were two individually wrapped packages. She opened the first and it was a baseball that had all the 1947 Yankkee signatures on it. The second one was a baseball signed by Bobby Brown. She held both of these balls and said, "these are the best, where did you find them?"

William said he went to a collectors show and found a dealer who had Yankee memorabilia. The collector told him these were two of the rarest Yankee baseballs. "I felt that you not only deserve these baseballs but you have earned them. Rose will take care of them while I am away but they will always be part of our family."

Dan and Jackee went out to the porch and talked for a few moments. She had not received a present from Dan and now he was about to hand it to her. He told her he wanted this to be between only them. It had been carefully wrapped and she carefully opened it. There was a gold locket with her and Dan's picture inside. A gold chain was attached to the locket and Jackee said it was beautiful.

"I want you to wear this near your heart so that I'll always be close to you."

They were hugging very tight when she said "this is so expensive and you need the money for college."

"I wish it was 100 times more because you deserve to have the best."

She said, "I already have the best in my arms and I'll never need more." They kissed for a long time. Rebeeca and Rocco wanted to go home but they would not open the door and interrupt them. Finally they could not wait any longer and rattled the door to warn them that someone was coming out. Jackee said good night to Dan and thanked him for another great date. She said goodbye to Rebecca and Rocco and went inside. She told her parents that Kim had shared a secret with her and asked if they wanted to hear it.

They said "if it is a secret why will you tell us?"

"It's not really a secret but Kim and Bats are going to have a baby near the end of December."

William said he was pretty sure of that when he saw the look on Bats face. "He never could hide his emotions, that is why he could never win in poker." They all laughed and then went to bed.

It was Saturday and Dan came over early for their usual date. Jackee hadn't told him that she had a speaking engagement at Travis high school. The girl scout leader, or whoever she was, had called her and asked if she was available this Saturday. Jackee told her she would be honored to come but not to expect too much since she was not a good public speaker. When they arrived at Travis they were greeted by the woman who called, and a group of girl scouts. Dan was impressed by the way the girls treated Jackee, it seemed like she was their hero or idol. They led her to the head table and gave her a seat usually reserved for a person of honor. He was completely ignored until the woman in charge offered him a seat at her table. This table was for her family and guests. Mrs Charles Johnson, who seemed to be in charge, gave an opening address thanking everyone for coming and said that this was by far the best turnout they ever had. She told everyone that the food and drinks had all been prepared by volunteer mothers and a few merchants. She then introduced a zone leader who spoke for a few moments and then helped give out the awards. Usually at these events once the awards are given out, parents pack up and leave but no one left. Mrs Johnson now introduced Jackee. She told the audience that she took her daughter to see Travis play Reagan at the high school. She thought her daughter had finally acquired some school spirit and interest in sports. "To my surprise she only wanted to see a young girl who was playing for Reagan. All she did was cheer when this girl batted or fielded a ball. It now dawned on me that my daughter had seen something I totally missed.

There was a girl doing something that has never been done and doing it very well. I told myself that if she agreed it would be my honor to have her speak at this awards dinner. She graciously agreed. Let me now introduce the MVP of section 6 and the MVP of the baseball state championship, Jackee Jenco."

Dan could not believe what he was seeing, everyone was on their feet clapping and cheering for Jackee. After what seemed like forever, Jackee got up and stood by the mic and started to speak. First she thanked everyone for the warm reception and Mrs Johnson for inviting her. She looked over the audience and said that each of the young girls here has the power and ability to do great things. "No one has the right to tell you that you can't do something. Your talent whatever it is was given to you by God and only He has the power to take it from you. When I was young it seemed to me that only men were given credit for achieving great things. Then I found out that most times, women were told they couldn't do something. I made up my mind that I was going to do something no other woman has done. Since I was very young, I have loved baseball. Not only because my father loved it but because I found that I was good at it. My parents encouraged me to be the best at anything I did. You probably have not heard yet that I have been accepted to a new 6 year program for medicine. I have also received 3 separate offers from division one schools to play baseball for them. Most people believe that my being on a baseball field was some kind of a gimmick or publicity stunt. My being on the field is because I earned it. In baseball, if they find someone better, you're out. My coaches started out very skeptical and ended up supporting me. Two of the best things I have learned I am going to share with you. First, if something is easy, everybody could do it . The harder it is to do, the greater the achievement. Second, America was founded on doing the impossible. It is our unique heritage that Americans do the impossible and that is why this country is number one in the world. Each of you young ladies was born to do great things. Let no one stop, abuse or tell you that you can't. One more important thing to remember, success is not always 100%. The greatest hitter in all of baseball made outs 3 of every 5 at bats. Thank you and may God bless you and always be your guide."

For the next hour she spoke to girls and signed autographs. Finally Mrs Johnson took her aside and asked when she finishes medical school will she come back and speak again. Jackee said "you have my home phone and God willing my parents will be there to update you on my status." She then took Dan's arm and let him lead her to the car.

While driving he said what a great job she did talking to all the girls. He now understood what makes her keep going against such great odds. One more important thing he told her, that she was the most dedicated individual he had ever known. She sat close to him and said how sorry she was that they were not seated together. Dan started laughing, "they didn't even know or care who I was. Everyone came to see you, not some boy who drove you there."

"Does this bother you that most of these people are interested in me and what I have to say?"

"I could never relate to them the way you can, they realize how much it took for you to be where you are. I never want you to feel that I am jealous of your success. From our first date I knew that I would always be in your shadow. What did surprise me was that you had feelings for me. I figured a beautiful girl like you had many boyfriends and would eventually tire of me."

Jackee moved closer to him and he could hear her softly crying. He pulled the car into a secluded area and just held her. She stopped crying and he dried her tears and kissed her gently. She told him that some day he may "decide it is too hard being with such an object of attention and get rid of me."

Dan said, "I just want you to know that I will always respect and love you no matter what happens. On new years eve when I took you home and we kissed good night, I knew then that I never wanted to lose you. He kissed her again and said it was time for their ice cream."

Although she was very disappointed that he didn't continue to kiss her, she knew that going for an ice cream was a protective device. He was protecting her from herself and it felt good that he cared that much for her. In the ice cream store of course Jackee was the center of attention and as soon as she walked in a crowd started to gather. Her ice creams were always on the house or someone else paid. Dan had kiddingly told her he may never have to pay for an ice cream again. A few autographs later they left and drove to Jackee's house. They parked at the far end of the driveway and did a little necking. Dan just held her and they began talking about the senior prom that was next Friday. Every year the PTA and some parents decorated the Gym at the high school into whatever theme the seniors had decided . This year's theme is cruising down the Mississippi. Parents and PTA had one day until 6pm to get everything ready. From 6 to 7, food and music had to be set up because the doors opened at 7 sharp. It would be a four hour affair and no one was allowed to leave and come back in. There was no liquor allowed and the punch or soft drinks were never spiked. Years ago a car loaded with prom attendees was involved in a serious accident. No one died but many were seriously hurt. This new format offered better control over drinking and driving. Between dance sessions, senior awards were given out. Most of these are funny and only relate to the seniors. These awards were voted on by the class, Class officers tallied all the votes and then got fun prizes for the awards. Only one award was not their choice. Faculty usually chaperoned the prom and they selected a couple for the king and queen or best couple award. It could be called either one but king and queen is the usual name. That couple selected, would lead off the last dance session, and after a minute or so of their dancing everyone else joined them on the dance floor.

Jackee told Dan that she had her gown from Rebecca's wedding cut down to a prom dress. She thought that the seamstress had done a great job and she saved a lot of money. Her mother thought that the dress looked very good on her. Dan said his tux was in the style of what could be worn on a riverboat. He then asked if she planned to play baseball this summer. Bats asked her the same question. Everything depended on her school visit and if she decided to go, and when she would have to be there. "If it is fine with you I would like to play at least part of the summer."

"Never ask my permission for anything you want to do. I told you once and I'll tell you again, you make all the decisions about what you have to do. I am part of your support group and not a decision maker."

"I know what you told me, but I feel that helping me decide is a big part of our relationship."

He got out of the car and opened Jackee's door and helped her to get out, then he walked her to the front door, kissed her tenderly and said "I'll be here at 6:30 on Friday so we can take pictures before going to the prom."

Dan walked in exactly at 6:30 with a Roses corsage in a box. He was dressed like a riverboat hustler. Jackee was coming down the stairs as Dan was talking to William. They both looked at Jackee and Carmela, who had been helping her dress, walking slowly toward them. William said aren't they beautiful, but Dan said nothing at first as he handed Jackee the corsage. Finally, he looked at her and said "there are no flowers that can compare with your beauty. You will be the most beautiful girl at the prom and I am the lucky one to escort you."

All Jackee could do was blush and whisper "thank you." It was a good thing that he had the corsage made so that it could be pinned on, or wear it on the wrist. There was no place to pin it since this was now an off the shoulder evening dress. Everyone in the house had a camera and Rose, Evelyn, and even Rebecca took what seemed like one million pictures. When everyone had their fill of pictures the prom couple said goodbye and headed out.

The parents knew it would be a late night since more often than not seniors had after prom parties that lasted most of the night. Jackee had mentioned that Dan had been invited to at least three such parties. William asked Carmela if she saw the look on Dan's face when Jackee came down to meet him. She said it was pretty much the same look you had for me.

"That is what I am afraid of. If the same thoughts crossed his mind that crossed mine, Jackee could be in over her head."

Carmela smiled at him and said "it is not Jackee I am worrying about, it's poor Dan that I feel bad for."

William shook his head and told her he could not understand what she was saying. Carmela told him she trusted Dan to keep his emotions under control but she could not trust Jackee to do the same. She knew he still did not understand what she was trying to tell him. She said, "Jackee has been aggressive her whole life and this emotion has not come up before, so she may not be able to handle it properly. Dan has already proved to me that he is capable of handling it for both of them."

When they entered the prom, most everyone was looking at them. No one there had ever seen Jackee formally dressed. Dan thought to himself that the senior girls were lucky only seniors were eligible for the king and queen award. Jackee had the queen award uncontested if she was in the running. Decoration of the gym was perfect and the food was plentiful and delicious. Soft drinks went from water to punch and most everything else. Music was by a DJ who had been selected by the dance committee. He seemed to be very attentive to what the dancers wanted. Jackee and Dan danced the whole night. Except for the time between, that involved speeches, awards, eating, and powder room trips, they were either talking to people they knew or they were dancing. At 10:45 or so couples started to leave and close to 11:00 Dan asked if Jackee was ready to leave. He had been invited to a party at one of the football players' houses. It was a large house with a large backyard. The patio consisted of a heated pool, deck area, sauna and a big dance area.

While driving to the party, Dan explained that the house had only prom attendees there. The rest of the family was gone for the evening and the graduating senior is incharge. The neighbors had been warned, and a DJ had been hired to play for 3 hours until about 2:30. Food and drinks had been laid out. This food looked to be more expensive than that at the prom and the drinks did include Beer and some wine. After dancing for over an hour Jackee and Dan sat on a very comfortable swing. He asked if she wanted something to eat or drink. Jackee told him that she would like to try the fruit and maybe some water. Dan left and soon returned with a fruit dish, some finger food and a bottle of water and a lo-cal drink. Jackee kept seeing couples going into the house or basement. Others were just making out in different areas of the patio. More and more, the party goers seemed to be shedding clothing. Some had bathing suits and shorts that they brought with them. Jackee did not remember Dan saying anything about a pool or change of clothing. She was shocked at some of the swimsuits that were being worn. She heard about bikinis and had even seen a few but none compared to these. She knew that there was no way she could fit her body in such a small piece of cloth. With her arms around him she said "do you think those girls in bikinis are sexy?" He looked over and said how could he not. She said "I could not wear something like that in public."

Dan answered, "I hope not. You can wear one of them when we are alone or on a deserted island."

She finally asked Dan where the other people who were here earlier were. He said many are inside making out and do not want to be seen doing it. "Are you going to take me inside? No! Not here, not now." Just as he was saying this a girl ran out of the house wearing only underwear and jumped into the pool. More followed the first girl into the pool, some with much less clothing on. She had heard about skinny dipping but had never actually seen it done.

Dan said he thought it might be time to leave. Jackee wanted to know if he was tired or just ashamed of her. He put his arms around her and told her he could never be ashamed of being with her. That she was the most important thing in his life and will take care of her forever.

"Then why don't you want to take me inside, am I not good enough or am I too much of a prude."

"Jackee, I told you before there is nothing I would want more than to take you someplace and love you until you tell me you had enough."

"Then why don't you do it?" she asked?

"Because when we are done, I would hate myself for not loving you enough not to take you inside. Jackee I swear to you that there will be a wedding day and a honeymoon when we will be together body and soul forever. Just hug and kiss me now and wait for that day."

Jaqckee said she did not fully understand but as long as he held her she would follow whatever he wanted. A while later they took their leave and headed home. They walked hand and hand to her door, kissed passionately and Dan left. Jackee quietly went to bed and once again had a turning, tossing kind of night.

Next morning she was up before Carmela came down. Carmela knew something was wrong but played it cool. She calmly said "you're up awfully early the day after a prom night." What Carmela had not expected was for Jackee to start crying. She took Jackee's hand and led her to the porch where they could be alone and no one could hear. "Now tell me what this is all about."

"The prom was fantastic and we left at the end and went to a gorgeous house. We had the whole house to ourselves since the family was gone, and it had food, music and a heated pool. Later in the night couples were going into the house to make out and I assume other things. Later some came out to jump in the pool, and some were skinny dipping. I asked Dan why he did not want to go inside with me and he just said that he loved me too much to do that. In fact, he said that it would happen on our honeymoon."

"I knew it, I was right about him all along. He is my knight in shining armor."

"Mom, what are you talking about?"

"Jackee, it is exactly as I told you before, Dan is protecting you from yourself."

"You said that before and I thought I knew what you meant but I really don't understand. I wanted so much for him to take me inside and love me."

"You have to understand what he did, he thought so much of you that he didn't have sex with you. Any other boy or man for that matter would have taken you, got your clothes off and had sex with you. That person would not have cared about who you are but only wanted to satisfy a sexual urge. After he was done, you would be like any other girl that he had sex with. You would have meant nothing more than that to him. Jackee, the way you look last night, and the way Dan looked at you I can tell you for a fact he wanted to have sex with you the whole night. The reason he didn't is because he knows you are striving for something that is more important than sex. He knows that if you don't try to reach your goal you will blame him for not achieving it. This will eventually cause you to hate him even though you were partly to blame. Now do you understand what he did? He sacrificed his own personal needs for you and your dream. That Jackee is a man you will never meet again. Never hurt him or ever let him go because he loves you more than he does himself."

"Oh, mom, how do I show him that I care for him? What can I do or say?"

"Just be yourself and continue to do what you are doing. He fell in love with that person and respects her above all else."

Olympus college invited Jackee and her family on the Monday after the Prom. Jackee had only talked to Dan on the phone and told him about the visit and how she wanted to talk with him. He told her he had some family obligations to take care of and that he would see her for his graduation next Saturday. She had a sinking feeling that he was blowing her off. Her college visit was very important so she decided to concentrate only on that rather than on what Dan had said.

When they approached the college, after a five hour drive, the campus seemed to open up like a scene from a movie. The grounds were very large and well kept. Most of the buildings seemed to be fairly new. They drove by a number of science buildings that looked very modern and newly built. Upon arrival at the administration building, Coach Zimmer, Dean Grant and two others were waiting for them. William had called ahead when he was 15 minutes from the school. They had not anticipated a welcoming committee like this. Mr Grant introduced one as the president of the school, Mr Washington, and the other as head of the medical school, Dr Hopkins. After the introductions they entered the president's office and sat down. He asked if they wanted anything to eat or drink. Carmela asked if they could use a rest room. President Washington looked embarrassed, said of course and had his secretary show the ladies to a faculty room. William got to use the president's private john. When all were seated and had something to drink, president Washington told them how proud the school was to have a candidate with Jackee's near perfect rating apply for our new program. He admitted that this was an innovative program that he hoped would be a successful one. "We are looking for the best to give our program its best chance to succeed."

Dr Hopkins spoke next. He told them that when Mr Rogers contacted them, they knew he was offering the very best he had. "From what he sent us and the recommendation he included, I could not help but want to meet this young lady. When he also mentioned how beautiful she was and also a star baseball player, I thought he was talking about three different people. It is very clear he underestimated her beauty and according to Coach Zimmer also her baseball ability. We can only hope he also did the same with her science potential."

Coach Zimmer spoke next. He said they worked out a plan for her as far as baseball is concerned. "If it is your intention to play baseball, we as a group recommend that you be redshirted the first year. This is to give you time to adjust to the heavy workload you have in science. You would workout with the team just as if you were to play every day. However you will not be allowed in a game but can play in our fall program, Spring practices and our summer league if you wish. Our baseball facilities at the field house will be open to you 24 hours a day 7 days a week."

Dean Grant now took over. "Your family is welcome to visit at any time and we have guest rooms available on a first come first serve basis. There will be no cost to you for room, board, fees, or books. In fact Dr Hopkins seems to feel you can work on his research projects so we will pay you a small amount of money when you do assist him. Lastly we would like you to consider being a poster image and speaker for our program. Money can not be given to you directly because of your amateur status, but until that happens our accountants will make some other arrangement. Please think our offer over and if you have any changes let us know and we will tell you if they are acceptable. Now let us show you around the school. You will have your choice of dorm room. You can have a single, double, or group room."

Jackee was taken all over the campus. The field house was fairly new and had almost every type of training apparatus. There were at least four variations of iron mikes, indoor pitching mounds, and an artificial grass partial infield for ground balls. Three full circuits of weight machines and plenty of free weights. Other apparatus that looked like torture equipment was set up in one section. These were special machines to work out specific parts of the body. They went to see the dorms next and one in particular caught Jackee's attention. It was a new complex that consisted of double occupancy rooms, and had a study/computer room and a lounge room with the two bedrooms. Immediately Jackee knew it was ideal for her needs. Library, cafeteria, gym, and student union buildings were all well above average. Lastly, they visited the science buildings. One whole building was for nothing but lab and research work. There also were two additional buildings for science classes and meetings. All in all, the Jenco's were very impressed by the tour. Upon going back to President Washington's office, they asked if a final decision could be given to them in about a week.

President Washington said they were already making plans for this young lady and would be waiting for her acceptance to activate them. "Thank you for coming and have a safe trip home."Olympus college was the big item discussed on the trip home. Jackee could not wait to tell Dan all about it and what they offered her. William was more concerned about how they were going to use her in regards to promoting their college. First he wondered how their accountants would not show monies paid to Jackee for her endorsements and speaking engagements. One thing he knew was that if they were giving her so much, they must be figuring out how to get it back. As an accountant he understood there were many ways to be creative. Sometimes you can be too creative and go over the line. He did not want this to happen to Jackee. She was a brilliant student but very much lacking in street smarts.

Carmela had been interested in the environment Jackee would be living in. She thought the college rooms were great and she loved the one Jackee said was her kind of room. Food at the cafeteria impressed her and she believed that mostly good wholesome meals were served. Each dorm had a laundry room and it was secured from outsiders coming in. There were security cameras all over the place and a 24 hour security service montering the equipment. Although this was an open campus, there were security patrols 24/7. Any stranger on campus was immediately reported to security. If they didn't have a pass or reason to be there the police were called. Each female student was offered free of charge a security device that would alert security that you needed help and it gave your location. When she thought about it, Carmela decided this was one of the safest schools she ever heard about.

Next day Jackee called Dan and told him about the school and that she wanted to talk with him. He said he would see her after work later that day. Around 7:00, Dan rang the bell and Jackee answered. As soon as the door opened she threw her arms around him and they kissed. She led him into the living room and sat down next to him and started to explain the trip to Olympus college. She talked the whole time while Dan just listened. When she finished, Dan looked over at William and asked, "what did you and your wife think of the school's offer?"

William told him, he and his wife thought the school and their offer were extremely generous. "I have one or two reservations but the overall conditions are acceptable."

"Do you know how they intend to use her?" Carmela looked at William and asked Dan how he knew they wanted to use her for something? He told them, "from the moment I became aware of what a fantastic person she really is, I have seen people trying to use her for their own benefit. It's not for me to say who or what is right, but I never want to see her hurt or exploited."

"How did you know that the college wanted to use her?" Carmela asked.

"It's rather obvious that if the school is giving her a blank check scholarship they want a lot in return. Mr Jenco you are a lot smarter than I'll ever be, but if I shook hands with these people, I would count my fingers after we were done. I would tell Jackee never to sign anything without a lawyer reading it first. You should get as much as you can from them, in other words, use them more than they are going to use Jackee. If they do not follow what they agreed to, then I would threaten to pull Jackee out of school and go public with what they did. Jackee originally had only a local following. Since she won MVP of the state baseball tournament she not only gained state recognition but now it has gone national. According to baseball weekly she is in the top 100 baseball candidates in the country for the draft." He took a magazine out of his pocket and handed it to William.

When all the dialogue was finished the parents got up to give them space for talking. Before Carmela left she approached Dan, who had stood when the parents got up, put her arms around him and said, I was right about you from the very beginning and knew my daughter could never be in better hands. She kissed on the cheek and thanked him. Dan was at a loss for words, he just stood there looking at Carmela leaving the room. Sitting next to Jackee he said "I don't understand what happened here."

"My mother just told you she approves of you being part of my support group and that she values your opinion." She put her arms around him and said, "so do I." The rest of the evening was spent talking about both their schedules and future dates. There was graduation on Saturday and a party that Jackee, her parents and Rose were invited to. Dan had made it a point to have Rose come with them.

Saturday was a beautiful summer day and a large crowd came to see graduation at Reagan high school. Dan received his diploma, student athlete award and a $500.00 scholarship from the American Legion. Jackee knew she would have been presented with the student athlete award next year if she graduated with her class.

About 7:00 the Jenco's arrived at Dan's house with Rose leading the way. Dan introduced the Jenco's to his parents and then took Rose to where the younger adults were and introduced her to the group. Rose knew a few from school and track so she fit right in. Both sets of parents were talking so he took Jackee around and introduced her to family and friends. Jackee was the center of attention as soon as she walked in. She talked to many people and after a while excused herself and looked for Dan. He was talking to other graduates and asking what they were doing now that school was finished. When he turned and saw Jackee, he went to her and asked if she was ok. She grabbed his arm and held on tight so he could not run away. Later in the evening, her family went home but Jackee told them that Dan would drive her home. Cleaning up after the party was quick and Dan told his parents he was taking Jackee home. When they arrived at Jackee's house they sat in the car and talked about what the next step would be. She mentioned that Bats had asked her to play on his summer team. There was still a room available at his house. Lastly they spoke about when she has to start college and how he could visit. Jackee mentioned the free rooms that were available for guests. Later she said that playing baseball for the next 6 weeks on Bats' team seemed to be the right thing to do. "It would provide good competition and keep me active until school starts. I suppose you will be working as much as you can so we wouldn't have much time together anyway. I'll miss you but you will be in my thoughts and heart all the time." Sitting in the car and holding each other was all that they were doing. He later walked Jackee to the door, kissed her and said he would try to make some of her games.

Sunday morning the family headed to Dutch Hill and the Dukes. Kim was waiting for them and said how happy she was to have Jackee stay with them. Carmela wanted to know if it would be too much for Jackee to stay with her. "I told you before that Jackee will be a big help to me and it gives me someone to talk to while Bats does all his work." William gave her a check for $1300.00 and forced her to take it. She thanked him and said she would use the money for decorating the baby's room. Jackee settled in and the Jenco's drove home.

Within a week Jackee had worked and hit her way back to mid season form. For some unexplained reason she was hitting with more power. Her upper body seemed to have more strength and her swing was more controlled and compact. Arm strength and fielding were a bit better but it felt like she wasn't as quick. When she was timed running the bases they were similar to past timings. A thought came that she might not be getting the usual jump on the ball. In practice she now found that was the case but did not know how to correct it. Bats brought in an infield coach he knew and he looked and watched Jackee in a game. After the game Jackee came to him and he told her she was as good as any one he had worked with, and that her only problem was that she's not concentrating enough. Jackee quickly realized that was the problem and she had to get Dan and the school out of her head when she was on the field. It was not possible to forget Dan but the school might be. Since she had committed the Sunday they left for Dutch Hill, it had been on her mind as to when she would hear from them. That night she took a picture of Dan he had given her and said to it, "during games you can stay in my heart but must get out of my head. When the game is over you may reenter my mind."

Jackee felt free and she played the best ever. Her hitting was the best since junior high, fielding was a step up from last year and her relationship with the other players was the best. The team was winning 80% of their games and getting better. For some strange reason Jackee was having the time of her life, it seemed everything had come together and only Dan was missing. She called him one night and told him how much she missed him. "I am doing my best ever and after the game I have no one to share it with." He told her how much he missed her and that he had gone out with some of the football players and came home more depressed than when he left. One Saturday after work he just drove down to see her. She was playing a night game at home, since they won, it was only 8 1/2 innings. The game ended at 8:45 and as she was walking to the parking lot she saw Dan standing by the car. Dropping everything she ran at him and jumped into his arms. Dan almost fell over but he righted himself and began kissing her. That lasted a very long time and finally they relaxed and Dan went over to get her equipment and put it in the car. Bats came out and saw she had a ride so he just left. Jackee got into the car and they drove to Kim's house where she could shower and change. When she was getting out of the car with her equipment she said "you can wait inside while I shower and change."

He said "do you need any help washing your back?"

"There is nothing more that I would want than you washing my back."

He smiled and said "I am looking forward to that day." She went inside, and then upstairs. 20 minutes later she was down and ready to go out.

Dan looked at her and again still could not believe how beautiful she was. Here is a girl who spent 20 minutes getting ready and she still comes down looking beautiful. He could remember his pre Jackee days when he waited an hour for the girl to get ready and they never looked like this. "How hungry are you and what do you want to eat?"

She said "I just want to hold you and kiss you but if you are hungry there is a great place two blocks from here." After being seated in a booth they order food and soft drinks. While waiting for the food they caught up with the things that had happened since they last saw each other. Dan told her about his job and he heard from his college and had to go to orientation the last week in August. She told him about the season so far and that she was waiting for the final decision by Olympus college. When she receives the date for reporting to the college, she is coming home a few days before to spend time with him.

"I'll be looking forward to that day." Food and drink finally arrived and they ate like they were starving to death. Both had not eaten all day and they really were hungry. While they were at the restaurant people kept coming up to Jackee for her autograph. She was a local hero in this area and had become almost a legend. The manager or owner came over and said "there is no charge for the meal, just leave a tip for the staff."

With a big smile Dan said "I may never have to pay for our dates ever again." He left a twenty dollar bill on the table and thanked everyone they could find before leaving. Ten minutes later they were kissing in front of Kim's house. When Jackee started to fall asleep in his arms, he told her she had to get some rest for the game Sunday. She told him that a bed had been set up in the living room and he could come inside with her. He followed her into the house and saw the couch had been converted to a bed. When their good night kiss ended she went upstairs and he took off his pants and shirt and went to bed. Next morning Kim was up early and started breakfast for everyone . When Dan awakened he asked if he could shower and shave before he ate. Kim set up the bathroom with clean towels and new soap. Just as he was coming out of the bathroom Jackee had come down and was ready for church. Kim and Bats had started going to church right before their wedding so this was a normal Sunday thing. Dan's family were known as A and P catholics. They always went for ashes and palms and most other big religious holidays but not on a regular basis. He had attended most Sunday Mass since he started seeing Jackee. Now, because he wanted to please her, he became a regular church goer. After church Bats and Jackee got ready to leave for the game. Kim had to prepare all the things she would need during the game. She was happy that Dan offered to help her get ready and bring her to the field. Five minutes before game time they were sitting in their reserved seats.

Jackee put her game on the next level. In fact, she dominated the game. Not only did she go 3 for 3 with two walks, but she made two spectacular plays in the field. One was a diving catch on a pop up behind second base. After she caught the ball she got up and fired a throw to first that completed the double play and one step before the runner from third touched home. Since the third out was recorded before he touched home, the run did not count. Instead of a tie game the Dukes were up by one run. The game was over by 2:30 and Jackee was at Dan's side soon after. She told him that he should start for home. He readily agreed but not before telling her how great she had played and how proud he was to be part of her life. She hugged him so hard he could feel the sweat from her uniform. She started crying and told him she loved him so much and she will never let him go. He said "don't worry i'd be a fool to let the greatest woman ever get away." He then kissed her and said goodbye to Kim and Bats and thanked them for taking care of him and Jackee. Bats told him to please come back soon because he never saw Jackee play better. They shook hands and Dan left for home.

Bats could not explain it but the Dukes now we're playing unbeatable baseball. With Jackee leading the way, the team won its next 10 straight games. They went out to the field every game with the "we can't lose" attitude. If it wasn't their-hitting then it was their fielding that won the game, and when both were working, they destroyed the other teams. Soon every member of the team was at the field early. It seemed they could not wait to play and win the next game. This attitude in a team was very rare, and Bats had never had it happen to him before. The truth was that he wasn't sure how to handle it. So he just kept a low keyed atmosphere in the dugout and just let them play. Other coaches knew what to expect when playing a Bats team but this was something no one could explain, not even him. When Bats asked the ball players how they felt about what was happening, all they would say was, "isn't this what you trained us to do."

CHAPTER TEN

Jackee Plays Third Year of Summer Ball and New Lab Research

*D*utch Hill Dukes were in first place and had already clinched number one seed in the playoffs. The only problem they had is that Jackee had been told to report to a special orientation at Olympus college the following Sunday. Their season would end on Wednesday and the playoffs would start on Thursday with the championship game on Sunday. Jackee called Dan to inform him but he told her William called when the letter came. Bats had expected that something like this might happen. He planned for this exact thing. He called Jackee into his office on Tuesday and told her that William was on his way to pick her up. She was to say goodbye to the players and someone would drive her to Kim's. She was to pack and wait for her Dad. She did not know what to say. Bats grabbed her by the shoulders and told her she was the best player he has ever coached and he was proud to be one of the coaches who she played for. It was time for her to move on to the next chapter of her life. "There is nothing more that you can learn here, if you want more you have to go find it. The whole world is waiting for you, don't let them down. Jackee, you have a chance to affect real change, let nothing stop you from doing it." She hugged him and thanked him for all he had done for her and that she would never forget him and what he taught her.

She went to say farewell to her teammates. She thanked them for their support and how great they were taking the abuse because she played on the team. "I want you to go out and prove that this team did not win because of one player, instead we won because we worked and played together as a team. Win the championship because we are the best team and one more thing, win it for Bats, he deserves it." She turned and left before the tears started to fall. A car was waiting, and took her to Kim's.

When William arrived she was packed and ready. She thanked Kim and kissed her before leaving. William also thanked and kissed her. He said to give Bats a big kiss for him and to win it all. While driving home he told Jackee that they had made all the plans to attend the playoff games and even Dan was scheduled to go with them. She told him "this is the first time I ever put baseball second to something else. I feel like I let my teammates down."

William told her that "in life, you have priorities, and sometimes you have to make a decision that may hurt other people. No matter what the decision is, someone wins and someone loses. That is what people have to do and they must live with their decision." They sat in silence the rest of the trip.

Dan was waiting on the porch as they rolled into the driveway. Jackee ran from the car and into Dan's arms. He held her while she cried. Finally he said "I have to help your father unload the car. Rose and your mom are waiting for you."

She went into the house where Rose and Carmela were waiting. Rose asked 10 questions while dragging her into the trophy room to show all the awards she has won since Jackee has been away. Carmela stayed in the background knowing that she and Jackee would have a long talk later. She had prepared a little meal for everyone and eventually all sat down to eat. Conversation during the meal was very light and centered around just family catching up on things. After a time Dan said he had to leave and get some rest for work Wednesday. He told Jackee he would see her after dinner tomorrow. They said their good nights and Dan left. Only the two of them were unpacking Jackee's bags when she stopped and said, "Mom, I am scared. This is what I wanted but the six year commitment seems like forever. Do you think this is too much for me to handle?"

"Your father and I are both scared for you but we both know that if you put your mind to doing this we have no doubt you will be the best candidate they ever had."

Sometime after breakfast, Carmela and Jackee were back in her room getting everything ready for their Sunday trip to the college. They had to pack for both the Fall and winter. There was no schedule for them to plan anything. The letter said that a full description of Jackee's schedule will be discussed when she arrives on campus. Jackee trained a few hours with Rose as she was getting ready for a summer invitational track meet this Saturday. Jackee saw the fire in Rose's eyes as she trained and knew that Rose had that inner drive to win, just as Jackee had.

Dan showed up right after Jenco's finished dinner. Carmela told her to go with him as Rose could help clean up. She and Dan walked for a time as they were discussing how to spend the next few days together. They both knew this was going to be the longest time they had ever been apart. "We can make plans for Thanksgiving and Christmas but neither one of us has a true picture of what to expect. I'll write to you as soon as I know my new address. You will have to do the same when you settle in at college, our parents will know our new address first, so we can contact them first." Now they were back at the porch catching up on their kissing.

Dan had to work late on Thursday so the next time he saw Jackee was Friday evening. They went to a movie that neither one was interested in and when it ended, they went for their usual sundae. Jackee was still a major attraction but Dan had to pay this check himself. Later they parked in a secluded area and talked for a while. She finally asked him a question she was afraid to ask, "Dan, since I'll be away for so long do you still feel the same about me."

He smiled at her and wanted to know what brought this up. She told him that my mom said that men have different needs and desires. "Your mom is 100% correct and my needs and desires are all about you and not anyone else. There are very few people in this world who get to achieve their dreams and I know you are one of those people. You have that one chance in a million and I want to see you do it. You have the necklace I gave you and I will always be with you for support and assistance, but I will never interfere."

Jackee hugged him and said "I want you to be more than a support. I need your strength inside me and your arms holding me. I love you and want to be your wife and lover forever."

"You will be but now you have to be Jackee the baseball player and Jackee the medical student. Just think, someday I will be able to make love to a baseball player or a doctor or both. How many people can say that?"

She kissed him and said, "please don't ever hurt me and I'll give you all that and more. "

He held her close and said "we better go. You have a track meet to attend and I have to work so I'll see you tomorrow night." He took her home and left.

The invitational track meet included some of the best runners in the state. These included high schools, runners clubs and colleges. Rose was one of the youngest if not the youngest runner registered to compete. Coach Flagon thought this would be a good experience for Rose. She would get to see what real competition looks like. He entered her in the mile, 5000 meter and the long jump. He decided against the shot put for fear she would be under too much pressure. In her first event, the one mile race she finished Fourth but set a new high school record if this was a high school meet. Her time of 4:34.10 was better than the state record by over 5 seconds. For the long jump she finished third with a jump of 25.00 feet. This was .02 feet off the state record. Her last event was outstanding; she did the 5000 meters in 15:40.23, and this would have been a new state record for high school by over 5 seconds. Coach Flagon was so proud of her that he told her he was going to train her for the Olympics. Jackee held Rose and told her she was going to be "better than I'll ever be." Rose told her she was her idol and she could never do what Jackee has already accomplished. William just let the girls have their time together and later told Rose what a great athlete she had become. Carmela heard about what Rose did and she had her favorite meal waiting for her. Macaroni and cheese was not one of Carmela's well balanced meal foods, but for Rose's sake everyone enjoyed the special meal.

Their last night together was spent first at a fast food drive in and later in their secluded parking spot. Dan, for a reason Jackee could not understand, just wanted to look at her. He touched every part of her face very gently and finally told her how beautiful she was. She did not know what to do or say and just let him continue touching her. She finally asked, "If I am so beautiful, how come you don't want to kiss me?"

He said "I want to kiss you forever but to see and touch something so beautiful should not be spoiled with a kiss." He pulled her to him and kissed her more passionately than ever before. She melted in his arms and felt so warm and safe being there. She kissed him back to let him know that she was his whenever he wanted her. As it was getting late and Dan could not stand any more kissing or felt he would lose control, he suggested they go home. The Jenco's were leaving early, right after 8:00 mass. To Jackee's surprise Dan was waiting at the church when the Jenco's pulled into the parking lot. She was never more happy and told him so before the Jenco's drove to Olympus college.

The Jenco family arrived at Olympus college at around 2 pm. They did not expect the reception committee that was waiting for them. William called them and gave them his ETA with one qualifier, depending on traffic. These were the same people who talked to them on their first visit. Dr Hopkins spoke first. He told Jackee that he laid out a one year program for her and if she agreed it would immediately be put in effect. "You will be the first freshman to be registered for class. I also put time in your schedule for assisting me in the research center. You and your roommate will be the only new researchers in the lab. She arrives on Monday and has already agreed to interview for the opening. We hope the two of you will be the backbone of this new program. Dean Grant will show you to your dorm and as soon as you are ready a small lunch has been prepared for you in our faculty cafeteria."

They emptied Jackee's luggage in record time. The room itself was the best looking dorm room that William ever saw. He told them this made his old college dorm room look like a closet. Carmela immediately started putting things away and as they were finishing bringing in boxes she had most everything sorted and away. When they arrived at the cafeteria a buffet had been carefully prepared. It was basic simple food and since everyone was starving they dug right in. Coach Zimmer gave Jackee a key to the locker room and told her to use the field house anytime she wanted. "There is a separate female changing area and shower."

President Washington came by to see if there was anything else they needed from him. William thanked him and said everything had been better than expected. Rose had said very little all day. It was hard for her to realize that Jackee would not be there for her. She did ask coach Zimmer if they had a track team and a track. He told her the track team had some national recognition this year and two team members were going to the Olympic trials. Rose told him "cool," Carmela thought they should be starting for home. They thanked everyone and said farewell to Jackee. She hugged and thanked both her parents and told Rose to keep her informed of her meets and times.

Monday morning Jackee was up at 5:30am and went to the field house to work out. She ran around the track for 30 minutes and did some light weights and then the step machine. On the other side of the field house was an iron mike. This was a new type but since they all work the same she decided to try it the following day. Her bat was still packed, but it would be unpacked and available from now on. After a shower, she decided to have breakfast and went to the student cafeteria. As of yet she did not have a meal card but instead had a card from President Washington. The line at the cafeteria was very small and she got some funny looks when she showed her card. Many foods and drinks were available and they were all very good. She was allowed to take some fruit back to her room and was told that there was something to eat here from 6am to 10pm. Monday through Friday. Weekend food is served from 8am to 7pm. About 10am Jackee went to the science building to see if Dr Hopkins was there. As she entered a secretary called her by name and said the doctor wants to see you. She asked the secretary how she knew her name. Miss Willis, the secretary, said that "she was told a beautiful young lady named Jackee will be coming in and she is one of our new research staffers." There could be no mistake as to who you are.

Dr Hopkins showed Jackee around the lab and the various projects they were working on. A locker with her name and all the protective gear was shown to her. She was amazed at the equipment and supplies that were available. It made her high school lab look like a cheap imitation. Miss Willis came in to say that a new student, Miss Barachelli, had just arrived. Jackee and Dr Hopkins went over to the administration building to greet her. She had arrived with her parents and was talking to Dean Grant. Dean Grant introduced her to Dr Hopkins and Jackee, then said to Jackee, "meet your new roommate Andrea Barachelli."

Jackee shook her hand and told the family she would show them to the dorm room. "My mom put my things away yesterday. It had been a hectic day so we were rushed. If there is something you want to change, feel free to speak up." Andrea loved the room and had plenty of space for her belongings. When all her things were in the room, her parents said they had to leave and they kissed Andrea, said goodbye to Jackee and left. Andrea apologized for their rude behavior but she said this is the first time I have been away, and it is hard for them to accept this. As they were getting to know each other, Jackee asked if she had a nickname or a name she wanted to be called. Andrea told her that she really loved her name and refused to have any other. Jackee replied, "I fully understand where you are coming from and see nothing wrong in wanting to use your given name."

They talked as Andrea was putting her clothes and things away. When she was reasonably settled Jackee asked if she was hungry or if she wanted to see the lab first. The thing she was most interested in was science and the lab, so maybe that should be first. Jackee led her to the lab, introduced her to Miss Willis, and then they went into the laboratory. As they were nearing Jackee's locker she noticed the locker next to hers had been set up. Andrea was taken back when she realized her name was on the locker. Opening the locker she just said "WOW".

Jackee mentioned that is how she felt when she saw all this. "This equipment is top of the line and state of the art." Andrea thought that it would take her a great deal of time to learn how to use these things. She then told Jackee she was hungry. Together they went to the cafeteria and had an early dinner. As they were walking back to the dorm Jackee asked if she had a boyfriend. Andrea said she had four close male friends but only two really mattered. A bit surprised, Jackee asked how do you handle four boyfriends at the same time. The answer was very simple, Andrea said "when you are smarter than they are it's easy."

"Someday you will have to explain that to me. I have only one and there is no one who could take his place."

"Only one boyfriend, that is not civilized, a woman needs to grow, experience, and extend her horizons before selecting a permanent significant other." All Jackee could do was laugh with her and said this could be the start of a great friendship.

Wednesday was orientation day for all new students. When Jackee and Andrea were called they both were handed schedules and complete folders with everything already processed. They sat down and compared folders. Each had 18 hours of class time and 3 hours of lab work. That took care of regular school work, in addition each of them had 6 hours a week set aside for working with Dr Hopkins. These were volunteers and had some flexibility built into the program. Jackee noticed that she had plenty of time for working out and studying. Andrea could not believe how organized this was and she felt like her life was being programmed. She made a comment to Jackee and asked what she was told about the new 6 year program. Jackee explained to her all she could remember and Andrea said she was told pretty much the same thing. Looking at Andrea she wondered out loud if they were the only two new assistants to Dr Hopkins and both had been asked to be poster and speaker candidates for the program. They were both females, tops in their class, outstanding science students, and considered beautiful looking. A chill went down Jackee's spine, and she wondered what she had signed on for.

Classes began the next day. The two women both had very similar class schedules and lab times. As each entered, class text books were provided for them. All other students were told that they could buy the books at the school bookstore. Every class and lab had the same approach to these two students. Even in the labs any additional items that the students normally paid separately for were already given to Jackee and Andrea. The Girls figured from who they saw in their classes that about 25 to 30 other students were in this six year program. Naturally these other students were wondering *who the hell were these two girls?* Most of the classes were what Jackee and Andrea had expected. There was one course Called the history of medicine which seemed to have only these 6 year program students attending. This class would be 12 semesters long. The next 11 would deal with specific areas of medicine. Two other mandatory classes which were included in the curriculum were a business course and a legal and ethics one. Their work in the research lab for the first week will be getting familiar with how it operated and what was going on. Their responsibilities would increase as they become proficient in handling the material.

Jackee mentioned that she worked out every day, if possible. She wondered if Andrea would like to join her. Andrea told her she liked to swim and run, however she was not much of an athlete and had not played a sport since junior high. "Let me tell you what I do. I run most every day, outdoors on good days and indoors on bad ones. I do weights, exercise and batting most days."

"Batting you say, batting what?"

"Baseballs of course I am a better than average baseball player."

"Why would a beautiful girl want to play baseball?"

"Because I can and they tell me I am better than most boys."

"Well if nothing else it must be a great way to meet boys and men."

"I don't know about that since I never tried. My relationship is strictly being a teammate and not a trophy for someone."

"What a waste, I'd have a new date every night and enjoy every minute of it."

"I have been very lucky in that I have earned their respect and was treated as an equal on the field."

"Next, you will be telling me that you intend to play baseball here."

"I could have played for many other colleges but chose this one because of the special program."

Both were exhausted and decided to go to bed early. Jackee was up at 5am and by 7:30 she had completed her running, batting, and drills. After she showered they went to breakfast. This is how the first week continued and a routine developed for the rest of the semester. Starting the second week Jackee worked out with the baseball team before or after going to the lab. Her first day at fall baseball, she was mostly ignored by the other players. Coach Zimmer had not told anyone about her being or even trying out for the team. She finally found someone to warm up with and he was a walk-on who had no chance to make the team, even as a benchwarmer. The second day, the coach asked her to hit. She got her bat and settled in at the plate. Her first swing produced a ground ball but after that line drives started going all over the field. Near the end of her swings she hit one ball over the fence in left center and one ball against the center field fence. None of the boys said anything but the coach hollered, "great round!" He later hit her some ground balls at shortstop and she fielded every one and threw a strike to first base each time. Next day every candidate wanted to talk with her and find out who she was. One of the Players had the sports magazine that had picked her as one of the high possible draft picks. There also was a small story explaining why she was picked. Coach Zimmer explained why she was redshirted for this season but would be on the team next year.

The first semester was flying by. Every day was planned out and most times it was followed to the letter. Their big decision was whether to go to church at 5pm Saturday or 8am on Sunday. St. Michael Roman Catholic church was one block off campus and it was a very short walk from their dorm. In inclement weather a bus on campus would take you there and pick you up. Jackee and Andrea formed a very close relationship since most times they would do the same things and more importantly had the same interest. Both were neat freaks and kept their dorm room immaculate. There was never an argument over cleaning the bathroom, they always cleaned up after themselves and on Saturday the dorm room was cleaned from top to bottom. Since they were very similar in size their clothing was marked accordingly. Personal items were shared but no personal space was violated without permission. One major benefit was for the first time they had someone who could correct their mistakes and give new ideas to a project. When one of them hit a mind block the other would be there to help break through. Together they proved to be superior to any other assistants in the lab. Dr Hopkins found them better than anyone he has ever had working with him. His projects were on track to be completed ahead of schedule. This gave him more time to properly prepare a presentation. Since both his new assistants were doing A+ work in all their courses he decided maybe a few more hours of lab work could be added to their schedule.

One incident did come up that really bothered Jackee. Andrea had one of her friends visit one Saturday in early November. His name was Brett Haywood and he was an outstanding looking boy. He was introduced to Jackee as a very close friend of Andrea. When they were going out Saturday, Jackee was asked to go with them. She said no, they did not need a third wheel on a date. They insisted and finally she agreed to go eat with them but said she would leave right after dinner. Brett took them to a Texas something restaurant that had peanuts all over the place. They ordered wings and potato skins first and then hamburgers for dinner. A pitcher of light beer was ordered and some soft drinks. Jackee only had the soft drinks and water. This was the first time she was eating anywhere but the school cafeteria. All the food seemed to be perfect and since they had skipped lunch, they consumed all of it. Jackee asked to be dropped off before they continued their date. She was and immediately went inside to write Dan and get ready for bed. An hour or so after she had fallen asleep she heard strange noises coming from Andrea's room. At first, being half asleep she did not realize what she was hearing. Finally it became very clear what was happening. She rolled over, covered her head and went back to sleep. 6am Sunday, Jackee left to work out. Around 7:30 she returned to shower and then go to breakfast. There was no one stirring in the room so she went to breakfast by herself. Other students were eating and Jackee joined a few instead of eating alone. It was after 10am when she got back to the room. Brett was up and looked like he showered. Andrea was still getting dressed and came out a few minutes later. She said they were going to breakfast and then Brett had to leave and get back to school. Jackee thanked him for the dinner last night and was glad to have met him and to have a safe drive back to school. Andrea said she would be back by noon and would see her then. They left and Jackee called home for the weekly talk with her parents.

When Andrea came back to the dorm Jackee was studying at her desk. Andrea said she was back and was going to do laundry. She offered to do any laundry that Jackee had but Jackee said if you wait a few moments I'll go down with you. While they were waiting for the laundry to finish Andrea told her she was sorry for last night. They had started making out in the car and it went too far. It was her idea to come up to the room because she was very uncomfortable doing anything more in a car. "I promise I'll be more discreet next time." Jackee told her it was her room and she had a right to entertain in it. However there has to be rules or guidelines that should be observed.

"Although I never walk around naked, there are times we do need privacy. We should not have drinking or smoking since the school does not permit either in these rooms. You kept whatever you were doing confined to your room which is as it should be. Sleepover guests are acceptable but their movement within the room has to be limited. Both of us must feel secure in our room." Andrea agreed and apologized if she offended her.

Thanksgiving was only a few days away. Jackee found out that the lab would be closed from Wednesday through Sunday. They had early classes on Wednesday and would finish by 10am. Andrea arranged to be picked up by another student on the way home so she told Jackee they could drop her off near her home. There was just such a place about an hour from her home. Jackee called home and arrangements were made to pick her up. Henry Campo pulled up in his pathfinder just before 10am. He got out of the car and said "get your things and we are out of here." Both girls had their bags packed and were ready to travel. They had taken extra food from the cafeteria at breakfast and Henry had a bunch of snacks in a box so except for gas there would be no stops. Henry stopped for gas about 60 miles from Jackee's pick up spot and Jackee called home to tell them where they were. Less than an hour later they arrived at the designated pickup area and Carmela was waiting in the car. Jackee got out, thanked Henry, wished them a happy Thanksgiving and took her traveling bag to where Carmela waited. She hugged and kissed her mom and said how much she missed her. All the way home Jackee talked about school and everything she was doing, especially in the lab.

As they arrived at the house Jackee noticed that no one was home. "Evelyn will be home later and Rose has a track meet at 4pm." Carmela told her. "Your father had a special meeting that had to be finished before the weekend or else he would have come for you at school." They went inside and in a few moments Jackee's bag was emptied and the contents either put away or in the wash. Carmela went to the kitchen and started to prepare dinner. Since they were alone Carmela asked how her room mate was. She told her that Andrea was a lot like me with many of the same interests. There is one thing that bothered me, and she explained what had happened with Brett. Jackee said she knew some girls were sexually active but never saw or heard someone doing it.

"Were they in a closed room or out in the open?" Carmela asked.

"They were in Andrea's room with the door closed."

"Then it really was none of your business."

"Mom, are you condoning what they did?"

"No I am not but neither am I being judgemental. What they did may have been morally wrong but it does not give anyone the right to judge them. What do you think was going on at the prom party and what do you think would have happened if Dan took you inside the house that night? Remember the night Dan stopped kissing you in the car and decided to take you home? Think back about how upset you were and now you see what could have happened if he had not stopped."

"Mom, thank you, I never put the two incidents together. Now I also know why you like Dan so much."

Evelyn arrived home with Jon and Rose came home after winning all her events and setting new school records. William arrived later than usual saying that everything was completed and he was free until Monday. Rose was with Jackee the whole time asking her about college, her roommate and how her workouts were going. She wanted Rose to tell her about all the meets and her school activities, but Rose only wanted to hear what Jackee was doing. Later on Rebecca and Rocco stopped by to say hello and find out the schedule for Thanksgiving. Carmela asked them to stay for dinner and Rocco without hesitating said they would. Dan called the house to find out if Jackee was home from school. He hadn't heard from her since Sunday. He had been at a special football camp with no communications off campus. The camp ended Wednesday at noon and from there he started his Thanksgiving break. Jackee took the phone and wanted to know when they could see each other. Dan told her he would be free in one hour and he would come by for her.

One hour later he came to her house. She was waiting on the porch and jumped into the car as soon as he stopped. He was taken by surprise and asked if there was a problem. Jackee said "no, I just want to be alone with you before we mingle with other people." Now he really was confused but he decided to go along with her for the time being. The best thing to do was go to the place where they usually are alone.

After parking the car he turned to her only to be attacked. She threw her arms around his neck and kissed him so hard, his lips hurt. when she finally stopped kissing him, but still holding him tight, he asked, "what is the matter?" She told him she loved him even more than her mother.

"Your Mother! How is she involved in this?"

"My mother thinks you are the greatest guy ever and she told me never to lose you. I just want you to know that I am never going to lose you and I want you to feel the same as I do."

"Jackee, you haven't been smoking any funny looking cigarettes at college have you?"

"No, you know I don't smoke. I just found out what you did for me and I love you more than I ever thought was possible."

"What exactly did I do for you?"

"Prom night when everyone was going into the house and the skinny dipping thing. You could have taken me inside and I would have probably willingly done whatever you asked. Another time in the car when you stopped kissing me and I got angry with you for stopping. You could have gone further and I had no resistance left in me. In both situations most other boys would have taken advantage of me, and you didn't. Why?"

"Jackee, you are the only person I have ever met who has a dream and has dedicated herself to fulfilling it. For at least 10 years before I met you, you have worked toward that dream. Once I got to know you I made up my mind that no one is going to take that dream from you. I will support you until you either reach the goal or decide to give it up. All I ask in return, is when either one happens you then transfer that dedication to me."

"Answer me one question, how can you love a girl who dosen't have sex with you when you need it?"

"Jackee, if I asked you to have sex with me would you do it."

"You know I probably would. I am fully aware of this, so it is my choice not to have sex because you mean much more to me than satisfying some needs. When we are both ready it will be the greatest happening of our lives." She held him so tight for so long that she felt a part of him. He loved holding and kissing her. When he thought she had settled down they went to her house and talked to the family.

Thanksgiving day had the whole family, plus Jon, Kim, and Bats around the table. Carmela out did herself because the food was terrific. Desserts were the best ever, as all the girls helped make them. Each girl picked out their favorite dessert and then proceeded to make it. Dan came over after dinner with Italian homemade desserts. Everyone had to try a cannoli and a very small piece of cassata cake. They all raved how moist and tasty this cake was. Dan told them it had a special rum imported from Italy as one of its ingredients. Bats and Kim left early but not without some food and dessert. Rebecca and Rocco also had a big bag of food and desserts. They had to go to the Manelli's and would end up with a second bag of goodies. Evelyn and Jon went for a walk while Dan and Jackee took Rose to see the tree lighting in town. Later they dropped Rose off at home and sat in the car talking. From her letters and calls, Dan knew most everything Jackee did in school. He filled her in on some of the things he failed to include in his letters. They had another night before heading back to school on Sunday. William drove Jackee back to school right after church on Sunday. They just dropped her off, said their goodbyes and headed for home.

The time between Thanksgiving and the Christmas break is basically preparation for final exams. Most of Jackee's courses had hands-on finals. She did have two written exam finals but she already had an A plus in both and she would be exempt from the written final. Andrea had exactly the same thing except for a gym class that Jackee was excused from because she is in a sport. Even though she was redshirted it still counted as participating. Their lab work with Dr Hopkins had gone better than expected and they were ahead of schedule. Dr Hopkins had told everyone that these were the best assistants he ever had and one of his major projects should be complete before Christmas break. Andrea and Jackee had spent all their extra time working in the lab. Their work has been so good that they were given a key and could work any time they had available. Miss Willis sometimes found them working when she arrived at 8am. She was usually the one who opened and prepared the lab. Both of the girls took a personal interest in this skin disorder project. Most of the testing and results had been completed before they came into the lab but the results had to be coalesced and put into a usable program. This program would become part of a presentation to medical students, interns, and practicing doctors. Although their names would be listed last, it still was a great first recognition for the girls.

Jackee continued to workout with the baseball team and every day she felt her game coming together. The starting shortstop was a senior and a good all around ballplayer. Jackee compared the two of them and decided that her arm was stronger and more accurate. She made better contact at the plate and was definitely a better game control person in the infield. This was never said out loud to any one, but Jackee knew that she would be the starting shortstop next year. There was a backup second baseman who was a freshman and looked to have excellent potential. In fact she thought he was better than the senior second baseman but had not seen enough of either one to justify her conclusion. One day she introduced herself to him and asked if he would like to work out with her. He told her his name was Jack Gillian and he would love to work with her. "Why are you not going to play this year?" he wanted to know. She told him about her 6 year program and she assumed the coach wanted his senior to finish his last year. "Coach Zimmer told me that I would probably play second but I am telling you once he sees us in action, we will be his middle infielders." Jack said he wished he were better but promised to work hard for her. Jackee told him that he will make her better and she will make him better. "The team of Jack and Jackee can't miss. The JJ's will be the best in our conference. We will be called the double J's".

CHAPTER ELEVEN

Jackee Has Christmas Vacation and Speaker Engagement

*S*even days before Christmas Dr Hopkins made his presentation at a big medical conference. Both Jackee and Andrea were present and had their names included in the final report that was submitted to the AMA. When they arrived back at school a party was prepared for Dr Hopkins and his staff. All the big wigs were there and many friends of Dr Hopkins. He introduced his staff and previous assistants who could make the party. His wife Gloria took one look at his two new assistants and said "there is no way you can work late with these two beautiful young ladies." They both blushed and thanked her for her kind words. Neither girl knew what to do at this party so they made some lame excuse about having to prepare for finals and left. All their finals were finished and their straight A pluses had been recorded. They really had to pack for the trip home two days from now. Andrea had her usual ride. Jackee told her that her father was coming early to pick her up so she didn't need a ride home. Andrea said she will miss Jackee and wished they lived closer so they could spend some time together over the holidays. Jackee told her she would stay in touch and maybe something could be worked out.

William arrived early and Jackee was ready to go. Since they were not due back until the middle of January, she packed all her fall clothes to take home. She also brought home her workout clothing and of course, the bat. The Jenco Christmas schedule still included the Vets and orphanage as well as Kim, Bats, and George Herman, who was only two weeks old. They had twelve people going to mass on Christmas day. After church they came home to open gifts and have brunch. While gifts were being opened Carmela prepared a very light snack, just enough so as not to interfere with Christmas dinner. "If all goes well, dinner should be ready by 2:30." This time is set so Kim and Bats could start home early and Rocco could make his family dinner at 6:00pm.

The girls said grace before dinner and William made the toast. He thanked everyone for being there and wished them all a blessed, happy and healthy Christmas and New Year. Rebecca and Rocco made an announcement. It seems that Carmela and William are going to be grandparents. Everyone at the table congratulated them but William appeared to be not too excited. Rocco asked him if he was upset by the news. William with a straight face replied, "how would you feel if you had to go to bed with a grandmother?" Everyone burst into laughter except Rose who could not figure out why everyone was laughing. He then got up and kissed Rebecca and shook Rocco's hand. Carmela wanted to know if Rocco's parents knew about this. Rocco said they will be told at dinner tonight.

Jon was not eating and Carmela wanted to know if there was something wrong. He told her the food was the best he has ever had but there was something he had to ask them. William said to him if you want to borrow money I charge 6% interest. Jon smiled and said, "I do not need money, I need Evelyn and I want your permission to get engaged to her." Carmela asked what Evelyn said.

Jon said it is customary to get permission first and then ask the young lady. "Well Jon, how much will you pay us for her?"

Carmela kicked William under the table and told Jon he was kidding and "you most definitely have our permission and blessing."

He turned to Evelyn, who appeared to be in shock and asked her to be his wife. "I have three more years of interning and residency but when I finish I want you beside me as my wife."

She finally spoke and told him she would be proud to be his fiancee now and "in three years if you still want me I'll be even prouder to be your wife." He took a small box out of his pocket and handed it to her. She opened the box and a gorgeous diamond ring was inside.

He took the ring and put it on her finger and said "remember I have all these witnesses to prove you said yes." She got up and kissed him and told him he didn't need any witnesses that she felt exactly the same about him.

By the time Dan came over with the desserts from his mother all the conversations had ended and everyone was silent. Dan looked around and said what did I miss? They all looked at him and started laughing. He wanted to know if they were going to include him in as to what happened. Jackee got up, hugged him and filled him in on what had taken place. He congratulated Rebecca and Rocco, then turning to Jon told him he was getting a great young lady. "I feel it is my duty to make you aware that William told me that if anyone hurt one of his daughters, he'd take his gun and make her a widow." Smiling, he reached out to shake Jon's hand and told him he was just kidding. William said, with a straight face he never told Dan that but it was a great idea.

Dessert was being served so Dan included his mother's goodies to the table. When everyone finished the table was cleared and the cleanup began. Later, the two couples sat on the couches and Jon talked about his family but he sounded like an outsider rather than a son. He had always wanted to be a doctor but not like his parents. They liked the excitement of traveling and aiding people all over the globe. "There is enough need right here in this country for doctors." Jackee told him. He still had years to decide which field of medicine he really wanted. She told him about her new program and asked if he had any thoughts that may assist her.

"The lab work you are doing is the best start for any medical student. If I hear anything I'll get the information to you. For a start, I can give you the names of two books that may help: 1. The Brigham Board Review in Infectious Diseases. 2. Skin Diseases EBook diagnosis & Treatment Edition 3." Jackee thanked him and asked Dan if they could go for a walk.

While walking Dan was unusually quiet and Jackee asked him to tell her what he was thinking. Dan said "a lot of good things happened at your Christmas table. Your two sisters gave great gifts to your Mother and Father but I am in no position to offer you anything right now."

"I don't understand what you are saying."

"Jackee, it is very simple I can not get engaged right now and the only commitment I can make to you is that I love you and at some future time I want to be with you forever."

"You silly guy, do you think I want something more than I have right now?"

"Most young girls do want more of a commitment from their boy-friends."

She grabbed his arm tighter and told him all she wants is exactly what she has right now. "Having you by my side and knowing that you support me in what I am trying to do, is more than I could ever ask for. Our joining together happened the night of the prom and nothing can come between us unless we decide to break up. You are the second and last man I will ever love. No matter what you do or where you go as long as you come back to me that is the way it will be for me. You are going to be my first and last lover." They turned to each other and kissed for a long time. Then It was time to go home and look forward to their weekend date and his family New Year party.

The week went so fast and all of a sudden it was December 31 and Dan was coming at 7pm to take her to the party. She came down and asked her parents how she looked. Carmela said "you look fantastic. That dress looked as if it was custom fitted on you." William still could not believe how beautiful she looked and except for a few pounds, just like Carmela. Dan arrived about 6:50 and Rose let him in. He wished her a happy New Year and kissed her on the cheek. Then he told her that if he did not have a date with Jackee, he would be begging her to go with him. She said that Jackee would really be upset if you ever broke a date with her. He saw Jackee walk into the room and all thoughts of any one else disappeared immediately.

William saw that look on Dan's face and said "I hope Carmela is right."

Carmela whispered to him "should we put Rose to bed and really celebrate the new year?"

William turned to her and just said, "hussy." They both smiled but William thought that was not such a bad idea.

When Dan and Jackee arrived at the house, the party was in full swing. The food was really good and there was plenty of it. Most of it was home made by the women who were in attendance. There was plenty to drink and the music was perfect dance music. Dan introduced Jackee to the guests but most knew her already. His parents spent some time with them and later wandered off to greet newcomers. So they just danced or talked to some friends. There was a gentleman present who was the school principal of an inner city junior high. When he was near Jackee he asked if he could speak with her. Dan left them to get Jackee something to drink. He told her he was Alec Fisher and principal of Robinson junior high. His wife told him about Jackee as she was at the Travis speaking engagement. Mr Fisher wanted to know if she would speak at his school and if there was a fee. "I would be glad to speak at the school but my time is very short and I only have a few free days available. As for a fee, just make sure there is water available. Give me your name and number where you can be reached and I'll give you what I think my free time will be."

Dan returned with the drinks and Mr. Fisher excused himself. "He wants me to speak at his school and I told him if he could fit my schedule into his I would do it."

"That was very nice of you but don't cut your free time too thin." They danced most of the night and when midnight came they kissed and wished each other a happy new year. This lasted for many minutes as they made their way around the floor. Dan's parents joined them on the dance floor and were especially gracious to Jackee. The Fisher's greeted them and Mr Fisher handed Jackee a piece of paper saying that I hope to hear from you. Half an hour later, Dan and Jackee were parked in their favorite place and doing their favorite thing. Jackee had to report back to school for lab work and have Miss Willis order her two books. They would have one more weekend together before Easter break. Jackee wasn't sure if she would even have a break but somehow they would see each other

Mr Fisher called and told her the Friday before she was to leave would be perfect for her to speak at his school. He said the board of education and the superintendent had agreed to her speaking at 11am in the auditorium. She confirmed that the time and place were acceptable and she would see him there. Dan was working over the break but he asked for the day off so he could drive her there. William was committed but Carmela wanted to go. 10am on Friday, Dan showed up and Carmela and Jackee were ready to go. They arrived at the school 30 minutes early and were greeted by Fisher and a host of board members, administrative personnel and teachers. She introduced her mother and Dan, and acknowledged the reception committee as Fisher introduced them. They took her to a room to store their things and use the necessary facilities. When Jackee was ready she was led to the stage and seated in front of about 600 boys and girls. Principal Fisher introduced her by telling the audience all the awards she won and most important she was the state baseball M.V.P. in this year's tournament.

Jackee rose and went to the microphone, thanked Mr Fisher and all the others who invited her there. Looking out over the students she said her talk will be directed to the young ladies in the audience. "I can never claim to know what goes on in the mind of a male teenager but I can relate to the female ones. Principal Fisher listed some of my accomplishments but what he could not know, what it took to achieve those things. I had a lot of help. It is my belief that God was always by my side looking out for me. I believe He gave me the things I would need to accomplish certain results. I love the game of baseball but was told that girls did not play baseball. Well I am 18 and I have had offers from 3 division 1 schools to play for them. Do you know why they made these offers to me? Because I earned them. On my way up to this level there were times when people thought they would use me as a gimmick, but what they didn't know was, I was using them. Every one of you young ladies is more powerful beyond your wildest dreams. Each one of you was made in the image of God, and He is the most powerful force in the world. There is a four letter word that I want you to think about. No, it's not that one. It is the word RARE. All of you know the word and have an idea of what it means. Some of the meanings are Extraordinary, Precious, Scarce and Unique." Jackee left the stage and walked to a young girl in the first row. She asked her to stand and if she would face the audience. "I want all of you to look at this beautiful young girl. Do any of you know any other young girls who look like her? Therefore she is rare, unique, scarce, precious and extraordinary. Never let anyone tell you differently, or belittle you or tell you you're not good enough. No one can make you feel worthless unless you let them. By the way some of you may have said, how about twins or other multiple births, they all look the same. Even twins are different from each other. Remember one very important thing, success sometimes comes in strange ways. Failure can drive you to greater levels, it's all up to you and not someone else. I'll use baseball as a perfect example, the greatest hitter in baseball made out 65 out of 100 times at bat. So he failed 65% of the time and still is considered the greatest hitter in baseball. I want to apologize to all the young men here today for not being able to relate to you. However I will tell you this, if you don't find a way to do what I told the girls to do, some day you will be working for them. Now if time allows, I'll answer any questions you may have."

For the next 30 minutes Jackee answered every question directed at her. Young girls wanted to know everything about her. Even some boys raised questions about how she was treated. Finally principal Fisher told the students the first lunch period was starting and the others had to go to their classes. He explained that in some cases this would be the only real meal that they will get today. Jackee said she wished she was a better speaker and role model. Mr Fisher told her she did a fantastic job and the students listened to every word especially the female ones. If you helped one young lady today, then this was a great success.

Before getting into the car to leave the school grounds, Carmela put her arms around Jackee and told her what a great talk she gave and how proud she was of her. While driving home Dan told her she was getting better with every talk she gave. He told her he now realizes that he does work for her and probably always will. Carmela smiled and said she would not touch that statement with a ten foot pole. "Mom, Dan always feels that way but the truth of the matter is if he wasn't by my side I couldn't go out and give these talks. Him being there gives me the courage to speak."

"The two of you are a great pair and I hope you never lose each other." Jackee told her mom that she has committed herself to Dan for as long as he'll have me. Dan told Carmela he feels the same. "You are the weirdest couple I ever heard of but I think you two can make it happen." Dan spent the rest of the day with Jackee including having dinner with her family. He again saw her the next night which would be the last one before she returned to Olympus college. They talked about many things but the fact remained that they would be apart for at least two months.

CHAPTER TWELVE

Jackee Assists the Baseball Program and Visits Dan

*S*unday, Dan met the family as they entered church. He held Jackee's hand during the entire service. Dan offered to take Rose and Evelyn home so William could start the trip immediately. William thanked him, and they were off to Olympus college. Evelyn offered to make breakfast for Dan and Rose. Both agreed and they headed for the Jenco's house. Rose had a big breakfast, but Dan just picked at his food. Evelyn asked if he missed Jackee, then realized it was a stupid question. Just as he was about to speak, Rose told him that whenever she felt sad, she did a workout. "Why don't you join me later and we will workout together." He told Rose that may be a great idea, suppose I come back about 11. "Cool," she said "I'll be waiting."

They arrived at the college and unloaded all Jackee's luggage then headed for the cafeteria for some late lunch. After lunch they helped Jackee get settled and prepared to start back home. Jackee told them that Andrea should be coming at any time. There was no exact time for them to return but both knew that the lab had to be prepared for the next round of research. When her parents left she finished putting her room in order and then headed for the lab. Miss Willis had started to prepare the lab for the next project Dr Hopkins wanted to work on. Jackee asked her if she could order the two publications Jon had recommended. She said they will be ordered "as soon as the doctor signs off on the order. It will take a few days after that for it to come. We do have priority shipping on anything we order." Jackee thanked her and asked when she expected Dr Hopkins to return. Lucy, Miss Willis, told her he was already back and had been here earlier in the day. "Dr Hopkins did say he would be here regular hours starting tomorrow." She left the lab and went to dinner. Two hours later she was sound asleep.

At 5am, she was up and headed for the field house. When she got back to the room she discovered that Andrea was back and sound asleep. Half way into breakfast Andrea walked into the cafeteria and sat next to her. While Andrea had a cup of coffee they talked about what they did over the break. Jackee asked if she was going to eat and Andrea told her she had too much food over the holidays and now needed to lose 5 pounds. They went back to the dorm and then to the lab. Dr Hopkins was waiting for them and set the parameters for the next project. For the next two weeks the girls worked 10 hours a day on the new project. They were dealing with diabetics and their reaction to certain types of insulin. Diabetes ran in Andrea's family so she was very interested in this study.

Classes started the following Monday so lab time reverted to their usual schedule. Jackee worked out with the baseball team every day. She spent as much time as possible with Jack and it proved to be time well spent. Jack was a quick learner and within a few practices it seemed like they had been playing together for years. He was a natural lefty but his mother insisted he write and eat with his right hand. When he first started playing catch with his father and brother, he threw with his right hand. There was no explanation for his batting left handed except he said it always felt more comfortable and he saw the ball better. When he was in little league his father tried to make him a switch hitter but he could not get comfortable hitting right handed. She heard he was taking a great deal of abuse from the other ball players regarding his working out with her. Some of it was sexually orientated about them. Jackee asked him to come to her dorm so they could talk. He agreed and would come over after dinner. He came over about 7:30 and Jackee let him in. As soon as Andrea saw him she started to leave but Jackee told her to stay. Andrea was confused but curiosity forced her to stay. First Jack was introduced to Andrea and told who he was, then Jackee asked him what was happening in the locker room. He said it was nothing he couldn't handle.

"I want you to tell me exactly what is going on because I have lived with this since junior high."

"Usually the guys tease me about playing with a girl and if I continue I'll become to feminine. Lately a couple of wiseguys started saying we were having sex and what is it like to have sex with a dyke." Jackee said to him she was sorry he had to go through this and if it was too much they could stop practicing together. He said "not on your life. I feel sorry for you. You are by far the best player I ever worked with. I am a better player than I thought I'd ever be and as long as I work with you I'll keep getting better."

"Jack, I want you to know that I have a boyfriend and that I have never been intimate with any female. Many times I have heard these slurs and a lot worse but I swear to you none of it is true."

"You don't have to tell me because I don't care. Without a doubt you are the best teacher of baseball I have ever had and the finest young lady I ever came in contact with. It would be a great honor for me if you were my girlfriend, but I know for a fact there is not one boy I ever knew, who is worthy enough to even carry your glove off the field. You are a one in a million and too good for this school or team."

When Jack left, Andrea turned to Jackee and said "who the hell are you and how do you get these boys to grovel before you." Teach me because I want to learn how to be put on a throne. Jackee told her that these boys can not understand how a girl can compete with them and even be better. Their egos are hurt and they lash out, out of frustration. What they can't understand intimidates their manhood and they revert to gutter remarks. Andrea said that may all be true but "that boy who left here worshiped and probably had a crush on you."

"Now he knows that I have a boyfriend and that sexually I am not a switch hitter."

Andrea said "it's a good thing I like men or I would fall in love with you myself."

The school year was moving toward spring break and the baseball team was having a bad year. They were 6 and 14 after the first 20 games. Jackee attended all the home games and a few of the nearby away games. She could see that they were not a team, just a collection of ball players finishing out the year. Jack had started a couple of games and had done really well but the coach always puts the senior back at second base. One day a player on the team had a black eye and a puffy face. Magically, the rumors about Jackee seemed to stop right after that. Jack appeared to be more relaxed and was turning himself into a real fine player.

Spring break came and Jackee found out that Dan had lacrosse games and would not be home. Lab work had ceased because one person in a control group died and they were waiting for the autopsy results before starting again. Her mid terms were all finished and she had A pluses in all her classes so there was really nothing to do. Andrea asked if she wanted to go see Dan at his school. Jackee asked how it was possible since neither of them had a car. "Brett is about 20 miles from Dan's school and he could pick us up and take you there." Jackee asked why would he do that? Andrea said she would make him an offer he could not refuse.

"You're a bad girl" Jackee told her but Andrea said "everyone has their own way of working out."

Brett arrived one day later and told them to hurry. He had a tennis match at 4pm today. It was a four hour trip back to his school and another 30 or so minutes to Dan's. He told them he would take Jackee after his match to Dan's school. They watched him win his match and Jackee thought he was a pretty good player. He played number two so that is usually a very high position on the team. Once all the matches were over he showered and they were off to see Dan. It was getting dark when they arrived at the school and Jackee had no clue how to find

Dan. Brett said he had an idea and drove to the field house. He went inside and a few moments later came out and said "Dan will be coming out in a few minutes. They just came back from a game and he was taking a shower." Just as Brett had said Dan came walking out with a few other players. Jackee jumped out of the car and ran right at him. Dan did not recognize her until she was a few feet from him. All of a sudden she ran up to him and threw her arms around him and held on for dear life. All Dan could do was hold her so they would not fall. The three players he walked out with were just as stunned as he was. Finally they just smiled, wished him luck and moved on.

Andrea turned to Brett and said "I hope that's Dan."

Brett said "no matter who it is, he is one lucky fellow."

Dan recovered from the shock of being attacked and kissed Jackee very passionately. Andrea told Brett she wished he kissed like that. All he said was "practice, practice, and more practice." Jackee brought Dan to the car and introduced him. Dan thanked them for bringing Jackee to him and wanted to know for how long they were staying.

"I'm being picked up on Wednesday so we have to be back by Tuesday evening."

"That means I have to pick her up after practice on Monday. We will meet you right here on Monday. Call and tell me about what time you intend to come and we will be ready. Figure it will be around 6:30 and if there is a change I'll call the school."

"Jackee, have you thought about where you are going to sleep?"

"The only place I had considered was in your arms."

"You are tempting me beyond my control so let's be realistic. A few of the female athletes are still on campus so you may be able to bunk with them. My roommate dates a girl who is still on campus so let's ask him." They went to Dan's dorm and asked his room mate about the possibility of getting a place for Jackee to stay.

Raymond, his roommate, told him that was an easy fix. "I'll bunk in with Scott next door, he has an extra bed since his roomy quit school. Jackee, you make the final decision as to where to stay."

She said the arrangement Raymond suggested would be perfect for her. "I have everything I need in my overnight bag." Raymond took what he needed and went next door. Jackee arranged Raymond's room and told Dan she was hungry. Dan suggested they pick something up and bring it back to the room. They walked down to a fast food store on campus and took the food back to the dorm. After eating and cleaning up, they sat on the couch and held each other.

She Told Dan that she never felt more comfortable and safer in her life. "I missed you so much and just needed to be hugged and reassured that you still needed me."

He told her he felt the same but this was not something she should ever do again. "Your parents think you're at school and if they try to contact you and can't find you, what would they think?" She agreed with him and said she was sorry and would not do it again unless prior arrangements are made. Since now they were on the same page, he felt more relaxed and gathered her in his arms. She snuggled closer to him and he could feel her heart racing. Moments later they both fell asleep in that position.

Jackee woke up first and just stayed perfectly still. An hour later Dan opened his eyes and saw Jackee looking up at him. He smiled and kissed her before trying to get up. Both had a problem since they hadn't moved the whole night. They went to breakfast which on weekends featured a buffet rather than the usual walk through line. After a shower, that they took separately, they dressed and Dan showed her around the campus. He told her he had Practice at 11am and would be back by 2:00.

She watched his practice for a while, then just started walking around the campus. Most of the buildings were locked for the weekend, but the library was opened. After reading the local newspaper she went back to Dan's room and waited for him. He came back and asked her "is there anything you want to do?"

"Can we just sit and hold each other for a while?" Dan quickly agreed and sat with her. He told her there was a show on campus tonight that might be fun.

"Anything would be fine as long as it was with you," she told him. As they were getting ready to leave, she told Dan she was sorry but she brought only one change of clothes and they were not dressy. "I don't want you to be ashamed of me."

Dan said, he could never be ashamed of having you by my side dressed in anything. After the show, which turned out to be a bluegrass hoedown, they ate something and went back to the dorm. The TV was on in the lounge area so they watched it for a while. Around 10:00 they went up to his room. "Tonight we will sleep in bed rather than the couch." Jackee teased him as to which bed they should sleep in.

He told her that "one is yours, this one is mine."

Sunday at 9:30 there was a Catholic service on campus at the school chapel. Dan always attended that service so he and Jackee went. Afterwards, they once again had breakfast at the open cafeteria. Since there was no game or practice Dan could spend the whole day with Jackee. Mostly they just walked around the school grounds. The girls softball team had a doubleheader at home so they watched some of the game. Some of Dan's teammates were going out to dinner and asked them to join in. They agreed and went to a local sports bar. Other athletes male and female, joined them and about 16 people were now gathered around one big table. The food was very good and the service even better. Before they knew it, it was 9:00 and they had to leave.

Going back to the dorm for their last night together. Before going to bed Jackee asked Dan if she could stay in bed with him. He told her that may be too much to ask. "Dan, I just want to hold you for as long as I can. If you say no I'll accept it." He agreed and they went to sleep in each other's arms. In the morning she woke up and kissed him and told him it was the best sleep she ever had and can't wait until I can do it forever.

Dan told her he felt the same but they are never to do this again until they are married. "It's much too hard on my self control." 6:30 Brett was there to pick her up and take the two girls back to school.

When they were getting ready for bed back at Olympus college Andrea asked Jackee if she had a good time with Dan. She told her it was the best ever and she really hated to leave. Jackee then asked Andrea how her stay went. Andrea said the sleeping arrangements were "very crowded but we eventually found a good sleeping position. Brett had no complaints and got a lot more than I originally promised. Some day you may have to teach me some of your tricks."

"I can't believe how you treat your boy friends and how they keep coming back."

"Jackee, are you good at what you do?"

"Yes, people say I am very good."

"Well I am very good at what I do and these boys are my witnesses."

Next Morning Henry came by to pick them up for the trip home. Four hours later Jackee thanked Henry for the ride and wished them a happy Easter. She walked inside and was greeted by her mother. After putting all her stuff away she came down to get something to eat and help get dinner ready. While they were preparing dinner Carmela wanted to know why Jackee hadn't called on Sunday. She told her how they drove down to see Dan and that she spent three Days with him. Carmela asked what the sleeping arrangements were. Jackee told her the truth as she always did. Carmela did not say anything, so Jackee continued and told her the last night she stayed in the same bed as Dan. "I was the one who asked to do it and Dan finally agreed. Mom, nothing happened. I just wanted to hold him and that is all we did. He told me we could never do that again. Although I don't agree, I'll try to honor his wishes."

"Jackee, do you have any idea what that boy went through? A beautiful girl in his room for two nights and then on the third night sleeping with her arms around him in his bed."

"But mom, that is all I needed to do."

"But Jackee, that is not all that he needed..You raised his sexuall desire to its highest level and then you asked him to respect you. I can't believe he actually did not have sex with you. You tempted him beyond belief and he still resisted you. He is either impotent or the greatest guy ever. Don't ever do that to him again."

CHAPTER THIRTEEN

Jackee Helps Coach Zimmer and His Wife

*J*ackee spent most of her time working with or watching Rose. Rose had become one of the best runners in the state and she still had two more years in high school. She had set most of the records for females in the state. In addition, she also was becoming very good in the decathlon events. Her chances of competing in the Olympics were now excellent. They went for a run and Jackee could not keep up with her. It was amazing how she grew and how much wider her stride had become. When William came home, Jackee told him she was better than I ever was at that age. Rose told Jackee that she will never be as good as her. Jackee grabbed her by the shoulders and told her she was better right now and that someday she will be the greatest female athlete ever. As Carmela came into the room Rose was crying and hugging Jackee. "You, Mom, Dad and my two other sisters gave me life when my biological parents treated me like a piece of trash. I promise to make all of you proud of me or die trying. The family gathered around Rose and Carmela said to her, we are very proud of you. You chose to be part of our family and you have given us much more than we have given you. Your sisters decided before we did that they wanted you. William and I had been trying to have a child but it just never happened. We thought our prayers were not heard, but then you happened and we could not have been happier. There is no doubt in my mind that God sent you to us and we thank Him every day."

Easter Sunday, which is a joyous occasion in all Christian churches, was not a happy one for Jackee. Evelyn had Jon, and Rebecca had Rocco, but Jackee didn't have Dan. His school was playing in a tournament over Easter week and the players had to stay with the team. She would talk to him later that night but she missed him being there. Carmela could always use some help preparing for Easter, so Jackee became her assistant. They prepared a seven course meal with plenty of desserts. Any other free time was either spent with Rose or studying. William did drive her to see Dan's parents so she could wish them a happy Easter. They also were upset that Dan was not home and resented the school entering a tournament over Easter week.

Rebecca was in her seventh month and told Jackee the baby should arrive around your birthday. Jackee said she would be happy to share her birthday with a niece or nephew. The dinner went very well and after dessert everyone helped clean up. Later Jackee spoke with Dan, who told her he really missed her and wished the team hadn't been committed to this tournament. They were doing well but most of the players rather be with their family. The team would be getting back to school when classes are scheduled to resume. This ment there was no time off for them. Andrea was picking her up Monday afternoon as they had a lab scheduled for Tuesday. They talked a while longer, then Dan said he had to go to dinner with the team and will call her during the week.

Andrea arrived with Henry at 12:30 and they headed back to school. Henry helped them take their travel bags into the dorm and then left for his school. An hour later the girls had everything away and decided to get something to eat. Getting back to the room, the girls started planning for the next two plus months. Most of the class work was well taken care of. Both of them were doing A plus work in school but the lab remained a problem. When her workout and breakfast was finished Jackee headed for the lab. Lucy was at her desk and told Jackee a new program would be starting next week. Dr Hopkins told her the new program would be an additional one added into the schedule. Since there was nothing to do in the lab, Jackee went back to her room to study then get ready for a workout with the baseball team.

Jack was already on the field when Jackee got there. She asked him how he thought the season was going. He said it was a disaster and he had never played on a team that was this bad. She agreed with him and said the leadership was poor and the coach had to take the blame for it. "I personally checked out the coach before committing to play for the Olympus and everybody raved about how great a coach he was. Not one person or previous player had a bad word to say about him. Something happened between last season and this one." Whenever you want to hear the truth about an athletic problem you ask the equipment manager. They hear everything about everybody and they are right most of the time. So Jackee went into the field house office and found Robert Harris behind his desk. No one else was around so Jackee asked him flat out if something had happened to coach Zimmer. Mr Harris told her that Zimmer's wife had a miscarriage and probably will never be able the have a child. Both of them took the news very hard and Mrs Zimmer has not been able to break out of her depression. It has really taken a toll on the coach as this would have been their first born. Jackee thanked him and asked if he would keep this conversation just between them. He agreed.

When practice ended Jackee waited until the locker room was empty and entered the coach's office. Coach Zimmer was alone and Jackee asked if he had a moment to speak with her. He told her to please come in and is there a problem I can help you with. She said there was no problem, she just wanted to say how sorry she was to hear about what had happened to your wife. "I always believed that God works in strange ways and usually provides an answer to most problems, if we listen." Coach asked her what she meant. "Do you remember meeting my sister Rose?"

"Yes, the girl who asked me about the track team. She looked like a great young dedicated athlete."

"Well she was adopted by my parents when they were having problems having another child. The family loves her because she has brought so much more to our family. My mother and father love her more because she chose to be a part of the family. My sisters and I did not have that choice. You see God provided an answer to my parents and I believe He has one for your family. My parents have been going to this orphanage, where Rose was, for over 25 years. Maybe your answer could be found there. It's not far from my home and my parents would be glad to recommend you to the Sisters in charge." Coach thanked her and said he would mention it to his wife and see if she would consider it.

Andrea was waiting for Jackee so they could go to dinner. As soon as Jackee changed they were off. While eating Andrea said that Lucy told her there would be nothing at the lab for at least two weeks. This would give them plenty of time to study and complete their school lab experiments. "I'll spend more time with the baseball team if you can check in with Lucy from time to time."

"That is a good idea, this way we will know the current status of the lab. Maybe I'll invite Brett to come and take up some of this free time." Jackee reminded her of the promise to be discreet.

"Brett really likes you and I doubt he would do anything to offend you."

"I think Brett is a really great guy and I can not understand how he is so controlled by you."

"It's because I made him an offer he can't refuse. For years men have been using women, now women have found ways to use men. What's good for the goose is good for the gander."

"Your logic escapes me but if it works for you it must be right."

Jackee spent more time with the baseball team and really started to see many of its problems. Comparing Bats' teams with this team, it was easy to see where all the weak points were. This team was weak up the middle and very poor defensively. There seemed to be no communication between the fielders. They had a team captain, but he could not lead a thirsty horse to water. With every game they played it only got worse. One day the coach noticed Jack and Jackee working out together and for the first time realized what they were actually doing. When they were resting, he went over to them and asked where they learned to play like that. Jack immediately said "she taught me." Jackee told him about Bats and how he improved her game.

Coach told them that they show professional ability and that "right now you are my starting combination for next year." Coach Zimmer seemed to change and really got into the games. There was more discipline and better coordination between the players. The team started to win a few games and actually had a 6 game winning streak. Although she did not play in a game, she did assist in practice by hitting to the fielders and keeping score during games. Many times during games, Coach Zimmer asked what she thought in certain situations and took her advice more often than not. They became very close because he never met anyone else who knew more about baseball than he did. One day while they were alone, he said his wife would like to look into that orphanage you mentioned.

"My father has already talked to the sisters and they would be happy to interview you. When you can take a break from your duties, arrangements could easily be made."

While the season was coming to a close, very little was happening with Dr Hopkins and the lab. Some workups had to be completed but the two girls finished them in record time. Brett did come for a weekend and they had a good time together, just the three of them. Later on in the evening around bed time the third wheel went her way and the two went to the other bedroom. There was never a problem and Brett was the perfect gentleman in every situation. Things were all coming to an end. Baseball finished about the same time that final exams were about to start. Neither Jackee or Andrea had any exam to take since again each had A pluses in every course. Their lab experiments lasted longer because of the time frame that controlled their start and finish. Their final lab class was to be completed on Tuesday and both girls would be headed home on Wednesday.

Coach Zimmer asked Jackee if she was playing summer Baseball. She told him she was but had not decided where. He said that he was coaching a summer semi-pro team and would like to have her play for him. She asked how the quality of the competition was. He said it was made up mostly of college and ex professional ballplayers. "Would I be the shortstop?"

He told her "not only will you be the shortstop but Jack will be your second baseman."

"How long does the season last?"

"It lasts seven weeks beginning the first week in July."

"How are the players and do the umpires control the game?"

"You will get some bench jockeying but the umpires will control it. Since the fans have to pay to see the games, control is extremely important."

She told him that comments don't affect her game but they sometimes hurt her teammates and put them off their game. "They must know ahead of time what to expect. Where is the home field and when do you have to report for tryouts?"

"This is our home field and the players should all be here by June 22."

"Lastly, where will I sleep and when we travel what will my sleeping arrangements be?"

"You can stay in your dorm room if you want and we have two female athlete trainers who travel with the team."

"I'll let you know in about 10 days."

CHAPTER FOURTEEN

Jackee Starts a New Season and Finds a Brother

*J*ackee arrived home Wednesday, Brett picked up Andrea and since Jackee was using the dorm over the summer, they both were traveling very light. In fact, Jackee only had one small bag plus her glove and bat. Carmela was the only one home and the two women had a real long talk. School was the most important item and Jackee told her mother that every course had an A plus grade. This pleased her mother and impressed her more when she heard about the lab work with Dr Hopkins. At the dinner table, she told them about the baseball team and how she was invited to play baseball with coach Zimmer's summer team. "He said the competition would be equal to or greater than Bats league." William had heard from Bats and he expected Jackee to play for her college coach over the summer.

"I still want you to call Bats and thank him, also you never know if the new league will appeal to you. Bats could be a safety net in case coach Zimmer's team doesn't work out."

Later that evening she called and talked to both Kim and Bats. She told Bats that it was important that she find out what type of player she would be in contact with. Coach Zimmer promised her a great deal, now she would see if he was a man of his word. Bats fully agreed with what she intended to do and said "if it doesn't meet your standards call me immediately." She thanked him and wished him luck for his coming season.

Dan had been on her mind all day and she hadn't heard if he got home yet. Just as Jackee was preparing for bed, Dan called. He told her he would be home late Thursday or early Friday. His last exam was Thursday but he had to pack everything since he would be in the athletic dorm next semester. Saturday night would be his best chance to see her, so they made a date for 7:00 that night. She was so excited that she forgot to ask him about his finals. *Well*, she thought, *there will be plenty of time over the weekend.*

Jackee started to work out and began hitting on Thursday. She felt there was enough time to be game ready by June 22. Rose still had one more state meet before she starts her summer invitational meets in July. Running clubs all over the state had called her to compete and she has turned them all down. She just wanted to work with Jackee until baseball starts. Coach Zimmer called to ask Jackee if her father could make an appointment with the orphanage for this coming Saturday morning. They both would like to see if adoption was right for them.

"I'm sure my dad will do this and I'll have him call you as soon as he contacts the Sisters."

Coach thanked her and gave her a number where he could be reached. The last thing he said, with his fingers crossed, was "see you on the 22nd." Carmela called William at the firm and told him about coach Zimmer's plan to come up on Saturday. William said he would stop at the orphanage on the way home.

When William walked in the door both women were waiting for him. He told them the Sisters had a little girl and a baby boy that may be available. "The mother is a crackhead and there is no father in the picture. They are waiting for the mother to sign a release form giving up her rights to the child. There is also the possibility that she has overdosed and may not recover."

Over dinner, Jackee explained what the Zimmer's had been through and how it had affected the wife. Carmela said to lose the first baby was not a good sign and adoption may be their only option. "We have a tentative appointment at 12 noon, so I'll call them right after dinner."

Mrs Zimmer, Nancy, answered the phone when William called and she started crying as she talked to him. All she could say was "we will be at your house at 11:30 and thank you about five times before she hung up."

William looked upset but Jackee told him that she has been crying almost nonstop since losing the baby. They all decided to go with the Zimmer's on Saturday to show their support. Carmela whispered, "if they don't want the boy I'll take him."

They all stared at her dumbfounded, then Rose screamed, "YES"! Carmela walked into the kitchen smiling and William went to get a drink.

Saturday at 11:00 the Zimmer's rang the bell. Carmela answered the door and asked them to come in. Mrs Zimmer apologized for being so early but she had been up most of the night and they decided to get an early start. William called ahead and the Nuns were waiting at the door. They did not expect so many but they were used to all the Jenco's coming together. The Mother Superior explained that the little two year old girl had been abused both physically and sexually. "The doctors seem to think that no physical damage has been done and that she will not even remember any of it. The boy has some narcotics in his system but that should disappear soon and there should be no physical damage."

As soon as they showed the baby boy, Jackee had to grab Rose by the shoulder to stop her from picking up the boy. Rose looked at Jackee and said "he's ours." Jackee said not yet. All the women stayed with the baby boy as the Nuns showed the Zimmers around the orphanage. Finally the Nuns, William and the Zimmers went to a conference room while the girls still stood guard over the baby boy. One half hour later everyone came out smiling and the Mother Superior told them that the Zimmers had decided to take the little girl. They already signed the papers to start the proceedings for adoption.

Rose screamed out "He is ours". She picked him up and was dancing around the floor. William took Carmela in his arms and asked if she really wanted to start all over again. She put her arms around his neck, kissed him and said why not? Now all the Jenco's sisters were dancing with Rose. Rose finally let Evelyn and Jackee hold him. The Nuns wanted to know what was going on? William told them that this poor boy is going to have 5 women spoil him rotten. William, Carmela and the Nuns reentered the conference room.

Dan and Jackee went out on the usual Saturday date. However one thing was different, this time they talked more than they kissed. The separation of the college year gave each of them a chance to reflect on the future. Jackee wanted to know if his year away at college had changed his thoughts about her. She knew that there must be many girls who find Dan extremely desirable. She saw girls at her college entice boys by using their bodies. Andrea had explained to her that it was one of the best methods to get what you want. He held her and said nothing has changed. "For as long as you want me, I will be yours. I will not tell you that there haven't been offers made to me and some have been very interesting, but all they did was inflate my ego. None of them could ever replace what I feel for you. Your mother told you I was one in a million, well you are 10 times that to me."

She started crying and kissed him until she had to breathe. She told him she loved him and to please always love her.

He said that "5 Years from now we will be married and we will be one forever."

When he took her home and kissed her good night, she told him in "5 years we will not have to say good night."

June 21, Carmela and Jackee were preparing for her trip back to Olympus college. There was not much to pack since Jackee had left most of her clothes in her dorm room. William was surprised that the college let her use the same room for a summer baseball program. He had never heard of a college doing that. So far the college had not asked Jackee to do anything extra. Early the next morning they took Jackee back to the school. When they arrived coach Zimmer and Dean Grant were at Jackee's dorm, William had alerted the college that they would be entering the campus around 11:30, a heads up went to the coach and dean. Coach thanked the family again for their help and told them the adoption was right on schedule. He also told Jackee that she had a physical to take tomorrow before practice. Dean Grant mentioned to Jackee that "there will be a large group of students coming on campus this Saturday and we would like you to be one of the speakers."

She told the dean it would be an honor to speak with them. He said she would be notified as to time and place. William correctly assumed that the pay back was beginning. The parents had lunch with her and then kissed Jackee good-bye and left for home.

Every pre-season physical is about the same and she never knew anyone who failed one. Immediately after, she changed into her sweats, got her glove and bat, and headed for the field. Beside her there were 21 other players trying out. Four were from the college team including Jack. Jack knew a few others and introduced Jackee to them. There was no doubt that the coach had not yet told them about her. Coach Zimmer called everyone into the infield and gave them information about the coming summer program. Lastly he made everyone aware that there was a female playing on the team. "You will soon find out that she is one of the best in this state, as shown by the fact that she was the MVP in last year's state champion series. Jackee, would you talk to the team?"

She told them to never answer back if someone on or off the field cast slurs her way. "Never get into a fight over what they call me. I have had pros rip me to pieces and I never needed any help. I would deeply appreciate it if you would refrain from using certain curse words. Not that I haven't heard them many times but because it makes the team look classless. We will be a class team and will answer all insults with base hits and great plays. I apologize to you now for any insults that are directed at you because of me. I have heard them all before and still achieve great success." The meeting was over and the players went to their positions. A batting order had been posted behind the home plate screen.

Jackee and Jack were due to hit near the bottom of the list so they started infield drills. Infielders were directed to go to a position of choice. Two pitchers were asked to assist the two J's working the infielders. Jackee took third and short while Jack hit to second and first. Each fielder got 25 ground balls. Two first basemen were set up along the first base line and the left side of the infield threw to the first one and the right side threw to the second one. When that was done the players switched positions on the field. The other shortstop saw how Jackee fielded ground balls so he thought he might move to third. When Jackee batted she was in midseason form and hit line drive after line drive. She drove one over the left center fence. The other potential shortstop now said he was a third baseman. There was no doubt in any player's mind who was in charge of the infield. Whenever a practice started they looked to her for what to do. Coach Zimmer thought it was strange that almost everyone on the field was older than Jackee but she was the one they listened to. He saw immediately that she was a leader who wasn't given the right to lead, she earned that right. Friday night she had a message from Dean Grant that she should be at the school large group instruction room at 1:00pm. She finished practice at 12 noon and had plenty of time to shower and dress.

She arrived a little before 1:00 and Dean Grant filled her in on what was happening. This was a group of hand picked science majors who wanted to apply for the six year program. Each administrator gave a short talk on their responsibilities in the program. Dean Grant then introduced Jackee as one of the leading students who by the way had a straight A plus GPA. Jackee, who was wearing a dress and had surprised the administrators when she came in thanked dean Grant and welcomed the crowd. This group consisted of both parents and students. Jackee centered her talk on the students but tried to include the parents when possible. "Here is a program that offers you the best opportunity for a medical degree. Everything here is top of the line and if something is needed, the science department goes out and acquires it. Every teacher I had here has gone out of their way to make me a better student. Teachers, and especially Dr Hopkins have spent extra hours making sure all things are covered and understood. When you eventually leave here you will have one of the most rounded medical minds in the country. I told you what is here and what you can achieve. It can only be done if you commit to it. This is not a party school or program. If you can not dedicate 100% of your mind and body go somewhere else and save your parents a lot of hard earned money. You owe them a lot more than you could ever give. This program provides you the opportunity to start paying them back."

"If I might take one more minute of your time. To all the young ladies here I want to tell you one very important thing. Here you will be treated as an equal. My parents always told me that I can do anything I put my mind to. Others tried to hold me back. Let no one take away your God given right to be a success in any field you choose. Our constitution guarantees to everyone this right and many people before us have died to protect these rights. I am free all afternoon and would be glad to answer any questions you have." Administrators were speechless as Jackee returned to her seat. They never expected her to give such a talk and did not know how the audience would react. As soon as Dean Grant ended the talk and told the people they could look over the campus, they got their answer. Jackee was mobbed by the parents and especially the young ladies. She spent the next hour answering as best she could parents and students' questions. People were later directed to a reception in the cafeteria where light refreshments were served. Jackee followed along and was still talking to the people.

Around 4:00 people started to leave and most were gone by 4:30. A parent with 3 daughters asked if she would join them for dinner. Jackee resisted at first but the girls begged her to come. She agreed and later was seated at the restaurant with them. When the girls found out she had 3 sisters they wanted to know all about them. The oldest daughter hoped to be selected for the program. Jackee said she will be, if her grades are good, and "you will be an example for your sisters to follow. Look me up as soon as you get on campus and I'll show you around." She thanked Jackee as the parents dropped her off, and the potential student was reminded to contact Jackee when she arrived on campus.

Baseball tryouts were over and the team had been selected. Coach Zimmer was a totally different coach then the one Jackee saw in the spring. He was more relaxed and really into preparing the team. She had to think that the loss of the baby and the new adoption proceedings had a lot to do with it. She decided to hold judgment until she saw him in game situations. Coach was considering letting Jackee bat first. She makes contact and has much better than average speed. He consulted her and she told him anywhere he wanted her to bat was fine, but she felt more comfortable batting third. Jackee mentioned to the coach that Jack had good speed and a good eye at the plate. Coach said that Ross would be a good second hitter and Bo a good number four. Bo or Harris because each one hits for power. "That gives us more than half the lineup and the rest should fill right in. We are strong up the middle and our pitching is very good. Anyone of our first four starters could be our number one. Which of our outfielders would you consider for center field?"

Without hesitating Jackee answered "Ross."

"I agreed, he gets a jump on the ball, has a strong arm and speed."

Games were played on Tuesday, Wednesday, Friday, Saturday and two games on Sunday. The Olympians first four game series started on Friday against the Eton Eagles. Game time was 7:05pn and the gates opened at 6:00. Olympians took infield at 6:40, Eagles at 6:50. There was a meeting at home plate for ground rules and exchange of lineup cards. Starting lineups were announced, Zeke Baker threw 8 warmups, catcher threw to second and the umpire hollered play ball at exactly 7:05. Zeke retired the side in order. Bottom of the first Jack walks after seeing 10 pitchers. Ross flied out but Jackee hit a line drive double to left center. Jack scored and Jackee took third on the throw to the plate. She later scored on a long fly ball off the bat of Bo Taylor the catcher. This was a lead the Olympians never lost. The final score was five to nothing. Once again the crowd was into Jackee being on the field. She heard some applause when she came to bat but when she doubled the fans were on their feet cheering. Jackee did not disappoint them, she had a perfect night with 3 hits, two walks and two rbi's. Zeke had pitched a complete game 2 hit shutout and Jackee felt he deserved the biggest applause.

A local reporter interviewed Jackee after the game and told her most of these fans came to see the wonder girl in action. "You did not let them down."

"I am one ball player on this team, you should be talking to our pitcher who pitched a near perfect game. No one player wins a baseball game. It takes nine players, it takes good defense, it takes offense and of course good pitching."

"All that may be true but many of these fans are here only because of you and neither you or I can change that."

Jackee talked to the coach and asked him if this crowd was a normal size. He told her it was "at least double what we normally get. You will have to get used to this because every club is using you to draw bigger crowds."

"What do we tell the other players, that I am the star and they are my side show?"

"Jackee, you should not feel that way. Because of you they play in front of many more fans, because of you the team gets much more recognition."

The team crowded around Jackee and Jack told her that he had never played in front of so many people and it felt great. All of them echoed Jack's statement and Bo told her "please don't get hurt, because if people know you're playing the stands will be full."

Jack was right, each day more and more fans showed up for their game. Over 90% of the extra fans were females, and there was little doubt who they came to see. The Olympians won the first three games of the series. Just as the coach expected the big crowds elevated everyone's game and the team played like champions. He did notice one thing, Jackee seemed to be pressing. Her fielding was still fantastic but her hitting was off. Before the final seven inning game of the series, he spoke to her prior to the game starting. She told him that most of these people were here to see her and she was trying too hard to please them. Coach told her that if she stays within herself the talent will come out naturally. Shaking her head, she thanked him for reminding her what her father always said. "If you stay within your own ability, the talent will rise to the occasion." In the final game Jackee had three hits. All were line drives and all were extra base hits. Since it was Sunday night and still early the fans stayed to mingle with the players. They had never experienced anything like this and they thanked Jackee for making it happen.

Sunday evening, after dinner, she called home and Dan. Her parents only talked a short time but Dan's call lasted almost an hour. They talked about many things but it all came down to how much they missed each other. Next week the team was on the road so she would be late getting back Sunday night. If it's too late she will call him on Monday.

Tuesday morning they headed for two games against the Cresswood Cyclones. They also played their games at a college field but it was not as nice as Olympus's field. After they had something to eat, they put on their sweats in the field house and headed for the practice field. Two hours later the team entered the field house to get ready for tonight's game. While they were working out the ground keepers were moving portable stands next to existing ones. Sure enough when the game started, only standing room was available. The Olympians won the first game and the fans got their show. Jackee hit an inside, belt high, fastball right over the 310 foot sign down the left field line. When the 6 to 2 game ended Jackee was surrounded by fans and stayed for an hour signing autographs, taking pictures and just talking. Coach Zimmer asked the Cyclones coach how he rated the crowd. He said "this is almost triple what we normally get and most of them were cheering for your team."

"No, they were cheering for my shortstop and she deserves every bit of it."

"Where did you find her?" The Cyclone coach asked.

"She is in our 6 year medical program and just happens to play baseball. Talent she showed on the field did not just happen. Behind that young lady is years of practice and determination."

Olympians spent the night in the athletic dorms. Jackee had a special room with a bath for herself and loved it. Next morning at 5:00am she was running and lifting some weights. Three hours later she was having breakfast with the team and other athletes. There was some time to kill so she went to the library until lunch time. She fell asleep for a few hours then dressed for tonight's game. While taking infield, they noticed more stands had been added and they were filling up. When the game started most of the seats were filled. Once again in a 4 to3 win over the Cyclones, Jackee had a triple, a single plus two walks. The game ended when Jackee went far to her left, fielded a ground ball, stepped on second and threw a strike to first. Olympians spent the night at the college and their bus would be there at 9am on Thursday. They will be on the road this weekend for their four game series against the Hasting Hustlers.

Friday after breakfast the team bus was on its way to Hasting. Arriving at noon they had lunch in the college cafeteria and then rested for an hour. After a short practice they rested for a while then dressed and headed for the baseball field. This was a stadium where the double A team played all their home games. Facilities at this stadium were top of the line and the Olympians took advantage of it. Whirlpool, sauna and steam room were all used. While taking infield, Jackee noticed that the artificial turf was very fast. Hit baseballs got to you very quickly. She mentioned to Jake and Casey, who played third, to play a step or two back. By playing back you can cover more ground but the throw to first is longer. All the travel must have caught up with them because the team seemed to have no energy. Their winning streak came to an end in a 4 to 2 loss to the Hustlers. Saturday was a new day and a new team. Olynpians came out swinging and scored 10 runs to win the second game 10 to 1. Jackee had a great game with 2 doubles and a triple. She also made the play of the game by catching a ball in foul territory down the left field line. She had to catch the ball as she was sliding into the fence. This was the final out of the inning so the cheering lasted until she left the field. Again a crowd gathered around Jackee and although she was hungry, she stayed and mingled with the people. No matter how hard she tried she could not resist talking to the girls after the game. Sunday's double header was a disaster for the Hustlers. Olympians two starting pitchers, pitched complete games and between them they allowed a total of 10 hits. Jackee had 4 hits including a double and three walks. Sunday had the largest crowd and it was hard to tell who they were routing for. Since the team was spending the night there, Jackee spent a great deal of time with the girls after the second game. A bus was due at 9:00am Monday to take the team back to Olympus college.

Upon their arrival back at school the players were told to get some rest and report to the field for a short practice at 4:00. By 6:00 they were in the cafeteria having dinner and then going to their rooms. Jackee went to her room, showered and prepared for bed. She called home first and then called Dan. It was not a long call since Jackee was exhausted and falling asleep as they spoke. Dan realized what was happening and said "you need to get some rest so I'll call you tomorrow at 7:00." She was asleep as soon as her head hit the pillar. At 5:00am the alarm rang and she got ready to work out. The cardio and light weights were most important and she made sure they were done every day. Since she was hitting off a live arm almost every day, the iron mike was only used on rainy days or if she felt her mechanics were off.

The Gotham Tigers were the next team on Tuesday and Wednesday. Attendance was even greater than the first home series. The local TV station asked if they could broadcast one of the games to the community. With the school's permission the league's administrators agreed. Through her coach, Jackee told them what the rules were for an interview. They were only to be conducted after the game and nothing before a game. The TV station was not happy because they would have to stay after the game. Coach Zimmer told them it was a take it or leave it decision. They agreed.

Whatever drew the crowd, it was the biggest ever at Olympus college. Not only were the parking lots filled, there were also cars parked all over the campus. When Jackee's name was announced there was a loud cheer, but when she came to bat now everyone realized who it was and the cheering was deafening. If you could think of the best thing that might happen, you would be almost right. Jackee lined an over the plate belt high fastball over the centerfield fence for a two run homer. As she rounded the bases Coach Zimmer thought *it can't get any better than this*. None of the Tigers had ever seen anything like this on a baseball field. Hometown fans cheered until Jackee came out for a curtain call. The Tigers coach knew his team was intimidated and it would be a tough game to win. He was right. All Jacke's teammates were pumped up and they scored 12 runs to win the game 12 to 1. Game two was not too much different. Only the score was. Olympian's won the game 10 to 0. The Tigers coach could not wait to leave town. Jackee had 5 hits and 6 runs batted in, which was only one hit less than the Tigers got in two games.

Rosewood Robins would be the weekend opponents starting on Friday. They were not a good team but did have good pitching. Scouting report was right on. Pitching in the first game was dominating the hitters. Olympians scored two runs and that was enough for a 2 to 1 victory in game 1. Game two Saturday was on local television. In the first inning, Jackee drove in the first run with a single to left center. The crowd at about the same size as the previous three games erupted in wild applause. The Olympians won going away and the final score was 8 to 0. Jackee accepted a short interview after the game. Only one question was on the point. "Why would a girl want to play baseball?"

Her answer was on the mark, "because I can. In baseball the best players play." Since they had no comeback to this answer the interview ended and the crew went home. Jackee was asked to go out with some players after the game but she said I have to get up early for church. Some other night would be great. Sunday's double header ended in identical losses for the Robins. Both games were 6 to 1 and Jackee and Bo Taylor had great games. Later that night she called home and also talked to Dan.

Tuesday and Wednesday they will play the Summerfield Swingers. This team is one of the best in the league. They proved this by beating Olympians 3 to 0 in game one. Game two Zeke helped return the favor by pitching a one hit shutout. Jackee either drove in or scored 3 of the 4 runs Olympian scored. The next morning they were on their way to play the Bayview Pirates, a weekend series. This would end the first half. The crowds at Summerfield were very big, but the crowd on Friday night at Bayview was standing room only. Bayview had their own TV agreement with the local station. Each game will be televised and huge crowds are expected for all the games. Game one went 10 innings with Jackee scoring the winning run on Bo's sacrifice fly. Jackee had doubled and stole third and just did beat the throw home from the left fielder. Game two on Saturday was all the top of the order for the Olympians. The first four batters had 7 hits, 3 walks, 5 RBI's and 6 runs scored. Josh Dunright pitched a 4 hitter and allowed only 2 runs. Sunday's double header was a standoff. The Olympians won the first game 6 to 4 but lost the nightcap 6 to 2. It was a tired team that sat down to dinner Sunday night. Jackee finished eating and just went to bed. She showered in the morning and never got to breakfast. In fact she was late for the bus taking the team home. Most of the players slept on the bus and not a voice was raised the whole trip back. Upon arrival back at the school, first they went to eat, and then to their rooms. Coach Zimmer had told them, there will be no practice today, just get some rest.

Second half began with a Tuesday trip to play the Eton Eagles. Both games were won by the Olympians by 5 runs. Tuesday the score was 6 to 1 and Wednesday it was 7 to 2. The crowd was big but not as big as they were used to. Still, after each game Jackee was asked to talk to the fans, especially the girls. This became a ritual after every game and Jackee became very good at it. She loved talking to the young girls and answering questions about her mother and sisters. Coach Zimmer was her guardian Angel. When he felt she did enough he would say she has to have dinner now. Thursday morning the bus left for Crestwood to play a weekend series against the Cyclones. Here the crowds were very big and on Saturday set a new record. Although they lost the first game on Sunday, Olympians won the other three. Coach Zimmer had the team winning baseball games and he loved his double play combination. No other team had anything close to his double J's. Jackee and Jack had completed 10 double plays so far. Their defense was the glue that held the infield together. They both directed the infield and outfield together and it seemed there was no need for them to look because they knew where the other would be. Coach Zimmer could not wait until his college season arrived.

Hasting Huslers were coming in for the mid week two game series. Since they were well rested the Olympians swept the two games. Thursday was a travel day as they had to play a weekend series against the Gotham Tigers. Olympians won big on Friday before a huge crowd but lost on Saturday in a tough 3 to 2 game. Jackee made the last out when she hit a line drive right at the third baseman with the bases loaded. The ball was hit so hard that she never left the batter's box. After the game she was surrounded by at least 50 young girls and spoke to them for over an hour. Finally the coach came over and told the crowd to please excuse her. "She really has to eat and get some rest. I'll let her talk to you after the games tomorrow." Sunday's 9 and 7 innings games were totally different. The Olympians won the first game 8 to 0. Game 2 was scoreless in the first four innings but after the Olympians failed to score in the fifth, the Tigers scored two in the bottom of the inning. Top of the sixth Olympians rallied and were trailing 2 to 1 with runners on second and third and only one out. Ross squared around to bunt on a squeeze play and was hit in the stomach by a fastball. Now the Olympians had the bases loaded and Jackee coming up. She was looking for a pitch above the belt that she could drive to the outfield. In came a hanging curve, belt high on the outside of the plate and out it went over the right center field fence. This was Jackee's first grand slam of the season and it finished off the Tigers 5 to 2. As promised, the coach let Jackee talk to the girls for over 90 minutes. Even though she was exhausted, the adrenalin kicked in after the grand slam and she had a great time with the girls. Two hours later she laid down on the bed still in uniform and did not wake up until 7am Monday. Having showered, packed and gobbled down some breakfast, she barely made the 8am bus.

The two games away at Rosewood Robins were a big success behind the pitching of Zeke and Josh. Both would be pitching for Olympus college in the fall and spring. Each one had a live arm and shut down the Robins with only one run in both games. This late in the season saw most of the crowds cheering for Jackee. It was highly unusual to see a home crowd cheering for the opponents. The Olympians to a man enjoyed and admired playing beside Jackee. Her desire to be the best was infectious and gave them something most of them never had, respect on the baseball field. Thursday morning found them heading home for the final four games at home. Summerfield Swingers came in riding a 6 game winning streak. Coach Zimmer anticipated big crowds for the four final games. He was not surprised when they had a sellout crowd on Friday. However the Swingers would not cooperate and won their 7th in a row. Jackee did have two hits, one being a long double off the left field fence. It was not enough to make up for a poor pitching performance by Larry. Saturday was a different story and the Jenco family and Dan were on hand. Jackee led the team going 4 for 4 and playing great defense. Zeke pitched a 6 hitter and allowed only one run. Jackee told the girls who were waiting to see her that her family was here and she hadn't seen them in almost two months. She said she would meet with them tomorrow after the double header. There was a moan from the girls but the parents took control and thanked Jackee. She immediately ran to her parents and then to Dan. She hugged him so hard that it knocked the breath out of him. William was taking the family out to dinner when Coach told him he would take Jackee home on Thursday since he and his wife had to pick up their daughter from the orphanage. Carmela congratulated him and said Saturday they were picking up their son. Rose chimed in and said "that's my brother William."

They selected a restaurant close by. William dropped Jackee off at her dorm, drove the others to the restaurant, and then went back for Jackee. It worked out perfectly as she was ready when William came back for her. After dinner the family said good night to Jackee at their hotel. Dan then took her back in the car and they were alone for a little while. She took Dan up to her room and they sat on the couch. They talked for a time and then kissed for a longer time. Jackee fell asleep in his arms and he just held her close. He woke her gently and said she had to get to bed. She locked the door behind him and prepared for bed. Before Dan was halfway to the hotel, Jackee was in a deep sleep. She was up at 7am and ready for church when the family arrived at 7:45. After Mass they went to breakfast and at 10:30, Jackee had to get ready for the double header. There never was a larger or more enthusiastic crowd at an Olympus's College baseball game. They even cheered the ground crew when they had to come out and fix a problem on the mound. The Olympians were into the crowd and showed it at the plate. Both games were dominated by the home team. In the first game every Olympian player had at least one hit and the team had a 14 hit game. Game two both teams emptied their benches after the third inning. Jackee for the first time this season missed an inning of play. When she went out for the top of the fourth, Coach sent in a new shortstop before one pitch was thrown. Naturally the crowd gave her a standing ovation that continued even after she went into the dugout. After the second curtain call the game went on. Next inning one by one the coach removed all the starters and each one was individually acknowledged.

When the second game ended the team was told a buffet dinner was waiting for them in the faculty cafeteria. Jackee of course would be late as she met with a group of girls immediately after the game. Her family stayed with her for a while but left and would see her in the cafeteria. It took some 40 minutes before she could get something to eat. As she entered the cafeteria her teammates all stood and clapped followed by all the other guests. Jackee had a big smile and tears in her eyes as she approached the family and Dan. Coach Zimmer made the announcement that the last two games against the Bayview Pirates were being canceled so he would collect all the baseball uniforms and gear starting tomorrow at 10am. He also told them that if the league designated a champion team for the season, it would be the Olympians. "We had the most wins, highest batting percentage, lowest ERA by our pitchers and the leading batter in the league. Jackee, congratulations, you won the batting title for the summer." Before the dinner ended Jackee would go to each player and thank them for being such great team mates. No matter what they thought of her before the season started, they were 100% behind her by the time the season ended.

William gathered up his family and told Jackee good bye. She reminded them that the coach would be taking her home on Tuesday. When Rose came over to say goodbye Jackee gave her a baseball and told her it was her grand slam baseball. Coach Zimmer had sent one of the players to get the ball. He had to give the kid who finally found the ball 5 dollars but it was worth it. Jackee mentioned to Carmela she thought the coach canceled the games so he and Nancy could pick up their new baby. Carmela reminded her that their new baby would also be legally theirs this week.

Just after the Jenco's and Dan left, the coach told all the players that "the Lions Club is having dinner for us at the local country club. It's scheduled for 6 PM Monday. All are invited and any family or guest that may be here for you as well." There was no workout on Monday morning, Jackee just cleaned the dorm room. She did not want Andrea to find a mess when she arrived. She finished about 10:30 and headed for the field house to turn in her uniform. Coach Zimmer said he would pick her up at 8:30 Tuesday morning. Since she only had one piece of luggage and it was already packed there would be no problem. Most of the other players were going to lunch so Jackee decided to join them. About mid afternoon they broke up and started getting ready for the evening. This was the first time that she was really dressing since summer baseball started. Everything was done with care as she wanted to look her best. Coach Zimmer and Nancy were to pick her up at 5:45. They were late and it caused them to arrive at the country club's banquet hall at 6:30. When Jackee entered the room there was complete silence. Her teammates had never seen her dressed up. She always wore a uniform or sweats. They were stunned at how beautiful she was and they also wondered how she hid that body under a uniform. Sitting with the ball players was the sensible thing to do. Jokingly she said to them, "you knew I was a female, so why all the fuss."

"We knew there was a female ball player in that uniform, but we did not know she had the body of a goddess," said Ross.

The Lions Club had permission from the college to sell refreshments at all the home games. Because they had so many spectators at games the club made a great deal of money. Their wives suggested this dinner to thank the players, especially the female one. It was agreed by the club that the wives would run the dinner. After eating but before dessert was served the ladies spoke. First they thanked all the players and coaches for the great season the team had. Next they told them how all the money would go to local charities and people in need. This is what Lions clubs all over do with all monies raised. Lastly they asked Jackee to come up and accept this small gift for all the time she dedicated to the girls after the games. Every year the Lions club honor's one person who in some way helped enrich the community. An engraved plaque was given to Jackee as the person of the year. The speaker explained that "everything you see here has been donated by someone and that includes the plaque. No money came from the Lions club." Jackee thanked everyone and added that coach Zimmer and the players on the team deserved to be part of this award.

Tuesday, Jackee was sitting on the steps with her bag as the Zimmer's pulled up to her dorm. She could understand how excited the couple must be. Coach told her the doctors felt their chances of Nancy giving birth were less than 50%. This alternative, for now, represented their best chance to become parents. Jackee asked if she could go to the orphanage with them. They agreed and when they stopped for gas Jackee called home and asked her mother to meet at the orphanage. Sure enough, Carmela was waiting with the Sisters when they arrived. 15 minutes later, after signing all the legal documents, the Zimmers had their little girl named Maria. Nancy had asked her husband if she could name the baby after her grandmother who had raised her. Coach agreed if the middle name was Anne after his mom. So Maria Anne entered the arms of Nancy as her daughter. The Sisters provided the baby with a Bible, Christening outfit and a change of diapers. Carmela gave them a miraculous medal on a gold chain that she and William had picked out. The Zimmer's thanked everyone and told the Sisters they would be in touch. Without even stopping to eat, they left for home. Carmela and Jackee did the same after conferring with the Sisters about when little William will be available. Mother Superior said they were expecting final papers any day.

When they got home Jackee found Carmela had prepared lunch in case the Zimmer's wanted something to eat. Together they had a small lunch and just talked until Rose came home. Rose saw her plaque and asked where they were going to put it. Carmela suggested on the wall next to the showcase. Jackee wanted to know how Rose was doing, and Rose told her about all the events she now enters. Her coach was preparing her for the decathlon. "It's a lot of hard work but I really enjoy the variety."

Jackee said how proud she was of her and "someday we will see you on that stand getting a gold medal." Looking at Jackee and Carmela she said if it happens it will be for the whole family.

After dinner, Jackee called Dan at school. He said he was coming home Friday after practice but had to be back on Monday morning. She had to be back at school on Monday so they would probably leave after church on Sunday. "I'll call you as soon as I get home Friday."

She got the call about 4:00 and he would see her after dinner. The family wanted him to eat with them. Dan arrived and Jackee immediately kissed him in front of her family. At this point the Jenco's were assuming he was part of the family. They went to their favorite parking spot and talked for a long time. They had at least two months to catch up on. When they finished talking, Jackee just folded herself in his arms and said how much she missed him. He held her tight and finally kissed her. It was a long passionate kiss that told her he felt the same. Jackee asked him not to be mad at her but she had to tell him that she loved him so much it hurt. He told her, "The hurt tells you that the feeling is real." Later he took her home and said he'd see her tomorrow night.

Saturday was a red letter day. The Sisters called to tell them that little William was ready to leave their care. At 9:00am the Jenco family was at the orphanage to pick up the baby and take him home. All the necessary papers were signed in the conference room and would be filed with the state. Carmela received a birth certificate, legal name document, bible, Christening outfit and the baby's medical records. An appointment with the family doctor for little William had already been made. All the girls wanted to hold the baby on the drive home. "The baby can not be held all day long. He needs time to sleep and time to get used to his new surroundings, "Carmela told them. When they arrived home Rebbeca and Rocco were there with their new son, who was born June 4th and named Frank Joseph. Frank's uncle William had been born February 12th. Now pictures were taken of both children, together and with every family member. Lunch had been completely forgotten so preparations were made to have an early supper.

Dan arrived and was introduced to Little William. He looked at the father and said, "if you teach him to play baseball as you did Jackee, he'll be one hell-of-a baseball player."

William said, "I just hope I have enough left in me to help him be whatever he wants." Jackee and Dan left for their last date until maybe Thanksgiving.

For the last hour before Dan arrived, Jackee had tried to make herself look as sexy as possible. She wanted Dan to think she was desirable. As they walked to the ice cream parlor Dan held her hand. When they entered, all male eyes went to Jackee. She looked absolutely stunning. He guessed she had what they call natural beauty. No matter what she wore, she looked good in it. Once she was recognized, the girls came over to talk. When their order came everyone returned to their own table. This was one courtesy Jackee's admirers afforded them. One hour later they were headed for their special parking area. Neither one mentioned anything about leaving tomorrow and they just enjoyed their time together. When Dan said they better go as it was getting late, Jackee said just one more kiss. She had tears in her eyes when she entered the house and ran to her room. Carmela followed her and knocked on her door. She went into the room and found Jackee face down on the bed crying.

Gathering Jackee in her arms she asked what was the problem. Jackee told her they have so many long absences and she misses Dan so much that it hurt her mentally and physically.

"You are both trying to make a life for yourselves, and to do that you must be apart for a time. This is the best way for each of you to strive for your goals. Any other way might jeopardize one or both of your goals. A lot sooner than you think, the two of you will be together. Just look forward to that day and take each day one at a time." Jackee held her mother and thanked her for being there for her.

CHAPTER FIFTEEN

Jackee Starts Second Year of New Program and Fall Baseball

*S*unday morning as the Jenco family was getting ready to enter the church, Dan showed up and held Jackee's hand for the entire service. Immediately after Dan left to go back to school, William dropped Carmela and his new son at home, and he, Jackee and Rose headed for Olympus college. Four hours later they were in the cafeteria having lunch. Andrea was just finishing but she sat with them while they ate. William and Rose left right after and the two girls went to their room. Andrea mentioned how great the room looked and was surprised to hear that Jackee had been in the room all summer. Jackee told her about the baseball season and how the school let her stay in the dorm, instead of the field house. All Andrea wanted to know was, were there any hot boys on the baseball team? With a slight blush on her face, Jackee told her she had no way of knowing since she did not date any of them. "You mean to tell me that you had 20 male athletes with you all summer and you didn't show an interest in any of them. What are you, some kind of a nun? There must have been at least one that you wanted to rip the clothes off and check his credentials."

"I told you before that I have a boyfriend and he is the only one I ever want to be with. We are committed to each other and I see no reason to lead someone else on."

"That is so unnatural but if that's how you want to play the game, so be it." Just then a call came in from Dean Grant asking the girls to speak to the new freshmen class at 11am Monday.

Both Andrea and Jackee looked like models as they waited to speak to the new students. They mostly stayed talking about the science program. Jackee was able to add some insight for the other amenities offered at the college. When the group gathered informally in the cafeteria many wanted to know about Jackee playing on a men's team. Andrea was pushed to the background as Jackee was the center of attraction. Only the real science candidates wanted to hear more about the curriculum and Andrea talked to that group. When they were done Jackee and Andrea headed back to their room. They later decided to walk over to the lab and talk to Lucy as to there being a schedule for the coming year. Lucy had not heard anything yet from Dr Hopkins but some new material had come in but hadn't been analyzed. Their classes were starting tomorrow and they had wanted to prepare a workable schedule. Jackee especially needed one so she could fit in fall baseball. As the girls were walking back to the room they decided to make their schedule and Dr Hopkins would have to accept the time they set apart for lab work.

Classes were programmed for them and they had the choice times for classes and labs. Since they completed history, and ancient remedies, this semester was about pre 19th century medicine. The first two semesters were very interesting and they hoped this one would be as good. Fall baseball would only have 15 games. All local schools will be opponents. This is mostly getting to know new players and seeing what they can do. Coach told Jackee that she could plan her own fall schedule. He wanted her fresh for the spring so she should complete as much school work as possible before February 1st. Jackee told him her schedule was all laid out and there was enough time for everything. She then asked about Maria Anne, and he told her he had never seen his wife happier since their wedding day.

Andrea and Jackee were doing great in their classes but had not heard anything from Dr. Hopkins. Jackee worked out every morning and with the team every afternoon. The double J's were a big success and the team was really rounding into shape. Pitching candidates were fantastic. Beside hold overs Zeke, Josh, Evan, Sal, Thomas there were freshmen Brady, Drew and Stan. All had excellent pitching ability with an above average fastball. The infield had a huge addition. Bo Taylor, the summer catcher, liked coach Zimmer so much he transferred from his college to Olympus and as a sophomore has 3 more years of eligibility. There was also an outfielder who was one of the fastest runners Jackee has ever seen. His name was Sonny Lightfoot and he is full blood Indian. The tribal council sent him to college so he could become a doctor and eventually return and care for his people. As a player he was a fair outfielder with an average arm but not much of a hitter. To say he was quiet would be a big understatement. When talking with him all answers were one word or less. In one of Jackee's classes she remembers seeing him but except raising his hand to acknowledge his name, never spoke one word. Jackee and Jack approached Sonny and asked him if he was comfortable in center field. A nod of the head was all they got in return. Jack told him they were trying to get a strong team up the middle and the last piece is a center fielder. "We would like to help you develop into that person. A center fielder must cover a lot of ground and be the leader in the field. Do you think you can be that person?" Sonny just nodded. Jack shook his head and said fine.

Every day before practice actually started the two J's worked with Sonny. He appeared to be a quick learner because every day he seemed to get better. After about a week of this he even talked to them. He told them "thank you". It was a breakthrough, A two word sentence. Jackee arranged to meet him in the field house at 5am and had him hit against iron mike. His bat was slow entering the hitting zone. She showed him two exercises that would help speed up his bat. Coach worked with him on keeping his weight back and not hitting off the front foot. Since he worked hard every day these two adjustments made a big difference in his hitting. One day after class Jackee introduced him to Andrea and she told him that they are willing to assist him with any science school work. Andrea had been a willing participant and even said she thought he was cute. To Jackee's surprise, a little while later, Andrea was tutoring him and they were actually talking to each other.

The Olympus baseball team played games against any 2 or 4 year college that was nearby and had a fall program. There were 5 of these schools and a 20 game schedule was arranged. They played 4 games a week for 5 weeks. It was a short but productive 5 weeks. They won 18 of the 20 games and the team played really well. Coach was very happy with the results and was now anticipating the spring season. Jackee had hit extremely well and had been on base over 65% of the time. Sonny hit almost .300 and was improving when the season ended. Jack, Bo and Casey had really good stats. The double J's combination pulled off 10 double plays and neither player made an error. Bryon, a sophomore first baseman, had a bother playing football on Dan's team. He asked Jackee if she wanted to see one of the games. Without hesitation, she agreed and asked if Andrea could come. There was a home game the last Saturday in October, so they agreed to go. When classes were finished that Friday they grabbed some lunch and snacks and headed for the college. They arrived just as the football team finished their usual light workout before a game

Bryon went inside to find his brother while Jackee and Andrea waited outside. When he found his brother, Bryon asked if he knew Dan Silvio. His brother pointed to Dan and Bryon introduced himself. He then asked Dan if he would come outside with him. Dan agreed, and they walked out and there was Jackee standing in front of the field house. She ran up to him and without realizing where she was, kissed him. Dan was shocked but recovered enough to just hold her for a minute. Then he asked how she got here. "Bryon is on my baseball team and his brother plays football with you. Since he was coming to the game, Bryon asked if I wanted to come. Andrea came along to chaperon and to make sure you don't take advantage of me. However, if you want to, it's fine with me."

He smiled at her and said hello to Andrea. After he put away his gear they all went out to dinner. Most of the football players went to a pizza place on Friday nights. Andrea thought she went to heaven as she had a huge crowd of football players all around her. Anything she wanted was immediately brought to her. She didn't need her purse because everything was paid for by one of the young men. Jackee and Dan watched her reign over her new kingdom. It was amazing, in less than an hour she was the center of attraction. Dan mentioned that he had a bed check at 11 and they needed to find a place for Jackee to spend the next two nights. He went over to a few other football players that had their campus girl friends with them. After introducing Jackee to everyone at the table, he asked if any of the girls had room for the girls to spend two nights. One girl said that her roommates were away for the weekend and there was room in the community room. The two bedrooms would be off limits but the rest of the apartment is available. Jackee thanked her and asked when they could meet later.

Cynthia said "we have to put these football players to bed by 11, so we'll meet at my dorm at 10:45." When they went over to tell Andrea the good news she said that all her sleeping arrangements had been made and would see Jackee at breakfast.

"It is very difficult to find any kind of a room on football weekends, and this week being homecoming makes it even harder. Maybe I should ask to room with Andrea," Jackee said to Dan. He told her that may not be a good idea. Then they just went off to do their thing. Eventually they walked over to a group of dorm buildings and found Cynthia and her boyfriend in front of one. Dan handed Jackee her overnight bag, kissed her and walked back to his dorm.

Cynthia asked if the other girl was coming. Jackee said "no she made other arrangements."

"I'll bet she did, every boy that was at her table could find her accomodations for the night."

Not being sure what that meant, Jackee just said "I hope she will be safe."

Smiling, Cynthia said she will be well cared for. Showing Jackee around the suite, it was decided that the couch would make the best bed. "If you want more privacy you could sleep on the floor in my room. I hope you understand that I can't let you use any of the other girls' rooms, we agreed to this when we first moved in together."

"I totally agree and this is the exact same agreement Andrea and I have." Jackee found the bathroom facilities to her liking, so she took a shower and got ready for bed. The couch had been carefully set up like a bed and Jackee thanked Cynthia for being so considerate. "This is the same arrangement that we make whenever one of us has a guest overnight." Jackee woke up about 7am when she heard Cynthia stirring around. She washed and started getting ready for breakfast.

A while later Cynthia came out and asked if she was hungry. They walked to the cafeteria where Cynthia used her card and put enough food on her tray for both of them.

"All the football players and staff have breakfast set up in the athletes cafeteria. You can not believe how much food is prepared for them. The game starts at 1pm but the homecoming festivities begin at 12pm. I tried out for cheerleading but never made the cut. For three years in high school I was a cheerleader and a captain in my senior year. I'll try again next year but my chances don't look good." Jackee wanted to know if she did any sports in high school. "Softball was the only other thing that interested me, but I was not that good. Do you play any sport at your college?"

"Yes, I play baseball."

"You mean you play softball not baseball."

"No, I play baseball and am very good at it."

"How did you accomplish that?"

"By working my butt off since I was 5 and being able to take a bunch of garbage for the next 12 years. Two years ago I was voted MVP of the state tournament."

"You are that Jackee? I heard about you and figured that person was half man and half female. It can't be possible that a beautiful girl like you can do that."

"Please just keep this between us as all I want to do is see Dan."

"Your secret's safe with me, so let's get ready for homecoming."

Homecoming was a bunch of floats, decorated cars and the band. It lasted 45 minutes along with a king and queen riding on a fancy decorated trailer. As far as the football game went, Dan's school won by 17 points and the game was never in doubt after the first half. It took the players over an hour before they left the locker room. Dan finally came out with the other players and for the first time Jackee saw Andrea. Jackee asked her if she saw the game and she told Jackee that she was in the special boxes reserved for donors. One of the football players has very wealthy parents who use the box for all home games. She was invited to watch the game with them. "Jackee, I was treated like a queen and I loved every minute of it. They want us to have dinner with them and I said we did not bring clothes that would fit in a country club atmosphere. The father said all the arrangements have been made and we could go as we are. Dan, you, me, Cynthia and her boyfriend would be welcomed. There are many other football players and their dates who also will be there. Well what do you say?"

Dan said "why not, let's see how the other half live."

None of the group in Bryon's car had ever experienced anything like this before. The club was elaborate and the food was the best they ever tasted. Music was outstanding and the band could play any tune you wanted to hear. Around midnight the football players started to fall asleep. They agreed that it was time to get back to school and Bryon, who did not have a drink, would drive them back. Before leaving the group thanked the couple who had arranged all this. The parents were very gracious and told them "any time you are here for a football or basketball game, you will be our special guests." Mrs John Benson, the wife of their benefactor asked Jackee if she would speak at one of her charity events.

Jackee wanted to know how she knew that she had given a few talks. Marilyn, Mrs Benson, said her son who played on the football team last year learned about her from Dan. "He spoke highly of you and how dedicated you are to young girls. You would be perfect for this charity. All transportation would be taken care of and all you have to do is tell me where you want to be picked up."

"It would be an honor to speak at your charity, if there is no conflict on the date. Here is my name and the numbers that I can be reached. Also Dan would be an excellent coordinator." Back at the school the group broke up and went different ways. Cynthia had given Jackee a key so she could come and go as she pleased. Jackee knew that Dan was exhausted and needed to get some rest so she asked him to walk her to Cynthia's dorm. When they got to the dorm Jackee invited him in. Cynthia was not back yet so they sat on the couch and started kissing. That only lasted for a few minutes because Cynthia came home with her boyfriend. Dan told Jackee he was all in and had to get some sleep. They agreed to meet at 7:45 to attend Mass at the local Catholic church. Dan left, and Jackee prepared for bed. When she came out of the bathroom Cynthia and her friend were in her bedroom so Jackee just went to sleep on the couch. Next morning Jackee got up, showered, dressed and waited for Dan in front of the dorm. He was right on time and they walked to church. After the service they went to breakfast at the local Ihop. Jackee wondered how everybody was going to get together for the trip back to Olympus college. Dan said Byron is staying with his brother and he lives on the second floor of Dan's dorm. Later, when they found Byron. He told them Andrea knew to meet him at his brother's dorm at noon. A little after noon everyone was together so the girls got into Byron's car and headed back to school. Before leaving, Jackee could not find Cynthia so she left the key and a thank you note for her in the room.

There was very little talking on the way back because it had been a long weekend. Byron dropped them off at their dorm and then headed for his. Once inside, Jackee asked Andrea what had happened to her. All Andrea would say is that she had a great time and looked forward to going again. They went to dinner, then prepared for next week's classes. Since fall baseball was over, Jackee went to her winter workout. This time she had Sonny to keep her company. He was eager to learn and really got into weight lifting. At first he could only do wimp weight but after a few weeks he had built up to 125 pounds on the bench press.

He developed excellent form and had natural farm boy strength. She figured before he taper off, two weeks prior to spring training, he should be benching 250 or more. The more they worked together the more he talked to her. His mother passed away when he was 10 and he was educated at the Catholic school near his home. His father remarried and he had a brother and sister from this marriage. He attended the local high school but hated it. Track was his best sport since he could be alone and not have anyone bother him. He played baseball because the track coach also coached baseball. "He needed players to fill out his team so I was picked. I wasn't too good but I worked hard and learned fast."

Jackee told him that she saw those two things immediately, "that is why Jack and I picked you for center field. Coach Zimmer saw the potential in you even before we did and gave us permission to work with you." She asked if he had always wanted to be a doctor.

Sonny said "I never thought about it but because my science grades were extremely high the tribal council decided to pay my tuition if I agreed to become a doctor. One other condition is that I practice for at least 5 years on the reservation upon completing my medical degree. Since there is no way I could have paid for this myself, it was my only option."

"Sonny, I promise you that Andrea and I will be with you for the next 4 years." He thanked her.

Dr Hopkins called a meeting of all his lab people and told them that they were going to work on PRP platelet-rich-plasma. "Using a patient's plasma to treat one's self dates back to around the last decade of the nineteen century. We will not start this until next fall because new equipment has to be set up and trained on. We will have some lab work so keep in touch." After the meeting both girls approached Dr Hopkins and told him they would be available whenever he needed them. He said they are the ones he is counting on to lead this study. This statement by Dr Hopkins inflated their ego and made them more anxious to begin the lab work. The college had a grand Halloween bash for the local children. It was similar to the safe halloween Jackee had at Reagan high school. Jackee and Andrea were asked to assist both in the preparations and the happening. This was a well planned activity that included schools, parents, organizations, local merchants, and even first responders. The public relations for the college was outstanding. People raved about it and it was covered in all the media both local and nationally. When it was over, a halloween dance was held at the school for just the students and some guests. Wanting to look their best Jackee and Andrea went back to their room and prepared themselves. Both looked like they just stepped out of a fashion magazine. When they entered the college gym, which had been set up for this event, most eyes were on them. Andrea told her "good luck," and drifted over to the science group.

Jackee saw a few of the baseball players so she joined them. She danced with the baseball players most of the night and even got Sonny to dance with her once. He surprised her by being a very good dancer and he explained how the Nuns made the eight graders learn to dance before they graduated. She saw Andrea with a crowd of boys around her and the only time she wasn't dancing was when nature called. Jackee wished that Dan could be here but she knew it wasn't possible. Toward the end of the evening, other boys came over and asked Jackee to dance and she did. It felt strange and felt worse when two asked her out for a date. She thanked them for asking but said she had a steady boyfriend. One of the boys said if that ever changes to consider his offer still open. Andrea was still going full blast when Jackee decided to go back to the dorm. Sonny offered to escort her and she agreed. As they walked she asked Sonny how he planned to get home for Thanksgiving. He said his parents would not be home as they were going to his step mother's parents house. So, he decided to stay at school and catch up on some studies.

Back at the dorm, Jackee got ready for bed and fell asleep immediately. She never heard Andrea come in and stayed asleep until her alarm went off at 5am. The workout with Sonny was not as strenuous since they were both tired from the dance. When they finished she thanked him for walking her back to the dorm. He told her "anytime you need something you are to call on me." Back at the dorm Andrea was getting ready for breakfast so Jackee took a quick shower, dressed and they both went to the cafeteria.

As usual they sat with the science students. It was then that Jackee realized that no new science student has dropped out yet. Last year two or three had already left the program. Since Sonny wasn't there yet, Jackee asked them if they could get to know Sonny better. She continued, "he came here all alone and from a culture far different from this one, so I would appreciate it if some of you could find some common ground with him. He is on a tribal council arrangement to become a doctor for his community. Andrea and I are assisting him with his studies and he is an excellent student. What we need is to see his social network expanded." Most everyone there agreed to help.

The Sunday night before Thanksgiving Jackee was talking to her parents. Toward the end, she told them about Sonny being at the school with no place to go. Carmela said there would be "plenty of room at our table for one more and we could arrange for him to bunk with Jon."

Jackee said, "that is why I love you two so much, neither of you would ever turn your back on someone in need."

After her Monday workout with Sonny, she told him that her parents invited him to Thanksgiving dinner and he was to come home with her. He started to protest but she said everything has been arranged including sleeping quarters. "My parents would be insulted if you refused their offer." Wednesday, William was there at noon and both Jackee and Sonny were ready to leave.

Jackee introduced Sonny to her dad and Sonny immediately thanked him for the Thanksgiving invitation. "My wife and I are glad to have any friend of Jackee come to our home." All the way home Sonny joined in the conversation and to the surprise of Jackee, actually spoke about his past life. They arrived just as Carmela was finished preparing dinner. Evelyn and Jon were already home from school and Rose had just gone up to shower. When Rose came down, she was the last to be introduced to Sonny. Sonny stood as she came in and said he was glad to meet her but he kept staring at her. Jon asked Sonny many questions and that turned out to be the main dinner conversation.

Sonny kept looking at all the women and finally Jackee asked if there was something wrong. He apologized and said that you three women really resemble each other but Rose is so different. Rose smiled at him and said, "I picked Mom and Dad to be my parents because the whole family wanted me. You see little William there, he just joined us a few months ago and see how happy he is to be here."

"I'm sorry, I didn't mean to pry into family matters. It just seemed strange to me that there are 4 beautiful women and only three of them look so much alike." Sonny remained mostly quiet for the rest of the meal.

William did say that more than a few people have said the same thing when they see the whole family together. "Carmela's genes are in all the girls and that is a very good thing."

While the girls were cleaning up Rose asked Jackee if Sonny had a steady girlfriend. Jackee was very sure he had no one at school and he never spoke about a girl back home. Rose told Carmela, "I want him. Can you and Dad adopt him for me?"

"No we can't, so you will have to win him over on your own." She looked at Jackee and said "how?"

"I hope you weren't making a joke here, but I can tell you he likes to run track."

Rose asked Sonny if he would like to see some "awards Jackee and I won." He readily agreed and followed her into the den. He could not believe how many top awards the two girls had won. Since he knew about track he was really impressed with what Rose had won.

Rose told him "I run every morning and maybe you can join me tomorrow." At 5am the next morning he found himself running five miles and then some weight training until 7am. She said they have to get ready for church and then breakfast. Since Sonny had gone to Catholic school he had no problem with going to church. In Fact he enjoyed the fact that Rose sat very close to him during the service. Again at breakfast she sat next to him and they shared some of the meal. When they got back to the house, they packed three cars full of gifts.

Rebecca and her family had joined them at church but were not introduced to Sonny until after Mass. The caravan headed for the orphanage where Rose told Sonny "this is where little William and I came from." He was introduced to the Nuns and helped give the children some goodies. From there it was off to the VA hospital /home. This was similar to the stop before it, but these were much older children. Here were men who have served their country in war and peace. This was their final stop before meeting their maker. Babies William and Frank proved to be the best medicine and gift for them. Sonny thought that seeing new life made it easier for them to give up their old one. He found a new respect for the veterans back at his reservation. Carmela left early with Rebecca and Rocco to feed the babies and to get dinner started. William finished his inspection of the facilities a short time after, and started for home.

The cars pulled into the driveway and the girls sprang into action. First they changed clothes and then helped Carmela and Rebecca with dinner. Sonny did not know what to do with himself. Dan, Jon, Rocco, and Sonny were led into the den by William. He said "unless you stay out of their way, you have an excellent chance of getting run over." There was a football game on the TV, also soft drinks and munchies were spread around the den. They were warned by Evelyn not to snack too much or it will spoil their appetite. Dan left to go home but said he would be back for dessert. Around 4pm the table was set and prayers were said. William raised his glass of eggnog and gave a toast. Like Jon, Sonny had never experienced anything like this. It seemed to him that this is how everyone should celebrate Thanksgiving. He tried a little of everything and found it to his liking. Some food he knew, some he guessed what it was and others he didn't have a clue. Rose never left his side and made sure his plate was always filled.

Jon asked him if he ever had a meal like this? He said one tribal celebration had "a great deal of food but nothing like this." Holding up his glass he looked at Carmela and said, "Mrs Jenco you have achieved the greatest honor that can be bestowed on a chef, you have made a total stranger feel like part of the family," thank you.

"Our home is open to relatives and friends and all are welcome," Carmela told Sonny. Rose moved her hand onto his and thanked him for saying nice things about her parents. For the first time since his mother died he felt a part of a family. Dan came back as they finished dinner. Carmela asked the men to go into the den so they could clear the table and reset it with desserts. Rocco, Rebecca and the baby left for his family's dinner. Dessert was outstanding. There were at least 10 different varieties of food, not including some dessert that Dan had brought from home. Sonny, like Jon, tried a little of as much as he could get down. He finally gave up and told Rose, if he eats another bite his stomach would explode. Jackee and Dan went for their usual walk after the table was cleared. Rose took Sonny into her workout room. She sat down next to him and wanted to know more about his life.

He told her about his mother and how much he missed her. "She was very beautiful like you, in fact you remind me of her. Not in your looks but in some of your mannerism." Rose put her arms around him and kissed him as best she could. Since she had never really kissed a boy before, she had no way of knowing if it was good or not. She decided to ask Sonny and he said he would have no way of knowing since no adult woman had ever kissed him.

She laughed and said how weird it was that it was the first kiss for both of them. "I guess we will have to practice until we get it right." She then kissed him again and this time it felt more natural.

Jackee and Dan made it an early night since they were planning longer ones for the weekend. Tomorrow there is the tree lighting at the village square. Dan walked her home and kissed her at the front door before heading for home. Jackee walked into the house and wondered where everybody was. Evelyn and Jon were in the living room while William and Carmela had the baby in the den. She asked her mother where Rose was and was told they are in the workout room and have been there a long time. "I think Rose has her first crush on someone."

"Believe it or not mom, I believe this is his first experience with a girl. If I am right, he is in way over his head." William had no insight into what they were talking about so he just did not say a word. The three of them decided to get some sleep. While Jackee was preparing for bed Rose came into her room. She wanted to tell Jackee that she really liked Sonny and would like to be his girlfriend. She thought he was the most wonderful boy she ever met.

"What do I do next to make him aware of my feelings?"

"I believe the next thing you should do is talk to him and find out how he may feel about you. You should also talk to Mom, she is very good at giving advice."

Friday's date turned out a little different for Jackee and Dan. Before they left for the village square Jackee asked Dan if it would be alright for Rose and Sonny to tag along. Dan said it might be fun because he took a liking for Sonny as soon as he met him. Rose kissed Dan on the cheek and thanked him for taking them. At eight sharp the Christmas tree was turned on. It was a thirty foot evergreen fully decorated. All the children were excited when Santa came in on a fire truck. Sonny had never seen this type of thing in real life; he only saw it once on television. He said it is so much more exciting when you are a part of it. Later, they went to get ice cream. When they were finished Rose suggested Dan drop Sonny and her at home. A suggestion was made by Dan, that they go to the movie on Saturday with them. Sonny was very hesitant but Jackee insisted and he agreed to go. When they were alone in the car, Jackee told Dan that Sonny does not have any money. "He gets an allowance from the tribal council each month but it barely covers his needs." Dan said he would cover the bill including pizza after the movie.

Jackee put her arms around Dan and told him "that is one of the reasons why I'll never let you go."

Back at the house, Rose had Sonny in the workout room and told of her feelings for him. Sonny said he was in "no position to have a beautiful girl like you. I have no money and I am at the mercy of the tribal council. When and if I finish medical school and do become a doctor, I owe them 5 years of my life. As a man I could never turn my back on that obligation."

"I'm not asking you to do anything that might hurt you, all I am asking is, can I be your girlfriend. I will go along with whatever you say. If you feel I am wrong for you, so be it."

"Rose, how can you feel anything for a person who can not even pay for the movie we are supposed to be going to see on Saturday."

"What I believe my feelings are for you have nothing to do with money. It has to do with who we are and what we can do about our future."

Holding her he said "if that is how you feel about us, I promise to dedicate my whole being to make you happy."

While they were driving to the movie Dan told them that his summer boss gave him 4 tickets to the local movie house. He had 8 tickets he bought for his daughter's birthday party but the girls decided to go roller skating instead. After the movie the local pizza place was very full but they finally got a table. Jackee was recognized immediately and a crowd gathered around her. When the food came the crowd wandered off and allowed them to eat. After they finished Dan went to see the owner and later returned, put 10 dollars on the table and walked out. In the car he told them that because Jackee always draws many admirers the meal is on the house but they would appreciate tipping the waitress. Once again Rose and Sonny were dropped off. They were in the workout room when Rose asked Sonny if he was coming here for Christmas. He said the break is 3 weeks and he hadn't been invited. "I already have permission from my parents for you to stay here for as long as Jackee stays."

"I will accept the invitation and I still can not believe how great your parents are."

"Having you here for three weeks will give me a chance to really get to know you."

Jackee and Dan were in their favorite parking spot, talking about the Christmas break. Dan would come home two days after Jackee. In all probability Dan would work for most of the break. They both would leave for school on the same day in January. She finally told him enough talk, please kiss me. Next morning after Church William, Jackee, Rose and Sonny were packed and ready to head back to Olympus. Dan kissed Jackee, said goodbye to everyone and left for school. Evelyn and Jon drove Carmela and little William home. Before leaving Sonny hugged Carmela and thanked her again. Driving back to school Jackee sat up front with William while Rose and Sonny sat close in the back. Sonny was dropped off first and then Jackee. After a quick use of Jackee's bathroom, William and Rose left for home. Andrea was not back yet and Jackee did not expect her until much later in the day. She did some housekeeping and then went to collect her mail and messages. Only one message was important and that was the one from Marilyn Benson. She listed three dates that the conference could be held and she wanted to know if Jackee would be available for any of them. The only day and the best one for Jackee would be the Saturday before Christmas break. She immediately wrote a letter to Mrs Benson informing her of the best date. She also wanted a complete description of the event time, place and expected guests. She walked the letter back to the post drop and decided to have dinner. Back at the dorm, she studied for a time and then went to bed.

Waking from a sound sleep, she shut off the alarm, dressed and jogged to the field house.

There was a chill in the air and it started to feel like winter was on the way. Sonny was stretching out and ready to start the workout. Jackee limbered up and suggested a mile run to warm up. They threw, hit and ran for about two hours. It was a normal workout with less weights. They will be included from now on. Sonny told Jackee what a great family she had and how it felt to be part of it. Jackee thanked him.

He mentioned the fact that he found Rose to be very interesting. He said there never was a steady girl in his life. There were girls who messed around with the boys but none that interested him. "She is the first one who wanted me unconditionally. When she put her arms around me I felt safe, loved and cared for all at once. Does that make any sense to you?"

"It makes all the sense. You have discovered what unconditional acceptance really means. Rose had been hurt very badly and she would never cause anyone else to suffer as she did. When she put her arms around you she was taking you into her special world. Believe me when I tell you no one outside of her family gets that special hug. You were chosen to be part of her family."

"You don't mind that some strange Indian boy thinks your family is fantastic and your sister someday may be his wife."

"My sister is going to be an Olympic champion and whoever she selects will also be a champion. If you can accept that, you have my backing 100%."

Back at the dorm Jackee showered and heard Andrea getting up. "Hey girl, I'm starving. How about we get something to eat."

Andrea asked "how can you be so cheerful so early on a Monday."

"I have been up since 5am ready to begin a new week."

"Hold your horses, I'll be with you after a shower and get some clothes on."

While eating breakfast they each told their stories about Thanksgiving. Jackee's were exciting, especially the part involving Sonny and Rose. Andrea had done nothing except date boys she hadn't seen for awhile. Upon their return to the dorm they laid out the week's work. Finals were coming up and both girls had straight A's. That automatically meant they would have no written finals. Lab work for classes had to be finished and an oral exam was to follow. This was nothing more than proving that you really did your own lab work. These two girls made great lab partners because they knew what the other one would do even before they did it. Every lab that they turned in was perfect, infact their labs were used as a guide for other students. One thing that they did notice was Sonny was now turning in quality work and it was unbelievable how fast he learned.

Most of the days were flying by. It seemed they woke up on Monday and before they realized, it was Friday. One Saturday after her workout Jackee visited with coach Zimmer. She asked about his wife and little Maria. Coach told her she is the joy of his life, and his wife has not shed a tear since we brought her home. "You and your family saved her life and our marriage. We have never been happier and Nancy has been a new partner to me. She loves our daughter and can't love me enough. Our marriage has gone up at least two levels. I suspect she thought about what might have happened and is so grateful for what we have now."

Jackee told him that his coaching greatly improved after Maria came into their lives. "I saw a different person in the summer as opposed to the one during the spring. You know, every morning I workout with Sonny Lightfoot. He is getting stronger and is really hitting the ball. We are going to be very strong up the middle. Barring injuries we should have a good team."

Coach told her about a new program he has set up for very early in February. He has different speakers coming in to talk about individual parts of the game. These talks would also be open for local players from little league to minor leaguers. "It will be held in our Gym as soon as basketball is over."

Andrea and Jackee made sure that Sonny was ready for his finals. His lab presentations pulled down his grades to B+ but they planned to have him doing A work next semester. The Saturday before Christmas break the school had a Christmas party in the arena. There was a decorated Christmas tree, great varieties of food and snacks and many soft drinks. All the music was performed by the music department. Mostly the band played but in-between there was a rock group and some individual performances. Every teacher and administrator seemed to be present and the students enjoyed their company. Once again Andrea had a partner for every dance. Jackee was asked to dance and she did many times. Later in the night she danced with Sonny. While they were dancing she asked if Sonny was still coming home with her. He said when he told his father, the father seemed disappointed but accepted it because his wife would be happy. "When I thought about it, there was very little for me at home, but possibly a better future with Rose. I'll have to go home sometime in the summer to talk to the Tribal council about school but I should be back for baseball."

It was hard for Jackee to follow and digest everything he said but she could understand his talk of a future. Final arrangements would be made when William knew what day he was coming to get them. As usual Andrea and Jackee achieved all A+. All their school work and programming next semester would be completed by December 21. A phone call home alerted William and he told her he would be there around 10am on the 22nd.

William and Rose were right on time and Jackee had all her stuff ready to go. On the way off campus they stopped to pick up Sonny who was waiting in front of his dorm. He had only one big bag and a carry-on. That was just about what Jackee expected since she knew his room did not have many luxuries. He thanked William for allowing him to spend Christmas at his home. He smiled at Rose and said "it is a pleasure to be in your company again." She put her arms around his neck and kissed him.

Everyone in the car was surprised except Rose. It was hilarious when she said "your damn right". Jackee and William acted like nothing happened but poor Sonny was still in a trance. "Dad please tell him it's alright before he has a heart attack."

"Sonny, you have to excuse Rose, she is not much on holding back her emotions."

Rose said to Sonny, "didn't I tell you I had the greatest parents ever. I am only passing onto you what they have given to me. I know you don't understand but believe me it is beautiful." The rest of the drive home was small talk. Rose told Jackie about little William and all the new things he is doing. She even mentioned that one night she baby sat while her parents went out. It was the first time they trusted me with the baby. "Little William and I had a great time and he was sound asleep when they got home."

Jackee for the first time realized why Rose was so taken with the baby. It was because they were the same, total strangers taken into a family. They had nothing and now they have everything because someone really wanted them. She looked at William and thought, *Rose is right, they really are the best parents in the world.*

As the car pulled into the driveway they saw Carmela holding the baby and waving at them. Rose bounced out of the car and ran toward her and Carmela was saying to "hurry because he really missed you." Approaching the three, they heard Carmela saying to Rose, "he has not stopped looking around for you all day." Rose was holding the baby and kind of dancing and talking to him. Entering the house they found dinner on the table and since they were hungry it looked and smelled fantastic. While eating, everyone was catching up on family news. Sonny could not believe the dynamics of this family around the dinner table. Anything and everything was discussed and all had a say and nothing was held back. It was absolutely beautiful that a family could do this. Around his family table only his father said anything. Occasionally his step mother might say something. Children were to be seen but not heard. William saw Sonny taking in everything but not saying a word.

Finally he asked Sonny if he had anything to add to the conversation. Sonny just said, "I want to thank you for allowing me to join your family this holiday season."

"We are happy you could be here and you have especially made my daughter happy."

Things had to be put away and Sonny had to be shown up to the room he would share with Jon. Since he was staying longer his gear could be put into drawers and a closet. Rose helped him as the baby was taking a nap. When the putting away stuff was done she took him into her workout room and kissed him properly. She explained her workout schedule with Jackee and how he could join them if he wished. He explained that Jackee had been working very hard with him and he hoped it did not hurt her training. "Nothing interferes with Jackee 's training, if she is helping you, she is working harder someplace else. We start at 5am every day. Over Christmas break I have an invitational meet and you must come to see me do my thing."

"You know darn well I would not miss it for anything."

"I'll bring home a medal just for you and you may kiss me again." Jackee later joined them and made sure their workout schedule was set to begin tomorrow.

The day before Christmas eve was the most hectic of all the days. Everything had to be prepared for the visits to the orphanage and Vet's home. Jon and Evelyn were home and they were involved. Jon brought a car load of things from his home that he and his parents did not want any more. Most of it was expensive and almost brand new. They spent hours sorting and wrapping. There were even things that the Nuns could use. Sonny went up to his room and came down with some small indian dolls that his Tribal Council had sent to him. He had requested them for the orphanage and they were glad to accommodate him. He brought them down and the family was ecstatic. They never saw such beautiful decorated dolls. The girls were sure that the children would love them. Sonny had been afraid that they may consider these things to be cheap trading posts, made in China items. There was a freshly cut Christmas tree in the living room half decorated.

William had set the tree and put on the lights; the rest was a family tradition of adding hanging things and garland. By supper time all work had been completed and everyone was exhausted. Dan had called to say he was home and would see Jackee after dinner. Carmela made a huge prime rib with all the trimmings for dinner. She told everyone that they worked so hard, it was the least she could do. There was nothing left over when they finished dinner except a few vegetables.

Dan walked in as the family finished and was getting ready for dessert. Jackee invited him to sit next to her. He said hello to everybody and sat. Carmela asked how his school year is going. He said "football had a good season but the school stopped us from participating in any bowl games. That is why I am here instead of getting ready for a game. Is there anything I can do for your annual visits to the Vets and orphanage?"

Rose said "you are a little late, we finished a little before dinner." He said he was sorry because he enjoyed getting everything ready. After dessert Jackee and Dan were going to go for a walk but the night was very cold so they got into Dan's car and went to their favorite parking area. Jackee had her arms around him before he shut off the engine. He just held her tight and let her kiss him. When she relaxed he let her go and they talked about many things. They both had to report back to school on the same day. He was also working during the Christmas break but it should not interfere with their time together.

Christmas Eve started for the Jenco's about 2 pm as 3 cars headed for the orphanage. The Nuns had everything prepared and the recreation hall was decorated in the real Christmas spirit. The older children played instruments and sang Christmas songs. Everyone helped bring in the presents and goodies. All the girls helped distribute the presents while the Nuns were setting up the goodies. Sonny's Dolls were the hit of the day. Every little girl received one and for the first time since his mother died Sonny had tears in his eyes. A Nun was standing by him and Rose and asked if something was wrong? He said to her he wished his mother, who had passed away, could see how happy the dolls made these little girls.

"We believe that she is standing right beside you and is enjoying the happiness on the faces of these girls and also thanking God for what a fine young man her son turned out to be." Rose just wanted to hold him in her arms but was afraid of what the Nuns might think.

He told her, "Indian boys are taught not to show emotions and here I am with tears in my eyes. Back home they would laugh at me."

"Here," Rose said, "is a girl who not only is proud of you but loves you." Carmela witnessed this but kept it to herself. Around 4:30 they went to the vets home/hospital. They also were waiting for their usual visit and were very happy just to have company. Having a huge family come with presents and goodies was a big plus. Jon's presents to the Nuns had been a huge success but his presents to the Vets were bigger. His father was a big man so all his sweaters were large or bigger. There were 25 brand new sweaters never worn, a gift from a city he helped during an epidemic. All were hand made and each was a different style. Since most of these Vets are always cold, these were very well received. When this visit was completed the family headed for their favorite restaurant. Jon's father had already wired the restaurant that all charges were to be put on his american express credit card. William would only find this out after dinner.

Christmas morning always seemed to be complete confusion. Getting ready for church, opening presents, feeding the baby, getting dressed and finally getting everyone into a car seemed like an impossible dream. However, by 8:50, Dan's, Jon's, and William's cars were filled and headed for St Mary's. There was a time when Carmela and William sat in one little section of a pew, now the family took up a whole pew and the ushers made sure one was available when they arrived. Monsignor Nicholas gave his usual short and to the point Christmas service and he later waited at the door and shook every hand and wished all a Merry Christmas. Beside giving his congregation the final Blessing at the end of the Mass he also individually blessed each child on their leaving the church. Carmela and Rebecca each thanked him and then the family went directly home. All the women except Rose prepared breakfast for the family. Rose had the babies and was helping them open gifts. She had all the men gathered around and laughing at her antics with the gift unwrapping. Most of the meal had been set up the night before. The batter was mixed and put in the refrigerator, so as soon as the grills heated up, pancakes and waffles started to stack up. Ham and sausage was in the microwave, while eggs were frying in a huge pan and toast was popping up every minute or so. Rebecca called out that breakfast was served and the family devoured almost everything. Everyone helped clean up and the breakfast dishes were done in a hurry. It was now that the whole family could open gifts. Jon's parents sent a baby swing that automatically rocked the baby for a set amount of time. Little William and Frank loved the swing. All the girls gave their parents a weekend escape at a casino. Rose had the largest amount of gifts including one from Sonny. She saved his gift for last so they could open both together. Sonny also gave her parents a gift. Carmela opened the package and it contained an Indian vision of the holy families' first Christmas. A miniature stable with Joseph and Mary dressed in fine Indian clothing and a child wrapped in an Indian blanket. It was the manger setting but according to Indian Culture. It actually was a beautiful handcrafted piece. Carmela got up, thanked and kissed Sonny on the cheek then placed the piece in the center of the dining room table.

Sonny and Rose exchanged gifts. Rose picked out a pen and pencil set with a holder for Sonny. He gave her a locket that belonged to his mother and had a picture of him inside. At first Rose said it was something Sonny should keep. He told her "my mother told me you should have it."

You could hear a pin drop, only the baby was making noise. She was crying when she put her arms around him and held him tight. Dan and Jackee opened gifts from their parents and each other. Jackee walked him to the door, kissed him and said "I'll see you for dessert." Evelyn and Jon exchanged gifts and then wandered off to the living room. Rose took Sonny to the workout room.

Jackee and Rebecca told the mother, "we are the only ones left so let's get started on Christmas Dinner."

Kim, Bats and George Herman came about noon and their baby loved the swing. Bats wanted to know about Jackee's team and the summer program she played in. She told him the competition was not as good, especially the pitching. However she played with some team mates from college and is better prepared for the coming season. "Coaching wise he is nowhere as good as you but he is young and learning more each day." She told him about the new lecture clinics he is having and how it may positively affect the team.

Bats thought it was a great idea and how he may attend one. "When the schedule is set up, send me a copy."

All the men eventually ended up in the den while all the women were preparing dinner. Rocco and Bats took care of the babies. Both men were very good with feeding or diapers. Bats talked to William for a while and Jon and Sonny joined them. When Bats found out that Sonny played baseball with Jackee he wanted to know all about it. Sonny told him what Jackee had done for him and how she was making him a much better player. "William, do you still have the batting machine still set up outside?"

He said it was ready to go weather permitting. It was suggested by Bats that Sonny should change and they could go outside and hit a few. Not long after Sonny came down ready to hit and the men went outside. Jackee heard about the batting lesson so she dressed for outside. Actually, she fed the iron mike while Sonny hit. Bats said his swing was good but he needed to get more hips involved. He suggested that Sonny cock his hips more and keep his weight back. With a little more compact swing you should be perfect. While Sonny was standing at the plate, Bats took his hips in his hands and showed him how they should work. Sonny immediately felt the difference and after a few swings was hitting the ball harder than ever before. Jackee took a turn in the cage and after a few swings she was hitting the baseball really good. Bats told Sonny, "that is one of the sweetest swings you will ever see." Actually seeing Jackee hit, he now saw what Btas was telling him. Carmela called them to come in as some light snacks were put out for everyone.

Jackee and Sonny went up to shower and change. When Jackee came down she was wearing a very revealing dress. It left no doubt that this was a very beautiful young lady. William said she looked like a person preparing for a major event. She said, "I just want to look nice for Dan. Most of the time he sees me in casual wear but I want tonight to be special."

"Well if he doesn't appreciate this he's got to be deaf,dumb and blind." She hugged her dad and thanked him for the compliment. Dinner was scheduled to be ready about 4:00. Glasses were filled with whatever people asked for. Shrimp was a special treat prior to the main meal. Carmela prepared a roast beef, a turkey and a small ham. There were two types of potatoes, six veggies and three offerings of bread. Since most of this was too heavy to pass around, a buffet table was set up and everything was laid out. The women were to go first followed by the men. Finally everyone was seated and Carmela offered grace.

After the prayer, William offered a toast. He thanked all for coming to share this special day and meal with his family. He also wanted to thank God for giving us these fantastic children and friends who are here at our table. " Salute". Everyone thanked him and drank something. Some went back for seconds because the food was delicious and they had to try a little of all the meats. There would be plenty for Rebecca to take home and still enough left for the rest of the family to enjoy. A separate dessert table had been set up so only the dirty dishes had to be removed and new plates set out. When Dan rang the bell, Jackee answered and when he saw her, he still could not believe how beautiful she actually was. He brought more dessert from his mother and added it to Carmel's

Kim and Bats headed for home after dessert but not before Sonny had thanked him for his help. After cleaning up Rebecca and Rocco left with a large bag of leftovers. They still have to bring the baby to his parents house and celebrate Christmas dinner with them. Another bag of goodies would go with them when they finally leave to go home. Rose and Sonny went to the workout room and Evelyn went with Jon to the living room. William, Carmela and the baby were in the den relaxing. Jackee and Dan decided it was too cold to walk so they just drove to their parking spot.

As they were cuddling in the car, Jackee asked Dan if he still wanted her.

"Do you have any idea how beautiful you looked tonight?"

"I made a special effort to look my best so you would want me."

"Well, you outdid yourself. You are getting more beautiful every time I see you." They kissed for a long passionate time.

"Finally Jackee said the coat is making this more difficult so I should take it off."

"Do you want to completely drive me crazy?"

"What do you mean Jackee asked?"

"Your coat is the only thing keeping me from taking your clothes off."

"Do you want to take my clothes off?"

"Yes and no. Yes, because I want to share everything with you and not because it would be wrong for our future together."

"Dan, why is not being near you hurting me so much?"

"Jackee, if I knew that answer it would make it so much easier. The only likely answer is that I love you too much to interfere with your destiny."

"If my destiny doesn't include you I don't want it."

"No! You had this destiny before you met me. I will not allow you to give it up because of me. It would completely destroy our relationship."

"Dan, please promise you will always be there to hold and kiss me."

"I promise!"

Rose, Jackee, and Sonny worked out every day. William hired the indoor batting cage for two weeks. So Sonny and Jackee hit every day inside and on good days outside. Rose and Sonny ran every day. Jackee was considered a very fast runner but she had a hard time keeping up with Rose and Sonny. He was the best training partner for Rose because she had to keep up with him. He was very fast and had great endurance and it seemed he could run all day. The competitive nature of Rose forced her to try and keep up with him. By doing this, she became faster and even more competitive. This Saturday was her meet and the whole Family was going. She was entered in the mile, and 5000, as well as the long jump and Shot put.

Saturday the family had an early breakfast because Rose had to register and get her number by 10:00AM. William, Jackee and Sonny took her there early and William would drive back home to pick up the rest. Jon had already left for his rotation at the college's medical school. Carmela, Evelyn and the baby had to be taken to the arena. They arrived back at 11:30 and the meet had already started but none were Rose's events. Her first event is the shot put. Her best throw in that event was 54.6 feet. The mile run was her next event and she was timed at 440.2 minutes. A short time later she competed in the long jump and recorded a jump of 22.10 feet. Her last event was the 5000 and it was the last event of the day. Rose finished the event in 1530.65minutes. When all the events were over the judges tallied the scores of all the candidates. In the girl events Rose won three of her four events. She won the mile, 5000 and the long jump. She lost the shot put by 6 inches. She received those four medals and then was awarded best female athlete trophy for the invitational. Sonny could not believe what a great athlete she really is. When she approached the family. She hugged and kissed her parents Jackee and the baby then turned to Sonny and gave him the best hug and kiss.

"Sonny told her this is the best victory since Little Big Horn." The family cracked up and

Jackee said "this is the first time I ever heard him make a joke."

One week later Jackee and Sonny were back at school. Evelyn was entering her last semester and left two days before Jackee. It was felt that she went back early to be with Jon. Rose was to start her last semester in February and the family was looking at all the offers she was getting from colleges. Jackee could not believe that 5 Ivy league schools had made her tentative offers. Sonny and Jackee immediately got into their morning workout and both were ahead of schedule. They were soon joined by Bo, Casey and Jack. Andrea had come back right after Jackee and checked in at the lab. Some new equipment had come in too, but no manuals or schedule for training accompanied them. According to Lucy, things would be on hold until at least the summer. This meant the two girls could be available for other assignments. Mrs Benson had finally reached Jackee and had told her that the day she selected in December had to be canceled. There were two new dates, one in early February and one at the end. Jackee told her the one in early February would be better for her because baseball starts February 15th.

Around 3:00pm a limo came to Jackee's dorm and picked up the two girls. They had no idea where the driver was taking them. Mrs Benson called one day and said "a limo will pick you up at your dorm at 3."

Jackee asked about bringing Andrea and was told that would be fine. The limo pulled into a home and garden landscaped country club. Waiting at the front door was Mrs Benson and five other extremely well dressed women. If it were possible to tally the cost of the jewelry they wore you could probably feed a third world country for at least one month. With the finest clothing Andrea and Jackee could wear they still looked like wash women compared to these women. Andrea and Jackee did have one very big advantage, they were young and each had an outstanding figure. Even with their clothes Stevie Wonder would still call them gorgeous. Entering the main dining room of the country club not one male in the audience failed to notice them. Mrs Benson directed them to the dignitaries table. After dinner was served there was a welcoming address and a few other speeches before Jackee was introduced. When Mrs Benson did introduce her, she was given a standing ovation.

She started by thanking all the dignitaries and especially the young women who came out in the cold to honor her. "Yes it is an honor for someone like me to speak here. My talk is directed to the young girls in the audience. I can only speak as a woman to women. You want to know how I got here? I worked my tail off since the age of 5. When I was not working out, I was studying. This will probably sound like bragging but I must tell you that I have never received less than an A in any class, from grammar school to college. You know how I got those A's, I earned them. You know how I won the state MVP in the baseball tournament? Yes, I earned it. My mother and father are the number one parents on this earth. You know why? Because no matter what I wanted to do, they backed me 100%.

I believe in my heart that even if I was an orphan God would stand beside me as my support. Whatever talent I have came from Him. It was my responsibility to make it work for me. Each and every one of you has God given talent or talents. With His help you must make it work for you. I have heard women say, I'll marry someone who is rich or I just want to get married and stay home. Being a good mother is the hardest job in the world. No other profession even comes close to it. God gives you that baby to protect and nurture, but that's the baby's life not yours. I want each of you to look in the mirror and ask that beautiful woman that you see what is my dream for the future. Let no one take that dream from you. No one has the right to interfere with your dream. We sometimes let others make important decisions for us. Not any more. I will live with my decisions, good or bad. If they are good, I'll make them better. If they are bad I will correct or improve them, but they will be my decisions and not someone else's. You know that the culture of America is your culture. The great women of our history had to overcome unbelievable odds to achieve success. Sometimes it even cost them their lives. We have a great heritage to live up to and because we are Americans we can and will achieve success. Thank you and may God always be by your side."

The country club was rocking and even Andrea was on her feet cheering. It was 2 hours later before Andrea and Jackee went back to school in the limo. It seemed that every girl in the room had to talk to Jackee and shake her hand. While on the ride back, Andrea said,"girl where did that come from? That was the most uplifting speech I ever heard. I wanted to jump up and start looking for my destiny."

Jackee told her "isn't that the whole idea of who we are and what we want to be." After that, both of the girls remained quiet on the drive back to the school.

CHAPTER SIXTEEN

Jackee Starts Spring Training at Olympus College

*C*oach Zimmer called an unofficial meeting for all baseball candidates. He told them that a baseball seminar was to be held in the gym starting on Monday and probably lasting all week. "It will deal with all aspects of the game. It is my wish that every player attends all the sessions. You will be a better player if you understand all the elements of the game. First part will deal with pitching. This part of the clinic will be mandatory for all pitching prospects. We have invited coaches from little league, high schools, colleges and even professionals. Parents and players at all levels have also been invited."

Coach Brady, who is the head baseball coach at Western college and pitching coach for a minor league team, gave the welcoming address. He then gave this qualifying statement, "what I am going to tell you are the things I have discovered about pitching over 30 years of experience. You may accept all of it, some of it or just say he doesn't know anything about pitching. Holding up a baseball, he said let us start with the basics. This is a baseball. It must weigh between 5 and 51/4 ounces. It is between 9 and 9 1/4 inches in circumference, it is 2 7/8 to 3inches in diameter and has 108 double stitches holding the ball together. There is a cork center surrounded by a special cord wound tight by a machine. The leather covering is put on last. Hold the baseball in your hands, feel it, rub it, find where your fingers are the most comfortable. With the seams, against the seams, across the seams. Each method you use may cause the baseball to move differently. Even though baseballs are machine made, you may find that they vary. It could have a high seam or a broken seam. It might be smooth, scuffed or may have a different size or weight. Professional baseball has a very high quality control but even they still may have defects. You will find more problems on the lower levels and by different manufacturers."

"Remember this important fact, no baseball game starts until the pitcher throws the ball. A pitcher controls the pace of the game." Coach Brady posed this question to the pitchers present, "Who is the best pitcher on the team?" All the pitchers looked around to see if anyone volunteered. Naturally no one wanted to say they were the best. Coach Brady told them that "every pitcher here has to believe that he is the best. A pitcher stands 60 feet 6 inches from the batter, when he actually releases the ball, he is 55 feet or less from home plate. He must have the courage of a river boat gambler. He has to believe in himself and have confidence in his pitches. Fear is for the batter to have not the pitcher. Remember this, the greatest hitter in major league baseball made out over 65% of the time. The odds are always with the pitcher. You have one player in front and seven behind you so let them play. I watched a boy pitch a perfect no hitter. Not one batter on the other team swung and missed any pitch. They hit 21 balls in play. The infielders and the outfielders made every play. From the 5th inning on, the hitters were so frustrated that they swung at anything and usually hit easy outs. The so called number one pitcher on that team never pitched a no hitter much less a perfect game. Your main job is to throw strikes. In a nine inning game the opposing team is entitled to 27 outs or 81 strikes. You have to throw as many strikes as you can. Throwing balls is boring, nothing is happening. When you walk batters your fielders lose concentration, which can lead to errors or failing to get a jump on hit balls. Weather plays an important part in a game. Heat, cold, drizzle, rain or fog has a direct effect on a player's concentration. You start walking batters and you will find that the players are now thinking about something else and not the game. Work a little faster in bad weather your players and even the umpires will be more into the game. Covering bases is a big part of pitching. Any ball hit between first and second requires you to cover first base. Even if you think that the ball should be played by the second baseman you can't be sure that the first baseman doesn't try to field it. You can always stop if the first baseman is there but you must be ready if he is not. You must work on pickoffs to every base including third. A pickoff at third is very rare but just showing the move may keep the runner closer to the base. The closer you hold a runner on a base the better chance you catcher has of throwing out a base stealer. Also it gives the outfielder a chance to throw a runner out at the plate or third base. There must be a sign as to who is covering second on a steal or a comebacker to the mound. This sign should not be obvious because you do not want the batter to know who might cover."

"Before you pitch in a game you should know which direction the wind is blowing. When you warm up it should be in the same direction as the mound on the field. This way you will know how your pitches are going to be affected in the game. Example, your curveball should break down if you're throwing into the wind. It makes no matter which way the wind is blowing, it will have some effect on your pitches and you should know this before you make the first pitch. You always warm up by throwing to a plate. Make sure no matter where you go you have a plate to throw to. I recommend you practice throwing to a smaller plate. Instead of a 17 inch plate make one 16 or15 inches and practice on that. Make the catcher get into a crouch and throw to a set strike zone. If you do not know a batter the safest pitch is at the knees and on a corner preferably the inside corner."

"Keep your head in the game. Watch where a batter stands and what he swings at. See if they make adjustments on your pitches.(ex a batter who chases a curve might tend to crowd the plate next time up. If he does he sets himself up for an inside fastball. In between starts you can work on two things. Pressure fingers and accuracy. Putting pressure on the pointer or middle finger will make the ball move, practice that and see if you can make the ball move. Control is very important to a pitcher, the more strikes you throw, the less walks you give up. if you're around the plate the chances are the umpire will give you the close pitches. Whenever you throw a baseball, throw it for effect. Hit the catcher in the knee, shoulder, heart, inside , outside and down the middle. When you throw off the mound in practice or game, look hard at where you want the ball to go and then throw it there. If you concentrate hard enough it will go there."

"Change speeds, slow curve, straight change up, Slider(fast curve) these pitches will increase your arsenal of pitches and give the batter something else to look for. Many pitchers don't throw the ball 90 miles per hour and yet they still win games. This happens because they have become pitchers and not just throwers."

"A pitcher should never make an error. He has the shortest throw of any fielder. Practice throws to every base under every possible situation and get them perfect. When a player makes an error behind you, ignore it, your job has not changed. Concentrate and keep throwing strikes. Most pitchers until they build up their arm strength peak at 65 or 70 pitchers. The less pitchers you throw early in the game, the stronger you will be in the later innings. Throwing is the best way to build arm strength. Light weights can also help build up an arm but you must be careful not to over do it. Baseball is a loose sport and not a tight one. Coach Brady took questions for the rest of the session and at the end, told the players that any problems you have, feel free to get in touch with me, your coach knows where I can be reached."

Jackee did not fully understand everything coach Brady talked about but it made sense. She never considered how weather could affect a game. Because she trained herself to always concentrate on the game, she never let the elements affect her game. Now she knew she was kidding herself. Weather does and will enter into the game whether you like it or not.

Coach Martin came the next day and his expertise was infielders. He coached Sacred Heart college and had played the infield all his playing days. He played mostly triple A ball but had a two week callup in the show. Jackee and Jack were very interested in what he had to say. His talk was very basic and simple.

He first said, "no one expects you to make great plays, when you do make one it is a big plus for the team. Making the ordinary plays is what is expected of you. Each play you make means your opponent has one less out in the game. If you turn a double play that either breaks the back of an inning or ends one. Every out is critical and you failing to record an out gives your opponent a big advantage. Remember a mental error, although it's not recorded as an error, may have the same effect. Example, you drop the ball instead of throwing to first to complete a double play. The inning is still going and if there was a runner on third, he scored because the play wasn't completed. Errors of omission or lack of concentration gives a free gift to your opponent and means your pitcher has to work more than he should have. Always make sure you get one out. Let's say there is a runner on first and a ground ball is hit to third, the third baseman is going to start a double play but bobbles the ball. There should not even be a thought of still trying for the double play, just pick up the ball and get the out at first. Instead of hurrying a throw to second that could be either late or wild, you got the sure out at first. You have now turned a possible disaster into an acceptable outcome."

Infielders should work as a cohesive unit not as an independent piece. Bases must be covered at all times. Different situations require different coverage. It is very difficult to diagram it on a blackboard, it should be done on the field so everyone on the team has an idea of what their responsibility would be. He and coach Zimmer set up the field house with a simulated infield and everyone moved to that location. Coach Martin started with no one on base and what happened with a single and then an extra base hit. Next with a runner on first, runners on first and second, bases loaded, runner on first and third, runner on third, and finally runner on second. Each one of these situations required a different defense. It took a long time to go through each one but to Jackee it was worth doing. Lastly he went through run downs which is when you have an opposing player trapped between bases. He painstakingly went step by step through each one and emphasized how outfielders should participate. He told them that they are players and not spectators. "If you want to watch the game buy a ticket, your job is to help out on every play. I am sure the outfield coach will cover this. Also you should watch the ball hit the bat so that you can get a jump on a hit ball. The more you watch the better you will get at judging where a hit ball will go." He then asked if there were any questions.

Jackee was the only one to have a question and she asked if there was a different defense for grass or turf. He said "thank you for asking, I forgot to mention the difference. What I usually recommend is a step or two back on turf because the ball comes at you quicker. With grass you have to judge the conditions on the field. If the grass is cut short and it's a dry day the ball will be quick. If the grass is high the ball will be slower and if it's wet, even slower." He forgot one other thing, there is one leader on the field and is usually the shortstop or second baseman. "Thank You for coming and I hope you got something out of all this."

Coach Berry who coached at Sagamore college was a catcher all his life. He still caught in the over 60 baseball league. He started out by saying that catching is the most difficult position on the field. "A catcher basically controls the defense once the pitcher releases the ball. He is the only player who is in foul territory during the game. No other player in the game can be in foul territory. He is also the only player who sees the whole field of play. no one else has his view of the game. One of his jobs is to keep the team alert and prepared for the next pitch. Pitchers are your main responsibility. Before the game you should go over strategy for the game. If there is a scouting report, it should be discussed. Field conditions may have to be considered. When warming up the starting pitcher you should make sure he is throwing in the same direction as the mound on the field. There should be a home plate and you should insist he hit your glove with every pitch. When his arm is loose, you direct him to concentrate on watching where you set the catcher's mitt. Move the glove around and see how his pitchers are reacting. Make him throw all his types of pitchers from both the stretch and windup. Never let him over throw or over stride because this could cause him to lose his control or rhythm or both. Let him know what pitchers are good and what ones may need more concentration. When the game starts, watch what the umpire is calling and on what hitters. He may like the inside corners on a lefty and high pitch on a righty. You have to remember, pitchers are sometimes lazy or lose concentration in a game. Keep talking to them and demand their full attention. There are two situations that you should be aware of. One is when he loses the strike zone and the other is when a fielder makes an error behind him. The later one is especially more accute if it would have ended the inning. One other situation is when he feels the umpire is not giving him the close pitches. Talk to him and make him reconnect with you and concentrate on hitting the glove. Calling a timeout and going to the mound may help give the pitcher time to settle down. You have to practice pickoffs at every base. Nothing perks up a pitcher more than getting an out without throwing a pitch. If nothing else you keep the runners closer to the base. Keep the infielders on their toes and make sure they know how many outs there are all the time. You only catch a popup if it's a low one around the plate or a popup behind the plate. Let the infielders catch the rest since they would have the best angle. One other very important thing, try not to tip off pitchers. Sometimes an infielder will move when a certain pitch is thrown. Maybe a curve ball to a righty on the outside of the plate may cause a shortstop to cheat toward second base. Now let us go over to the field house and try some situations. "

Outfielders were handled by Coach Snider who retired a few years ago but still assisted local coaches. He played the outfield in pro ball and was at the triple A level when he blew out his knee. He walked with a limp because when he injured the knee medical technology did not have the means to repair it. He told the outfielders "you should be required to pay for watching the game. Most outfielders below the college level stand in the field and are bored to death. There are certain rules you should follow: Number one, the centerfielder is in charge of the outfield. He catches every ball hit between left center and right center. Number two, when two outfielders are running at each other, always move to your right. If you follow that method, collisions between outfielders would be almost nonexistent. Talk to each other and know where everyone is on the field. On shallow hit balls the player coming in has the advantage because the ball is in front of him. That doesn't mean that the infielder is not going to try for it. If you feel you have no play on the ball, let the infielder try and you just backup the play. Whenever an outfielder is going toward the infield to make a catch some other outfielder should be backing up the play. When a ball is hit down the right field line, the left fielder should be backing up third or second. The opposite should happen on a ball hit down the left field line. If there is a relay to be started, the fielder with the strongest arm should throw the ball. Qualifying this fact is who gets to the ball first. A left fielder is closer to the ball even though his arm is not as strong as the center fielder he must make the throw. In a time of the essence situation the one who can make the play quicker should always make the play. A delay of 2 or 3 seconds means the runner can probably take an extra base. Any time there is a round down, the outfielder should be involved. The fastest runner should be there to help. The others should be backing up the play or covering a base. Every ground ball should have an outfielder backing up the player handling the grounder. When there is a try for a double play the outfielders should protect against a wild throw. A pop fly over the infield with runners on base, means one or two infielders may be going for the ball, which means no one is covering the bases. Every play you should be in motion. You know it is possible that an outfielder never touches a ball in a game. There are no fly balls or base hits to his field. So moving on every play keeps you alert and keeps you warm on cold days and keeps you loose during a game. One point I missed while talking about relays. It is a blessing to have a strong arm but more important your throws have to be accurate. Even if your arm is average, making accurate throws to your relay or cut off man is just as important. Work with your shortstop or second baseman and get to know how they like the ball thrown and what their signals mean. One thing that might happen, if one of the usual relay infielders has a sore arm the outfielder might make a good relay player. Let's go over to the field house and work on a couple of drills I'll show you. Any infielders who are here can join us." Jackee and Jack were ready to go.

The last day of the clinic was to be a short one. It dealt with team organization, discipline and signals. Signals were the most interesting. Coach Zimmer said he would use the K.I.S.S. method. "This means, keep it simple stupid. Signals may be oral or by some action. If he uses the words look, see or take I want you to take the next pitch. If none of these words are used, you're on your own. We never swing at a 3 and 0 pitch unless I say go for it. If you swing at a 3 and 0 pitch and make out you give the pitcher a big lift. Whatever he throws you on 3 and 0, you are probably going to see on a 3 and 1 pitch. When you are ahead of the pitcher in the count make sure you only swing at a good pitch. Chasing a bad one in that situation helps the pitcher. Every 3 and 1 pitch is an automatic hit and run situation. The pitcher must throw a strike or the batter takes a walk and we have another runner on base. I want us to be an aggressive team, always putting the pressure on the other team. Let them try to keep up with us. Force them to play our game thereby putting even more pressure on them. I am going to stop now and finish this when the team is picked. Have a good weekend and be ready to start tryouts on Monday in the field house."

Before tryouts were to start, Jack and Jackee asked the coach if they could work independently with the other infielders and later, in a week or so with the pitchers. Coach wanted to know what they had in mind. Jackee said that the two of them had to know where the other one was going to be under all situations. "There is only one way to do that and that is by working together until we become a unit. It will take about 2 weeks of intense work but I have done it before and Jack is willing to try. You saw how we worked in the summer, we are just going to expand on that."

He told them to keep me informed if you need anything. The field outside was not ready for use so the field house infield was their only option. Jack got all the infielders together and laid out the method of practice that was going to happen. Soon ground balls were being hit and fielded. Jackee reminded all the infielders that this infield was a perfect one and all balls would take a true bounce. "This is not true on grass and not true on some artificial turf, Weather plays a large part on how the ball comes to you on turf." The coaches were very happy with how hard the infielders were working. It would not be hard to select the best and let the others go.

By the time the team was finally picked, the double J's were working very well together. In fact they already had started working pickoffs with the pitchers and also with the catchers. Sonny had become a very good hitter and with the added muscle with more power. Working him in the outfield was easy, he was the fastest one on the team and could outrun almost any fly ball. On both sides of Sonny they had good fielders Augie Hoff, a sophomore, was in left and Peter Jinx, a freshman was in right. PJ as he was called had an above average arm and good speed. This trio gave the team a strong outfield. Bo the sophomore catcher was even better than he was in the summer. He lost some weight but added good muscle. His throwing was stronger and more accurate. When he did pickoff drills almost every throw was right on. His hitting was better than in the summer. He seemed to have added more power to his swing. This gave the team a very strong up the middle nucleus. Casey Jones, a junior on third and Bryon Harp a sophomore on first rounded out a pretty good starting team.

Pre season games and scrimmages were very successful. The team's defense was fantastic and the hitting started slow but after a few games and a bit warmer weather seemed to be ready. Sonny who was working with one of the coaches on base running and leads off bases has been a huge surprise. He has even stolen some bases standing up and others where the opposing catcher didn't even throw the ball. He also caused two pichers to balk. The pitching has been excellent. There is only one senior and two juniors all the rest are Freshmen or sophomores. Two sophomores, Zeke and Josh are the best. Both did not give up a run in the non league games. Thomas, the senior and our two juniors Sal and Brady, also gave very strong performances. So Coach Zimmer said this was the best team he has ever put on the field.

In the early part of the season it was easy to see which team was ready to play and which one was just rounding into shape. Olympus College was on a roll and won its first 8 games. Whenever it was publicized that a girl was playing, much larger crowds attended the game. When Jackee did something on the field or at bat the cheering grew louder. The umpires association had warned all the schools in the conference that they would not tolerate gender related jockeying from the dugout. So this helped explain why she was receiving more noise from the stands than from the dugouts. Coach had asked the team to treat Jackee as just another player and to watch their language. Jackee told them not to defend her on the field. She did not want anyone to be thrown out of the game or suspended because of her. "I have heard it all and no one can disrupt my game unless I let them. My answer is with my bat and glove and I have been successful so far. Most media people think that the story is me and they try to make me the centerpiece. The other 8 players on the field are just as important but most times they will be ignored."

Jackee was having a great year both at bat and in the field. She was hitting over .400 and had not made an error. The double J's had completed 8 double plays and both of them had made fantastic catches of balls blooped toward the outfield. Jack made a catch down the right field line and ran into the fence. He appeared to be hurt but never said a word and just went back to playing. On the bus going home he had a knot the size of a baseball on his leg. He told Jackee not to worry, he heals very quickly. Next day was a home game and she knew Jack was hurting but he never mentioned it. Later in the game Jackee started a double play and just after Jack released the ball toward first, the runner slid into him and knocked him to the ground. Jack could barely get to his feet and there was no way he could continue. The backup infielder was put in and Jack was helped off the field. When the player who slid into Jack inquired as to his condition, Jack told him it was a clean slide and it's part of the game. Jackee had practiced with Hal, who was the backup during tryouts, and although he did not have Jack's skill, was good enough to fill in. Hal had practiced at all the infield positions for just this happening.

After winning their first 12 games, Olympus lost a close game at Regis College 4 to 3. In this game Jackee hit her second home run. She had not hit one in a long time, but now felt that her power swing was coming back. This gave her 10 extra base hits for the year. Jack returned after a four game hiatus. The team's aggressive approach in the game still appeared to give them an edge over their opponents. Jack's return ignited the team, especially Jackee. She went on a hitting tear and in the next 12 at bats got 8 hits, two of them home runs. Olympus team record was now 21 and 1. The weather was getting nicer each day and they would have a break for Good Friday to Easter Monday. Dan, who she had not seen since Christmas break, had a similar break in his lacrosse season. Jackee's last game before the break was on Wednesday at home, immediately after the game she left for home. William had driven down to see the game and had Carmela and the baby with him. Jackee and most of the team gathered around little William. William had just arrived before Olympus came out to practice. Carmela had just finished feeding William when Jackee came out. As soon as she saw them she ran to where they were waiting. After hugging her parents she took the baby and was dancing around with him. She got a warning from Carmela that he just ate so be careful not to get him too excited. Coach calls the team to practice and to get ready for the game. Both coaches agreed that the game should be seven innings and not nine. Game time was scheduled for 1:00pm. There was no doubt that Olympus would win their 22nd game. Jack added three hits to his total and Jackee added two, one of them being a triple. The game was over in 2 hours and by 3:30 they were on the way home. Jackee had packed a bag and just had to pick it up at the dorm. Andrea was already gone and Jackee quickly changed into sweats.

A little after 8 they pulled into their driveway and Rose came running out, hugged Jackee and carried her bag into the house. Rose prepared a light meal that Carmela had started before she left that morning. Little William was fed first and then the family sat down to eat. Jackee finished eating and then went to shower and put her pajamas on. She was tired and would not see Dan until some time Friday. She also had to explain to Rose that Sonny had to go home and see his father and both had to appear before the tribal council. She wasn't sure exactly why this was but she knew it had to do with the tuition and his stipends. Needless to say, Rose was heartbroken, she wanted to see Sonny and be with him on Easter. Jackee said good night to her parents, little William and Rose. It took her all of three minutes before she was sound asleep.

Next morning at breakfast Carmela told her Dan called last night to say he would be home late Thursday as they had a 4:00pm game at home. Jackee wanted to know how a school could have a game scheduled for Holy Thursday. Carmela reminded her not every college observed religious holidays.

Jackee and Rose worked out in the morning and the family went to church services Thursday evening. She waited until 11:00 for Dan to call but when he didn't she decided to hit the sack. Friday while she was having breakfast, Dan called to tell her he didn't get home until past midnight and would see her after lunch. Sure enough, Dan rang the bell about 1PM and Jackee answered. She did not say a word, she just threw her arms around him and they kissed.

He looked at her and said, "I guess you're glad to see me."

She poked him in the stomach and said, "I suppose you're not?"

"Well you know I only came here to see Rose and for your mother's cooking."

"I guess my kisses are wearing off and you don't need them any more."

"You know very well that will never happen" and he kissed her again.

She broke away and said "that's better." They went inside and Dan said hello to Carmela and Rose. He took one look at Rose and asked what happened to Sonny. Rose told him he had some meetings about school back home. Dan told Rose he was sorry and she could hang out with us for the weekend.

Rose said, "who needs a grumpy third party on a date?"

They headed for church and the 3:00 pm services on Good Friday. Back home after the service they had dinner at 6:00. Jackee and Dan then drove to their favorite parking area to get reacquainted. Saturday the couple spent together and basically stayed home with the family. Easter Sunday, Evelyn joined the family for church. She had come home on Saturday after a short visit with Jon's parents. His parents flew her home in their charter plane and saw to it that a car was at the airport to take her home. Jon was on shift and had to work the weekend. Rebecca and her family joined them at church and had breakfast with them after services. Easter dinner would be at 3:00 so Rocco could get to his parents house by 5:00. Dan would show up for dessert later. Everything went according to plan, and by 7pm Jackee and Dan were once again getting acquainted. Dan had to leave for school early Monday while Jackee had to go by noon. They talked for a while, kissed for a while, and then decided to go home. They would not see each other until school ended in June.

Back at school Jackee found Andrea already there. Andrea had been to the lab and found that Dr Hopkins was still in the process of setting up a training schedule for the lab on the new equipment. She said "they are also scheduling a new format for us to give talks to new possible medical students. In addition, I don't know how true this is, but we are supposedly going to make appearances in different parts of the country for the college in general. This is what I heard from one of the secretaries."

Jackee had heard none of this and it came as a complete surprise. It would seem that a complete itinerary should be formulated before we go any-where. "Maybe this is the pay back we owe them for everything they gave us."

One other observation Andrea made, that it was all about Jackee and "I am just an added piece. After all, you are a national face right now. Women's groups all over the country are looking for you to endorse them or speak at their meetings or conventions."

"You know Andrea, you may have hit the nail on the head. It hadn't dawned on me before but Dan had warned me that something might be in the planning stage."

Jackee had a bad night thinking about all she and Andrea talked about. Her early morning workout with the few baseball players and later the full team practice was distracted by this uncertainty. She asked the coach if he had heard anything that might interfere with her playing baseball. He told her there better not be since she was the backbone of the team in addition to the team's leading hitter. Normally a distraction has little or no effect on her studies or game. This one really bothered her and did affect her game. In the next few games she made one error and one omission error. A mental error is usually hard to detect but Jackee knew immediately that she did something wrong. This forced her to go see Dean Grant.

He told her that a tentative tour was being discussed but as of yet nothing is official. "I can promise you that whatever it is, it will not interfere with your baseball or studies."

When they went to dinner Jackee explained to Andrea what Dean Grant told her. She qualified her understanding of what he said by saying, "if he is telling the truth."

Andrea asked Jackee "what other choice do we have but to believe him?"

The next few games showed Jackee at her best. Whatever had bothered her since the Easter break was gone and the pre break Jackee was back. She went on a hitting spree and made up for the 1 for 11 slump she was in. The next 5 games she was 10 for 18 and was on base 16 out of 24 plate appearances. She now had a total of 5 home runs in 32 games and the team had only 2 losses. They were sure to be included in the division 2 national tournament. Their position in the tournament would be decided by a power rating and not record. The final 10 games they played their record was 8 and 2, giving them a 38 win season. When they heard from the committee, they were ranked 6th of the 32 teams selected. This means the 27th rated team will have to travel to Olympus college in the first round. Clarkston college showed up for the 4PM game on Thursday. Zeke Baker pitched the game for Olympus and threw a 4 hit no walk complete game. Not a Clarkston runner reached third base as Olympus rolled to a 5 to 0 victory. Jackee, Jack and Bo combined for 6 hits, 3 runs scored and 3 RBI's. Round two they were to play a team rated number 11 at home on Saturday. For the noon game, Layland college visited Olympus. Sal Presto, a junior, started for Olympus and pitched well before tiring in the eighth. Brady Hall, a freshman, relieved him and got the save. He pitched to 6 hitters, struck out four and walked one and the other batter popped out to Jack to end the game. Sonny had the best day, he was on base three out of four at bats. He scored two runs and drove in one. Jackee, Casey and Bo each drove in a run In fact seven players drove in a run and Olympus won the game 7 to 4.

The next round Olympus had to play the third ranked team but in this game they had to be the visiting team. On Monday they traveled to Siden college for a 4:00 PM game. Here Olympus ran into a grinder. Siden had their number one pitcher, who was a prospect that was slated to be one of the first ten picks in the major league draft. August Coles was a senior with a 100 mile an hour fastball and a curve that dropped off the table. He stood 6'6" was over 225 pounds and to make matters worse he threw directly overhand and the icing on the cake, he was left handed. Josh Dunright pitched for Olympus and pitched a great game. He gave up only 3 hits and walked only one batter in 8 innings. The only problem was that Olympus got only 2 hits and no other players reached base. Jackee did get a double with two outs in the 4th inning and Sonny beat out a bunt in the sixth. Josh's one walk turned out to be the winning run. He was bunted to second, moved to third on a grounder to first and scored on a hit up the middle that Jackee dove for but could not get up in time to throw out the runner. Season over, wait until next year. That saying is as good today as it was in the 40's and 50's to describe the Brooklyn Dodgers.

When the team got back to the school there was a big crowd waiting for them. The fans came to cheer for their team that had come within 3 games of the championship. There was a dinner celebration waiting for the team in the athletes dining hall. Most of the players were hungry but not in the mood to party. Andrea was waiting for Jackee and joined her in the dining hall. While they were eating, Andrea told her the schedule for our speaking engagements was in. "The bad news is we leave Wednesday at noon. All our classes are done and all A pluses have been added to our transcript. We will be gone for a week to 10 days."

Jackee told Andrea that she had only one dressy change of clothes.

"No problem, we are both pretty close in size and I have plenty of dessy stuff. Besides we can take different clothing to do a mix and match to create a different look. We must pack everything that goes home for the summer and the school will deliver it to our homes. When we finish the tour, they will fly us home and a car will take us from the airport to home."

"Sounds good and have all the travel arrangements been made?"

"As far as I know, a car will be here at 12 noon Wednesday to pick us up. We have 14 speaking engagements in 10 days."

Wednesday at noon, a limo pulled up to their dorm and once luggage was put into the car, they were off to the airport. Fly to an airport, get into a limo and head for the hotel. This was the same everyday. All the hotels were triple A rated and the service outstanding. They could have all three meals at the hotel or order in. Every speaking engagement had some type of refreshment for the people. Their schedule was very tight because planes do not wait. Every audience consisted of possible students and their parents. The boys could not get enough of the two speakers. Andrea's very sexy clothing must have had a great deal to do with it. Since both girls have almost perfect shapes they really presented one sexy image of the school. Andrea played the role perfectly and even the fathers were interested. The mothers and the girls usually asked the important questions. Most fathers were only interested in the cost and if the other girls at the college all looked like them. At one of the stops Jackee was surprised when a man put a piece of paper in her hand. It was a first name and a cell phone number. Andea had one better: she had a woman do the same thing to her. They discussed having some fun and calling the numbers but later thought better of it.

This went on every day and every night. Andrea still found time to go out on a date. One of the parents invited them to dinner. Jackee said no but Andrea said she had enough rubber chicken to last her a lifetime. She later claimed to have danced all night at a country club and had a great meal. She also mentioned dancing with an older man who she claims had at least six hands and all of them were on her.

Finally they were at number 14 and the end was in sight. They were told that this last one would be the biggest. It was by far the best attended. From their view it seemed all the students had their parents and some grandparents with them. The main talk went over very well, as they were now experts on Olympus college. Jackee was responsible to talk about the six year medical program and Andrea spoke about the rest of the programs. They made it a point to tell the audience that they roomed together and both had straight A+ averages. Jackee would always be introduced as a student in the six year medical program, and also the shortstop for the varsity baseball team. Some of the people in the audience had heard or read about Jackee. One man at one of the stops wanted to try putting Jackee down for playing baseball. He asked if she was as good as the boys were on the field. She told him she was better. All the women cheered. He said "I can't believe it."

"Believe this" Jackee countered, "I led every team I have played on except one in batting average. This year I batted .468, had 6 home runs, stole 16 out 17 bases and only had 1 error in the field. According to major league scouts my fielding is considered a 5, which you should know is the highest rating possible." At almost every stop the women want to know why Jackee played baseball. She told them she loves baseball. Next, she started practicing baseball at age 5 and practiced every day 364 days a year. She hit in a batting cage in her yard or in bad weather at a local baseball arena. She runs every day or uses the treadmill or steps in a gym or football field. Her arm has been rated as a 4 1/2 and in all the years she has played, that include spring , summer and fall, committed less than 10 errors. In 3 years in secondary school she committed exactly one error. Everytime she steps on the field there is someone who says she can't be that good. She has proven them wrong.

She added this, "I have taken the talents that the Almighty has given me and used them to the best of my ability. Isn't that the American way we should all believe in?" The audience stood up and applauded her. Andrea went over and hugged her. They asked if there were any questions and reminded them that they could stay for an hour before leaving.

A man jumped up and screamed "you think you're good enough to play major league baseball?" Now Jackee was really pissed, she looked at him and said the question is are they good enough to keep up with me. Now the place was a madhouse as the women were cheering and crowded around the two girls. After about 45 minutes the crowd started to leave and the girls left them with this pledge. Those of you who are interested in the medical program will see us at orientation so feel free to come to us for help. Two hours later the girls were on a plane heading home. Jackee and Andrea really bonded on this tour. They had been close before but now they had been through a great adventure together and that made them as close as sisters.

CHAPTER SEVENTEEN

Jackee Starts Second Summer Baseball Program at Olympus

*W*hen Jackee arrived home she was surprised to find Sonny at the house. William was persuaded into driving down to pick him up. Rose had talked Sonny into staying at the house then going back with Jackee for summer baseball. She reasoned that it makes little difference if dad has to take back one or two. Originally she sat on his lap and hugged him when she asked if he would pick up Sonny for her. Carmela was laughing so hard, she was crying when she told William to give in, "you know eventually you're going to do it anyway." Rose became dad's best friend since the other three girls were not at home. She was also Mom's right hand helper and basically little William's mother in waiting. This made Jackee very happy. Her parents never looked happier than they did right now. Between Rose and little William their life had meaning and Rose alone gave them more joy than their first three girls. The last two children have added a spark to their lives.

Rose was to Graduate next Saturday and would commit to a college the following Monday. She now holds the record in 11 different events. If her conference had a heptathlon she would have won it easily. This was an event she hopes to pursue in college and later in the Olympics. There are over 40 college offers and most are full rides to the school. One school told William that a car dealer was willing to sell William a model of his choice for a single dollar if Rose attended his former college. Rose would also have his limo at her disposal 24/7, 365. One Female clothing store wants to give Rose a complete wardrobe with updates every year if she will endorse their line of clothing. Jackee had received a similar offer but rejected it for fear of being called a professional. She has sponsored a few charities but has never accepted anything for it. The college's lawyer has verified all the events before Jackee would accept them.

The three of them worked out every day. Sonny and Jackee hit off iron mike and sometimes William threw some live batting practice. Jackee asked Sonny how his meeting went over Easter break. He said the council was very pleased with his grades and even gave him 10 dollars extra each month. "I know it sounds like a small amount to you but the council is on a very tight budget. They even told me that when I am a doctor and practicing my trade, since I will be the only doctor in the area for many miles, they will charge the non Indians a fee for my services. They will also give me 10% of the money they collect. You have to understand these other people are even worse off than the Indians. There will not be much money collected."

The entire Jenco family was at Rose's graduation. When Rose was given her diploma The superintendent told the audience that Rose had been voted female athlete of the spring season. He also mentioned she was the first female to hold 11 state records at the same time. The most any female ever held was 2. "Our spring awards ceremony was moved from last Friday to Sunday night because the awards were not ready. Please try to attend so that we may properly recognize our fine athletes." He then continued to hand out diplomas. When the graduation ceremony was over the students had to run home and get ready for the prom. Their prom was a week late because everything locally had been booked and the PTA did not want the students to drive a great distance on prom night. They did get the local country club because one of the parents made an offer to the directors that they couldn't refuse. Not only did they have full use of the club, swimming pool and hot tub, they only paid half as much as it usually cost. The high school gym was under construction because of some structural damage, so the prom had to be moved out of the school.

William saw to it that Sonny had the proper tux for the affair. A member of his Vet's group owned the rental store so Sonny received a personalized fitting when William took him there. The owner was told that Sonny had nothing so all the accessories were included with the suit. When they went for the final fitting and to pick up everything, Sonny could not believe how many different items he needed. He had never been or seen a formal dress affair and had no idea how anything was worn. As they were driving home, William told him he had the exact same problem when he went to his first formal dance. He said not to worry and that he would help him dress. "You may feel uncomfortable at first but I guarantee that when you see Rose you will realize that you are properly prepared."

A little after 6pm Rose came down fully dressed in her gown. The whole family including Sonny was waiting for her. Her three sisters started screaming and Carmela was crying as she stepped off the last step. The men in the room could not believe their eyes and Sonny stood with his mouth opened and his eyes bugging out of his head. Finally he said "you are the most beautiful girl I have ever seen," as he handed her the corsage. Rose had on a navy blue three quarter length strapless gown with special trim and designs that fit her to perfection. Rose thanked him and kissed him on the cheek as the family started taking pictures. Fifteen minutes later a team mate of Rose and her date stopped by to pick up Rose and Sonny.

Carmela told the family that "8 years ago we thought we were saving a child but in reality she was saving us. How much happiness has that girl brought to this family? Each of you three sisters have another sister you can be proud of. Your dad and I have another precious moment we can add to our lives. God gave us the opportunity to see a poor unwanted child turn into another beautiful daughter. Without you three sisters pushing and standing with us it would never have happened."

While driving to the country club, Sonny told Rose how beautiful she looked and that he hoped he would not do something shameful to ruin her special night. She told him not to worry and that he never could do anything to hurt her. She gave him a kiss and told him there will be more later. Upon entering the club they could not believe what had been done. The entire club was decorated in the school colors and the motif setting that the class had voted on. It was absolutely outstanding. All the servers and staff had school shirts on and not their usual formal dress. Only the graduates and their guests wore formal attire. Certain food was selected by the class but the club added things like shrimp, selected cheeses, meats and hors d'oeuvres. All the fountains were really soft drink dispensers and many assorted punch bowls were all over the room. Music was provided by the house band and a special rock group hired by the class. Each musical team played for alternating half hours starting at seven. While dancing a slow dance Rose asked Sonny if he was having a good time. He told her he had never been to a formal dance and was enjoying himself. She hugged him and thanked him again for coming to her home for this occasion.

When the dance was over they were invited to a friend's home for a pool party and later for breakfast. The home was in the best area of their town and had all the bells and whistles on a two acre piece of property. Rose and Sonny had not brought bathing suits with them so they just wandered around until they found a good place to relax. Other graduates had not brought bathing suits but that did not stop them from going swimming. Sonny was a little shocked but Rose told him that it was a ritual for most summer proms. They were by themselves, just enjoying each other's company. She said how much she missed him and he told her that he missed her just as much, even more than his mother. "I want you to know right now you are next to my mother in my heart."

She started crying and hugged him so hard that neither one could breathe. They had an early breakfast and headed home for some sleep because Rose had to attend the sports award ceremony at the school.

Everyone in the Jenco family, including the children, were at the awards ceremony. Awards were given out for all spring sports and all the league, county and, if any, state awards. Rose received all her track awards for the league and county. Both of these included athlete of the year for track in each section. Finally a state representative for the governor was there and awarded Rose the state athlete of the year award. When the award was given to Rose she was given a standing ovation and had her picture taken for the local, state, and national papers. This was the biggest story for the school since her sister, Jackee, left. In the history of Reagan High school only the Jenco sisters made state recognition. Rose came down from the stage, with her award and gave it to her mom and dad. She told them that they deserved the award as much as she did.

After hugging and thanking her sisters she saved the last hug for Sonny and told him it would make a good start for our home. He told her "we already have a good start."

Jackee and Dan had only a few days before she and Sonny had to go back for summer baseball. They spent as much time together as possible but the time seemed to fly by. Before they knew it, their last weekend was coming up and it seemed like they hardly saw each other. Friday night's date was short because Dan had to work late and he was working Saturday half a day. On Saturday Dan was at her house by 6pm and they decided to just have a sundae at the malt shop and then go to their favorite parking spot. They talked about the future and what it looked like. Both were entering their junior year and although Dan would graduate in less then two years, Jackee had four more years to go. Dan had finalized his major to international accounting. He was good with numbers and had a knack for languages and negotiations. He would apply for internships with 10 possible international companies. His professor and advisor had some pull and seemed sure his resume would be very well received. In Jackee's case she would not begin her internship for two more years. Everything is supposed to be done in the college or in the medical teaching hospital connected to the college. She wasn't sure how baseball was going to be affected but she was sure it would be. Eventually a decision would have to be made for either medical or baseball. The college had promised that it could be worked out for both. When all the talk ended, they settled down to just holding each other and sometimes kissing.

Directly after church, which Dan attended with them, Jackee and Sonny left for summer baseball. They arrived back on campus and after William had lunch with them, he and Rose drove home. Rose got a job offer from the local sports complex. Of course she knew that they were only trying to cash in on her being named state athlete of the year, Also she was to announce her decision on college and there would be at least 10 colleges attending this event. She talked to William the whole time driving home. He told her to select the school that she felt would do her the most good. "Don't let anyone affect your decision. What is best for you should be your only concern."

"If I go to Olympus college I could be with Sonny and Jackee."

William made the point about how that will affect their programs. "Will you be a distraction to them or them to you? One more piece of advice I am going to give you, look at your greatest dream and which college gives you the best chance to fulfill that dream."

Rose looked at her dad and threw her arms around him and thanked him for making the choice so easy. William had been startled at first since he was driving at 70 mph but regained control and was happy he could help.

To accomodate all the interested parties, the athletic director offered to hold Rose's announcement at the high school gym on Monday at One pm. This provided all the college's and news people enough room to properly see this announcement in person. Rose, with some of the family present, spoke to the people in attendance. She thanked everyone for their generous offers and wished she could accept all of them. Her decision was a very difficult one "but a brilliant person gave me the solution to my predicament. I will commit to Rockwell University." Again I want to thank everyone for their offer and director Mr Weeks for letting us use the high school gym. Jackee and Sonny would learn of Rose's decision later that night. They could have learned earlier because it was on all the sport shows as soon as Rose announced her decision. They were eating dinner together when they heard the announcement. Both agreed it was the right choice for Rose to make. Rockwell offered full tuition, room and board, travel vouchers for every break, choice of accommodations, pick of meets and invitationals. She would also have free accommodations for all her guests on campus.

Baseball tryouts for the summer team was scheduled for 2pm Monday. Coach Zimmer had decided to keep as many of his starting players on the summer team as possible. Only the third baseman, Casey, the two DH's and one pitcher could not make the tryout. There were a few new faces on the field but only four looked as if they could make the team. Buddy Catera was an excellent infielder and Gabe Polski could play either infield or outfield. The other two were pitchers who had some pop on the ball. Jackee was not 100% sure but she thought both threw over 90 miles per hour. Jack immediately worked Buddy out at third base and he looked really good. Gabe worked out at all the infield positions and proved he could be the backup for all of them. In less than a week, the coach had his team picked and everything was looking good. The double J's were functioning better than ever and with Sonny in center and Bo behind the plate the team was very strong up the middle. The pitching was far superior to anything Jackee had seen before. At least four pitchers could be called number one. The two best relief pitchers were lights out for at least two innings. Both threw hard and had excellent control. Tom also threw a slider that is not hittable if he gets it in the strike zone.

Their five warmup games were a big success against fair to good opposition. The Olympians scored 52 runs while the other side scored 6. The pitching was unbelievable since none of our top five pitchers gave up a run. Every pitcher on the team pitched at least 5 innings. Our relief pitchers did not give up a run and struck out 60% of the batters they faced. More important neither one of them issued a walk. Coach had told the team that he scheduled the best teams he could get and the team will be making a trip to 6 different teams in a one week time frame. "We have complete use of the athletic bus for the trip and sleeping accommodations are being arranged as we speak. These would all be away games at top colleges or universities with almost no rest between games. Three of the six will be night games. This school has never played this caliber of team before. Every schedule usually has a few easy teams to play. This is not that schedule. Every one of the six is rated very high in the country. I believe we can sweep this schedule, and we have the team for the first time that can do it. We will have to bring our A+ game for every one of these games. My double J's will lead our team since they are the team captains." Jack and Jackee heard this for the first time and had no warning that it was to happen.

The double J's took their new leadership role seriously and put the team to the most strenuous training possible. They took all the things that the coaches the year before had stressed and even added a few of their own. A warmup of a one mile run in under 6 minutes followed by stretching and some calisthenics then throwing to loosen up the arm. There was no wasted time on the field. One player was hitting off a live arm while the next hitter was hitting off iron mike in an enclosed cage. Each hitter had a number and they knew when their turn at bat would come up. Pitchers were throwing live batting practice or warming up in the bullpen or doing drills like hot box or covering bases. Each pitcher had to take some swings in the iron mike cage in case they had to hit in a game. Outfielders usually hit first and then rotate to the outfield for covering batted balls. One outfielder at a time would be drilled in outfield practice. Each hitter on live pitching got 10 fastball swings, five curveball swings, and five swings at pitches called by the catcher. One day a week they practiced bunting on 15 pitches. 5 fast balls, 5 curves, 5 called by the catcher. Infield practice is 25 ground balls thrown to first, 25 ground balls thrown to second, and 5 to third. Third baseman would throw their last 5 by going over and stepping on third then throwing 2 to first and 3 to second. On a day that had some wind Jackee took the iron mike and elevated it for pop ups in the infield. She put an iron mike between home and the pitcher's mound and put the balls in. There were many staggering catches and many misses before the infielders got used to the wind. It wasn't long before every infielder could catch a popup in the strongest wind.

Jackee asked the coach if they could try Bats' infield pre-game warmup. She explained how it was done and the effect it had on most opposing teams. He told her he was used to a certain way but it sounded like fun, so he would try it out. The first time they did it nothing went right. Coach would have stopped it there but he saw the team having fun trying to do it. By the fourth day it was perfect and the team loved it. Coach liked one important part of the drill, each player had to be aware of when his turn was and what he had to do. There was no communication on the field, not a single word was spoken until the last segment and then each player shouted the whole time. Coach noticed that even his team watched the drill when they did it.

First 8 games were against the same teams that they played last year and the results were even better than last year. Going into the first of the 6 big games the team was more than ready. It was to be a Sunday afternoon game starting at 3pm. The school athletic bus would leave at 6am for the four hour trip. Jackee, Sonny, and a few other members of the team attended church services Saturday night and had a light dinner after. There were boxes of food for each player already on the bus before it left school. One small item the coach hadn't mentioned was that each school that they were to play had been told that Jackee would be playing. Previous to this year the coach had to mention that a female was on the team and certain courtesy should be given to her. This year he only said "Jackee is playing on his team. Every college and university knows about Jackee. They all use her as an attraction to draw much bigger crowds." Last year every school they played had at least an attendance boost of 50%. This year some schools were counting on at least another increase of between 25 to 30%. This increase in ticket sales, refreshments and other souvenirs, more than paid for the cost of the season and still left additional money for next year.

Riding an 8 game winning streak, Olympians pulled into Randolf University a little before 10am. Team members were taken to a set of dorms that they would use for the night. After storing their gear they were taken to a cafeteria where lunch had been prepared. The food was better than any of them had seen at Olympus or any other college. Around the table, the players wanted to know how Jackee rated a room by herself while they had to sleep 3 in a room.

She jokingly told them that she was better looking than they are and because of that she rated a special room. "If you don't believe me, ask anyone on the other team who they would rather have a date with." Even the coach thought that was funny and found it very interesting that his team seemed loose and ready to play.

After lunch the double J's lead the team in their pre game warm ups and drills. Batting practice lasted about an hour and then they left the field while Randolf took their pre game practice. Olympians took the field immediately after and went through their pre game practice. It was done to perfection and had not only the other team watching but most everyone in the stands was paying close attention to what they were doing. They all seemed to be waiting for a player to make a mistake, but none did and when the team completed it most of the people in the stands applauded. Coach thought to himself, so much for the home team advantage.

Zeke Baker was given the call to start the game and according to Bo, he looked unhittable. Jack led off for the visitors and after a long at bat drew a walk, Sonny lined a single to right center sending Jack to third. Jackee came to bat amid a big round of applause, She did not disappoint them, and on the fourth pitch, a hanging curve she lined a triple down the right field line. All the women in the stands were cheering because this is what they came to see. Was this girl for real or just a publicity stunt? Before the inning was over Jackee had scored and Olympians led 3 to 0. Bo was right about Zeke and he dominated Randolf hitters. He allowed two runs and 6 hits and he struck out 10. Their defense was great and included two double plays by the Double J's. One of the double plays was a standard 4-6-3, but the other was when Jackee dove for a ball behind second and while lying prone flipped to Jack who stepped on second and fired a strike to first. Jackee was thankful that she was wearing the chest protector that Kim had gotten for her. This protective undergarment saved her many sleepless nights. She also had two other hits and a third RBI. Final score Olympians 6 Randolf 2.

Coach and double J's ate together and discussed the game and how they could improve it. One thing the coach wanted to know was if Jackee was comfortable with spending an hour after the game talking to the girls. "You never seem to disappoint them but it's always an hour or more."

"Coach, talking to the girls gives me the desire to play harder and do better. It is part of what drives me on. Do you think I could have done this if those girls weren't behind me every step of the way? I have great desire and have worked hard to bring my body and mind to this level but because it means so much to them it drove me beyond being just good. Without that support I would have never thought the next level was possible."

"Jackee, the women will be at every game because each team is using you to get a bigger crowd. Did you notice today there were more women in the stand than men."

Jack said "it is a shame you're not getting a percentage of the profits, after all you are creating the excitement."

"That would ruin my amateur status."

"By the way coach, how did you like the reaction of the crowd when we did our infield, outfield warmup. He said it was the best ever and the team looked like the Rockettes performing at Radio City Music Hall."

At 6am Monday they had breakfast and headed for Raider University for a 7pm game. This was a 6 hour drive but it was mostly highway. They arrived at Raider and basically had the same routine they had at Randolf. Stow baggage in dorms and get something to eat. This was followed by a short rest then practice and after the home team took their infield, the Olympians took theirs. Once again it was faultless and the crowd being bigger gave a bigger cheer. Josh Dunright was selected to pitch the second game. Bo told the coach that during his warm up Josh looked as good or better than Zeke. Coach told Jackee to look into the stands. What she saw was a full house and the vast majority were females. Jackee told the coach she would give them their money's worth. With one out in the top of the first Sonny bunted for a hit and beat it out without even drawing a throw. Jackee came to bat knowing that the pitcher was going to throw all her fast balls to give the catcher a chance to throw out Sonny stealing. Sure enough the first pitch was a fastball belt high toward the outside of the plate. There was no doubt as to where the ball was going. The right fielder took two steps back, stopped and watched the ball clear the right center fence by more than 50 feet. This was a line drive that kept going up. As Jackee was rounding the bases most every female in the stands were on their feet roaring their approval. Her teammates had to push her out of the dugout for a curtain call. With two outs in the bottom of the first, the number three hitter hit a shot up the middle. Because their scouting report said that this player never pulls the ball, Jackee was cheating toward second. With a dive and a flip to Jack who in turn fired a strike to first to get the runner, the inning was over. It was an unusual 6-4-3 out but the two J's had used it many times before. Olympians added single runs in innings 5 thru 7 so they led 5 to 0 in the bottom of the seventh. Raider scored two runs and had the bases loaded with two outs. Hitter number two in the lineup, hit a pop up to short right field. Jack now became the hero as he dove headlong for the ball and caught it in the webbing of his glove for the final out of the inning. Tom Shaffer was called in to get the final 6 outs. All he did was strike out the first five batters he faced and the last one hit a comebacker to him and he outran the batter to first ending the game. Just like the game before, Jackee spent the next hour talking to the crowd of females who gathered around her. She signed from Baseballs to hats and never failed to talk to every young girl there. Finally the coach told the women that they would be back later in the week and Jackee would be available then but right now she had to get something to eat.

Food was laid out in the cafeteria family style and the Olympians dug in. Most were starved because they only had a light lunch. There was no food allowed in the dugout; only energy bars, gatorade, and water were available. The teams had a nice time together as there is only one cafeteria open this time of year. Raider's players were curious about Jackee and made it their business to talk with her. What they found was a very open and lovely young woman. She answered all their questions and even joked with them. They of course would not see her dressed up so they only knew half the story of Jackee Jenco.

Next school was Wallans University which would be another 6 hour ride on Tuesday. This was a night game scheduled to start at 7:30pm. Team members were getting tired of this bus trip every day but the coach had promised that Thursday would be a rest day before they played their last two games on this trip. Close to 1pm the bus arrived at Wallans University, just in time for lunch.

Olympians enjoyed a 10 game winning streak and their confidence was sky high. Baseball players are very superstitious and would never change anything while on a winning streak. Players sat in the same seats on the bus, at lunch and dinner, in the dugout and even in the same order for batting practice. Once again the crowd was huge, the mix was about 50/50 and this field had a very large seating capacity. Pre game rituals went well but when Olympians did their fielding drill the crowd loved it. This was the third day in a row that it went perfect. Sal Presto was the starter and Bo told the coach that Sal looked very sharp. He did not have an overpowering fastball but his curve and change were the best on the team. Jackee who had a triple and a home run in the first inning of the last two games and did not disappoint these fans. She doubled to left center and drove in Sonny who had beat out an infield single. Bo doubled Jackee in and he later scored on a hit by Augie the DH. Once again they scored first in the three games and now led 3 to 0 in this one. The first 6 batters for Olympian had at least two hits each. Bo, Augie and Buddy had home runs and the team scored 10 runs. Coach let Sal pitch 6 innings then had Brady and Drew pitch one inning each. For the last inning he brought in Arnold, the other reliever, who proceeded to strike out the side. This made it 3 for 3 on the trip so far. Coach originally thought if he split the 6 games the team would have done well.

Food was laid out for both teams in the main dining room. Jackee would be late as once again, the usual crowd of women gathered around her. Later the coach and Jackee were eating when the coach got a message from the athletic director of Raider University asking if Jackee would speak at a girl scout convention when they went back to Raider. "It seems the scouts are having a four day convention and one of the mothers attended the game and spoke with you. They know we are off Thursday and want you to speak Thursday afternoon."

"Coach I did not bring any dress clothes and can not face these girls in sweats or baseball uniforms."

"The mother already thought of that and has a female clothing store willing to dress you for your talk. If you tell me it's ok then I'll do it. Jackee this was supposed to be your down time for rest and relaxation, only you can make this decision. It should not affect the team one way or the other. We will play Harriston at 2 pm Wednesday, have supper and drive to Raider and sleep there."

Olympians arrived at Harriston at 10:30am. There was a pre game meal available for the players but most just had some drinks then went into the locker room and dressed for the game. Everything was right on schedule until they took their pre game infield drill. When the drill for the outfield started there was a mixup and it took awhile for the team to regain their composure. Coach blamed himself for not having a solution in place if such an occurrence happened. This was the first time the coach saw his players lose the confidence edge they had all trip. Prior to the game he tried a pep talk, but it seemed to fall on deaf ears. By the

5th inning Olympians were losing 4 to 0. Top of the 6th, the coach went ballistic and told the team, if you're going to throw away an 11 game winning streak, at least go down fighting. His words shook them up and they started coming back. When they came to bat in the top of the ninth, the score was 5 to 4 Harriston winning. With runners on second and third and two men out, who do you want to see coming to the plate? Jackee of course. Jackee had a full count when she lined a ball headed to left center field. Today was not her day to be a hero because the shortstop jumped as high as he could and caught the ball in the webbing of his glove ending the game and their 11 game winning streak. Walking back to the dugout, Jackee had her head down, but the people in the stands and her team-mates were clapping for her effort. After showering and dressing the team had dinner at Harriston before heading to Raider.

Olympians arrived at Raider late that night and were immediately shown to their dorm rooms. Some snacks were available in a conference room in the dorm. Most players just took one or two items back to their rooms and went to bed. Jackee had something to drink and went back to her single room. The baseball game will be a 1pm start on Friday so the Olympians had off until 9am Friday. Mrs Beth Ballard left word for Jackee that a car would pick her up at 10am and take her to the clothing store. It would take her back to Raider and pick her up again at two for the speaking engagement. After breakfast Jackee prepared herself to be picked up. Sure enough at 10am sharp a car pulled up to where she was staying and took her to the shop. All the help at the store could not do enough for Jackee. In less than an hour she was fully dressed. The workers were saying how beautiful she looked. Jackee was not sure if they were sincere or if it was just workers saying nice things for sale purposes only. Two shops down from the dress store was a hair and nail shop. As Jackee was leaving the dress shop she was escorted to the hair and nail shop.

A woman who appeared to be the owner approached Jackee and told her that she had been directed to prepare her for a speaking engagement. "First we will prepare your hair and then your nails." One hour later Jackee exited the shop and was driven back to the school. She was hungry so she walked over to the caf-eteria where all their meals were to be served. When she walked into the dinning room all talk stopped and all eyes were on her. The only sound being made was her high heel shoes tapping on the floor.

She saw the coach and Jack sitting at a table so she joined them. Looking around she asked what was going on. Coach told her these gentlemen have never seen a shortstop who was so beautiful. Blushing, she said "they always knew I was a female."

"Yes, but you have never been dressed like this before."

"Well it must be the clothing and the new hairdo."

Jack said "and a gorgeous figure that was hiding under a baseball uniform."

"Thank you Jack for thinking your shortstop is pretty."

She ate with them and then went back to her room to wait for her transportation. She asked Sonny, Jack, and the coach to come with her but only Sonny was free.

Entering the center, Jackee was met by Mrs Ballard and her committee. She then was escorted to a special table set up for the speakers. Most of these speakers had already spoken to the scouts. After she was introduced to the other speakers and Sonny had been assigned a seat close by, Jackee was introduced to the audience. As usual she qualified her remarks by saying she can only speak from a female point of view. She gave her background of school, family and career so far. Then she broke it down for them.

"I found a love for baseball when I was 5. My father saw my desire so he nourished me all along the way. He spent time with me when he should have been resting. He never once said he was too tired or maybe we could do this some other time. The more he paid attention to me the more I wanted to be the best, just for him. It's easy to say that I have worked for 15 years to get where I am today. That is a total of almost 5500 days, and except for maybe 100 of them, I have worked out and practiced baseball. Every choice that I have made was made by me with the support of my family. Never once did I hear the words no or you can't. My goal has been very simple, be the best baseball player on the field or work harder. Two years ago I was declared the Most Valuable Player in the state championship baseball tournament. That in itself was a great honor but I can't let that be the end. Right now I am continuing my dream by playing for Olympus College and we are playing Raider at 6 pm Friday. I wish I could give you all a free pass but Raider is incharge of the gate. I am going to school to be a doctor and I want you all to know that I carry a Perfect 4.0 grade point average. You can have more than one dream. The only thing that is stopping you from your dreams is you. I am not telling you that there will not be hard times ahead. Every dream you have will be hard to achieve. The bigger the dream the harder it will be. Dream small and your rewards will be small. If you have the dream and the drive, let nothing and nobody stand in your way. Do not ever give an excuse for failing. You will fail most of the time. Failure is not the end, it is a learning experience. A champion picks herself up and tries harder the next time. Unlike most other countries you have a heritage for doing the impossible. This country was founded by people who risked their lives everyday. Who worked with usually not more than their hands, and carved out the greatest nation on the face of this earth. We had great women in our history that risked everything, including their lives so that this country could survive. That is our legacy, to honor them by carrying the torch forward for the next generation of women. Each of you has God given talents, it is for you to decide how to use them. I have seen too many women let others make important decisions for them. Don't let that happen to you. You already have a great start by belonging to one of the finest female organizations ever founded. The girl scouts give each of you a good start for self esteem and self reliance. Use that as a building block for your future. I will be here until they throw me out, so I will be available to speak with you after the formal part of this meeting is over."

Some time later the meeting ended and Jackee had a crowd of women and young girls around her. The questions were pretty much the same no matter where they spoke. She tried to answer every question as honestly as she could. Her family was always a big topic. Now they were asking about a boyfriend. Dan was almost always on her mind so it was easy to talk about him. She explained how hard it was for both of them to be apart. "However, we both have dreams and we are 100% helping the other to achieve that dream." One older girl wanted to know if sex was a problem for her to achieve her dream. "Jackee told her everything could be a problem but it was up to you as to how it will affect your dream. Remember, many of our greatest women achieve success after being married and raising a family. We have no idea what obstacles we may have to face in the future, all that can be done is to face each one head on as they occur." Finally Mrs Ballard came to the group and said Jackee really should get some rest for Friday's game. Jackee told the crowd that "I Pray that God will always be by your side and direct you toward your dream. I'll see you after the game if you come. God bless and thank you for having me."

Sonny and Jackee got back to Raider about 8pm because Mrs Ballard took them out for dinner. Mrs Ballard asked Jackee and Sonny many questions and eventually became interested in the fact that Sonny was a full blood American Indian. When she dropped them off at school she said that "if you're here next year I hope we can get together again." They agreed but were not really sure if she meant it.

Jackee went right to bed as she was exhausted and could barely keep her eyes open. Next morning at 9am the Olympians had a practice to prepare for the game. The practice went well and the fire seemed to be back in the team. Zeke was to start, and the team was fired up about having their number one ready to pitch. Coach at the end of practice told the team he was sick and tired of this losing streak the team had and he wanted it to end tonight. The whole team was laughing and this helped put the edge back in them. After lunch the team had time to rest before reporting to the field. Many members of the team told Jackee how great she looked last night and one suggested that he hoped the baseball Jackee was back and not the girl they saw yesterday. "We need our leader and not some model."

She told him "the player is always there but sometimes I have to remind myself that the other Jackee needs to be seen." Later when it was their turn to take fielding pre game practice it went perfect and the fans in the stands reacted to their precision performance. As Jackee looked into the stands for the first time she realized that the stands were packed and all the girls from the previous night must be here. She mentioned to the coach that she asked the girls from last night to attend the game.

He told her that they must all be here because this is by far the biggest crowd Raider has ever had. The Raider coach told coach Zimmer that their stands had never been full even for championship games. Zimmer told him he could thank Jackee because she spoke at their meeting and she invited them to attend. There was no doubt as to why the female crowd was there. When Jackee was announced in the pre game ceremony, she was given a standing ovation that greatly impressed the Raider team.

An umpire shouting play ball, starts every game and this one was no different. Jack and Sonny each got on base with a single and a walk before Jackee came to the plate. She hit a bullet toward the center fielder who tried to make a shoestring catch and missed the ball. It rolled all the way to the fence and Jackee rounded the bases before they could get the ball back to the catcher. Still no one out and Jackee had a three run homer to her credit. The fans were roaring and once again her teammates pushed her out of the dugout to take a curtain call. Zeke was the recipient of all these runs and he lived up to his number one status. Jackee came up again in the third inning and doubled down the left field line. She scored on Bo's single to right. She batted in the seventh inning with Sonny on second and this time hit a drive down the left field line that hit the foul pole for a home run. The whole time she was rounding the bases the crowd was cheering. They would not stop until she came out and tipped her hat to the crowd. Zeke had a two hitter going and in the bottom of the seventh with two outs a batter hit a short pop up toward center, Jackee with her back to home plate dove and caught the ball as she hit the ground. She rolled over and held her glove above her head. Sonny, who had been coming for the ball, got to her first. She tried to catch her breath but was having a problem. He grabbed her belt and lifted it and lowered it a few times. This aided Jackee in catching her breath. Jack and Sonny helped her to stand and they all walked off the field to a great deal of cheering. Once again Jackee was saved by her chest protector but she still had pain in both her breasts. Coach asked if she was able to continue and she claimed to be fine. Thomas replaced Zeke in the bottom of the eighth and just before he made his first pitch, the coach replaced Jackee at shortstop. She trotted off the field to a standing ovation and tipped her hat and formed the words thank you on her lips. Thomas once again was locked in and retired all six batters he faced, striking out four of them. Olympians broke their losing streak by a 11 to 0 score and now were 4 and 1 on the trip. There was no way Jackee could leave the field with the crowd of young girls around her. She held court for over an hour and although she was in pain, talked to all of them. Coach finally came over and asked if they would excuse Jackee as she had to shower and get something to eat. He also told them that they would be playing Raider again next fall.

Coach told the team at dinner that "we will sleep here, have breakfast in the morning and at 8am be on the road for Jefferson University. It is a three hour trip and we have a 1pm game after which we will have a three hour trip home and dinner when we get there."

While eating dinner many of the Raider players came over to congratulate Jackee and two of them offered to marry her whenever she would have them. She told them she was spoken for but "if it doesn't work out I'll look you up." Coach had never had a team that played this well and with this win attitude. He realized it was all because of Jackee. The boys tried harder to keep up with Jackee and she worked harder to keep ahead of them. It was a win, win for the coach. Jackee took a long hot shower and rubbed some of the cream that Kim had given her over her breasts. They hurt and she thought that more is never better in some things. She went to sleep and didn't wake up until 7am. She showered again and felt some of the tension leave her body and the pain had been reduced. She applied more of the cream, dressed and went to breakfast after she packed. It was evident that she had lost some weight on this trip and her appetite was still missing. She tried to eat as healthy as possible but many times it was eat and run so healthy intake was limited. Bus trips are not usually this bad because it is only for a day. This was a long trip to far away teams with very little quality down time. The team was tired but they had one more game in them.

Coach asked them on the bus to make this game an example for the rest of our season. "We have three home games coming up so we should be back on our usual schedule when we start the rest of this summer program."

Once again their pre game drill went off like clockwork. The crowd, which was a big one, clapped when the Olympians finished and cheered louder when Jackee was introduced. Bo came back from warming up Josh and told the coach he looked better than last time. It would be impossible for Jackee to play better than her last game. Two home runs and a double plus 5 RBI's and at least 3 very good fielding plays. It still was a scoreless game with each pitcher retiring 9 batters in a row. Jack was the first base runner for either team when he drew a 12 pitch walk in the top of the fourth. Sonny followed with a drag bunt that he beat out easily. Jackee was due up next and she signaled Jack and Sonny to try a double steal. When the pitcher moved toward home both runners broke for the next base. Jefferson's infield moved accordingly with the second baseman covering second and the third baseman covering third. Seeing where the holes were Jackee proceeded to hit a ground ball exactly where the second baseman was before he went to cover second. Jack scored and Sonny went to third and all the right fielder could do was throw the ball to second holding Jackee on first.

On the first pitch to Bo, Jackee was stealing second and when the catcher threw to second Sonny stole home. This must have really upset the pitcher because he left a fastball over the heart of the plate and Bo took him down town for a home run. In just 5 pitches Olympians led 4 to 0. The game stayed that way until the bottom of the seventh when Jefferson put a rally together. They had one run in with only 1 out and runners on first and second. Next batter hit a slow ground ball to Jack who flipped to Jackee and knowing she had no play at first, jumped over the sliding base runner and fired a strike to third and Buddy tagged out the runner from second who had taken a big turn rounding third. Coach brought in Arnold to pitch the last two innings and he continued the excellent relief work. He retired all six batters he faced, striking out four. Game ended at 3:15 and Jackee spent an hour with all the young girls. She had a 5pm bus to catch but all her gear would be packed and put on the bus by Sonny.

On the way home, the coach told the team he had hoped that they would win maybe three games. He felt that the competition was the best they had ever seen and even feared getting swept. Now he just wished that Jackee had hit the ball 2 inches higher against Harriston. Most of the team had started teasing Jackee about how she was the reason they lost their winning streak. She sarcastically told them she really had to try harder so it would not happen again.

Jack stood up and said, "I can see why she has to practice more. She is leading the team in hitting, doubles, triples. runs scored, is second in RBI's and has a 1000% fielding percentage. Only thing left for her to do is sell tickets. By the way she is the reason we play to mostly full houses every game. There is one fear I do have and that you will be eligible for the draft after your junior year. There is not one major league team that would not make a fortune drafting you. Every woman in the country would pay to see the greatest women baseball player." She thanked Jack for his kind words and said she hoped to live up to them.

After dinner Jackee went back to her dorm and after a hot shower she called home. First, she talked to Carmela and asked about Little William and Rose. Carmela told her William was fine and getting big, as far as Rose was concerned she won her first summer meet in the mile and 5000. William was next and Jackee asked him to do her a big favor, she explained why she needed it. He thought about it and said it would be taken care of. She did take the time to tell him about the trip that was just completed. It sounded to William like Jackee had reached a level that even surprised him. Finally he said for her to get some rest and they would talk more when she comes home. Just as she was about to call Dan, he called her. They both said the same thing, how much they missed each other. She told him that 2 baseball players from Raider University proposed marriage to her and how she had to turn them down because of him.

"Was it a hard choice to make?" he asked.

"There has never been a doubt in my mind as to who I want to spend my life with. Do you still want me?"

"Jackee, there has never been a time that I didn't." They talked for a half hour more and Jackee started to fall asleep so they said good night and went to bed.

Sunday, Jackee went to church with Sonny and went back to the cafeteria for lunch. Sonny told her he called Rose last night and they talked for an hour. "She sounded wonderful on the phone and is having a great summer doing track. She wants me to come home with you after baseball but I do not want to be a burden to your parents."

Jackee told him that Rose can have whatever she wants because their parents would never refuse her almost anything. "We are just so happy she found herself. If you had seen her when we first did, it would have shocked you. She found a family in us and a soul mate in you. Sonny, I love Rose and I'll tell you right now, you will never meet another girl like her. There is no partial drive in Rose. She is 100% in everything she does. Do you want a companion for life? Well, Rose is the one since she picked you out just like she picked us."

Having a record of 13 and 1 with 16 more games to play represented a high point in the Olympus summer baseball program. Since they have already played the best teams, the remaining games should be somewhat less competitive. They won 15 out of the 16 games and finished the summer with a 28 and 2 record. This was by far the best summer baseball record in the history of Olympus college. Coach Zimmer had to rethink his summer schedule because he would have the same team coming back and they would have to play better teams to keep their edge. He took the core of the team and held a meeting to discuss this very thing. Coach mentioned to them that they were locked into a spring schedule because of the school's commitment in their league. "However, in the summer we are basically freelancers and can play anyone. Players wanted to know what our restrictions are in the summer as far as our budget. We can not fly but we have a bus with a driver at our disposal. Can we make two 10 game trips covering two weeks each. Make a circle with the schools closest to us for the first and last game. The furthermost teams would be games 5 and 6. Then we swing toward home for games 7 thru 10. We can book our home games the weeks before, after and between the trips. It would fill seven weeks and leave us a little more time at home." Coach thought that was a good approach and he would send out letters requesting dates. He did mention that no division one school wants to play down. "It's not only the competition but also if they are beaten by a lower division school, how it would look on their record for NCAA seating. Speaking of seating, I am asking our league if we can be included in a division 2 or 3 baseball championship. Since we do play teams playing in both of these divisions we may be eligible for either one. Division 2 would be the best competition but division 3 has the most schools. My secretary and I will start working on this immediately and before we start the spring season we should have some answers." Players who were present were very excited about both plans.

Jackee told Sonny to be ready to leave by noon on Thursday. William was coming with Rose and he will pick both of us up. "Rose told me to tell you that if you don't come she is coming here to be with you."

Sonny said "I guess her wish is my command." They were sitting on Jackee's porch when William pulled up. Rose jumped out and kissed Sonny before he could say a word. She then put his bags in the back and got back into the car's back seat. With Sonny's help Jackee put all her stuff in and sat up front with her dad. Rose sat very close to Sonny and whispered how happy she was to have him visit. They talked about the summer program and what the coach was trying to do. Since Jackee would not say anything, Sonny told Rose and William what a great year she just had. "We thought she was great in the spring but in the summer she had her finest moments. She batted over .450 leading the team in hitting, fielding, doubles, triples, and runs scored. There were plays she made that no one else even came close to making. Also, she spoke to at least 3000 girls and even spoke to the girls scouts. Mr Jenco you would have been proud to see her speak and the reaction of the girls after her talk. Also she had a special dress for that speech and looked like a model but much more beautiful."

"You're only enforcing what I already know about her and by the way, I took care of that favor."

"Thank you dad, and I knew I could count on you taking care of it." They arrived home and Carmela had a feast ready for them.

Dan called all day to see if Jackee arrived yet. Carmela had the good news that they would be home in half an hour. As they started to eat dinner Carmela told Jackee that Dan would be here at 7. Jackee finished eating and went up to shower and dress, she wanted to look her best when Dan came. Just as Dan arrived she came down and ran into his arms. They kissed and then he said hello to the family and Sonny. He asked if she wanted to go for a walk and she agreed. When they got outside Jackee told him she would rather drive somewhere as she was still a little tired. He said he knew a place where she would feel completely relaxed. Of course, they drove to their favorite parking area. Usually they talked first and then kissed but this time it was reversed. She told him every time they are apart the hurt she feels for him grows stronger. He admitted it is the same for him.

Jackee said she found that "all the young girls who come to see her play are the only reason for me continuing this baseball dream. When I found you my dream was compromised but the adulation bestowed on me by these girls drove me to a new level. I never want to disappoint them, but not having you near is hurting me awful."

"Right now," he said, "there is no answer that may not ruin our dreams forever. You and I both know that we can't have everything we want right now without compromising something."

"I know you are right and it is just a silly girl's way of saying I love you."

Meanwhile back at the ranch, Rose had Sonny all to herself in her work-out room. She told him how much she was looking forward to college and her future in track. He told her that with the help of Jackee and Andrea his grades were good enough to get into med school. "When you graduate, I will be starting my internship and we can really make plans for our future."

She told him that there has to be one Olympic performance in her future "but after that I am all yours."

"You do remember that I owe my people 5 years of service after becoming a doctor. Yes, I remember, and I will be by your side every step of the way."

Lucy sent word that Dr Hopkins wanted everyone back by the Wednesday before school starts. Before leaving campus, Jackee asked if there were any openings in the lab. She wanted to see if Sonny could get some part time work. Lucy had said she would talk to the doctor about him and let her know. "Sonny does qualify for aid in the form of an on campus job. But all lab positions are awarded to exceptional students like Jackee and Andrea." Lucy included in her message that Sonny should report with her. Jackee broke the news to Sonny and he was speechless. He never would have applied because he knew only a select few ever were considered for those jobs.

Rose knew that Sonny would leave with Jackee because it would be hard on William to make two trips a few days apart. Besides, he had to take her to college just about the same time. Jackee sat down and talked to Rose about her school schedule. She told her to get her classes early in the day so that they never interfere with her workouts or meets. Not to get involved in parties and never say anything to your roommates about their lifestyle. "You will see many strange things on campus but don't let any of it change who you are and what your dream is. Whenever you are not sure of something, call me or mom and dad."

The two couples spent as much time together as possible. It turned out that Dan had to leave first for football. He had been doing very well as a tight end and his coach had some plans to use him on more plays. Jackee saw him off and then proceeded to work even harder with Rose and Sonny. Rose received a call from her new college coach who asked her to report to school a full week early because the school had a meet the first week of school. Since they knew her times and qualifications, it was important to see her workout and schedule her in the proper events. Rose was a little heart broken but she knew from watching Jackee, this was a normal occurrence. One Sunday after mass, the car was packed and off they went, everyone except Carmela and little William. William had called Rockwell when they were about an hour away. So it was no surprise to see the coach waiting for them. But there were many people including newspaper people waiting with him. Rose was treated as if she was a dignitary of some kind. Many pictures were taken, interviews were made and finally everyone was brought into a reception area where food and drinks were available. Coach Holland introduced Rose to everyone and gave a short talk about her and how happy the school was · to have her attend Rockwell. Jackee asked if the baseball coach was available. Coach told Jackee that he saw him a while ago and he will have his assistant see if he could find him. Coach Cherrie, the Rockwell baseball coach, came into the reception area and was introduced to Jackee. She told the coach that she was the sister of Rose but she was also a baseball player on the Olympus college team.

"You are the Jackee that all these scouts are raving about." She told him that she knew nothing about raving but she was Jackee Jenco and she does play baseball. "Well I am happy to make your acquaintance and if you're thinking of transferring to Rockwell I'll have the papers prepared in one minute."

"I really appreciate your offer but all I want to know is, can I give your name to my coach and have him contact you about playing a game in the future."

He told her "before you leave my secretary will give you all the information your coach will need to contact me." Later, as they were getting ready to head for home, a young girl came and gave Jackee a packet for her baseball coach. She thanked the girl and asked her to thank coach Cherrie for acting so quickly. They said their goodbyes to Rose and steered the car for home.

Two days later Sonny and Jackee were back at school. Andrea was already in the room and had prepared it for Jackee's return. She had also received a packet from the lab, laying out the groundwork for their new research. Jackee thanked her for cleaning the room and carefully studied the contents of the packet. When she finished, both of them talked about the proposal. They were excited that for the first time they would be working on a new concept rather than upgrading an existing one. Dr Hopkins' first meeting confirmed what they thought about the project and he laid out the training on the new equipment. "The manufacturer will send a scientist to live on campus and educate all of us on the new equipment. Because the scientist will live on campus, our training can be held any time of the day or night."

Coach Zimmer had told the summer team that he was going to play most of the new prospects and some of the players who had not played during the year. He knew that the other schools would be upset that Jackee would not always be in the line up, thereby reducing the possible attendance. All the captains were asked to attend as many games and practices as possible to aid him in getting the team up to our level of play. Sonny, Bo, Jack, and Jackee set up their workout at 5am each day. Others were offered the opportunity to join them at any time. Sonny felt he needed more power and better contact with two strikes. Jackee told him he needed another session with Bats over Christmas break. Sonny smiled and said he forgot about his offer to help him anytime he needed it. Bo and Jack only have this year left so we have to find replacements for them.

CHAPTER EIGHTEEN

Jackee Starts Third Year and New Science Projectc

*T*he first semester of the year was fantastic. Classes and programs were a perfect match and both labs fit right into their schedule. Class labs were right after the classes and Dr Hopkins research lab was fitted into their down time. Training on the new equipment was done when they were available. A young research scientist named Claire was sent to train the staff. She spent hours training the staff and she made herself available except for the hours of 10pm until 6am. Those 8 hours were her time but the other 16 she was available to train anyone in the lab. Jackee became very close to Claire and many times she joined the staff at the cafeteria. There was even a weekend when they had dinner off campus. Claire paid because she said all her meals were being paid by her company and she almost never used all that she was allowed. Claire also had the responsibility of giving some training to the hospital staff. Since the hospital helped pay for the new equipment, they wanted their hematologist and endocrinology department personnel to also be trained on the new equipment. It took Claire many hours to train all the hospital staff but she never complained and still used any free time to assist Dr Hopkins staff. One of the hematologists just happened to be a single male who was rated number one in his field at the hospital. He and Claire became very close as he was actually using what he learned for the good of his patients. He had already improved his procedure by being able to pinpoint exactly where to treat his patient. This gave the patient faster and better healing. She notified her company and they used this information in their ads to sell this new equipment. Just before she was to return back to the company, Claire was offered a job at the hospital, working with the hematology department. This offer would mean a 25% cut in pay. Her doctor friend spent the weekend with her and, would you believe she agreed to work for the hospital, but first had to give two weeks notice to her company. Claire's working at the hospital was also a big plus for the lab because they now had her available if a problem came up.

Working in the lab, with the baseball team plus all the classes made the time fly by. First there was the Halloween trick or treat/dance and a short time later it was Thanksgiving break. Dan could not get home because his team was playing in a bowl game on Friday after Thanksgiving. Jackee and Sonny drove home with Andrea's ride and returned the same way. Christmas break was to be from December 21st until January 15th. Rose had won all of her races and events. Her grades were excellent and her adjustment to college life was very good. She was the biggest sports story in that area and it seemed like everyday a picture or story or both appeared in some news media. Her school had a special charter plane take her home and back. William only had to go to the airport to pick her up. With Sonny by his side William was waiting for Rose at the airport. They saw her leaving the charter carrying her bags. Sonny ran to her and took the bags. Rose kissed her dad and thanked him for picking her up and then kissed Sonny. At Sonny's insistence, Rose sat in front with William so she could tell him about her first semester. She told him her GPA was 4.0 and that she has won every event and race she has entered. William asked if she was being trained in other events. Rose told him she had a promise from the coach to train in every track and field event. The javelin, pole vaulting and hammer were to be taught to her over the winter season. "In fact some of the male athletes have offered to help train with me."

When they arrived home everyone was there to hear how school went. At the dinner table, Rose told them how she was treated like a queen at the school. Every coach made it a point of talking to her. "The softball coach is my new best friend because she thinks I must be as good as Jackee. She also believes that I can do both spring sports at the same time. One day I did hit with the softball team and hit three balls over the fence. The coach is now after me every day to come out to their practice. I like hitting but it doesn't affect me like track and field does. It was always fun to work with Jackee but running is what gave me the most happiness."

William told her that her decision is easy to make, "track is your passion and you do not have to let anything interfere with it."

Rose said "I know you are right but it is very hard to say no when you are the new kid on the block."

Jackee told her that the new kid on the block is being used by the school but should never be abused by the school. "Tell them, in order for you to compete in track you must be 100% dedicated to that goal. Anything else will interfere with my ability to compete."

Thinking about it. Rose said "you are 100% correct and from now on that is the way it will be."

After dinner the family began decorating for Christmas and the season came into full swing. The Jenco visits to the orphanage and Vets home were a big success. Sonny had his council send many dolls for the children which they all loved. Since the council was told about the Vets, they added new items especially for them. Good luck charms and warrior statutes were also included in the shipment. When the two visits were finished William had a family meal planned at their favorite restaurant. Dinner for 10 plus two children was a big deal but William made the announcement that the gifts from Dan, Jon, Rocco and Sonny made this the best Christmas ever for the orphans and Vets. Rocco and Dan's family supplied many fantastic desserts, enough for both groups. Jon' family provided the orphans with special tee shirts and the Vets with special sweatshirts. He thanked one and all and told them to order whatever they wanted as long as it was under three dollars. Later, when William asked for the bill, the owner whose father was in the Vet's home, told him the meals were on the house and he and his family should have a Merry Chriatmas. The owner knew what the Jenco's do this every year and this was the only way he knew to thank them. Carmela and William thanked the owner and William left a 150.00 dollar tip on the table.

Christmas eve all four girls and Carmela prepared for Christmas dinner and desserts. Only Rebecca tried a new dessert the others made their usual. Once again Carmela had to have a separate table just for the desserts and that did not include the ones to come from Dan and Rocco. Next everyone decorated the tree and each year it was more beautiful then the year before. Mistletoe was hung in the archway entering the dining room.

Christmas morning was the usual mad house and it is a good thing that there are two showers in the house. Rose mentioned to Sonny that they could save time and water if they showered together. Sonny only blushed while Rose was laughing her head off. Church went as usual and the ushers had a row set aside for the Jenco's. 10 adults and two children take up a lot of room in a very crowded church on Christmas day. After mass and all holiday greetings were finished the Jenco's returned home for breakfast and to open gifts.

Jon told the other three men that his family had a villa in Italy and the Jenco's where to pick a week in March to go there. All arrangements had been set and all they had to do was select a date. The villa will be opened in March but his parents can not get there until April at the earliest. Plane fare and other costs are fully covered. "Rocco, if you and Rebecca wish to go, there is plenty of room and the children can go with you. There are enough trained staff to care for the children if you want to go out for the day or evening. Carmela and William might feel better about going if you go with them." Bats, Kim and George Herman came just as they started to open gifts and included their gifts to the pile already under the tree. Sonny saved three special dolls for the three children. He also gave Carmela and William hand made jackets and Rose a sweatshirt with the tribal crest on it.

Jackee asked Bats if he would check Sonny's swing and see if he could add some power to it. Bats agreed and watched Sonny bat for about 15 minutes.

He finally stopped Sonny and told him that he was only hitting with his upper body and needed to get more of his hips in his swing. Although his swing was good it needed a minor adjustment. Taking Sonny by the hips, he showed him as he did last year, how by cocking his hips he would get more leg and back muscle into his swing. Sonny tried 10 practice swings and then went back into the cage. A few swings later Sonny was hitting the ball with more authority and could feel the power he was generating by cocking and uncurling his hips as he made contact. Then they all went inside and prepared for dinner. Prior to taking their first bite, prayers were said and then William gave a toast. He thanked everyone for helping Carmela and him have the best Christmas ever. He heard someone once say that if you have one good friend, you are a wealthy person, when I look around this table that must make us the richest couple on earth. Carmela said, drink up and I hope everyone enjoys the meal. Dan came just as Rocco and Rebecca were leaving. He brought dessert from home and got into some family pictures.

Dan's parents' New Year party was on for this year. Last year Mrs Silvio was in the hospital for an emergency appendicitis and just came home on New Year's eve. This year everyone was healthy so the party was ready to go. Jackee had a great time just being with Dan and later that night spent the remainder of the party with him alone in the sun room. Jackee looked especially beautiful that night and he was jealous at how the men at the party were looking at her. She did not tell him that this was the clothing she received when she spoke to the girl scouts at Raider. He decided that he didn't want to share her with anyone else so they went to a room that was only used in the summer. It was fine with Jackee as she only wanted to be alone with Dan. She knew something was different when he started kissing her and she could feel the passion in every kiss. As far as she was concerned it was the best ever. For Dan this was trouble, he found it very difficult to bring this passion under control. Finally he told her, he had to stop as she was driving him crazy. She asked him to just hold her tight and tell her what he was feeling.

"What I feel for you can not be put into words, it can only be expressed in physical contact. I don't want to hurt you so let me take you home."

"Dan, I know you could never hurt me, so please let me stay in your arms a little longer." He agreed and just held her for the next couple of hours.

Rose and Sonny were also at a party for New Year. It was a friend of Rose that was on the track team. The parents were well to do and had been invited to a very exclusive hotel party. The party was to go all night and the parents were to spend the evening at the party and sleep in the rooms provided by the hotel. Since most knew that the parents would not return home until later on New Year's day, it was a no holds barred party. There was an indoor swimming pool which had most of the swimmers wearing nothing but a smile. Neither Rose or Sonny was comfortable with this so they went off to another area. What they found was more of the same but these guests were not swimming. They didn't find a room not occupied until they got to the den. When they were inside Rose locked the door and she and Sonny sat on the couch. Rose was definitely the aggressor and Sonny knew he didn't have to say a word.

10 Days later Rose had to leave for an invitational meet, and 4 days later Jackee and Sonny were picked up by Andrea and taken back to school. Andrea said she only got to half the boys she planned to see over the break. Jackee said it was a great holiday break and Dan was terrific. Sonny told them that Rose was in complete charge and we had a great time together.

"You do know that you should have a say in the relationship" Jackee told Sonny.

Shaking his head, he said "I can't hurt her in any way so I just let her lead me."

"You would not be hurting her by telling her how you feel about something. There should be communication between couples and always an honest exchange of thoughts." Sonny told them he would think about it.

Back at school Jackee and Andrea dove into the lab work and a week later classes started. Every morning the group worked out. As the other players found out about the 5am workout they joined them. Soon Jackee and her group had almost all the team from last year and all the new freshmen coming every day. Their normal 2 hour workout was now 3 or more hours. Jackee decided to do her cardio later in the day because now there was no time. Coach Zimmer could not be happier because he never had a team so dedicated to preparing for the coming season. He also received word that division 2 accepted Olympus College for their year end tournament if their record qualifies them. Coach knew that they would be invited because Jackee would be the biggest draw in the tournament's history. He also knew the deeper his team got into the championship round, the bigger the crowds and the more tickets that would be sold. If they made the finals, he would guarantee that there would be national coverage. Last year's record even with the power rating would have had them in the top five teams. This year because of Jackee he guessed it might get us in the top 3. This is a tournament with 32 teams invited.

Sonny was the perfect lab worker. He used every spare moment to be in the lab. Dr Hopkins took him under his wing and even gave him extra hours so he could earn more money. Jackee had mentioned to Dr Hopkins that Sonny was living on an allowance from the council back home and that it was very little. When she spoke to Dr Hopkins about it, he told her Sonny earns every dollar he makes. "You and Andrea are excellent assistants but his mind is like a sponge. He never forgets a single thing I tell him."

Jackee now realized what was different in Sonny. Since the day that her and Andrea started tutoring him, he started getting A's. He had trouble reading but if he heard something his mind absorbed it. When she told Andrea about Sonny, Andrea told her that she tutored a girl who had the exact same problem. "It was my fault for not putting the two together and seeing the problem immediately."

CHAPTER NINETEEN

Jackee Plays Spring Baseball & Finishes School Year

February 1st, baseball team tryouts officially began. The 5am workout was still going strong and most players did both. Casey, who was now a senior, would have a tough time beating out Buddy. This was a team that had everything, they were strong up the middle and their pitching was fantastic. There were 4 pitchers who would be the number one pitcher on most other teams. Add to that the two closers, Thomas Shaffer and Arnold Napper, and you have the ingredients for a near perfect season. As a team, they worked very hard on the pre game drill. It seemed that someone always made a mistake. Every time a mistake was made the coach put in a new wrinkle. An example would be if an outfielder missed a ball, the shortstop or second baseman would run toward that fielder and set up a cut off play with the catcher making the final call. Only one word would be heard and that is the catcher saying, Third, home or hold. Then the drill would continue as if the previous play never happened. Then one day it worked to perfection and the team never had a problem again. Coach made final cuts and now the team was set.

In all the scrimmages and pre league games the team looked unbeatable. The starting pitchers and the two relievers did not give up a single earned run. Hitting and fielding were just as strong as the pitching. They won the 4 pre league games and then proceeded to win every league game. When they played a weak league team, the coach tried to book a division one team to fill in the week. That competition was better but it did not stop the team from going undefeated for the season. Olympus College baseball team finished the season 36 and 0. First undefeated season in the school's history and the first one ever in the league. The Olympus baseball team always had a big following because of Jackee, but their winning streak drew bigger and bigger crowds.

Coach called for a meeting of all players for 4pm Monday. At the meeting he told the players that "we have been invited for two post season playoffs. The division 3 committee has offered us a number one seed. Division 2 has offered us a number two seed because their rules state that the best power rated team must receive the number one seed. I want you to vote and tell me which one I should accept." The team members all agreed that the division 2 would have better teams and we would get wider coverage. Coach told the team that "because of Jackee, we can expect maximum coverage no matter where we play. We would be the home team for the first three games. The finals will be held at the minor league stadium. Final championship is 2 out of 3. So we have to win 6 games to be division 2 champs. I believe that the finals were moved to the stadium because they needed more seating if we were in the finals."

First 2 games against the numbers 31 seed and 19 seed were not competitive. Olympus had huge crowds for both games. Game three would be against the number 9 seed. It was scoreless for the first 3 innings but Olympus scored 2 runs in the fourth and broke it open with 5 runs in the seventh. Sal Presto pitched the first seven innings then Arnold and Thomas pitched the last two. Coach found out after his game that seeds 1, 4, and 7 also made it to the finals. Olympus will play seed 4, Patterson University in the second game on Friday. Saturday at 10am the two losing teams from Friday will play for third place. The two winning teams will start the first game of their best 2 out of 3 series at 2pm Saturday. Both teams will play again at 11 am Sunday, if each team has a win the final game will be played at 3pm. Coach decided to gamble and he started Stan Weeks against Patterson. Bo came to the coach and told him Stan looked nervous but his pitchers were very good. Stan fell behind the first batter when he threw three pitchers out of the strike zone. Jackee called time out and went to the mound to talk to Stan.

She told him to "relax, take a deep breath and just play catch with Bo. Let him hit one to me because I need some practice. I'm tired of you pitchers striking everyone out." Stan smiled at her and told her to get off his mound. After one strike the batter hit the next pitch right at Jackee and she threw to first for the out. She then thanked Stan for keeping her in the game. In all the games so far very big crowds came to see Jackee play. She had not disappointed them. For the first three games she was hitting over .500 and it seemed she was always on base. In the bottom of the third with Sonny on second she lined a shot that went over the left field fence for her first homer run of the playoffs. She added a RBI double in the fifth and a single in the seventh. Stan finished with a 4 hitter and only allowed 1 run. Olympus won the game 6 to 1. Number one seed Braden University won their game so the first two seeds will play for the championship.

First game on Saturday, the consolation game to determine who finishes in third place, was boring. Both teams had that let's get it over with attitude. The coaches complained that the tournament should have ended with a double elimination format. The committee had thought about that but did not want to add an additional game to the tournament. It would be a consideration for next year. Patterson won the game and would stay for the rest of the tournament while the losing team was packed and on their way home before the next game started. Olympus had a short batting practice early on Saturday. They took batting practice very seriously but most everything else was taken lightly. It was now 5 months into the season and all they wanted to do is to get on with these final games. Winning the next two games would not only give them the division 2 championship but also give them a perfect season. Winning 42 straight games for any team is a coach's dream, and a feat none of the players will ever forget.

Braden won the toss and took the home team for game one. Olympus would be the home team in game two and if a third game is necessary a coin toss will be used again to decide the home team. Braden took their pre game drills first. The Olympus followed with a perfect pre game drill. The crowd loved it. It was an exceptionally large crowd for a division 2 playoff game, but since the crowds had been large in every game Olympus played, this was to be expected. Bo came in and told the coach he felt sorry for the Braden hitters because Zeke looked great. "He must be pumped up because his fastball was hopping."

The coach told the team to "just play your normal game and make every at bat count. There are no ties in baseball so let's get Zeke some runs." Jack got a single over the third baseman's head. Sonny was bunting for a hit but bunted it right at the pitcher. He smartly threw to first for the out as Jack went to second. Jackee was not given a pitch to hit so she walked. Jackee sent a signal to Bo who relayed it to Jack and on the next pitch squared around to bunt. When the third baseman broke for the possible bunt the two J's stole third and second. This upset the pitcher and he left a fastball over the plate. Bo lined a base hit to left center scoring both runners. Zeke was having his best game as he retired 18 batters in a row striking out 9 of them. Jackee hit a double leading off the 5th inning and scored on Bryon's sac fly. In the bottom of the seventh after striking out his 10th batter, Zeke broke off the mound to field a check swing ground ball. He caught his cleat where the grass started off the mound and twisted his ankle. Limping to the ball he did throw out the runner for the second out, but he was done for the day. After they finally took Zeke off the field, Thomas was allowed to warm up until he said he was ready. Thomas did allow one hit, that lone runner never even got to second. Retiring 7 of the 8 hitters he faced, while striking out 4 he earned himself a save.

Jackee's family arrived while the game was going on and they just found their seats and never tried to let Jackee know that they had arrived. After the 3 to 0 win Olympus players were on the field celebrating. Jackee went over to find out how Zeke was. The trainer said he was done for at least two weeks. As she was teasing Zeke, she spotted William who was waving at her. She ran over, but before she could reach them a crowd of young girls and women surrounded her. She talked and signed various items, but after twenty minutes she said her parents were here and she wanted to see them. Before walking to her parents, she promised to see them before the game and immediately after the final game. Carmela brought little William to Jackee and she agreed, he had grown a lot. William congratulated her on the game and also on their undefeated season. He told her that is a once in a lifetime achievement. The team knew this and were looking for the final game on Sunday.

Sunday was a gorgeous day as had been every day of this champion series. Jackee was up early and was looking forward to the game ahead. Last night, after church, she had dinner with Sonny and the family. She could not believe how relaxed she was. She showered and went to breakfast. Most of the players from both teams were at the designated place where all the meals were served. This had been arranged by the organizers of this tournament. There was a distinct feeling in the room that there will be only one game today. Olympus players were cool and confident, while the Braden players had their heads down as if waiting for the axe to fall. The two coaches were having breakfast at the table set aside for the committee and other special invitees. Umpires were not allowed to eat with them so they had special arrangements at the local hotel where they were staying. When Jackee was finished eating she went back to the room to get ready for the game.

By 9am all the Olympus players were on the field loosening up. They had a short batting practice hitting against a lefty, because Braden was starting a left handed pitcher. Coach felt the team was at its peak and showed it in the pre game drill. It was perfect and the crowd reacted. Braden took the infield next because Olympus was the home team in this game. When the two drills were compared Braden could pack up their bats right after they finished. Bo walked up to the coach and told him Josh looked even better than Zeke looked yesterday. Coach told Bo, keep him in the game and don't let him wonder off his game plan. The umpire shouted "play ball" and the game was on. Josh missed with the first two pitchers. Jackee called time out and went to the mound. She took the ball from Josh and started to rub it up. Then she said, "Braden is entitled to 81 strikes and if you throw one more ball I am going to kick you in the you know what. Now cut to the chase and pitch us a game to remember."

Josh smiled and said "yes master I will try to do better." He then proceeded to throw 9 straight strikes, striking out the side.

As they were walking off the field Jackee casually said "that's better".

For the first two innings Olympus hit the ball hard but had little to show for it. Bottom of the third. PJ Jinx led off with a solid base hit. Jack followed with a walk. Sonny, who faked a bunt, lined a base hit to left center scoring PJ and sending Jack to third. The first pitch to Jackee was a pitchout but no one was running. Next pitch, Sonny broke for second and Jackee lined a shot into right center, scoring both runners and she slid into third with a triple. Bo was walked intentionally and Bryon hit a drive that curled around the left field foul pole for a three run homer. You could now stick a fork into Braden because they were done. It was just a matter of Josh getting 18 more outs. Jackee was 2 for 2 with a walk when she batted in the seventh. There were two outs and no one on base. With two outs and no one on base, you have to get into scoring position. She looked for a pitch that could be hit up the alleys. In came a hanging curveball and she drove it to left center, only this ball carried to the fence and hit the top railing and went over. Jackee knew she hit it hard but didn't know the ball was up. As she was running hard to second she saw the umpire making a circular motion with his arm signifying a home run. The crowd reacted and she received a standing ovation. In the top of the 8th, the second batter hit a pop up down the left field in foul territory. As soon as the ball left the bat Jackee was racing to the ball. The ball, Jackee and the fence all arrived at the same time. She caught the ball, hit the fence and fell into the stands. All of a sudden she was lying in the lap of a 250 pound man.

He said to her, "I know we can keep any ball hit into the stands, can we keep a player who falls into our lap."

Jackee showed the ball to the umpire who called the batter out, and then she handed the gentleman whose lap she was on the baseball and thanked him for cushioning her fall. She also said "you can keep the ball but everything else you have to throw back."

He smiled at her and said "you have to endorse this for me because I believe someday it will be a very valuable collectible."

"I promise right after the game I'll be back." As she was going back to her shortstop position, the coach noticed a limp. He called timeout and asked Jackee if she was alright. Buddy who was playing third told the coach that she hit her knee hard before flipping over it. Coach called out Casey and walked Jackee off the field. Everyone in the stands stood and cheered for her as she left the field. Braden's coach came out of the dugout and was clapping, soon the rest of his team followed his lead. Even though Jackee knew there was no crying in baseball, she could not help herself. She hid the tears as best she could but the pressure of the season just came out. Four batters later Josh finished with a two hit shutout, and the Olympus baseball team won the division two championship and completed a 42 and 0 season.

Finally the celebration on the field came to an end and Jackee hobbled over to the gentleman who had saved her from a bad injury. She signed the baseball with a date, game and final score. She also signed her full name Jacalyn Jenco to make the baseball more valuable. The committee was setting up the awards ceremony and when the fans settled down they gave out the trophies. Patterson received third place trophy and medals. Braden received second place trophy and medals. Olympus received the Championship trophy and each player received a special medal. The MYP pitchers trophy went to Zeke Baker. MVP for the tournament went to Jackee Jenco. She also was given a baseball from the home plate umpire for Rose. William and Carmela hugged Jackee.

Carmela crying asked if she was hurt? Jackee told her there was a bruise but she has had a lot worse. William asked if the thousands of hours of hard work was worth all this.

She answered, "God must really love me because he gave me great parents and enough talent to be one of the best. I will try to never disappoint Him or you." Jackee now did her thing with the girls who were waiting for her. She introduced her family to them and introduced them to little William. All the young girls wanted to talk to him and Carmela stood nearby to make sure he was courteous to them. Coach joined in and told the group that reporters and tv people want to talk to Jackee and we have to get ready to leave. They said goodbye and Jackee gave a short interview.

On the bus traveling back to Olympus College the coach told the team that they had completed the greatest baseball season of any school in the country. "Our record will live forever and it is something to be proud of. It is silly to say this record will never be broken because almost every old record has been broken. Ruth's 60 home runs in a season, Drysdale consecutive scoreless innings, Lou Gehrig 2130 straight games played, Ty Cobb 104 bases stolen in a season and finally Ty Cobb total hits, 4191. Someday our record may be broken but remember you were the first."

When they arrived back at school there was a huge crowd waiting for the team. Cheering started as the bus reached the dropoff area. It got louder as the players exited the bus. There was an extended cheer when the coach got off, and then Jackee got off and the fans went wild. Emotionally, Jackee was filled up and ready to shed some tears, but Bo and Jack just picked her up and carried her around and finally to the reception area. There was a microphone set up and after introductions they asked the coach to speak. Coach Zimmer told the crowd that this "was the best team I ever coached and it could be the best team anyone ever coached. These young athletes achieved one of the greatest feats ever and they deserve all the credit. There was never a team that worked harder than they did. Everyone of my starting players at one time had an injury yet none of them missed a game. Our winning streak meant that no one wanted to be the reason for losing a game. They played above their ability for the name on their chests and for our loyal fans who supported us every game. This was their way of saying thank you."

Next, they asked Jackee to speak and when the cheering stopped she told the crowd that "this was not only a team but that they were family. We were as close every day as you are to your family. Outside of my family I have never been treated better than I was as part of this group. You have before you an example of what this country has to offer. A group of young people dedicated to a goal and finally achieving it. It was my honor to be one of the team captains and an even greater honor to be accepted by them as a team mate. Thank you for your support and God Bless all of you." There was a big banquet setup in the large cafeteria with enough food to feed an army. It was basically an open house for the players, students, and local fans. Some media people were there but only the coach was interviewed.

As soon as she could Jackee went to her dorm for a shower and to get some rest. Andrea had followed her to the dorm and waited for her to finish her shower. She then congratulated Jackee and told her that she might be the most famous female athlete in the country. "Thank you for those kind words but right now this girl has got to get some sleep."

Grabbing a broom, Andrea said, "have no fear, I will personally see that you are not disturbed." Jackee laughed and went directly to her room.

It was noon before Jackee woke up and she was still tired. Andrea came in as she was dressing and told her we have to go to lunch. "You must be hungry and I missed breakfast so let us partake in the lunch specials." When Jackee entered the cafeteria the students there surrounded her. After a few moments Andrea dragged her toward the food line. Both filled their plates and trays and headed for an open table. While eating, Andrea explained all the classes were completed and all the labs were turned in. As of right now we both have finished the semester with perfect A+ average and our final lab reports are in the hands of Dr Hopkins.

"I recorded our findings just as we discussed them and hand carried everything to Lucy." Jackee thanked Andrea and apologized for not being there to help. Andrea said that Jackee had completed 70% of the work so it was only fair that she contributed something. "I am being picked up on Tuesday and heading for home. Do you want a lift?"

"Since Sonny told me he has to go home and meet with the council, I Will accept your offer. My dad will be glad he doesn't have to make a big trip again so soon."

CHAPTER TWENTY

Jackee Starts Summer Baseball and Speaking Engagement

*W*hen Jackee arrived home, only Carmela and little William were home. Carmela updated Jackee on the family news. "Evelyn is scheduled to graduate this Saturday at noon. We must leave at 6AM to get to the school on time. Rose is scheduled to fly into the local airport by the school. She will land at a private airport about two miles from the school and she has transportation to get to the ceremony. Rebeeca and Rocco are also driving down but will not go with us. This will be the first time we will meet Jon's parents. Evelyn has committed to a job at the hospital where Jon is interning. She will manage the scheduling of patients entering and leaving the hospital. A new computer system is to be installed and she is incharge of setting up the system and seeing that it works properly. Jon has an apartment that she will live at while he lives at the hospital for his internship. I suspect that they will announce a wedding date within the next year or so. You of course know all about Rose and her great year in track?"

"Sonny keeps me informed so Rose only calls me when she has a problem."

"Dan is driving to the graduation with us. He offered to be the second driver if your dad needs a break." Jackee was glad to hear that since they will have only a short time before she has to start summer baseball.

Dan came over after dinner and the two of them went to their parking spot to talk and other things. Jackee hadn't seen him since the week after the New Year party. Over Easter, both of them had games and could not get home. Although she talked to him a couple of times a week, she still described her undefeated season to him. He said there was a big article in the local paper about this team with a female shortstop that won 42 straight baseball games. I read it over and over and never found anything about you, except your name. She told Dan that the winning streak had a life of its own. "When it first started there was pressure game after game and then a funny thing happened. The team just seemed to relax, everyone was loose and just looked forward to playing the next game. We entered the tournament so confident that I was afraid we were being overconfident. The truth is we completely dominated the tournament. Jack and I were so proud to be captains of the team. There was not one incident of disagreement on the team. Even the players who did not get into any game, cheered their teammates on. One other thing, not one of the players ever disrespected me. In every situation they had my back and treated me as a teammate. Now I'll shut up and you can kiss me."

Saturday at 6am, they started for Welby university and medical school. Little William, Jackee and Dan sat in the back. Since Jackee hadn't seen little William that much, this was a get acquainted ride. For almost 5 hours Jackee and Dan kept the baby happy. Carmela just sat in front enjoying the ride. Jon was waiting and showed William where to park. There was special parking for selected people and Jon had two spaces set aside for family. Rocco and Rebecca were already parked and waiting for the rest of the family to arrive. Rebecca and Carmela used Evelyn's dorm room to change and feed the babies. Everyone else used it for a pit stop. Fifteen minutes before noon, they were all seated in the seats reserved for them. Rose finally found them and said she had been delayed because of bad weather. After she finished saying hello, she took the baby and sat with him during the ceremony. Right on schedule the graduation started. As usual, very little attention was paid to the speakers and only the valedictorian commanded some attention. Her speech was about the world of tomorrow and how the graduating seniors should be the ones to lead it. Evelyn graduated cum laude in her computer management degree. When the ceremony was over they all drove to Evelyn's new apartment and found most of her things had been moved in. William and Jon carried in some more of her clothes from home. She will not have to officially leave the dorm until Sunday at 6PM. At that time she will check out and settle with the school when she picks up her diploma.

Jon had arranged a dinner for 5PM at the local country club. "My parents should be there as they would be flying in and going directly there." Sure enough doctors Jonathan and Bianca Zarrelli were waiting at the club. Introductions were made and then they all sat down for dinner. The menu had many items but steak and fish were their specials.

During dinner, the Jenco's and Zarrelli's got acquainted. William and Carmela thanked them for all the gifts they sent for the orphanage and Veterans home. They especially thanked them for the use of the villa in Italy that they and their daughter stayed in. Jonathan said he was glad that someone used it because they hadn't had the time themselves. He thanked them for having Jon over the holidays and especially for letting him find Evelyn. "She is so fantastic and since Jon has known her he is like a new person. For the first time he is applying himself and doing so well as an intern." William told them that he had three more daughters just like Evelyn. Each one is unique and totally different from each other. Both doctors agreed that if they had more sons it would be mandatory for them to spend time at your house.

When dinner was over, Jonathan and Bianca had to leave for an assignment in the Congo. There was some sort of an outbreak of something and they were in charge of bringing it under control. Two things they did tell William and Carmela. "First you are welcome to use the villa any time. Second, we know a wedding date will be forthcoming, so whatever is decided we want to pay for half of all expenses. Our family has many connections and they are available to you. Jon is our only child and we have almost no family on either side so the arrangements we will leave up to your family and Jon. He has our full power of attorney and our full confidence in his decisions. We live on the edge in almost every emergency we face and many times the outcome is not always a good one. This goes with the life we have chosen and Jon is aware of our wishes." William and Carmela thanked them for the generous offer and said that Jon and Evelyn will be the ones to determine what is to happen. Jon told them that all bills had been paid including 5 rooms in the hotel next to the country club. They all took advantage of the offer since it was getting late. It was much safer to drive home Sunday rather than late Saturday night. There was a Catholic church a few miles from here and there was breakfast for all the hotel guests until 11AM.

Evelyn and Jon came over for breakfast and the family ate together. Rose had to leave right after, because she had a track event that Rockwell was leaving for on Sunday. This was a huge college invitational which included domestic and foreign colleges. Jon was working Sunday so he left for the hospital. The family got Evelyn settled and then drove home. Dan spent the whole day with Jackee and promised he would try to spend as much time with her as his schedule will permit. Jackee told him she was thinking of not playing baseball in the summer. He asked her why the change in plans. She told him that it was very hard to only see him for a very short time in the summer.

"I thought that we agreed that neither of us would interfere in the other's dream. You are making me interfere in your dream. You are very close to actually living your dream and I will not be the reason for you failing to achieve it. We have come this far no matter how much it affected our being together and now with it in your reach, you want to put it on hold. Jackee you can not do this. I love you and want to spend the rest of my life being by your side. But right now that doesn't matter. There are thousands of young girls waiting for you to show them that the impossible dreams are really possible. When you were 5 years old and could barely pick up a bat, you took the challenge and every day you committed your life to reach a goal. Girls all over this country are waiting and praying for you and I will not be an accomplice in letting them down."

She was crying so hard that he had to hold her tight to stop her shaking. When she stopped crying she said he was right and that she was just feeling sorry for herself. Dan left a short time later and Jackee went to her mother. "Mom, does the pain ever go away?"

"I believe I told you before that the pain is how you know it is real. If there was no pain, Dan would just be a friend. Because there is pain you want him to be more than a friend and the greater the pain the more you want him to be." She hugged and thanked her mother and said good night to her parents.

Rose called to tell them that she won 2 of the 4 races and had a very good showing in the other two. Jackee received word that she had to be back at the school by June 30th. One day later Rose called to tell them that she was going to see Sonny and meet his father. They would leave for Olympus College together and she would drive home with dad. During dinner it was being discussed and Jackee said she hoped that Rose would not be disappointed in how Sonny lived. "You know Jackee, when she took your hand, she changed all our lives. I thought our family was happy before Rose, but she raised us to a new level of happiness."

Jackee agreed but "Sonny just lets her do anything she wants."

William told them that Sonny actually found the secret of Rose. "He lets her be Rose and only steers her in another direction if he feels she will be hurt. There is complete control of Rose but she is not aware of it. Sonny lets her be herself because that is the Rose he wants and adores."

Jackee worked hard every day and some days she worked out with the high school team. Coach Begali loved having her work with the team because he did not have one boy who could carry her glove. They were all dumbfounded when they saw her hit and field. There was not one boy on the team that could out run her. She took her workout to the next level. Every night she went to bed exhausted and woke up the next day and did it again. Last Saturday at home, she did a light workout because she was seeing Dan that night. They ended up in their usual parking area and for a while just talked. Later their kisses were very passionate.

Dan finally said "it is getting late and you have to leave tomorrow." Jackee wanted to stay a little longer. Dan gave in but would just hold her and not kiss her. She was very happy being in his arms and had no idea how much it was bothering him. Once more he said it was time to leave and this time he started the car and drove her home. They both agreed to call each other and will have a week together before school begins. While packing the next day Jackee told Carmela that Dan seemed strange last night. She tried to explain what she meant and

Carmela interrupted her and said you are teasing him far too much. Mom, I just do what we always do.

"That my dear daughter is what I am talking about. The sexual desires in a man are very different from a female. We spoke about this before. Remember I told you the sexual drive in a male is much higher than in the average female. Which basically means that men reach these desires much faster than a female. Dan reached that peak and had no place to go except home. He could or would not take advantage of you. I assume the two of you made some kind of an agreement and he is trying to keep it." She asked her mother how she knew about their agreement? Carmela smiled and said, "I have been there." They finished packing, had breakfast, went to church, and then Jackee, Dan and William started for Olympus College.

When they arrived at the college Rose and Sonny were waiting for them. Sonny and Dan helped Jackee move her bags into the dorm. All the goodbyes were said and then Rose entered the car for the ride home. A few minutes into the drive William asked Rose how was her stay at Sonny's home town. She said his father and the family were very good to her. "The father seemed to have Sonny's temperament. His step brother and sister go to Catholic school but the school does not have as many opportunities as our school. The father works hard but there are few luxuries to be had. I was introduced to the Council and although they treated me very well, I felt that I was still considered to be an outsider. They mentioned in front of me that Sonny had a 5 year commitment when he becomes a doctor. We both agreed that I would be by his side the whole time and that everything he owes them will be completed. Dad, I have to ask you if it would be alright for me to become a nurse so that I could better help him."

For the first time, Dan offered a suggestion, "instead of becoming a nurse why don't you become a doctor so you could really help." William immediately said that was a fine idea.

Rose asked if mom and you would agree to her doing that. He told her "it's not what we want but what do you want to do with your life. We will, as always, be 100% behind you."

While he was driving, Rose threw her arms around his neck and said "I knew you were the greatest parents in the world."

5am saw Jackee and Sonny working out. In between drills Sonny talked about Rose. She was treated well but the Council was not happy about their relationship. "You must understand that many of our best young adults leave our community and never look back. There are very few young leaders left at home. It puts a big strain on the community and it also means that our population is dropping very fast. There are very few advantages in staying home. We have only a few role models for our youth to look up to. Rose has offered me 100%

commitment to our future but it is hard for me to believe someone would be so dedicated. There is something I want to tell you about Rose, she is the most dedicated person that God ever made. She lets nothing stand in her way once she makes her mind up."

"You are now what she wants and she will not let anything come between you. She will never allow you to be hurt and your word is now her word."

"Deep down I could feel that but it would take a super person to accept my responsibilities."

"Believe me when I tell you that Rose is better than super, she is in a class all by herself."

Baseball physicals and orientation was scheduled for Monday at 1PM. Coach had most of the players from the team that was undefeated. The pitching was still very strong. Even though Zeke was drafted and immediately sent to the double A team, all the other pitchers were back and three new ones added. Freshmen Lefty Al Rasko, John KO Sullivan and transfer Bobby Jo Dugan represented a big upgrade in the pitching staff. Rasko and Dugan were lefty and Sullivan a big right hander. Each one threw over 90 and Rosko had a 12 to 6 overhand curve. Bo complained that "when he throws the curve and it bounces before he catches it, he has no idea where it is going. I'll have black and blue marks all over my body every game he pitches."

Up the middle, the team was exactly the same as during the Spring season. Nothing changed and the infield remained the same. The first eight games were done in one week. Most of the schools were local or summer teams. Two of the teams were made up of all college graduates and two were rookie league teams. Once the tryouts were finished and the pre game drill was perfected, the team was ready to rumble. Olympians caught the rookie league teams just getting together and dominated them. The two college teams were not very disciplined and our team's cohesiveness proved to be too much for them. All the other remaining teams offered very little competition.

Coach felt the team was now ready for the first 10 game road trip. This would be a combination of division one and two teams. Olympians were playing some of the same teams as the year before. Since Randolf was the closest school, games one and ten would be against them. Randolf had basically their regular school team playing and although their pitcher was very good, Olympians pitching completely dominated them. Final score was 3 to 0. Josh and Brady combined for a three hit shutout. The Olympian hiting was horrible and they were lucky to score 3 runs. Jackee, although she hit the ball hard, only had one for three day and a walk. Bo drove in two of the three runs. Following the game the team spent the night at Randolf and left Tuesday morning for Raider. As soon as the team arrived Marilyn Benson was waiting for Jackee. She asked Jackee to speak to a group of women at a local catering hall that evening. With the permission of the coach she agreed but said she would have to wear her sweats since she had no dressy clothes with her. Mrs Benson agreed and said a car will pick her up at 5:30 tonight. Coach called a practice to begin one half hour after lunch. This was a full practice which included live hitting. Jackee finished practice at 5 and took a quick shower, dressed and was waiting for the pickup car. She took Jack and Sonny with her. When they arrived everything was pre arranged. Sonny and Jack were seated with other special guests and Jackee sat with Mrs Benson. There were two speakers before Jackee but it was obvious that most came to hear Jackee.

As usual, Jackee started her talk with a qualification, "I speak to and for only women who have a dream. There is no way that I could speak for or to a man who has a dream. My dream started at 5 because I wanted to be close to my father. After a time the dream changed and it became me against an accepted form of discrimination. There were many great female baseball players. They even had a league and played for a few years during World War 2 and even a few years after. Probably because of lack of attendance they were put back on hold and never heard of again. The boys were given little league, american legion, industrial league and many other organizations to play in. We females were given Bobby dolls and easy bake ovens to play with. Now there were some sports where women did compete but not against males. We have track & field, basketball, golf, tennis, swimming and many other sports but not in competition with males. My goal or dream was to play baseball on the same level as a man. My father encouraged me every step of the way and I had a great many men who helped me to continue. Some used me as a side show to sell more tickets or get more publicity and I used them to show my skills. I don't need them anymore, they need me. A few years ago I met someone that became a part of my dream. He is not intimidated by my success and he encourages me to go on and not give up. Right now my biggest encouragement comes from young women who are praying for me and developing their own dreams. You should see the letters I get from young girls who say because of me they now want to try for that brass ring. I have said this before but I'll say it again, there is nothing wrong with wanting to be a good mother, good wife or good anything. These are all very important and necessary jobs. What I am talking about is the God given talent that each of us was given at birth. This talent is yours to use or not to use as you see fit. You are given the choice to use it now, later or never. Never feel that you are too old to try something new and remember to encourage your young children, both male and female, to be the best they can be. My personal journey will continue until I succeed or break down. I will not quit and disappoint so many people. It is my belief that Almighty God is standing with me and wants to see how far I can take the talent He gave me. God Bless and love you all and may He always have you in the palm of His hands." She was given a standing ovation and even Jack and Sonny were on their feet clapping. Jackee sat down for dessert but she was surrounded by young girls who wanted to talk to her. Later the three players were taken back to the college.

The game against Raider was a blow out as the team just started hitting and never stopped. Final score was 14 to 1. Next game was against a division one team, Melon State. Lefty Rasko pitched and Bo was right about his curve. When they just fouled it off it was a big achievement. After 7 innings and no runs on one hit, Lefty was done and Thomas came in to finish up. He faced 6 batters and struck out 5. The other out was a foul pop up to Bo. Finale score 4 to 0. Jackee again went 1 for 3 and a hit by pitch. She did score two runs and had one stolen base. Saturday was a 1PM game at UMC state. This division one school had a very good athletic program.

Coach told the team that according to a scout who has seen them play they try to intimidate the other team. "So, we will be a very aggressive team. I want you to take every extra base, run on balls in the dirt and steal as many bases as possible. Keep putting pressure on them and see if they break."

Bobby Joe was the starter for Olympians and Bo gave him a thumbs' up to the coach. Sonny was on first with one out when Jackee got and gave the hit and run sign. Jackee grounded a single where the second baseman had been before he went to cover the attempted steal. With runners on first and third, Bo ducked away from an inside pitch but the ball hit his bat and was a pop up to the catcher. Jackee signaled Sonny and Buddy that she was stealing on the next pitch. The pitch was a curve and the catcher threw to second trying to get Jackee, the second baseman seeing Sonny break for home, cut the throw off and relayed it home. It wasn't close, Sonny could have scored standing up. On the next pitch Jackee broke for third and Buddy hit the ball where the third baseman was before he ran to cover third. Olympians led 2 to 0 at the end of one inning. UMC State was now the intimidated team. Olympians took advantage of this and scored three unearned runs in the fifth inning. The score was 5 to 1 when Jackee came to bat in the sixth inning. She hit a drive to left center that cleared the fence. The biggest crowd so far on the trip was on their feet cheering. Jackee had a following at all the places she played at. These new teams are all seeing bigger crowds and many more women. Coach was still amazed at how the females were there and cheering for Jackee. Bobby Joe ran out of steam in the eighth inning but Arnold came in and finished the game. Olympians won this game 7 to 4. After the game the team was to leave for Rockwell University and have dinner when they arrived. They were to play a double header on Sunday and sleep Saturday and Sunday night at Rockwell. The bus for Rockwell was delayed because the crowd of females would not let Jackee go. Finally the coach promised he would make the next trip to UMC with a longer stay over. However they had to leave now or the team would miss dinner at the next stop.

When they arrived at Rockwell coach Cherrie was waiting and directed them to the athletic cafeteria. Coach Zimmer said his team was starving and would probably eat everything in sight. Coach Cherrie said "plenty of food is waiting and if we need more I'll send out for it." Olympians did not eat too much because they were tired and dirty. There was no time to shower before leaving UCM. Jackee had more to drink than eat. She took some fruit and asked about her room. One of the female trainers showed Jackee her room and all she wanted to do was shower and go to bed. Before she went to the room arrangements were made with Sonny to go to Mass at 7:30am Sunday. Sonny was at her room by 7:15 and they walked to a Catholic church. 8:15 they were in the cafeteria having breakfast. 9:30 the team was on a practice field getting ready for the first game at 11. There was a nice size crowd and once again females were dominant.

Rockwell had a very good summer program. Every year for the past 10 years they have put a winning team on the field. This year had been no different in fact they played in the division one world series. In the third round they ran into a left hander who was the third pick in the draft. He shut them out and ended their season. Although this was not their regular team, there were always enough good ball players to fill out the team in the summer. Rockwell took their pre game practice on the field first. The Olympians were next and they performed the infield and outfield warmup perfectly. The large crowd loved it and applauded when it was completed. Coach Zimmer noticed that the Rockwell players were standing around watching the Olympians, rather than getting ready for the game. Coach thought to himself, they were intimidated. *Score one for us.*

John KO Sullivan started for the Olympians and looked really good retiring the first 9 hitters. The Olympians had only one base runner in the first 3 innings and it was Jackee who walked on 5 pitches. Sonny led off the 4th inning with a hit up the middle. He stole second on the first pitch to Jackee. The second pitch was a curve and Jackee lined it to right center and slid into third with a run scoring triple. She scored on a double by Bo and he scored on a single by Buddy. Rockwell got one run back in the bottom of the fourth but that run scored when Jack and Jackee turned a double play. Jackee batted one last time in the top of the eighth and had Jack on second with one out. Coach Cherrie brought in a hard throwing right hander to pitch to Jackee. First pitch was a fastball right down the middle and Jackee got it all. When the ball finally landed it was 30 feet beyond the left field fence. The crowd loved it and Jackee had to do a curtain call. Thomas pitched the last two innings and struck out three and had three popups. Final score Olympians 6 Rockwell 1. There was a small cafeteria adjacent to the field so a buffet was set up for both teams. Coach Cheerie had never lost a double header and he was not about to do it now. He started his number one pitcher in game two and that pitcher threw a two hit shutout at the Olympians. Jackee went 0 for 3 but did get hit with an inside fastball. She also stuck out for the first time this summer. Her other two outs were line drives. After the game Jackee did spend an hour talking to the women and men.

Coach Cherrie talked to coach Zimmer about Jackee. He told him he had never seen a more complete baseball player in a non pro setting. "I heard she was good but seeing her in person was a privilege. You should be congratulated on having brought her to this level of play."

Coach Zimmer said he could not take credit for her. "What you see is what she came with. This is a remarkable young woman who has dedicated herself to the game of baseball. She knows more about the game than I do and her instincts about the game are amazing."

After dinner most of the players were looking to relax because Monday night there was a game at Hanover University, another D1 school. Jackee saw coach Holland and they talked about Rose and how she was doing in school and track. Coach Holland wanted to get her ready for the Olympics because he felt she had a great chance to successfully compete. "She is the best female athlete that I have ever coached. There is nothing she doesn't want to try and her work ethics are exceptional. No athlete male or female, can keep up with her. She has raised the level of my program by at least two or three." Jackee thanked him for taking the time to talk with her and he should take good care of her sister. Rose was away for a weekend event with the assistant coach and would miss Sonny and Jackee's stay at Rockwell.

Next morning after breakfast the Olympians headed for Hanover and after a three hour trip arrived in time for lunch. Coach told his team that at 2 PM there would be a round of batting practice and maybe a quick infield. The Hanover coach could not take a summer division 3 school seriously so he started his backup players. In the top of the 6th inning the Olympians were leading by a score of 11 to 0. Hanover had a total of 1 base runner who got on first because Buddy did not pick up a short hop cleanly. Brady Hall, a junior pitcher, has a no hitter so far. Coach Greymore, the Hanover baseball coach, could not believe what he was seeing. When he heard about their pre-game drill he should have known that this team was different. But he still looked down on D3 teams. Well, he was getting an education and even his fans had turned against him. The fans were cheering everything that the Olympians were doing. When Jack made an over the shoulder catch they cheered like crazy. Jackee dove for a ball going up the middle, caught it, popped up and threw the runner out at first. The stands erupted and the cheering lasted until the Olympians left the field. When Jackee doubled in the 8th inning it represented her 4th hit and left her shy of a home run for the hat trick. Had the crowd come to see if Jackee was for real, she did not disappoint them. A triple, double, 2 singles, a walk and 4 runs batted in. Her fielding was the talk of the crowd and the women could not wait to meet her. Coach Zimmer took Jackee out just as the bottom of the 9th was about to begin. She received a standing ovation and was directed by Hanover's publicity director to meet with the women in the back of the press box. These fans never saw Arnold strike out the side to end the game. Final score was Olympians 16 Hanover had 1 hit and a total of 2 base runners.

Coach Zimmer had to ask the crowd to let Jackee get something to eat. Before anyone could say anything Coach Greymore told the gathering that Jackee's team is holding a 10am practice, and was scheduled to leave at 2pm for San Jenerra University. "Weather permitting, I will set up on this field an area where she can speak with anyone who wants this to continue. With Jackee's permission it will be available to her at 8:30am."

Jackee readily agreed but set the time of 9:45 as the end because she had to be at the team practice. The two coaches and Jackee then went to dinner. While at dinner Coach Greymore told Jackee that her performance was "one of the finest I have ever seen on a baseball field. I wish that I could instill in my players the fire and determination you showed on the field. If you never pick up or hit another baseball, I believe you are the greatest female baseball player."

She thanked the coach for his encouraging remarks but she said "I play this game because I love baseball and want to be one of the best."

"Tomorrow at 8:30 we will see if your fans truly believe you are one of the best."

Next morning, Jackee had an early breakfast and put on her practice sweats. Sonny and Jack were waiting for her and the three headed for the field. Coach Greymore met them and told Jackee that these people have been sitting here waiting since 7:30. "Remember what I told you last night, this proves you are one of the best."

Jackee could not believe the size of the crowd and they started shouting her name as soon as she entered the field. There was no way for her to stop the tears from flowing. Stepping to the microphone Jackee told them that this was "by far the greatest honor I have ever received. I pray that every woman here achieves this same honor in their chosen field. For 16 years or well over 5800 days I have worked to get to this level. My thousands of hours of running and exercising and hitting have helped make this moment possible. I have never smoked, used alcohol or any type of drug to achieve this. It could never have happened were it not for my great parents and sisters. My boyfriend helped me to understand why this was important to others. Also it was people like you who kept me believing that every step I took forward, more women would follow. Please make everything I have accomplished a part of you doing your best. Can you imagine what this country would be like if every female did her very best. What I did was not to destroy the male image but in fact to raise that image to a higher degree. I want everyone to take that God given talent and be the very best that they can be. Ladies forgive me for rambling on and I will now answer any questions you have of me. The very first question was perfect. How do you think all the males feel about your success in baseball?"

Jackee asked Jack and Sonny to answer that question. Jack said that she "has raised the level of all her teammates. No team could have a better leader or a finer person as a friend. We depend on her so much that I fear we are pushing her over the limit. There is not one person on our team who would not protect her. Can any of you imagine the abuse and vile remarks she has had to put up with. I personally would have quit years ago if I even suffered half of what she went through. Her drive and courage drove our school team to 42 straight wins and a division 2 national championship. The best part is she was voted MVP of the tournament. In my opinion she is the female Babe Ruth of baseball."

Sonny told them that his girlfriend is Jackee's sister and because of Jackee, "Rose is scheduled to become an Olympic champion." This continued until 9:45 and as agreed, it was stopped and the three players got ready for practice. Very few in the crowd left and they stayed to watch the Olympians practice.

Around 1PM the bus headed for San Jennera University and a scheduled 7PM game the next day. The team arrived in time for dinner and was then set up in one of the dorms. San Jennera had just moved up to division 2 baseball and did not have a very good team. They were a science dominated program and class work came before anything else. There was no football and a lacrosse team was still in the club category. This game offered an opportunity for Coach Zimmer to give some other players a chance to play. He had to start Jackee because many people only came to see her play. Coach let her play 6 innings and then she was free to speak to the young girls who were there. In her 3 at bats she had a walk and two hits, one being a triple off the fence in right center. Jackee spoke to the group and once again stressed that they should do their best. These women were the most reserved group ever. They listened to every word and never interrupted. When the game ended they assumed so did the talk. They wished her well and thanked her for time spent with them. Coach Zimmer was pleased and the whole team went to dinner. The game was never in doubt and Drew, Bobby Jo and Arnold pitched 9 scoreless innings. Last game on the trip was against Cordia University. This was to be a Thursday night game and Friday was to be a traveling day. Stan Weeks started for the Olympians and pitched very well. In fact this game was a nail biter, and it really wasn't decided until Bo hit a two run homer in the top of the 8th giving the Olympians a 5 to 2 lead. Thomas pitched the final two innings and allowed only two hits. Jackee spent about an hour after the game talking to some fans and then had dinner with the coach.

Friday around 4pm the team arrived back at Olympus College and the players were glad to be back. Most went to their rooms and then to the cafeteria. Jackee was famished as she had very little to eat over the last week. Sonny joined her at dinner and said he was looking forward to a quiet Saturday night. Jackee agreed that after the 1pm game they would have time to go to church and have a relaxing meal. Just as Jackee was heading to her room the coach called out her name.

He took her into his office and explained that Braden had "filed a complaint with the league that you accepted gifts and that you should be classified as a pro and we should forfeit all the games you played in after accepting these gifts."

Jackee told the coach she had accepted no gifts and that these claims were categorically nonsense. Coach told her there will be a hearing next Saturday at the division 2 league office. Jackee told him to get a copy of the charges and she and her father would attend with him.

The team played 5 more games against local teams and won all 5 games. The crowds were still very big and Jackee was still the main reason. Someone broke the story and now the local papers and newscast picked it up. The team and Jackee in particular were swamped with calls for interviews. No one was allowed to speak in public about the charges until after the hearing was held. Saturday at 11am, Jackee, William and coach Zimmer walked into the hearing room. 5 men representing division 2 baseball welcome them to the hearing. All the charges were laid out. It seems someone from Braden found out that Jackee was given very expensive clothing and free beauty treatment including hair and nails.

The chairman asked Jackee to respond. Jackee told them that Mrs Ballard had asked her as a favor to speak at a girl scout gathering at the convention center. "I told her It would be a privilege for me to speak to them. Since we were on a road trip I had only my uniform or practice sweats to wear. She said this was not a problem and she would take care of everything. A limo was to be my transportation since we had only the school's athletic bus available. She also told me that I was to be picked up at a specific time. The limo picked me up and brought me to an elegant dress store where I was fitted with a full set of clothing from head to toe. Next I was taken to a place where I received a hair styling and a manicure. I asked for none of these but I had to assume Mrs. Ballard wanted me to look nice for the event. I asked the clothing store where I should return the clothing and they told me that they never take back anything that has been worn." The chairman said "but you did keep the clothing."

William now spoke, when Jackee told me what had taken place I contacted the two businesses and paid for whatever she received. "Here are the receipts and a copy of the canceled checks. These people charge a great deal more than we would normally spend but Jackee said they did a great job on short notice. " All the members of the board looked at the exhibits and agreed that there was no proof of any wrongdoing. William continued, "since this accusation was made public, it is our wish that you make public the fact that there was no wrongdoing by my daughter." All the members of the committee agreed and a public statement was issued.

William stayed around for the game and then went to church with Sonny and Jackee and right after he took them to dinner. All of them caught up with family doings and William began his trip home by 9:30. The team was to start their second 10 game road trip Sunday at 2pm. The first two stops would be the same as the last trip. Randolf would be on Monday at 6pm and Raider would be on Wednesday at 7pm. The crowds at these games were even bigger than before. A statement from the division 2 league exonerating Jackee of any wrongdoing really increased her public image. Now everyone wanted to see her. Jackee also felt that a great burden had been lifted from her and as the coach said, "she was on fire". Jackee was hitting bullets all over the field and with excellent power. This brought the whole team up to a new level. Randolf was losing after Olympians' second batter finished his at bat, and it only went downhill for Randolf after that. Final score Olympians 18 Randolf 1. Jackee had a perfect day which included a home run. She spoke to a large crowd of females after the game. This lasted more than 90minutes and the coach had to pull her away. Wednesday it was Raider's turn to take a beating. Once again, Jackee had a big game and hit her second home run on this trip.

Mrs Ballard looked for Jackee before the game and apologized for what had happened. She said that one of the scout leaders had a son who played for Braden. "It was that mother who told the coach of Braden what happened with your talk to the girl scouts. Please do not hold this against the Scouts. The girls love you and even offered to testify at your hearing as did I." Jackee told her that she knew it wasn't their fault and that "these girls are my biggest fans. Thank them for me and tell them I love them too." Mrs Ballard said "you can tell them yourself because they are all coming tonight." Sure enough after Jackee hit her homer all the girl scouts in the stands were on their feet cheering like crazy. After the game almost every scout had to hug Jackee. It took at least one half hour to finish the line of girls waiting for a hug. The coach pulled Jackee in the 7th inning so she could talk to the girls. Almost half the stands were empty when the girls found Jackee waiting to talk to them in the back of the press box. Stan Weeks pitched a two hitter and the final score read 15 to 0.

Melon refused to play them a second time so coach Zimmer had to book a division 2 team. Fulton State agreed to play after coach Zimmer told them of the large crowds that came to every game Jackee Jenco played. The Baseball coach at Fulton made all the arrangements for housing and meals. The game will be played at 6:30 on Wednesday. Since they were only one hour from Raider this would be an easy trip. With permission from Raider the Olympians practice at 9:30 on Raider's field. They had lunch at Raider and at 2 left for Fulton. At Fulton they were assigned rooms and then came out ready for the game. Fulton had a good team but was no match for Lefty Rasko. He completely dominated the hitters and he struck out half the hitters he faced. Lefty's pitching line was 12 strikeouts, two hits, no runs, no walks and not a runner for Fulton ever touched third base. Meanwhile Jackee was still on fire and almost had her third home in three games. The ball hit the top of the left field fence and became a double. Final score 8 to 0. Fulton's coach now realized what coach Zimmer was saying about Jackee. His stands were full for the first time ever. Even though most were women cheering for Jackee it still felt good to play in front of a full house. He also was surprised by the large number of girls standing behind the stands while waiting for Jackee to emerge from the field. Jackee spoke to them for 40 minutes before coach Zimmer asked that they end the talk so Jackee could get something to eat. They would stay overnight and practice at 9AM, have lunch and then leave for Rockwell. Coach Cherrie set up a four team tournament. It would start on Friday and finish on Sunday. Chester and Heartland Universities were the other two teams. Every team except Olympians was a division 1 school. Olympians would play the first game against Heartland and Rockwell would play Chester. Friday the first game will start at 5:30pm. The second game at 9. The two losers will play for third place on Saturday at 10am with the winners bracket at 1:30pm. Second game of the winners bracket will be played at 11am Sunday. If the teams are tied at one loss apiece a final game for the championship would begin at 2:30. All the teams will be housed at Rockwell.

Heartland University was a farm country team. They were farm boy strong and hit for power. Most of their hitters tended to over swing and their strike outs were very high. Josh had his curveball and change up, working to perfection. He did allow two very long home runs but with no one on base. Except for four other hits that is all the offence they could generate. Meanwhile the Olympians came out swinging and scored 9 runs on 14 hits. This ment the Olympians were going to the finals. Rockwell won their game and will meet the Olympians in the finals.

Chester and Heartland played on Saturday morning and Heartland hit 5 long homers with some teammates on base. The final was 9 to 7 as Chester made it a close game by playing small ball. Both teams stayed to see the second game. Coach Cherrie started his number one pitcher once again hoping to get a quick one game edge over the Olympians. Coach Zimmder reminded his team that this pitcher is the only one who has beaten them this year. He used a phrase that was used many times in Vietnam, "We need some pay back".

When it was their turn to take the pre-game infield, they had a perfect round. The crowd, which was very large, applauded and this gave the Olympians an additional incentive. Top of the first and Sonny was on second with one out. He walked and stole second on the first pitch to Jackee. She sent a signal to Sonny and on the next pitch he started for third. The third baseman went over to cover third and Jackee bunted up the third base line. Before, either the pitcher or third baseman could get to the ball, all the runners were safe. Two pitchers later Jackkee broke for second and Bo hit a single to right center. Sonny scored and Jackee kept on running. Because the center fielder had been playing Bo to pull the ball, he had to chase the ball down. When he got to the ball his only thought was to hold Bo to a single. The throw to second held Bo on first but Jackee was trying to score from first. With a head first slide she beat the throw home and Olympians led 2 to 0. Bobby Jo was the starting pitcher for the Olympians and he was outstanding. Over the first 6 innings, he allowed one run on three hits. His secret is that he walks very few batters and in fact he is always ahead of the hitters. This allows him to make the hitters swing at his pitches thereby giving him the edge. In the top of the seventh Jackee had her third hit, a double to left center. At this time the score was 3 to 1 and coach Cherrie ordered Bo to be walked. Buddy and Augie each had a hit and each drove in a run. With Olympians leading 5 to 1 Peter Jinx sacrificed the runners to second and third. Rocky Gilardi the DH hit a soft line drive down the right field line to clear the bases and he ended up on third. That hit finished Rockwell and when the game ended the final score was 9 to 1. Jackee had her usual meeting after the game but coach Zimmer stopped it after about 50 minutes. He told everyone that Jackee will be available after the game Sunday.

The Olympians needed some down time and the coach insisted that all the players turn in early and get a good nights' rest. Sonny and Jackee decided they would go to Mass early Sunday. They met by the field at 7:45 because the church was 2 blocks from the field. There was a light breakfast after church and a quick change into their uniforms and out to the field. At 11am the umpire called "play ball". Olympians were the home team since Rockwell was the home team in the first game. Brady started the game and after a shaky start settled down and pitched 6 great innings. He left the game with a 3 to 2 lead. Since his relief pitchers needed the work coach let them each pitch 1 inning. Jackee hit in the bottom of the eighth with one out and a runner on second. She drove a 2-0 pitch over the centerfield fence which made the final score 5 to 2. Arnold allowed one hit and struck out 3, Thomas allowed no hits and struck out 3. KO Sullivan needed some work so he pitched the last inning and struckout two while retiring Rockwell in order. Coach Cherrie had ordered trophies for the teams and ordered a special one for the winner. He had intended for it to be put in his trophy case but right now the Olympians were the proud recipients of the championship trophy. Once again Rose had a meet over the weekend and would not return until Monday night. Sonny and Jackee had missed seeing her again.

Monday morning the team left for Hanover for a 7pm game on Tuesday. The Hanover baseball coach was there when the bus arrived. He and his assistants showed them to their rooms and then to the cafeteria where lunch was being served. Coach Zimmer asked if his team could hold a practice starting about 2 o'clock. He was told the field was his since his team had a morning practice and was gone for the day. This was to be a full four hour hitting and fielding affair. It turned out to be just what the team needed. Overall the hitting was sharp and the fielding was very upbeat. All the pitchers threw batting practice or had a bullpen session. Tuesday, John KO Sullivan was to be the starting pitcher for the Olympians.

During dinner Jackee was asked to do an interview with a local TV station. She agreed if her coach could be included. The station agreed and the interview was held in the athletic office. All the questions except one were directed to Jackee and she answered each one as best she could. When coach Zimmer was asked how he felt having a girl on the team, he said she was probably the best player he ever coached. "She is the glue that holds the team together. There is not one other player who is looked up to more than Jackee. There has never been a time when a ball player, admirer, fan or even an opponent asked for help, that she did not go out of her way to help them. Do you know that she has spoken to over 5000 young women in the last two years. Many times she is hungry and exhausted after a game, but she never disappoints these women. This ladies and gentlemen is a woman in a class by herself." With that, the interview was over and Jackee went to her room.

Tuesday they had a light workout starting at 10am, then lunch and rested until 4pm. The team was assembled and dressed for the game at 4:30. Just prior to the game they went through their pre game drill and wowed the crowd. Hanover's starter did not get out of the 4th inning as the Olympians exploded for 6 runs. John KO was just throwing strikes and pitched the first 7 innings. He allowed 3 runs but the score after 7 innings was 9 to 3. Arnold completed the last two inning and he gave up his first run of the summer. Tuesday night was spent at Hanover and the next morning they headed for Kingston College and a game Thursday at 7pm. Kingston is a division 2 school and their summer baseball program is rated very high. Coach Zimmer had saved Stan because coach Littlefield at Kingston had said he may consider playing a doubleheader on Thursday or single games both Thursday and Friday. When Olympians arrived at Kingston they found out that Coach Littlefield had invited two other schools to play in a single elimination tournament. One of the teams was the last team that coach Zimmer had booked on this trip. This made it much better for the Olympians. They would spend the next two nights at Kingston then return to their college. Kingston was scheduled to play Mooney College one half hour after Olympians plays Howthorne College starting at 6pm. All the teams are division 2 schools except the Oympians.

The pitching schedule changed when the coach found that they would play Howthorne first. Josh now gets the start and at 6 PM Thursday he threw the first pitch. There was a large crowd on hand and they were very loud. They cheered the execution of the Olympians pre game drill. There was also a cheer whenever Jackee did anything. She did get a hit in the first inning that drove in a run and she made two fine plays in the field. The second one was a diving catch on a foul popup down the leftfield line. Since this was the last out in the inning the crowd was cheering as the trainer went out to Jackee. It was a combination of a sore leg and the wind knocked out of her. She batted in the bottom of the sixth and had her second hit, a double to left center. With the score 7 to1 after 6 innings the coach took Jackee out and put Gabe in to play short. Josh pitched 8 innings and Thomas pitched a perfect 9th. Kingston beat Mooney, so the Olympians will play Kingston the second game on Friday.

The first game of Mooney versus Howthorne was won by Mooney. Kingston lost the coin toss, so Olympians were once again the home team. Bo told the coach before the game that Stan looked unhittable. It was a good thing because there was no score after 6 innings. In the bottom of the seventh Jackee and Bo had back to back homers for the first time ever. Stan completed the shut out with the final score of 2 to 0. Jackee spent time after the game talking to her fans. Since the team was spending the night there, there was no rush to finish talking to the young girls. Coach did come over later to say that the cafeteria was closing in 15 minutes and Jackee had to eat. She just grabbed a sandwich and some fruit and went to her room. Sonny and Jack joined her and they talked for a while before going to bed. Next morning the bus arrived and after everything was put in the storage area, it headed for Olympus College.

Saturday at noon they arrived at the fieldhouse and every player helped bring equipment inside. Last thing was to take their personal gear off the bus and get it to their cars or rooms. Jackie turned in her uniform at the fieldhouse before going to lunch. Sunday it would be cleaned and laid out for her to be used in their 1pm game. Wallans College would be the Sunday opponent. Their summer program is stronger than their regular school program. This was true of almost all the summer teams that they played. Many baseball players wanted to play in the summer and usually join a local team so they can be near home. Olympus College did the same thing for years until Coach Zimmer changed and decided to fill the roster with only Olympus students. Olympians pitching was still its strong suit. Fielding was a very close second and hitting was third. There were 4 more games to play in this summer program. Jackee just wanted to get home and hold Dan in her arms. They beat Wallans College on Sunday behind the strong pitching of Sal Presto. Harriston was on Tuesday, and the coach selected Drew Driscal to pitch. After 6 innings the coach used Thomas and Arnold to finish the 6 to 1 win. Wednesday, they traveled to Johnson college, Bobby Jo and Lefty split the game. In the end, the Olympians won 8 to 4. Mooney College traveled to Olympus College on Thursday. This was a very close game but Josh and Stan held on to beat Mooney 2 to 1. The game was tied at one run each when Jackee walked with two outs in the bottom of the ninth. She was trying to steal second when Bo hit one in the gap in left center allowing Jackee to score the winning run.

Coach Zimmer called a meeting after the game and told the team that their Friday opponent canceled the game and the coach decided not to book someone else. "This means that everyone will turn in equipment starting at 9am Friday. I want to be finished collecting equipment by 3pm." Jackee called home and asked William if he could pick up her and Sonny Saturday. Carmela called Jackee later and told her to be ready between 8 and 9am.

William and Rose were there at 8:15. Sonny and Jackee had everything packed and were waiting for them. As soon as the car stopped, Rose was out the door and kissing Sonny. Jackee was smiling because she would have done the same thing if it had been Dan. She was also smiling because Sonny was blushing.

To help Sonny survive this moment, Jackee said to him "and she was always the shy one". Finally, they put everything into the suv, Jackee sat in the front by William and Rose sat in the back with Sonny. All of the conversation over the next 4 plus hours was about catching up on the past seven weeks. From the phone calls back and forth pieces of what happened were already known but a lot more needed to be said. When they arrived home, Carmela and the baby were waiting with a big lunch laid out in the dining room. Jackee and Sonny put their bags in the bedrooms then came to the dining room for lunch. Carmela was shocked to see Jackee so thin and told her so.

Sonny said that she never had time to eat because the women were always waiting for her after every game. "Most times the coach had to beg them to let her eat and get some rest. She truly is an amazing person. She never refused anyone a chance to speak with her and never refused to play a game. There were guys on the team who didn't do half of what she did and had trouble getting up for a game. She never complained and played every game as if it was game seven of the world series." Both William and Carmela were proud of Jackee but to hear Sonny talk about her this way made them understand what a truly great daughter she was.

While she ate, Jackee had the baby on her lap and he was just loving it. Carmela told them that unofficially Evelyn and Jon had set a wedding date for the Saturday after Thanksgiving. "You and Rose will be home and Jon's parents have cleared their schedule so they will also be available. Everything is supposed to be finalized by this weekend."

Dan called and Jackee explained that she was home and anxious to see him. He was at work but would be at her house by 6:30. There was no way she would see him in everyday clothing. Around 5 she started getting ready. By 6:15 she looked like she just stepped out of a fashion magazine. William took one look at Jackee and said he felt sorry for Dan. Carmela said to Jackee that she looked beautiful and "unless Dan is blind he should be very pleased."

Both Rose and Sonny complimented her but Rose added that she is every bit as beautiful as mom, "and I always thought she was the most beautiful mom in the world." Jackee hugged and thanked Rose beside telling her that all the Jenco girls are beautiful just like mom. Sonny got his two words in by saying he agreed.

CHAPTER TWENTY ONE

Jackee Has Her Sisters Wedding & Spring Season

*W*hen Dan rang the bell, Jackee ran to the door, threw it open and hugged Dan as if her life depended on it. He was taken back at first but soon recovered and kissed her. He then came in and said hello to everyone. William suggested that he wipe the lipstick off before people think you are bleeding. Dan told them that he likes shy, laid back girls and that is why he likes Jackee. Dan looked at Jackee and said to her that she is the most beautiful girl he has ever seen. She thanked him and said she made a special attempt to look like a woman and not a baseball player. It was agreed that she did not look like a baseball player. Everyone settled down at the dining room table and tried to catch up on the happenings of the last two months. Jackee told everyone about the summer season, especially the road trips. Rose talked about her meets and how she was learning all the Olympic events. She said the huddles were the hardest for her to learn. Carmela mentioned to Dan that she was "99% sure that Jon and Evelyn will be married on the Saturday after Thanksgiving. If possible try to keep that time open."

Dan said his team would likely be in a bowl game but did not have a clue as to where they would play and when. Williams told the two boys that "Evelyn wants both of you to be our daughters' partners in the wedding party. Tomorrow I would like to take both of you to the tuxedo store so that your sizes are registered with the store. If and when this wedding happens, I will be able to get a tux for you and have it waiting if you make the wedding." Dan said that sounds like a great plan and would make himself available anytime William setup.

Sonny agreed to the same thing. He did say that one trip home to meet with the council was necessary but that had to be anytime before the end of the year. "There is a budget that has to be submitted by January 1st and my costs have to be included."

Jackee and Dan were about to leave when Rebecca and Rocco came in. They had gone out for ice cream and decided to stop here on the way home. Rose and Jackee immediately took Frankie and little William into the den and started playing with them. Moments later you could hear the babies laughing and the girls laughing with them. Rebecca had not heard anything from Evelyn but she thought that this weekend everything would be finalized. "It is my understanding that both of them will be here on Sunday."

Carmela looked at William and asked if this was enough time to prepare a wedding. He answered that with his and Jonathan's connections it all can and will be taken care of. Carmela went over and kissed William and then she and Rebecca went in to see how the babies were doing. Rocco was filled in on what the other ushers were doing. He liked what William had told the other two and said to count him in whatever they decide. Not long after Rebecca came into the dinning room to tell Rocco they had to go since it was near the babies bedtime. After they left Dan and Jackee left for their favorite parking area and Rose took Sonny to the workout room.

Evelyn and Jon showed up at 11am Sunday with the news that the wedding is on for the Sunday after Thanksgiving. She had already set the date with Father Nicholas at St. Mary's. "There will be a 4pm mass followed by a 6pm reception at Big Pines country club. Between 6 and 7 will be a cocktail hour and at 7 a sit down dinner in the reception hall. Dinner will be a choice of meat, fish, chicken or vegetarian. Each one will have at least two separate choices. The invitations, favors and D.J.have been set up. Mom, dad, you have an unlimited number of guests you may invite. We just need a complete list and who is actually coming. You will have to help with the seating. The country club provides the flowers, cake and photographer included in the cost. We will have a special dessert hour after the meal and the cutting of the cake. I will give a piece of my bouquet to each of my three sisters and there will be no garter throwing. Dad, we want to ask you a big favor." William told her "anything below a million dollars is fine with me." "No, it has nothing to do with money, Jon and I are paying for everything. We just want to ask if you will allow Jon's father to walk down the aisle with us. Jon feels that since he is an only child, his father will never have this opportunity to ever do it." William said "I would consider it an honor and I think that both of us kissing you on the check before handing you to Jon would make a great picture." Evelyn immediately threw her arms around William and told him that "this will make his parents eternally grateful to you."

William called his friend and they agreed to meet at the tux store at 1pm. Evelyn formally asked the boyfriends and husband if they would join the bridal party. All three said yes and now all the men would be measured at the same time. Jon knew the formal wear he wanted for his ushers. His dad had a full line of formal wear since he must attend many formal affairs every year. His mother probably would coordinate with Carmela since her wardrobe ranges from hundreds to thousands of dollars. Her three sisters and a close friend would be the only bride's maids. Their dresses will be simple but elegant. The local bridal shop is part of a chain operation and they have a store not far from where Evelyn works. It would be a simple matter for both stores to coordinate the dresses. William told Evelyn that he would host the rehearsal dinner immediately after the rehearsal at the church. Jon and Evelyn both agreed this was a good idea. "As a member in good standing my American legion hall would be a great place to hold this non formal dinner. One of our members is a fabulous caterer and he owes me a favor. We would have all of Friday to prepare the hall." Carmela said the last thing would be a guest list and invitations to send out. Enelyn told them, "the invitations are being prepared as we speak. Rocco, Dan and Sonny, if you want anyone in your family to attend, just give the names and addresses to my mom, they are all welcome at our wedding." The whole family now sat down to Sunday dinner.

Dan and Jackee had very little time together since both had family matters to take care of. The following Sunday, Dan had to leave for football and Sonny and Jackee had to meet Dr Hopkins for the start of their new research. Saturday night Jackee cried almost the whole time they were parked. She complained that she sees more of Sonny than her boyfriend. Dan promised her that "over Christmas vacation you will see so much of me that after a while you will be bored seeing me." She hugged him as tight as possible and told him she will never have too much of seeing and holding him.

Rose on the other hand had Sonny's complete attention as she slowly kissed every inch of his face and then slowly zeroed in on his lips. Much of their talk was about their future. Sonny was now entering his senior year, which meant for him a college degree and first year of medical school. Rose was now a pre med student and when she completed the year she would be right on track as far as necessary courses are concerned. She reminded him that "next year it is a year divisible by 4 so that makes it a summer Olympic year. My coach thinks that my times in many events would qualify me today. He hopes they will improve and that will give me good positioning in most events. He is planning for me to do two Olympics as well as something called world games. These world games are held between Olympic games. I guess this is so the athletes can see who they will compete against at the Olympics." Sonny still hadn't said a word but he thought to himself, *we will probably have to get married between events at some meet.*

Back at school Sonny, Andrea and Jackee started in the lab on Monday morning. Work had been laid out by Dr Hopkins and his instructions were easy to follow. Sonny and Jackee still worked out each morning and after a new student orientation, workouts with the fall baseball team will begin. This team had all the returning players from the spring team and many new candidates. It seems last years' championship and undefeated season encouraged a great number of candidates who wanted to be part of the team. Coach told all the participants that everyone will get a fair chance to make this team, but only the best will actually be picked. The double J's were introduced as team captains and all were told that if they wanted you to do something, assume it was a direct order from the coach. "As you can see, one of the captains is a young woman who knows more about the game and how it is played than most coaches. Learn from her because she is the very best teacher. I have never heard her say a dirty word to or about anyone so I do not want to hear any such words used on this team."

For some strange reason, even though Jackee was completing her college degree and starting pre-med, it seemed like she had a lot of time for other things. The college courses needed to complete her college degree were easy and required very little work. All the new pre-med courses were a bit harder but still did not challenge her. She seemed to have a lot of free time and spent it talking on the phone or writing letters. Sonny and Jackee did accomplish one big thing, they arranged to have the Monday after Thanksgiving free to be used as a travel day.

As a courtesy to some of the away schools they played in the fall, Jackee made every effort to play in the games. She was still the biggest drawing card and any game she played in usually had a large crowd. Sonny and Jackee still worked hard every morning, infact, Jackee had been working on increasing her stamina and strength. Many other team players joined in the early morning workout. One in particular was a big addition. Hands Donovan, Bo's backup catcher from last spring, started coming every day. He told them he had to hit for more power if he was to take Bo's place. Jackee helped him with his hitting and conditioning but she went one step further, she contacted Bats and asked him if he could spend one day there working as a batting instructor. Bats agreed and a Saturday was picked as the day he would come to Olympus College with one condition: He had to be invited by the baseball coach. Jackee realized she had made a mistake in protocol. If Coach Zimmer did not extend the invitation, Bats coming would suggest that the coach was being bypassed. Jackee immediately went to the coach's office and asked him if he thought it would be a good idea to invite Bats' as a guest hitting instructor. She explained how he had helped her over the years and how Sonny increased his average by 40%. Coach thought it would be a great idea and immediately had his secretary send out the invite. Bats accepted the invitation and set the following Saturday as the day. There was no game that day since they were scheduled to play a night game the day before. Bats showed up at 9:30 and spent the next 8 hours working with Jackee's team mates. Sonny had a minor adjustment but Hands needed 3 adjustments and Bats would only give him two. He told Hands that he would help him with the third when Hands felt comfortable with the first two. Bats explained that too many adjustments at one time can lead to no help at all. He also made a suggestion to Jackee reminding her that baseball was a loose sport and you appear to be tight at the plate. She wondered how he knew that she was weight lifting again?

All the lab assistants were called to a meeting with Dr. Hopkins. He just wanted to congratulate them on a job well done. " A paper was being prepared to be presented to the Medical Academy and they were all invited to be there. Also there will not be any work until the spring so all of you except Mr Lightfoot, who will assist Lucy in making an inventory of all our equipment. We will probably resume work after Easter break." When they were leaving the lab both Andrea and Jackee kept calling Sonny "Teachers Pet". They were all laughing and Sonny told them that he was selected "because Dr Hopkins knows I need the money."

The Halloween affair was once again a huge success, more and more volunteers and merchants allowed the college to put on a great safe party for the children and the dance later that night, for the workers and students. Both Andrea and Jackee made a great effort to look their best. Andrea was dressed very sexy but Jackee looked absolutely sensational in her modest dress. When they walked into the room every male noticed them. Even if Stevie Wonder was there he would have noticed them. Their intention was to hang with the medical group. That was their plan but every single male at the dance was interested in the two stand out young women. There was not one dance that either girl sat out. Their only rest was when the music stopped or if they went to the powder room. Jackee danced with many of her teammates and had at least 15 offers to go on dates. Two medical students offered to marry her anytime she said. One young man had to be put in his place when he developed roaming hand syndrome. She made it look casual so that he would not be shamed in front of his fellow students, but the message was clear, you can look but you can not touch. Andrea was having her usual good time. She danced with many of the doctors, who were invited by the faculty. Olympus college and the adjoining hospital maintain a very close relationship. This six year medical program could never have happened unless both had worked very hard to create it. When the party was coming to an end Sonny offered to walk Jackee back to her room. Jackee accepted because she was worried that someone might follow her if she left alone. She said good night to Sonny and locked her door. On the way out Andrea had whispered that she made other arrangements and would not be coming back to the room tonight.

With only 3 weeks before Thanksgiving many little things had to be finished. The one big item was Dr.Hopkins' presentation to the medical academy which they were asked to attend. This was to be held on the Thursday before Thanksgiving. Since the fall baseball program ended just before Halloween, there were no other commitments except school work. All the lab work was done for her classes and only had to be turned in. Sonny had arranged with his professors that the Friday before Thanksgiving would be his last day of classes until the Tuesday after the break. This would give him time to go home and still be able to join the wedding party of Evelyn and Jon. He called Rose and told her his plans and said he would get to her home as soon as he could. Andrea made arrangements with Brett to pick her up on Tuesday and offered to take Jackee with them if she needed a ride. Jackee agreed and told Andrea that it would take some of the pressure off her father since both parents were involved with her sister's wedding.

While they were waiting for Brett that Tuesday morning, Jackee asked Andrea what was her relationship with Brett. Andrea replied that he was a very close friend and she thought a great deal of him. "Is he a boyfriend or just someone you see from time to time." She told Jackee that he was very special to her but she did not want to be tied down to anyone right now. "We both agreed that we could date anyone we wanted and that it would not affect our personal relationship." "I don't understand what you are telling me, how can you not feel bad if you know he is with other women." "Jackee, let me ask you a question. How many other people have you dated besides Dan?" "Dan is the only boy I have ever dated." "Then how do you know he is the right one?" "Because when I am not with him it hurts me a great deal, but when I am in his arms it feels so perfect." "How do you know you would not have an even better feeling with someone else if you never tried." "Why would I test other relationships if I already found a perfect fit? Beside my sisters, you are my closest friend but I don't understand all the sleeping around you do. Mind you, I am not passing judgment on you, I am just afraid that you might run into a bad or dangerous relationship."

Andrea said, "most times I can pick and choose who I am with and there have been times that I did not like how it turned out. But I enjoy the excitement and have learned a great deal about what a relationship should be. The time may come that I would want to settle down but not just yet." Brett just pulled up to their front door and both of them picked up their belongings and went to the car. When they reached Jackee's house she got out, thanked Brett for the ride and wished him a happy Thanksgiving. She then went to the passenger side and Andrea got out of the car and they hugged. Jackee said to Andrea "I love you and so does God so please be careful." Andrea said she loved her too and "thank you for looking out for me." They parted and Andrea got back into the car and off they went. Jackee stared at the car until it disappeared, said a prayer for Andrea and then entered her house.

Only Carmela and the baby were home and Rose was not expected until Wednesday. Carmela told her all the wedding invitations were sent out and all but two have been returned. "Evelyn and Jon will be here Wednesday to finalize the seating arrangements and country club schedule. Flowers and limo have to be coordinated along with the DJ. We need to go for the final fitting on the dresses and the men have to get the tuxedo's. Dad has the hall all set for the rehearsal dinner and they are being paid to decorate and clean it. Dan's parents are coming and so are Rocco's. Father Nicholas will say the prayers before and he will stay for the dinner. I have also hired a hairdresser to be here early Sunday to do all the bride and bridesmaids hair. Dad and I decided to have breakfast and a light snack for lunch. There will not be any drinking before the dinner at the country club. There is a room at the club where the bridal party can have something to eat and drink while pictures are taken. Evelyn and Jon will be introduced for the first time as man and wife when the reception room has everyone inside. Ushers will be told how to excort special people to their seats. Rocco has all the gratuity money for church and limo drivers. There will not be a gratuity jar at the reception. All staff personnel will be given an envelope containing their gratuity. There will be two professional babysitters to take care of the young children during the reception."

William walked in and after kissing Carmela, he got a big hug from Jackee. When they sat down to dinner, Jackee told them about fall baseball, school, her lab work and how Bats made an appearance at her school.

Wednesday was a hectic day. Evelyn and Jon arrived about 10. Rose was delivered at 11 and Rebecca came for lunch. Around 4pm there was a knock on the door and Jackee went to answer it. When she opened the door, Sonny stood on the other side. He was invited to come in and said hello to everyone. Rose was upstairs getting dressed and did not hear him come in. Jackee asked him who dropped him off. He told them no one. "Well, how did you get here?" "I walked from the bus depot." Carmela said "the bus depot is over 5 miles away, why didn't you call us?" "I know how busy you are with the wedding and all and I didn't want to inconvenience anyone." "Sonny it is never an inconvenience to pick someone up. We have many drivers in this family and other options are available to us at any time." "The walk did me good since I did not have a chance to workout today." Rose heard voices down stairs and came running down. She screamed "Yes " and ran into Sonny's arms. She kissed him and asked how he got here. Everyone said together that he walked there.

William finally stepped in and told them to "leave the boy alone, he is tired from his long journey. Let him wash up and get ready for dinner. He must be starved from traveling all day." Rocco walked in just as Carmela was putting food on the table. A few minutes into the meal the doorbell rang and Jackee jumped up and shouted it must be Dan. Carmela went to get another plate as Jackee was kissing Dan at the door. When he came in he said hello, kissed all the women on the cheek and sat next to Jackee. William looked around and said "the gangs all here."

After dinner, the girls prepared everything for the visit to the orphanage and Vets home. Sonny told William that his community was sending gifts for the children and the Vets but that would come the week before Christmas.

"You have to give me the names and address for your council because I want to send them a thank you note. Also I am going to ask my Veteran's association if any members have things they could give to your village. I know for a fact that many times there are things that become outdated but are still usable." Sonny thanked William and felt that this could be a good thing for his village. After church, a visit to the orphanage and a stop at the Vets home, the Jenco family settled down for their Thanksgiving dinner. First Grace was said, then William gave a toast, but before the actual toast, he thanked everyone for coming and he said how lucky he and Carmela were to have 5 great children who have. added wonderful people to our table. Raising his glass he said God bless and happy Thanksgiving.

Friday was a blur. Everyone was running in different directions. All the women, including Evelyn's friend Catherine, had to go for their final fittings. Only Jackee's dress needed some small adjustment as she lost some weight and firmed up part of her body. Three hours later all the women had their dresses hung in Jackee's room. The men took a real detour. Once all the tuxedo's were stacked in the car, William arranged for a mid day bachelor party at the local restaurant. There was a private dining room in the back and it was set up for them. Carmela and William had talked about this and since there was not enough time for a bridal shower and bachelor party this is what they decided to do. Carmela would have all the women at the house and Evelyn would open all the gifts Carmela provided. These were things she felt every bride might need. A few fun gifts included. William would do his things outside of the house so that the girls would not be distracted. William also provided gifts he bought for the party and most were fun types. He gave Jon two sets of boxing gloves so they don't hurt each other when they have a fight. A small whip in case Evelyn will not listen to reason. Also a best seller book in case he is bored on his honeymoon. One of the other gifts was similar to what he had given Rocco at his bachelor party. It was a belt buckle with a very rare American silver dollar. This silver dollar had a San Francisco mint mark. The men could order anything on the menu but they wound up ordering just the appetizers. This was a very unusual bachelor party because not one alcoholic drink was ordered. Back at the ranch the women were teasing Evelyn about how all the young doctors have affairs with the nurses and how all the female patients fall in love with their doctor. Evelyn told them that if she ever caught him doing something like that she would perform a radical circumcision on him. When both parties were over everyone gathered at the house and for dinner, pizza and other assorted appetizers were bought in.

Dan and Jackee only had a couple of hours together. They did drive to their favorite parking area but all Jackee wanted was for Dan to just hold her. She told him "It just feels so perfect when I am in your arms." Later, she asked him about what Andrea had said and wanted to know if Dan felt that way. "Jackee, I told you that I dated many girls before I asked you out. When I got to know you I knew that you are the perfect girl for me. Why would I need to look any further if I found a perfect match?" Jackee said "that is exactly what I told Andrea. Andrea said I have no experience in relationships with boys. But I only want to have a relationship with you and trust that we can learn from each other." Dan kissed her passionately and told her, "we have a plan and in a year or two it will all come together."

Rose had hardly any time with Sonny. Evelyn and Jon did take a ride to the country club with William and that is when she took Sonny into the workout room. As usual she was the aggressor and Sonny had very little to say about it.

The Jenco family attended church at 5pm Saturday and immediately after they had the wedding rehearsal. Following the Mass and the rehearsal, they would go to the rehearsal dinner . Jon was surprised when his parents showed up in church just as Mass started. Father Nicholas started the wedding rehearsal as soon as the church emptied. He thought the idea of both fathers walking the bride to the Altar was a unique idea. One half hour later the bridal party and families were headed for the veterans hall. Decorations were outstanding and the food was impressive. Everyone got to know Jon's parents and they seemed to fit right in. Carmela had been in contact with Jon's mother, Bianca, to coordinate the proper dress for the wedding. She had worked with Carmela on the invitations and guest list and even some seating arrangements. She also sent a gift for the bridal shower and it was a set of silverware for 12. There was also every other accessory included. The chest that held the silverware must have cost as much as the silverware. Evelyn loved the gift but asked when she would have that many people at a dinner party. Carmela told her that an important doctor may have to entertain many people. Around about 10pm the babies were getting cranky so the party started to break up. Catherine and her fiance Fred, who was also in the wedding party, were the first to leave. This was the first time that the other ushers met Fred. He could not make the bachelor party and he picked up his tux just before coming to the dinner. Jon's parents were staying at the local hotel and would dress there and meet them at the church. Rebecca and Rocco went directly home. Dan went home after dropping Jackee off at her house. Everyone else stayed at the Jenco's. Since Rebecca was the maid of honor Jon had asked Rocco to be best man. This worked out perfectly because in the morning Rocco would bring Rebecca to the Jenco's to get her hair done and pick Jon up and take him home to dress at Rocco's house. When it is time, the two of them will drive to the church and wait for the rest of the family. This changed when Jon's father called him and asked if he would join his parents for lunch at the hotel. Both should bring their formal wear and they could dress at the hotel and then all of them can drive to the church.

Sunday was a clear day with a forecast of 50 degree temperature. William was up early and prepared a big breakfast for everyone. There were fresh bagels, rolls, and pastries. He made a batch of pancake mix and had bacon and sausage on the side. There was a gallon each of milk, orange juice and an urn of fresh coffee. Half awake people started drifting into the dinning room one at a time. By 8:30 everyone was around the table. It was decided that all the women would shower in the parents' bathroom and then dress in Jackee's room. All the men will shower in the hall bathroom and they will dress in Rose's room. There were 6 women who had to shower so there might have to be an adjustment during the day. Evelyn thought that Catherine wanted to get her hair done but had not made a commitment as yet. Fred would not be at the house at all. He was scheduled to drop Catherine off, then go home and meet at the church at 3:45. Jon called Evelyn earlier and said he was going to where his parents are staying to have lunch with them and he and Rocco will probably dress there before going to the church.

The hair dresser came and brought a nail person to take care of the hands and feet. They both worked in the kitchen where there was more light and room. Maggie the hairdresser had a type of hair drop cloth that caught all the hair that was cut. This operation started at 10:30 and was complete by 2:30. Catherine was dropped off at about 1:00 and was the last one to have the hair done. Rose was the last sister to shower and Catherine got into the shower a few moments later. That meant only Carmela and William had to shower because the other men were done. Carmela finished her shower and started to dress. Jackee and Rebecca had the babies all dressed and packed, ready to go. William followed Carmela in the shower and finished dressing 20 minutes later. All the men were now ready and the photographer was starting to take pictures. Slowly the females started drifting down. First it was Rose followed by Jackee, then Catherine, William and Carmela came down together now everyone waited for the two sisters. Dan came over about 3:00, took one look at Jackee and wondered how it could be possible that she would look more beautiful on her wedding day. He didn't dare kiss her because if he messed up her make up there would be hell to pay. So he just went to her and kissed her hand while saying how beautiful she looked. Carmela for the first time realized that Sonny had the one bathroom all to himself. She forgot that Rocco and Jon were at Rocco's house and that Dan was at home. Here all the women were killing themselves to shower and get out so the next one could get in and a full bathroom was just sitting there.

Rebecca helped Evelyn get ready, but they had to slow down when the photographer wanted some early pictures of Evelyn dressing. They also had to take pictures with the mother and just before coming down some had to be taken with the father. Many family pictures had to be shot and because Rocco was missing they had to be finished at the reception. Finally the limos pulled up and William hollered game time. Dan took his car to the church and everyone else got into the two limos. As soon as they arrived the mothers were escorted to their seats. Bridesmaids lined up with their partners and the two fathers assisted Evelyn in the rear of the church. Everyone stood and the organ began playing, here came the bride, Rose and Sonny, Dan and Jackee, Catherine and Fred, Rebecca followed and finally Evelyn, William and Jonathan came down the aisle. They both kissed her on the cheek at the same time and a perfect picture of that event was taken. The crowd in church burst into applause. Then she walked to Jon.

Father Nicholas welcomed all in church to the uniting of Evelyn and Jon. He mentioned the fact that he had Baptized Evelyn and given her first Holy

Communion. He also Concelebrated at her Confirmation. "I want you all to know that I have heard most of her confessions and truly they were boring compared to some others. It is good that this couple choose to take their vows in the house of God. That they are willing to express their love for each other before God. More importantly they are asking God to watch over them and their commitment to each other for as long as they may live." The service continued until the last command,"you may kiss the bride." They then turned to face the people, who were now applauding. After a few pictures they walked down the aisle and out to the vestibule where they waited for their guests to file out. Once everyone was out they walked past their bridesmaids and ushers who were lined up on the steps. They were greeted with hands full of rice and confetti. A limo was waiting in front of the church and it took them to the reception. It was 5:40 when the full wedding party arrived. The Mass had taken over an hour because it was a high Mass. Now they were in a special room set aside especially for the wedding party. There was food and drinks and a waiter standing by to get whatever they may need. Most just wanted something to drink. Fred and Catherine had a beer but no one else took an alcoholic beverage. The photographer was taking many pictures and some included both parents. The babies were also included in the family ones. Sounds of the DJ could be heard so the cocktail hour must have begun. Jackee was holding Dan's hand and would not let it go. Rose was with Sonny and for a change he was talking to her. Dan and Rocco went out to make sure their parents had arrived and were introduced to others.. They should not have worried because William was seeing every guest who entered the room. He made a special effort to welcome both their parents. Both parents had been assigned the same table for dinner. Jonathan and Bianca were tending to their guests and introducing them to the host.

The wedding dinner always begins with the introduction of the bridal party and the new Mr. & Mrs. Bridal couple. After their first dance was underway all the guests joined them on the dance floor. Evelyn had selected her parents' favorite song for her first dance with her new husband. An oldie but goodie entitled "Because of You." Following this dance the best man usually gives a toast. Rocco asked everyone to stand with a drink in hand for the toast. His toast was a short one. "May Evelyn and Jon have a long and happy marriage, may they always love and honor each other and may they be blessed with children and most importantly may their union be blessed by God and may He keep them in the palm of His hands." He then asked everyone to toast the new couple with a drink.

A full 5 course meal was served over the next 3 hours. Guests had a menu of over 15 different dishes to choose from and each was individually prepared. The DJ played music during and between courses. Early music consisted of both slow and fast types of dance songs. Many of the older generation still liked the 60's and 70's music. As the night wore on the DJ slowly added the newer music for the young people. Bats and Kim were guests and seated at the next table to William and Carmela. Now that people were scattered all over, there was room for Bats and Kim to be near their hosts. Bats asked William if he liked to dance to this modern music. William told him that it is only dancing when you get to hold the girl. If you are dancing and not holding a girl, you're really doing aerobics. Bats agreed, it is definitely much more fun to hold a girl. Later, William danced with Evelyn to Daddy's little girl and Bianca danced with Jon to Mr. wonderful. Evelyn was supposed to throw her Bouquet to all the single girls but instead told her guests that she was dividing her Bouquet into 3 parts and giving them to her sisters.

"This is to show my love for them and for all the great times we had together." She asked her sisters and mother to come forward. As they did she gave the 3 sisters their share of her bouquet and as Carmela came up she gave her a special rose bouquet. She hugged and kissed each of them. All five Jenco girls present were now in tears, in fact many of the guests present also shed a few tears. She did not throw her garter but instead gave her husband a special garter she had made for this occasion. Together, they did a ceremonial cutting of the cake and the 5th course of the meal was being served. There were 5 dessert tables and an ice cream station that resembled an old fashioned ice cream parlor. Just before the venetian hour ended Jon and Evelyn said goodbye to everyone and went to a dressing room to change. Her gown and his tux were given to William and they went to the hotel for some needed rest. The next morning they were going to Aruba for their honeymoon. Jon's father had arranged a honeymoon suite overlooking the Caribbean for two weeks. All expenses were prepaid. This was their wedding present from his parents.

Carmela took the leftover wedding cake home. She would freeze it and exactly one year from now she would give it to Evelyn and Jon. Many of the guests were invited to take any dessert they wanted, bags and plastic boxes were provided. William asked if the desserts that were left could be delivered to an orphanage. The manager said all he needed was the name of the person in charge and the address. Before he left the club all the necessary information was provided for the manager. All the gifts were put into a special storage truck that had been delivered to the country club earlier that evening. William had the key and drove the vehicle to the side door of the club. The staff at the club help load the gifts and other items into the truck. William then took Rose and Sonny with him and drove home. Carmela and the baby went home with Rocco and Rebecca. Dan drove Jackee home and everything else that needed to be taken home. Many envelopes probably containing money were in a special bag that Carmela carried with her.

It took awhile for all the gifts to be stored in the workout room. They would sit there until Jon and Evelyn returned home to open and record them. A thank you note had to be sent to every guest and it would be a nice gesture to mention the gift. There was a strong possibility that it would be Christmas before all the gifts could be opened. The bag containing the envelopes was put into a safe that was secured in the basement. It was time to get to bed as it had been a long day. Jackee and Dan stood by his car. "I wish it was us going to that hotel tonight", she said to Dan. He agreed and told her "our day will come and when it does all our sacrifices would be worth it." She kissed him and he left for home promising to see her before she left for school.

The next day William had to drive Sonny and Jackee back to school. Andrea was already back because Brett had classes on monday, Dan kept his promise and before he left for school he spent an hour or so with Jackee. William made the round trip in 8 and one half hours. He had dinner and went right to bed. Rose had left earlier by limo and chartered plane. Carmela and the baby were the only people left awake in the house.

Sonny joined Jackee at 5am for their usual workout. Jackee said she felt bloated and sluggish. Both agreed that a light workout was a better idea so that we can gradually get back to normal without fear of pulling something. She told Sonny she would see him at lunch or dinner but she was skipping breakfast today. Her classes today consist of a lab and two other pre med classes. Andrea was in all her classes including the labs. She told Jackee that "there was nothing new in any class and you didn't miss a thing not being here yesterday." All the previous labs that they had completed together Andrea turned them in on Monday. "We do have two more labs to complete and Sonny has three. If we work on them everything should be finished by next week. There is one very important thing I do want to talk to you about. Remember our little talk about my dealing with so many men." "Yes I do," Jackee replied. "Well Brett asked me if we could get engaged for Christmas. He told me that every girl he dated could not compare to me and that since he could find no one better, he concluded that I must be the best. The truth of the matter is that I knew that he was the very best for me over the summer break. I could not admit it because if he didn't feel the same about me I would have been devastated. Without knowing why. I told him I always loved him and would be proud to wear his ring." "Andrea, you don't know how happy I am for you. My greatest fear was that you would one day run into a situation that you could not control." "There were a few that scared me but that is all behind me and I will never look back. There is one more thing, Jackee, if Brett asks me to marry him, I want you to be my Maid of Honor.""I would be proud to stand by your side when you and Brett take your vows."

Jackee was now committed to the Spring baseball season. She pushed her fellow players hard and she told them every team will want to stop our streak. "That means we will always see the best that each team has to offer. Because of that, we will have to be better than last year. I know it may sound impossible but we have to raise our game at least one level and that may not be enough." Most of the other players had not thought of that but then they realized that Jackee knew what she was talking about. Even at this informal practice they had to prepare their bodies and minds for the coming season.

It was hard for her to believe but her teammates were working harder than she had ever seen. They all seem dedicated to prove that last year was not a fluke. This intensity continued until December 21st which was their last day of informal practice. They all agreed to be back in school one week before school starts. Coach Zimmer notified the school that his baseball players would be back early and he wanted the school ready for them. Administration gave them the green light for their early return and all preparations were officially set in motion.

Brett and Andrea took Jackee home on December 22nd but Sonny went home to see his family. He said it was important for him to speak with his dad. Rose already knew she would not see Sonny until Christmas Eve. Yet when Jackee walked into the house, Rose gave a quick look to see if there was anyone else. She knew there would be only Jackee but she still felt hurt. Sonny was becoming the most important thing in her life. Even her Olympic ambition was no longer as important as Sonny. Rose had talked with Carmela about this. She remembered what Jackee had said about asking Carmela if there was ever a problem. She and Carmela had a long talk and Carmela gave her perfect advice. Her mom said the Olympics were a one or two shot deal but Sonny was a lifetime commitment. "You have pledged yourself to Sonny and his work while still wanting something for yourself. The problem you have is separating the two desires. Sonny could be put on hold while you pursue your Olympic goal. It is nearly impossible to reverse the two goals. So the choice is actually very simple. Give up the Olympics and your dream or put Sonny on hold. No other human being can make the choice for you. If I were you, I would go to St. Mary's, sit in the back and ask God for Help. When you leave the church you should have your answer."

First Rose did her workout without Jackee and then she went to church. She prayed for some time and began to cry. She looked at the cross above the altar and said "please God help me". A few moments later her crying ceased and it felt like a great weight had been taken from her shoulders. She stood up, got out of the pew, knelt down, looked at the altar and said "Thank You," then left the church. It was a 25 minute jog home but for the first time she knew exactly what she had to do. Jackee and Carmela were waiting for her as she walked into the house. Rose kissed Carmela, told her she loved her, apologized to Jackee, and went up to shower. Jackee looked at Carmela and asked what just happened. Carmela mentioned that Rose was looking for an answer and I believe she received one. "The only time I had that look was when I felt God answered one of my prayers." Carmela just said "there you go."

CHAPTER TWENTY TWO

Jackee Plays Spring Season at Olympus College

*S*onny called to tell Rose that he would be at the bus depot at 6pm on the 23rd. She said they would be waiting for him and for him not to be late. The bus pulled in a few minutes early and Rose was out of the car and by the door before it opened. A few people got off the bus and then Sonny stepped off. The passenger side of the bus was treated to Rose throwing her arms around Sonny and flat out kissing him. A round of applause from the passengers was followed by such words as, "you better marry her" and "I hope you two are friends".

Rose couldn't care less what anyone said but poor Sonny was blushing and said "let's get into the car." William welcomed Sonny and told him he had no intention of kissing him. Rose told Sonny that they had to talk later about some very important matters. William had no idea what she was talking about but he knew that Carmela would fill him in at bedtime. When they got home Carmela had prepared a dinner for Sonny and just asked him what he wanted to drink. Jackee had mentioned to Carmela that Sonny would not eat on the trip unless he brought food with him. He had very little money and was very frugal with it. He kissed Carmela on the cheek for the first time ever and thanked her. Jackee, seeing the kiss, thought to herself, *another breakthrough*. Dan arrived just as Sonny was finishing dinner and he said hello and asked him about his trip. A few moments later Jackee asked Dan if they could go for a ride. This was just an excuse to visit their favorite parking space. When they parked, Jackee told Dan about Andrea and Brett.

Dan told her that most relationships work out between couples who are sincere about each other. "Some are good, some are bad but few of them are perfect. When I had a few dates with you I realized that I found that perfect someone. You on the other hand had very little experience dating so I was surprised when you selected me to be your one and only." Jackee told him, "my mother said you are one in a million because you have protected me from myself. Now let's get reacquainted." ·

Rose took Sonny into the workout room and sat him down and then sat on his lap. She told him about going to church and getting the answer she was praying for. She said there were world games this year and then the summer Olympics next year. "My coach thinks I should be ready and at the top of my game when the tryout rolls around. After the next summer Olympics I will take a year off from any meets except school ones. This will give me time to catch up with my studies. Then I will train for the world games again and should peak in time for the next Olympics 6 years from now. I will retire after that and become a full time wife and doctor by your side forever." Sonny held her tight and told her "if that is your plan I will support you. Just be sure that it is what you want. You will still be young enough to compete 10 years from now." "No, It will be time for me to have achieved my dream and then help you to achieve your dream." They spent the rest of the night holding each other.

Evelyn and Jon arrived the next morning and Rebecca and Rocco came a while later. Now the whole family was preparing to visit the orphanage and the Vets. Dan arrived as the family was leaving for the orphanage. He took Jackee, Rose and Sonny in his car and followed William. The Sisters and children were waiting for them and started singing Christmas Carols as the family was walking in. They had to make a few trips to bring in all the packages. Jonathan and Bianca had sent about 40 toys from around the world. They also included some warm ladies coats for the Sisters. Sonny's council had sent all the leftover Indian dolls that were decorated for Christmas. William asked Sonny "if your people are so poor, how are they able to send these beautiful dolls here for free."

Sonny said all the material is supplied by merchants who can no longer use this material. "We have a business that handles all our mailing at their expense. So basically there is no overhead and all the labor is supplied by us. When an item is not selling any more it is usually given away. These dolls will not be sold again so they gave them to the orphanage."

"You should be proud of your people, even though they do not have much, they still are willing to help those in need." Sonny said he was indeed proud and grateful for the things his people do. "Putting me through college and medical school does put a strain on the budget, but I hope to pay them back many times over."

Once the baked goods and other goodies were passed around, it was time for the Vets home. Again Jonathan and Bianca sent dressing gowns for the Vets. These were warm and very well made. Jonathan sent a box of cigars for the New Year's eve celebration. There was no smoking at the home but certain places were designated smoking permitted areas. Again the council sent some items that the Vets could pick from, like a grab bag. Other Vets were also there handing out presents or just assisting the older Vets. William looked around the common area which is used for all celebrations and told Sonny that this group of men and women had over 200 medals for serving their country. These were combat earned medals and they did have one congressional medal of honor in this group. Originally William wanted to tape the combat that each of these Vets had experienced. This was not to be since most of the men who saw a great deal of combat refused to speak of it. One Vet made the statement that 'there are some things better left unsaid.'

Carmela, Rebecca, and the babies left early. They left to put the children to bed and also to lay out the snack Carmela had prepared that afternoon. When the rest of the family arrived home all the food was on the dining room table. It was meant to be a very informal snack. Rebecca was incharge of drinks and she had soft drinks and eggnog. The main discussion was about the Vets and how so few visitors they have. William explained that most had outlived their family and friends. It is not unusual for some of them to never have a visitor except for other Vets. "Remember that for 99% of them this is the last stop before meeting their Maker."

Sonny made the comment that "when America called millions like the ones that we saw, they answered the call. Now all we can do is put them in a holding area waiting for their final call to duty. We have many Vets in my village and they are treated about the same as they are here. My father used to take me to see one of the men he served with in Vietnam. He was with him when he was wounded but he would never tell me anything about what actually happened. I know my father has some medals because I sneaked a look at them when I was little. I have no idea what they were or for what they were awarded. Once he told me that if I wanted to go to West Point, it could be arranged but we never spoke of it again."

William thought about what Sonny said and asked if any of the medals had a type of ribbon that could be worn around the neck. Sonny answered he was not sure but one appeared to be different from the others. "Why do you ask?" William said that children of the Congressional Medal of Honor winners can attend the military college of their choice. "It is one of the rewards for earning that medal." He looked at William and said, "my father would never talk about this so is there any way of finding out what medals he does have?" "I could go through the Department of Defense records because all veteran organizations have access to most military records. I'll check into it later this week." Sonny thanked William.

Christmas morning was the usual chaotic time at the Jenco's. Little William was up early looking for presents. If left unchecked he would open all the presents but Jackee and Rose had just returned from their run so they guided him. Others drifted down slowly and both Rose and Jackee got the chance to shower and dress for church. At church the Jenco's were saved a full pew for their family. Father Nicolas gave his usual Chriatmas sermon and blessed everyone but he then asked his parishioners for their prayers and donation for the local orphanage. "It seems the orphanage has had it's funds cut off from the state and local governments. That is about 40% of their budget each year. The Sisters have asked the Bishop for help but the cut also affected all the parochial schools. Our church is full today because there are many here who only visit us a few times each year. Christmas, Easter, Palm Sunday and Ash Wednesday seem to be the favorite days for our church. For the next 4 weeks we are going to have a basket by each entrance labeled 'Orphanage', and all the contributions put into these baskets will go directly to the orphanage. I pray that all who are here will give whatever you can for the Sisters and the children. So we ask those who we will not see until Ash Wednesday, to come one more Sunday in the next 4 weeks. Of course you are still welcome even if you can't give anything." Father Nicholas was greeting everyone as they left the church and William asked when he heard about the orphanage. Father said the Bishop called him late last night, just after he heard from his sources that budget cuts were coming.

While driving home all the talk was about how to help the orphanage. "I am sure many groups will assist them in any way they can, it is just a matter of will it be enough."When they arrived home, getting something to eat and opening presents were the main concern. Pancake batter was already mixed, the coffee urn was ready, juice was put on the table and two girls started cooking eggs and bacon. Toast and fresh bagels were put out with the butter, cream cheese and jelly. It took 10 whole minutes and everyone had something to eat. Not long after, presents started to be opened. In the middle of all this Kim, Bats and the baby walked in and joined the present openings. All the gifts had been opened and there was nothing from Sonny to Rose. Sonny then stood in front of William and asked him if he had his permission to ask his daughter's hand in marriage. William told Sonny it was her decision not his. Sonny said it was the custom he grew up with that the fathers had to give permission before the proposal could be made to the young maiden. When he asked his father, he was told that the young woman Rose was the perfect match for him. He also said my mother would have approved and loved to accept her as a daughter into the family. "Now I need your permission before I can ask your daughter." Not a sound other than Sonny and William was made. This was the strangest situation because everyone was looking at William and they were waiting for his answer. Rose was in a state of shock and looking at her dad when he said, "yes, you have my permission to ask my daughter for her hand in marriage." Sonny stood before Rose and said, "this ring is the only thing I have left from my mother. I give you this as a pledge that I will take you for my wife for as long as we shall live and that I will love, protect and cherish you all the days of our lives." Rose ran to him and said "Yes!" threw her arms around him and kissed him passionately. Everyone in the room was moved by the outward profession of love by this quiet young man. Jackee was the most surprised because she never heard him say this many words at one time. She knew it must have taken him great courage to do this in front of so many people.

Dan came over later for dessert. He brought the present Jackee left for him under his tree and she had the present he left for her. They both opened the presents together and each received a watch. Jackee told Dan what Sonny had done and he too was surprised. The following Sunday as they were entering church Sonny took 3 wrinkled one dollar bills and put them into the basket for the orphanage. Rose saw him do it and whispered, "that is why I love you so much." Jackee who was walking behind them also saw what he did. After church she told Dan and William that he only had the three dollars because he does not get paid or receive his stipend until the end of the month. Dan said he got this and proceeded to ask Sonny and Rose if they had plans for New Year. They said no, so Dan invited them to his house as he was having some friends over while his parents had their party. William also invited them to his amvets New Year party but he made them aware that mostly older people would be there. Rose accepted Dan's offer but mentioned that they had no transportation available.

Dan told them not to worry as he would do all the driving and he would pick them up the same time he picks up Jackee. He told them about the movie and show tickets he got from his summer boss. "There will be a huge holiday show the Saturday after New Year at the convention center and I have 6 tickets."

On New Year's Eve everyone had some place to go. The Sisters at the orphanage sometimes baby sat to earn extra money. There was no set amount and the people gave what they could afford. The Sisters were always pleased to have one of their own come back as it gave them an opportunity to see how the child was progressing. Carmela and Rebecca both felt that leaving the children with the Sisters was even safer than leaving them at home with a babysitter. Dan picked up Jackee, Rose and Sonny around 7:30 and took them to his house. After all the introductions were made he took them to the finished basement where his party and friends were. Rose and Sonny fit right in and Rose did know some of the other young people. There was plenty of food and drinks and a music system that held over 500 different songs. You just had to select a key and a group of songs would appear and then hit the number of a song and it would be the next one to play. It was possible to program up to 25 songs at a time. There was very little hard drinking at Dan's party. Only one or two people had a beer or two. Most of his guests were athletes and since most were driving alcohol was not a drink of choice. Midnight brought on some singing and many hugs and kisses before the party settled down to just couples dancing or making out. Around 1am, people started to leave and one couple offered to take Rose and Sonny home. Jackee wanted to spend more time with Dan so she stayed when they left. When Rose and Sonny got home she took him into the workout room and sat on his lap. Dan and Jackee spent the rest of the evening dancing and later on cleaning up before he took her home about 3:30. Carmela and William had made it home before 1am so they were already in bed when Rose came home.

Next morning, Rebecca came and took Carmela to the orphanage . Both children had been washed, fed and dressed. A monetary gift was left for the Sisters, then Rebecca headed for her parents house. As they entered the house Rose and Jackee took the children and started playing with them in the den. William and Sonny were still up stairs but they could be heard stirring around. Carmela wanted to know if anyone wanted to eat. All three of her daughters said yes and offered to help. By the time breakfast was on the table Sonny and William had come down and they too were hungry. The weather was too cold for outdoor workouts so the three athletes made a schedule for outdoor running (weather permitting) and indoor hitting and working out. Dan had to work a few days over the vacation as his boss needed a few more hands for the seasonal rush. Whenever Dan was free he spent the time with Jackee. She felt this was the happiest time she ever had with him. It seemed so right when they were together. She was happy for Rose but she was jealous that it was not her getting engaged. She hated herself for feeling this way because she did not want to envy Rose, she wanted to be happy for her.

Naturally the next step was to ask Carmela what she thought. Carnela started out by saying that "Rose became part of our life. We love her as a daughter and probably gave her more than our other children. This was the right thing to do since she needed more because she had nothing. Now she still wants to be part of our lives but she wants a life of her own. She feels that Sonny and her could start their own life and still be part of both families. She has dedicated herself to Sonny and is willing to do whatever is necessary to achieve that life. This is right for Rose but it is not for you. You and Dan made some kind of an agreement. I have no idea what it was but I bet it involved your dream and not too much of Dans'. When he feels the time is right he will do the right thing. Just be smart enough to let him make this decision and not force one from him." She thought about what Carmela had said and all of a sudden she realized how perfect her mother really was. Crying, she put her arms around her mother and said "I love you and dad so much." Carmela held her until she stopped crying. William started to walk into the kitchen, took one look and thought to himself, *I'll hear about this in bed tonight.*

William had given Rose $50.00 in small bills and told her to use this money if you and Sonny want to do something or go somewhere. "Let him think it is your money and if you need more just let me know." She hugged and kissed her dad for understanding that Sonny is too proud to ask or accept anything but he may accept something from his future wife. There was a little back and forth but Sonny finally agreed to have Rose pay if they needed something. The holiday show at the convention center was a great show and after, Dan suggested they go for a pizza. While the girls were busy signing autographs and talking to everyone because both were celebrities, the boyfriends just sat there and enjoyed the pizza and soft drinks. It was exactly the same the following date, when they went to the movie and then for their sundae.

Jackee was having the best time with Dan. He spent every free day by her side and she was enjoying every minute of it. One fear kept her awake some nights. She had always been able to separate herself from all outside interests when she was playing baseball. This was a quality that all great baseball players have. The ability to focus for the entire length of the game takes great concentration and she always had the ability to do that. Now there was a dent in her armor and that was Dan. Would she be able to play at that high level if she had him in the back of her mind? This doubt scared her because she never had to deal with it. Their time together was running out, since Dan had to leave for lacrosse camp next Sunday. Friday night was not too bad but Saturday night all she did was cry when they went to their favorite parking spot.

Dan began by saying that this was his final year and he was going to make it his best ever. He had no place else to go once his college days were over. "You still have another year if you want to play and you do know that some team will draft you to play in the minors. This is the chance you worked for all your life and nothing, not even me, should stand in your way. For the last two seasons you have achieved more than any other female ever has. You have a following that is in the millions and you must never let them down. Promise me that starting Monday you will dedicate yourself to being the best baseball player you can be. Dedicate this next year to all the girls that had a dream but were never able to try for it."

Jackee looked into his eyes and told him that she would do it if he told her that he loved her. He held her close and told her that "someday soon you will be my wife for the rest of my life." He then kissed her and took her home.

Dan left for school immediately after church. He drove his own car to school. There were two other players he had to pick up on the way. Jackee was glad that he would have company on the drive. Last night she came to terms with herself and now felt that drive that she thought was lost. Starting Monday the three of them worked hard on their individual skills. Sonny and Jackee started strength training and both were getting much stronger. Both their hitting was close to mid season form. The high school coach let them throw in the gym and hit in his indoor batting cage. Rose had them running with her and they were building up their stamina. Coach Begali had some of his pitchers throw indoor batting practice to them. By the time Jackee and Sonny got back to school, they were both in great condition.

The 5am practice was now attended by almost all the returning baseball players. Even some candidates for tryouts came down to workout. Tyler Rosier, a freshman infielder, was being groomed to fill Jack's shoes. Jackee had been so comfortable with Jack that now it seemed strange that he would not be there. She asked Tyler and the backup infielder, Matt Murray, to start working out with her. Both came and she was pleased by their positive attitude. It wasn't long before Jackee decided that Tyler was the better of the two candidates. Tyler had a stronger arm, was faster getting rid of the ball, and seemed to be a more disciplined hitter. Coach Zimmer felt Tyler should be the lead off hitter since he had good speed and seldom struck out. There was also the fact that he enjoyed working with Jackee because Jack had told him that she will make you a better player. Matt would be the backup second baseman if Tyler or Jackee could not play. Tyler would play short if Jackee did not play because he had the stronger arm and the better range. Tryouts officially started February 1st and as most years it meant indoor practice. If Tyler played well the team should be very strong up the middle. Hands Donovan looked to be in excellent condition and his arm is stronger than Bo's. The outfielders were all very fast but Sonny was still the fastest runner on the team. Pitching had to be rebuilt since 4 of the top pitchers graduated. The team did add two good short relievers in freshman Hook Carson and transfer sophomore Sid Lunker. A very important transfer was sophomore Specs Glasser. He was a big lefty with a big kick and an overhand fastball close to three digits. His only problem was that he was not sure where the ball was going after he released it. Coach has set up a special string strike zone that the old Brooklyn Dodgers used for their pitchers. Dexter Wright and Toby Knight are two promising freshmen who should be excellent pitchers once they gain some experience. One very important addition was Roscoe Renalds. He was a backup outfielder, pitcher and DH. There was a rumor that he can also catch in an emergency. Supposedly he was an excellent hitter with absolutely no speed. There was a joke around that when they timed him from home to first, instead of a stop watch they used a calendar.

First day of outdoor practice was sunny but cold. In less than 10 days the coach made his final cuts and the team was ready to scrimmage. Brady, Drew, Bobby Jo, Lefty and John would be the starting rotation. If the team scored some runs these pitchers should do very well. In the 5 scrimmages prior to opening the league season the starting pitchers allowed one earned run and the two relievers allowed none. Hook did not even allow a base hit. He faced 15 batters and got 15 outs. Sid allowed one hit and one walk but otherwise shut the opposing team down. Hitting was a problem, the team seemed to struggle to drive in runs. There were plenty of men on base but too many were left on. Jackee was talking to coach Zimmer and suggested that maybe the team needed another Bats' day. Coach told her that was a great suggestion and he would call Bats as soon as practice was over. Later he saw Jackee leaving the field house and said Bats will be there on Sunday for a clinic. Jackee was happy because she knew that Bats would get the team's hitting on track.

Sunday at 9am Bats was on the field, ready to go. First he watched the players hit in the batting cage. He then watched them hit live pitching. Three of the starters were trying to hit a homerun every time up. That means they were not getting good wood on the outside pitch and hitting weak ground balls on the curve ball. The adjustment was simple especially when they learned these balls could be hit to right center with power. Bats asked Stretch Ward if he ever wore glasses. Ward said he did but not for playing baseball. Bats told him to get his glasses and come out to hit again. When he finally came out with his glasses, Bats put him up against live pitching and he began hitting the ball. As he adjusted his swing it was like a miracle. He said the ball looked like a softball instead of a golf ball. Bats told coach Zimmer that the pre-season physical does not always pick up an eye problem. "You should have a hand eye coordination test because they are more accurate." There were other minor adjustments here and there but nothing more serious. Coach Zimmer thanked Bats for his time and told him the school would send a stipend for your travel. Jackee hugged Bats and beside thanking him asked about Kim and the baby. He said "Kim and the baby are fine and George Herman is going to have a new playmate this summer." "That is great news and I'll call Kim soon to congratulate her."

The league opener was set for Monday but it rained so the game was moved to Tuesday. Randolf showed up for the first of three games they were to play for the season. Brady started for the Olympians and pitched six shutout innings. Toby, Specs and Dexter threw one inning each to finish the game. Specs had a weird inning, he walked three and struck out three, no one hit the ball. Dexter allowed two runs before getting the final out. His first college inning and it showed. Final score was 8 to 2. There was a large crowd for this time of year and as usual Jackee was the reason. She had a perfect day with 3 hits and two walks, two stolen bases, three runs scored and one RBI. She spent over an hour after the game, in the cold, talking with the women and the media. Olympus college has never had so much media coverage. Everyone was interviewed from time to time. Players, coaches, administration and even the fans had some media coverage. Game two against Melon State was on Thursday. The Olympus team got there early and for the 4pm start. When it came time for their pregame fielding practice the team performed the drill to perfection. This as usual drew applause from the crowd. Jackee was the center of attraction and she reacted early by hitting a home run with one on in the first inning. As the Olympus team was to find out over the course of the season, most teams held out their number one pitcher to face them. Melon had a hard throwing right hander who was going to show Jackee who was the best. He tried to throw a fastball by her but got it belt high and over the middle of the plate. Jackee just used her coordination and his speed to send the ball over the left field fence. The ball was retrieved for her collection. The next time up the pitcher gave Jackee a I'm not happy about you showing me up pitch. The inside pitch hit the top of her helmet as she hit the dirt. A warning went out to both benches. Drew was the starter for Olympus and he pitched seven fine innings allowing only 2 runs and no walks. Sid and Hooks finished the game with 6 straight outs. Final score 5 to 2. Jackee had 1 hit, two walks and one hit by pitch. Next was a three game series against the Raider. Double header on Saturday and a single game Sunday. Olympus won all three easily and was now 5 and 0 for the season. They played 5 more games the next week and won all 5. On Tuesday they traveled to Hanover, a D1 school to play a 4pm game. This game drew a very large crowd and a lot of media coverage. Hanover was ready with their number 1 and 2 pitchers. The game was well played and neither side made an error. In the fourth inning Jackee led off with a double and after one out she stole third. Peter Jinx hit a line drive near third and the third baseman dove for the ball, caught it and fell on third base before Jackee could get back. Hanover scored two runs in the sixth to take a 2 to 0 lead. In the top of the eighth with one out Sonny and Jackee singled to put runners on first and third. Hands hit a ground ball up the middle but the shortstop got to it and flipped it to the second baseman who started to throw to first but Jackee slid into him and knocked him off his feet. The run scored but Olympus never had another base runner. Their winning streak ended after 56 games and the Hanover crowd went wild. Jackee's only comment was that Hanover played a great game and should be congratulated. Coach Zimmer said all streaks come to an end and Hanover played a great game. He also said that a new streak starts tomorrow.

Coach had been right, for the next 10 games the Olympus baseball team was on fire. Jackee had talked to the team before their next game against Randolf. She told them they were every bit as good as last year's team. "The only way a team as good as we are can lose is if we beat ourselves. Let's show these teams who we really are. Only together can we do this. Today starts the rest of the season and a new winning streak."

Come out they did. None of the games were even close. Pitching was outstanding, their earned run average for these 10 games was 1.15. Every hitter in the line up was hitting above their usual average. Fielding was spectacular, there wasn't a fly ball that fell safely in the outfield. It appeared that they had seven players in the infield instead of five. No ground balls or pop ups became hits. No starting pitcher threw more than 100 pitches in any game. Infact Brady and Lefty pitched complete games throwing under 100 pitches. Coach could not have been happier. Last years' team had the winning streak to keep them up for every game. This team had to assume their own identity. Once the streak ended, it forced them to set their own goals. Jackee was the captain and leader of the team. She was leading the team in hitting, walks, hits and had not made an error or struck out. Even opposing team players showed respect for her. There were no more off color remarks and it seemed that now she was just another player. The fans saw it totally differently. Crowds of females came to see and talk to her. There was not one organization who didn't want her to speak at their event. Coach could not understand how she accommodated so many of their requests and still brought her A game to the field every game. Coach did notice that she lost some weight. When he suggested a rest might do her good, she refused saying, "the team expects me to be there every game." Coach asked the nurse to look her over to make sure everything was alright. The nurse came back and told him she had multiple bruises,scrapes and black and blue marks but she was good to play.

For the next two weeks they would be on the road playing 10 games in seven different colleges. They won all 5 games the first week including a double header on Sunday against Cordia University, a D1 school. Next week got a little harder. Game on Monday was easy but in the game on Wednesday, Jackee dove for a foul pop fly down the left field line and hit her chest very hard. She finished the inning but the coach took her out of the game and sent her to the dispensary. After the game he talked to the nurse and she told him that Jackee had a bad bruise on the left side of her chest. It made breathing very difficult. Since there was an off day on Thursday, he told Jackee to rest until Friday. She wanted to play but the coach insisted that she could coach first and get ready for the double header on Saturday. She did mention to him about Tyler playing shortstop and Matt starting at second. Coach thought that it was a good suggestion. Friday's game would be the first start for Specs. While he was warming up before the game, Jackee was watching and talking to him. She mentioned that he should pitch exactly like he did warming up. "Just make believe you are playing catch with Hands." That is precisely what he did. He did walk 5 batters but he also struck out 14 and did not walk anyone after the fifth inning. Coach let him pitch 7 innings but took him out after 110 pitches. This gave Olympus their 18th consecutive win. Jackee had rested all day Thursday except for a treatment that the nurse gave her before she left for Friday's game. Saturday was special to her because they were playing Rockwell, a doubleheader and she would see Rose.

Rose was waiting for Jackee and Sonny as their bus pulled up to the field house at Rockwell. She hugged both of them and had a special kiss for Sonny. Jackee introduced her to the team. Rose already knew the coach and some members from last year. Coach Cherrie welcomed them and showed them to the locker room where some light food was set up. It was 11am and the double header was to start at 1:30PM. They would spend the night at Rockwell before heading home on Sunday after breakfast. Most of the players drank more than they ate but some food was consumed. Rose took Jackee to the female locker room where she changed into her uniform. She could not wear her chest strap because when she put it on, it was difficult to breathe. The nurse had given Jackee a soft cotton padded bra and although it caused some discomfort she could breath but more important she was able to run. There was no doubt that she still had some pain or at least some discomfort but she was determined to play. Major league scouts had been following the team since early April. Jackee was eligible for the draft since she was a junior. Many teams had shown some interest in her but none had yet made any kind of offer. When Olympus went out to practice they noticed a large group of scouts standing behind the backstop. As usual Jackee ignored any activity before the game except her preparation for the game ahead. Coach Zimmer told the group about Jackee's injury and hoped that they would not hold it against her. Game one was to start as soon as Olympus finished their pre game field drill. This drill was perfect and Jackee showed no signs of slowing down. Coach Cherrie had saved his best pitchers for these two games. He was not about to lose two more games to this division 3 team.

Jackee was up with two on and no outs in the top of the first inning and she caught a 2 and 0 fastball and drove it over the centerfield fence. The Rockwell crowd again, mostly women cheered until Jackee made a curtain call. This first game was supposed to have the number one pitcher on each team pitch. Coach Cherrie held back his number one for the second game. He had hoped to sweep both games but decided that even a split would be better than a double loss. Brady started for Olympic and gave up only one run in seven innings. With the score 5 to 1 coach Zimmer decided to give Toby and Sid some work. Both pitchers retired the side in order. Game two was a pitchers duel and the game was tied at one going into the ninth inning. There had been great plays on both teams to keep the score tied. Jackee made an over the shoulder catch with runners on to end the 6th inning. In the top of the 6th Jackee hit a line drive that was headed down the leftfield line and would have scored Sonny from first except the third baseman dove and caught the ball in the webbing of his glove. Top of the ninth Sonny walked with two outs. Jackee put the hit and run on with Sonny and she hit a ground ball where the second baseman had been before he went to cover second on the steal. With runners on first and third and two outs, Jackee broke for second as the catcher threw to second Sonny broke for home and scored before the second baseman could return the throw. Jackee had stopped short of second because she wanted Sonny to score before she was tagged out. Hook Carson struck out the side in the bottom of the 9th to nail down the 2 to 1 victory. Jackee had 3hits, 4walks in 8 at bats and now with Rose by her side she had to talk to the fans after the game. This talk was different because some of the young ladies wanted to hear what Rose had to say. Rose has built up a big following of her own. The local papers are full of her Olympic potential. Jackee gave Rose her home run ball and Rose would add it to her collection of over 50 balls all carefully labeled with date, team and score.

Dinner was served at the athletes dining area. Rose joined Sonny, Jackee and their teammates. Since this was Olympus first real meal of the day, they consumed a good amount of food. Jackee asked Rose about Sunday's Mass schedule. She said "usually I go to the 7:30 Mass Sunday morning. It still leaves me time to have breakfast before the 9:30 closing. Coach thinks your bus will leave at about 10am, so there is plenty of time." Jackee was to sleep in Rose's room. She had a private room with two beds and a bath. Sonny would be with them until they decided to go to bed then he would go to the dorm rooms that were set aside for the team. Jackee decided to go with some team mates to a local college hang out so Rose and Sonny could spend some time together. About 11:30 she could not keep her eyes open so she went back to Rose's room. Sonny was already sleeping on a sofa and Jackee was going to leave but Rose told her that there was plenty of room in her bedroom. Since she was too tired to argue she got into bed and was fast asleep in less than a minute.

Next morning Jackee was up early and showered and dressed before anyone else was awake. Rose was up next and followed Jackee's example. Sonny was up as Rose finished so he readied himself for church. It was only a ten minute walk to the chapel where the mass was held. After church they went to breakfast and got ready to leave. Jackee thanked Rose for everything and wished her luck in her next qualifying events. Sonny was with Rose until it was time for him to board the bus. The trip home always seems like a long one but winning all 10 games makes it a very happy trip. They arrived back at Olympus College just before dinner, so they had time to unpack and change clothes. Andrea was not in the room but there were signs that she had been there not too long before. Sonny escorted Jackee to dinner and there was Andrea sitting with some of their teammates. She had been at the lab to see if anything was doing but Lucy said everything was quiet. "It has been very boring since you left and I have just about completed our labs for the year. You have some catching up to do but it should not be a problem for you or Sonny." They talked about the trip and Sonny mentioned Jackee's injury. Andrea asked how bad the injury was and Sonny said Jackee could hardly breathe. "It's still a little tender but it has improved every day" Jackee told them.

They moved on to how Andrea was coping with the fact she had not had a date since coming back to school from Christmas break. "Not since I was twelve years old have I been this long without some kind of dating. The weird thing is I have so much time that all my work is done and I even cleaned the bathroom."

This made Jackee laugh because she knew how much Andrea hated cleaning the bathroom. "Now you have some idea what I have been going through not seeing Dan."

Andrea told Jackee that she was used to abstaining since she was part nun, "but for me this is total withdrawal." On that note they had dessert and went back to the dorm.

The last ten games were mostly at home and except for one division one team, they were conference games. Coach Zimmer used these games to prepare for the invitational tournament. He approached each game as if it was critical to win. This kept the fire and edge in his team. When he felt it was safe he substituted freely and gave a chance for the others to play. Road trips are very hard on the team and the two week trip had most of the starters exhausted. There were two weeks to rest and then bring them back up to the fine tuned team they had been. Jackee knew what the coach was doing because she saw Bats do it to his team. Good coaches instinctively know when to push and when to ease off. She talked to the coach about a fun drill that Bats used to get his defense ready. "Players take their normal positions in the field and a batter hits the ball themself, wherever he wants. They have three outs in any inning and you count how many runs they score. Pitchers are usually the hitters." Things were going great until Toby tried to bat. He must have tried 10 times and never hit the ball once. Finally he threw the bat down claiming he never gets to hit anyway. Usually pitchers are some of the best athletes on any team and most hit very well. This was hardly the case here. The most important thing was, the team had fun and the defense did get to practice many possible situations. Only one of the last 10 games was reasonably close and that was the game against a D1 team.

A call came from the tournament committee the Saturday before the tournament was to start. Olympus college was seeded number one because of their two year record. They would be the home team in the first three rounds if they won. Round 4 would be played at the triple A home field on the following Friday. Saturday would see the consolation game for third place and the first game in the best two out of three. Sunday the second and third game (if necessary) would be played starting at 11am. Seeded team 32 will play at the Olympus field on Monday at 4pm. For all of its remaining games Olympus will always play the lowest seeded team still left in the tournament. Since they were the number one seed, any of the remaining 31 teams would be below them. Home field always goes to the highest seeded team.

Monday at 12pm Tyler University showed up for the first playoff game. They were shown to the looker room where food and drinks were available. They were scheduled to take their infield practice 20 to 4. Lefty Rasko was to start for Olympus. Over his last three starts he has had an earned run average of .075. One other reason for him to start is because the scouting report on Tyler is that their three big hitters are lefty batters. Jackee still had a tender area but she could breath without any discomfort. She led the team onto the field and the over crowded stadium was on its feet cheering. After Rasko retired the side in the top of the first, Olympus drew first blood. Sonny walked with one out and scored on Jackee's double to right center. She stole third on the second pitch to Hands and scored on his deep flyball to center. That would be enough runs for lefty but Jackee added a two run homer in the fourth inning. Coach Zimmer removed Lefty after seven shutout innings and Sid and Hook pitched the last two. Final score Olympus 7 Tyler 0. Olympus heard later that number 28 had defeated number 5, so that ment on Wednesday they will host Byton university at 4pm.

Byton was a D2 school and had an excellent record in most of their sports programs. Their baseball team did very well for the year finishing with a 30 and 6 record. The scouting report said that the team hits well but their pitching is suspect. They like to run and play a lot of small ball. Bunting and the hit and run are a big part of their game. They arrived on Tuesday and spent the night at the Olympus. Next day they took a full morning practice in preparation for the 4 PM game. Jackee and a few other players watched their practice to see if they could spot any weakness. One outfielder had a weak arm and the catcher didn't seem to throw well. Coach Zimmer selected Brady to start. He was having a great year and he is the oldest pitcher on the staff. Just like Monday, the Olympics took infield at 3:20 and Byron at 3:40. Once again Jackee led the team onto the field and the overflow crowd cheered. This game remained a close affair because Jackee and Tyler had Byton off balance. In the third inning Byton tried the hit and run, but Jackee covered second and the batter expected Tyler to cover since the batter was right handed. Tyler faked going to second on the steal and had a ground ball hit right at him. By getting rid of the ball fast Tyler was able to barely get the runner at second and Jackee, even though the runner slid hard into her, she was able to throw to first for a double play. Byton tried the same play in the fifth inning but this time Tyler actually covered second and the batter froze at the plate, allowing Hands to throw the runner out. Meanwhile Olympus scored single runs in the third and fourth innings. Hands drove in Jackee who walked and stole second and Stretch Ward the first baseman drove in Joe Gilardi. Byton scored their only run in the sixth inning that ended when Jackee made one of her over the shoulder catches in short left center. After Brady finished the top of the seventh, Olympus had four straight hits starting with Jackee and ending with Gilardi. Sid and Hook finished the game and Olympus won 6 to 1. Later that night coach Zimmer received a call that number 23, Stockton College, a D2 team would be Olympus' opponent on Thursday.

Scouting report on Stockton is that they are rich in pitching but weak on hitting. Most of their wins are because the pitchers have held the other team to very few runs. Coach Zimmer figured that they had to use their numbers one and two in the first two games. Olympus had Drew ready to go and the coach felt that he was better than any other team's number three. Much like Monday and Wednesday the schedule was exactly the same except Stockton did not arrive until 10am Thursday. Stockton took a short practice then had lunch. Coach Zimmer had a 9am hitting practice but nothing else, he wanted his players rested for the game. At exactly 4pm Jackee led the team onto the field before the largest crowd in the school's history. There was no parking within 6 blocks of the school and cars were parked all over the campus. If you saw grass there was a car on top of it. Campus security was overwhelmed and just did what they could to keep people safe. The fans knew from various media sources that this could be Jackee's last home game ever. When she led the team onto the field the cheering from the crowd was ear shattering. Coach Zimmer thought that if we needed an edge, this was it. Olympus infield drill was one thing that shocked Stockton players but the large crowd and their cheering was very intimidating. Drew was pumped up and he retired 15 straight batters. Olympus batters did get two runs in the third inning, one driven in by Sonny and one by Jackee. Stockton got their first base runner when Drew walked the first batter in the top of the sixth. He retired the next three so he still led 2 to 0 when he started the seventh inning. With one out, he gave up his first hit, a bloop that Tyler could not reach in short right center. The next batter hit a one hopper to Jackee who started a double play. Sid and Hook took care of the rest and the game ended Olympus 2 Stockton 0. After the game, the team and especially Jackee were swamped by the fans. Jackee remained on the field for two hours after the game. Media, both TV and reporters, were talking to every player but most wanted to hear from Jackee. Coach Zimmer heard later from the committee that teams 2, 4, and 10 also had won. So Olympus would be playing the second game on Friday against Jefferson University, a D2 school. The other two teams, Brockport College and Stevenson University, both D2 teams, would meet in game one.

Both these games should be pitcher's duels because all four teams have their number one pitcher ready to go. All the teams have won between 30 and 35 games this year. Game one started with both teams being introduced and after the Star Spangled Banner was played, the umpire said "Play Ball". This game turned into a pitchers duel and the game was still tied at 0 to 0 after nine innings. Finally in the top of the eleventh Stevenson scored 2 runs. Brockport scored one run and had the bases loaded with two outs in the bottom of the eleventh but a pitch hitter struck out to end the game. Game two started exactly on time as the first game finished in three hours. Olympus College was the home team in the game and took infield first. The crowd, which was a full house, applauded the performance. Jackee led her team onto the field at exactly 4 PM. Drew looked unhittable and retired 21 of the first 22 batters he faced. He gave up a single to the second batter he faced. Jefferson's starting pitcher did allow some base runners but none reached home plate. Sid came in and pitched a perfect eighth inning. Jackee singled with one out in the bottom of the eighth and stole second on the first pitch to Hands. Hands hit, what looked to be an extra base hit, to right center but the center fielder made a diving catch. Jackee got back to second and tagged up and went to third. Jefferson's coach called a time out to talk about the next hitter.

Jackee met with Coach Zimmer and the next two hitters. She told them that "this pitcher was slow delivering the ball to home plate. They will probably walk Jinx intentionally and pitch to Gilardi. Joe if the first pitch to you is a strike, this pitcher usually throws a curve on the next pitch. On this second pitch I am going to steal home. I want you to swing at the pitch but not hit it. Swing from the belt up just to keep the catcher honest. If all this happens I want you to touch your cap so I know you're ready to follow the plan." Joe said "I signal you by putting my left hand on top of my helmet." The pitcher threw two well off the plate pitchers to Jinx before intentionally walking him. His first pitch to Gilardi was called a strike on the inside corner. Gilardi put his left hand on top of his batting helmet and took his position in the batters' box. As soon as the pitcher started his motion Jackee broke for home and startled the whole team. She was more than half way home when the pitcher released the ball. She easily slid under Gilardi's swing before the catcher could catch what was now a fastball. He hesitated because he was looking for the curve he had called for. The umpires conferred on the play and the second base umpire had called a balk which would have scored Jackee anyway but they decided to let the steal of home stand. Everyone at the game was surprised that Jackee had stolen home. Most had never seen a steal of home on this level of competition. There was a buzz around the whole field about what they had just seen. Hook came out to pitch the ninth and retired the side in order.

Consolation game for third place was to begin at 11am. Brockport was to play Jefferson and immediately after their game Olympus would play Stevenson. Olympus would be the home team in game one and Stevenson would be the home team in game two. If there is a third game, a flip of the coin would decide the home team. Neither team in the consolation game really cared if they came in third or fourth. If you're not playing for the championship there is very little to brag about. Jefferson did beat Brockport by a 4 to1 score and thereby finished number three in the tournament. Brady started for Olympus and he pitched very well. Jackee, whose uniform looked like it had been in a war, continued to lead by example. She walked, singled, tripled and doubled in her four at bats. She drove in two runs and scored two runs. Of the six runs that Olympus scored, she was involved in five of them. It made life a bit easier for Brady as he pitched 8 innings and allowed only 2 runs. John KO Sullivan pitched the ninth and walked one of the four batters he faced. He struck out two and had a comebacker that he ran to first and tagged the base himself, ending the game. Game two was scheduled for 11 am on Sunday. William, Carmela and Bats were at the Saturday game. They arrived just before the game started and did not want to bother Jackee. After the game she saw them and immediately went to them. Interviews had to wait until she said hello to her family. One scout had offered to treat the family to dinner at a local restaurant but Jackee refused saying she had to be with the team. William and Bats fully understood what she was saying and agreed with her. She told them that there was a local Catholic Church two blocks from here that has a 7:30am mass on Sunday. There is also a big reception for the teams Sunday night at 6pm. All the awards will be handed out at that dinner. She spent the next hour talking to reporters and other media people, then went to dinner with the team and told William to pick Sonny and her up for church at 7:15.

After church the next day Jackee and Sonny were dropped off at the hotel for breakfast. Since many of her teammates were eating with their families she asked Carmela, William and Bats to join them for breakfast. She and Sonny had to be on the field at 10am. Neither Jackee nor Sonny felt like eating so they had some juice and headed for the locker room. Jackee dressed in the aid station. Her uniform and equipment had been stored there for the night. Once on the field Jackee warmed up with Sonny and felt a bit tired but otherwise, ready to play. This would be the first game in the tournament that Jackee would not lead her team onto the field. Once all the pre game ceremonies are done the game will start. Coach Zimmer told the team, "this is the game we have waited for all year. Let's go out there and show the world who we are. You are the best team in this tournament and I want you to prove it to everyone."

Today the crowd was almost all Stevenson or Olympus fans. Media coverage grew and the number of scouts more than doubled. The four umpires were the highest rated ones in the section. Game two started exactly at 11am after all the pre game events were completed. Tyler was the first batter and he drew an eleven pitch walk from the big lefthander for Stevenson. Sonny bunted him to second and Jackee was walked intentionally. Hands delivered a single to center that scored Tyler but Jackee stopped at second. Peter Jinx hit a line drive back to the pitcher who threw to first completing the double play. Bobby Jo Dugan Started for Olympus and retired the side in order. The game stayed 1 to 0 for the next three innings. Gilardi led off the fifth with a single and Gabe Polski bunted him to second. Stretch Ward grounded to second and Gilardi moved to third. Al Temple, the DH, singled to right, driving in Gilardi. With the score two to nothing in the bottom of the fifth Stevenson had runners on first and second with none out. Ther number four hitter hit a line drive to the shortstop side of second. Jackee at full speed and with a headlong dive, caught the ball, rolled over and flipped the ball to Tyler who stepped on second and fired a strike to first completing the triple play. Jackee had to be helped off the field. She hit the left side of her chest again and was in some pain. Jackee was due up second in the top of the sixth and right now she was with the female trainer under the stands. The trainer sprayed the left side of her chest with a freeze that masked the pain and gave her a chance to continue. Jackee batted with one out and single to right on what appeared to be a very deliberate swing. Coach Zimmer had detected that if the pitcher was going to throw to first, he dipped his left shoulder, otherwise he went into his high kick and delivered the pitch. As soon as Jackee saw the shoulders staying level she took off for second and stole the base easily. Hands was walked intentionally and Peter Jinx Lined a ball to left center scoring Jackee and putting runners on second and third. A new pitcher walked Gilardi intentionally and Gabe unintentionally. Stretch Ward cleared the bases with a triple to right center. He later scored on a sac fly by Al Temple. You could stick a fork in Stevenson because they were done. Bobby Jo pitched the sixth but the last three innings were shared by Toby, Specs and Sid. Coach Zimmer did one thing in the bottom of the ninth, Jackee went out to short but before the first pitch, he sent Tyler to short and put Matt at second. Jackee slowly jogged off the field to a standing ovation that did not stop until she made two curtain calls.

Carmela was on her feet and crying. William and Bats were pretty much doing the same thing. William told Bats he was partly responsible for this. Bats said Jackee earned every bit of the applause she was getting. Everyone of her teammates was applauding and the Stevenson coach and all his players were out of the dugout and clapping. All the scouts were on their feet and joined the rest of the crowd in honoring this exceptional young woman.

Once the game ended the celebration continued. William and Bats tried to shield Jackee from the crowd until they were sure she was not in danger. Jackee was just accepting congratulations from everyone but was thankful when her dad and Bats offered some protection. Carmela made her way to Jackee and while still crying hugged her. Jackee told her she was sore but not as bad as the last time. She also told her mother that breasts were not good for baseball players. They both laughed and Carmela asked, "what alternative do you have?" Scouts wanted to talk to the family but William told them that nothing could be discussed now. Next week Jackee would be home and then arrangements could be made. People asking about endorsements were told the same thing. Later that night at the awards dinner, the championship trophy was given to coach Zimmer. The MVP of the tournament was also announced. Jackee was the unanimous choice and this was decided by not only the committee but also by the media. Every player that attended the dinner came up to Jackee and congratulated her. Many asked her to autograph a baseball for them. They celebrated well into the early hours of the next day and finally Jackee got to bed at 4am. At 11am the bus took the team back to Olympus. The crowd at the school was far more than they had ever had before. The dinner and reception at 6pm was the most outstanding event in the history of the school. When the dinner was finished President Washington spoke and introduced all the coaches, trainers and lastly the players. Jackee was the last person called and everyone in the room stood and applauded.

The president asked her to say a few words. She started out by thanking the school for all they did and then she told them that baseball above all else was a team sport. "No one player wins the game alone. Coach Zimmer is an outstanding coach and he has not received the credit he deserves for putting this team together. He also should be given credit for molding this team to be a winner. We played many teams who had very good ball players but coach Zimmer made us better and gave us the incentive to beat all of them. Look at the nucleus of this team, Tyler, Sonny, Hands, Peter, Joe, Gabe, Stretch, Al, Matt Casey, Brady, Drew, Al, Bobby Jo, John, Hook, Sid, Toby, Specs and Dexter and you tell me which one could we had done without. We are a team. We won together, lost together and became Champions together. God gave us the talent and the desire but Coach Zimmer gave us the spirit to come together and be a winner. Thank you for your support over the years and I hope you will be behind us next year and for years to come. God bless you all."

CHAPTER TWENTY THREE

Jackee Plays Summer Baseball and Fall Semester

*J*ackee finished school and still maintained her perfect 4.0 GPA. Sonny went home for a week and then saw Rose at her house. Andrea also had a perfect score and will graduate Summa com lada same as Jackee. Sonny will have a 4.0 average but did not do as well before he started getting help from Andrea and Jackee. He qualified for the Hospital affiliated with Olympus College and also with the help of Dr. Hopkins. He starts medical school and some internship on July 5th. Jackee missed Dan's graduation from college as she was playing that Saturday in the tournament. She is all excited as to how she is going to make it up to Dan. She had spoken with him the day before graduation and he told her it was supposed to rain and they moved the ceremony indoors so the tickets for guests were limited. Next evening Dan called her and told her how bad the graduation actually was. "The place was hot, the speakers were boring and even handing out of diploma's was just an assembly line affair. As soon as it was over people just left. I was with my family and the family of other athletes so we just headed for a good restaurant." He and the family did not leave for home until the next day because he still had to pack, sell or give away the stuff in his room before he could leave. There was also the picking up of the real diploma and settling any debts to the school. Jackee was scheduled to be home the following Wednesday. She would pick up her diploma before leaving but she did not have to move her belongings because Andrea would be there next year and the room was reserved for the special medical students.

Dan came over later that evening after Jackee got settled. She wanted to go to their favorite parking area because she had to talk to him. First things first, and after a prolonged kiss she began telling him what was about to happen. "There are scouts from at least 20 teams that want to talk to me, and a similar number of companies want her to sign on to do commercials for their products. This could be worth over 3 million dollars per year. If I decide to do something with these companies, I want you and my dad to be my agents. I spoke to my dad on the way home and both Rose and I will need someone looking after our affairs. Rose can turn pro any time since the Olympics is no longer an amateur sport. Dan, I know that you have done everything to help me and not once complained about how I have ignored your dreams. Rose and I need a person we both trust, beside my dad, looking out for our interest. We all agreed that you are the only choice. I also told them that I am asking you to marry me whenever you select a date. There is nothing more important than being your wife and the mother of your children. This is the final part of my dream and I need your guidance to decide what happens next. There is going to be a family meeting when Rose comes home on Sunday. At this meeting all matters will be fully explored about our future." He held her close and said that he will be the one to propose and she will make the final decision. "Right now I believe we have to wait a year or a little more to see how you and Rose feel about turning professional. And one more important fact is that your father and I will have to hold a meeting to see if we are on the same page."

William and Dan did hold a meeting after church on Sunday. And just before Rose arrived home, they shook hands sealing whatever agreement they reached. They decided that on Monday at 10am the family meeting will start. Dan had dinner with the Jenco family and after that he and Jackee went for a drive. When they parked, Dan told her how impressed he was with her dad and how much he respected him and his ideas. Jackee was happy that the two men she loved the most would be working on her future. After the couple left, William told Rose and Carmela how impressed he was of Dan's knowledge of the business world and how much he cared for Jackee. Carmela was happy that someone else will be helping to shape the future of her daughters. It had been the custom that William would seek her approval in such matters but things have become too complicated for her to give quality advice.

Monday at ten, all interested parties were sitting around the dining room table. Rose spoke first and told Dan that she and Sonny were happy that "he and my dad were looking out for their interest."

Dan said "the normal payment for an agent is 10% but William and I agreed to take 5% to represent both the girls. Is this agreeable to each of you?" Both girls agreed that this was more than fair. He told them that they will have final say before any commitment is made to anyone. "It was agreed that before any commitment is signed by either of you, it must be agreed to by at least one of us. If and when one or both of you marry your spouse must sign on to this agreement and he can not make any agreement without our approval, and that means both of us. This is to protect Jackee in case she marries someone beside me. If that were to happen Jackee could ask for my resignation and I must comply with an agreed buyout. Both of you will be employees of a corporation William is going to form. For the next two weeks we will schedule meetings with baseball clubs and business people to hear offers."

There were business offers for both girls with most being for Jackee. The baseball clubs had only Jackee in mind. There were 12 major league teams and one expansion team who made appointments to talk with Jackee and her agents. None could make offers since the major league draft will not be held for two more weeks. Business people came from all over to seek an endorsement mostly from Jackee. Rose's value would be better determined after her Olympic appearance. The more medals she wins, the higher the bid. Jackee on the other hand is a proven commodity and her offers were very big. In fact they were more than double what was originally thought. Jackee saw one venture that interested her and that was a baby clothing company. She asked William if the company donated the money directly to the orphanage would she still be considered an amateur while doing their commercials. She wanted to keep her options opened and not lose her amateur status.

She also asked William to contact the Major League Baseball Commissioner's office to see if she could select the team instead of being selected in the draft. "Because of the nature of this signing, a special contract must be agreed to and some concessions made by the league. You could mention to them that the Japanese League has made inquiries as to her availability." Press conferences, dressing facilities, traveling accommodations and public appearances are just a few of the items that must be hammered out before a contract could be agreed to. Dan and William jotted these things down along with other things that they considered critical. This meeting ended after 7 hours of solid give and take by the four main players. Rose and Jackee were very impressed with Dan's approach and recommendations for their future. Jackee for the first time realized just how very much Dan loved her. She fully understood that in their hands her future and working conditions would be protected.

For the next two weeks mornings from 9 to 12 a different baseball team was scheduled to present their outlines for an offer. From 1 to 4 companies looking for endorsements would present their offers. There will be no meetings on Sunday, this will be a family day to relax and maybe to review some things. This schedule went extremely well and at least 5 companies outlined offers that included both sisters. These offers excited both girls since they would be working together. William had taken two weeks vacation and he and Dan spent most evenings sorting and cataloging each day's offers. Rose had to leave for some special meets and needed time to train properly for these events. Jackee had taken part of the summer off and would not see competition again for at least 3 weeks. The Monday after all the offers were made saw the three people analyzing what took place. On Wednesday, they heard from Major League Baseball. Commissioner

Higgons had granted Jackee's request to make the final decision as to which team, if any, she would play for. There was one stipulation, that the final contract would be within the bounds of what the contract would have been if she had been drafted. William acting as her agent gave his word to the Commissioner's office that his stipulation will be respected. Everyone realized that if and when Jackee signed and finally made a major league team, her first swing through the league, teams would add thousands of fans to every game until her novelty wears off. If she has any kind of success the trend could continue for a very long time. Sorting out the commercial offers was not so easy. There were one or two that did not appeal to Jackee and she raised her doubts about them. She liked most of the ones where She and Rose could participate together. Rose had asked William to do the same thing for her as he was doing for Jackee, namely getting a company to donate directly to the Indian council so she still keeps her amateur status. William had contacted the NCAA about this issue and was still waiting to hear from them. He knew that some professional athletes did something like this, but they did it for tax purposes and not athletic standing. Jackee decided to start playing summer baseball and contacted Coach Zimmer and it was agreed that she would be back at school by Sunday night.

She spent her last weekend with Dan and Saturday night they just parked and talked. She laid out her plans and asked him what he thought about them. He said he fully agreed except for one thing. She said "whatever it is, I'll agree to go along." "Well it seems that there is a Saturday in October next year, looking for a special event and I would like to fill it." "That sounds fine to me because I probably will be free at that time. What is it you want?" "Will you marry me on October 20th next year and really be my partner for the rest of your life?" "YES, YES, YES!" She cried and held and kissed him. He told her he wanted to get engaged on Christmas Eve and we can start then to make our wedding plans. Jackee smiled at him and said "remember I asked you first."

Dan drove Jackee home and when they pulled into the driveway, Jackee realized that her parents were still up. She asked Dan if it would be alright for her to tell her parents about their plans? He thought it would be better if they did it together. They then proceeded into the house and saw her parents in the living room. While they were holding hands, they approached the parents and asked if they could talk to them. William, who had been working on his company affairs, looked up and saw two blushing young adults. He told them "whatever it is, remember we can't afford it." Dan came right out and told the parents that he has asked Jackee to marry him and she has agreed. "Now we need your permission and blessing." Carmela jumped up from her sofa and hugged Jackee and said "What took you so long". William said he would give his blessing as soon as he found out what Dan was going to pay him for his daughter's hand in marriage. Dan's response was that he had an old car, a few dollars in the bank and the rest of his assets he carried around with him.

Carmela said "you can never be sure how a marriage will work out but you two leave no doubts in my mind. I have never seen a couple who have given so much of themselves in a relationship. From the first time I met Dan, I knew that Jackee found the one person who would mean more to her than her dad and baseball. Never let anyone tell you that prayers are not answered. Today my faith has been reinforced." Dan kissed Jackee as he was leaving and told her he would see her at church before she leaves for summer baseball. Jackee went back to her parents and thanked them for being such great understanding parents. William reminded her that her parents have always been proud of her and knew that she would always try to do the right thing. "This is the right way for you and you found the right person to be your spouse."

"Dad, I will tell you honestly that we have done a great deal of kissing but never once has Dan tried to take advantage of me. This has not been my choice because I am not sure if I would have stopped him. This was totally his decision and there were times that I felt hurt. I had the feeling that maybe I wasn't good enough for him to even try. Mom explained to me that he was protecting me from myself. That also confirmed to me how much he really cares about me. Dad, I'll tell you right now, that after we are married I will spend the rest of my life thanking him for how he has protected me. I may not know now what I have to do, but I will learn how to make him happy." "Congratulations" Carmela told her, "because you are now a woman who understands what every marriage needs."

Jackee left for school right after church and upon arriving at school went to see Coach Zimmer. She heard the curve ball, slider and split finger were the hardest pitches to hit in the majors. So she wanted to know if he could devise a program for her to practice on those pitches. Coach said he would look into it but now wanted to know what condition she was in. "My conditioning is fine, but my hitting needs to be fine tuned." He told her "we will start taking care of that tomorrow." In just two days Jackee was hitting at a mid season level and it was with some power. She had lunch with Sonny and told him about the new corporation and how Dan was working with her dad. Sonny heard all about this from Rose but there were things that Jackee filled him in on. He was very happy to have Dan working with William because he not only liked him, but trusted him as he would a brother. "Please don't say anything to him but I am going to ask him to be my best man when Rose and I get married." Jackee was very happy about this because Rose had told her she would be her maid of honor.

Coach called her into his office one day, to tell her he located a battling machine that threw curves and sliders. No machine can duplicate the split finger but they are working to create one. This machine has seven or eight adjustments for various curves and sliders. "One unit will be installed on Thursday so we will have it for the weekend." There was a game scheduled for Friday at 1pm so the team started hitting off the new machine at 9am. It took awhile but Jackee started picking up the rotation of the ball as it left the machine. The tight curve was the hardest to detect. Most of the freshman players had never practiced watching the spin as the pitch left the pitcher's hand, so all this was a learning experience for them. Tyler was working with Jackee and was a fast learner. Jackee wanted him to be the leader of the team because he had the ability and respect of the returning players. She suggested to the coach that if she played, the positions in the field should be switched. Matt would be her backup and they could develop another player to be Tyler's backup. Coach told Jackee it was her choice as to where she wants to play, adding that she has earned that right. Jackee thanked the coach and said that she was considering signing a professional contract by the latest July 1st.

Coach knew that it was going to happen but he thought it would be sooner. "I am leaning toward the expansion team. Their offer guaranteed me just about everything I was looking for. Money was not a consideration, since my endorsement offers would more than double any salary that was offered." Coach wanted to know what this new expansion team was to be called. Jackee said "it's not official yet but they are leaning toward Vegas Gamblers. It will be the first major league baseball team in Nevada. They are building a billion dollar enclosed baseball stadium with a retractable dome roof. When the dome is closed it will be a perfect climate controlled environment. The stadium is scheduled to be completed 19 months from now. This winter they will select players from major and minor league clubs to fill the six teams that they will begin with. One major league team, one triple A, one double A, two single A teams and one rookie league team. I could be assigned to the Double A team and later brought up to triple A. I figured this would be the easier transition for me, seeing that all the players would be new to the team. Some resentment is to be expected but it should be much less than with the established teams."

Jackee was having a great summer baseball season. She was playing mostly second base and tutoring Tyler in his new position. Tyler listened to every word Jackee said and could not respect her more. Here was a great player dedicating all her time so that he could take her position and never asking anything in return. He knew he could never be as good a shortstop as she is but he made up his mind that he would never disappoint her. One more thing he knew was that he loved her. Not the love between a man and woman but the love one has for his mother. Matt Murray was also one of her pupils. He will be the starting second baseman when she leaves and she wanted him and Tyler to be a great double play combination. She had no problem with either one and the coach loved having her coach them. Personally, Jackee was having a career season. She was hitting over .500 and leading the team in hits, runs scored, extra base hits and walks. She did have one strike out and one error. Still every game saw more and more women and girls wanting to talk with her. The coach made her the DH in some game so that she could rest and have time for her fan club. Scouts and fans were upset when she did not play but the coach sent out a schedule as to when he was going to use her as the DH. Coach Zimmer had been asked to arrange for Jackee to speak at a huge women's convention. They were going to honor her and wanted it to be a surprise. He asked Jackee to do him a favor by speaking to a group of women. She readily agreed since she would never refuse him anything. He got in touch with the organizer and all the arrangements were made. A complete schedule was laid out for her at a beauty parlor and clothing store on the morning of the event. Coach Zimmer had the college pay for everything. He did not want an incident like the one they had before.

A limo arrived at her dorm at 10am. She had already showered so she was set for the beauty polar. Jackee was dumbfounded by the attention she was getting, but just went with the flow. Once they finished with her, the limo took her to a clothing store. She originally said it wasn't necessary since she had dress clothing at her dorm. Coach told her this was a special gift from the college for her speaking to this group. This explanation was accepted, but she said she would have spoken to them without this fanfare. The women's boutique was the top of the line and Jackee was treated like a queen. After more than two hours she looked into a mirror and could not believe what she was seeing. They all complimented her on how beautiful she looked and all Jackee could do was cry and thanked them for all their work. When she started to cry they all shouted "NO, you'll ruin the make up." Everyone laughed and Jackee stopped crying and went to the limo.

Coach had asked the ladies if some school administrators and some of his players could attend. They agreed and a section in the back of the auditorium was set up for them. The limo arrived at five minutes to five. Jackee was escorted to the back wing of the auditorium and heard a voice say her name along with an invitation to join them. She walked out unescorted to a standing ovation from about 800 women and young girls. She was in a state of shock and it got worse when she saw her parents and teammates. The speaker turned to her and extended her hand. Jackee reached out and held her hand as the speaker told the audience that they are here today to honor a great young woman. "She has broken yet another barrier that has excluded women. Like the old Star Trek show, she has gone where no woman has gone before. It is difficult for me to believe that this beautiful woman has competed in a men's only sport and won the respect of not only the other players but millions of fans. Without further ado, I give you Jacalyn 'Jackee' Jenco." For a full 2 minutes the audience clapped and cheered. Jackee saw her parents, sisters and teammates standing and cheering like everyone else. Dan stood next to Sonny and both were also cheering her.

When the audience finally was seated, Jackee began speaking. "It is not hard doing something that you love. I love baseball. From the time I was five all I ever wanted to be was a baseball player. I am not saying that it was easy but as a player once said if it was easy everyone would do it. The truth is that the more difficult it is, the greater the achievement and reward. There are hundreds of women out there who deserve this honor. I personally know a woman doctor who just the other day took a tumor out of a five year old boy's head in an operation that every other doctor said could not be done. She should be here getting an award. I met a police woman who saved a child from a burning building and then gave the child artificial respiration and brought him back to life. She should be standing here. You have stories like this every day and these are women just doing their job. You honor me but the real honor belongs to my parents. Mom, dad would you please stand up. These two people gave me life, love and everything I needed to be a success. God gave me the talent and His love to show me the way. All I had to do was work hard and not lose that desire to be the best. Everything we do requires choices and these choices make us what we are. Sometimes these choices are easy and sometimes they are seemingly impossible. The Almighty gives all of us many talents, it is up to us to either use them or not. I have, what I believe, taken a talent and used it to achieve my goal or if you will, my dream. All along the way God provided me with people who helped and supported me. It is impossible for me to thank every coach or person who helped me. It is also impossible to thank every fan who encouraged me on the field. There were times when I was hurt and could barely dress myself let alone play but when I saw all those young female faces in the stands and heard them cheering for me, I could not let them down. Their cheers carried me onto the field, their cheers helped me hit and catch the ball and more importantly, they made me want to give them something back for all the love and encouragement they gave me. I want you to know that now I understand how Lou Gehrig felt when he was honored at Yankee stadium. Here are you honoring me for doing something that I love to do. I should be honoring you for giving up your valuable time to come here. There is also someone I want you to meet. He made my final decision to make this dream possible. We have agreed to spend the rest of our lives together and on October 20th of next year we will be married. Dan please stand." He stood up and the audience clapped until he waved and then sat down. Jackee continued by saying that "the Nuns used to tell us that we all had a guardian angel. Well I found one that I could see. I hope each of you can find someone you can call a guardian angel and a partner for life."

"For the next few minutes, I wish to talk to the young ladies in the audience. You have an unlimited ability to be whatever you wish. Each of you have God given talents. It is your choice as to how you want to use those talents. Never let anyone take away your dream, tell you it can't be done or call you a failure. Remember one very important thing, not achieving something is not failure. It only becomes a failure if you don't keep trying. The greatest baseball player who ever lived, hit under .400. This means that in every ten at bats he made 6 outs. He failed 60% of the time. Willie Mays made outs his first 23 at bats in the major leagues, but today he is in the hall of fame at Cooperstown, New York. Just think what would have happened to him if he quit after those first 23 failures. It is exactly the same with you. Never let anyone take a right from you. Let no one say you are too tall, too fat, too old, too slow, too skinny, not pretty enough or not anything else. You are all made in God's image and if anyone has a problem with that, have them take it up with the Big Fellow up there, as she pointed straight up. Thank you for honoring me today and may God bless you and love you."

She walked back to her seat as the audience was standing and clapping. Carmela was crying as were the sisters. William could not speak and Dan just wanted to hold Jackee in his arms. Jackee spent the next hour signing baseballs, papers, hats and anything else they put in front of her. The crowd finally thinned out and she went to her family. She hugged her parents and sisters and kissed Dan. She told him she was sorry for putting him in that situation but she wanted everyone to know how much he meant in her life. Before the school officials left they all told Jackee how proud they were to have such a wonderful young lady represent their school. It was also mentioned that a special dinner for her and her family was now being prepared back at the school. Coach Zimmer and the players he had with him were also invited.

Next morning Jackee had reviewed in her mind all that had taken place yesterday. It all seemed surreal but it actually happened and she loved every minute of it. Each time she was honored it made all the hard work and pain worthwhile. There was never a thought that she was breaking some kind of barrier, she was just doing what she loved, playing baseball. One very definite decision was formed in her mind, she would sign to play baseball for the Vegas Gamblers. She will call Dan tonight and confirm that after her last game in the spring it will be time to go to the next level. The main idea now was to finish summer baseball, go home and prepare for a wedding and the following school year. When she told Coach Zimmer, he thought it was a workable plan and readily agreed to help her in any way possible. There was also a mention that while she was finishing her medical school program, he could use her as a coach or special assistant. Jackee loved the idea and felt it would keep her baseball skills sharp. Dr. Hopkins was the next person she had to speak with. He would plan her medical school program around her playing professional baseball. This had been one of the original promises that Olympus college had made to her. Periodically, she would still have to do endorsements and talks for the college and the 6 year medical program. Those would all be at her convenience. There were so many things that had to fall into place for this plan to run smoothly. Lucy did all the scheduling for Dr. Hopkins and she had become an expert on how to keep things running efficiently. It would take a miracle to make Jackee's proposed schedule work but if anyone could do it Lucy was the one.

Jackee called Dan that night and explained the tentative plan she had decided on. He thought it was a good start and would confer with William on her thoughts and a few that he would add. William for now would be the final word on the various steps Jackee has to take.

His expertise in the business world had to be respected and followed. One thing William did recommend is that this Lucy Willis person be given some kind of stipend from the corporation they had formed to handle the two sisters' money matters. This way she would take a better interest in handling Jackee's affairs. "A person getting paid is more dedicated to your needs than one who is working for nothing."Dan thought that was a great idea but wanted to know how this could be done since she was already working for the college. "It is not unusual for an employee handling a special condition outside their duties to be rewarded with something extra. As long as it does not interfere with her normal work duties, I am sure Dr Hopkins would not mind."

Dan asked about the timing of Jackee signing a professional contract. William thought the first or second week in June should be the perfect time, unless Jackee decides to do it earlier. "We will negotiate the contract in April, or May the latest and have everything settled by the time Jackee is ready to sign in June. There are some endorsements that Jackee has to do over the summer, but that money is going to the orphanage and not Jackee. The orphanage will now be independent and not have to beg anyone for money and the company will get a good writeoff on their income tax. We also have to discuss how endorsements will be handled. Do we go after them immediately or wait to see if Jackee is a success in pro ball. Her value after she has made it to the majors will be at least double what it would be prior to that. Someone has contacted me for a possible book offer and a studio wants to do a movie about her life. They even said she would act in the movie since it is very unlikely they could find a girl as athletic as she is to play the role. We must be careful not to put so many things on her plate before she gets to playing in professional baseball. I'm thinking that we should put all endorsements on hold until the two of you are married. We would have the whole winter to decide on the next steps to take. There should be enough money from her signing bonus to keep the corporation running for many years."

Dan asked Carmela if she had any thoughts on this discussion. Carmela said she did not want to get involved with the business end but she did ask that Jackee be given time to enjoy her wedding and honeymoon. Immediately William agreed and Dan knew Jackee would love the idea. He wanted to take Jackee where they would not be hounded by autograph seekers, but there was little chance of that most anywhere in the USA. Media coverage alone would follow her everywhere she went. He finally decided that she would make the final decision on the honeymoon. There was little doubt in his mind that Carmela would be involved and he was glad to pass this one to her.

Jackee was continuing her great summer in baseball. Every one of her 5 baseball skills were working perfectly. She also was never more popular with her teammates and the teams they were playing knew Jackee well, so not a bad word was ever heard on the field. Most opposing coaches tell their players to watch her play. In the field she always knows where to go when the ball is hit. At bat, she very seldom swings at a bad pitch and with two strikes becomes a dangerous hitter. Coach Zimmer claimed she was close to a .400 hitter with two strikes. That alone is an unbelievable statistic. She worked very hard with the infielders and the players enjoyed working with her. With Jackee playing, the coach thought he had the best infield in the league or just about anywhere else. When Jackee does not play, he still thinks his infield is one of the best. Catcher Hands Donovan was getting better every year and he threw out over 50% of all the possible base stealers. The replacement for Sonny was the lightning fast Fredie Prince, who was a great fielder with a better than average arm but weak with the bat. Jackee recommended some weight training. Coach Zimmer could not believe the number of boys who wanted to play baseball at Olympus College. Applications had more than doubled since they won their first championship. Coach was thankful for Jackee because he had to spend most of his time with the pitchers. He had 12 pitchers but would only keep 10 for the Spring season. Therefore it was crucial that he got some kind of a read on all the pitchers so in the Spring he could get them ready for the season. By mutual agreement, Jackee left the team with one week left in August and came home

When she arrived at the house, everybody was waiting for her. Rose asked about Sonny, but he had been so busy at medical school that Jackee only had dinner with him one time. All the other conversations were short since both their schedules never matched. Sonny worked 16 hours a day 6 and sometimes 7 days a week. When he had a spare moment, he was either studying or resting. She did tell Rose he is very happy and doing very well in the program. William started to ask Jackee about some things related to the corporation and she asked him to stop. Jackee apologized and said for the next two days she is spending them with Dan and not discussing anything else except their being together. Carmela said "you are 100% right and you and Dan go off and have a reacquainting time." One look from Carmela and William knew he had been shot down and he should keep his mouth shut.

Dan came over after work and before he could say hello, Jackee had her arms around him. She mentioned that the next two days were for just us and she wanted to spend as much time as possible with him. He agreed but said it would have to be after 1pm as he was committed to work. Since she hadn't told him about coming home early, he had agreed to work for his old boss. She said that was fine but "at 1:01 you better have your arms around me or else." Dan kept his word and the next two days they spent together. A large part of their conversation was related to their wedding and honeymoon. Her three sisters will be her maids of honor. She wants all three of them to be standing with her when she takes her vows of marriage. "I know it is unusual but I can not select one over the other. I also want both my parents to walk me down the aisle and give me to you at the Altar. If you agree I want the choir from the orphanage to sing at our wedding. Father Nicholas, before God, our families and all the people in attendance, will administer the vows that I pledge to you for the rest of my life. Then he will marry us and we will be one forever. Dan asked, "what about my vows to you?" "I am sure Father Nicholas will ask you the same vows he asks me. You can take the vows or not. As far as I am concerned, it is not necessary since you have already proved how much you love me many times over."

The honeymoon was a different story because she would be in the last year of the six year medical program. There would be a few days or maybe five days that she could miss but more than that would not be acceptable to the administration. It was finally settled that they would leave on Sunday after the wedding and come back the following Saturday so she could be back in school by Monday. Jon had offered to let them use a timeshare his parents owned in Acapulco. His parents had five weeks that they could use at any time as long as they gave one month's notice. However, Jon said that his parents are always accommodated no matter when they call. Dan agreed that it might be the perfect place for them since not too many people vacationing there would be interested in a baseball player, even if the player is a female. Jackee did not care as long as they were together. William will make all the travel arrangements through the new corporation. The Jenco family had opened a savings and checking account in the name of the new corporation by putting $3000.00 in each. There would be a joint family meeting so Dan's family would know what was going on and could offer some input. Most families have certain traditions that they would like to see included in the preparations and the Silvio's and Jenco's would not be any different. Jackee would not be throwing her bouquet, it will be handed to Rose and her one garter will be given to Sonny, the other will be for Dan. This had all been settled in Jackee's mind a long time ago.

William updated Jackee on their plans to negotiate with the new expansion team. He showed her a list of recommendations and wanted her input for any additional ones. Normally in negotiations both sides make demands and go from there. Dan and William felt that by calling them recommendations it would make the negotiations less stressful. Jackee thought that the most necessary thing was for her to have a private dressing area before and after any game or practice. When the team traveled she would gladly share a room with a female who works with the team, otherwise she wanted her own accommodations. She would participate in any and all team activities but would not be used for a publicity stunt. "I will not accept anyone sexually harassing me. If a member of the team does something like this I want that player disciplined. All my press conferences should be recorded and the recordings saved. I never want to be misquoted or lied about what was said at an interview. Also there may be times when I will want tickets for a group or guest. If tickets are not available, the request will be withdrawn. An extra carrying case will always travel with me. It will contain dress clothing that I may wear if a special occasion arises."

Dan copied all this down and promised it would be included in the negotiations. William mentioned that her bats would be very valuable "especially the ones that were used for your first major league hit, home run, at bat or game winning hit. It might be wise to have them kept in a secured area." "Dad, one very important thing that I forget to add, I never talk or do interviews prior to a game. Once I am at the park or field it is strictly preparation for the game and nothing else. I will accommodate anyone after the game as long as I do not have a previous commitment." William answered, "I'm glad you reminded me, I totally forgot about that. It will be on top of the recommendations but it will not be a negotiable one."

Before Jackee goes back to medical school she has to do a commercial for the baby clothing company. Carmela and the baby went with Jackee and William to the recording studio. It took several hours and little William was included in one of the segments. The director told them that all three segments were excellent. He complimented Jackee for being so accommodating and how easy it was to work with her. The baby was a surprise but he was sure the company would love what the baby added to the commercial. Samuel Hitch the director of the studio wanted to know if William would be available for other baby commercials. Carmela said that she would make him available if the commercial did not take too much time. Mr Hitch told her that "all babies are handled with care and they are never used for more than a certain amount of time. Also all working conditions are well within the child labor laws." "All subject matter in any commercial must be approved by me or my husband before any shooting can begin." Mr Hitch told them that is the only way he works with any child.

Jackee had her last date with Dan before leaving for school. They finalized most of the recommendations that the corporation would give to the new franchise. Later Jackee began crying about leaving but Dan told her that in about 13 months we will be married. "Just keep that thought in your mind and let that be what keeps you going." She loved that thought and admitted it has always been on her mind since they agreed on the date. It made her next year much more exciting and gave her something to look forward to. Dan took her home and made plans to be with her at church before she leaves. Andrea was coming to pick her up and arrived at Jackee's house about 11am. On the way to school both girls discussed their weddings and what their future might be. Andrea was looking to become a general doctor or a researcher. She found that research excited her and the fact was, that she was very good at it. Dr Hopkins had offered her a full time job at his lab but most of the time she will be working at the affiliated hospital research lab. She knew that the hospital lab was top of the line and its reputation was world wide. Jackee wanted to work in the pediatrics field and felt she could do her best in that field. Another big factor was that children would not be interested in her baseball career. Their main concern would be if she could make them better and not her autograph. Andrea said "this could be a very lucrative business, you not only get paid a fee but you also charge the parents $50.00 or more for your autograph. Now that will make medical history." They both laughed, but like Bobby Brown, she wanted to be respected as a doctor as well as a baseball player. When they finally reached the dorm, they both had messengers waiting for them. Jackee had the coach, president of the college, and Dr Hopkins trying to contact her, Andrea had Dr Hopkins and the president of the college leaving messengers. Dr Hopkins had a new research grant for them to start on. The president had two speaking engagements for them. One of the speaking engagements was right at the school but the other was at the big convention center and involved hundreds of students. The one at the school was easy because it was for students already accepted into the program. All they had to do was give these new students some insight into what was expected of them and what they could expect. The one at the convention center was much more detailed since they were competing with other programs that would be offered by other schools. Andrea and Jackee talked with the president as to how he wanted the school presented. He told them that the school was looking for the best and not for quantity. Jackee said that is the way she would have thought to present the school's program. "The standards in our medical 6 year program must be the highest in the country. This would help turn out the best possible doctors since only the best students will be selected to the program." President Washington emphatically agreed with her and wanted them to present their talk exactly with that in mind.

Around 8:30am, and after her workout and breakfast, Jackee and Andrea were at the lab. Lucy had their folders ready and all material laid out for them. They dug right in and two hours later had their lab schedule all worked out. Fall baseball had to be fitted in for Jackee, but once her class schedule was set everything should fall into place. Cach Zimmer knew that she would have little free time but he also knew she would be there as much as possible. School work was by far the easiest part of Jackee's day. The course text books were always available to her over the summer and she read most of them cover to cover. All the lectures were taped so she could listen to them over and over again. Lab work for the courses were very easy for Andrea and her since they had a more efficient lab at their disposal. Many times they completed lab work in the research lab because there was more opportunity to really check the results of their findings. Baseball still consisted of a 5am practice and a full workout or game later in the day. Jackee did not mind the schedule since it made the time fly by. Before she knew it the halloween party was there and then they were preparing for Thanksgiving. She finished fall baseball with her best stats ever. Now she had more time on her hands to do school work and research lab work.

Andrea drove her home on the Thanksgiving break and it was two days early since they both were caught up on everything. Carmela met her at the door and could not believe how great she looked. Jackee proclaimed that it was the best first semester she ever had. "Everything just fell into place and there were no bumps in the road."

Since no one else was home Carmela felt it was a good time to speak personally with Jackee. Not 100% sure where to start, Carmela went right to the point. "I am not interested in your premarital relations with Dan, that is between you and him, but I am interested in preparing you for your life together. Marriage is two people working together for a common goal. Anyone who tells you it is a fifty, fifty relationship has no idea about marriage at all. It is extremely rare that any relationship can be a fifty, fifty arrangement. Most disagreements can be resolved by some form of mutual consent in which both parties are happy. There are times however when one party has to give more because the other party can't or wouldn't. On many occasions one would have to give between 60 to 100% in order to make the agreement work. It may not be fair but it is the reality of a good and lasting marriage. You know each other's limits and you make decisions or adjustments accordingly. It is not unusual for one of the parties to make most of the important decisions while the other party has little input. Does that mean one party is dominated by the other or does it mean that they are in full agreement with the decision. The key is helping your spouse make the decision you want without their knowing it. This way everyone is happy and no one feels the decision was one sided." Jackee said to Carmela, "you have given me a good insite as to how a marriage relationship should be but you have avoided any direct mention about sex." "That is because it is between the married couple. There is no one size fits all category in a sexual relationship. It is between the couple to decide what is best for them. There are times when fantasy makes the real thing a disappointment. If you really care about each other, it will be the greatest experience of your life. Otherwise it will be just going through the motions." Jackee thanked her mother for her usual down to earth advice and said "I hope Dan and I will be as happy as you and dad are."

Dan came over later that evening and he and Jackee spent much of the night going over what Carmela had told her. One thing was very clear, Carmela knew both of them better than they knew themselves. Her approach was not a mother trying to protect her daughter but a mother trying to show her daughter how to make a successful marriage. Dan always thought his parents had a very good marriage yet he saw a totally different marriage for Jackee's parents. Since both seemed to be a success he wondered which one is better. Finally they both decided that maybe a combination of the two, plus a few new ideas of their own may be a good way to start. Later on, just being in Dan's arms was enough for Jackee to just fall asleep. She had not felt so relaxed in a very long time. A large part of her future was beginning to take shape and for the first time she was sure about many things. Dan woke her up and kiddingly said how boring he must be for her to fall asleep. Jackee told him that because it felt so good and so safe in his arms she just totally relaxed and thought this is what I want for the rest of my life. She smiled when he said "it will be my pleasure to supply these arms for the rest of your life if that's what you want."

The family Thanksgiving visit to the orphanage and Vets home was again a big success even though Evelyn, Jon and Sonny were missing. Rebecca's family, Dan and Rose were able to make it and as usual the children were a big hit with both places. Rose, Jackee and Carmela decided to really dress up for thanksgiving. They were so excited about going to the hairdresser and called Rebecca to meet them there. At the Thanksgiving dinner the four women were a beautiful sight. William had gotten wind of what the women were planning and he ordered special corsages for them. As they came to the house he gave Rocco and Dan the flowers to give to their partner and he and Carmela gave Rose her flower. Carmela pinned it on Rose and told her Sonny asked her to stand in for him and do the honors.

Rose was crying when she kissed her father and mother and said "I love both of you so much." Rocco got a quick kiss but Dan got a long passionate one. They all laughed as he was blushing when Jackee decided he had enough. Dinner was the best ever but the food was secondary to the four beautiful women at the table. William thought back to how beautiful he thought Carmela was when he first met her. She still was as beautiful now as she was then. Rocco realized that he had just been taking Rebecca for granted and had forgotten how much he really loved her. He thought he would tell her tonight when the conditions were more appropriate in bed. Dan thought maybe a 30 minute cold shower might erase the thoughts that were going around in his head. He realized that it would not work since Jackee was always on his mind. He never thought that a woman could be more beautiful as she gets older but Jackee was living proof that it does happen. Poor Rose could only think how happy Sonny would be to see her now, and how much she wanted him to see her. She promised herself that at Christmas she would look even better for him.

Jackee did have a commitment to do a commercial for the childrens corporation and little William had a shooting at the same time. Saturday the family went to the studio for the takes. Mr Hitch was waiting for them and when he saw William and Frankie together he thought they would make a great take. The make up artist prepared both the children and Jackee for their commercial. Mr Hitch did the children first and within 90 minutes he had 4 great shoots that he felt the principals of the ad corporation would like. He then prepared Jackee for her shoot and in less than two hours had 3 outstanding commercials to show the ad people. When all the shooting was over he complimented all of them for how easy it was to complete his work. One last bit of information he needed. Would Rose and Rebecca be interested in posing for a few stils. He thought about how beautiful the family was and how he might use some of them in the future. Rose said she would be interested but she had to retain her amateur status for a while longer. Rebecca said she would think about it and ask her husband but she saw no reason why he would say no. Mr Hitch was thrilled and mentioned to Carmela that I may have a perfect spot for you and the baby.

Sunday after church Andrea picked up Jackee at her house and they left for school. The two girls had their school work well under control and they would finish the semester at least a week early. A strange thing about Andrea and Jackee, neither one of them has ever taken a final exam. Because they always had an A or A plus the school excuses the holder of such grades from any exams. They had to take a quiz in a health class but that was a pass or fail class just filling in the social science requirements. Their lab assignments were finished but two still needed write ups. Dr Hopkins research was almost done except for coalescing their findings in a final report. Jackee could now spend extra time on her baseball and conditioning programs. More than half the team would be at the field house at 5am, 6 days a week. Tyler and Matt never missed a morning practice and the two of them were really getting good. It occured to Jackee that they might one day be better than the two J's were. She made arrangements to be back in school a week before the school is scheduled to go back in session. This gave them a full 10 days of preparation before spring tryouts. Andrea once again dropped Jackee off at her front door, wished her a Merry Christmas and off she went. Carmela and little William greeted her at the front door. Jackee kissed her mom and carried William into the house. When they entered the kitchen, Jackee saw a small lunch had been prepared for them. Not having eaten anything all day, Jackee was starved and after saying grace she attacked the food. This thrilled her mother because she never felt Jackee ate enough to maintain her normal weight.

Jackee called Dan and left word that she was home. He called back later to tell her he would be at her house about 7. When William came home he filled Jackee in on what had happened with the corporation. "The Vegas baseball team has scheduled a meeting with us on July 1st. A tentative offer including some things that they want included in any agreement will also be submitted to us. We are to read the offer and make any changes or additions and send it back to them. We may have to lose some of the offers for commercials because there may be a conflict with the baseball team's commercials. They have mentioned the condition that the signing bonus must be allocated over a three year period. If you are pregnant and can not play any time during those three years you would lose a percentage of the bonus. That is one condition we are going to fight because even pregnant you still will be able to represent the team in some capacity. Dan and I have worked up an alternative proposal which we think will solve the problem. Frankie and William have done two new commercials together and both have been a success. Rebecca has done one and even your mother has completed a special commercial with the two children. Everyone is doing commercials and Mr Hitch claims they are very good at it. William has over 100,000.00 dollars in his trust fund. We have even had to open a special account for your mother. Our corporation is now handling four additional clients. Mr Hitch wants to talk to Evelyn over Christmas and we got the go ahead to put Rose in a commercial with the money going to Sonny's Indian council. We are now also handling the orphanage account as well as the Indian council. We are taking a 5% fee from each of them. They are receiving 90% of all monies earned. My accounting firm is handling all the paperwork and another 5% is taken for administrative costs."

Visiting the orphanage brought a new surprise to the Jenco's. Each Nun thanked Jackee for the great gift she had bestowed on their community and then they showed her a new wing that held runaway young girls. Another section of the orphanage had been remade into a safe haven for battered women and their children. This was a dream of the Mother Superior for years since she originally came from that type of home. Mother Superior asked the Jenco family to come back on December 28th for the dedication of the center. William and Carmela agreed and everyone got back to the children and their party. As usual Sonny's council sent gifts and Jon's parents sent boxes of toys and clothing. The last thing said to the Jenco family as they were leaving was that everyone is remembered in our daily prayers. William thanked them, wished them a Merry Christmas, and headed for the Vets home. Gifts from Jon's parents were also sent to the Vets. One exceptional gift was a motorized wheelchair, this was to be used by a Vet that had to leave the home for a special reason. Administration had ordered just such a chair but due to budget cuts and red tape it had not been approved yet. William and his committee were in the process of asking for a new administrator to run the facility. There were just too many complaints from the Vets and their families on how things were being run. The committee felt a change of personnel was necessary.

When the family got home they found Evelyn, Jon and Sonny waiting for them. Jon stopped to pick Sonny up at his hospital before they drove to Jenco's house. Jon apologized for being late and missing the annual Christmas visits but he told them he could not leave until one of his patients was stabilized. Evelyn had started to bring out the usual snack that Carmela prepares when the family does not go out to eat. She knew that William would not go to a restaurant unless the whole family was there. With the table set and most of the food out it took only a few moments to get everything ready. Finally after everyone was seated, grace was said and everyone just started filling their plates. Rose had run up to Sonny, hugged and kissed him before he even had a chance to say hello.

Sonny told the family that the council has made Rose a member of the tribe because of the money she had sent to them. "No Indian child will go hungry or not have some warm clothing to wear this holiday season. A portable hospital has been set up to update every child under 16 medical records. There will be no new outbreak of the winter flu or children dying needlessly. Rose, you have no idea the number of people you helped or the lives you have saved. Whatever you want I will do everything in my power to give you." Rose walked over to him and out loud said "I want you". He hugged her and said it's not enough. "It is for me," she replied. They talked and ate and finally Rocco said they better be getting home so Frankie could get some rest. Before long everyone was saying good night and heading home or to bed. Sonny now slept in Rose's room while she slept in Jackee's room.

At 5 am the girls were in the kitchen with a hairdresser. Carmela was the first one showered so she had her hair done first. Each head took only about 25 minutes to complete, so in a little over two hours all the women were done. By 7:30 the women were ready for church. Men started coming down at about 7. William went to his car, lifted the trunk and took out the corsages. He gave Carmela hers and whispered to her that no flower could compare to her beauty. "That was the best Christmas present I ever received," Carmela told him. As the other men came down William handed them a corsage.

Sonny gave it to Rose but first he just looked at her, stunned at how beautiful she looked. "How is it possible that so much beauty can be in one family?" Rose told him, "it is because we are happy and love each other. Now pin the flower on me without sticking me." Sonny did as he was told but kissed her after it was pinned on. Jon was next and when Evelyn came down from dressing in Jackee's room, Jon was surprised at how beautiful she looked. Jackee came down last and William had to take some pictures. Rebecca and her family came just before Dan arrived. Rocco gave the flower to Rebecca and Dan gave the last one to Jackee.

Carmela called out that they had to leave now or miss church. Packed in three cars they pulled into the church parking lot at 7:50. An usher was told about the Jenco's and escorted them to their reserved pew. There was one new piece of information that Father Nicholas added to his sermon. He started off by reminding the people about the problems they were having with the local orphanage. "It seems that the orphanage is not only doing well now but has added a battered women section and a runaway or abandoned child section. A certain young woman in our parish had donated all her modeling fees directly to the orphanage. That doesn't mean that they no longer need your support. It just means for now they do not have to beg for help." Jackee was basically hiding behind Dan and she was not prepared for Father Nicholas telling everyone about what she did. It wasn't a great stretch of the imagination to figure out who did it. When Mass was over Jackee felt the weight of Father Nicholas' talk. She was surrounded and congratulated for this wonderful donation. It took an hour before she was allowed to leave. Carmela and Rebecca took the little ones home and set up for breakfast. Dan and William stayed with Jackee and as soon as possible wished all a Merry Christmas and finally headed for home.

As they walked into the house, it was clear that some people were opening gifts and others were eating. Dan wanted to eat and so did William. They went to the dining room table and sat down. Jackee joined them but she ate very little. Most of the presents had been opened and family members were just waiting for them to all be finished. Dan received his present from Jackee but now it was his turn to present her with his gift. He said to everyone in the room, "you all know that I have asked Jackee to marry me and she has accepted. It is now time to seal this proposal by giving her a ring." He then handed Jackee a small box. She opened it and inside was an engagement ring with the inscription, Jackee & Dan Forever and Always. Dan took the ring and put it on the fourth finger left hand and then kissed her. Jackee was looking at the ring and had tears rolling down her cheeks. All the women pulled Dan out of the way and surrounded Jackee. Dan looked around and said to no one, "I guess I can leave now." Once all the discarded wrappings were cleaned up the family just sat around and talked.

Jackee gathered her sisters and mother and explained how she wanted all three sisters to be her maids of honor and be on the Altar while she took her vows with Dan. She then asked her mother if she "would accompany dad and me down the aisle and up to the Altar. I want a picture of both you and dad kissing me and giving me to Dan." All the sisters agreed that they would do anything she wanted. Carmela agreed to her request if your father says it is fine with him. William quickly told them it was a unique idea and he was excited to do it. Jackee lastly said her bouquet was to be divided into four sections but would appear to be a normal bouquet. Before cutting the cake I will separate the bouquet and each one of my sisters and mother will receive one of the sections. My two garters hold up nothing but they seem to be symbolic in a wedding so I am giving one to my dad and another one to Dan.

At this point Dan stood up and said he had only two things to ask, "Sonny will you be my best man and if it is alright for my parents to stand with your parents as we take our vows." "Oh, Dan, I should have thought of that. It would be like the icing on a cake, and it makes a perfect picture added to our ceremony. Do you think your parents would feel comfortable doing it?" "I'll just tell them you demanded that they do it or else!" "Don't you dare, I'll ask them and beg if I have to. It makes everything come together but we still have to get permission from Father Nicolas to actually do it." William said not to worry because he will make Father Nicholas an offer he can't refuse. Everyone laughed but knew that Father Nicolas would never refuse something that the Jenco family wanted. Jackee and Carmela had already reserved the wedding date at the church and Father Nicholas had agreed to perform the wedding at a high Mass. His singer and organ player will be there to assist the orphanage choir.

Jon's father, Jonathan, suggested they go see a personal friend of his that runs a country club near the Jencos. Carmela and William said, as a courtesy to Jon's parents, they would investigate the country club but they knew the price would be way out of their income bracket. With Dan, Jackee, Rose, Sonny in tow William and Carmela drove to the club. From their house the drive took 35 minutes. It was well within the distance you might have to travel for a reception.

They were met at the door by the friend of Jonathan and he introduced himself as Harold Longsted. He insisted that they call him just Harold. "Jonathan has given me a complete rundown of your family and I am to cater to your every wish. Let me first show you what we have to offer." He then took them on a full tour of the accommodations that were on premises. Even the Bathrooms (called male and female lounges) and kitchen (called food preparation site) were inspected. Plates, napkins and silverware were examined and found to be top of the line. Special silverware was available for children since the adult ones were too heavy for them to use properly. The wedding party table could be expanded to hold as many as 30 adults. Guest tables could be set to be together or surrounding the dance floor. "We can accommodate up to 400 adults or open up the main dining area to accommodate up to 750 adults. There is a florist whom we work with that will do all the flowers for the party at about 40% of the usual costs. Jonathan saved the florist's life and sponsored him for citizenship in the USA. The florist, who took the name John Smith so he could be more American, will set a time to come to your home and arrange your flowers from boutonniere to bridal bouquet. I am to give you his number and you only have to say Harold asked us to call and everything will be taken care of. October is usually a great month to hold a wedding because the weather is cool and there is usually not much rain. We could hold a cocktail hour, which we call, pre-dinner appetizer, on our patio, that also has shade covering. You can select all the food, some of the food, or just tell us to go ahead and prepare it. When the time comes for the people to move into the reception room the leftover food will be wrapped carefully and brought to your orphanage. I was told that had to be one of the conditions. Four of my best people will bring and serve the food to the Nuns and children. Don't tell anyone but macaroni and cheese along with hot dogs and our homemade nuggets will be added to the food. We do not serve that here unless it is requested. About an hour later we will serve the salad followed by an appetizer then a palate cleansing sherbet. Personally I think that it is overkill but the mainstream people expect it. You will have the option. There are over 30 meals to choose from so we wish you to ask your guests what they would like for dinner. Your invitations will include a space for selecting their entree. This is so we have an idea what food to order. All our meals are made fresh, just prior to serving, so we need to know what and how they want it cooked. By the way, a company whose name I'm not at liberty to say has given us a check for $60,000.00 as an advance for this wedding. No records will ever appear of this transaction so the young lady need not worry about her playing status. Someone is to give me $10,000.00 in cash and not another nickel from your pocket. By the way we have both a 4 piece band and a fabulous disc jockey for this wedding available. You can have both or if you prefer to bring in your own people. Since both would be already paid for it seems silly not to have both play. Liquor wise, whatever we have in our three bars are available to your guests. It is our policy that if we determine someone is under the influence, they will not be served any more alcohol. They also will not be given their keys back. We have a sobriety test kit and if they fail, the law says we have to take their keys away. Our final treat of the evening will be after the bride and groom cut their cake we will present our old fashion ice cream and cake hour. All leftover cake will be packaged for the Orphanage or the Vets home if you prefer. It is my under-standing that the Vets can not eat these rich deserts so most of the staff gets the goodies. As I told you before, this is all up to you as to how things happen. We have some examples of the invitations you can send out to get the information we need. Exactly 90 minutes after your wedding mass, food will be coming out for the cocktail hour. Before you leave a brochure will be given to you which has all this information in it. My personal phone number is written inside and I will be available to you anytime day or night. My best time to talk during the day is between 10 and 2, or at night after 10 but before midnight. Read the brochure, talk every detail over and call me if you have any questions. My secretary can help you with most of the questions that come up but you have to make a final appointment with me to finalize the wedding. September 1st will be the last day you can have my full attention after that my schedule is full. Does anyone have a question or are we done here?"

William thanked him and said we have enough information to last us a lifetime. "We will definitely be in touch." Carmela and Jackee both thanked him for the walk through and the presentation and wanted to know one more thing, would he be supervising the wedding. "I am here 16 hours a day mostly 7 days a week so you will see me around. My staff is well trained and well paid so I actually do very little directing. I have found if I stay the hell out of the way things run better." He said goodbye and the Jencos left for home.

On the way home all the talk was about what they had just seen. William could not believe how organized the club was and how much they offered to the guests. This sentence in the brochure must be their guide. Carmela read it to them, "If your guests are happy you will be happy and your gathering will be a huge success". "Our price is about one third of what I expected to spend. I don't see how we can not accept that offer. Even the Vets hall would have cost much more than that."

Dan had not said a word the whole time and Jackee wanted to know what he thought about the club's offer. His first words were, "only in a movie could something like that exist." In his wildest dream he never cast himself in something like that. "Jackee, this is the most important day in our lives and since you will definitely be the center of attraction, it is up to you to decide how you want to spend the day. Jon's parents have called in a lot of chips for our special day and I would hate to disappoint them. Mrs Jenco, how do you feel about this?" Dan asked. Carmela thought the place was beautiful but the choice was theirs to make. "No, Dan said, I believe we need a more mature woman's opinion." She did say that if the family accepted this offer, 80% of all the preparations would be handled by them thereby taking a great deal of preparation and stress from us. "On the day of the wedding I want Jackee free from any and all decisions" Dan said. "I want her to just enjoy the family and more important the whole day. My best man and my brothers in law will handle all the guests at the church and the payments to the church and the people involved. Since no one in the wedding party drinks hard liquor it should be the most sober wedding party in history. The club handles everything from when the wedding starts until it ends. Putting the reception in the hands of Harold is a no brainer." All agreed that the brochure's outline will be followed and Harold and his staff will be in charge.

All the Jenco women decided to select the store where their gowns would be made. They had 5 names including one that was recommended in the club's brochure. One by one they eliminated possabilities and finally settled on the gown shop recommended in the brochure. Miss Grant, the owner, knew that this family would return for their gowns. She was given a heads up from Harold and told to make them a good deal because this wedding is personal. Miss Grant's presentation is usually enough to win the bridal party over. She is the very best because she treats every bride as if she were a queen. The bride is usually the one who is won over by Miss Grant. Jackee was no exception, she loved the way she was treated and how each part of the gown seemed to become part of her body. There was no doubt in Carmela's mind that all the gowns would be purchased from Miss Grant. Andrea would have to come for a fitting but that should not be a problem for her.

Jackee asked about prices and Miss Grant said "I am only allowed to make a 10% profit according to Harold. So the price would depend on material cost and labor. You are not to worry, my work usually makes the bridal party more beautiful but in your bridal party that would be very difficult to accomplish. I will guarantee you one thing, once you have seen my work, you'll never buy a gown from any other shop. I'll need at least one month before the wedding to make sure everything comes out perfect." Jackee said that in June we all will be able to come for the first fitting. Miss Grant agreed, June would be a perfect time to start preparations.

John Smith, the florist, was contacted and a date had been set for a visit to his flower shop. When Jackee and Carmela arrived at the florist a full display was laid out for them to choose from. Jackee explained what she intended to do with her bouquet and Mr Smith informed her that he would make a special arrangement just for her. "You will have your bouquet and there will be four exact miniature bouquets available for your family. There will be no charge. It will be my wedding gift to you." He advised them that no flowers should be selected until you have the colors of your gowns finalized. "You will then decide if you want the flower colors to follow gown colors or have all the bouquets exactly the same. All the men get the boring white carnations unless you have another idea." "Right now we are relying on your expertise," Jackee said. Mr Smith said, "your flowers will be beautiful and the church and reception at the club will have perfect arrangements." Carmela and Jackee thanked him and as they were leaving he gave them a very large daisy to take home. While driving home they talked about how easy Harold made it for them. "Mom, I feel like I am in a dream and everything is perfect." "Jackee, I have never heard of anything like this. These people are the best at what they do and are making sure we only have the best. This makes me wish that the date was closer rather than in 10 months."

Later that night Jackee explained it all to Dan, and he was happy that she was having a good time doing all this with her mother. He mentioned that she had another semester and a baseball season coming up in two weeks. That should more than keep her busy and her mind off the wedding. She agreed to fully dedicate herself to those two things for the next 5 months.

"While you are doing that your father and I will be preparing your transition from amateur to professional. Considering the amount of time your father is dedicating to this, it should be a smooth change. Once it happens everything should fall right into place. No additional endorsements will be committed until after Thanksgiving. Your first professional baseball experience will be free of anything else. There will be no endorsements or speaking engagements until your first season is over. Your father is hoping that speaking engagements can also wait until after Thanksgiving. When final negotiations with the Gamblers are complete there should be an exact time table for you to consider. Your mom has made your father promise that on our honeymoon we will not have a single commitment." Jackee cuddled in Dan's arms and told him that "one whole day was to be spent just like this." "If that is what you want I will be glad to accommodate you, but there will be a 5% fee," he laughed.

The next two weeks flew by and only Andrea called to ask if she could take Jackee back early. It came as a surprise but then she thought it would be a good time for Andrea to see Miss Grant and get her first fitting. Andrea spent the whole day with the Jencos and slept in Evelyn's room for the night. The two girls had spent the day going for the fitting and later to see the country club where the reception was to be held. Since Andrea committed to Miss Grant that she wanted her to do her wedding dress, Jackee took her to see John Smith about the flowers. When the two girls arrived back at the Jenco's, Carmela had dinner all prepared for them. All Andrea could talk about was how great the people were for the gown and flowers. The women talked the whole night and it was after 12 when they finally got to bed. Next morning, after a breakfast prepared by Carmela, the girls left for their final semester at Olympus College.

CHAPTER TWENTY FOUR

Jackee Plays Last Year at Olympus College

$\mathscr{C}$oach Zimmer was glad to have Jackee back at school and ready to practice. He was having many problems scheduling the spring activities. "Many new schools want us to schedule a game with them. Most times the dates don't jive because we have to play certain league games. It seems they all know this will be your final swing through the league and they are trying to cash in before you leave. For the first time in our league history most schools are in the black with their baseball program and it is because of you."

"Coach, do what you think is best but be careful not to put too much pressure on the team trying to accommodate these teams. It would be good if we could be invited to participate in the division tournament." Coach was pretty sure, because of Jackee, the team will be asked to participate. "If what you say is true then we want the team to be fresh and ready to compete." She also told him that Monday will start the 5am workouts and as soon as her lab schedule is finished some afternoons will have workouts.

Jackee met Andrea after her meeting with the coach and they sat down and went over the schedule Lucy had prepared. They thought that Lucy must be a genius because their lab schedule did not interfere with school or any other activities. It was very clear that this schedule was made around Jackee's baseball commitments. Lucy had mentioned that William had been in contact with her and they reached an agreement to work together. "Dr Hopkins has agreed to this as long as his work is not affected." Lucy said that it was a pleasant surprise since she was getting married in 16 months and could use the money. William explained to her that she would receive a 1099 as an independent worker because the corporation has to account for all monies spent. It does not have any employees, it only has clients. While Jackee is finishing school and later when she is just at the hospital Lucy will coordinate all her activities from the lab.

Now baseball workouts were really getting started. Morning workouts were optional but the afternoon ones were mandatory. Jackee found her morning workouts were fully attended. It took a great deal of coordination to get everyone involved but soon they had a schedule that was perfect. One very windy day, the coach took the team outside and had all the pitching machines set up to do pop ups. This was the funniest thing ever. Here were boys trying to catch a ball that was caught up in the wind. Players were spinning and falling and one got hit in the head going for these balls. After a while most of the boys got the hang of chasing down these pop ups but one boy did not have a clue. Coach finally asked him what he would do if a pop up was near you. He replied he would just call Jackee's name and let her catch it. The third time the team did this drill everyone did fantastic. They practiced avoiding collisions by making sure they always stayed to the right. When in doubt go right and this would avoid serious injuries. Relays and backing up plays were also stressed. Whenever there was doubt as to who would field the ball, the person with the best arm would take charge. Coach asked Bats if he would put on a hitting clinic before the season started.

Bats agreed and one Saturday in mid February he came early in the morning. He stressed the importance of preparing to bat. The key to being a good hitter is to have a plan before you step to the plate. He made suggestions as to the different approaches that a batter could take. Then he made some suggestions to improve batting stance, bat position, hip gyrations and watching when the ball leaves the pitcher's hand. When talking to Fredie Prince he made an adjustment to his bat coverage and later told the coach that a second adjustment should be made and he told the coach what to do but not now. "Let him first get used to the adjustment I just gave him." When Bats was finished he and Jackee talked about his new daughter and son.

She missed having them come at Christmas but "I guess it is much more difficult having two children to prepare for a trip." "Kim really missed seeing you but George Herman had a ball playing with his presents most of Christmas day. Besides the fact that this was our first Christmas with Kim's family. You know I follow your every move and am waiting for the big day when someone will draft and sign you." Jackee told him that she has special permission to select my own team. "The commissioner felt it was fine because of all the unusual circumstances my signing will create. We hope to negotiate with the new expansion team from Nevada." Bats thought that it would be a good move because there would be less loyalties among the players. "There still will be some prejudice because of your gender but it should be much less than if it were one of the other teams." "That is exactly what we concluded." Bats left and told her to call if she needed anything at all.

Jackee now started to concentrate on her game. She had to get ready because everyone would be depending on her. It did not take long for her to get bat speed, conditioning and arm strength up to par. In fact she now felt that she was near mid season form. While hitting, she felt the best ever. The ball appeared to be bigger because she was picking it up as soon as the pitch left the pitcher's hand. To her surprise she was hitting with power. Coach asked her if she wanted to still hit in the third slot of the batting order. She loved hitting third and told him so. When the team had their 5 scrimmage games Jackee was playing at her peak level. She hit two homers and four other extra base hits. Everything she hit was a hard line drive. Even her outs were balls hit hard right at a fielder. March 21st they played their first game. Jackee had two hits and only played 5 innings. Coach took her out because the weather was bad and he was afraid she might get hurt. Pitching was outstanding and they allowed the opposing team a total of one hit and no walks. The game was stopped after 7 innings because of darkness. The next 5 games were a carbon copy of this game. Hitting was good, the pitching was better. The first four batters in the lineup were all hitting over 400 and Jackee was over 600. Later, with a 6 and 0 record they went to play Cordia University, a division one school. This is a team they had played before so there was some history between them. Cordia was also undefeated and their coach ment it to stay that way. He had his three best pitchers ready to go and they all had quality arms. What coach Zimmer did not know was that the Cordia coach had someone scouting his team for the last 4 games. A scouting report similar to a major league one was given to the Cordia coach. The main theme of the report said if you neutralized the top 5 hitters numbers 6 thru 9 are not a threat. Additional information included weaknesses of all their hitters. Only the number three hitter appears to not have a tell tale weakness. It is recommended that you pitch her low and inside, leaving nothing in the strike zone. Pitchers were also rated and any tipping off of the pitchers were also indicated. Luckily all their games were being put on video because the school wanted a permanent record of the season in its archives. Cordia pitching held Olympus to just 3 runs but Olympus pitching gave up 6 runs. Jackee walked 4 times and did get one hit. She scored two runs and drove in one but it was not enough to beat Cordia.

Driving back to school, the coach asked Jackee what she thought of the game. She said "it appeared that they had an excellent scouting report on us. I personally saw only one strike all game. Hands never got a pitch he could drive and Matt and Tyler were kept off the bases for the most part. Whatever it was, it was well planned and they played it to perfection." Over the next eight games the team bounced back and even though they played some division one teams all the games were in the win column for Olympus.

Jackee was still hitting over .600 but her walks almost doubled. Coaches were now saying "don't let her beat you." She had not hit a homer and had only a handful of extra base hits. Her hitting showed that she was only taking what was offered to her. Her on base percentage was almost .800 and her runs scored was very high but her total hits had dropped dramatically.

Coach had been over the Cordia tape over and over again. He had sent a letter, along with a copy of the tape to Bats asking him what if anything can be concluded from it. At first Bats had not noticed anything unusual but on the fourth viewing he knew exactly what the Cordia coach had done. He traveled on Sunday morning to Coach Zimmer's house and they both sat down and viewed the tape. In two hours they had broken the game down to its individual parts. Coach Zimmer felt he should have seen it immediately but Bats told him "unless you suspect something you have no idea what you are looking for. You must also assume that the coach at Cordia might have contacted other coaches."

Bats had to leave because of a family commitment and the coach thanked him for all his help. "Without your great analysis I would still be in the dark about what happened." At 5 am Monday the coach was waiting for the team to show up. Jackee walked in early and the others straggled in a few at a time. He sat everyone down and went over Bats' analysis of the tape. "Only one player thought there might be a reason for losing to Cordia, and that was Jackee. She instinctively knew that they were pitching around her but she didn't realize there was a plan for all their hitters. Coach told Tyler and Matt that they had to get on base more so Jackee and Hands don't have the bats taken out of their hands. Every batter has to be more disciplined and force the other team to make good pitches to you. Take whatever they give you and make sure you put the ball in play. I broke down how all of you were pitched to in the Cordia game. It will be in my office and all you have to do is put in your name and your at bats in the Cordia game will come up. Look at the tapes and we will talk about adjustments that have to be made." Jackee knew she would not see better pitchers unless Tyler and Matt got on base more.

Later in the week, they played Melon State and it was obvious that Cordia had spoken to them. Since Olympus was ready for them, it did them little good. The team just played small ball and had base runners on all the time. The score was lopsided and the team loved it. Jackee received a call from Bats asking her to call back. When she did he tried to encourage her to stay within yourself and not let what the other team was doing affect her approach to hitting. She explained how it was taking a toll on her ability to stay focused. "But that is exactly what they are trying to do, get into your head and make you chase their pitch and not wait for yours. You are better than that and when they see it isn't working they will have nothing left to throw at you." She thanked Bats and knew he was right and she had to get back to her strengths.

In the very next game against a division one school, Jackee was walked twice and had one single going into the top of the eighth. With the score tied at 5 each, Olympus had the bases loaded and two outs with Jackee coming to the plate. The first two pitches she saw were off the plate, low and outside. Jackee knew that the pitcher had no choice but to throw a strike or fall behind 3 and 0. She was looking fastball from the belt to the knees possibly toward the outer half of the plate. Coach had given her the hit sign as she waited on the pitch. In it came a fastball thigh high toward the outer half of the plate, Jackee attacked it and sent it flying toward the right center field fence. The ball was still going straight when it went over the fence for a grand slam home run. As usual the crowd was large and many were women who came to see the female phenomen. Today they were not to be dissapointed. This was the best feeling she had in more than two weeks. Even though she was a big part in the team's wins, it never seemed to her that she was doing her share. Today was different, every one could now see her value to the team. The title of team captain was now an honor she truly deserved.

Bats had nailed exactly what would happen and from that game forward things started going Jackee's way. Her batting average was still over .600 but now power had been added and it seemed a new dimension to her overall game also had been added. There still were many after game meetings with fans, mostly women, but there were more and more media people looking for a story. Since it was impossible to accommodate every media person, many stories were now being made up about her and her family. There would be no speaking engagements until the season is over, but these rogue stories were starting to affect her.

Coach saw that she was losing weight and sleeping very little. He decided to take a stand. "There will be only one media gathering and it will be on Sunday afternoon and only at Olympus college. After games her fans will meet on the field in front of our dugout for no more than one hour. If any of these rules are broken, there will be no media coverage or after game talks." Jackee's incoming calls were now being screened and only family and listed people will be able to speak with her.

Jackee felt that a fifty pound weight had been taken off her and she started to respond. She gained some weight and began to sleep better. Andrea was a big help because she screened all calls to the room before handing the phone to Jackee. Her defensive play which had suffered because she was tired now became one of her strong points again. Her team in turn responded by stepping up in game situations and seeing that after the game she had time for herself. Coach never had a team that was so close and caring about each other. He loved that all the members of the team were now trying to protect Jackee. His one big problem was that the team would peak too soon and not be at top form for the division playoffs. Because of their schedule he tried to rest the starters as much as possible. Every player had to play out of position at times to accomplish this. Matt had to play third, Jackee played short and third, and Tyler played second and third. They all DH one or two times. Coach juggled his lineup but it made very little difference, they continued to win and in most cases, win big. Pitching had finally stabilized and now everyone was turning in quality outings. They finished the regular season with just one loss, so they ended up 41 wins and 1 loss. It was expected that they would be chosen to be the number one seed. This year the committee decided to have 64 teams in the tournament, so there will be one extra game and a shorter down time between games. The games will start on a Saturday and the finals will be the following weekend. Final four teams will be housed at a university very near the triple A stadium where the final four teams will meet. This University has room for the 100 or so players and coaches. Locally there are many hotels and motels to accommodate the followers of the four teams. Food service at the university received the rights to sell refreshments at the stadium during finals. They were also given the rights to sell souvenirs and such. There were estimates of up to 10,000 people attending the final four and about 10% more for the championship games.

Game one for Olympus was against the number 64 seed, a small division two school named John Adams college. Their pitching was good but their offense was not up to Olympus pitching. Bobby Jo held them to two hits and then Toby, Hook and Sid finished the last three innings. Jackee had a run scoring double and two walks. The home fans knew that any loss in the next four games ment that Jackee had played her last game at Olympus. The many fans who followed Jackee did not want to miss her last home game. For this opening game the stands were packed and cheered every move Jackee made. After the game the women knew that Jackee would talk to them. Coach finally told the group of women who were left, that they would have to excuse Jackee because she had to prepare for Sunday's game. League representatives called to tell the coach that Olympus was playing the 59 seed, Brennden college. Brennden was a good baseball school with an excellent reputation. Lefty Al Rasko was picked to start this game and when the coach asked Hands how he looked, Hands responded by saying he was glad that he was pitching for us and not against us. Olympus still did their no talk infield drill before the game and it always seems to impress a school who has never seen it. Brennden stopped everything that they were doing and watched the entire drill. Their coach finally called out to them that they had to take the infield next. After the ground rules were laid out the umpire called play ball and the game began. Rasko came out on fire and struck out the side with 12 pitches. Brennden's pitcher retired the three hitters he faced but two of them were on line drives right at an infielder. Except for Hands Donovan's home run, the next two innings produced nothing else. In the top of the fourth Lefty Rasko walked the second hitter and that was the first base runner for Brennden. In the bottom of the fourth, Matt had a hit and Jackee followed with a double down the left field line. Matt had to stop at third as Jackee slid into second. Hands was intentionally walked and Joe Gilardi hit a sac fly to right center scoring Matt. Top of the sixth Rasko gave up his first hit but then retired the next two hitters. In the bottom of the inning Tyler singled and Matt walked to bring up Jackee with none out. With both runners in motion Jackee hit a single to right. Tyler scored, Matt went to third and Jackee held first. She saw no sense in stealing second because they would probably walk

Hands. Her thinking paid dividends later when Hands doubled to right center and scored both base runners. Olympus added more runs as the game wore on but Rasko completely dominated Brennen players and finished with a two hit shutout and a complete game.

Since the next playoff game would not be until Tuesday, Jackee spent extra time talking to the Olympus fans after the game. She was feeling real good and wanted to let the fans know how grateful she was about their being there. A few minutes was spent talking to the media. The rules had been set by coach Zimmer. Any question about the tournament would be answered but all personal questions will not be addressed. That restriction was breached in 10 minutes so the coach broke off the interview and walked Jackee to the locker room. A call from the committee told the coach that Olympus will play the number 50 seed, Springton College at 2pm on Tuesday. Zimmer had heard about Springton college from one of his former players. They had a good baseball program but very undisciplined leadership. They followed a motto of "We will win at any cost". Their athletic director called the Olympus college and told them that Springton will arrive about one hour before game time. Coach Zimmer could not for the life of him figure out why they would arrive so close to game time. There has to be a logical reason but for now the reason escaped him. After much thought, the coach decided to start his big right hander John Sullivan. Sullivan had been pitching lights out. In his last 4 starts his earned run average was under one earned run per game. He had averaged 10 or more strikeouts per game and his arm had been getting stronger as the year wore on. Monday there was a light team workout and a short team meeting. Coach had talked to some other coaches and found that Springton was not the nicest team to play. They try to intimidate the opposing team and will come into a base cleats high. "Throwing at a batter is in their playbook and they use it frequently. They play very aggressive baseball so you can count on them to try and steal and they always look to take the extra base. They have good speed and are very good bunters. Look for them to try and bunt for a base hit." All this information was given out during the team meeting. One change was made in the infield. Jackee was to play third to cut down on bunt possibilities. She was the best they had on getting to a ball and throwing accurately to first base. Matt moved to second and he would cover all attempted steals of second. Outfielders were reminded to backup all infield plays.

The Springton team bus arrived 5 minutes after one. That ment they had 55 minutes to game time and 35 minutes until they took infield practice. When finally leaving the bus they headed to the outfield for their pre game warmups. At 1:25 Olympus started their infield warm ups. It went like clockwork and the field was turned over to Springton. Springton never took the infield and just came into their dugout and prepared for the pre game ceremonies. Introductions were first, then the ground rules and finally the National Anthem followed by the cry of play ball. Only one of the first three batters tried to bunt and he totally missed the ball. Coach wanted to score first and maybe take them out of their game plan. The first three innings saw 18 players bat and 18 outs were recorded. Top of the fourth Springton scored the first run. The number one hitter hit a sinking line drive to left field that Joe Gilardi tried to catch but missed and had the ball rolled by him. Before Freddie could back up the play, the batter was on third. Three pitches later they pulled off a suicide squeeze. With the runner on the move, Jackee had no choice but to throw to first to get the out. Bottom of the fourth saw Jackee up with one out and a runner on first. The first pitch to Jackee was high and inside. It was a "don't get too comfortable at the plate or I'll stick one in your ear" pitch. Jackee got up off the ground, did not dust herself off and dug in the batter's box. The very next pitch Jackee knew would be one in your ear, or a curve ball to try and freeze her. This pitcher had a good fastball but a so so curveball. Jackee sat on the curve ball and sure enough it came and she got all of it. The right fielder started going back but just looked up as it went over his head and out of the field. Olympus now led 2 to 1. Sullivan allowed a runner on in inning 5 and 6 but did not yield a run. Jackee came to bat in the sixth inning with one out and two runners on base. She did her usual preparation before stepping to the plate. Once she was ready the umpire signaled for the pitcher to pitch and in came a pitch slightly behind her head and at the same level as her head. She used the Dodger method of avoiding a pitch and it saved her because if her reaction was to step back the ball would have hit her helmet. Without hesitation the umpire ejected the pitcher and warned both benches that any future errant pitches would cause the player and manager to be ejected from the field. Springton's coach argued that the ball was not directed at the batter but rather was just an errant pitch.

"If I believed that then I would be willing to buy that bridge they sell in Brooklyn," the umpire said. A new pitcher was brought in and allowed to warm up as long as he needed. He took about 10 minutes. Then told the umpire he was ready. Jackee guessed that he would try to get ahead of her so she believed that a fastball was coming. She was now 2 for 2 in guessing because in came a belt high fastball. Fans could hear the contact Jackee made as they saw the ball hitting the wall in left center. Two runs scored and Jackee easily got to second with a double. She later scored and Olympus had a 5 to 1 lead. Sullivan now had enough runs for him to relax and just throw strikes. He did allow one more hit and one walk but ended the game by striking out the side.

Now everyone knew that this next home game would be Jackee's last one at Olympus. The coach heard that seed 34 Paxton had upset seed 5. Paxton would be coming to Olympus at 2pm on Thursday. Whoever wins that game will be one of the four teams left in the tournament. Pitching rotation was now critical. If he could get by this game, the coach would have a full rested staff for the championship games. A decision had to be made and the coach selected Toby. Toby had come a long way since fall baseball. He has the best assortment of pitches on the team. His control, although not perfect, is still good. He may walk two or three in a game but he will also strike out a large number. At Wednesday's practice the coach went over what information he had on Paxton and it was not much. Their pitching was used up in the games they won to get this far. Coach told his team that Paxton had to use their top three pitchers in every game. "If I was a betting man I would say that they will try to do the same thing on Thursday. Paxton's coach must not trust any of his other pitchers. These three pitchers have carried them this far so why make a change now. According to some information I have received, their hitting is just fair and their fielding is very suspect."

Coach made his final adjustment to the team. He decided that they should go back to playing the original positions, where Jackee was on second, Tyler was at short and Matt played third. He asked Jackee if that was ok with her, suggesting that "If you want to play shortstop you have earned that right and I'm sure Tyler would agree." Jackee put her arm around Tyler and said "he is our shortstop and I can't improve the team by playing there. This is our best defensive team." Immediately after this was settled they had a team practice. It was one of the best the team ever had and the mood was loose and upbeat. Coach now felt confident about the team and what their chances were in the tournament. Just as they were leaving the field Paxton pulled up in their team bus. The athletic director met the bus and directed them to their sleeping quarters. He also told them that lunch was now being prepared for them and the practice field and playing field would be available to them for the rest of the day. Coach Zimmer introduced himself to the Paxton coach and said, "if there is anything you need call my office and you'll be helped."

Olympus had a light workout Thursday morning and then an early lunch. Around 11am the stands started to fill up. By 1pm there was not a seat left in the stands. The Olympus ground crew took some movable stands from other fields on campus and put them down the two foul lines. As fast as they put the stands in, that is how fast they were filled up. Behind the center field fence it was sectioned off so that no one would interfere with the batters while they were hitting. However all the area behind right and left field was slowly becoming occupied. Cars were being directed to other parking areas all over the campus. William had Carmela, little William, Rose, and Dan in the car when he pulled into a private parking place just set aside for VIP'S. A special area had to be set aside for the media. Olympus College had made arrangements for local media but was surprised to find that some national media was present. The press box, which usually has a few people in it, was now filled to capacity. Scouts and VIP's had a section behind home plate sectioned off. That now had twice as many people as planned. The school had never seen anything like this before and their accomodation was stretched to the limit. A call went out for portable bathrooms and every close to the field building had its facilities made available to the crowd. A PA system was set up for the game as well as for a special tribute to Jackee. Players could barely make it to the field because of the large crowd, and people were still coming in.

Both teams completed their pre game drills on the field and now a ceremony was to take place. President of the college Mr Washington welcomed all the people and said beside this being a tournament game "we also want to honor one of our own. On this field there is a young lady who has dedicated herself to the school's medical 6 year program, graduated with the highest awards this school has to offer and has led this baseball team to three consecutive baseball tournaments. Just to add a bit more she has been voted the MVP of the first two tournaments. She has set an example for every young girl in this country to follow. She has spoken to thousands of people and in my humble opinion should be women of the year. Ladies and gentlemen I am proud to introduce to you Jacalyn Jenco or as she is known to us as Jackee." The cheering was so strong that in some of the buildings things fell off shelves. "It is one of the team rules that they don't speak to the media or people before the game. To honor this rule we will have Jackie speak after the game."

When everything was ready to go the home plate umpire called "play ball". Toby was ready and his first pitch hit 97 miles per hour on the radar gun. He struck out the side on 10 fastballs. Tyler led off with a single to center, Matt bunted for a base hit but just got beat to first by a great throw by the pitcher. Jackee came to the plate to a standing ovation and it lasted a full two minutes. Paxton's coach was having none of this and he intentionally walked her. He later paid the price when Joe Gilardi singled to center and scored Tyler with the first run of the game. Stretch Ward also single scored Jackee and Casey doubled to left center scoring Joe and Stretch. Olympus had a 4 to 0 lead after the first inning. Toby went out in the second inning and just kept throwing fastballs. He walked one hitter but retired the others without any damage. Olympus had runners on base every inning and did score a few more runs. When Toby went out to pitch the top of the seventh he had an 8 to 0 lead. That inning Paxton got its first hit, a double to left center. Fredie tried to run it down and did make a diving try but it was a clean hit. Going for the outs the runner scored from third later in the inning, on a ground ball to Jackee. Toby struck out his last batter to finish his seven innings allowing 1 hit two walks and had 12 strikeouts. Hook and Sid pitched the last two innings to finish the game. Jackee had three walks, a single and a line out to the shortstop. In the top of the ninth with two outs, Coach replaced her with Oscar Olando, the backup infielder. As Jackee walked off the field she was given an ovation fit for a queen. It took three curtain calls before the crowd would let them finish the game. The Paxton coach stood in front of his dugout and clapped just like everyone else and within a few seconds all his players were doing the same.

Before Jackee spoke after the game, the coach located the final ball and had every player sign it and then give it to Jackee. No one seemed to leave as they waited for Jackee to speak. Jackee thanked everyone for being so kind to her. She thanked Olympus College for allowing her to fulfill her second dream of becoming a doctor. "I love the game of baseball, it is by far the fairest team sport ever played. There is no clock to stop you and no one can take away your right to bat or even one strike. In a nine inning game you are entitled to 27 outs and the game will not end until you have had every one of them. I thank God every day that He gave me the talent to do the thing I love most. Thank you again and may God always be by your side."

She waved and went to where her family was. Carmela and Rose were both in tears and Rose kiddingly said "where is my ball?" Jackee handed her the just signed ball that the coach had given her. Rose threw her arms around Jackee and told her she loved her the first time she held her hand. Now they were both crying. Dan came over and hugged both of them. William was with Carmela and little William but he could never imagine the little girl who could barely pick up a bat would turn into a beautiful woman who is about to make history.

Later that evening Jacket and her family were treated to dinner in the faculty cafeteria. Coach Zimmer and the team joined them along with other selected people. All the food was top of the line. Dan held Jackee's hand most of the time. Coach had one announcement and that was which teams are still alive in the tournament. He told them that they play Cordia at 1pm Friday. "At 4 pm Hairston plays Olmstead. Losers play Saturday at 10am while the winners play at 2 pm. Sunday at 11am the second game will be played and if a third one is needed, it will start 30 minutes after the end of game one. Boxworth College is putting up all four teams and their extended helpers. There are plenty of hotels and motels in the area and there is plenty of parking at the Triple A sports complex. It takes about 5 hours to drive there so our team bus will leave at 4:30am Friday."

Dan walked Jackee back to her dorm and since Andrea was not there he stayed the night with her. They cuddled on the sofa and Jackee was asleep in less than 2 minutes. Around 4 the phone rang and it was the security desk notifying all players that the bus will leave in 30 minutes. Dan had been awake and when Jackee woke up she apologized for falling asleep on him. She said being in his arms was so relaxing she just drifted off. "I have not had that kind of sleep since baseball started in the spring. Watch out Cordia. I am fully rested and raring to go."

Dan smiled at how beautiful she was in the morning. *She doesn't need any makeup or fancy clothing to show her beauty. Her innocence is such that she never thought that something may happen to her when she fell asleep in a man's arms.* He heard her getting ready and a few moments later gathered up her baseball gear and she was ready to go. Dan walked her to the bus, gave her a kiss and said he'd see her at the game. He stood there and watched the bus leave and continued to watch until it disappeared from his view. He had to find the motel William was staying at. He assumed it was the same one he usually booked so he just walked there. Sure enough William's car was in the lot but it was still only a few minutes to 5. He went to the managers office and explained what happened so the manager told him he could use the office until his people woke up. Dan saw William go to his car about 8am, he told him what happened and how he couldn't move after Jackee fell asleep. He had no thought about how he was telling the father of the girl that they slept together the whole night. Carmela did ask later if Jackee slept well and Dan told her what Jackee said to him. All Carmela could say was she was glad. At 8:30 the family was on the road to the Triple A stadium. They arrived at the stadium at about 1pm.

About 9am the bus arrived at the complex. They were directed to Boxworth College and they were met there by a member of the student council and directed to their rooms. Twenty minutes later all Olympus players were having breakfast. Not too much longer after that they were on the field practicing. Since Olympus college was the highest seed they became the home team. All the players were introduced and finally the words Play Ball was heard. Rasko started for Olympus and according to Hands he had all his stuff. Cordia had one base runner but Al left him stranded. Bottom of the first Tyler made out but Matt worked out a walk. Jackee came to the plate. On the first pitch Jackee hit a ball over the fence but foul. The next pitch hit Jackee square in the middle of the back. There was no way to avoid being hit. Before Jackee could talk, the whole Olympus bench poured onto the field. The pitcher was running for his life as the bull pen came running from the left field line. None of Cordia's players on the field was trying to help the pitcher. The three umpires were doing their best but 3 against around 20 was not good odds. Home plate umpire had ruled that it was on purpose therefore the pitcher was disqualified for the remainder of the series. He also warned each coach and bench that any other incident like this and both player and coach will be disqualified. Jackee went to first base but still could not believe that every player on the team was willing to protect her. At first she had trouble breathing but now it was just a pain in the back. Whatever advantage Cordia might have had in giving Olympus their only loss was gone now. All Olympus players now wanted to destroy them. Hands came to the plate and promptly took the new pitcher downtown. The ball exploded off the bat and landed fifty feet behind the left field fence. Olympus jumped out to a three to nothing lead. Rasko had good control and never went to a three ball count on any batter. Jackee stayed in the game until her third at bat. That is when she doubled with the bases loaded and cleared the bases for an Olympus 6 to 0 lead. Coach sent Orlando to run for Jackee and to play second base. Rasko finished 8 innings allowing 3 hits, no walks and no runs. Codia was dead; you could stick a fork in them because they were done. Jackee was getting treatment when the game ended and soon returned to the dugout to be with them as they celebrated. Coach told the team to go and relax and he would see them after the second game. He and the other coaches were going to scout the other teams.

Jackee met her family and they decided to have an early dinner, but they also wanted to know how Jackee felt. Not one to complain, Jackee just said she was glad it had not been in her chest. "There you have real pain. Most of the pain is gone now but the trainer told me it would be very sore tomorrow." She had some problems eating but did eat pretty well. The milk shakes were easy to get down and they really made her feel good. Dan did not even try to hold her because he had no idea where it would be safe to touch. Her father had been upset until he saw the whole team going after the pitcher. He had not seen that before and in fact never heard that such a thing happened. William wanted to know if it hurt for Jackee to swing the bat. She mentioned that when she hit with the bases loaded it hurt until she saw the ball roll to the wall, after that she just felt fine. After dinner she heard there was to be a short team meeting at 8:30am. Dan stayed with her and she wished she could sleep in his arms tonight, but the dorm rooms were restricted. The trainer came up to her room and gave her a sonic treatment to help keep the swelling down and to take away some pain. It helped Jackee get to sleep and she stayed that way for the next 8 hours. At the 8:30am meeting the coach told the team that they would be playing Hairston. They beat Olmstead 5 to 4 in 10 innings. Hairston is a good all around team but we match up well against them. All of the three important things in a game, we are better than they are. If we play our game no one beats us. Later that morning Olympus had a light workout and a short batting practice. They were ready and showed it in their infield drill. In the game for third place Olmstead blew out Cordia by a 10 to 1 score. Cordia left immediately after their game and had their athletic director stay to pick up their trophies.

Being the number one seed gave Olympus home field in the first game. Hairston will be the home team in game two and a coin toss will determine the home team if a third game is necessary. Sullivan was selected to pitch game one in the best of three. Hands told the coach to sit back and enjoy the next two games. Coach did just that. He decided that the team does better when he just lets them play. Olympus line up was exactly the same one the coach used for the first game of the season. He handed it to Jackee and asked her to take it to the pre game meeting at home plate. Prior to taking the field, Hands held a meeting in front of the dugout and told the team that they have come a long way together and had just two more games to play. "I want this team to dedicate these last two games to our coach and to the player that started Olympus baseball on the road to success, our captain Jackee." With a loud yell Olympus took the field. Jackee looked around at her team mates and thought to herself, *there is no way any team is going to beat us.* Sullivan, Sully for short, did exactly what lefthanded Toby had done except Sully did it right- handed. He just reared back and fired fastball after fastball. There was one very big difference, Sully had excellent control. He did not try to pace himself because he knew that both Hook and Sid were well rested and both were lights out pitchers. Hairston's starting pitch kept everything scoreless until the bottom of the fourth inning. Matt led off the inning with a single and went to third when Jackee had a hit and run single to right. Hands were intentionally walked to fill the bases. Gilardi, the next hitter, was hit on the elbow by an inside pitch. Stretch drew a 10 pitch walk. As Jackee was crossing the plate she told Casey, who was the next hitter, to look for a first-pitch fastball since the pitcher just walked a run in. Sure enough, Casey got a fastball and lined it to centerfield for a two run single. Fredie bunted both runners over and the DH, Al Temple drove both runners in with a single between short and third. Starting the top of the fifth Olympus led 6 to 0. Sully allowed one hit in the fifth and two hits in the sixth but none of the runners scored. In the bottom of the sixth Olympus scored three more runs, one each being driven in by Jackee, Hands and Joe Gilardi. The seventh and eight innings, Sully retired Hairston in order. Coach Zimmer replaced the starting line up with players on the bench. Coach asked Sully if he wanted to finish the game and Sully told him, "Hell Yes". The first game in the best two out of three was won by Olympus by a score of 9 to 0.

Jackee took a quick shower and the Jenco's with Dan in tow went to the local Catholic Church which was located not two blocks from the field. William took the family out to dinner after and they ate at a restaurant that was packed with Olympus fans. Jackee was the center of attraction. This was not expected although she knew that the school had hired 6 buses to bring the fans to the championship finals. Now she realized that no matter where they ate, the same thing would probably happen. By 10pm Jackee just had to get some rest so they apologized and drove back to Boxworth College.

She so much wanted Dan to stay with her but knew that Boxworth had set a special room for her in the female dorm. She had her arms around him and whispered "4 more months" and kissed him good night. Jackee was in bed and sound asleep before William entered the parking lot of his motel. Plans for Sunday had already been made. Jackee would have breakfast with the team and then get dressed for the game. Around about 10am both teams began warming up for the second game. Hairston took infield first since they were to be the home team in this game. Olympus went through their infield drill without a hitch. Hands once again called the team together and said "this is the final game of the season, so let's make it a great one. Bobby Jo will pitch us a great game so let's back him up with good run support." Players were introduced, the Anthem was sung and finally the umpire called, "Play Ball."

First two batters for Olympus made out but when they pitched carefully to Jackee, she drew a walk. Jackee took a good lead off first and on the second pitch took off for second. She was just wasting energy because Hands hit one a mile over the fence. She waited for Hands at home plate, when he arrived, she said "you got all of that one." "It felt really good," he said. Bobby Jo retired the first 6 batters but ran into problems in the bottom of the third, the first two batters singled. The next hitter bunted them up a base. Their lead off batter hit what appeared to be a hit between first and second but Jackee with a full out dive, knocked the ball down, recovered it and fired a strike to Bobby Jo covering first.

Bobby Joe retired the next hitter so Olympus still had a 2 to1 lead. Top of the fifth Fredie led off with a bunt single and on the second pitch to Al Temple, sole second without a throw. Al hit a ball to second moving Fredie to third. With the infield playing in, Tyler hit a single up the middle. Matt followed with a hit and run single to right. Jackee pushed a bunt toward the second baseman and beat the throw to first. Tyler scored and Matt was on second. When the Hairston coach came out to talk to the pitcher, Jackee told Matt not to steal third because they will walk Hands intentionally. Hands has a hot bat and he loves runners on base. The pitcher, being very careful, fell behind Hands 3 and 0. Hands signaled to Jackee and Matt that they should be running on this pitch. During the Hairston conference , Hands felt that the pitcher was told to keep throwing curve balls and not to give him anything good to hit. So Hands was looking for a curve ball and that is exactly what the pitcher threw. Both runners were on the move as soon as the pitcher started his pitch toward home plate. The pitch came in and it was a below average curve with nothing else on it and Hands hit a line drive that hit the center field fence on a fly. Both runners scored easily and Hands had a double and two more RBI'S. He later scored on Stretch's single which increased the Olympus lead to 7 to 1. Bobby Jo now had a big lead so he just kept throwing strikes and let his defense become part of the game. After he completed seven innings, the coach used his dynamic duo to complete the game. He took Jackee out of the game with one out in the ninth. She of course received an ovation from the large crowd. When there were two outs he took Hands out and of course he received an ovation.

After the game, Olympus fans and the baseball team were congratulating each other in the middle of the field. The pitchers were telling everyone that they were the real MVPS of the tournament. It took some time before the commit-tee had everything set for the awards ceremony. Olympus College was given the championship trophy for the third straight year. The MVP of the tournament however did not go to Jackee but it did go to Hands Donovan. Spokesman for the tournament said the choice was unanimous. Jackee hugged Hands and said he was the perfect choice. "You are the reason we so dominated the other teams and our pitchers just followed your directions. All three games of the finals, you called three perfect games."

Many of the Olympus fans were still waiting for Jackee to speak with them. She did come out and spent about an hour with them. After the hour, William and the coach came over and told the people that Jackee had to change before going back to Olympus. Jackee thanked the fans for always supporting her and she hoped God would always be by their side. She then went to shower, packed her stuff, put it on the bus and then got something to eat with the team. One hour later the team bus was on its way to Olympus College. William took the family and Dan for something to eat then started the trip home. Olympus Col-lege was waiting for the bus when it pulled in at 10. About two thousand people were there to welcome home their champions. Coach was first off the bus and the players forced Hands to get off next. Someone speaking into a portable PA system called out his name and the fact he was the MVP of the tournament. The team was cheering for Hands from inside the bus. All the other players started exiting the bus. Cheering got much louder when Jackee excited and she once again was the center of attraction. Andrea was there and she offered to help Jackee carry her bags back to the dorm. Someone announced that there was a buffet in the faculty cafeteria and will be there until midnight. The two girls dropped off the bags back at their dorm and then headed for the buffet. Actually they did not dine in but took some food back to the dorm. Jackee told Andrea that she was exhausted and could barely keep awake. While Andrea cleaned the snack up Jackee got ready for bed. She sat with Jackee until she was sound asleep and then went to her room. Next morning they had breakfast and took some food for the road. Back at the dorm they took what was already packed, put it in the car and started for Jackee's house.

CHAPTER TWENTY FIVE

Jackee Turns Professional

*A*ndrea pulled into the driveway and parked behind Carmela's car. Carmela and Rose came out the front door to greet them. Rose hugged Jackee and started helping Andrea carry baggage into the house. Two trips and everything was inside. All the bags except the one containing dirty clothes were taken up to the bedrooms. Evelyn's bedroom would be Andrea's for the night. A call went out to Miss Grant and a 3:30 appointment was arranged for Andrea. As usual Carmela had prepared a lunch for the homecoming and she and Rose waited for the girls to come home before they ate anything. So now the four women sat down to lunch. Jackee talked about school and the medical program as well as the baseball season. "I want to do as much as I can for the wedding. As soon as we recorded that last out, all I could think about was seeing Dan and making sure all our plans were properly laid out."

Carmela told Jackee that "Mrs Silvio and I tentatively selected a format for the wedding invitations. We just need your input and final OK to start having them printed. Harold Longsted called to tell us that two limos have been reserved for the wedding date. The only thing we have to pay is $200.00 for each driver. They will be at our house one hour before the church and they will be finished when you are dropped off at the country club. Jon's parents have arranged transportation for both of you to the airport on Sunday and the same limo is picking both of you up when you return. You can use Dan's car from the country club to the hotel after the reception. Only the guest list, final selection of flowers and color selection, fittings for the gowns and seating chart for the reception remain to be done." "You and Mrs Silvio will have to give Harold the food choices that come back on the invitations. Dan did say he would like certain food available for his friends but I think Harold has that all covered."

Dan came over after dinner to find that Jackie and Andrea had selected the colors for the gowns and that his mother and Carmela were going on Saturday for their first fitting and color selection. Sunday the two mothers and Jackee would select the flowers. It seemed to Dan that once he had his tux all he had to do was show up.

July 1st, there was to be a meeting with the Gamblers. This was their first year playing as a team. Players had been selected from all the other clubs last November. All six teams were now playing but the major league team was struggling and attendance had taken a downturn after memorial day. They do have the number one selection in the draft but it usually takes a few years for that player to reach the majors. Their five other teams are doing as well as can be expected. Four of them are in cities that never had professional baseball so they are still doing well at the gate. Jackee wanted to know if she would be at the meeting. William said he wanted her at all the pre negotiation meetings but when it was time for bargaining he did not want her there. "For the final meeting you should be there to give a final OK."

Dan told her that he and William had been on the same page since day one. Your father is a great organizer and a tough negotiator. I firmly believe that he is the right person to handle this. Jackee went over to hold Dan's hand and said she could not be better represented by any one else.

Right after this meeting, Jackee and Dan went for a walk and they talked the whole time about the next few months. They walked back to the house and got in Dan's car and drove to their favorite parking area. Jackee was in his arms before the car was turned off. She just wanted to be held and feel the security his arms gave her. One thing did come out, she said she was scared for the first time about playing baseball. All the other times at every level most people thought she would fail. She knew that was not an option for her. The playing level, as she moved up each level, had only been a one jump deal. Since she was at the top of her game at every level, it was easy to produce at the next level. "The jump now is playing with the best players in the world. The Major league teams have over 800 baseball players. Just using the United States as an example, that comes out to about 1 major leaguer every 500,000 people. If you include all the countries that our players come from it's probably more like 1 player out of every 2,000,000 people. Dan, I need you more now than ever before." He held her tight and could feel her shaking. Never before had she ever questioned her ability to play at any level and now it seems her confidence has been shaken. In the moonlight he could see the tears on her cheeks and he slowly kissed away each one. He let his lips slip down to hers and it seemed to be magic. She responded and her tears stopped and she held him so tight that he could feel her heartbeat and now he just wanted her to be part of him.

When she let go of him it was after midnight. He drove her home and just before he kissed her good night, he said that she had nothing to worry about "because the woman who kissed me had enough strength to face any obstacle and overcome it. I love you and it's you who gives me some of that strength she told him."

First meeting with the Gamblers was very informal. They introduced themselves and laid out their plans for the future of their teams. They wanted Jackee to play at their single A club starting July 15th. "We want you to be part of our family, in fact we want you to be the face of our family. No one who scouted you told us how beautiful you are. We do know about the talks you have given and when we received notice, one of our people attended the talk. It has come to our attention that you gave all the money you earned doing a certain commercial to an orphanage. Jackee, you are the person we want and we hope your baseball skills are as good as your character. If for some reason you can not play baseball at this level, we still want you to be the face of our family. A young lady like you comes once in a lifetime and my organization wants you with us. We will accept any reasonable demands in the hopes that this can be settled by the end of this week. We have a full campaign ready to go at our single A facility."

William said "we are demanding only a few things, the rest are recommandations we would like to see in a contract." Mr Bragan who seems to be the main person in charge asked what non negotiable items are we talking about. William listed them and then talked about money. He said that "the average number one pick goes for about 5 million. We want 2.5 million up front on a non refundable basis. 1 million more is to be put into a retirement account for her and her family. The remaining 1.5 million is to be given to Jackee on a three year plan. Every year she plays, half a million is to be given to her. If she only plays 1 year the other million is forfeited. If Jackee were to have a pregnancy, the payment would be frozen until her return. Most important is her privacy especially prior to a game. There can never be an interview while she is preparing for the game. After the game they are fine but the organization should have some standards that have to be met. Her privacy when preparing for a game and after the game is a must. She should have her own dressing area and her equipment must be kept secure. You know that if she is successful her personal things will be very valuable. She will make a great spokesman for the team especially with women and young people. We will never compete with the team as far as commercials are concerned. She will not advertise alcoholic beverages or any type of drugs. Even if certain drugs are legalized she will still not endorse them. We know there is no way you can control what is said by the other teams. Media coverage and how she is treated can almost never be controlled so we hope the organization will do its best. Controlling what goes on in house can be and should be handled by the organization. What might be said by the sensational papers or scandal sheets will affect the organization so we want your backing by providing legal assistance. We also suggest that you limit Jackee's endorsements so other team members are not cut off from earning extra money. Jackee learned baseball from the very best. She will always put the team and her teammates first. Nothing is more important than protecting the game of baseball and that will always be her goal. She is getting married on October 20th and the minor league season should be over. If you intend to bring her up when major league teams can extend their rosters please keep that date in mind. It would be nice if she has at least from the Monday before the wedding free from any other obligations. Here is a written presentation of most everything I have just said along with some other recommendations. Read them and then give us any changes and any other things you need to have included in the agreement. As soon as I have your changes, within a day or two you will have our response. This can be settled in a week and both sides will be satisfied before any agreement can be reached."

Mr Bragan thanked William and Jackee, he told them he is "meeting with the owner and legal staff at 9am tomorrow and I will get back to you right after the meeting. I believe your offer is very generous and if this was anyone else it would be a done deal. That is not the case here. We are entering a whole new change and it will be even more difficult than the ones that came before this." As Mr Bragan was leaving he told Carmela that her apple strudel was the best he ever had.

William asked Jackee if everything was said properly and "did I cover all that you want?" She told her dad that he was fantastic and asked for more than she expected. "Dan, at the next meeting, I want you in on the conversation. This is going to be a big part of your life too." Dan said, "there was no way that I could have entered the conversation. You were unbelievable in how you handled this. I know I'm supposed to be a voice in this corporation but there is still much more I need to learn before I can improve on your presentation." "Dan, you know more already but you are holding yourself back by letting it intimidate you. Jackee is going to be your wife and what happens to her has a direct bearing on your life together. I will protect her legally but you must protect her physical well being. Carmela and I want you to handle all the commercials that are going on in the family. There will be a family meeting over the July 4th weekend on this but when I talked to them they all seemed to agree. Sonny even offered to have some Indians available if you needed them for commercials."

Dan smiled and told them that he has been studying books on the great negotiators and he does believe he could handle this part of the corporation's business. "I intend to expand the corporation's interest in commercials because I truly believe we can grow into that part of the business culture. This will open a new door for us when and if Jackee decides to stop playing." William had not thought about that but now realized that Dan was making sense. He knew he was right about Dan's ability but now realized it was even better than he thought.

Two days later Mr Bragan had requested a noon meeting with the Jenco's. When he arrived with a lawyer and secretary he was shown into the dinning room and a lunch was set for his staff and the Jenco family. William told them, "Carmela prepared this so we could just sit, eat and talk as a family would over lunch." Bragan and his staff had never been treated like this in a negotiation setting but he knew better than to do anything but accept what was being offered. Everyone ate and had some non-alcoholic drink with the food. There could be no more relaxed setting than what existed right then. Bragan asked if he could take off his jacket and Carmela said please make yourself comfortable. After taking off his coat, he looked at Jackee and asked his assistants if they had ever seen a more beautiful baseball player. "William, as a negotiator I am supposed to make the best deal for my client as possible. I can not do that. Everyone in my organization including our ground crew wants this wonderful young lady on our team. I have a contract here that was supposed to be altered as we negotiate a final deal and then a new copy made for signing. We have basically accepted everything you wanted however we did improve on some of your suggestions. Jackee will be protected 24/7 while she is with the organization. The owners insisted that no harm is ever to come to her. We have hired the best female bodyguard as her companion for the season and any event that she has to attend for the organization. She is on our payroll for the year. If Jackee in the off season feels uncomfortable about attending an event all she has to do is call and her bodyguard will be there. Let me tell you how much the organization thinks about Jackee. We understand that she is scheduled for a honeymoon in Mexico. If she feels threatened by going there, her bodyguard will accompany them. Personally I thought it was overkill for the organization to do this. But one of the owners told me about baseball players who were shot or attacked. He also told me about an American baseball player who was kidnapped playing summer ball someplace and he had to be ransomed to secure his return. I am now one of the big supporters of this condition in the contract. Within 24 hours of the signing, the 2.5 million will be deposited in any bank you say. While you are reading over the contract I would like to speak with Rose about something."

William took Dan and Jackee into his office to read the contract. Rose could not figure out what she might have to do with a baseball organization. Mr Bragan said to Carmela "please feel free to sit in, it may help Rose to relax. Neither of you may be aware that before we sign any player or worker, we do a full background check on the person and their family. Our investigators found that you are adopted by the Jenco's. One of our owners is also an adopted child and he sponsors an orphanage he built and paid for. He wants someone to be the spokesperson for that orphanage. Since your family checked out so well he hoped you would consider his offer. He will guarantee that your amateur status will not be affected and he wants you on the board of directors as his personal representative. He knows about your Olympic trials coming up and he can wait for an answer until after the games are completed."

Two hours later William, Jackee and Dan came out of the office and approached Bragan telling him that the contract was acceptable. "Jackee wants to know if there is going to be a media photo opt at the signing." Bragan said "a signing this important has to have coverage. This represents a once in a lifetime signing event and by its very nature has to be preserved for the archives." William said she knew that, but did not want it turned into a media circus. "Also she wants the people who helped her get to this level to be there."

"The organization anticipated that this would be one of the biggest sports events in history. The organization has to do this not only to recognize Jackee but to energize its fans. Jackee can have as many people as she wants. Your whole family is invited. There is a big dinner the night before to introduce Jackee to our people. Whoever you want to invite is fine with the team. At the hotel where this dinner is being held we have reserved 100 rooms and a suite for Jackee. Right now it is possible that the main ballroom at this hotel may be where the signing will take place. They have everything we need and can accommodate over 1000 people. July 8th will be the dinner at 6pm, on the 9th at 10am Jackee will sign her contract. If this schedule is acceptable to you we have a deal." Jackee said "I have five guests and their families plus my family and Dan." Bragan told her fine, "just call my secretary and give her the names and numbers. A private plane will be at your airport for an 11am flight to Vegas. A charter bus will take you to the hotel."

Jackee called all 5 coaches and invited them to the signing. Within an hour she had all five saying they would come with the families. Jackee called the team secretary and told her the numbers and names of the people. Carmela had contacted all her daughters and gave them the information. Jon could not attend because he was scheduled to perform surgery that day and it could not be postponed. Sonny could make it because he was between rotations for those days. Dan went down to pick him up and also picked up Evelyn.

10:45 on the 8th, all the people going to Jackee's signing were boarding the private Gamblers team jet. There was an inflight lunch served on the flight. There were steaks and lobsters for the adults, and franks, hamburgers and chicken nuggets for the younger travelers. By 2pm they were all registered and given their rooms. Jackee could not believe the suite she had. It was bigger than any room she had ever been in. In the bedroom there was an elaborate bathroom with a steam room. It also had a kitchen with a fully loaded refrigerator, and a living room big enough to hold a dance. A bar fully loaded with soft and hard drinks. The hotel manager personally showed Jackee to her suite and let her know if there is anything she would like, it would be provided.

"If you wish, our beauty saloon has an appointment for you at 4pm today and 8am tomorrow. Here is my card: call me anytime for assistance." Dan came into her room and told her the whole family could move in here.

William and Carmela came in and said "is this the best the Gamblers can do?" Jackee did say it really did not have everything because the 18 piece band was missing.

Later, they went to the hotel's private dining room where all Jackee's future employers and staff were waiting. Bragan did all the introductions and never missed one person's name. Jackee, who was dressed beautifully and with her new hair-do, was introduced to the owners of the team and their wifes. There was one major and two minor owners. Mr Brickly was the major owner and the money man. His wife was much younger and could be a professional model. He reached for Jackee's hand and told her how proud he was that she selected his team as the one she wanted to play for. "I'll personally see that you never regret your decision. If for any reason you have any doubts, please come to see me immediately. My staff has been told that you always have a direct line to me." It took at least 30 minutes before everyone was introduced. Much to Jackee's surprise the staff went out of their way to congratulate her and most said it was the most courageous thing any woman could do. Bragan requested everyone to find a seat because dinner was about to be served. This so called dinner was over the top as no one could possibly eat like this. You could get a steak, lobster and chicken on the same plate. Pork and lamb were also available. Caviar was made available upon request. Pizza, hot dogs, mac and cheese and french fries were just some of the things that were made available for the children. There is nothing that can be said about desserts because if you could name it, they served it. The children were all going to be sick.

Jackee stood up and thanked everyone for being here with her. She told Mr Brickly that this was not necessary. "I hope your staff enjoyed it because they probably deserve it much more than I do. You have made me and the people I love most, feel that you care about us. I hope and pray that I can repay you by making your fans love the Gamblers. I will dedicate myself to keeping that promise because I love baseball and want all our fans to feel the same way. From my heart I want to thank you again and from this day forward please treat me as one of your players. When I am wearing a uniform it will be much easier to do."

Mr Brickly told her that "your family and friends will receive one of my gold cards which gives them the right to attend any gamblers home game. My private box is always available to my friends. We hope that your relationship with us will last a lifetime. Thank you for wanting to be part of my family."The party broke up a while later because the staff had a great many things to do before the signing tomorrow. Jackee and all her family and friends went to her suite. Only the children and one parent went to their rooms. Most everyone has had a long day so most left after a few moments to go to bed. Jackes parents left next followed by Rebecca and Rocco. Evelyn and Rose stayed for a time but finally Sonny said he was tired and going to his room. Rose left with Sonny and Evelyn followed. Dan was going to leave but Jackee asked him to stay a few minutes more.

He did and Jackee said "can I sleep in your arms tonight, please?" Dan did not know if it was the right thing to do. Jackee said "tomorrow is the most game changing thing I have ever done and I need to feel secure for just a few hours now." Dan agreed and they went into the bedroom and settled on the bed. Jackee curled up in his arms and fell asleep in less than two minutes. Being tired himself it wasn't much longer before he was out. Five hours later Jackee stired and the both woke up. "That was the best sleep I have had in the last two weeks. Your arms are a magic elixir for me. I'm sorry if you were uncomfortable and I promise to make it up to you but last night I needed the strength of those beautiful arms. Today I am ready to face the world knowing you are there for me. Thank you," and she kissed him as passionately as she could. She then ran off to shower, get her hair done and dress for the signing.

Bragan came to Jackee's room and briefed her on what was to happen. "You will not have to wear a uniform or even put on a team hat. Mr Brickly felt you were too much a lady for that old gig. He wants you to be yourself because he found that to be perfect. At 9:45 I'll meet you and your family downstairs and I will get them seated behind you. Once they are ready and the front office is seated, I will introduce you to the media. There are over 500 people waiting to see you. I have never seen so many media people. This is twice what we had when we first introduced the team." He told her not to worry because "you will handle it just like you did last night." Bragan left and she put the finishing touches on how she was going to present herself.

William and Dan came to her room and said it was time. Her family and friends went to the signing room and Bragan was waiting for them. He laid out where they were to sit and a few moments before 10 the organization people filled in their chairs. Bragan finally said to the audience that "I am going to introduce not our selection but the one who selected us as the team she wants to play for. Also this beautiful young lady will be the first woman ever to sign a contract to play professional baseball for a major league team. Ladies and gentlemen, I give you Jacalyn 'Jackee' Jenco."

Jackee came out to a wild round of applause and it lasted for a few minutes. When it stopped she thanked everyone for coming and took the opportunity to thank the Gamblers organization. She then went on to say "what a great country we live in where a five year old girl had a dream and many years later that dream became a reality. You never achieve great things alone. I had a great deal of help. My parents were the reason I had the dream at all. Without their love and support none of this could have started. Along the way people had to have faith in me or the dream would have died there. My first little league coach for softball, Mr Chuck Summers, please stand, he saw the possibilities in me and helped make me a better player. He took the chance and it was up to me to prove him right. The next barrier was jr high and would the school let a girl play baseball instead of softball. Coach Dan Wangel please stand. This coach told everyone one simple truth, he will play the best player no matter who it is. He took a great deal of heat because we were approaching a new frontier. We proved he was right. Next in high school, Coach Mickey Begali, please stand, had to endure abuse from our school and most every school we had to play. He simply told everyone if you can find a better baseball player, show him to me. No one took his challenge. Once again we proved he knew what coaching was all about. Next was summer baseball and I was lucky enough to play for this man, Coach Bats Howard. My father told me he was the best man he ever served with. Dad also said he had the best baseball mind. Coach Howard came to my house to tell me to forget this impossible dream. He worked me out until I thought I would drop but he saw in me a desire that was so great he had to see if it was real. For two summers I played for him I saw his team dominate their summer league. He is the best and he made me believe I could be the best. Most of all, his love for the game drives him to help any player or coach who seeks his help. They will in turn receive the very best help and advice they are looking for. Each level of play has a standard that has to be met in order for players to achieve success. The college level provides the link between amateur and professional. Since there are so many colleges we have many baseball coaches. You can easily separate the good ones from the others by seeing if they respect the game. Baseball is not just any game, it is America's game. It tells you what America is all about. Baseball is the fairest game ever played. Everything about it shows how fair it actually is. There are no time clocks to stop play. No game can end in a tie and every team has to get the same amount of outs and at bats or else the game is not over. There have been players 5 feet tall and some close to 7 feet tall. You have players who can run to first in close to 3 seconds and others who are clocked with a calendar instead of a stopwatch. You have pitchers who throw 100 MPH and others who throw in the 80's. Both seem to win games. College coaches have to sort all these differences out in order to put a good team together. Race, religion, gender, or size have nothing to do with playing the game. Good coaches will put the very best players on the field, because that is the right way to play the game. When coaches came to speak with me, I was always worried that they may try to use me as just someone who might help them draw attention to their team. Similar to what Mr Finley did years ago when he signed a little person to play on his team. He tried many gimmicks, some good, others distracting. I did not want to be a gimmick or a distraction. I have worked since I was 5 years old to get here and nothing or no one is going to stop me from trying. Coach Zimmer, my college coach, gave me the opportunity to reach this level. He never once tried to use me as anything more than a baseball player. All these coaches here took varying degrees of abuse because they let me play baseball. I hope that what I have accomplished justifies their faith in me, and makes up for all the abuse that had to take because of me. I will make one promise to the Gamblers and their fans, I Will give 100% in every game I play and the day that I can not, will be my last day in uniform. Thank you and God Bless you all." Everyone in the audience and everyone on stage stood and clapped until they finally had to be stopped.

Mr Brickly told the audience that the team was honored to have a player like this on their side. "Now I want to sign her before the other clubs realize what they missed and try to steal her from us. Jackee, if you will please come forward with your agent to sign our agreement. You will notice I have already signed all four copies. The Hall of Fame has called me to ask for a copy of the agreement, and it be sent to them so that they can display it in their museum. This will probably be my only connection with the Hall of Fame."

William and Jackee approached the desk that had been set up near the podium. Bragan gave Jackee a gold pen to sign the contracts but after she signed the first one he took the pen and put it into a special display case and presented it to Jackee. He then took 3 additional pens and had her sign the other three copies. William signed all four copies with one pen. All four copies were put in special envelopes and one was given to William, the other 3 were put in the hands of the organization's legal counsel. One of the envelopes was already addressed to the Hall of Fame.

Jackee answered questions for the next hour. Very few were about baseball. Most were about her personally. She tried to say as little as possible because she did not know these people and had no way of knowing what they would say or write. She did introduce her family and her fiance Dan. All questions about a pending marriage were given an off limits answer. When the questions started to get repetitive Bragan stepped in and said lunch was being served in the main dining room, all were invited. William told Jackee that she handled this signing as if she had done a hundred of them. "This organization really loves who you are and what you can do. I truly believe you made the right choice." Dan was waiting for her to have lunch and when she entered the room, immediately went to her and said how proud he was of her and how great her talk at the signing was. She kissed him and said she was glad it was over, now all she had to do is prove that she can play baseball at this level.

Before Jackee left to come home she was given an itinerary by Mr Bragan for her trip to join the single A team in Terre Haute. The Hustlers are starting a seven game homestand on July 15th and the organization wants her there the day before. Their private jet is to pick her up at 9:30 on the morning of the 14th. They will have her in Terre Haute before 11:30 and someone from the team will be at the airport to meet her. She then will be taken to her quarters to unpack and have something to eat. Later she would be escorted over to the baseball field where she would meet the manager and coaches. Sometime after that, she will meet and be introduced to the other team players. "It is our wish that this will be a smooth transition for everyone. Our coaches and manager have been given the responsibility to make that happen. The front office discussion with them made it clear what is expected. Have a safe trip and once again welcome to our team." The itinerary was signed by Mr Bragan but also countersigned by Mr Brickly.

Dan asked Jackee if she was nervous about this and she said "yes, but not any more than I was at other beginnings. Of course it's a giant step but it is the step that I have worked for all my life. This is what is called the moment of truth. I will either succeed or I will have wasted many years for nothing." Dan said "you are wrong. You have opened new doors for every young girl in junior high, high school and college. Not to mention little league, summer baseball and many other sport possibilities. All over this country young women are using your victories as a reason for them to be playing some sport or other life program. Sports may have been the start but now many more opportunities are open to them and it is all because of your dream at age 5. You can never be a failure because your whole life has been one huge success. For you this should be the easy part, all you have to do is play the game you love." She kissed him and thanked him for being there for her.

CHAPTER TWENTY SIX

Jackee Plays First Professional Season

*S*omehow the local paper heard about Jackee leaving to join the Hustlers and printed the story. The airport was now filled with well wishers especially women and young girls. At first Jackee just assumed it was a normal airport crowd but soon realized it was for her. She looked at Dan and her parents and they knew what just went through her mind. *Please God don't ever let me disappoint them*. It was impossible for her to talk so she smiled and waved to them. The receptionist on the jet came down to escort her on the plane but also to make sure her luggage was properly put on board. Jackee at the top of the boarding steps turned and waved to the crowd once more and to her family. She mouthed the words "I love you" to them and turned to enter the plane.

The receptionist introduced himself as Walter but said she could call him Walt. He showed Jackee to her seat, made sure she was buckled up and prepared for take off. When the plane reached cruising height he explained what his orders were for her. First he gave her the names of everyone affiliated with the Hustlers, from the manager to the locker room attendant. Next he described her accomodation for living in Terre Haute and when the team travels. He also thanked her because this was the most fun he has had since joining the Gamblers. "I have been ordered to buy lunch for you and the crew and was given a voucher for more than my salary to pay for it. Now you are either someone special or I have died and gone to heaven."

She told him we are supposed to be going to Indiana, "which may be heaven to some, but I just consider myself to be a baseball player not an angel. Please ask the crew where they want to eat and that will be fine with me. You have been very helpful but please just treat me as a fellow employee of the Gamblers." "I am an employee of the Gamblers, Walt said, and when I have to travel it's by car, train or bus. This is my first time on this plane and I never knew we had a private jet. My usual travel money is $25.00 a day."

Part way into the trip, the pilot came into the cabin and introduced himself. He gave her their ETA and advised her that flying conditions were perfect. Walt wanted to know where he and the other pilot wanted to have lunch. He said there was a small restaurant they usually went to on trips here but it was nothing fancy. Walt looked at Jackee and she just nodded. "That will be fine and when we get there, I'll put in a call for the limo."

The pilot reminded Walt that he "needs to know when you are ready to return so he can file a flight plan with the airport." Walt asked if they wanted to spend the night here or go back later tonight. "I would rather fly during daylight than at night. There is no rush to get back so let's plan on staying the night." Walt agreed and this would give him time to prepare his report and make sure everything went well. During lunch Walt called for the limo and gave his location. When it arrived Jackee thanked the pilots, wished them a safe trip back and left with Walt. Jackee was quartered where most of the players stayed but had a room all to herself. It was much like the average dorm room, nothing fancy but had all the necessities. Walt helped her with the luggage and also some of the unpacking. Jackee changed into practice clothing and tried to look like a ball player and not a lady. Walt came in and informed her that the manager and coaches will all be at the field by 3pm.

Walt and Jackee reached the stadium at 2:45 and looked around the field. A few minutes to three they walked into the manager's office. Walt introduced Jackee to the manager Bob Ferris and the other two coaches, Herb Higgins and Donnie Dingle. She said hello and the manager welcomed her to the team. Jackee looked at the faces of the three coaches and knew exactly what thoughts were going through their heads.

Making a bold move, she started talking to them. "I know you are all in a ticklish situation but let's be very clear as to what I expect. I am a baseball player and I have proven over the years that I can play on a high level. You have doubts and well you should. Unless I prove myself on this level there is no reason for you to accept me. All my life I have played for coaches who have said, I play the best baseball players available to me. That is all I expect of you. If after a fair chance you feel I don't belong here, I will accept your decision. If I feel this level is too much for me, I will quit and give up baseball. Is what I have just said a fair assessment of where we are right now?"

Manager Ferris said "I like and approve of what you said and I welcome you to the team and guarantee you will be given every opportunity to play on this team. You have called the game. I only play the best baseball players on this team. I do have a secret to tell you, Bats Howard called me and threatened to make me a eunuch if I didn't give you a fair shot. On top of that ticket sales have almost doubled since the local paper wrote a story about you playing here. We hope you do great because we also want to improve our standing with the organization.

There will be a team meeting at 4 and all the players were told to be on time. My players know that a fifty dollar fine is the standard fine for violating one of my rules." They showed Jackee where she was to change before a game. "Your temporary shower has not yet been installed but we do have a promise it will be done by August 1st. If there is an emergency or if you want to shower before going back to your room, you can use my shower and I will personally see that you are given all the privacy needed. Your size was sent to us and four uniforms have been purchased for you. There are two home and two travel sets and 3 pairs of baseball sneakers have been put into your locker. We were told that number 7 was the number you wore all your playing days so that number has been put on all your uniforms and equipment."

She thanked them but said it was not necessary. "I would hate to have someone on the team give up their number for me". "Actually the number was not being used and no one has requested it." "That number was worn by my father's favorite baseball player so when I started playing softball I took that number and kept it ever since."

Coach Ferris said he will personally address the team about how he expects them to treat our new female baseball player. "They know that I keep my word so what I tell them is the law." "The last time I saw Bats he told me no player on your team will respect you if they think you are hiding behind the manager. You have to show them that if it becomes necessary you are capable of taking care of yourself. He gave me a few options and I think there is one to fit this situation. If it is on board with you, I would like to speak to the other players." Manager agreed, and told her "it would be a better arrangement if it did come from you."

The whole team, coaches and players were together in the locker room when manager Ferris introduced Jackee to the team. He told them that this was going to be a new experience for everyone involved. "This is just another situation you have to adjust to. You all have made these adjustments in the past and it will be the same now. All cursing in this locker room and anywhere in this complex is to be kept to a minimum. Jackee is to be treated as you would any other teammate. If you have a problem with that either quit or we will suggest a trade be made. You will take abuse from the other teams in the league and even some fans. It will only last once around the league. I will not tolerate any disrespect from any player on this team or any other team toward Jackee. Are there any questions?" One player wanted to know if this is a real ball player or a gimmick to sell more tickets.

"Jackee will answer that question." "Thank you manager Ferris. I intend to take a position from one of your starters. Not because someone says it's mine but because I will earn it. There are two basic rules I follow and one is that any teammate that has my back, I will have theirs. Second rule is that I will not tolerate anyone abusing me physically or vocally. Now I did not say I will not take a joke. That is accepted in most every looker room. You all know the difference. Let me make my position very clear. This is my all time favorite bat. With this bat I have hit many balls one at a time. Now if I am ever abused I intend to use this bat to hit 2 balls at one time. Just like all of you, all I ask is a fair and honest chance to play baseball on this team. If I can't cut it no one will have to ask me to leave. Guys, I have worked since the age of five to get where I am standing now. I have taken more abuse in one month than you have taken your whole life. You can not understand how it feels to be the only different player on every team you played on including this one. All I ask of you is to be treated as you would any other new teammate. I am looking forward to playing for manager Ferris and beside you on the field." When Jackee finished, the manager told the team that "we open a seven game home stand tomorrow at 7pm. Everyone here is 4:30."

Jackee had dinner with the coaches and Walt. Walt picked up the check and told Jackee he was leaving in the morning and wished her luck. He told the coaches that he would report back to the organization on how this was handled and "I am sure they will approve." After Walt left the coaches thanked Jackee for the meal. She hadn't paid for the meal and she told them so. Coach Ferris explained that "the organization never bought us a meal but because they felt you should have one we were "colateral" guests." Jackee was dropped by her room and made a few calls. Later she started reading the medical textbooks she would be using next semester.

Her first day in professional ball started pretty much as every day starts. She got up early and ran for about one hour. Around 11 she had a light lunch and headed for the baseball field. The equipment man was there and he directed her to the weight room and batting cage. She used the weights first then did some stretching and finally the batting cage. There was some rust in her swing but the contact was good. Luckily her hands were still tough so although they were a little sore there were no blisters. Now was the time to rest and change into her home uniform. Everything fit perfectly, even the hat. You don't break in new shoes during a game, so she wore her own shoes until her new ones were ready for game use. She decided to run the next few days with the new baseball shoes and hoped that no bruises or blisters would appear on her feet. The noise from the hustlers locker room indicated that players were getting ready to go out and practice. She followed a group out to the field. Most were either playing catch or some other loosening up exercise. Jackee jogged around the perimeter of the field and then started playing catch with another player. He introduced himself as Buddy Banta, the shortstop on the team. Jackee thought he looked like a baseball player but noticed his arm was not much more than average. She wasn't sure but it seemed that she would play second tonight and a coach probably told him to get acquainted with the new player. Just before taking batting practice she saw the lineup card and slotted in the number three batting order was her name and second base next to it. Actually there was number 4 next to her name and not a written word. Teams usually hold a team meeting prior to starting a new series to go over the team they are playing and signs. These signs are used during the game to communicate with the players on the field or at bat. It was no different here. During her live batting practice she did really well. When she got the timing down, the balls started flying all over the field. One of them cleared the left field fence and one was a line drive off the right field wall. Ferris had been warned by Bats that Jackee had good power. The other players didn't get that message until now. Most stopped whatever they were doing and watched her hit. Buddy looked at Sid Hemus who was the second baseman before today and told him to find a new position or a new job. When she finished hitting she took a position near second and field ground balls as well as those hit in batting practice.

When Jackee first came out to warm up very few people were in the stands. Now as the team ran out the stands were packed. Coach said this was the biggest crowd since their first game. Jackee heard her name and saw more women than men in the stands. Hustler's starting pitcher, Clyde Kress retired the side in the first inning. Jackee came to bat with two outs and drew a 10 pitch walk. Jackee saw that this pitcher took a long time getting the ball to home plate. She signaled to Ferris the steal sign and he returned the signal. The next pitch Jackee was off for second and stole the base easily. On the next pitch to catcher Teddy Bartoli, singled to center, scoring Jackee with the team's first run. The fans were cheering and no one was sure if it was for Teddy or Jackee or both. In the third inning Jackee batted with runners on first and third and sent a long drive to right center. Center fielder made a nice running catch but the runner on third tagged up and scored the second run for the Hustlers. Clyde held the visiting team scoreless until the fifth inning. Top of the fifth, the Waterloo Warriors scored two runs and had the bases loaded with two outs. The next batter hit a blooper to short right center that appeared to be a sure hit. Jackee ran at top speed to the place she felt the ball would drop and as she got there she saw the ball just in front of her. Instinctively she dove for the ball, catching it just before it hit the ground. For the third time she came down chest first. With the ball clutched in her glove, she rolled over holding her glove in the air. Second base umpire gave the out sign and the top half of the inning was over. Jackee tried to get up but she had the wind knocked out of her, and the pain in her chest was very bad. Right fielder Tommy Foster and center fielder Hank Dryer helped Jackee get up. Still trying to catch her breath and in some pain she slowly walked toward the dugout. Although the fans were cheering for her, she later claimed she did not hear any of it. Coach Ferris took one look and told her Sid Hemus would take over at second so that the trainer could check on her. She entered the main locker room which was empty except for the equipment manager. The trainer being a male didn't have a clue as to how to examine her. He just asked what hurts the most?

Jackee told him that this has happened more than once and she had a creme but it was not with her. "What actually hurts, the trainer asked?" She told him that her left breast was hurting more than her right one. "I am wearing a special protective device and I should be fine for tomorrow's game. After I shower I'll put my creme on and most of the sting should be gone." The trainer said he did have a creme for surface injuries but I feel it would be unwise to use it in that area of the body. "However, before you play again I will have every medication you might need in my bag. Please accept my apology for not being prepared, it's my job to be prepared for emergencies." Jackee told him, it is not your fault, It's mine for being so careless.

Coach Ferris came in between innings to check on her condition. She told him not to worry, I"ll be ready to play tomorrow. Coach just said we will see what tomorrow brings. He did ask her to come out and sit on the bench because "the crowd wants to know if you're OK. Did you hear the ovation you got after catching that blooper?" "No I did not." "Well they continued to clap until you left the dugout." Jackee said she didn't hear a thing. "Trying to catch my breath and assessing my damage was all I could think about. Coach thought that her catch was one of the best he has ever seen. This team has never had defensive play of that caliber. I believe you will take this team to at least the next level."

Jackee went out to the dugout for the last few innings and showed herself to the crowd. After the game she did spend about 30 minutes with the fans before the coach came out and told them that she had to be treated but she will be back tomorrow. Jackee went into her dressing area but just took her uniform off and changed into street clothes. Coach Higgins drove to her room and made sure she got in safely. Jackee immediately prepared for a shower and checked on her injuries. When the hot water hit her chest she jumped, after a few moments it began to feel better. Stepping out of the shower she looked in the mirror and had some black and blue marks. She rubbed her creme on both breasts and about one hour later most of the pain had left the area. Thinking about calling home and Dan brought one funny situation to her mind. What if Dan were to see her right now with these black and blue marks, *would he still think I was sexy*. She made up her mind that he would never see her like this.

A concession at bed time had to be made, she could not sleep on her stomach as she normally did. It really did not make much difference because she was so tired that once she had her head on the pillow it was lights out. Next morning she felt pretty good and decided to have a big breakfast since the only food she had was the small buffet that the club provides in the locker room after the game. She had to wait until all the other players were dressed and that meant there was not a lot left. Coach Higgins recommended this breakfast, lunch, and dinner place he said was very good and reasonable. Jackee ordered the special with juice and fruit. It was a small steak, two eggs, hash browns and a choice of drink beside all the coffee you could drink. She put a dent in the meal and took the fruit with her for later.

Coach Higgins would pick her up at 3:30 for the next game against the warriors. He was there on time and on the way to the park, he said "a package meal would be given to you after the game. They hadn't realized that you had to wait until everyone was dressed before you could come into the locker room. Coach Ferris corrected that this morning." Arriving at the field she sought out the trainer and showed him her special creme. He said "I'll order it right now and have a second bottle added for when you're on the road."

As soon as the coach saw her, he said "do I pencil you in or do you want to rest one more day?" Jackee told him that she was good to go and would like to play today. He said "fine and I'll pencil you in the three slot." As Jackee was preparing to go out and warm up, every player on the team came over to ask how she was feeling. This surprised her since she thought it might take more than a month or even longer for her teammates to accept her.

The crowd tonight was even bigger than the night before. When Jackee was announced the applause was loud and long. In the batting practice before the game, Jackee had some problems swinging. She decided to take a short stroke because that gave her very little discomfort. If she really had to drive the ball she could and would take a full swing. George Glen started for the Hustlers and he threw very hard. He walked one batter but retired the other three. Jackee batted with a runner on second and one out. She took a fastball and hit it to right center for a single, scoring Hank. She then scored on a double by the catcher Teddy Bartoli. Teddy eventually score on a hit by Butch Davis. Hustlers led 3 to 0 after one inning. Jackee lined out to the third baseman in the Bottom of the third. The at bat in the fifth saw Jackee leading off the inning. She reached for an outside curve ball and hit it over the first baseman's head and down the right field line. By the time the right field got the ball back to the infield Jackee was sliding into third. She later scored on a sacrafice fly by Butch. Coach took her out of the game to give her some rest. This game eventually turned into a blowout. After the game Jackee stayed for over an hour talking to the fans and signing various objects. As was promised, the caterer provided a great meal for her. She took it with her when Coach Higgins brought her home. She showered, put on her PJ's and had dinner while talking to Dan and her parents. This is how the next 5 days went. The Hustlers were on a roll, their hitting and pitching were outstanding. They won all seven games of the homestand and Jackee was hitting over .500 with 10 runs scored, 8 RBI's and 7 walks. Her defensive play was the best on the team and the ticket sales were going through the roof. Coach Ferris told the team that the bus was leaving tomorrow at 8am for the start of the next 8 games on the road.

Coach was worried about their first four games with the Madison T Birds. They were a good team but not one that you could grow to like. To them, winning anyway you can was acceptable. Coach took Jackee aside and explained his analysis of the T birds. Jackee mentioned that she has played against unruly and dirty teams before. "There are not too many places on my body where I haven't been hit. As long as I can expect some help from the team, it should be OK. The umpires are the key. If they are in control of the game it should not be much of a problem."

The Coach of the T Birds met the bus and directed them to the visitors locker room. Although they were advertising Jackee to increase ticket sales there was no private dressing room for her. The female trainer for the T Birds took charge of Jackee and provided her with a private room to change in. They talked for a while and she told Jackee to be careful because her team has a bunch of S.O.B's on it. She found them to have national hands namely Russian hands and Roman fingers. "They tried to grope me every chance they had. Last week I put an end to it by breaking one of the offending players' hands. Just to add some icing on the cake, I refused to take care of him. Luckily the manager saw what happened and backed me up. Just be very careful around them." Jackee thanked her for the heads up. Hustlers batting practice was from 4 to 4:30, their infield was at 6:30, and game time was 7. During the T Birds hitting and fielding, Jackee noticed that the left fielder had a weak arm and two of their hitters had late swings and a third one pulled everything. She mentioned it to the coach and he checked it out and agreed with her assessment.

Umpire called, play ball and Hank led off and flied out but Buddy singled and that brought Jackee to the plate. Even though she was a visiting player, the crowd gave her a big hand. The first pitch was a fast ball high and tight. Jackee just did get out of the way. The catcher said "welcome to Madison honey. You should be home playing softball."

She stepped out of the box and asked for the tar rag. While she was rubbing the bat she said to the catcher, "hey bad breath there are two things wrong with that. First I'm not your honey and would never even consider it, second if I weren't here you would be playing in front of empty seats." She got back into the batter's box and figured a curve ball was coming. So it was, a curve ball breaking over the plate. She got all of it and it hit the wall in right center on one bounce. Buddy scored easily and Jackee slid into third with a triple. Teddy drove her in with a long fly ball to center. The next time Jackee batted was the top of third and the first pitch was at her head. She did the Dodger tuck but the ball still hit the top of her helmet.

She expected that the umpire would issue a warning. He did nothing. On the way to first the pitcher said "you're lucky I feel sorry for you." Jackee went to first and on the next two pitchers stole second and third. Now the pitcher was pissed off and tried to pick her off third but threw the ball away allowing her to score. Jackee batted in the eighth inning against a different pitcher but his first pitch was at her feet. She got herself ready for the next pitch and when it came in she swung and the bat went flying over the pitcher's head. He was shook up and finally he glared at her and she told him it slipped out of her hands, "but next time I'll be a lot more accurate." The crowd loved it, but the umpire still said nothing. After the game the umpire approached her and said he was proud of her and that he intentionally waited to see if you were going to respond.

"You were perfect and I doubt when word gets around, and it will, only a fool would now go after you. Welcome to professional baseball." She thanked him and when she looked around there was a huge crowd of women waiting to talk to her.

That night she not only called her parents and Dan, she also called Bats to tell him how his advice helped her. He said he was very proud of how she was handling herself and that he had been given an update on her playing from Coach Ferris. He told her he knew about her injury and "I'll bet your parents don't know."

She also told him that she had expected much better pitching than she is seeing now. They are no better than division 1 pitchers. "Any pitcher with some talent is usually moved to a higher level," Bats told her. "Most of the pitching you are seeing now are pitchers that are filling a roster and have little chance of making the show (a major league team)."

Next 3 games against the T Birds had the same results, the Hustlers won all 3 games and were heading to play 4 games against the Rock Island Robins. Coach Ferris told the team that the Robins were an excellent baseball team and that the manager is one of the best. He will probably be the next manager of their big club. "Coach Brady has done a great job with the Robins."

Jackee said that "he spoke at my college about pitching and was an excellent speaker." Coach Brady had his top two pitchers ready for this series and Jackee saw good pitching. The Robins won the first two games and held the Hustlers to 10 hits so far in the series. Jackee did have 3 of the hits but they were all singles. Good fielding kept the Hustlers in both games but it eventually came to driving in runs. Crowds were very large for both games. The Robins usually drew a good crowd because they put a quality team on the field. These 4 games drew as many as on opening day. Jackee was still the object of interest with the fans. After each game, mostly women gathered near her dugout and waited for her to join them. She always spoke for a minimum of an hour. Coach Brady joined her and when she had to leave he personally thanked her for being so cooperative.

Game 3 was a different story, the Hustlers came out swinging and they scored twice as many runs as they did the first two games. George pitched a great game and his defense played like pros. In fact the last out Jackee dove for a ground ball and from her knees threw the runner out at first base. She also made an over the shoulder catch in short right center but did not have to dive for it. Her usual gathering after the game was even bigger than at any other game. She spent most of the time speaking with younger women. Jackee had resisted talking to the media and the club backed her on this. Game four was a nail bitter as both starting pitchers were at the top of their game. The score was still tied at one run apiece going into the eighth inning. Each team had three hits and each team had someone hit a home run for their only run. Buddy grounded out and Jackee batting next had an infield single. She stole second and went to third on a grounder to second by Butch Davis. Jackee noticed that with two outs the pitcher went into a full windup. She signaled coach Ferris about a steal and he signaled back an OK. The third base coach gave the take sign to Teddy and he understood what was coming. Taking his sign the pitcher never checked Jackee on third and split his hands to start his throw home. By splitting his hands it meant that he had to throw home or commit a balk. When he finally saw Jackee out of the corner of his eye she was half way home and he tried to speed up his delivery. It became so awkward that he stumbled off the mound and never threw the ball. Second base umpire signaled that a balk had been committed and the base runner was awarded home plate. Hustler's starting pitcher Roger Mc Shea completed the game adding a 1,2,3 eight and ninth inning. Jackee's fan club after the game was more excited than ever. Most of the fans who see Jackee play realize she does have a chance to make the show. Women who had been praying for her to be successful were now asking themselves when it was going to happen.

When coach Brady joined the group the question was asked directly to him. Coach Brady responded by saying "the final decision rests with the front office but if he had a say in her future I would say within two years. She appears to be at the peak of her game and a finer young lady would be very hard to find." Jackee was blushing a little and she thanked him and the fans. She told them she was sorry but had to leave as the team was leaving for home early the next day.

On the bus ride home, coach Ferris had Jackee sit next to him part of the way . He told her he would send in an evaluation to the home office. "It is no secret that you can play baseball, what has to be seen is if you can play on a major league level. At first I was really scared that recommending you might reflect directly on my chances to move up in the organization. This is no longer the case. You have made a believer out of me, and my analysis of you is an easy matter. You are the most rounded, dedicated and baseball wise person I have ever met. There is no 100% telling what a person might do in a given situation, but you, just being on the team makes it a much better team. There are only a handful of baseball players who have fit the description. I originally thought that bringing you along would get me a higher rating with the organization. Instead of me teaching you, you have taught me what it takes to make it to the show. Jackee I heard coach Brady say in two years you should be ready for the show. I personally think he underestimated you. I believe that next year you will be called up from triple A to finish the year with the big club."

Jackee thanked him for his kind words and said "I have never given less than 100% any time I was on the field. That is what I was taught and that is what I always do. The day I can not give 100%, I will leave the game forever."

The first two weeks in August were a tough fourteen days. The days and nights were above average in temperature every day. Night games weren't to bad but day games were devastating and double headers on Sunday were share torture. In the second game of a double header Jackee thought she saw two batters at the plate. She realized that she was dehydrating. Luckily that was the last batter of the inning and she just drank two big cups of gatorade. Every inning after that she kept on drinking but the side effect was she had to use the "john". Her weight had come down a few pounds as it normally does during a season but on this day alone she lost 5 additional pounds. They played 14 games in 14 days but that was pretty much standard for summer baseball. It appeared that the heat had not turned off the fan base and most games had large crowds. Coach told Jackee it was because of her, from his past experiences teams usually lose some fans to other summer activities. "Your fans have been here every day and most days you don't disappoint them." She was still hitting over .350 and even had two homers added on to her 18 extra base hits. The minor league president had warned the clubs about Jackee in a memo and had listed some don'ts. Most times the unwritten laws are respected but there are always a few who try to push the envelope. One team had two bench jockeys who were really getting on her case. They called her many names not heard around the dinner table. One of her coaches called them out but Jackee told him to relax and she'll take care of it. What was most disappointing was that the home plate umpire in charge of the game said nothing to the players or their coach. When Jackee batted later in the game she was looking for a way to get even. The pitcher was not even good enough to pitch in college so when her count went to 3 and 0 and she had, you are on your own sign from the manager, a plan took shape. She was looking for a fastball down the middle and she got one. Not only did she get it but she got all of it and before landing it was on the outside of the center field fence. As she was turning third and heading for home she looked into the dugout and right in their eyes and said "maybe you should be home baking cookies." When she reached home plate, her fans were cheering and most of her teammates were out of the dugout to meet her.

Coach said "you gave a perfect answer to your detractors."

William had contacted the organization and requested that Jackee be sent home the last weekend in August. "Her medical school program begins the day after Labor Day and she needs some time for wedding preparations." Her last game would be the Sunday before Labor day.

Mr Bragan called William and said the organization has agreed since every report on her has been positive. "We have decided that Jackee will play Triple

A next year and that the only thing we are doing now is keeping our fans happy by playing her. They will be upset that they will not see her anymore but we will make a big show of her last few games. By the way, we are very proud of her because she not only is a fine baseball player but she is a great spokesman for women and the team. We want your family there on opening day in triple A and when she is brought up to the parent club."

William said it would be our pleasure and honor to attend any game she plays. William went to tell Carmela and of course she started crying. When Jackee comes home the whole family will be told of the arrangements made for both events. William and Dan started preparing for Jackee's promotion to triple A. It should greatly increase her fees for endorsements and the jump to the Gamblers should nearly double that. Dan asked William "how do we handle money when there are multiple clients in the commercial?"

"In most cases so far the sponsor has sent money to the individual people involved. The children had the money sent to their trust accounts. Any client that we handle, who is a minor, we will probably recommend the same method be used. The adults will be offered different recommendations."

Jackee was told by the coach that her last day with the Hustlers will be the Wednesday before Labor Day. "Next year you will open the year with the triple A team. Mark Wright is the manager of the Roseville Rollers and he is a very good one. He is an excellent baseball man and I think you and him will really hit it off. Jackee, I will hate to see you go but the fact of the matter is there is nothing more you can learn here. Triple A and the big club are the only things that can offer you a challenge. They are planning a night for you on your last game. It is supposed to be a surprise but I think this heads up will give you a chance to prepare. Don't tell anyone."

Jackee responded by saying "I didn't hear a word you said." For the next two weeks Jackee played spectacular baseball. Both hitting and fielding improved and her fan base became even larger. With one week remaining before she was to leave, word was given to the local media. They of course used it for headlines and it created a stir in the community. From that point on every game was sold out. Jackee spent as much time as possible after the game with her fans. She offered to come back sometime to speak but she could not make a commitment at this time. Wednesday before Labor Day was a beautiful summer night. A baseball picture card of hers was given to everyone in attendance. Many fans wanted the card signed by Jackee but that was impossible at this time.

Jackee was given a complete set of luggage and many small mementos for her time spent with the Hustlers. She thanked everyone for coming and told the crowd that her parents had to come down here just to get a picture of me. "I am sorry that I can not spend time with you after the game but I must leave immediately after the game." Once the game was over, Jackee went to where her parents were waiting, after the usual hugs and kisses, Jackee told them all her gear was packed ready to go. This new luggage had to be added to the SUV. She said goodbye to her teammates and to the coaches, especially coach Ferris.

On the way home, Carmela filled her in on all the wedding plans. "When you approve, the wedding invitations will be mailed out." A tentative seating plan had been worked out by Mrs Silvio and Carmela but of course until the return cards are back no final seating can be completed. Dan would meet her at home because one of us had to stay back and take care of business. Jackee had been very disappointed when she did not see Dan but her father explained that he was spending the whole day in meetings dealing with family commercials.

"Mom, dad please don't take this wrong but I have to spend a night with Dan for my personal well being. I need his strength to get me through the next two months. You may find this difficult to understand but right now I need to feel him close to me so that I know he loves me." Carmela said she fully understood and "whatever you need we will not stand in your way." William again had no idea what Jackee was saying but he knew Carmela would probably tell him tonight.

When they arrived home they found Dan working in William's office. He had been there since early afternoon putting the finishing touches on commercials for almost all members of the family. Little William and Frankie were the most popular but Carmela seemed to have caught the attention of the sponsors. He had been at a 4 hour meeting with Mr Hitch and sponsor representatives in the morning but was not in full agreement with their offer. While he was hugging Jackee he mentioned to William that they had to talk about what happened at that morning meeting. Carmela immediately stepped in and said "nothing will be discussed until tomorrow. You and Jackee go off by yourselves and get reacquainted."

Jackee whispered ``please in his ear and he said "it can definitely wait until tomorrow." Since it was already late, Jackee said she was tired and had to get some rest. She took Dan by the hand and took him up to her room and closed the door. Dan did not know what to say but he was holding Jackee and could feel her shaking. He finally said, it's "OK, tell me why you're upset."

"Next year I'm to start the year in triple A with the Roseville Rollers. That is a two level jump and I am scared I may not be good enough." "Your father and I heard about this from the organization. We both felt it was the right move and Bats concurred that you need to see better competition so this is the next logical move. We all believe you will be fine and we hope the big league team will call you up to the show before the year is out."

Jackee just held him tighter and Dan could feel her heart pounding. She said "everyone is depending on me to be a success, you, my family, friends, the organization, and every woman that has seen me play and many thousands more who are using me to improve their lives and future." She was crying and said "I can't fail, I can't let them down oh God please help me."

He was now holding her up and he said "you will not let them down, in all your life there has never been one person who you have disappointed. Failure is not in your code and the day you step out on any field is the most successful day of your life. No living female has accomplished what you have in baseball. I am very jealous of baseball because it competes with me for your love. But I also know that if I can get just some of your love of baseball directed to me, it will be the truest love of my life. Jackee your love for baseball showed me what could be accomplished by a person with that amount of love and desire. It is one of the things I love about you. I am going to be by your side because someday all that love will be directed to me, and I am looking forward to that day."

"Dan, will you stay with me tonight and hold me until this fear leaves me."

"Jackee, what will your parents say about that?"

"My mother told me it will be fine with her and my dad."

"How do you know that?"

"My mother will make him an offer he can't refuse." They both started laughing so hard that the tension just left both of them.

"Dan said you better make me an offer I can't refuse."

"In less than two months I will make you an offer for the rest of my life. Just lie on the bed with me and hold me for the night."

"I'll do it, but I want you to know it goes against nature." They took off their shoes and Dan just let her curl up in his arms. Both were so tired that in 3 minutes they were fast asleep.

Dan woke early and left Jackee sleeping. He entered the bathroom down the hall and washed up. When he went downstairs he found Carmela in the kitchen. Still not sure what to expect. Carmela said "thank you for staying with Jackee last night. I know this has been a tremendous strain on you but you have handled yourself just like the great guy I thought you were. You were the only one who could have saved her last night. We would have helped some but you were the perfect choice. I truly do not know how you do it. You have put her first above all normal male desires and the only conclusion I can make is that you actually love her more than you do yourself." Just then Jackee appeared, kissed Dan and said thank you for last night. "I don't think I would have made it without your arms around me." "Any time, I'm always available for personal service." William walked into the kitchen and wanted to know if everything was alright. Jackee said "there is no way I am going to disappoint millions of women. My goal has been and always will be to play in the major leagues. With God's help that is exactly what I will dedicate myself to do."

William asked Dan if he wanted to discuss the commercial contract now. Dan agreed and they went into William's office. Later, Carmela called them for breakfast and both came out to eat. Both men were hungry because neither one had dinner the night before. When they were done Dan said he had to make a stop at home and again meet with a sponsor. He kissed Jackee and said he would see her later.

After Dan left, William told Jackee and Carmela that "Dan right now is better than the negotiator I have in my office. He is like a sponge and absorbs everything you tell him and even makes it better by adding his ideas. I believe that this corporation will be bigger than my accounting firm. Jackee, you have found yourself quite a man."

"Dad you don't know the half of it," Jackee said as she was leaving the room.

William turned to Carmela and asked "what did I miss?"

"Not a thing, Jackee found a new drive and Dan guaranteed that he and Jackee will be together real soon. Now I have to talk to Jackee about the wedding." Carmela found her in the den and they went over the invitations. Jackee agreed that they were perfect and she and Carmela prepared them for mailing. Next they went over the flowers, last fittings, and tentative seating plan for the country club.

"All the food, entertainment, photographer, and times have been set. Limo times have been set and hairdresser and final fittings have to be made. Dan will speak to the ushers and I will speak with my sisters and Andrea. Tonight Dan and I will discuss where our guests are to sit. You and Mrs Silvio can arrange the other tables as the invitations come in. I need to stop at the church and personally invite father Nicholas to say grace at the reception. Would it be agreeable to you if I invited Mr Hitch to take some pictures of the wedding?" "I think that would be a great idea since he has hinted toward that a few times." "Can you think of anything else mom?"

"No, I think we have covered everything."

Jackee stopped at the church and spoke with Father Nicholas. He agreed to say grace at the wedding reception and to stay for some of the reception. "You will be seated at the head table right next to the parents. If you have a dietary problem let us know so we can inform the caterer." Jackee asked if the church singing has been coordinating with the Sisters at the orphanage. Father told her everything has been taken care of and "God forgive me but I eat everything."

"Good, we will see that you get everything."

Their next stop was to the florist and that only took a few moments because all the flowers had been selected except the one for the bride and Jackee had that one covered. She gave Mr Smith a color scheme for her bouquet and the flowers she wanted. Last was the fittings, Carmela was easy since she has been the same size since she got married. The only exception was when she was pregnant but a while after giving birth she would go right back to her regular size. Jackee had a problem because of the weight she lost during the hot summer. She told Miss Grant and was informed that her final fitting will be the day before the wedding and all alterations, if any, would be done on the spot. "We will make the dress as beautiful as you are, I promise."

Carmela and Jackee left the shop and decided to have lunch at a local restaurant. While they were waiting for their meal, Carmela asked "if Jackee was happy?" She answered, "I am not sure. All this is like a dream and it seems to be playing out faster than I can keep up with it. Mom, I am the first woman to sign a major league baseball contract. In less than 2 months I am going to marry the greatest guy in the whole world. My father and future husband are creating an almost perfect life for me. Why should this all be happening to me? God has been extremely good to me and the only way I know to thank Him is to do the work He gave me the ability to perform. I hope in His eyes it is enough. My other problem is how am I going to make Dan happy. I owe him so much and just want to show him how much I care."

Carmela said "I will talk to you before you get married but I want you to know that both of you will find ways to make each other happy. In finding those ways it will be the most exciting part of being married and you will grow even closer than you are now." Jackee reached over and took her mother's hand and thanked her for all she has done for the family.

Dan and William were huddled in the office when the two women arrived home and after a time they came out and told them about the deal that was on the table. Dan had negotiated a family deal lasting three years, with a two year option. "The offer for the three years is 5 million dollars a year. If the sponsors want to pick up the option the dollar amount has to be renegotiated. We have to create a conference call so it can be discussed and a final agreement made. How Dan got them to agree to this is beyond me but we both think this is very good for the family. We have also signed four other people who want us to represent them. Dan may not be able to go on his honeymoon because we have so much work."

Jackee stood there in shock with her mouth open but Dan told her "nothing is going to stop me from spending that week with you."

She ran over and kissed him and said "never make a joke about our honeymoon again or I will not marry you."

"You will marry me because there is no one who loves you more than I do."

He kissed her and she just said "YES."

William explained how this agreement will eventually affect every member of the family. "If all goes well, there will be enough money for each person to retire. Rose has pledged most of her earnings to Sonny's people but I will put some in reserve for her and Sonny. Evelyn and Jon will have a source of income from his parents but Evelyn will earn money from this new deal. I will set up a trust fund for her and she can eventually transfer it to her children. Rocco and Rebecca will have their own account. Frankie will be separate so that when he is 21 any decision on his trust will be his to make. Dan has created a source of income that could last for years. "

Jackee and Dan had dinner at his house. His parents were very happy with the wedding arrangements. They hadn't expected to have so much say in the wedding preparations. Both his parents thanked Jackee for letting them participate. They also mentioned that her parents

could not have been more accommodating. "It took your father to tell us about how Dan is now part of a corporation handling your family finances."

Jackee corrected them and said "Dan is not just handling my family finances, he is also handling our affairs. We will officially be married soon but Dan has been handling our affairs for a very long time. I am where I am today partly because of him. There is no way I can repay him for all he has done for me. I can promise you that I will spend every day after we are married trying to make him happy."

His parents were speechless but they both realized that Jackee meant every word that she said. Dan held her hand and mouthed the words "I love you." His parents knew that he felt the same way as she did and that is all any couple could ask of each other. They left after dinner and went to their favorite parking area. Jackee had to leave on Sunday and Andrea was picking her up to go back to school. This will end their 6 year program and they will graduate May 1st.

Dan woke Jackee up as it was getting near midnight. He had gently nudged her and she hugged him harder. She said "I just want to stay with you the rest of the night."

He said "no, you have a long day tomorrow and a trip back to school the next day. Besides I need my rest because I also have a big day tomorrow and another on Monday." She complained but knew that he was right. They drove to Jackee's house and he kissed her goodnight and left.

Carmela was waiting for her because Andea had called to say her boyfriend was on a trip so she asked if she could come on Saturday. "I told her to come as she could get her final fitting before you leave for school. I called Miss Grant and she said to bring Andrea in." Jackee said she did the right thing and Andrea will have more rest leaving from here on Sunday.

Andrea reached the Jenco's by 10am. She only brought her overnight bag into the house and left the rest of her belongings in the car. Jackee welcomed her and showed her to the room she would use for the night. After she unpacked

Jackee took her down to the kitchen where Carmela had a snack set up. Andrea talked about her wedding and said the date was to be the Saturday after Thanksgiving next year. "Most of my wedding party is free that weekend so it's a perfect time to hold a wedding. My father agreed for Miss Grant to make my dress and those of my bridesmaids. Since Grant already has all your measurements you will only need one fitting or maybe two but no more. My parents agreed that it was the best time for us. Brett did not have a problem with the date but he did suggest only a one week honeymoon the following week. He is on the road most of the time but that will come to an end by the end of the year. After that he should be working from the main headquarters. Dr Hopkins said I could work from home but would have to come into the lab one week a month. Brett agreed that it would be fine with him and he would try to plan his road trips with mine."

Jackee gave Andrea her schedule for today. We will leave in a few moments for your fitting and then to a studio for a commercial I have scheduled for 1:30pm. Andrea only had to spend 10 minutes with Miss Grant and Jackee about double that to pick out her dress and get the first fitting. She would need only one more fitting to complete the gown. They arrived at the studio right on time and Jackee completed the shoot in less than two hours. Mr Hitch looked over at Andrea and said to Jackee, "are all your friends this beautiful? Young lady, how would you like to join Jackee in doing a commercial for me right now." Jackee wanted to know what commercial he had in mind. He had a face cream client who wanted one or two young women to endorse his face cream.

"You two are perfect and you dressed pretty much like I wanted the women to look. In 15 minutes my staff can have you ready and in less than an hour I'll have two or three takes to show my client. Please Jackee do me the favor." Dan can handle Andrea's contract for now and I will see she gets the same treatment as your family." They agreed and in less than two hours the takes were completed and they were on the way home.

Andrea was so excited that she would be in a commercial. "Do you think the sponsor will accept one of the takes?: Jackee felt that Hitch had done a really good job and it did feel right to her.

Jackee suggested that Andrea talk to Dan tonight and set up a client agent relationship. "You mean to tell me that I need an agent for what we just did? Yes and if they want you to do more, Dan will see that you are paid scale for your services."

"Jackee, are we going to get money for what we just did?"

"If they use one of the takes you will receive money for the commercial and more money each time it is shown."

Andrea said "God, don't you just love America".

Dan was a little disappointed that Andrea was here, because he did not need a third wheel on their last date before Jackee leaves for school. While eating dinner the girls told Dan about what had happened. He agreed to handle Andrea's interest for the same 5% but told her never to tell anyone else because they were charging other clients double that. "Do you want the corporation to handle all your interests? She said yes and he told her a contract will be drawn up and sent to her for signing. Return it as soon as you can because it is unethical to represent someone if there is no contract." She readily agreed and business was over for the evening. Jackee and Dan were going for an ice cream and asked Andrea to come.

She said "no I'm going to hang out with your parents if they don't mind. I need to find out more about the wedding so that I can plan mine. Your mom is a fountain of information and can really help me. Your dad can also fill me in on what agreement I just made."

When they left, Andrea said they needed to be alone and not have a third wheel ruin their last night together. Carmela told her she did the right thing. William and Carmela did talk to Andrea about the wedding and her adventure into the world of commercials. Jackee came home about 11pm and the three of them were still talking in the living room. Next morning after church, and all the goodbyes taking care of the girls headed back to school. The whole conversation revolved around two things, their boyfriends or the wedding. Back at school they collected their messages and began to plan their last year together. Jackee mentioned that her season at triple A begins with tryouts starting on April 1st. She must finish all the requirements for graduation before April 22 which is the first scheduled game. Spring training would be over and I would have missed all of it. "I am sure that will make me very popular with the manager and coaches. Add in the fact that I will be trying to replace a player who has been there the whole pre-season."

Andrea proposed that they complete all their work by April 15th and make Dr Hopkins responsible for the early completion. "I am very sure he will back us up. Since I decided to be his new assistant, it should give our early completion credibility. If they can arrange for you to complete your medical training at the local hospital you will be able to still use this room."

"I'll be a married woman by then and how will you feel about that?"

"Listen Jackee, you put up with my indiscretions for years and never once complained, so now it's my turn to be horny when Dan is here. Remember the year after I'll be married and we can play swap or whatever else you can think of."

Jackee was blushing and laughing at the same time and said she waited a long time for Dan and she will never share him with anyone. "Whatever he needs I will provide or he will do without."

Andrea was laughing so hard that tears were rolling down her face and all she could say was, "you are such a prude but I still love you." Dinner was next and both had healthy appetites since they had not eaten since breakfast.

Monday at 5am Jackee was working out and a few school baseball play- ers joined her. Two were freshmen and wanted some help with their hitting. She watched them and gave some advice. She saw a new machine and asked what it was. They said It's a new batting machine that throws split finger pitches. Jackee had the regular batting machine up to 100 MPH. She was seeing the ball and hitting it really hard. Her timing was excellent. She had some work to do on the curve ball machine but after a few days her sweet swing will come back. Then and only then will she try the split finger machine. Even before that she will have to speak with coach Zimmer to find out about the machine.

When her workout was finished she showered, dressed and went with Andrea for breakfast. Later they went to see Lucy and got all their instructions for the coming semester. There was one project and two studies to work on. Lucy spoke to Jackee about making a schedule for her. "Your father has hired me to make sure your schedule and all your affairs are always in order. You must let me know if you scheduled something so that a conflict never exists. Your schedule will appear on your computer Jackee, and I will update it every morning as need- ed. You and Andrea are scheduled to speak with potential students and their parents on Friday at 3pm. There is a request for you to speak at a young women's conference on a Sunday at 1pm. It will be at the convention center in the capital. All transportation will be paid for by the organizers."

"Lucy you are to blackout from October 14th to October 30th for my wedding."

"It has already been done as per your father's orders."

"I should tell my father to give you a raise but I have no say in the oper- ation of the corporation."

Lucy said "forget it, your father has been very generous in his offer to me. One more thing, if it is possible, always include Andrea in my commitments. This way I will have company going and coming."

The scheduling that Lucy prepared for them included classes, labs, and work at Dr Hopkins lab at school and hospital. Some of the equipment they will need is only at the hospital so staffing privileges had to be arranged with the hos- pital. Andrea will receive permanent privileges because she will be working with Dr Hopkins but on staff with the hospital. Jackee will receive temporary staff privileges until she is accepted as an intern by the hospital. Both women had the text books for their courses over the summer and both read these books at least once. At this stage of their education most of the courses overlap and have more substance dealing with the subject matter. Once they were satisfied that their classes were set, an appointment with the college president had to be arranged. Mr Washington agreed to meet with them on Wednesday before the parents and students came. He pretty much gave them the same talk as the year before, Quality not quantity was the main talking point. "So far we have not lost one student selected by our staff. We are preparing the best doctors and other schools are trying to copy our methods. You two prepare your own talk and present it just as you did last year. Our school has no better example than the two of you for our program. You are the best investment this school ever made. I wish you can be here forever but I know that is not possible so this year we are going to tape your talk and keep it for the future. So we will see both of you on Sunday."

Jackee asked Andrea if she had any ideas as to what she was going to say. Andrea said "we have to say something about the school and especially the program."

"Agreed, we should also mention the staff and facilities available. We can work something up and include it in our presentation."

Sunday came and at 3pm sharp the two young ladies fully dressed walked out on that stage. Andrea and Jackee both looked like professional models. Andrea was introduced first and gave a great talk about the 6 year program. Jackee spoke next and reinforced the study needed for the program. She told the audience that the two of us have received nothing but straight A's. "The school excuses you from final exams if you have an A+ in the course. Andrea and I have never taken a final exam. This program only turns out the very best doctors. Our students have never been denied acceptance to any school that they have applied to. Is it hard work? Very hard work. If it wasn't, everybody would want to be a doctor. If you are serious about becoming a doctor then this is the program for you. If you're not serious, please don't apply and waste your parents' money. Only the best make it here. You must decide!"

Jackee was about to sit down when President Washington spoke to the parents and potential new students. He told the audience that "this young lady has signed a professional baseball contract and is still a candidate to become a doctor. She has been pursuing two very difficult careers and has been extremely successful in both. Not once has she asked for a single assist from us, in fact she has worked in science projects and studies for one of our doctors and has achieved acclaim for her work. If you have half the fight and desire that this young lady has, come join us for the experience of your life."

There was a reception immediately following the presentation and all were invited. Andrea and Jackee were the center of attention. Everyone wanted to talk to the young girls and to find out if they were for real. Jackee told all the people who gathered around her that she has dedicated herself to God, country and family. "All three have been very good to me. I just hope that I can give back some of what I have been given. I do not mean to insult the young men here but I want the young women to know there is nothing holding you back except yourself. Dedicate yourself to whatever you want but never forget that God is there to help you if you ask."

Questions and answers went on for the next hour or so. Andrea spoke up and said "we have to go and get ready for tomorrow, please excuse us." They left and went back to their room and changed for dinner.

CHAPTER TWENTY SEVEN

Jackee Marries Dan

*M*onday started at 5am and it included her workout with the baseball team. After, she showered, dressed, and went to breakfast. Classes were easy for both the girls since each had a working knowledge of what to expect. They worked in the lab and Jackee still found time for the fall baseball program. Coach Zimmer worked with her on the slider and split finger. Jackee reached a point where she did hit most of the pitches and was no longer fooled by the pitch. She very seldom swung at a bad pitch. Her fielding was getting sharper and she was building up her stamina. Before she knew it September turned into October and she and Andrea worked very hard to make up for their future time off. Andrea only would lose 4 days but Jackee needed 12. Lucy had fixed the schedule and all her teachers were in agreement, so on October 17th Andrea and Jackee drove to the Jenco residence. When they arrived, only Carmela was at home. As was her custom Carmela had a snack waiting for them. They ate and went for their gowns. Miss Grant had everything ready and the three women were fitted at the same time. Within one hour they were on the way home with three perfect gowns. When they arrived home Carmela started dinner and then sat down with Jackee to go over the final seating plans. All the invitations had been returned and only two couples said they couldn't make it. All the children of these families had been invited because the country club provides a daycare room for the children. There are professionals who watch over and entertain the children. For the little older children a section has been set up for them with a special server who will introduce each person at the table. There are 310 guests including the children and all but a few of your friends have been put into the seating chart. Jackee wanted to know why Dan hadn't seated the remaining guests.

Carmela thought he was waiting for your input. "We have a possible shoot with Mr Hitch on Friday morning but that is up to you. He wanted the three of us there for no more than two hours. Andrea, Dan needs to talk with you in person so you can take care of that tonight."

Dan came for dinner but before he ate, he huddled with Andrea. He spelled out her contract and what she was paid for the two commercials that the sponsor accepted. She could not believe what they had paid her and that it was already in her account that Dan set up for her. Naturally the corporation's 5% was taken out. He also told her that if the commercial goes viral it will mean more money in your account. He then sat down with Jackee and in 10 minutes they finalized the seating plan. Now there was no more to do except get to the church on time.

Family members started to arrive and the house felt like Christmas. Rose, who was getting ready for the Olympics next summer, came with Sonny. She had her jet pick him up at the airport near the hospital and then on to her local airport at home. Rose and Andrea will sleep in her room, while Sonny sleeps in Evelyn's room. Evelyn and Jon will sleep at Rebecca's. All the meals will be at the Jenco house and supervised by Carmela. Carmela had laid out a big buffet, for Thursday's night dinner, and that will be the last big meal before the wedding. Friday night would be the rehearsal dinner, which will be held in the Vets hall. This would be catered by the country club as part of their wedding package. The members will supply all the drinks, decorations and cleanup will be done by the auxiliary personnel. William has already told them how it is to be decorated and they have been promised a nice bonus if everything goes well. "Rehearsal at the church is scheduled for 5pm and the dinner is to start at 6:15. All the bridesmaids who haven't done so are to have a final fitting at 10am Friday. All the ushers and fathers have to pick up their tuxedo's some time on Friday."

Thursday night the family had a great time. Brett surprised Andrea by showing up in the middle of dinner, Sonny was told he now had a roommate to keep him company. Carmela could not believe all the food that was consumed. She had added about 30% more than she figured they would eat. It turned out that almost all the food was gone and only some vegetables were left. Carmela had made deserts and almost all of them were gone. She never saw a more fed and happy group of people in her life. Jackee was happy for Andrea because she hadn't seen Brett in two months. Everyone pitched in and helped cleanup and in no time the house was pretty much back in order. It was now getting late and Rebecca told Evelyn they should leave soon. Evelyn agreed and they left a few moments later. Dan told Jackee he had to go because he had an early meeting in the morning but would see her in the afternoon. She was disappointed but knew he was working very hard for their future life together. Brett and Andrea went for a walk which actually meant they were going to his car. Sonny and Rose drifted into the workout room while Carmela put little William to bed. He had been playing all night with Frankie and appeared to be totally exhausted. That left William and Jackee alone and they were seated in the den. William asked if she was happy and excited about the wedding.

Jackee said "I'll tell you a secret that I have never told anyone. The first date I had with Dan, I fantasized about what it would be like to be married to him. When he kept asking me out, the fantasy got stronger and stronger. I finally reached a point where I would have done anything he wanted me to. He never demanded anything more than holding and kissing me. Mom later explained how much he loved me and what's really going on. From that day on, all I wanted was to show him how much I love him. Dad, most people are happy if they have one man in their life but I am truly blessed because I have two. Dan is going to be surprised after we are married because he has no idea how long I have planned for this, especially our wedding night."

Carmela came down and Jackee said she was tired and had to get some rest. She also told Carmela she would be down early to help with Breakfast. After hugging and kissing both of them she said thank you and went to bed. Carmela sat next to William, fell into his arms and began crying. "We are so lucky to have 4 wonderful daughters but Jackee is in a class by herself. I hope you are going to speak to her about her wedding night because she told me she has plans. William, trust me, I will talk with her but I believe they are so much into each other that it will just happen as if it were the natural thing to do."

Friday morning Jackee came down and found Carmela preparing breakfast in the kitchen. She had the big pot of coffee brewing and was just setting the table, so Jackee helped her. Drifting down one at a time the table was soon filled with hungry people and all the girls were trying to help.

Carmela finally told everyone to sit down and start eating. This was to be the final day for preparations so everyone had a job. All the tuxedos and gowns had to be picked up by noon. A stop had to be made at the country club to confirm the seating and make sure all else was in order. The hairdresser had to be contacted and the final time set up. Shoes had to be shined. The dress for the rehearsal dinner was to be casual. "There will be cold cuts in the fridge if anyone needs food before dinner tonight. Please feel free to help yourself because I am out of service until tomorrow morning. William, you are to take the men for their tuxedos and I don't want to see you until 3pm understood?"

William replied, "yes master, whatever you say master we will obey." William and Carmela had planned this last tradition for Jackee and Dan. After getting the tuxedos, William took all the men to the vets bar and a bachelor party was arranged for Dan. Carmela had all the girls back at the house at noon and while they were gone a few friends of her's prepared the den for a bridal shower. Rebecca and Carmela had prepared for this and had contacted the other girls. Gifts and fun things were laid out for them. A few other women were invited and were waiting for them to come home. Jackee was totally surprised because she felt there was not enough time to do this. Dan was also surprised because his friend had taken him out one weekend to celebrate his coming nuptials. William had only one room set up for the bachelor party and there was some food and anything they wanted to drink. No one had anything except a soft drink and the food was mostly finger food. These gifts were mostly jokes and the guys had a good time kidding Dan.

One of the gifts was an old playboy magazine with a note that said, "Just in case you get bored on your wedding night". There was a blow up naked girl with an instruction booklet with it. The final gifts he received was a briefcase with his initials on it and the belt buckle with the silver dollar that had the double "C" mint mark. He thanked everyone and since it was close to 3, they packed up and went home. Jackee's party was just wrapping up as the men came in.

Dan went over to Jackee and gave her a kiss and told her in a whisper that he loved her, she replied "but not as much as I do you." Carmela told everyone to help clean up and get ready to head for church.

Father Nicholas was waiting for them and he went through the whole wedding verbally. After that he went through a dry run of how it was supposed to happen. He mentioned the rings and the license since beside the participants they were very important to the ceremony. Dan said his best man Sonny will have the rings and "I will give you the license before the ceremony. All the gratuities for the church will be in envelopes and they will be given to the altar servers, organ player and singer. The orphanage will be taken care of and a gift will be given to you with the license. Did I miss anything?"

Father Nicholas told him he covered all the bases and a gift to the church was not required. When they were satisfied that they knew what to do, it was time to go to dinner. The parade of cars made it over to the vets hall and other invited guests were already there. Bats, Kim, Emma and George Herman along with Jonathan and Bianca were among those inside the hall. For 15 minutes people were meeting and talking with each other. A voice came from the main room inviting everyone to enter and prepare to eat. Salad bar, barbecue ribs and chicken, Roast beef, sushi, cheese and crackers, three types of pasta, two types of potatoes, mac and cheese and finally mixed vegetables.

Anything you wanted to drink was available at the bar. Part way through eating, Jackee stood up and said, "my parents, sisters, and especially Dan and I wish to thank you for sharing this dinner with us. Tomorrow Dan and I will pledge ourselves to each other with you as witnesses. I wish all of you could be as happy as Dan and I are at this time. Thank you and may God bless you." When the people appeared to be finished eating, the servers began to bring out desserts. There were cakes, pies, cookies. pastries and 4 different flavors of ice cream. Not long after the dessert was served people started to leave. It had been a long day for most everyone there. Jon and Evelyn said good night to Jon's parents and went home with Rebeca and Rocco. Bats took his family to the hotel rooms William had provided for them. Andrea and Brett would end up at Jenco's house as did Rose and Sonny. Dan dropped Jackee at her house after they had talked a while about the next day. Carmela and William closed their eyes around midnight after checking their schedule for tomorrow.

Saturday morning rolled around and Carmela was ready for it. Her kitchen was set up for the hairdresser and the living room for breakfast. The girls were the first ones down and were soon joined by Rebecca and Evelyn. Sofia the hairdresser brought two other girls and equipment with her. 10 minutes after entering the house they were working on one of the girl's hair. All the hair, nails and feet were to be completed by 1pm. Breakfast was prepared by whoever was not being worked on. The three men came down and just stayed out of the way for fear of being run over. They had whatever food was available in one corner of the living room. William took all the men's shoes to the shoe repair shop and had them shined. The tuxedo's were laid out on their beds with all the accessories. As each woman finished with the hairdresser she went to take a shower. After that they either put on a robe or some casual clothing. The makeup artist from Mr Hitch's studio was to come about 12:30 to do the makeup on all the women. Mrs Silvio was to drive over at 2:00 to get her makeup done. Bianca decided to have the beauty shop at the hotel take care of her needs. Things were going along right on schedule. Jackee was the last one to be finished by both the hairdresser and makeup artist. As the workers were leaving, Carmela gave each one an envelope containing cash. None of them wanted to take it because they said it had been taken care of. Carmela would have none of that and insisted that they take the money and not say a word to anyone. All agreed and with that, Jackee and Carmela personally thanked them for a job well done.

Miss Grant knocked on the door around 2:30 to help dress everyone and to make sure her gowns were a perfect fit. The photographer was now at the house and started taking pictures. He was different from the one they had talked to and they asked if a change had taken place. "Mr Hitch gave me this address and told me to take pictures of everyone including the young boy. What he said he would do to me if I screwed up is not to be mentioned in public."

This photographer took pictures of everything and everybody but never once interfered with all the other things that were going on. Just before 3:30, Jackee was completely dressed and ready for the church. At 3:00 the flowers arrived and all were distributed. Carmela had Jackee's and was waiting for her to come down. Jackee came down with Miss Grant close behind holding her train up so she would not have trouble walking down the stairs. The photographer had never seen Jackee before and just said in a whisper, "my camera would never do her justice. She is the most beautiful bride I have ever seen." Miss Grant told the photographer that she wanted a full picture of Jackee and the gown for my studio. Her sisters always knew that Jackee was the one who resembled Carmela the most, but they now saw a very young Carmela walking down the stairs.

William held his breath and whispered to Carmela, "I remember you then and you are even more beautiful now."

She nudged him with her elbow and whispered to him that he can prove that later tonight. Her mother gave Jackee her bouquet. And the photographer was taking pictures from every angle. Two limo's were outside the house and a large crowd had been gathering since 2:00. 3:45 every one in the house started leaving the house and getting into the limos. Earlier in the day they had dropped off three cars at the country club and Brett had driven the men back to Jenco's house. The only exception was Dan. He had to go back to his house and would be driven to the church by his dad.

Two limo's were now filled with the bridal party and the parents. The crowd outside was wishing Jackee the best and taking a great many pictures. They arrived at the church with 5 minutes to spare. Miss Grant had driven to the church a few moments earlier and was waiting for the limo's. She helped Jackee out of the car and arranged the wedding dress in the vistabule of the church. She also made sure that all the other gowns were properly arranged. When everyone was seated and the ushers had escorted family members not in the wedding party to their seats the bridal procession was started. First one slight change had been introduced, Dan was escorted to the Altar by his parents. With a parent on each side they walked him to where the best man was waiting and they stood with him and Sonny. Her three sisters were escorted by the ushers to the altar and Andrea and her escort walked to the altar and stood on the side. Lastly, here comes the bride's music started and Jackee escorted by her mother and father on each side started for the Altar. When they reached the step to going up on the Altar, they stopped and Dan's parents escorted him to Jackee. Dan kissed his mother, shook hands with his dad, kissed the cheek of Carmela and shook hands with William. Jackee kissed her mother and father and whispered something to each of them, went over to Dan's parents and kissed them both while also whispering something to them. Dan's parents stood next to Jackee's parents and then Dan took Jackee's hand and led her to the waiting priest.

Father Nicholas began by saying, "the couple must have wanted to make sure that there were enough witnesses present for their vows because this is the largest number of people I've ever had for a wedding on the Altar." He started with the dearly beloved and began the ceremony. Later he told the people in the church that he has known Jackee since he Baptized her. "If I started talking about her we would run into the 5:30 Mass. Just let me say this, I feel blessed that this young woman is a member of my congregation." When he asked who gives this girl to be wed, Jackee's parents in unison said we do.

Father Nickolas first asked Dan to make his vows to Jackee, then he asked Jacalyn Mary Jenco, alias Jackee, to make her vows to Dan. He blessed the rings and read the sacred words as the rings were put on their fingers. When the service was complete, he asked God to bless this union, his last words were you may now kiss the bride. Dan did just that and they stood for a moment as the people in the church clapped. Since the license had been witnessed prior to the ceremony, the church service was complete. Rocco handed the priest and the altar servers envelopes. The children's choir had begun singing the Ave Maria while the bridal party posed on the Altar for pictures. Father Nicholas had told the people in the church that this Mass could be used as their obligation for Sunday Mass. When the recessional song started playing, the couple knew it was time to leave. They proceeded down the aisle and were outside of the church as the people threw confetti and rice at them. Of course the bridal party followed close behind and after many congratulations they began entering the limo's for the trip to the country club. The photographers told them that pictures would be taken at the club because there were many good background things on the club's grounds and inside.

It was almost 6:30 by the time all the pictures were taken. The bridal party was escorted to a private room where food and drinks were available. Jackee just wanted something to drink but the others were either eating something or have gone outside to where the cocktail hour was happening. Jackee's and Dan's parents left after the pictures and were greeting their invited guests in the lounge. Their guests were all unanimous about one thing, the food was fabulous. Harold had so far done exactly what he promised. A few minutes before 7, the staff of the country club began advising the guests that it was time to enter the main dining room. Once most of the guests were in the room Harold invited everyone to rise and welcome the new married couple. He first introduced the parents, bridal party and lastly for the first time as man and wife Mr and Mrs Daniel Silvio. Dan and Jackee entered the room walking between the bridal party and their parents. Harold said that the couple selected "There'll never be another" as their first dance together as man and wife. Rose took Jackee's bouquet and the newly married couple danced. Part way through the song Harold asked the parents to join them on the dance floor, then the bridal party and finally all the guests.

When the dance ended everyone sat down and Harold asked Sonny for the traditional wedding toast. First he asked everyone to please stand and then handed the microphone to Sonny. Sonny, a man of few words, raised his glass and said, "To Jackee and Dan, May their life together be full of happiness, good health and much success, but most important may they always be in the palm of God's hands. "

Salute!

All present drank and started clapping until Dan kissed Jackee. They sat down and the first course was served. For the next 3+ hours they ate, drank, danced and partied. When all the tables had been cleared and cleaned, Harold had the wedding cake brought out. It was four feet tall and had a bridal couple standing on a baseball at the top. Jackee and Dan together cut the cake and a small piece was given to them for the traditional feeding each other a taste of it. Jackee took her bouquet and told her guests that she was not going to throw the bouquet but instead give a part to her sisters and mothers. The fifth bouquet she gave to Dan's mother after giving her sisters and mother the other four. She then discreetly took off her two garters and gave one to Dan and one to her father. Harold then asked William to dance with his daughter to 'Daddy's little girl'. When they finished, Harold asked Dan to get his mother and they danced to "Mr wonderful". These two dances took just long enough for the servers to set out the venetian hour display of desserts. The cocktail hour food that was left over had already been delivered to the orphanage and the deserts would follow later that night. The Nuns had been warned that it would be 11 or so and a refrigerator and freezer had to be prepared to take the food. Mother Superior and her group were ready and willing to accept the food. Jackee had her usual sundae and Dan had the same. In fact they toasted each other with the sundaes. As the venetian hour was ending, people started to leave. Jackee and Dan went to change. The wedding gown was to be put in a special box and sent to Miss Grant so that it would be clean and boxed properly. Carmela was to pick it up when the cleaning and packaging were complete. Dan had to simply take off his tuxedo and give it to William who would return all of them on Sunday. The sisters said their good-byes to Jackee and Dan as did both their parents. Then the new married couple headed for their room for the night.

Dan observed the tradition of carrying the bride over the threshold and then they were in their room. There was a bottle of champagne and a quart of coke zero in an ice bucket. Harold had known that neither one drank alcohol so many other soft drinks were also available. They kissed and the new Mrs Silvio said it was time to get comfortable. She went into the bedroom and changed into a very sheer negligee that her mother had purchased for her. Carmela had given it to her at the shower but she hadn't opened it until later when she and Carmela were alone. Carmela gave her the wifely duty talk as she opened the box. Jackee now looked at herself in the mirror and thought *if this doesn't get a rise out of Dan nothing would*. She also had made up her mind that she was going to make up for the times he went home unsatisfied. Dan knocked on the bedroom door and she said to come in. He entered and saw her for the first time as his wife. While he was taking it all in she casually walked to him and threw her arms around his neck. Her body was pressed against his and she kissed him with her whole being. He gently picked her up and carefully placed her on the bed and after taking off his clothes he joined her.

Next morning, Jackee woke up and found herself naked and in Dan's arms. She just laid still until he started to wake up. She kissed him and asked if she carried out all her wifely duties. He told her that he never considered anything less than perfection from her. "You were perfect, it was the best wedding night any man ever had."

She said it was "very kind of you to say that but I want you to know that I will keep trying until I do get it perfect."

"If it gets any better we will never leave the bedroom."

"I was treated like a queen and many times I have fantasized about my wedding night but you were 100 times better than anything I dreamed about."

"I Would love to continue practicing with you but we do have a plane to catch and it is getting late." Jackee went into the bathroom to start her shower and just as she was adjusting the water Dan slipped in with her. He said this was my way to conserve water and it makes it easier to get to those hard to reach places. Jackee giggled and said she fully agreed with this conservation method. One hour later they were getting into the limo for the trip to the airport. Their flight was on time and they were soon on their way to Mexico. At the airport in Mexico a limo was waiting to take them to the hotel in Acapulco. When they arrived at the hotel they were escorted to their suite and never even signed in. The suite was beautiful, not as great as the one in Vegas but pretty close. There was a bottle of chilling champagne but also many soft drinks. They put all their things away and Dan asked what she wanted to do until dinner time. Jackee started taking off her clothes and went into the bedroom to pull the sheets down. Dan followed and asked what she had in mind. He soon learned that she meant this to be a real honeymoon. About seven they went down to dinner and found the food to be excellent. While eating dinner, Dan had a strange feeling about the two men they had passed on the way to dinner. They were alone but showed a strong interest in what we were doing. Later when Jackee went into the bedroom to change Dan called William and asked him to tell the Gamblers to send the bodyguard to their hotel. William had the bodyguard's number and called her directly. She answered and told him she would be on the next flight to Mexico.

When Jackee and Dan went down to breakfast she joined them at their table. It was as if a fan had asked for her autograph and had been invited to sit down. She introduced herself as Rona Ripley. She arrived last night and is having the two men checked out as we speak. "Dan, you were right to call me and I see why you were suspicious about them. They are not travelers but are here on a mission of some kind. Stay on the grounds of the hotel and always be near people until we check them out. By dinner time I should have the full information on both men. I believe that one of them is in law enforcement and the other is the most dangerous. Meet me in the game room before dinner." They spent the rest of the day on the beach and had a great time. The ocean was calm and clear and the weather was perfect. They just had to be careful not to get sunburned. Late in the afternoon they went back to their suite. They showered, separately, and dressed for dinner. Before eating they stopped in the game room and talked to Rona. She told them that she was right about the one man, "he is a Mexican undercover cop but has nothing to do with you. The other is a small-time criminal who sometimes works for the local cartel. In one hour he will be picked up by the local police and held in isolation for your stay here. I have checked all the tapes for the last week and everyone else seems to check out as safe."

Dan told Rona we decided not to leave the hotel except to go home. "Our accommodations are such that we have everything we need right here."

"Rona said that may be the safest thing to do but I will still be here if you change your mind. When you leave, I will leave." They ate dinner and went back to their room.

Jackee smiled and told Dan "by staying in our room she thinks we will be safe. She doesn't realize, it is what I would rather do. Being forced to be secluded with you is what I have prayed for." Dan smiled at her and told she was a hussy and probably a sex maniac in disguise. "I'll be whatever you want me to be," she replied.

Every day was near perfect and the beach was the best but the nights were especially exciting. The hotel had different entertainment almost every night. A table had been set aside for the Silvio's as part of Jonathan Zarrelli's agreement with the hotel. It had a perfect view of the stage but also was away from the crowd. After the show and a short walk on the grounds of the hotel, they went to their suite and finished the night exactly as Jackee had planned. One morning they realized that this would be their last full day of their honeymoon. Jackee asked Dan if they could just spend it lying in each other's arms. He told her if that is what she wanted it would be fine with him, "but remember we have a whole life to look forward to."

She thought how she would feel to get up in the morning and not find him next to her. "I have to go back to school until Thanksgiving, then again until Christmas break and maybe a few days off until Baseball begins. We waited so long to be together and now that we are together, we have to be apart again."

"There is one big difference, we now have a future that has to be fulfilled and when we are together it means we don't have to sneak away in a car and park somewhere. We can go to our bedroom and as your mother put it, get reacquainted. We can have a new honeymoon every time we are apart and get together again. You must never lose sight of the fact that your dream is very close to becoming a reality. I will not stand in your way in making that dream come true. My wife will be the first woman to do something that people said could never be done. She will be a professional baseball player and a great doctor. Add to that she is now a wife and eventually a great mother. God gave you the talents but you work to make them come alive. I am here to do whatever you want me to do."

Jackee started crying and Dan just put his arms around her and kissed away her tears. She knew he was right but she felt so alive when he made love to her. Could she adjust to being a part time wife and lover?

Their last night of the honeymoon made it easier for Jackee to accept what was ahead of her. That last morning in Acapulco was a very relaxing one.

They went down to a late breakfast because they first packed their bags. Rona joined them and said she was going back on their plane and asked if she could hitch a ride with them to the airport. She was quickly invited and thanked for her great service. Rona explained to Jackee that "every talk you give from now on, I need to be there. If you take a trip other than going home, I need to be there. You get a call to meet someone someplace, I need to be there. Do you understand what I am saying? Whenever you have a doubt, no matter how trivial it is, I need to be there. Dan picked up on a possible problem because he has some street smarts, Jackee, you don't. I am not trying to make you afraid to do things and I get no extra pay for being at your side. My job is to protect the Gamblers organization's interest in you to the best of my ability. The salary I receive is equal to me spending 24/7, 365 days with you. You are looking at your new best friend. When you get back to school Lucy will already have given me your schedule and everytime she updates it, my network will pick up the change. Work with me and you will feel free to do most anything, but most important Dan will know you are in good hands."

Boarding the plane to go home, Rona got on last as she checked every person boarding. Dan saved the third seat in the row for her. When they landed Rona saw them to their limo and then just disappeared. They had decided to stay at Jackee's house for the night as she had to leave early the next day. A limo had been hired to take her to school and a short time later a message from Rona said the limo and driver had checked out OK. All Jackee had to take back was her overnight bag. She had talked to her mom as they were preparing dinner. She told Carmela that her honeymoon was the most exciting time she ever had. She always wondered how her mom was always with a smile in the morning, now she knew how that smile got there.

"Being in bed with that perfect someone can put a smile on any face."

Carmela laughed at her and said, "remember all the good times but remember there are also hard times ahead of you."

"Yes, I know, one is coming up in a few hours."

"I should not be asking my daughter this question, but I just have to know. What did Dan say when he saw you wearing that negligee I bought you."

"He was dumbfounded and couldn't say a word. I had to go and throw my arms around him to wake him up. He woke up in a hurry and we had the greatest night of our lives. Mom, I never wanted it to end, is that how you felt on your honeymoon."

"Exactly, and every woman should have that experience at least once in their life."

The rest of the family sat down to dinner and after everything was done Jackee said she was going to bed because she was exhausted. Dan told her he would be up in a little while as he had to speak with William. An hour later he went to Jackee's bedroom and quietly let himself in. There was only a dim night light on so Dan striped down to his shorts and slipped under the covers. To his surprise he found Jackee naked and half asleep she quickly rolled into his arms. Next morning as she came down for breakfast her mother was preparing the food.

Carmela said "I notice a big smile on your face and I will not ask how it got there." They both laughed as Jackee hugged her mom and told her she loved her. An hour later she was crying and getting into the limo for the trip back to school.

CHAPTER TWENTY EIGHT
Jackee Finishes School and Prepares for Triple A

*J*ackee wasn't in the door 30 seconds when Andrea wanted to know how she liked her first roll in the hay. There was a huge smile on her face when she said, "it was great."

"Don't tell me any more because I am horny enough already. This being a nice girl is very hard on the nerves. If I make it through the next 13 months, I might as well become a Nun."

"Come on Andrea, you are now committed to a great guy, isn't it worth a little sacrifice to spend the rest of your life with Brett."

"I guess you are right and I am just feeling sorry for myself. Brett has always treated me as if I was someone special and it never registered with me until I realized how much I loved him. Forget all that because we have a lot of work to do in the next three weeks."

Andrea went over the plan she had laid out and Jackee agreed except for the order of one experiment. Jackee said "this one should go first because it will take about two weeks to collect and organize the data."

Andrea agreed and didn't know how she missed it. "Did you go to any baseball games while I was away?"

"I went to two home games this past weekend and we won both. It seems that the team is having a good year. Enough, let's go get something to eat because I am starving." After dinner the girls talked some more and studied for a while then went to bed. Before getting into bed, Jackee called Dan and they talked for a long time. She started falling asleep and decided to say good night.

Next morning at 5am, she was working out in the field house. Her arms were tired and her legs felt weak. After hitting she ran outdoors and completed

5 miles. It was a struggle to complete the five miles. After breakfast they went to classes and did one lab experiment. The baseball team had a practice day today and she joined them. All the players and coaches congratulated her on the wedding and Hands said "I guess our dating has come to an end."

Jackee told him that he never showed any interest in her so she figured she was not his type. Hands said, "the greatest and most beautiful young woman I have ever met, and you think you are not my type, that really hurts my ego. I will probably have bad dreams for the rest of my life."

She told him "you are going to give me bad dreams if you don't start hitting again."

He said fine. "I'll just hit .500 for the next few games." The team did look good and Jackee worked very hard getting them ready for the games. In the meantime she was gettin her edge back and she started feeling comfortable hitting and fielding. Jackee had missed the Halloween party at the school but helped with the Thanksgiving dinners. Andrea decided they would leave on Tuesday after class to head home for Thanksgiving. Jackee arrived home at Dinner time and everyone was waiting for her. The family had been preparing for their annual trip to the orphanage and Vets home. Dan was the last one to kiss Jackee but he was by far the best. She held him very tight and whispered I love you so only he could hear. They all sat down to dinner and Carmela told Jackee that there were wedding gifts that had to be opened and thank you notes that had to be written. After dinner wedding gifts were opened and a record kept as to who gave what. The thank you cards were selected by the two mothers and two hundred were ordered. Carmela and Dan's mother addressed and stamped all the envelopes and all Jackee had to do was write a little note, put it in the envelope and mail it. There were gifts that had to be stored or exchanged but most people gave money. There was about 19,000 dollars and Dan had a bank account set up and it will be activated as soon as Jackee signs the joint account card at the bank. All the checks were signed with a restricted endorsement which meant the checks could only be put into the joint account. Jackee now had a list of 198 thank you notes to write. So much for free time. Evelyn and Jon went home with Rebecca and Rocco so Sonny could use Evelyn's room for the four days. Little William was headed for bed as Sonny and Rose went to the workout room. Dan and Jackee talked a while with William but then went to Jackee's room for the night. Jackee was very clear as to what she expected because in a very short time she was ready for bed and forgot to put any pajamas on. Dan was not far behind her and he settled in bed beside her. Next morning when she came down, Carmela said "you got that smile back." Jackee told her it was the longest three weeks of her life but she was fine now.

Jackee spent the morning doing thank you notes. Most were fairly easy to write but when it came to an intimate friend, a special thank you had to be added. She finished 90 before lunch and another 60 after lunch but had to stop and help prepare for their annual visits. Rose and her brother William always took a special interest in their visit to the orphanage. For Rose it was the first place that ever showed her love. It is also the place that introduces her to Jackee. She never knew what love was until Jackee took her hand and she felt that this person really cares about me. Growing up, all she ever wanted to be was like Jackee. She wanted to be a success so Jackee would approve of her. When Jackee asked her to be the maid of honor at her wedding, Rose knew that she loved her. Jackee had told her that she could not hurt her other sisters, so all three would be maids of honor, "but you were my first choice."

William on the other hand was a very young child when his mom and dad adopted him. He also knew that Rose was the one who got her parents to consider adopting him. He never once asked about his birth parents, and the fact of the matter is he didnt care about them. His real parents were William and Carmela and that is all he needed to know. He has had 5 women take care of him since he could remember. They spoiled him rotten, but he loved every moment of it. He also knew that he would be the last child for his mom and dad because they told him so. He loved going to the orphanage just to talk to the children there. His sister Jackee, did something special for the orphanage but he never clearly understood what it was.

All the gifts were handed out and the food had more than doubled because people from church wanted to give something to the children. Dan and Jackee also received a big thank you for the food and desserts that were received from the country club. The Sisters said they never had a better meal in their whole life. "The desserts were unbelievable, in fact there were some that no one knew what they were. We finally finished them last week and Harold has promised to send more food whenever he gets the chance."

The Jenco's finished at the orphanage and then proceeded to the Vets home. This is always a sad time because the Vets are getting fewer and fewer, and the ones that are there have trouble getting to the day room. There is always someone who would push their wheelchair to the day room but most just fall asleep. William made sure it was a quick visit and then he took the family to dinner. While at dinner, William realized that there was a great deal of talking going on. Even Sonny was having a conversation with Rocco and later with Jon. This was the person who invented the one word answer and here he was speaking in sentences. It started getting late and William asked for the check. When it was paid everyone headed home. Jackee told Rose that she was running at 5am and then coming back to finish her thank you cards. Rose agreed to go with her if she was up, but if she were sleeping, do not wake her up. As soon as they arrived home Jackee went up to her room. Dan followed later after speaking with William. Carmela and William had just settled down in their bed when there was a knock on the door. Rose stuck her head in and said "Sonny and I want to talk to both of you."

Carmela said "what is so important that it has to be done now."

"This is the only time when both of you are free together," Rose said to them.

"OK Rose. You have our undivided attention."

"Sonny wants his father and siblings to be at our wedding so he wanted to know if we should get married at his village."

William and Carmela looked at each other and William said, "we can bring whoever he wants at the wedding here and put them up for three days. We can accommodate at least 30 people if that is what you two want." Sonny said OK, and thanked them for seeing them so late at night.

William told Sonny that he was saving a surprise to tell him before thanksgiving dinner. "However, I believe this would be a good time for you to hear it. Yesterday I received word from my veterans affair contact. It seems your father had a very distinguished war record. He earned a silver star, the purple heart with two clusters and finally the Congressional Medal of Honor, which is the highest decoration for bravery that our government issues. The purple heart with two clusters means he was wounded at least three times in combat. His citation that won the CMH spoke about his bravery under fire and the many men he saved. His military record is one any American would be proud of. It will be my honor to have him and his family as guests at your wedding. Here is a copy of his military record and his citations."

Sonny was speechless and took the documents and thanked William. He and Rose left the bedroom and went to the workout room. William turned to Carmela and said, "I believe Sonny has a new appreciation for his dad."

On Thanksgiving day Jackee was up at 5am and ran for 5 miles. She did some weights, then showered and prepared to help her mom in the kitchen. Carmela told her to finish the thank you notes and they could mail them later. Jackee was going to object but then she realized her mom was right again. Going into the living room she dove right into the last of the notes. Most of the remaining thank you's were generic but a few to close friends and family, she had to add something special. She had her mom look over the last batch just as she checked the ones done yesterday. They were then stacked and readied for the postal drop.

"Thank God that's done now I can help you with dinner." The 24 pound turkey was already in the oven just waiting for the gas to be turned on. Breakfast was well under way and only the eggs and toast had to be cooked. They will not be prepared until they are ordered. Orange juice is no longer freshly squeezed, it is far cheaper to buy the 100% orange juice in the bottle. No hassle or mess, just open the top and pour. When someone said do you have grapefruit juice they were told that they are both the same. Both come from Florida, both are citrus fruits and both have the vitamin D that is good for you, drink up. No one ever asked for grapefruit juice again.

Rose came down and asked Jackee to forgive her because she was up very late with Sonny. Jackee just said, "gee I hope it was Sonny." Rose and Carmela laughed and Rose hugged Jackee and said thank you. The look on Jackee's face was one of "for what" looks.

Rose looked at her and said "for my life and for giving me Sonny. What Dan means to you is what Sonny means to me."

Carmela told them that her wifely duty talk will be a waste of time for Rose. Rose held Carmela's hand and told her "every word you have ever said to me is right here," Rose was pointing to her heart, "and I'll never forget any of them. You are one of the five treasures of my life and the one I least expected."

Sonny walked into the kitchen while the three women were hugging, and he told them that his tribe has a dance for maiden girls exactly like that. Altogether they said to get out of here. Sonny found William standing next to him and asked if he thought IHOP might be able to feed them. Rose told them to sit and she will serve them some humble pie. Dan walked in and everyone sat down for breakfast.

This was going to be only Jenco dinner. Bats and Kim would not make Thanksgiving but would come for Christmas. Mrs Silvio was having a big dinner party later that evening. Jonathan and Bianca have an epidemic in Africa that will take 4 to 6 months to get under control. So William carved the turkey for only his family as Carmela laid out all the trimmings. When everyone finished there wasn't enough left to make a sandwich on Friday. An hour later the desserts were put on the side board, and it was a help yourself situation. Jackee made herself a sundae and shared it with Dan. The others took some goodies but most preferred to wait until later. Dan and Jackee had to go to Dan's house and take some of the desserts with them. Rocco told Rebecca they should go and maybe he could spend some time with his family. Little William who led everyone in saying Grace before dinner had enough desserts and was going to sit with William in the den. The men were watching football and the women were watching a tape of the Macy's day parade down New York City 5th avenue. The rest of the day was spent doing busy work. Jackee returned with Dan about 10 and talked to everyone now seated in the living room. Carmela gave her car to Evelyn for her trip to Rebecca's house. Evelyn was to bring Rebecca and Frankie back with her for the commercial shooting at 10:30 the next day. Jackee was the first to go upstairs and was soon followed by Dan. Carmela had put little William to bed earlier and now she was going to put herself to bed. She went to her bedroom and William just followed. That left Rose and Sonny with the whole downstairs to themselves.

Friday, Carmela had all the girls and the two boys in the SUV and was heading to the studio. Hitch was pleased that they all walked in because he had created a huge set that he hoped to use in these shoots. As usual he worked with the children first and in two hours he had all the takes from them that he needed.

He then worked in a family setting so the children would be completely finished. A room had been set up to feed the children when their work was done. Jackee had three shoots that had to be completed and they went really well. Jackee and Rose did one shoot and Rose did one alone. The five women did two shoots and they were perfect. A single shoot for Rebecca and Evelyn were also done. This completed the shoots for the day. Hitch had enough material to please any sponsor. The last thing Hitch said was "Rose, win a gold medal in the Olympics and I'll make you a household name." It was late in the afternoon and Carmela called William and told him to order dinner from some place. When they finally got home pizza and many other goodies were on the table.

Carmela told William about their day and thanked him for setting up dinner as she was too exhausted to prepare anything. After dinner the girls cleaned up and the family settled down for the night. Rebecca and Evelyn went to Rebecca's house while Jackee and Dan went up to bed. William and Carmela followed them right after little William was put to bed. Rose and Sonny once again were left to themselves. Before they got too comfortable Jackee had a question to ask Dan. "Dan, if it is agreeable to you, I would like to keep playing baseball under my maiden name. This would give us some privacy when we are in the off season. Also it may cut down on unwanted calls." He agreed that it was a very good idea, also for years he wanted to have sex with Jackee Jenco but it never happened but now it was possible. She hugged him and reminded him that it wasn't she who resisted. "There came a time when I would have done anything you wanted me to do. My mother had to explain what was happening. She loves you almost as much as I do. I was told in no uncertain terms that you were the greatest guy ever and that I should never lose you. Now you show me what exactly you would have done to that naive Jenco girl."

Saturday would be Jackee's last full day at home until Christmas break. Dan had cleared his calendar so he could spend the day with her. They stayed in bed longer than usual and talked about their future. Dan finally said he was hungry and was getting up. They both dressed and went to the kitchen to see what was going on. Carmela and the two Williams were having breakfast so they joined them. William will contact the Gamblers organization before Christmas to find exactly what their plans are for Jackee. "I think we will just let this play out because they need to take the lead in your timetable for advancement."

"Dad you are right I just hope they give me a little heads up before any major changes take place."

"You just worry about playing baseball and let us worry about everything else. Between Dan and me we should have all the bases covered."

"If you and my husband can do that, I will try to be the best player they have ever seen."

"I know you will, but we must try to avoid being blindsided by something we should have been prepared for. If trouble comes, it will be from the outside and not from the Gamblers."

William asked Dan, "why do you believe that?"

"The Gamblers have too much invested in Jackee to want to see her fail. If she is a success, they at the very least will triple their investment in her. Women all over the country want to see the ninth wonder of the world. They now become the most recognized organization in the country, if not the world. Do you really think they want to lose all that?"

"You are 100% right and I am glad I have you to keep me on my toes. Where do you think we should be looking?"

"Two possibilities more than any other seem likely: number one would be the newspaper media and second would be the talking sport heads on the TV networks. Maybe look for some guy trying to make a name for himself or a thinking outside the box person. No matter what comes our way we have to be prepared for it."

"Agreed!"

The newly married couple were just hanging around all day and Carmela told them to go for a ride to visit with Evelyn before she leaves. Jon has a surgery to perform on Monday so they are leaving tonight or early tomorrow. Dan took Jackee's hand and led her to his car and away they went. Evelyn was glad to see her because they had to leave in a few hours. "Jon received an emergency call to report back to the hospital ASAP. There was a factory explosion and many people still have to be extracted from the rubble. Hospital staff have been totally overwhelmed. A private charter has been arranged for us at three, and we have to be at the airport at two." Dan offered to drive them to the airport and Evelyn accepted his offer. "We were going to call for limo service but this would be better." When all their travel gear was loaded into Dan's car, the four of them headed for the airport. Jon found the private charter waiting for them and they immediately took off.

Jackee barely had time to say goodbye and was thankful that her mother had suggested going over to see them. They stopped for a sundae and then drove back to Jackee's house. Rose and Sonny had been out shopping for Christmas gifts. They returned home just before dinner. Sonny was going with Jackee and Andrea back to the hospital and Rose was being picked up by the school's jet at noon tomorrow. After dinner they sat around talking until it was bedtime. Jackee as usual went up first and Dan soon followed. Dan did say the magic words when he got into bed with Jackee, "just think in about three weeks we will have another honeymoon." That and a little TLC carried Jackee through the night. The Next morning after church Andrea, who had arrived early enough to attend church with them, drove Jackee back to school.

Andrea and Jackee worked 16 hours a day to complete their semester requirements and still keep up with their lab responsibilities. Jackee took three hours a day to work out, mostly under Coach Zimmer's watchful eye. The girls completed everything by December 19th. That was also the day for the school's annual Christmas party. After they had the car packed and ready to go they did attend the party. As usual, because they were dressed up, they were the talk of the party. They smiled, joked with people, danced with all the old guys, and said nice things to the wives but all they really wanted to do was leave. Between them they had 5 offers to go home with other men. It was getting late when they made their excuses and left the party.

"I was wearing my wedding ring and I still got offers. How could they do that?"

Andrea mentioned "maybe it was because they were also wearing their wedding rings. The ring may slow them down but it sure as hell doesn't stop them." After breakfast they were on the way to Jackee's house. Sonny could not leave until December 23th.

Carmela had lunch waiting for them. Andrea wanted only to make a pit stop but decided to take a break and have some lunch. She left an hour later and Jackee and Carmela were all alone. Dan was not aware that Jackee was home because she only called her mother that morning before heading home. A call went out to William who said he would tell Dan as soon as he got back from a meeting. All the bags were unpacked and soiled clothes were put in the washing machine. Everything was set for dinner including all Jackee's favorite foods. In the three weeks back at school she had lost a few pounds. Little William was home from school and immediately went to Jackee asking her about school and baseball. She was still playing with him when Dan walked into the house. She stood up and before she could say a word he was kissing her. When the kiss ended she told him "that is the perfect way to welcome me home."

William came home an hour later and the five of them sat down to dinner. Dan had cleared his schedule as of December 22 so he had a full schedule for tomorrow. He apologized to Jackee but she had told him they were coming home after class on the 21st.

"Andrea and I got all our work done earlier than expected so we seized the opportunity to leave early." She said it wasn't a problem since she had a full day tomorrow helping her mom. "I thought that she would have help here but for right now it's just the two of us". Dan wanted to know if he could have a sleep over tonight with her. Jackee said "I'll have to ask my parents if that is OK with them. Mom, dad, Dan wants to know if he can have a sleep over here tonight."

Carmela said "definitely not, what kind of house does he think we run here."

"He claims that he has only honorable intentions."

"That's what they all say," Carmela answered.

"I have changed my mind. " Dan said, "I'll just stay at my house. I guess this means a divorse is in the future."

"Well, we will make a concession, he can sleep in Evelyn's room, every-one else does."

"That's not good enough" Dan shouted, "you promise me heaven and you want me to accept purgatory."

That cracked everyone up and William said, "what the hell, he can stay but he must pay rent. That is my final offer." Dan accepted.

Carmela and Jackie prepared a plan for the next 5 days. It included all meals, Christmas decorations, the orphanage and Vets home, church, and Christ-mas day activities. When Little William said he was hungry the family sat down to dinner. Later the men were in the den and the women were still working on their schedule. Carmela asked William when he was getting the tree, he answered that the tree will be delivered tomorrow before noon. "I'll set it up after dinner and put the lights on. The rest of the decorations will go on when the rest of the girls get here."

Jackee helped get Little William ready for bed. Once his prayers were said he slipped under the covers and was kissed good night by both women. About an hour was spent talking about her promotion to triple A baseball and then Jackee mentioned that she was tired and was going to bed. Dan stalled for a time but soon followed her to their bedroom. He wasn't sure what he would find but knew it was going to be good. He found her under the covers and she said "hurry before my husband comes home." He took off his clothes and got into the bed. She immediately folded herself in his arms. His needs exceeded his will power. In the early morning, Jackee thought about going for a run but as soon as she turned toward Dan that silly thought left her head. Much later and after a long shower she came down to the kitchen and found Carmela preparing some breakfast.

Carmela looked at her and said "that smile is bigger than ever. You have no idea how happy I am that you found Dan. I was afraid that your obsession with baseball destroyed all your womanly instincts. Now I see Dan not only gave them back to you but has made them greater."

Dan soon came down fully dressed in a suit and clean shaven. He told Jackee he had a full day but will be home by six and should be free for the next 4 days. She said this was to be a long day with her mom but she might be available after 8 tonight. "It's a date and I'll see you then." He left after kissing her goodbye and kissing Carmela on the cheek.

"I love that guy and I hope your father never finds out. "

Her son had 2 more days of school before the Christmas break so she and Jackee had two full days to get things ready. William came down fully dressed and ready to leave for his office. He reminded Carmela that his company Christmas party was set for tomorrow night at the restaurant by his office. She had it listed on the calendar and would be ready by 6. He kissed his wife and told Jackee that the sleepover looks like it was a big success. She told him it was the best ever and she was looking forward to many more. "That is exactly what your mother said to me 25 years ago."

Jackee watched her brother get on the bus for school and she remembered those days when her mother stood in the same spot and watched her and her sisters do exactly the same thing. When she went inside the house Carmela had her coat on and told her let's go. Go they did. From one store to the next and then back to the house to unload and restock what they bought. Soon Carmela with her coat on said we're out of here. Jackee didn't ask any questions but was just along for the ride. Christmas shopping had just two hours before the Christmas tree was to be delivered. At 12 noon they were carrying presents inside the house and setting them on the living room table for wrapping. All the things needed for wrapping, Jackee found in the basement and she brought them up and put them on the table. Now Carmela joined her and they both worked on wrapping gifts. Part of the way into the wrapping the doorbell rang and it was the Christmas tree William had bought. Two young boys brought it inside and said it was cut and ready for indoor use. Each boy received a tip and a merry Christmas before they left.

Once all the gifts were wrapped and tagged, Carmela prepared a small snack for both of them. Before it was on the kitchen table Jackee had found the stand and apron for the Christmas tree. She asked Carmela where she should spread the apron and set the stand. Moving a few pieces of furniture around, a good space had been cleared and the apron and stand were set in place. Over lunch many family matters were discussed, not of the least being Rose's marriage to Sonny. "If the Indians thought they had trouble before, wait until Rose joins them. It will resemble a cyclone that they never dreamed was possible. Federal aid will not be asked for, it will be demanded."

"Mom, if she wins a gold medal in the Olympics, she will be the greatest spokesman for them since Jim Thorpe." Carmela wanted to know if Jackee felt she had a chance to win the Olympics. "I have seen her when she has made up her mind to do something and it is scary. She has the ability to ignore pain and anything else that may be in her way to achieve what she wants. Don't you remember what she was like when she first met Sonny. He never knew what hit him. Sonny is a lot smarter than anyone thinks. He only allows certain things to happen. When Rose wanted him, he was in full agreement or else he would have just gone away. Did you notice he never once had to ask Rose about helping his people but instead let her tell him about what they should do. Which is exactly what Sonny would have done anyway. Mom, Dan is the very best but Sonny is not that far behind. He will take Rose and show her love that she has never seen. It will be stronger than the love we have for her because it will not have to be shared with anyone else."

When lunch ended they started bringing up the decorations for the house. Carmela told Jackee that "this will be our best Christmas ever and you and I will begin it today." When William walked into the house he found Christmas stuff all over the place.

"A driver has been hired to pick up Evelyn and Sonny. Jon will come alone on Christmas eve." William said, "do you two know that he is one of the best surgeons in his field? His father has been in contact with me. I personally invited Jon's parents for Christmas but they could not leave Africa because of the epidemic. However, Jonathan did say they wanted Jon to join them but so far he has not committed. We will have to talk to Evelyn about this. There is talk at Jon's hospital that he is supposed to be made chief surgeon very soon. It is supposed to take years before that title is given to any surgeon but he did it in less than three. We have a positive response from Bats and Kim, also from Dan's parents. This does give us a full table of people for Christmas dinner. We will need all the inserts on the table and another table added to one end. We will need at least 16 chairs in fact we will need 16 of everything for dinner. There will be plenty of food. The problem is seeing that it is hot enough when served. Silverware will have to be washed between courses but that should not be too much of a problem. I purchased plastic glasses for the toast and then they will be replaced by our regular glasses. Dishes will not be a problem because we have plenty in all sizes."

Dan came home earlier than expected and he immediately changed clothes and assisted William in setting up the tree. They got it up and selected the best side facing front. Fishing line was used to make sure that the tree did not fall. Next the lights were systematically arranged on the tree for maximum effect. Now it was up to the girls to finish decorating the tree. This would not be done until all the girls are present. Ornaments, tinsel, and garland were left by the tree along with any new things that were purchased. Every year William likes to add a new touch to the tree. This year would be no different. Carmela called the two men and little William to dinner. They said Grace and began eating but after a short time, in walked Sonny and Evelyn. Evelyn explained that Sonny was let off early and she decided to leave as soon as the limo could get there. She had packed and was just waiting for her ride. On the way they picked up Sonny, who also was ready and waiting for them. "So here we are and what's for dinner."

Carmela had made extra and figured Sonny and Evelyn would eat much later. This would be more acceptable because they could now eat as a family and not piecemeal. A few moments later all were eating and talking. Sonny said that

Rose would be home tomorrow at around noon. Evelyn said she has great news but would only tell when they are all together. She also said Jon would be there on the 23rd but did not have a time except to say he would not miss the trip to the orphanage.

"Rebecca will come over tomorrow so all the girls and the children will decorate the tree. I want the inside of the house finished by tomorrow night. Because the next day will be for baking and preparing for Christmas eve." Carmela laid out the plan and it was followed in every detail. Interior and exterior of the house was completed on time and the baking went perfect. As usual all the girls did their favorite dessert and many cookies were created. Dan and Jackee spent their first night getting reacquainted and the next morning Jackee had a huge smile on her face. Carmela teased her but inside she was very happy for her daughter. Although nothing was said out loud it seemed that William found a new close friend. They both depended on each other and both gave complete loyalty to each other's needs. William never had anyone like Dan he could depend on. This relationship was so strong that neither would do something without the other's blessing. The corporation set up with Jackee in mind was now a multi million dollar business. It had been expanded by Dan, of course with William's blessing, and now people were asking to be handled by the corporation. Also the handling fees were now up to 10% which they should have been at the beginning.

One hour before going to the orphanage, Jon walked in. He apologized to the family and then took Evelyn in his arms and told her she was going to be kissed by the new head of surgery at his hospital. Evelyn kissed him as the family congratulated him. Sonny shook his head and said "you have to be years of being a surgeon before you can be considered for such a position. Yet here he is jumping over other surgeons to get this title. You have to be the very best to make a jump like that."

Evelyn, while still holding Jon, had an announcement to make. "I was going to wait until Christmas dinner but it seems this is the most appropriate time. We are going to have another Jonathan in the family. I'm sorry mom but you are going to be a grandmother once again. The girls all gathered around Enelyn and wished her the best." The men were congratulating Jon and were asking for the cigars. Carmela wanted to know when she was due and Evelyn told her in May and the new tests confirm it is a boy.

The family packed the cars and made their rounds for the orphanage and Vets home. Each stop produced a different response. The orphanage was a great outpouring of love and respect. Mother Superior could not praise the Jenco family enough. The new wing housing abandoned and unwanted girls was a huge success. "These girls will have a chance to make something of their lives. Considering what their choices were before, it was a tremendous change." The Nuns asked if Jackee and Rose would talk to them one day over the vacation. Both girls accepted. Jon's parents had sent gifts for the Nuns, children and the new young women in the shelter. All the other gifts including Sonny's were brought in and set under the tree.

Rose took little Williams' hand and took him to where the children were gathered. She reminded him that this is where their life had turned around. "These Nuns protected us until our parents found us. Jackee, God love her, selected me. I in turn selected you but it was our parents who took the responsibility for us. We owe God, the Nuns, and our parents more than we can ever give back to them. You and I must try to make them proud of the fact that we were saved by them. None of them needed to help us but they did it because they loved us when no one else did. Little William finally understood the meaning of family but more importantly, he now knew that love was more than just a word."

The stop at the Vets home was more a surprise to them than it was to the home. Jon's parents had sent a complete sound and TV system to the home. It had been installed the day before and it had the capability to have on screen communications, with pictures, for family members. If the Vet had family in California, he could see the family and talk to them through the TV. Watching a movie or sporting event was almost the same as being there. Even the hard of hearing person could select one of the remote pieces that came with it and put it right by his chair. The best feature of all was it had the capability to have a show in the community center and have it sent to every TV in the home. This included every office and rehab center in the building. A special tech person was coming tomorrow to demonstrate all the features of this new system.

William asked Jon "how can we possibly thank your parents for this?" Jon told him he knew nothing about this but his parents have a staff who keep up with anything new and they probably recommended it.

"My parents are world famous and deserve every bit of praise they get but they are not family. They want me to join them but Evelyn and our coming child is my family and I need them to be with me."

Jon turned away and William understood how hurt he was. All the material things in the world can not take the place of being with your child on Christmas morning, or birthday. Jon's parents will probably miss the birth of their first grandson. William promised himself that he and Carmela would be there when their new grandson is born. They finished at the Vets home and then to the restaurant for dinner.

Christmas eve was a beautiful day, it was cold but clear. Jackee and Rose ran together and did a little weight training. After a quick shower Jackee came down to see how her mom was doing. Rose followed a short time later but she hugged her mom and said what a great day this was. Carmela asked the girls if either of them had said anything to little William. Jackee wanted to know why she was asking. "Well late last night he came into our room and hugged both dad and me. He laid between us and fell asleep and that is where he is right now, next to dad. After the first few days he was with us he never showed any fear again. What he did last night made me think something was troubling him."

Rose took her mother's hand and related what took place at the orphanage. "He just did what I was always ashamed to do, get into bed with both of you and feel that I was a real part of you. You and dad plus my sisters gave me so much I was afraid to ask for more. I used Jackee for my reassurance because she was the first person who really cared about just me."

"Rose, I'm sorry Dad and I tried to treat you the same as our other daughters. It never occurred to us that you might have needed more than that. We just forgot that sisters provide a different emotional tie. We love you and your brother so very much that it is very difficult to show without hurting the feelings of others. What you experience before binding with us is something that is not easily dismissed. It is a part of you we could never understand or be prepared for. We allowed you to make the adjustment and I thought that both of you did a great job."

Rose said "my brother knew very little of his past but mine was much stronger. Every adult was bad, even the Nuns who did nothing but help me. It was Jackee, who showed me unconditional love, I could relate to. When she accepted you it was safe for me to do the same but there always was that doubt in the back of my mind about adults. I needed to get rid of that doubt but I never knew how. Over the years it slowly left me as I realized how much you did love me. Little William got that done last night when you let him sleep next to you. People don't know how the human touch makes a difference in a child's life. Jackee's hand your arms around me when I was troubled or sick. Dads hug after an event or when I brought home a good report card, they all helped change me. I see those girls at the orphanage and realize that could have been me. I swear to you, with Jackee's help I will not turn my back on them. They will have a chance or I will die trying."

Jackee hugged her sister and told her we will never let them down. They were all crying when William walked in and said "now what". "Don't tell me, I know, you will tell me tonight in bed." The women were laughing and crying at the same time.

Once breakfast was finished everyone had jobs to do. The men were watching a movie called "It's a wonderful life" and their job was to stay out of the way of the women. Carmela had trained the girls so well that they needed very little direction as to what had to be done. It wasn't long before the baking was going full blast and the table was set for their annual buffet for tonight and part of what was needed for tomorrow. The women were having a great time. Cake batter, icing, and even some fudge was smeared on different faces. Teasing and carrying on were the main things. In spite of all this, the jobs were getting done. William took one peek into the kitchen and told the men to pile into the SUV. They all complied and William bought them lunch at the local pizza palace. When their order arrived at the table, William placed an order for the girls back at the ranch. When the men got home the frenzy was still in progress. William found some paper plates and put pizza slices on them and handed them through the kitchen opening. Many hands grabbed the plates and then disappeared. He took some paper cups and filled them with some soft drink and did exactly the same thing, sticking them into the kitchen. The results were the same and now William felt he did his duty so he went back to the den with all the other men. Without knowing what happened the baking aroma that had been coming from the kitchen changed and a new aroma was slowly filtering into the den.

William led the men in moving all the Christmas presents to where the tree was. They were placed by name and of course Frankie and little William were the main beneficiaries. There were gifts for everyone including Bats' family and the Silvio's. Little William had shaken a box or two with his name on it and then looked at his dad and said clothes with a sad face. Jackee asked Dan and her father to help put the inserts in the main table. There were three and that table was ready for setting. A second table was arranged so that the entire arrangement seated 17 people. Chairs would not be arranged until they were going to be used. Rose came out of the kitchen with Rebecca and they went up to shower and dress for this evening. When the first two were done, Jackee and Evelyn did the same. Carmela was the last to get her shower.

Rocco and Frankie arrived just as Carmela went upstairs. Rocco said "everything smells good but where are the women?" He was told it had been a very hectic day and the women were cleaning up after all the cooking was finished. He said "I know what it was like because we just left my parents house and my mom was getting ready for the Italian eve. All day she has been cooking fish or shellfish. She was starting the pasta as we left. It was a lot of work but the house smelled delicious."

All five women came down together and the men were stunned. If you had to decide which one was the most beautiful, you would be wrong. William had his camera and said we have to take a picture of them. I wish Mr Hitch was here to take this picture because he could find 100 uses for it. Each man escorted his chosen one to the chair they had just occupied. When the women were seated they were each offered to be served. Carmela wanted to have a drink with her family. She had eggnog in the refrigerator and if anybody wants something with it you will have to add it yourself. Everyone was holding a glass when Sonny said to the woman in our lives and may God always bless them. Because it was Sonny, they were all speechless and when he finished the women said thank you and everyone drank. Rose, who was standing next to Sonny when he gave his toast, told everyone that our men deserve a kiss. So it was that the five men were kissed at the same time. Carmela was right. This was the best Christmas ever.

The buffet consisted of everything from shrimp to mac and cheese. It was all serve yourself but the men decided to serve their mates as a surprise Christmas gift. None of the women knew how to act so they just followed Carmela's lead. She told William that she wanted to try the shrimp, deviled eggs, chicken cutlet with the walnut salad on the side. She added, "please don't forget the napkin."

William acted hurt and said, "would I let a beautiful woman use her sleeve as a napkin?" Toco's, veal cutlet, baked ziti, Swedish meatballs, sausage and peppers and of course mac and cheese. There were salads, potatoes and cheeses to choose from. When all the women were served, the men served the children and themselves.

They even made an attempt at cleaning up but Carmela said "enough, we do not need any broken items." They talked for a while and even let Frankie and little William open one gift each. Rebecca made the first move by saying they had to leave.

Frankie wanted to sleep over but Rebecca told him that grandma had enough to do in the morning "but if you want, you can sleep over after Christmas." Reluctantly he accepted and said good night to everyone. Evelyn and Jon left with them. Carmela put little William to bed and to her surprise he had not visited them at night again. Rose had been right, the fear that he had left him never to return. Rose and Sonny stayed in the den as everyone else prepared to retire. Jackee was in bed first and when Dan came she said it was their first Christmas eve as man and wife. Dan slipped into bed and gathered her in his arms and said she looked absolutely beautiful coming down the stairs. We are so lucky to have each other.

Jackee woke first as usual and took a shower. She dressed in casual clothes to help Carmela with breakfast. By seven everything was ready and people came down in different states of dress for the meal. Little William came down and immediately was by the tree. Jackee went to him and asked him to wait till after church so that he and Frankie could open gifts together. He agreed although his heart wasn't in it. Everyone came down, got something to eat, and then headed back upstairs to shower and dress. By 8:35 Everyone was dressed and going out to the cars. Rebecca and Evelyn were waiting at the church. Once all the Christmas greetings were complete they went in and an usher showed them to an empty pew. Father Nickolas gave a little different sermon about Christmas but it was right on the money and the congregation loved it. After Mass, he waited in the back of the church to greet all the parishioners and personally wish them a Merry Christmas. The Jenko's drove home and found Bats waiting for them. A few moments later Dan's parents came and they all went into the den to watch presents being opened. The young ones went through their presents quickly then it was time for the adults. It wasn't long before all the gifts were opened and people began talking to each other.

Bats had some news that might interest them. "The Gamblers offered me a coaching job at their triple A team. Jackee is definitely the reason it was offered. They want her to feel more relaxed, they even promoted coach Ferris from single A to the triple A team. The money is very good and the contract will run for three years. They insinuated that if Jackee makes the show I would be moved up as a special coach."

Jackee was excited but wondered how Bats actually saw this. "Kim and I are still thinking it over and we have to make a decision by January 15th no matter what our decision is, I want to thank Jackee for making this offer possible."

"Bats, I would love to have you near but you must do what is best for your family. There is no doubt in my mind that you are better than 95 % of the coaches I have seen. Without me you will add a great deal to the Gamblers organization. You said it was your dream to make the show, maybe your dream was not as a player but as a coach." Jackee told him that it was her who should be thanking him "because you were the one who pushed me toward my dream. It would have died in college if not for your guidance and teaching skills."

Dinner was served at 1pm and all were seated at the makeshift dinner table. William asked Carmela to say Grace and after she asked God to bless and keep all present safe and healthy, William gave his toast. "A man once said if you have one friend you are a success, around this table my family and I have many good friends, that makes us the most successful family around. Bottoms up!" The food was delicious and disappeared quickly. It took 2 hours to get through the meal and another 30 minutes to clean. All the sisters started putting out desserts but most of the people were talking and just having a very casual after dinner chat. Carmela had put on coffee and it was done. Dinner dishes had been replaced by cups and saucers and dessert plates. One by one people started to select some desserts. The children were first and then the adults. Pies and cakes were selected first and cookies were last. Ice cream was put on the table but only the children took some. Dan's parents had to leave but not before getting something to take home. They had brought some of Dan's favorites and left them there for anyone to try. After they left the remaining people drifted to the den. The children were playing with their gifts and the sisters were helping them. Carmela and Rose had emptied the dishwasher and refilled it. Linen was in the washing machine and the tables had been separated by the men. Inserts to the table were taken out and put away. Desserts were left out for snacking on later. Bats was to stop at the Jenco's before going home to pick up some leftovers.

Jackee and Rose continued their working out. Running, weights, and agility drills were the staple. Jackee asked her mother if she could borrow the car to go to the indoor batting cage. This batting academy did have a fastball and curveball machine. Rose and Sonny went with her. She hit off both machines and decided to pay for two weeks of hitting. According to Andrea we would not be expected back at school before the second week of the new year. Rose and Sonny were another matter.

Sonny was going to leave with Jon as his next rotation was to start soon. Evelyn would go with them even though she still had a few more days of vacation time. Rose had a big invitational meet in California so she had to get back to workout with the team before it left for the west coast. This meet and two others would have all the potential Olympic runners competing. It was an opportunity to size up your competition prior to the trials to be held in late Spring. Rose had seen most of the runners who she would be competing against and was sure that at her peak she should do very well. Jackee pushed her every time they ran and never once could she even come close to beating her. One thing that Jackee did recommend was that Rose try to increase her upper body strength. Rose had let that part of her training nearly cease to exist. It would take time but she had plenty of that until the finals began. Jackee started her on light weights and Rose did very well. She set up a program for Rose to follow and also a small change in her diet. For a few days it was just like the old days when Rose helped Jackee to workout. The day after they had spoken to the girls at the orphanage, Rose had to leave on the jet that the school was sending to pick her up. Jackee, her brother, and mother went to the airport to see Rose off. They wished her good luck, gave her a snack to eat on the plane and off she went.

"The house is so empty when you girls leave, all I have is your brother when he is not in school. Our house was never quite like this when you girls were home. Your father says we have to make adjustments to all the changes but he has his work and now more because of you. Dan is creating a new field and now both of them had to expand their day. Your father thinks the world of Dan, and so do I."

"That makes three because I never want to be without him again," Jackee said.

Jackee hit an hour a day at the academy. First fastballs, then curves and she was getting her timing down perfect. She started drawing a crowd and the owner told her the hitting was on the house. His business jumped 500% since Jackee started hitting there. It was the least he could do to thank her for having so many people come in. Jackee hired a batting practice pitcher and four days a week he came to throw batting practice. He also did well because he was hired by others to throw to teams as well as individuals. Andrea called and told Jackee they had to leave on the 14th because the college wants them there on the 15th. Dan knew this day was coming and had prepared his schedule accordingly. He now was to spend the last two days with Jackee. She had a shoot with Rose before she left and now one was set up with Andrea on the 14th. Andrea decided that Jackee needed time with Dan so she was coming early on the 14th. After the shoot they will drive to the college. Dan spent the afternoon of the 12th until morning of the 14th by Jackee's side. After her brother went to school on the13th, Carmela left the house and did not return until 4pm. Jackee and Dan spent the whole time holding each other.

When her mother arrived home Jackee had that smile and told her mother she really appreciated having that alone time with Dan. "I hope it was enough time because now I have to prepare dinner for your father. However, we could go out to eat if you feel you need more time."

"I do not believe that will be necessary because Dan said he was totally exhausted and needed time to recuperate."

Carmela smiled and said "I know the feeling well, it has happened before." They both prepared dinner and at 6pm sat down to eat. Dan had seconds on everything and both Carmela and Jackee knew why. They went to bed early because tomorrow was going to be a long day. Jackee was up early and had all her bags packed and down by the door. Andrea showed up about 7:30 and gladly sat down for breakfast. Next the three women were working with Hitch on multiple shoots. By noon they were leaving Hitch to have lunch and get ready to leave for school. At 7pm they were unloading their bags and heading over to the cafeteria for dinner.

Next morning they checked their schedule and their message service. Lucy was waiting for them and had their schedule as well as Jackee's ready for viewing. There were two speaking engagements and a dinner appearance they had to make. Lab work had only one project that had to be verified. This would take weeks but there would be a great deal of down time while they were waiting for feedback. Jackee also checked in with coach Zimmer and a schedule was set up for her to hit. Her 5am workout was still going strong and more and more of the baseball players started to attend. Jackee worked with the hitters and coach Zimmer worked with the pitchers. She felt that the team was really starting to take shape. Hitters were making good contact. Next week we will start live batting practice and the coach wants to start taking fielding practice. Early morning practice and a full afternoon practice was now a six day week schedule. The pitchers looked really good for this time of year. It was surprising that the hitters were still making excellent contact. Pitchers were supposed to be ahead of the hitters in the early part of spring training. This was not the case here. Jackee continued her hitting and she started working on the slider and split finger pitches. The slider was easy because when she picked up the spin she knew what was coming. The Split finger was a whole new ball game. There was less time to pickup the pitch so you were already starting the swing before you were sure what the pitch was. Jackee decided that with less than two strikes, she would not swing at it. Most times, since the pitch is hard to control, it was out of the strike zone. With 2 strikes it becomes a different matter, you must protect the plate.

Their speaking engagements had two different audiences. One was for students wishing to enter the program and the other was strictly for parents. Both were actually easy if the school still maintained their quality not quantity ideal. Informing students that they are in for a great deal of hard work will scare most of the dead wood away. There are, however, some students who think they can slip by doing almost no work. Those need to be discouraged from even attending the talks. They think college is just going to be high school 13. That it will be a continuation of the 12th grade. For every hour of class in college there are 3 hours of study on your own. In pre med you can add on many more hours. There is no letting it slide in med school because you are turning out doctors not business people. An accountant makes a mistake, he erases it and moves on. A doctor makes a mistake and someone might lose their life. You can never eliminate all risks but you have to eliminate all the risks you can. The parents on the other hand have these notions that their child would make a great doctor. They never ask the child what they think and then they are in shock when the child fails.

The presentation to the students went really well. If they get 10% applications the school should be satisfied. Andrea was very disappointed in the parent presentation. She got the feeling that once the parents paid for the school, that it was a done deal. There was little understanding about the work the student had to do. Most of the fathers were paying more attention to their legs and other things than they were their words. Even though it was going to be a great deal of money out of their pockets, they were bored and just wanted to get it over with.

Last but not least was their appearance representing the school at a state convention of colleges'. They were introduced and then they were put in a booth and waited for people to show up and talk to them. It seemed to the girls that they were there because of their looks as well as their knowledge of the school. It was no coincidence that they had more propositions than questions about the school. Andrea kept saying we got a lot more than we had to give. She was 100% right. The college used us for what they needed and we used them for all that we got. The day at the convention center was the last time they would ever make a presentation off campus. There will probably be a talk to parents and students when they come to check out the school but other than that, they should be done. Saturday ended the convention and the directors of the convention supplied a huge dinner for the presenters. There was plenty of food and the variety was outstanding. After eating, the school's limo took the girls back to campus.

Andrea and Jackee got ashes for the start of lent. They had arranged for a five day break over Easter. It was to start on Holy Thursday and finish Monday night. Andrea figured to drive home after class on Wednesday. All lab work should be completed and they finish their last class at noon. All they would have to do is pack the car, grab some take out from the cafeteria and get on the road. Five weeks just flew by because both were busy, so on that Wednesday before Easter, at 12:30, they were on the way to Jenco's house.

Andrea was excited about seeing Brett because he would be home for Easter. "He also thinks his job at the main office will open up in the summer. That means he will be home most every night." They had decided to live at his house since Andrea would be away so much. His mother and father were both working and they have a cabin they use 9 months a year most every weekend. They have a room at the main house where all my equipment can be set up for my experiments when I work from home. As the journey was coming to an end, Andrea told Jackee that she was scared. "All my life I had relationships but deep down I made sure they weren't permanent. I truly believe that I love Brett but this is going to be forever and not for a short period of time. Will I be content to have just one relationship?"

Jackee told her, "one day go to a church, any church, and just sit in the back by yourself. You can pray, sing, kneel or stand. You can talk or just sit quietly but before you leave, you will have an answer. It may not be the one you hoped for, but it will be an answer. If it doesn't work we will talk about it."

Andrea wanted to know how Jackee got so smart in the short time she knew her. "I am book smart but I am not street smart" Jackee told her, "however I do know my family and friends. Because I know them there is a bonding that gives me insight to their needs. That beautiful girl I was living with was slowly losing respect for herself and I was helpless to do anything about it. This new girl has great respect for herself and will not revert back to the old one. The old one had no future and the new one has seen a much better life ahead of her. Try what I told you and see what happens."

They got to Jackee's house and Andrea wished her a happy Easter and thanked her for the good advice. She also said I'll see you on Monday at about noon and I do love you like a sister. Jackee took her bag and started for the house. Carmela came running out and Jackee hugged her. They carried the bag inside and little William gave her a big welcome home kiss. Dan walked in later on and was surprised to find her already home. She was not expected until after dinner. Dan was just hugging her and he finally stepped back and kissed her. She would not let go of him and asked him to stay like this for another minute. He did and after a time she let him go and whispered, later, in his ear. Carmela had dinner ready so that when William came home they ate and talked for a long time. Family news was that Rose would not be home until Thursday and Evelyn will also be here Thursday. "Dad hired a car for her because he did not want her traveling any other way. They will pick up Sonny on the way but both must leave early Monday morning. Evelyn will bunk in with Rose, and Sonny will have her old room. Jon will not make it because he is working. Evelyn was not going to come but Jon insisted since he would not be free any of the days. Word is that his parents have the epidemic under control but it will take two more months before they can leave. Jon said his mother wrote him a letter telling him his father has worked 75 days without a break except for a few hours of sleep most days. For the first time she said his health is a big concern among the other doctors. Jon wants to see them when they come home but Evelyn can not. They will have to quarantine about two weeks before going in public. A special medical plane will be sent to bring the staff home."

Dan talked to William about a new client who has cut a record that the studio thinks will be a number one hit. "The record company wants to sign her to a contract and she has no one to negotiate the contract. We were recommended and I put her on hold until we decided what to do."

William said, "I think you can handle it." Dan told him that the record company is just above a fly by night one. "You think they are that shaky."

"If I ask for 30% up front as my final offer, and they refuse, then I know they are not solid. I'll originally ask for half and let them bargain me down but nothing less than 30%."

"That is good thinking and I know you are right about the 30%."

Jackee said "enough of all this money talk, I have a homecoming to look forward to."

Dan told her there will be no more talk of business until you have been formally welcome home. "Is that fair?"

"I can live with that," Jackee answered. Dinner was over and everything was cleaned up. They sat in the den and talked for a time. Jackee said she was tired and was going to shower and go to bed. She left the room and helped Carmela put little William to bed before saying good night to her mother and then going into her room to prepare for a shower. Dan was still talking to William. William after a time, told him he better tend to Jackee or else both of them would be in trouble. Dan decided to shower before going to bed so it took a few moments before he closed the bedroom door behind him. Jackee was already in bed and wanted to know what kept him. He told her that a gentleman never interferes with a lady when she is preparing for bed. She told him she was his wife and not just some lady "now get in this bed so we can get reacquainted." He did as he was told.

Evelyn and Sonny arrived the next day, but Rose was delayed by bad weather. By the afternoon the pilot had his clearance and took Rose home. William and Sonny picked her up. On the way to the house Rose told them she has qualified for the Olympic tryouts. Her times in the last meet were her best ever. Jackee's upper body conditioning really did the trick. William said he was proud of her but expected nothing less. "Jackee has guaranteed that you will make the Olympic team. She thinks that your desire is even stronger than hers."

"Jackee was the best big sister a girl ever had. She is the one who showed me how to be a successful athlete."

Sonny finally said a word and he related what Jackee did for the baseball players at the college. "How many of them relied on her to improve their baseball skills? She not only is a great athlete, she is an excellent teacher, and she is definitely the greatest all round woman I have ever seen." William thought to himself that if Sonny is right, Jackee could very well be declared woman of the year. They drove home and had a big reception committee waiting for Rose. little William was the first to hug and kiss his sister as the two of them were different yet the same. Rose never let her brother forget that he was picked by her therefore they were soul mates. The rest of the family joined in and it was a very happy Holy Thursday. It was getting late before anyone talked about going to bed. Sonny decided to bunk in with little William. All the girls had their own room except Jackee who had a roommate. Carmela told everyone to go to bed because tomorrow will be a long day. They all went to their rooms and before long the house was quiet.

Friday morning there was a big breakfast for the whole family. William had to go to the office for about four or five hours but he would be home for church. Carmela had everyone else sitting around the kitchen table. All of them were trying to catch up on the latest news. Evelyn had said she was right on schedule to deliver in May. She asked Carmela to be with her a few days before and a week after. Carmela said "you know I get a fee to be a caretaker, but for you, I'll make a concession. Rebecca can have little William stay at her house and dad can care for himself. He and Dan are so busy, he won't even know I'm gone."

Sonny said his next rotation is obstetrics and prenatal care, "so I should be ready by May to assist if necessary." There was no way Rose or Jackee could be there because both would be in the middle of their greatest quest.

Dan asked if Evelyn would consider having the baby become one of the models for Mr Hitch. "He was looking for a baby when I talked to him. I think he wants Jackee to hold a baby while doing her commercial for the girls line of clothes. You know the one where Jackee doesn't get paid, instead the money goes to the orphanage."

All the girls went shopping with Carmela and the men stayed home. Dan worked on some contracts and Sonny played with little William. Three hours later the women came home with bags of groceries and other things. It took a time to put everything away and just when it was done, William came home. There was a 3pm church service and the family usually attends. So they got into the SUV and headed for the church. The service was solemn and short. All together the family was back home in less than an hour. Since no one had lunch, dinner was started immediately. Being Good Friday it had to be meatless. Lobster, shrimp, tuna salad, mac and cheese and pizza were available on demand. The mac and cheese along with the pizza were the first to go. Lobster was eaten and anything left over was made into a salad. Shrimp was more of an appetizer and was consumed early in the meal. For dessert Carmela bought ice cream, cheesecake and apple pie. After dinner the family just sat around and talked. By midnight they were all in their bedrooms.

Saturday morning Rose and Jackee worked out. This lasted for four hours and both were fully exhausted. It was 10am before they called it a day and went looking for breakfast. Rose and Jackee both ate a good breakfast. Dan and Sonny went for a ride and didn't return until after 2pm. William was working in his office and Evelyn was helping Carmela. Little William was getting the bowls ready for the egg coloring. Each bowl contained a different color. Evelyn was cooking up the eggs. When they were perfect for coloring she cooled them and set the three dozen eggs on the table to be colored. Eggs were colored by little William and the sisters. Each one tried to make their egg the best decorated. William decided he would take the family out for dinner so they called Rebecca and said to meet us at the Alamo Barbecue Pit at seven. He called ahead and reserved a table for 11 at seven. When they arrived the table was ready and Rebecca and her family were waiting. It seemed like they ordered the whole menu because the food barely fit on the table. The bill, with tip, was over three hundred dollars. Rebecca, Rocco, and Frankie left right from the restaurant to go home. William paid the check and the rest of the family went home. Since it was late the family just went to bed. Jackee was glad that Dan was in bed first because the sisters decided to put the brother to bed. When she entered the bedroom, Dan said "what kept you?" Jackee hurried and in no time at all she was cuddled next to Dan.

Easter morning Carmela was up early and so were her daughters. It was the family custom to hide the Easter eggs in the three rooms. The den, dining room,and living room. Little William was to find the eggs and put them back in the carton. When all the carton's were filled, all the eggs had been found, he would receive 25 cents for each egg he found. There was also a 9am service they had to get ready for so the time had to be watched. The little guy came down and started looking for the eggs. He found a total of 35 but had to stop and get ready for church This Sunday was different from all the others. Most people came in their Sunday best. Easter is basically the start of spring and represents a new beginning. Winter is finished and everything begins coming to life. Grass gets longer and greener, trees get their leaves, many birds are born and the dormant winter animals start foraging for food. It has great religious meaning because a Savior has risen from the dead and freed the world from the clutches of evil. A new light has opened the gates of heaven for the human race. Father Nicholas stressed some of this in his talk after he read the Gospel. Easter is meant to be a happy time of year, so his talk was uplifting. The congregation seemed very pleased and the many compliments he received after the Mass proved it. The family went home and little William kept looking for the last egg. He never did find it on his own, so Rose gave him hints and he found it. William gave him the nine dollars.

When Frankie came he told little William that he failed to find 3 of the eggs at his house. Carmela put the 36 eggs on the table and said there is a prize for the best decorated egg. The men are to pick the winner as none of them helped with the coloring. First, each man picked the egg they thought was the best. From the five selected they had to pick one. After much debate one egg was picked and it was decorated by Rose. Her mother pulled out a package and gave it to Rose. She opened the package and it was a bottle of Obsession by Calvin Klein. Rose loved the aroma because it was her mother's favorite. She hugged her mom and told her "when I need you near me I'll just open the bottle and take a sniff."

Dinner was started by the women, Carmela, Rebecca and Evelyn concentrated on the dinner, while Rose and Jackee prepared some snacks to carry everyone over till dinner was served. William was responsible for the drinks and of course they were all soft drinks. Eggnog was the first choice of most people. The annual Easter day parade was on TV and they watched for a time until they were bored with the floats and commercials. William shifted to the disk and put on the movie Ben Hurr. The men all gathered around and spent the next three hours watching the movie. Just as the movie ended, dinner was served. The roast was perfect and there was a selection from well done to rare. Side dishes covered anything a person might want. When all was said and done, the roast had very little left and most side dishes were near empty. Rose said for the men to go inside so they can clean the table and put out the desserts. Just as they normally do, the men followed orders and moved to the den. An hour later they were summoned to the dinning room for desserts. The last thing put on the table was the ice cream. Once again everyone had their fill of desserts. For some reason the table grew quiet and it seemed that no one had anything to say. This would be their last meal together for a long time. Everyone would leave at some time tomorrow, so in less than 24 hours this house would be back to just three people. The daughters started cleaning up and they would not stop until everything was back to normal. Dishes were washed and put away. Food was put in the refrigerator or freezer. Desserts were nearly all gone but there was enough left for the people who were left. Floors were cleaned and furniture put back in place. Everyone who had to pack did so. Rebecca and Rocco said good night and goodbye to everyone and took Frankie home. Jackee said she was going to bed and so did Evelyn. Rose was to stay up with Sonny for a time. But before this happens little William had to be put to bed. The three sisters took care of that and then retired to their rooms. Rose came out again after she changed. Jackee was in bed and was waiting on Dan. He came into the room and immediately joined Jackee who just said "hold me tight."

Next morning the limo was there to pick up Sonny and Evelyn and once their bags were in the car and all the goodbyes were done they were off. Rose had to be at the airport at 11am. Her parents and brother would see her off. Andrea arrived at 10am and Jackee put her bags in the car, kissed her parents and gave

Dan a hug and kiss and got in the car. They all said good luck and we will pray for you. She was smiling at them as Andrea pulled away, one block later she was crying. It lasted for almost an hour before she completely gained control of herself. Andrea did not know what to say or do, so she just drove.

Jackee apologized and said, "I am going to be asked to do what no woman has ever done before and my family will not be there."

"Jackee, you are wrong. Your family will be there. Millions of women have been waiting for this day all their lives. You are going to make them proud by opening doors that have been closed to them forever. Your sacrifice will be a signal to them that many new and exciting things can now be included in their dreams. Every mother and every female will now have a new hero to look up to. You did this, not your family. Whether you succeed or fail is not important. You have taken them to a new level and the higher you go, gives them even more goals to achieve. Just do the very best you can because we, the women of the world, will stand with you."

Jackee said it was a lot to consider but she knew Andrea was right. "This whole thing has gotten out of my control and it's no longer just about me. You made me see that many more people, especially women, are depending on me. It ceased being my choice when I committed to signing a professional contract". Now they were mostly silent for the rest of the drive. There was much to think about and the time was running out.

Monday after her workout and classes, Jackee was helping Coach Zimmer with practice when she asked if they could meet later that night. He agreed and they met in his office where they would not be disturbed. Jackee asked if he could help her prepare for joining the Rosevail Rollers on April 15th. He said it would not be a problem since he had already spoken to Bats and a program was formulated. She wanted to know how Bats was involved. Coach told her "he will be waiting for you when you arrive at the Rollers Field. He and his wife decided that this was an opportunity that he could not refuse. He was granted a leave of absence from his job so the risk is not too great. He expects to find you in perfect condition when you appear, so 5am tomorrow we begin." The plan called for a 10 hour day for 13 straight days including some minor adjustments as the training progresses. "I'll be in contact with Bats every step of the way and you will be at peak form when you appear at the Rollers field."

Jackee never worked so hard in all her life but after two days things started to fall into place. Her stamina was increased and she now felt new strength in her body. Coordination drills made her flexibility the best it has ever been. Reflexes on balls hit off the bat were better than ever. Hitting was right on target. She was hitting 95 to100 mile an hour fastballs with authority and the curve balls were almost as good. The split finger still gave her trouble but she very seldom swung at one in the dirt. Keeping back on all the pitches was still a work in process but it was slowly coming. Bats told Zimmer to keep her at it because she was on the right track. On the tenth day, which was a Sunday, only a very light workout was planned. Jackee was shocked when the coach said they were done for the day. She asked what had happened.

"Bats recommended tapering off and I agree with him, you need the break. Your next three days will be fine tuning and then it's off you go to make us proud." For the first time in more than a week she laughed at the coach and he hugged her and told her she was the best.

"My players hate you because you force them to work harder. Yet each one knows that you are the reason we are still undefeated. I am going to miss you because you have been like a daughter and close friend all wrapped into one. Thank you for all you have done for me and my family. Now get out of here and enjoy the rest of the day."

Andrea was waiting when she walked into the room. She asked what had happened and Jackee explained it was a light day. "We now have the rest of the day to do anything we want."

"Well let me see, Our classes are all finished including our labs, you are 98% packed for leaving on Thursday, the school has been informed and has agreed to your leaving and finally your acceptance to the medical program at the hospital has been confirmed. Could there possibly be anything else."

"Yes I could use a few hours with Dan right now."

Andrea said "you and me both."

Jackee kiddingly got that jealous look on her face, and Andrea said, oh you know what I mean. They both laughed and hugged each other. Jackee said "I am going to take a long hot shower to relax" and Andrea replied, "I am going to take a cold one later." Smiling at her, Jackee turned and went into her room. A few moments later Andrea let Dan into the room and she told him her overnight bag was packed and she was spending the night with her friend in the next dorm.

"You do your magic with her today Dan, and I'll have her ready to leave here on Thursday." Dan put down his bag and gave Andrea a kiss on the cheek and thanked her for looking after his wife. He then closed and locked the door when she left and he entered the bedroom.

Jackee nearly had a heart attack when she saw a male figure enter her room and then she realized who it was. Crying, she ran to him and hugged him as hard as she could. Dan could barely breath and soon became aware that Jackee was stronger than she had been. She was also thinner, and not as soft as he remembered. A few moments later none of this made the least bit of difference. Much later Dan suggested that they get something to eat. Food was not a priority for Jackee, all she wanted was to be held by Dan. He told her "we have the whole day and all night because Andrea has a sleepover planned with her friend next door. I don't have to leave until the morning so let's enjoy the day."

She agreed to getting some food especially after Dan said he had left home without breakfast. They went to the cafeteria since it was nearby and Jackee had guest privileges there. Dan took a full tray of food but Jackee just had her regular lunch. After eating they went for a walk and then back to the room. Their conversation was mostly about her appearance for the Rollers on Thursday. She mentioned that Bats was there as a coach so that was a big plus and she explained how he and coach Zimmer had prepared her workout schedule. "It is a great feeling to know so many people are trying to make my dream successful. Andrea made me see that many people that I have never met are pulling for me to succeed. I no longer feel alone but now know, beside my family, many more are behind me. You are my most important supporter but I no longer have to drain all your strength because there are others willing to support me. I took your dream and hopes and I used them for my benefit and you didn't ask for anything in return."

Dan told her you are not seeing what I received. "I have one of the greatest women who ever lived as my wife. She loves me and made my life better than I ever dreamed it could be. How can anyone ask for more than that?"

Jackee said, "I don't know how you could ever forgive me for what I did to you while we were dating. I truly did not understand because I was so naive."

Dan responded, "let me tell you that on the first night of our honeymoon you made up for all the anxiety you may have caused me. It was the greatest night of my life and I never wanted it to end."

"That is exactly what I told my mother and she agreed that is as it should be."

"You told your mother about our honeymoon?"

"Of course not in detail but in general. By the way, is it time to take away more of your anxieties?"

Dan left when Jackee went to workout. He did not know how she was so full of pep and ready to go. He figured he would have to rest up most of the day. He had a lot of work to do before heading to Rosevail on Thursday with the Jencos. Jackee on the other hand was working hard with the coach. Zimmer could not believe how much energy she had. He hoped she was not peaking too soon but decided that her night with Dan had been what the doctor ordered. They all had been in on Dan's surprise visit. It was agreed that she was working too hard and needed a break. It now seems that it was even better than they had expected. She was like a dynamo and sponge all in one. Instructions were followed to the letter and everything was done at a high level. This was the situation for the full three days. Wednesday was to end her training and a shorter day was planned. A special evening was planned by the college. They would honor Jackee before she leaves for Rosevail. She will be doing her medical training at the hospital affiliate, but still will be living at the same dorm. Her parents were not invited, it was just a college thing. They had dinner and made some speeches but the best one was given by her coach. He told the guests that the college made the choice of its life by selecting Jackee to attend the school. "Everything and everybody she came in contact with became better. No better spokesperson would this school ever have. No better athlete would this school have. We went from a nameless baseball program to one of the most sought after in four short years. She raised the level of this team so now some division one schools will not even play us. Some did because they figured to cash in on the fact that a female was playing in the game. They soon found that it was not only a female but one of the best baseball players around. Most found out the hard way. We lost a total of two games to division one schools while Jackee played. I want to wish her the best and as she once said to the young girls she spoke to, May God always keep her in the palm of His hands. Thank you for all you have done for the school. my family and me personally."

Jackee asked to say a few words. She started out by thanking everyone who has helped her. She followed that with, "on this campus I have always been treated with kindness and respect. This school has gone to the limits to protect and educate its students and has reached out to the community to be part of their life. In the six years I have gone from a young girl to a mature woman and that is because of this institution. My teachers and friends here, especially Dr Hopkins and his secretary, Lucy, have given me the knowledge and wisdom to move into the next phase of my life. Coach Zimmer and the athletic staff have strengthened my body and mind for what may lay ahead. May God Bless you All and as the coach said, always be in God's hands. She then shook hands and said her goodbyes. Andrea walked with her back to the dorm. For a change it was Andrea who started crying as she told Jackee that she would miss her. Having you as a roommate will make it difficult for me to live with anyone else. No one can live up to your standards. God knows you saved me more than once and I gave you so little in return. Jackee told her what her father always said: if you have one good friend you are rich. While I have you, Dan and my family, I must be the richest person alive. Thank you."

CHAPTER TWENTY NINE

Jackee Plays for the Triple a Team

*N*ext morning a limo from the Gamblers organization was there to pick Jackee up. Andrea and Jackee put the bags near the car and the driver put them into the trunk. Both girls were crying as they said goodbye. The driver held the door as Jackee entered, he closed the door, got in and drove for Rosevail. She asked if he was connected to the team and he told her he was the driver for the executive people. "My orders are to get you to the team safely or else."

They arrived at High Card Stadium at about 1pm. The driver had direct contact with the team and they knew exactly where he was all the time. Mr Bricky and Bragan along with the manager, Mark Wright, were there to greet her. Mr Bragan opened the door before the driver could get there. Jackee got out, thanked the driver and shook hands with the welcoming committee. Coach Wright said he has "heard a great deal about you and I welcome the chance to see you play."

"My only wish," Jackee said, "is that I can help the team."

"Your dressing quarters are next to the Rollers locker room and it does have a shower. You have a special locker to secure your valuables and you have the only key. Your uniforms and baseball bats are already in the room. This league uses wooden bats to prepare the players for when they make the show."

Jackee told them, "last week I was practicing with a wooden bat."

"That's good, we do have a game tonight but you do not have to play if you feel tired or rushed."

"Thank you but I am fine and will suit up for the game."

Within an hour Jackee was ready. She selected two bats to use in batting practice so she could determine which one is better. Coach Wright called a team meeting to introduce Jackee to the team. He also wanted to see if there was any kind of resentment. The player whose place she took on the roaster was called up to the show. The Major League team released an older player who did not cut it and he was too old for triple A. When all the players were assembled, coach Wright told them about the new player and what new rules were going to be enforced. He asked if there were any questions and only two, supposed to be funny ones, were asked. First was, why isn't she showering in the team locker room and the second was can I wash her back.

Coach asked Jackee if she wanted to answer those questions. She said "I will. If I showered in this locker room none of you would be able to get your jock strap on, and second my husband frowns on anyone helping me wash and he carries a pistol to make sure that doesn't happen. My rules are very simple, I will not be physically abused either verbally or by touching. I can take a joke but make sure it is funny and not pornographic. I am sure there will be some crude comments about my being a different gender but understand this, in my 12 years of playing baseball I have endored more insults than all of you combined. Since I first stepped on a baseball field, things have been said to me and about me. Some were bad, some I had no idea what they meant, some my mother and father, never even heard of. With a metal bat similar to this wooden one I have hit baseballs one at a time but it would not be hard for me to hit two balls at the same time, if you get my drift. I wish to be treated the same as you do. We are teammates and must protect each other when possible. I have never played for a team that had a losing season. I see no reason why this team should be any different."

Bats had come in just as Jackee was finishing speaking, and when he saw her he went and welcomed her to the team. Coach Ferris did the same thing and most of the team players followed. The clubhouse manager Bill Rizzo made sure that all her uniforms and gear had number 7 on them. This number had been put on hold when the organization started scouting Jackee. Coach Wright told the players to get out for batting practice.

A batting practice order had been hung in the dugout which was the custom for coach Wright. He liked to watch the starting players hit to see if they were ok. It was not unusual for a player to try and play hurt for fear of losing his position. Jackee stayed near the batting cage and did her stretching and loosening exercises before her practice swings. She also watched the pitcher and the two hitters before her. When it was her turn to hit most of the players stopped what they were doing and we're watching her. She first timed the pitcher then prepared to swing. The next pitch was lined to left center field and the next 9 pitchers were lined someplace on the field. Three curve balls were lined to center or right center. She was very comfortable with the wooden bat but it seemed that the ball did not travel as fast. She did hit one ball that she thought might go over the fence but it hit half way up. When she finished her round, she secured her bat and took her glove out to second base. Passing Bats she heard him say, "good job."

Dewey Jones, who was the team's second baseman told her to cover second while he went in to hit. She told him "it would be my pleasure to do just that." Bats started hitting Jackee ground balls. He thought she was as smooth as ever. He was used to seeing her at short but she was every bit as good at second. It seemed to him that her arm was stronger and she had better range but there was no doubt that she was better than anybody they had on this team. Buddy Banter who played with Jackee for the Hustlers was at shortstop so he immediately started working with her. They had been a good combination for the Hustlers so there was no reason why it would not continue here. It didn't take long before the coaches saw what Bats already knew, that Jackee was for real and Dewey would need to find a new position while she is here. As batting practice was ending, the gates were opened and the fans came pouring in. At first no one was paying attention but soon the noise had reached a very high level. Game time was usually 7pm for weekday night games. It wasn't even 6 yet and the stands were already more than half filled.

Bats mentioned to coach Wright it might be a good idea to pencil Jackee into the lineup. He said "if I don't, they will run me out of town on a rail." He rewrote his lineup card, and posted the starting line up on the dugout wall. Jackee was surprised that she was playing second and batting third.

6:55pm the lineup cards were exchanged and the ground rules were gone over. The umpires wanted to know if there was a special give away tonight because the stands were filled. Wright told them we were making history tonight and they were part of it. None of the umpires had been warned about Jackee playing tonight. They all had come from a previous city and had not read any local papers. Usually the league informs them of any unusual occurrences but no one contacted them about anything. When the Rollers took the field the noise was ear shattering. More than 60% of the crowd was female and the local media was all over the place. All the Jenco family who could make it and some friends were in a private booth. Jackee had no idea that her family was present and as her usual pregame meditation called for complete concentration on the upcoming game. Abe Singer, a lefty from last year's team, started for the rollers. As if someone wrote the script, the first ball hit was a grounder to second. Jackee fielded it cleanly and threw a strike to first base. The crowd loved it. In the bottom of the first with a runner on first and one out Jackee came to bat. There was so much noise that you would have thought that they had won the world series. She watched the pitcher and saw he had a good fastball but a lazy curve. One thing she was sure of, he was going to go macho on her. Throwing the fastball by her would prove he was the better of the two. She set for a fastball down the middle. The pitch came exactly as she had anticipated except it was to the outside of the plate, she got all of it, and the ball hit off the right center fence. When the ball was hit, the runner knew it was going to be a hit so he kept running and scored easily. This turned out to be Jackee's first extra base hit for her new team. Leading off second she later scored on a single by the left fielder Andy Pace. Abe had 5 scoreless innings and the score was still 2 to 0 in the bottom of the fifth. Leading off the 5th, Jackee drew a walk and two pitchers later stole second. Later in the inning she would score on a sacrifice fly by Roy Riple, the third baseman. They scored another run in the inning so now the Rollers led 4 to 0 after 5 innings. Karl Casper pitched two scoreless innings, and the relievers Nate Wilson and Doug Taylor pitched the last two. Final score was 4 to 0. Jackee added a single in the seventh, so she ended the game 2 for 3 with a walk, 2 runs scored and 1 RBI.

As was her usual custom Jackee talked to the fans after the game. What she didn't know was her family was working their way down to her dugout. Except for Rose, Sonny, Evelyn and Jon, all the other members of the family made it. About 15 minutes after the game ended, the family reached where she was. She stopped talking and ran over to them. There was crying and laughing all at the same time. When she asked how long they were here, she was told from about 3. Dan finally reached her and gave her a kiss. "You could have let me know you were coming."

"We did not want to interrupt your game plan or distract you in any way. You had Bats, and we figured he was the best at watching over you. We are only staying the night but the organization insisted we be here for your first game."

"That was a nice gesture on their part."

William said "you guessed right on that fastball in the first inning."

"Dad, you know if they have a fastball their ego is going to insist they throw it by me. By my very competitive nature you know I'm not going to let that happen."

"The scouts from the organization were impressed with your play and how you handled yourself." Jackee went to change and would meet them by the locker room. The three coaches were talking when the family came into the lobby area.

William walked over to Bats and asked "what do you think?"

Bats looked at coach Wright, and the coach said, "I believe she is the real goods. She will finish the year with us but after that I believe the organization has a huge decision to make. If I was a betting man, I would bet the farm that she is wearing Gamblers Gold next season." Bats and Ferris both agreed with that assessment. William carried the news back to the family.

When Jackee came out to join them she asked what they thought of the game, they all said, "not bad for a start."

All the coaches and her family were invited to have dinner with some of the Gamblers exec's. There was a big restaurant nearby and they all went there. Dan was sitting next to Jackee and he told her how great she had played. "You are like a dynamo on that field. Forgetting you are a girl, you were the best player on that field."

"I hope they never forget that I am a girl playing a man's game, and doing it very well."

Dan said, "I have proof that you are all women." The dinner had been great but the most important thing happened to Jackee, her fear of not being good enough was gone and a new burning desire was taking hold of her. She now felt this level can be a stepping stone to her final destination, the show. All the tools were in place, only the experience was needed. That could be completed this season. The off season would be spent with Bats and coach Zimmer getting ready for the show. *All that thinking is good but you can't get ahead of yourself. Right now I have to concentrate on playing and learning at this level. Forget next season and work hard on this one.* A plan that Jackee was formulating in her mind was the one she would follow until the end of this season. She had no idea what the coaches were planning but she knew that coach Wright had a new appreciation for her. It would automatically happen that the players would follow his lead.

Getting ready for the next game, which was 24 hours later, seemed to have a different feel. The players seemed to be more respectful and friendlier. There was more conversation towards her in batting practice and fielding drills. Her speed was tested against the fastest runner on the team. There was a debate whether she lost but the case was moot because no one else on the team had ever beaten him. Jackee asked if she could practice pop ups because she was not used to the winds in and around this stadium. Coach Ferris hit the short fly balls and Bat directed her chasing them. Posted in the dugout was the lineup for the game and it was exactly as the day before except Chris Barlow was the starting pitcher. Jackee noted that he threw hard and had a good curveball. This meant that more balls should be coming her way. Very early the stadium began to fill up and by game time there seemed to be only standing room.

Wright told the team, "you can thank this young lady for all these fans. After our opening game and a playoff game we have never had a full house during the season. Even on our giveaway games, a full house had never been recorded. You will feel the change because the fans cheering should raise the level of your play."

As soon as the team took the field, they knew exactly what the coach had been talking about. There was a different kind of excitement throughout the stadium. Every play, every hit, and ever run scored brought a roar from the crowd. When Jackee hit a ball down the right field line and slid into third safely she got a standing ovation. No matter what she did they cheered. She was the darling of the crowd and she more than deserved every cheer she got. Each pitcher for the opposing team tried to do the same thing, and that was to throw the ball by her. She was waiting each time and better than 50% of the time they paid a high price.

By the sixth game a pitcher threw a change up on the first pitch and Jackee was in front of the pitch and popped it up. That was her first weak hit ball. She had to prepare for that and she practiced hitting a soft liner to right field off her front foot. By July 15 the team was about halfway through their season and they were 40 wins and 31 losses. This was a dramatic change from last year when they were 26 wins and 45 losses. The coaches would receive most of the credit and it was well deserved, but the influence of Jackee could not be denied. She made the club better and led by example. Her hitting tailed off some but she was still hitting at a .365 clip. Amazingly she had only 3 strikeouts and 26 walks, both numbers were leading the team. Majority of the crude bench jockeying had stopped after the first swing through the league. The other clubs saw their attendance rise to the point of almost double for some of the teams. But more importantly, Jackee stayed after almost every game and spoke to their fans. She definitely was the shining star of the league. Speaking engagements requests were off the charts and they were impossible to fulfill but if it was on an off day, Jackee might accommodate them. Bats was a little worried because he had the trainer weigh Jackee twice a week and her weight has been going down.

He spoke to her and she said "I take my vitamins and all my supplements and I feel pretty strong."

"You are down 8 pounds and if you lose two more you are going to be benched."

"Bats, you can't do that, these fans expect to see me play every day. I can't disappoint them."

"You talk to them after the game but you can no longer do it for over an hour. You need your rest and to eat regular meals. You are slowly burning out and we have to turn it around now."

"Bats, I promise to eat regularly and to cut my after game pow wow in half."

He said "that is a start but as of right now you weigh in every day and I want a chart kept."

Jackee got a much needed break because the next day their game was rained out. Even though they had to play a doubleheader to make it up, the day's rest was a shot in the arm Jackee needed. She realized her game was at a higher level when she was rested so she made it a point to follow Bats' orders. One weekend her family came down for 4 days. The organization let them use the club's reserved suite at the local hotel. After the first game Jackee spent time with her family and the night with Dan. The next game Jackee was 3 for 4 with two extra base hits and two RBI's. Another night with Dan and she was a one man wrecking crew on the Sunday doubleheader. She was 5 for 7 with 3 extra base hits that included a home run. Her 4 RBI's helped the team sweep the four game series. When the coach took her out early in game four, she received a standing ovation as she left the field. She was told to leave the stadium before the game ended so that she could spend time with her family. She showered and dressed casually. Dan was waiting for her and drove her to where the rest of the family was waiting. William got a card from the organization's representative for the local restaurant and the meal was fully paid by the Gamblers. It was a great evening and got even better when Dan had a sleepover once again. Next morning the family left for home and Jackee was once again alone in her room.

July and August were very warm and the long days with travel and a game took its toll on everyone. Jackee had never played an extended season. Although she'd played many games in the year, they were spaced out over the year rather than all together. She did keep her weight steady because she knew that Bats would keep his word and have her benched. Sleep was the problem, even though she was exhausted it was hard to fall and stay asleep. Her fear of drugs kept sleeping pills out of the question. One change she did make, it seemed that if she brought her own pillow on the road trips she did sleep much better. One problem that never left her had to be solved. She wasn't sure what to do and finally she used her own cure.

This Sunday, she was up early and attended an early Mass. After almost everyone had gone, she sat in the back row and just closed her eyes and listened. After about 10 minutes a voice asked if she was alright. Jackee jumped and then realized that someone had spoken to her. She looked at the priest standing at the end of the pew and told him, he surprised her. She had been asking God for help and when she heard a voice she thought it was Him. "God does speak to us in many different ways but I am not one of those ways the priest said to her."

She looked at him and smiled saying "you might be wrong about that. I believe the answer came when you spoke to me. Thank you and God Bless you."

She left the church and a dumbfounded priest standing there with his mouth open. This was the first time she felt that a burden had been lifted from her shoulders. The plan she had been following now had a perfect solution. She would make contact with Dr Hopkins and put this new decision into action. Over the next week she started having fun playing baseball and it showed in her game. Everything seemed to get better, her hitting was going well but her fielding was outstanding. She caught two bloopers with over the shoulder catches that stirred the crowd. The combination of her and Buddy was turning double plays better than any other team that they have played. One game, Jackee caught a ball behind second, with her back to home plate and she flipped the ball to Buddy, he in turn threw to first getting the runner by half a step. It was very rare to see a play like that except in the major league.

Bats was talking to Wright and he told him that "if the organization wants to keep us working with Jackee, they are going to have to bring us up to the big club."

Jackee invited Dr Hopkins and Andrea, who was now working for him, to one of her games that was to be played by the college. They both agreed and Jackee set up game seating and lunch for them. Lunch was scheduled for noon so Jackee had three hours to spend with them. They picked her up at her room and went to the restaurant Jackee directed them to. When drinks were ordered and an appetizer was selected Jackee asked a favor of Dr Hopkins. She told him it was impossible to serve two masters. "I must concentrate on one to be effective. Right now that one must be baseball. Just playing the game is tough enough, but throw in speaking engagements, commercials, interviews and visits and you will have total collapse. I need to spend time with my husband and family. I need time to rejuvenate my body after a long season. Finally there is no way I can add medical school to that mix. I could never do justice to an internship and do everything else. So I am asking you, Dr Hopkins, to create a program for me where I can keep my hand in but push the full dedication to medicine down the road. If nothing can be done, I can live with that. But there is one thing I want you to know, as hard as I worked for a career in baseball, that is as hard as I will work to become a doctor. My dream for baseball included me eventually becoming a doctor.

Dr Hopkins shook his head but said "you are probably the only person that I know who could do that. I will create a program for you that will keep you up to date on all new medical changes and their effect on medicine itself. In addition, I will give you material and books for you to follow the internship program. Andrea and I will create exactly what you may need. I will contact you through Andrea and she will act as our go between." Andrea did not understand everything that was said but she did know that Jackee was usually right in what she did, so she was more than agreeable to be part of this new plan.

William called Jackee to inform her that Rose was at the summer Olympics and was scheduled to compete in the heptathlon which is a seven event held over two days. "There is no decathlon for women in the Olympics. Rose is the top qualifier for America in the event. She will be competing against the best female athletes in the world. She told me to wish you luck and that she will try to make you proud of her."

Jackee told her father that she "has been proud of Rose since the first day she held my hand. I feel sorry for those other women in the event because if Rose made up her mind to win, they better figure on trying to win the Silver medal." They spoke for another half hour about how she was doing but Jackee already knew that William talked to Bats after every game. She also asked about the family and was told they are all at the Olympic games with him and loving every minute of this colossal event. Jackee ended the call by saying "I love all of you and please keep me informed about how Rose is doing."

Two days later William called again to tell her Rose won the heptathlon with a score of 6975 pts. "Your brother was so excited when she let him wear the metal."

"Dad, that was perfect since the two of them are so closely bound together. They both deserved that medal. Tell Rose God has been good to both of us. Now it is time for me to put my new plan into high gear."

Jackee informed her manager that she will be there the whole season and will not ask for an early out to attend medical school. Coach Wright informed the front office, who in turn notified the league that she will be playing in all the post season games. The league commissioner's office was more than happy. When there was some doubt about Jackee finishing the season other clubs were upset because they feared that attendance would fall off. The crowd for the post season usually kept the league in the black if its attendance was good. This year with Jackee playing they anticipated that attendance would be a sellout. That would translate into a very successful season. The Rollers only had to come in fourth in their division to make the playoffs. Right now with 22 games left they were a solid third with a 66 and 52 record. Four teams from the two divisions would be eligible for the post season playoffs. First two rounds will be the best 2 out of 3. The finals will be the best 3 out of 5. All first games, up until the finals, will be played at the home fields of the team with the best record. Second of the three games will be switched to the other team's home field. If a third game is necessary a coin flip after the second game would determine the home team. Finals will start with two games at the best record team and the next two at the other team's home field. If a fifth game is needed a coin flip after game four would determine the home team. Over the last 22 games the Rollers played excellent baseball and the coaches used every player to see who would be best for the playoffs. Although it wasn't the same amount or even close to what the big league players received for their playoffs, any additional money was a big bonus for minor leaguers. They completed their season by winning 14 of the last 22 games to finish with an 80 and 60 final record. This was a 21 game difference from the previous year in the win column.

There had been some grumbling about this player getting all the attention, special treatment and a few other things. Coach Wright set the record straight. "Jackee Jenco has done nothing but make this team better. Because she is a woman playing a man's game all of you played better so that she would not show you up. Well let me tell all of you, if I had 8 more like her, a lot of those 60 losses would be in my win column. She has done nothing but play this game at a higher level than I thought possible. You played before the largest crowds in the league. We set the all time attendance record for this league. Every team we played away set records for our games. She put butts in the seats and money in your pocket. True, she received most of the endorsements but each of you shared when they gave stuff to the team. She even had them include some of you in the commercial. We were scouted by other teams so some of you may be drafted by these teams because they saw you while looking at her. She had an agreement with the organization to leave the team early but she opted out of it so she could finish the season with you. That means a bigger share of the gate in your pocket. The gate will be at least 50% higher because of her. The more games we win, the bigger cut we get from the league. You all should be thanking her for playing with us and not some other team. You do know that every major league team wanted her and that she selected the Gamblers as her first choice. She could have received much more money from some of the other teams but that was not what she wanted. I personally have never coached a more dedicated baseball player. Why she suffered all the abuse and insults over the years I can't understand, but I thank God that she played for me this year. All of you should do the same."

When Jackee entered the locker room she knew something had happened but was afraid to ask. Since nothing was said to her she figured it was not her business. She asked about practice and was told the team is going out very soon. Buddy came over and asked her to go out with him to warm up. They went out to the field, did a lap around the entire field, did their stretching and then started throwing. In the meantime the rest of the team had come out to warm up. Backup catcher and the outfielders hit first in batting practice. Word was passed down to the field that they would play the Brockton Bluebirds in the first round of the playoffs, away. Top four teams in each division were good baseball teams. There are no weak teams that are going to roll over so your team has to be ready to play. The best 2 out of 3 does leave room for error but it also could be a handicap. Going the full three games means you have used up your three top pitchers. There is only a one day break between series and no break during the finals series. So you could be playing 11 games in 13 days. Winning straight games does give you 2 days off before the next series. It also means your pitching rotation gets more rest. It was decided by the Rollers front office that they go the day before to the Bluebirds home field. Although they did play there during the season, it was still a good idea to have a rested team ready to go. Whenever there was a college close by the league tried to house the visiting player there. The league guaranteed that they would make good on any damage done by the players. It was a perfect solution for both. The clubs received good housing where they could keep their players together and the food at most of the colleges was good. There was no liquor sold on campus so that was a big plus for the staff. Cost was about one third of what it would cost at a hotel or motel. The college had staff working at the college all year round so it was no big deal. Also the league allowed free advertisement for all participating colleges at their home fields. One additional benefit was that the coach at these colleges usually had all the baseball machines and fields ready for them. The Rollers used the batting machines and fields to prepare for the first game.

It was a gorgeous baseball day when the first game was to be played. Introductions were made, all home plate meetings were finished, the Anthem was sung and the umpire shouted play ball. Winning the first game in any short series was critical and on the other team's turf even better. That is what coach

Wright stressed at the pre game meeting. He told them to play their game and have fun doing it. Jackee was a veteran of playoff games and she knew scoring first puts greater pressure on your opponent. Buddy got it started with a base hit. Sid Swift, the centerfielder, flew out, so Jackee came to the plate. On the second pitch to Jackee the hit and run was on and Jackee hit a ground ball where the second baseman had been. With runners at the corners, Teddy Bartoli flied to center and scored Buddy. Mission accomplished, the Rollers scored first. Abe started for the Rollers and he set the Bluebirds down in the bottom of the first. Both pitchers held the other team scoreless the next three innings. Gil Harris, the first baseman, started the fifth inning off by hitting a double down the left field line. DH Troy Turley hit a liner that the shortstop knocked down but had no play on either runner. Gil ducked back to second when he saw the shortstop jump to catch the liner. Leon Crest, the right fielder, bunted both players over and Buddy was intentionally walked to load the bases. Sid, the next hitter, hit a single to center, scoring Gil and Troy. Buddy stopped at second. Jackee guessed the curve ball after she fouled back a fastball, and that is what came to the plate. With perfect timing she lined the pitch to right center field and ended up on third base before the ball came back in. She later scored on a sac fly by Andy Pace. Rollers had 5 and the Bluebirds had yet to score. Abe pitched 7 strong innings but tired in the eight so Coach Wright brought in Nate Wilson, his top reliever to get the last 6 outs. That is exactly what he did, so the final score was 5 to 2. The Rollers team bus left immediately after the game for home. There was food and drinks on the bus supplied by the college. A little after midnight the bus rolled in and the players headed for their sleeping quarters. Jackee got to her room and showered before falling asleep on her bed. She slept a full eight hours and actually got up refreshed and ready to go. She had a good breakfast and then headed for the park. Dressed in practice sweats she did her pre game preparation. Other players started coming out for practice. Soon they were in full swing and two hours later had lunch served in the locker room.

Game two was scheduled to start at 6pm with Chris Barlow pitching for the Rollers. Chris was having a good year because he had excellent control and a better than average change up. This added miles to his already good fastball. This game would set the rotation for the pitchers. All the pitchers were well rested and if Chris has his usual game, only one or two might have to pitch a couple of innings. The crowd was the biggest of the season. Standing room was sold and that added about two thousand more people to the total. After the Bluebirds went out in order the Rollers came to bat and just took control of the game. Every player in the lineup had at least one hit. The first five hitters had 12 hits and 7 runs scored. In the eight innings the Rollers batted they scored in six of the innings and had runners on in the other two. After the fourth inning the Bluebirds just went through the motions. Chris threw 7 strong innings and Doug Taylor, the other reliever, pitched the last two. Jackee had 2 hits, one walk, and scored three runs. Teddy had a great day, with three hits and 5 RBI's. Final score was 13 to 1 and the Rollers were going to the second round. Word was sent to the Rollers front office that in two days they will play the Winston Mavericks in the second round. The Mavericks will be the home team in game one. Both semi final series have to start on the same day. This gives the Rollers two days off before they have to play again. One day will be used for travel but the other will be a practice day. Coach still has to decide which pitcher will Start for the Rollers. Both Marty Olsen and George Glenn are both ready to go. George has the best record but Marty was the most consistent over the last 4 weeks. Both pitchers had a bullpen session with Teddy and all the coaches. After the session both pitchers were told that one of them will start and the other will be the long man out of the bullpen. Practice day was pretty much what the team did all year but Jackee felt that the team spirit was very high. They were working hard but still kidding each other. Day two, they traveled to Winston for their game against the Mavericks.

Winners of 88 games for the season meant that the Mavericks were a pretty good team. Their pitching was better than their hitting. The Rollers would be facing their number three pitcher and Jackee felt that her team was more than capable of scoring some runs. There was no doubt that the Mavericks had a huge following. People came early and were still coming in at game time. Surprisingly, Jackee as a visiting player received the biggest ovation when her name was called. She thought to herself no matter how many times it happens that kind of recognition still makes her heart pump faster. It also sets her focus on the game. Pitching for the Mavericks was a big right hander with a better than average fastball. They hadn't seen him when they played them during the season so he must have been added from one of their other clubs. In the top of the first with one out and Sid on first base, Jackee thought he would try to impress the crowd by trying to overpower her. Her guess would be a high hard fastball. That is exactly what he tried to do and the ball came in on the outside of the plate and just under the letters. Jackee got all of it and drove it over the right center field fence for a two run homer. As she crossed the plate Sid and Teddy were there to greet her. The crowd reacted to the drive and continued to cheer as she crossed home plate and walked to the dugout. On the mound, the pitcher was ticked off and mumbling to himself. Now he forgot the first rule of pitching, to stay within yourself, and started trying to overthrow. This just made him lose concentration and control of his pitches. He hit one batter, walked a few others, allowed a few hits and you have the ingredients for a big rally. Before they took him out the Rollers had scored 4 runs and had the bases loaded. One more run was scored before the top of the first had ended. Martin pitched the first 5 innings and allowed only 2 runs. Meanwhile the Rollers scored single runs in the 3th and 5th innings. Starting the top of the sixth they led 7 to 2. Coach Wright put George in to pitch the last 4 innings and he did allow only one run. Final score was Rollers 8 and Mavericks 3. Immediately after the game, the organization's private jet took them back to

Rosevail. They were home by 11pm and in bed by midnight. Game two would be at home at 6 PM. Basically their routine was exactly the same as the first series. An early practice and a late lunch, a little rest, then go out and try to end this series with straight wins.

This game featured the two number one pitchers on both teams. It drew a crowd that seemed to be bigger than the second game against the Bluebirds. They were cheering from the time the team was warming up. They cheered the ground crew when they prepared the field for the game. At one point they were cheering the vendor selling beer and very surprisingly, they cheered the umpire when he dusted off home plate. Extra security guards were put on crowd control but they were not really needed because the crowd was just having fun and not one incident was reported the whole night. It turns out that these guards had the best seats in the house since no one was obstructing their watching the game. Both pitchers lived up to their number one status. The game was still 0 to 0 in the bottom of the seventh. Jackee was to lead off and she was having a rough night at bat. She struck out in the first inning and hit a weak ground ball back to the mound in the fourth. Maverick infielders were guarding the lines in an attempt to stop an extra base hit. Jackee was aware that the lefty pitcher came off the mound on the third base side after every pitch. She set herself in the batter's box and if the first pitch was a fastball that usually breaks away from the hitter, she was going to bunt the ball toward the second baseman. He was playing deep and close to second base. A fastball came in and at the last second she bunted it between first and second. All the infielders were caught flat footed and hesitated before going for the ball. Jackee easily reached first before anyone could make a play. There was a quick mound conference for the Mavericks and Jackee knew it was about her and the possibility of a steal. The lefty threw over 4 times to keep Jackee close and one time he almost got her leaning so the play was close. What really happened was the pitcher lost concentration on pitching to Teddy and he walked him. Now he was mad at himself. On a signal from the dugout the infielders went into a bunt defense. They used the Dodger rotation which tries to get the runner going to third. Third baseman and pitcher charge the bunted ball and whoever field's it, throws to the shortstop covering third base. What they didn't know was that with Jackee's lead off second and her speed, she could beat the shortstop to third. She was taking her lead and decided to gamble that Andy would get his bat on the ball and not pop it up. As the pitcher made his first move to the plate she broke for third. The pitch was intentionally high because they are the hardest to bunt. But the catcher had to reach outside for the ball and never really had complete control of it. Jackee stole third but Teddy remained on first. Now they played the infield in to stop Jackee from scoring on a ground ball. They were all on or near the grass part of the infield. Teddy easily stole second as the second pitch that was also called a ball. Andy was intentionally walked and Roy Ripple was the next hitter. Roy hit a high chopper over the pitcher's head, Jackee scored as the shortstop threw out Roy. The infield was still in the same defense, protecting against the bunt or getting the runner at the plate. Gil was the next hitter and he hit a seeing eye single between short and third scoring both Teddy and Andy. With a three run lead Coach used his two relievers to finish the game. Both pitchers had perfect innings so now the Rollers were moving on to the finals. Jackee and her teammates spent about an hour after the game mingling with the crowd. They were tired and dirty but were enjoying every minute with the fans. Next day during practice, coach Wright informed the team that the Hasting Bulldogs also won their second round so they will meet for the finals. Since the Bulldogs, winners of 90 games, will have the first two games at their field.

Game one featured the bulldogs number one pitcher against the Rollers Marty Olsen. The Bulldog pitcher, Chad Sumpter, lost only two games the whole year. Word was that he is to report to the big club as soon as the first game ends. Jackee could easily see how he lost only two games. He had control of all his pitchers and they were a step above anything she had seen this season. For some reason he had not been on the team when they played during the season. Later she found that he had been a first round pick but held out for more money and a higher starting level. He pitched two games in double A and was promoted to triple A and now to the show. He held the Rollers to two hits and no walks. Jackee took the collar with two strikeouts and a line drive the shortstop caught. Marty pitched a great game, allowing only two runs on 5 hits in eight innings, but the Bulldogs won game one 2 to 0. Game two was a different story. Abe started for the Rollers and was at the top of his game. He allowed one run in eight innings and Doug pitched a scoreless ninth. The Rollers were able to score 3 runs off the Bulldogs number two pitcher. Jackee did drive in one run and she scored a second run. The teams were now going to Rosevail for the next two games. Coach Wright told the team that he had no intention of coming back to Hasting so this ends in our house. We have Chris and George ready to go and any other pitcher we might need. Practice at 10am tomorrow and win the next two days.

Practice was very upbeat and all the ballplayers seemed loose and ready to play. The coaches were impressed by the spirited infield practice that the team had. Batting practice was the best ever, most of the players teased each other especially when they popped a pitch up or if they fouled one off. Bats had not really talked to Jackee that much because of his duties with other players, especially the pitchers. But instinctively she knew he was always keeping an eye on her.

He did stop by her locker area and told her he thought that this team needed someone to raise the level of the game, one step higher. "You know what I mean, they need one more push to bring out the best in them." She knew exactly what he meant but she was not sure how to do it. Every team has a certain makeup that makes it different from other teams. One thing may inspire one team and fall flat on another. Her bunt single against the Maverick's had been just such a play that inspired the team. Buddy came over and wanted to discuss how they were going to set the infield for the next two games. Jackee called Sid over and the three of them talked about a hitting plan for the next game. All agreed that it was their responsibility to get the team scoring started. If we can get on base and somehow score that would relax the team and get them moving in the right direction. Bunting, going deep in the count or even stepping into an inside pitch were all a possibility. The key to any good at bat is not swinging at a bad pitch. Don't help the pitcher out and don't over swing.

"We also should take advantage of our speed and maybe steal a few bases. If nothing else, it would worry the pitcher and force him to throw more fastballs." Sid also mentioned that with two outs and one of us on third, "we might consider stealing home."

Both Buddy and Jackee agreed that it was a good idea. "But not with Teddy at bat. He is a free swinger and could decapitate us." They laughed and agreed, not with Teddy at bat.

Prior to the game, portable stands were put behind the left and right field fence. This seating was a fixed price and you can sit anywhere in the stands. They still had the standing room crowd and the fans down both foul lines. No minor league team has seen anything like this crowd. It is true that the Bulldogs had a good following all year, and many of their fans did follow the team on the road but this was more than that. There was a rumor that some of the neighbors to the ballpark were selling parking for $20.00. They said our parking lot had been filled since 5pm. The opening ceremonies started at 6:10. Both teams were introduced and then the announcer introduced the winner of the gold medal in the heptathlon at the summer Olympics, Rose Jenco, sister of the starting second baseman Jackee Jenco. Rose came out from the home team dugout wearing her gold medal and a Rollers' baseball cap.

She ran over to Jackee and they hugged each other. Jackee said "I knew you would win and you and God didn't let me down. I just wish I could have been there because of all the times you cheered for me."

Rose told her, "you were right there with me every step I took and I could hear you encouraging me through the whole 7 events." The crowd was on its feet and the clapping got louder. She tipped her new Rollers cap and left the field the way she came in. The Anthem was sung and then the field was cleared. After the ground crew had touched up a few area's, the Rollers took the field with the fans cheering the whole time. Home Plate umpire shouted play ball and the game was on. Chris must have really been pumped up because he stuck out the side on 12 pitches. Buddy led off the bottom of the first and he did his job. 10 pitches later he was on first with a walk. Sid squared around to bunt and Buddy stole second base. The first baseman had started toward home to field a bunt but left first early so Buddy had a great jump and stole second easily. Sid was given the sign to bunt and he moved Buddy to third. With the infield playing in, Jackee hit a soft line drive just over the head of the second baseman scoring Buddy and giving the Rollers a 1 run lead. Coach Wright put on the hit and run on the second pitch to Teddy. He hit a ball to the right side of the infield but it was right at the first baseman. The play was made at first while Jackee was safe at second. With Andy at bat Jackee attempted to steal third and just did beat the catcher's throw. The pitcher was getting frustrated with two base runners and two steals, so he decided to watch the runner more carefully. He pitched out of the stretch to hold Jackee close to third. She took her lead and just as he was about to pitch she broke for home. Instead of continuing his pitch he hesitated and was called for a balk. Jackee was allowed to score and now the Rollers led 2 to 0. Chris continued to dominate the Bulldog lineup. They had 4 hits and a walk in 6 innings but did not score. Rollers did not do much better. They did have other opportunities to score but no other player crossed home plate. Top of the seventh the Bulldogs had scored one run and had runners on first and second with two outs. A pinch hitter for the Bulldogs hit what looked like a base hit up the middle. Buddy dove at the ball, knocked it down, and flipped to Jackee covering second. She stretched like a first baseman and caught the ball just as the runner was sliding in. There was a collision and both players were on the ground. The umpire asked to see the ball and Jackee held up her glove with the ball safely tucked in it. Umpire called "out" and the top of the seventh was over.

Jackee laid on the ground and had the wind knocked out of her and pain in her back where she was kneed. Buddy got to her first and asked how she was. She reached up and he helped her to her feet and she gingerly ran off the field. The crowd was still cheering the play when she entered the dugout. Bats told her to let the trainer look at it in the locker room. He and the trainer helped her to the locker room where the trainer sprayed the injured area with some type of freeze to mask the pain. Jackee went back to the bench and waited to see if she would bat in the inning. Bending was fine but swinging hard caused some discomfort. She had taken a bat and was practicing her swing while the trainer watched. She told him that everything seemed to be working fine. He could not tell if she was telling him the truth so he took her word about how she felt. Jackee did bat with two outs and runners at first and third. She received a very loud cheer as she entered the batter's box. Remembering her injury from years back she decided to just make contact. It proved very successful because the hit ball went to right center field for a run scoring single. This gave the Rollers a 3 to 1 lead. Nate was asked to pitch the eighth inning because the Bulldogs had two lefty hitters coming to bat. He not only retired the two lefty batters but also struck out the righty. Doug was brought in to pitch the ninth and he retired the three batters he faced striking out the last hitter. Rollers now led the series two games to one. A win tomorrow would give them the league championship.

Immediately after the game the whole team mingled with the crowd. The Jenco's finally made it down to the field and found Jackee with a crowd around her. Rose, still wearing her gold medal, ran up to her and they hugged and started crying. "I wanted to be there to see you win the gold metal. It must have been the happiest day of your life."

"No, it was the second happiest day, the happiest day was when you took my hand at the orphanage." Now the Jenco's had surrounded the two girls and the mother and sisters joined them in crying. Most of the executives of the Gamblers were at the game and they set a big dinner for the team after the game. It was locally at the hotel where they were staying. The Jenco's had reserved rooms from the organization for at least 3 nights. Dan had come alone because he was coming from a meeting with a new client who wanted the firm to represent him. He had arrived in the middle of the game after spending an hour looking for parking. Dan saw Jackee get hurt but was told by Bats over the phone that she seemed to be OK. Now he was waiting for the family to make room so he could hold Jackee. William slowly got the women to back off and Dan held Jackee for a few moments. Mr Bragan was asking people to go to the dinner at the hotel but almost all the starting players said they have to get some rest for the game tomorrow. Jackee asked Dan to spend the night with her. He said he never checked in at the hotel and he had his overnight bag in the car. While she was changing, he would go and try to find his car and would pick her up in front of the stadium. 30 minutes later Dan Pulled up, Jackee got in and they headed for her apartment.

On the way, they stopped and picked up two hamburgers, with all the trimmings and two soft drinks. At the apartment, first they kissed, had dinner, then decided to go to bed. Before he got into bed Dan rubbed a hemp type of healing cream on Jackee's sore back and then they cuddled in bed for the night. Jackee was up first and she took a hot shower letting the hot water hit the sore spot on her back. After Dan showered and shaved they went to breakfast as both of them were starving. There was a local pancake house that provided he-man breakfast plus just about any other breakfast item you may want. When they finished eating there was still a little time for them to talk, but not a lot. Jackee had to report to the stadium by 10am for practice, followed by a light team lunch and then prepare for the game. She hoped this would be the last game of the season and she could look forward to a restful fall and winter. Actually she intended to spend as much time as possible getting reacquainted with Dan. At 10am, Dan dropped her off at the stadium.

Jackee went inside and found the team waiting for her and wanting to know if she was going to play. "I would not miss this game even if both legs were broken. How could I not want to be with you when you win this championship. Our coaches deserve this because they put the team together and held us together the whole year. One more important thing, we worked very hard to get this far and no one can take that from us. Together we will be the best team on the field."

The local media was all over the place wanting to talk to the manager, players or even front office people. The manager did speak for a few moments to them but insisted that they leave the players alone until after the game. Well the media never takes no for an answer so they kept pestering front office people to get them access to the players. Coach and manager Wright told the front office that if they persisted with their demands, there would be no interviews even after the game. That settled the matter and no other attempt was made to get a player to talk to them. It was a perfect day for baseball and once again there was not even standing room anywhere in or around the stadium. People were amazed that with so many people, there seemed to be no disturbances. Someone jokingly said remember this is a baseball game not soccer or football. Similar to yesterday, the crowd cheered everything that happened even before the game. The four man ground crew received a loud cheer when they finished preparing the field just prior to the game. The crew in turn, tipped their caps and bowed to the fans. They received a louder cheer. A meeting at home plate for lineup cards and ground rules took a while longer because a rule had to be made for the standing room people down each foul line. Both coaches agreed that the ball would be declared dead and all play would cease as soon as the ball was touched or entered the crowd. All runners would advance to the base they were approaching. There were only three umpires, one had to leave for an emergency and no replacement could get here before the start of the game. League rules stated, no umpire can be added during a game so the league let it stand at three.

The call "Play Ball" started game four of this series. George Glen was the Rollers starting pitcher against the Bulldogs number four starter. Jackee felt her team had the momentum and team spirits had never been higher. George retired the side in the top of the first. Jackee batted with two outs and drew a walk. Before the game she mentioned to Teddy the other team will be looking for our team to steal when we get on base. We decided that our runners would try to act like we were going to steal by taking big leads off the bases and fake starts. This will make them throw more fastballs so that the catcher has a better chance of getting the runner. Look for the fastball with runners on. Teddy did just that and on the first pitch fastball he hit a drive off the left field fence. Jackee, running at full speed, rounded third as the fielder was throwing home. The ball and her arrived at home plate exactly the same time, but the catcher had to reach for the ball and as he did Jackee slid under his tag. That put the Rollers ahead 1 to 0. The Bulldogs scored single runs in the 4th and 5th inning. In the top of the fifth there was a bloop hit to center in which the center fielder tried to make a shoestring catch. For some reason both umpires went out to make sure if it was a catch or not. Both ruled it was not but neither one saw the play at second. Sid trapped the ball under his glove and had to get up and throw to second. It appeared from the dugout, and both Buddy, and Jackee that the runner was out. But the home plate umpire ruled he was safe.

Coach Wright jumped out of the dugout to challenge the call. He asked the umpire if he actually saw the play from home plate. The umpire said, yes and since there is no replay the play had to stand as called. Coach Wright said that he better have a big red S on his chest and a date with Lois Lane after the game to make a call like that from home plate. The fans loved the exchange but not the call. That runner for the Bulldogs eventually scored their second run. Leon Crest, the right fielder, led off the bottom of the fifth with a single. Buddy bunted to move the runner to second but beat it out because the Bulldogs threw to second and Leon was called safe. Sid bunted but it was too hard and right back to the pitcher so Leon was thrown out at third. Jackee tied the game with a base hit to left field that scored Buddy. Teddy was up next and he hit a liner that the short-stop caught as he was moving toward second and just stepped on second before Sid could get back for an unassisted double play. Game was still tied in the top of the eight when the Bulldogs had a rally going. The first two batters got on base so Coach brought in Nate to pitch. He got an out when they bunted the runners over to second and third. Nate struck out the next hitter but walked the following batter. Now with the bases loaded, the coach brought in Doug to pitch.

After he warmed up, Jackee and Buddy were standing close to the mound and Doug whispered to get the guy on second. Jackee knew exactly what he meant. Buddy was playing behind the runner making all kinds of noises and then stepped toward third base. The runner saw him move so he increased his lead just as Jackee broke toward second, Doug turned and threw a strike to second base. Jackee caught the ball and held the glove in front of the base as the runner slid back in. The umpire signaled out" and the top half of the inning was over. Jackee led off the bottom of the eighth with a single to center. With Teddy up next, she did not want to risk a steal since they would probably just walk him. When Teddy got to two strikes Jackee figured that he would see nothing but curves so she ran on the next pitch. It was a curve in the dirt so she stole second without a throw being made. Just as she expected Teddy was intentionally walked, so the Rollers had first and second with none out. Andy moved both runners one base with a perfect bunt. Roy was intentionally walked to load the bases. Gil came to the plate and was given the hit sign from coach Wright. He took one pitch for a ball but fouled off the next pitch fastball. Coach now put on the suicide squeeze where the runner on third tries to steal home and the batter bunts the ball any place on the ground. Jackee sees the sign and touches her cap. The batter also touches his cap telling the runner that he knows the sign. With the pitcher in a stretch position, Jackee takes a walking lead and just as the pitch moves his front foot she takes off for home. Part way through the delivery the pitcher realizes that the runner was headed for home. In this situation the pitcher and catcher should know that no matter what pitch had been called for, it was now going to be a fastball above the letters. It's the hardest pitch to bunt and the easiest for the catcher to control. The pitcher was trying to change his grip on the baseball at the same time as he was trying to throw it. The ball floated high and inside and the batter was hit on the helmet. This resulted in a dead ball. A run scores and the bases remain loaded. Troy was the next batter and he·hit a slow ground ball that scored Teddy. Leon flew out to end the inning but the Rollers now led 4 to 2. Doug finished the game by retiring all three batters in the top of the ninth and the Rollers were league champs.

The crowd poured out onto the field and the team gathered on the mound area to congratulate each other. After about 15 minutes of pandemonium on the field a path was formed to home plate and the leagues' trophy was presented to the Rollers. Teddy was named MVP for the tournament and it was a unanimous choice. Fans started to leave and as the crowd thinned out the Jenco's and the owners made it down to the field. Each member of her family got to hug Jackee.

Dan was last but he said "your dream will be fulfilled because you are going to Spring training with the big club. Bats and Wright are going with you as well as some members of this team." Mr Bragan told all the players and their guests that the dinner will be at the hotel they are staying in.

Jackee told Dan she was not going unless she looked her best. "Take me back to my apartment so I can change into a more proper dress." She met Dan outside and he drove her to the apartment. She showered and dressed, and even Dan could not believe the change. Here was his beautiful wife and not the baseball player.

They arrived at the hotel just after most of the other people had settled in. Jackee was not picked out by the media, so they entered without having to answer any questions. When she entered most people had never seen her in anything but a baseball uniform. The change shocked them. When the media got wind that they had missed her, there was a wild stampede to get an interview. Dan and Jackee joined the family at a table that was close to where the owner was sitting. Little William was having the most fun watching his sisters being the center of attention. Sonny and Jon could not be there and Evelyn was home caring for son Jon. Jackee wanted to be there when Jon Zarrelli the third was born but at least her mom was. Carmela had told her that Evelyn had a hard time at first but then the delivery was fast and she and the baby came through it in great shape. Evelyn was so good that after 4 days, Carmela left for home. At one point the three Jon's were in one room together. Carmela had pictures of Evelyn with Jon III, Jon II, Jon and Bianca. Jon III weighed in at 8lbs 6oz and a full head of hair. There was a plan to visit Evelyn next week. Nothing was finalized because no one knew how long these games would last. Dan had been asked by Mr Hitch to have Evelyn bring the baby with her so he could see if her and the baby would be suitable for a commercial. He had mentioned to Dan that he might like an exclusive with the whole family because they had everything his clients were looking for. The deals would have to be discussed with the whole family present so as not to leave anyone out. Right now they will enjoy the night and prepare for the trip home either tomorrow or the day after.

Jackee had to spend at least one more day there to clean out her locker and say her goodbyes. Dinner was anything on the menu and the family was hungry. After dinner and just before dessert was served, Mr Brickly welcomed everyone and told them that if there was a problem please see Mr Bragan for assistance. "This is our first championship at any level and I hope it is the start of something big for the organization. We would like to introduce some of the people that made this championship possible. Manager Wright and all the coaches, would you please stand up. Now will the whole Rollers team please stand. As they stood Mr Brickly told the guest that these are the people who turned the organization into a winner. Teddy Bartoli was declared the MVP of the tournament and as a reward he will be with the big club at Spring training. Jacalyn Jenco, better known as Jackee, will also be with the big club at Spring training. Others will probably join them but that remains to be seen. My sincere congratulations to the coaches and team for an outstanding season. Have a wonderful evening and thank you for coming." News was now out officially that Jackee would be on the major league roster in the Spring.

CHAPTER THIRTY

Jackee is Going to the Show & Rose and Sonny are Wed

*D*an and Jackee spent the night at the hotel and had their honeymoon all over again. There was no worry about being on time for anything. Just the two of them enjoying each other with no other commitments. Next morning after an excellent breakfast they first cleaned out her changing room at the stadium. While there, she had to sign two dozen baseballs for the people working for the club at the stadium. Every one of them came to the locker room to wish her success with the big club. Two of the women said they pray for her everyday because they are so proud of what she is trying to accomplish. Jackee hugged and kissed them and said she needs every bit of help she can get to do God's work.

Dan was surprised by the affection and admiration these people had for his wife. He knew she was special but this type of adoration was reserved for very special people. When they had packed all her clothes and equipment from the apartment and the stadium they started the trip home. He asked Jackee if she realized that these people were putting her on a pedestal.

She told him that since high school people have been praying for her and the higher she went the more people prayed for her. "Do you believe that I could have done this on my own? Without those prays I could not have made it out of high school. I was ready to quit 100 times or more but with so many people depending and praying for me I forced myself to take that next step. You know how many games I missed because of injuries? Just one. Every female who believed in me helped me swing the bat, run the bases, field the ball and more importantly, when I failed, they prayed harder for me to succeed next time. I was never doing this alone. First it was my family, friends, then you, and my growing fan base. But God was beside me the whole time, giving me the faith and desire to try. I believe He sent me you and you let me use your strength to go on. The first time you held my hand, I knew that you were my true love and that some day I would be your wife. I was afraid that you would not want some crazy baseball playing girl who was competing against boys. Most people would think, no one wants a tomboy for a girlfriend. When you asked me out the second time my heart was pounding so hard I thought it was going to burst. Every date I would come home and pray you would call me again. If you had dumped me, it would have destroyed a big part of me. It would have killed my desire to keep playing and there is the possibility that I would have never reached that level again. My dream might have died right there."

Dan had listened carefully to every word Jackee had said. He never realized that her inner strength was not enough to carry her for what she hoped to achieve. Now he knew how much the fans gave her to continue. He also saw how her faith gave her a supernatural power that can only be gotten from faith. "From our second date and every date after that, he told her, I realized what a special young woman you were. Your beauty, your drive and your desire was something special. There was only one like you and she was accepting all my offers for dates. You were the one who kept me going. The first time you really kissed me was the greatest feeling I ever had. It was so good, I never wanted it to stop. A thought ran through my head that I could have that feeling my whole life by marrying this girl. Then it hit me that this beautiful girl can attract any man she wants and it wouldn't be long before guys would be begging her for a date. At that time I would be nothing more than a memory. Once you started college I thought my days with you were numbered. There was no way I could compete with college guys. Then when I saw Andrea, I thought that the two of you would be the toast of the college. That the males on campus would be breaking down your door."

"Most of the men on campus were scared to death of me," she said. "Only the guys on the team really got to know me and a few did ask for dates. Andrea dated many guys on campus but that was her way of learning about life. She knew how to handle most of them. She did admit that there was a mistake or two but she said that's how you learn. That was not for me and I told her so. I knew exactly what I wanted and I found it all in you. Dan, you know you are the only person I ever had sex with. There were offers but I wanted to give myself only to the one I wanted for life. It may seem weird in the world we live in but it made perfect sense to me. It made our first night together exactly what I thought it would be. There was much that I did not know but everything that night felt perfect. You treated me like a queen and I loved every minute of it. When you fell asleep with your arms around me, I knew you felt the same way too. When I woke up the next morning still in your arms I knew then that we did have the perfect night." They continued to talk for the entire drive home and any doubts they may have had about their future together ceased to exist. One immediate decision was agreed to. They would live at the Jenco house for the near future. It made perfect sense, because the house was being used as an office for the agency business.

Carmela had prepared a big welcome home dinner for Jackee and Dan. Rebecca and her family were there but Evelyn could not come. Sonny had the same problem and although he would love to see Rose, his schedule was booked solid. Jackee had not seen her new nephew and told Carmela that if Evelyn can't come here, I will go there. Plans were made for a two day visit to see her sister and nephew. Dinner had all Jackee's favorite foods and it was the first good meal she had in a month. The organization's celebration dinner a couple of nights ago was good but she had no time to enjoy it. The interviews, thanking people, saying goodbye to teammates, took up the whole night. This was a sit down, talk to her family and not worry about anything else, dinner. Jackee started to clean off the table. Carmela told her to relax and talk to dad and Dan, but she insisted on helping. When everything was put away, Jackee asked her mom if she and Dan could live at the house for a while.

"Dad and I had discussed that possibility and both agreed that it would be wonderful to have you stay with us. We promise never to interfere with your privacy and dad will share his office with Dan. New furniture can be delivered in two days. Dad has two drawings of how the room will look and all Dan has to do is make any changes he wants and then give the signal to go and do it. Three days from now everything will be completed. Dan and your father should be going over it right now." Around 11 Jackee said she was going to bed but would be up early to work out with Rose.

When Jackee was talking to her mother in the morning, Dan came into the room and told Jackee "the Gamblers faxed me a list of events and asked if you could do any of them. I have a schedule for you and some commercials. One or two want Andrea to be with you and one is for you and your mom. You are to spend this morning going over the list and we can talk about it later. Jackee, pick and choose carefully, always saving time for yourself. Work out time and down time for you and the two of us should be the number one concern." Jackee took the information and began sorting it out. She asked Carmela to help her because her mother was very good at organizing things. Womens' organizations from all over the country want her to speak or visit them. There also was a possibility of speaking in front of the UN. She and Carmela agreed that it was not going to happen. They started making a schedule for appearances and speaking engagements. She also noticed that there were orphanages and children's hospitals on the list. Christmas week, Easter and Thanksgiving were blocked out because of family commitments. They had a schedule pretty much finished when Dan came home. He told them that he arranged the commercial that they were to make together and it would be shot tomorrow. Carmela said that was fine with her and she went off to prepare dinner.

Rose, who had been gone the whole day, came home to join the family gathering. She offered to help Jackee whenever she is available but tomorrow she had to report to school. She would graduate this June and had been accepted to Sonny's school for medical training. "Mom, I have a big favor to ask. Would it be alright for me and Sonny to get married this Christmas break? When we are at school, I want to live with Sonny and take care of him but I don't want you and dad mad at me."

"Rose, listen to me. Do you love Sonny?"

"Yes, with all my heart."

"Does he love you?"

"He better, because I am the one he is going to marry."

"Then I want the two of you to live together and take care of each other." Rose started crying and hugged her mother so tight that it was hard for her to breath.

"Mom, all I want to do is be near him. He is such a great person. I want to be his wife because he is all alone and never has anyone to care about him. Everybody needs someone and I really want to be his someone. Jackee, Rebecca and I will guarantee you a wedding between Christmas and New Year. Drugs took away my parents but God gave me the best parents ever. Mom, if God gives me children and one is a girl she will bear the name Jacalyn Carmela Lightfoot." William walked in at that moment and saw three women crying and Dan shaking his head.

He looked at Carmela and said, "I know you'll tell me tonight," and he walked into the den to get a drink

The next few days were very hectic. Jackee and Carmela did their commercial and had a great time with Mr Hitch. He liked working with the Jenco family but enjoyed Carmela the best. She was like the perfect mother and very photogenic. In less than three hours he had three shots finished and ready for his clients to see. Carmela mentioned her new grandson and Hitch wanted to know when Evelyn could come for a possible shoot. "The baby is only 4 months old and Evelyn is a very protective mother."

He told Carmela that he needed some out of studio work and would consider going to her if she agreed. "We are going to see her in a few days so we'll ask and I'll get back to you."

"That would be great because I have to do a baby food commercial by the end of October for one of my clients."

Lunch was next for the two women and Carmela had been trying to make sure that Jackee did not miss a meal. With all the working out and the schedule for speaking engagements, Jackee had not gained back the weight she lost during the baseball season. Neither of the husbands could drive them to see Evelyn so they drove themselves. Evelyn was surprised and happy to see them. They spent the two days spoiling Jonathan the third. Evelyn promised to call Mr hitch and make some arrangements with him. After the visit and before driving back home, they went to Olympus college so Jackee could see Dr Hopkins and Andrea. Jackee picked up the material that Dr Hopkins promised her and Andrea filled her in on the wedding plans for the Saturday after Thanksgiving. They in turn told Andrea about Rose's wedding on December 28th. Jackee was also interested in Andrea's research work for the hospital and Dr Hopkins.

She told Jackee that the work was exciting and she has already been promoted by the hospital to full staff status and the exclusive coordinator between the hospital and Dr Hopkins. On top of that, two big companies have offered her jobs in their research departments. "The offers are very tempting but I love it here and so does Brett." Andrea gave Jackee dates for gown fittings and rehearsal dinner. Jackee has already received a date for the bridal shower that was being arranged by Andrea's cousin. She had asked her mother to buy the same negligee that she had bought for her but one size bigger and in blue, which is Andrea's favorite color. After they packed all the material Dr Hopkins had for Jackee, the two women drove home.

William received the call that they would be home by 7pm so it became his job to get the dinner ready. The Texas Grub House had the Big Eats Burger special so William ordered four to go. This burger came with fries, onion rings plus many extras that you had to ask for. He also ordered Eve's Temptation which was a deep dish apple pie. They should be hungry enough to eat whatever he put on the table, and besides, it was what he and Dan liked. The women walked in a little after 7, kissed their husbands and sat down to dinner. Jackee later asked Dan to bring in her material from the car. Jackee put all the material by her old study desk and told Dan that tomorrow she will put it in order. He reminded her that on any speaking engagement Rona will be accompanying her. "She has a list of all that are scheduled and she will be with you from when you leave this house until you return. If you make any changes or add new commitments you must notify her ASAP." It was not what Jackee liked but she decided to make everyone happy and keep Rona nearby. She did like Rona because she was a very capable person but she didn't like the idea of a body guard.

Speaking engagements were going very well and all of them were full audiences. Her workout schedule was going well and she bought time in the batting cages. A study schedule was designed by her to fit into her every day schedule. Her brother worked out with Jackee whenever he could but he liked to sleep late and Jackee was out the door by 5am. He did play baseball but seemed to favor track much more. While hitting at the indoor batting arena the local high school coach asked her to help some of his players with their batting skills. She began working with them and found she loved to coach the boys. Those that paid attention and followed her advice began to show improvement and she soon had a following of believers. Word spread around that Jackee was holding batting clinics at the batting arena. She later suspected that the owner spread that rumor to increase his customers. All of the sudden young softball players were coming for advice. Mothers and fathers were bringing in their daughters who were playing for school or on traveling teams. Jackee decided to set up her hitting time when she would not be available for any type of instruction and two days when she would be if her schedule permitted. One thing she did find was that the younger girls learned much faster than the boys and they worked harder. The coaches could probably do the same thing Jackee was doing but they did not get the same attention that Jackee received. She also found that she had to stay away from the fathers involved because some seemed to be too friendly and one in particular tried to hit on her.

The last week in January was to be the last day for her being available. Her schedule called for a complete preparation for spring training sometime in February. That was a way off and the first big thing now was Thanksgiving and Andrea's wedding. The bridal shower the Saturday before the wedding was a big success. That special gift that Carmela and her picked out was the hit of the shower. Andrea had not thought to buy a special item to wear on her wedding night. Dan had taken her to the shower and then went off with the guys for a bachelor party. Jackee told him about the shower but Dan never said a word about his party. She wondered why? Andrea on the way home after picking up her wedding dress, picked up Jackee. Dan would later come to the wedding with her parents and take her home. The gowns were perfect, the rehearsal dinner went smoothly, and the wedding dress fit like a glove and looked fantastic on Andrea. While Jackee was helping Andrea dress for the wedding, Andrea hugged her and thanked her again for being such a good friend.

"Today is happening because of the talk that you gave me. You opened my eyes as to what is important in life. Brett is all I want right now and there is no doubt that I made the right choice. Jackee, if I am ever blessed with a daughter, I want you to be her godmother."

"Andrea, It would be an honor for me and I will be a real godmother to her not just in name only."

The limo picked them up and took them to the church. A wedding service very similar to Jackee's was performed by a young priest. He gave a beautiful sermon about what marriage was and how important it was for the couple to help each other in their life together. Jackee had never seen Andrea look more beautiful. She radiated a glow that brightened the whole church. When Brett kissed her after the ceremony there was no doubt as to how he felt. Their reception was very well planned and having Dan and her parents there made it even better. Since she was not going back to Andrea's house she packed and had her overnight bag with her. It was given to Dan after the pictures had been taken and there was time before the dinner for him to pack it away. Near the end of the reception, Jackee helped Andrea change and get ready to leave on her honeymoon. The wedding dress was packed for Miss Grant to take care of. The newly married couple said good night to their families and then left. Jackee joined her family after she changed into traveling clothes and packed her gown. Not too long after they were driving home, Jackee and Dan were snuggled in the back seat. When they were going to bed, Dan found Jackee wearing her wedding night outfit. She told him their wedding night had been the best and she wanted to see if he remembered. Next morning all Carmela could say to Jackee was "you got that smile on your face again."

The next 4 weeks were as busy as anyone in the family could remember. Getting ready for Christmas and Rose's wedding was a big job. Rose would get home a day or so early but everything had to be set. All the invitations were sent out and almost all had been returned. The local hotel had rooms set aside for Sonny's family and guests. His family was being put up by the corporation. Rose got her school to fly Sonny's family from their local airport to the airport near her home. A limo would make the trip from the reservation to the airport. Rose would pick them up in a limo at her airport and bring them to the hotel. Sonny would arrive at her house on the same day but later in the evening. Carmela prepared dinner for them that evening with a menu that Sonny had recommended. Sonny's guests from the reservation were traveling by chartered bus to the hotel. They would be arriving the day before the wedding and leaving the day after. A wedding dress had been selected by Rose and a picture was sent to Miss Grant. Miss Grant had all the sizes for the girls and basically had Rose's dress all ready for her to try on. All the other dresses except Evelyn's would be ready before Christmas. Rose did arrive home three days before Christmas. The next day she went for her fitting and with one minor adjustment the dress was a perfect fit. All the dresses were now complete except Evelyn's, she hadn't lost all the weight acquired during pregnancy. Miss Grant guaranteed that the dress would be ready the day she arrived for her fitting. Sonny had to work Christmas eve, Christmas day, and the day after Christmas. He then would have two weeks off for his wedding and honeymoon. Samuel Haslet, the part owner of the Gamblers and an orphan, arranged for them to have a week in Aruba at one of the owner's vacation sites. Their plane fare, limo service to and from airport and hotel, has been fully arranged and any expense generated on their honeymoon would be picked up by the Gamblers. Rose and Sonny sent a thank you note to Mr Haslet. With the visit to the orphanage and Vets home complete, the family spent Christmas eve getting ready for the wedding and Christmas day. With so much happening so fast it was time for the family to lay back and plan the next move. All the women planned the meals and had some input for the activities. Christmas Day Bats' family and Jon's parents were coming. Evelyn wanted to spend Christmas with her family and the Zarrelli's wanted to spend Christmas with their new grandchild.

The logistics were difficult at first but then William hit on a solution. "Evelyn could use her room for Jon 2 &3. Our Son will move into our room and the Zarrelli's will sleep in his room or he could bunk in with Rose until Sonny Comes. When Sonny gets here the Zarrelli's would be in their hotel room. They just want to spend the eve and Christmas with their grandson. It sounds like a great plan if everyone is on board with it." Rooms were set up and everyone had directions to bathrooms. Showers had to be planned so as not to run out of hot water.

Christmas eve night the plan worked like a charm. Christmas morning the women showered early and there was plenty of time for the others to shower. For the nine o'clock mass a full pew had to be set aside for the Jencos. Fourteen people came to sit in that row and Father Nicholas made the comment to the altar servers that he could remember when there were only two people now there are three generations. Father Nicholas gave his Christmas talk about family and said how lucky a priest is to have not only a possible blood family but to be a part of every family in his parish. "In the church today is a couple who started coming to this church 30 years ago. Today there are three generations here. I baptized, gave first communion, assisted at their confirmation and even performed the marriage ceremony for three of them. Just to add to that, I will perform another marriage ceremony in three days. I have watched over my families as they grew, moved away and even passed away. What greater Christmas gift can I receive than to have them spend Christmas mass with me. I can stand before them and ask God to Bless all our parish families, and keep them safe on this day of His Son's birth. God bless you all and have a very Merry Christmas."

There was no doubt that this service was a very happy and uplifting one. People went out of their way to greet others. It didn't seem to matter if they knew the person or not. Father Nickolas must have had at least 25 offers to attend Christmas dinner with some family but he declined because he was having dinner at the orphanage. The Jenco family had to get home because there were gifts to open and a huge meal to prepare. Carmela had most of it ready and while the daughters were to prepare some breakfast food, she would assemble the main event. Opening gifts and getting everyone something to snack on was a delicate matter. Jackee and Rose served while Evelyn and Rebecca prepared. Carmela insisted that Bianca stay with her grandson and not help. Jon's parents looked exhausted and according to Jon they average less than 4 hours of sleep a night. How they got this time off was a miracle. They would not discuss where they were or what they had to do. Bats and Kim came at noon. The children were still enjoying opening presents or watching others open theirs. Kim joined the women and Bats fit right in with the men.

William asked Bats how he thought Jackee would do in Spring training. His answer was, "she is the last one we worry about. Her being on the field has driven every team she played on to a new level. No one could understand it until I told them that the other players never want anyone to think that a girl is better than they are. Because of that, they work harder just to keep up with her. If she holds up, I believe you will see her improve. One thing no one can foresee is how the length of a major league season will affect her. I will make you a promise that I will watch her every move during the season."

"Thanks Bats, I knew you would be there for her." Carmela called out that dinner was served and everyone gathered around the makeshift table that was created. Praises came to Carmela from all directions because the food was fantastic. The Zarrelli's seemed to enjoy just about everything on the table. Jon was happy his parents were having such a great time and knew he could never be away from his family on Christmas. There was no way he would join his parents as part of their team. Jon thought that Evelyn could stop crying now because his mind was made up. He would put his family first and not the wishes of his parents. After everyone had finished eating, the main table was cleared of food. All the leftover food was put in the kitchen and set up as a snack if anyone wanted more later. The main dining table was now prepared for dessert. Cookies, pies and pastries were displayed on a separate table for each person to choose. Five flavors of ice cream would be dispensed by Rose when ordered so they would not melt if left out. Rocco and Rebecca were the first to leave since they had to put an appearance in at his parents house. Dan's parents joined the gathering just as Rocco and Rebecca were leaving. Mrs Silvio added more desserts to the table and brought presents for Jackee and Dan. Dan had put presents for his parents under their tree on Christmas eve. An hour later people started to leave and the family began the cleanup. Carmela insisted that Bianca and Jon stay the night and they could go to the hotel tomorrow.

Today was a big day for Rose. She had to pick up Sonny's family at the airport, settle them in at the hotel, and then take them to her house to await Sonny's coming. She would pick Sonny up at the bus depot when he called her. Their plane was on time and the hotel had been booked so their rooms were ready when they arrived. They traveled light so there was little to put away. They had decided to wear traditional wedding clothing so Rose, with assistance from Carmela, had it shipped to her and all of the clothing was professionally prepared for the wedding. The clothes had been put into the room and properly put away. A member of the hotel staff explained that she was responsible for them "so if you need anything at all, you call me," and she gave them her card with a phone number on it.

Sonny had told her that they were used to sleeping in the same room so Rose made sure that they had a suite. Rose, with the staff member's help, took the family all over the hotel and explained what was available. All the amenities were explained including the beauty salon. It would be for Sonny to explain how these things work because as far as Rose could see only the sleeping things interested them. After the tour of the hotel Rose took them to her house to meet her parents. Carmela had prepared a lunch for them with the favorite things Sonny had suggested. Jackee and little William each pitched in and helped serve lunch. Sonny's family were very shy at first so the Jenco's served themselves thereby showing them what to do. It wasn't long before they were eating and seemed to be having a good time. The children especially enjoyed the meal and absolutely loved the desserts. A call came from Sonny that he would be at the bus depot at about 4:30. Around 4:15 Rose pulled into the depot's parking lot and a few minutes later the bus came in.

Rose ran up to Sonny just as he got off the bus. Once again she surprised him by jumping into his arms and kissing him. While most of the strangers from the bus and those picking them up applauded, Rose totally ignored them. Sonny broke loose and said "I got to get my bag so we can go." Rose held his arm as they walked to the car. Driving home she told him about picking up his family and what had taken place at the hotel. He told her not to worry because he will inform them about what to do. It was a big relief for Rose because she wasn't sure if she did something wrong. When they arrived home it was obvious that Carmela had everything under control. His father and step mother were talking to William and Carmela like they were old friends. All the children were with Jackee who was showing the press clippings involving Sonny and his playing days. His family had never seen one article about him playing baseball. William explained about the commercial that Rose had done and how the money was going into a medical fund for the reservation.

He also tried to explain the wedding Mass and what their role would be. With Sonny helping him, William explained that all the travel and hotel expenses were being paid by a donor that was using Rose as his representative at an orphanage. Their family is to pay nothing at the hotel. All expenses including tips are fully covered. "Any item under 50 dollars is fine for you to take. Any female item, like getting your hair done, is fully covered." Rebecca and family were invited to dinner to meet Sonny's parents so when Dan came home the table had to be opened. Once again Carmela had prepared all Sonny's favorite foods, which he said were favorites of his family. Later that evening Rose and Sonny drove his family back to the hotel where Sonny explained many more things to them.

Sonny and Rose got back late and everyone else was in bed. Rose insisted that Sonny spend the night with her and he could get up early and go to his room. It was not something Sonny wanted to do but Rose told him not to worry as nothing was going to happen, she just wanted him near her for a few hours. Since he was totally exhausted, he gave in and went along with whatever she was planning. Next morning he heard Jackee going out to run and since Rose was sound asleep, he got up and went to his room. That night was the rehearsal dinner and

Sonny's family would have to take pot luck because it was catered. He spent the morning with the Jencos and then went to the hotel in the afternoon to be with his family. Weeks before he told the family about the hotel pool and how it was available to them. He introduced his step mother to the hairdresser·and asked for an appointment for her the next morning. She asked if her daughter could join her and two appointments were made. He took his father to the barber shop and introduced him to the head barber. Later the family went to the dinning room for a late lunch and he showed them how to order and how to sign the check. Deep down he knew they would never do this so he also showed them how to use room service. William and Carmela came by in the SUV and took them to the church rehearsal. Father Nicholas introduced himself to Sonny's family after the practice was over, he told them what a great son they have. He asked if their tribal holy man was coming to the wedding. Mr Lightfoot said he was, but would not interfere with the service.

"I want you to introduce him to me before the service." It was agreed that they would come early. A bus will bring all the hotel guests here before the service. William called out that the food was getting cold so let us get moving to the hall. His veterans hall had everything set exactly as Camela had laid it out. Food and drinks were available but only some beers were consumed. The bridal party, two families and some guests were the only people invited. As usual it went off as planned and the evening was a big success. That night Sonny spent time with his family at the hotel. Rose was not happy but some traditions had to be observed.

This December day was a little above average. It was sunny and the temperature was near forty degrees. Basically it was a repeat of Jackee's wedding day except the day was a little colder. Hairdresser, flowers and gowns were all the same providers but of course the price was much higher since William and Carmela were paying. Activities were a little less since only the sisters and their husbands were involved. When everything was ready the bride came down and the same photographer was taking the pictures. Hitch had told him to get as many of the women together and take a picture from all angles. Rose looked more beautiful than ever and a great deal of that was because of her hair and makeup. Because of her natural beauty very little makeup was used but her features were accented by a touch here and there. Her sisters crowded around her and finally agreed to have pictures taken. Rose took the last picture pinning a flower on her father. When that was finished they entered the limo for the trip to the church. When they arrived at the church, the family was lined up for their march down the aisle. Little William was first carrying the rings on a special pillow. Rebecca and Rocco were next followed by Evelyn and Jon followed by Jackee and lastly, Rose walked down the aisle with one parent on each arm. When she got to the altar she hugged both, thanked them and said I love you, then turned to Sonny, who led her to the priest. Standing next to Father Nicholas was the tribal holy man dressed in his native attire. Father Nicholas explained that no ceremony except those authorized by the dioceses can be performed inside a church. "A priest must perform the wedding ceremony that our religion allows. However, I do have permission for Big Sky to congratulate and give his blessing to this couple." He then began the wedding mass. The altar servers took Big Sky and showed him to a special seat on the altar. After his homily Father Nicholas performed the wedding ceremony and just before pronouncing them man and wife, he spoke to the church gathering. He told them that "when Sonny completes his medical training, he will work on the reservation and when Rose completes her medical training she will join him. You should know that Rose was adopted by the Jenco's from St Mary's orphanage, what you don't know is that Rose will not compete in the Olympics ever again. She needs to complete her medical degree so she can be with her husband as he helps his people and another orphanage. Now before I complete the marriage service, I ask Big Sky to bless this couple in his traditional way."

The holy man put their hands together and asked the almighty one to guide this couple on the path of happiness and love. Then he sang a verse while holding their hands, he whispered something to them and turned to Father Nicholas. Father came over and while they were still holding hands pronounced them man and wife. You may kiss the bride were his last words to them. Sonny did and the couple sat for the completion of the mass. 20 minutes later they were walking out of the church as man and wife. When the congratulations were done, it was now on to the reception.

William tried to have some of Sonny's native food prepared for the wedding reception but Sonny told him that his people are used to eating what is available or to go without. "Believe me, they will eat whatever is there and will enjoy it."

Carmela made sure that the cocktail hour had everything that was promised. She went out of her way to see that Sonny's family and friends knew how the cocktail hour functioned. Sonny finished with the pictures so he came out and helped Carmela. Rebecca, Evelyn, Jackee and their husbands came out to talk to the guests and help out if needed. Rose stayed back in the room provided for the bridal party. There would only be a few minutes before the guests were asked to find their seats in the dining room. The bridal party and the two sets of parents were being assembled just outside the dining room. The parents were introduced first and then the bridal party. Sonny and Rose were the last to be formally introduced and they danced to a song that was first heard in the movie of the same name. "You changed my life", It was an emotional ballad that had won the academy award for best song of the year. While the newly married couple were dancing, they were joined by the bridal party, the parents and then all the guests. When the dance ended everyone sat down.

Dan as the best man gave the traditional toast. He asked God to bless their marriage with children, love and happiness but most important that He always keeps them in the palm of His hands. He then added "let all of us drink to that and hope that God also includes everyone here." Jackee held Dan's hand and thanked him for the beautiful thought. Rose kissed Dan and told her sisters how lucky they were to have found such great husbands. Rose followed Jackee's example and after cutting the cake, gave half her bouquet to Carmela and to Sonny's step mother. A small arrangement of flowers were ordered and when Sonny's dad goes home he will get them fresh and he will put them on Sonny's mother's grave. The bouquet will have both Sonny and Rose's name on it. Rose never saw Sonny cry but when she told him what she was doing he hugged and thanked her and even though he turned away, she detected a tear rolling down his cheek. Her dance with dad and Sonny's dance with his step mother ended their night. A few moments later they were going to the bridal room to change. Jackee helped Rose change and packed the wedding gown so that Miss Grant could have it cleaned and pack it away.

They said goodbyes to the families and Rocco drove them to the hotel. A special representative of the hotel showed them to their suite. Once inside they saw that the family had prepared a special snack for them. Once they were alone Sonny kissed her and told her how much he loved her.

She kissed him back and said "in a few minutes you can prove how much you love me, all I have to do is change." Rose only had her sisters and mother at her bridal shower and that is what she wanted. Carmela took Jackee with her when she picked out the negligee for the wedding night.

Jackee jokingly said "if that doesn't cause an uprising in Sonny nothing will." Rose came out of the bedroom and stood in front of Sonny.

All he said was, he could not believe how beautiful she was and he picked her up and put her down on the bed. Much later he said, "I wish my mother could have seen you tonight."

Rose held him in her arms and said she did. Next morning they had breakfast with his family and guests including the holyman. Sonny wanted to know if anyone needed anything and if they enjoyed themselves. His father said he talked to all the guests and all of them said they had the time of their lives. "None had been to this type of affair and it is going to be hard to go back after seeing all this. You know it will be especially hard on the young people because they have so very little at home."

"Soon, Rose and I will be in a position to help make their lives better."

Jackee laid out her program that she hoped will get her ready for Spring training in Arizona. Bats had helped put it together and it was meant to make her lean and mean. Fighting for a spot on a major league team was a difficult thing to do. You travel first class, have everything handed to you, make money from base-ball cards to endorsing something and being idolized by an adoring public. The failure of not making it is long bus rides, poor sleeping quarters, handling your own luggage and equipment and probably having to find a job when the season is over. A major league baseball team consists of many different components. You may have different races, creeds, color, religions etc, except there is one thing that has always been the same, they are all men. Now Jackee was about to change that for good. Accepting change is not always easy, and sometimes there is a backlash against it. She has had good success in the Gamblers organization but she was not sure if the rest of the league is ready for change. Her father told her stories about Jackie Robinson's problems. He finally was accepted by his teammates because he could really play the game. He was a three hundred hitter with some power and a good fielder. This puts people in the ballpark and money in their pockets. Many teams around the league didn't care about that and resented his being on the field with them. Another challenge he had to face was that other team fans and communities resented him playing. This would not be her problem because the many women who came out to see her play were cheering for her. They often drowned out any boo's that were heard in the ballpark. One other major thing is that in 1947 there were only 8 teams in each league and they were all east of the Mississippi. Today you have world coverage of almost every event. William and Bats had stressed exactly what she had to do, stay within yourself and play your game. These are the words she would succeed or fail with. She was more than capable of preparing her body and mind for the new challenge ahead.

Most of January flew by and the week before she had to report to Spring training she kissed Dan goodbye and headed for Coach Zimmer and Olympus college. Andrea still lives on campus in a house Dr Hopkins provided for her so Jackee moved in with her for the week. She worked 10 hours a day on baseball workouts. Most of the time was spent hitting and with coach Zimmer. One day before she was to report, Bats came to pick her up and have a final skull session with her and Coach Zimmer. Basically they went over drills and situations and they tried to have her prepared for any possibilities. It was unrealistic to think every situation she would face could be discussed, but they gave her enough good advice to handle most anything.

CHAPTER THIRTY ONE

Jackee Reports to Spring Training

$\mathscr{B}$ats and Jackee arrived in camp one day early. Pitchers and catchers were to be at camp by Sunday. There were physicals and some small details to take care of before the first organized practice. The coaches and staff had a catered meal on Saturday evening. They basically went over the Sunday activities and the first practice on Monday. All the invitees were there except two holdouts who did not yet agree on a contract. Only one player failed his physical and that was because of high blood pressure. He will be under Doctor's care for the next week. Twenty pitchers and four catchers attended the meeting. Bats and Ferris were introduced as the new coaches. Ferris would be in charge of the pitchers and he would be supported by a bullpen coach by the name of Bobby Joe Carson. Mark Wright is the new head manager and Herb Higgins is his bench coach. Bill Rirby will be the infield and outfield coach assisted by Bats. Coach Wright started the meeting by telling them on the 25 man roster, he will carry 11 pitchers at the beginning of the season and 2 catchers. "That leaves us with 7 starters and only 5 backup players. As the season goes into better weather we probably will replace one of the backups with a pitcher. What you did last year has no weight for you being guaranteed a spot on the team. I will guarantee you one thing, you will be the best conditioned pitchers in the league. If it ever happens that you get out of shape during the season, you will be sent down in a heartbeat. I hate to see a pitcher give up a walk. That is a free runner for the other team and we never had a chance to get him out. Throw strikes, and give our fielders a chance to be a hero. The two catchers we select must be able to take control of the game. Keep the pitchers in the game. Don't let them get lazy. If you think their head is not in the game, go out to the mound and give him a swift kick in the you know what. No team should steal on us if our heads are in the game. You will be on the field starting tomorrow at 8am. You will have a lunch break from 12 to 2. From 2 to 6 or so will be the afternoon session. You will have this Sunday and the following Sunday off. Position players are to report that second Sunday. There will be 30 invitees vying for the 12 open spots on the roster. Any questions?" There were none, so he sent them home with this warning, "I advise you to get as much rest as possible because starting tomorrow your vacation is over."

Bats and Jackee were there at 7am. She used the gym for some warmups then went out to the field and ran about 2 miles. Pitchers started coming in at 7:30 but only 6 were on the field at 8am. Coach Wright was beside himself. He called all the players together and shouted at them that an 8am practice starts at 8am. That does not mean walking in the locker room door at 8am. If you are walking on the field at 8am you are 5 minutes late. "This team will be starting practice at 8am or you will be running until you step on your tongue." A conditioning instructor gave them 30 minutes of stretching and exercise. The next 20 minutes was strictly working on the pitching arm. He gave them exercises to do every day of the season and reminded them that "your arms are not game ready so your first 3 throwing sessions should be at half to three quarter speed. If you work on a new pitch, you must let us know so we can watch your motion. All of you will be filmed at various times to see if you are tipping your pitches. There will be a one mile run at the end of practice. This will be increased every day until you reach three miles. No one is excused from this run so mentally prepare yourselves for it." Now the coaches took over and they were divided in groups and each group was doing a different drill. One group was throwing to a stingy 15 inch plate, another group was doing pickoffs, another group was practicing fielding, the last group was doing backing up plays and run downs. This went on until lunch time. At 2pm sharp it started all over again and finally at 6pm they did the mile run and it had to be done in 6 minutes.

The following Sunday the rest of the invitees came in for physicals. Some had reported early and were already working out with the pitchers. Jackee knew some of the players because everyone who played for the Rollers and was invited to camp came in early. Buddy, Sid, Teddy, Andy, and Troy joined her for daily workouts. They were used to hard training camps so most of them had come prepared. All of them ran the mile in less than six minutes. They made a game out of it, with the winner drinking free that night. Jackee and Buddy each won three races with each one coming in second in the others. None of the pitchers or catchers came close to them in the run except Teddy. He had good speed and from what Jackee has seen of the other catchers had a good chance to be a starter for the Gamblers. The new manager wanted him to come in with the pitchers but he was overruled by the general manager. Buddy approached Jackee the second day he was here and asked her to work together as a double play combination. When they worked an infield practice many of the ball players watched them and forgot what they were there for. Coach Wright loved his combination because he saw them developing last year. He was sure that the combination from last year's

Gamblers season would find it hard to even make backup status this year. Bats and Coach Rirby worked with them and their improvement could be seen almost every day. Jackee was very happy with the team in general. Acceptance by the home fans she felt would not be a problem if she played her game. Acceptance around the league would be a whole new ballgame. Fans were still debating the role of the DH in baseball. Her fan mail has come from all over the country and in some cases the world. Included in the mail have been threats and some vile comments. Poor Rona has to read and assess each letter for possible follow up. Location was important so that if the team is playing near that postmark, Rona could prepare for some possibility. Some mail was very funny and the offers were unbelievable. Jackee has had over 500 offers for marriage and some sexual things. One request she will fill this afternoon is a young girl from the local hospital asked to see her.

Coach Wright gave her permission although she didn't need it since she was not officially due in camp until Sunday. Rona and Jackee arrived at the hospital between lunch and dinner, that is when the girl was not in any type of treatment. They checked in at the desk and were directed to the children's ward. They were greeted by a nurse and a woman who was crying. The woman grabbed Jackee's hand, kissed it and thanked her for coming. Her daughter wanted to see Jackee play but that is not possible now. They walked to a room and Jackee saw a teenage girl in a bed with tubes coming out all over. Her mother called out, "Roseann look who's here". The girl struggled to look and saw Jackee coming toward her. With all the strength she could muster, the girl turned and partially sat up in bed.

Jackee walked to the bed and smiled at the girl and said, "in your letter you wrote that you wanted to have a catch with me. I brought my glove and ball but I didn't realize what you meant was when you got better. Roseann, you know my sister's name is Rose and her middle name is Ann, so we do have something in common. Here, I want you to hold onto this ball, and when you are up to it, we will have a catch on the field before the game. You and your family will be my guests for the game. I will go one step further, you will sit in the Gamblers special box for special guests. Now how does that sound to you?"

Roseann smiled at her and said, "I want to be just like you and make people proud of me."

"I am proud of you right now and I don't want you to be like me, I want you to be better. I have a special baseball that is signed by me, it is the only one in the whole world signed this way and I want you to have it. Also, here is a signed baseball card with the proof that the baseball is authentic. Mom, see that no one takes these from her." Jackee said this as she was hugging Roseann's mother. The nurse moved the people toward the door as she was saying, Roseann has to rest now, she had enough excitement for one day. Rona asked the nurse what are Roseann's chances, the nurse just shook her head.

Once in the hall, the mother thanked Jackee and told her that "this was the first happy day Roseann has had in 6 months. God bless you, thank you for coming and we know you will be a big success."

Walking down the hall, Jackee turned to Rona and with tears in her eyes told her "someday I will be a doctor and help girls like that to live."

Rona took her by the shoulders and said "you just did."

Next day at the field, some of the reporters who followed the team got wind of Jackee's visit to the hospital. This would be a great human interest story. Most of the articles in Spring training are boring, because not much is really happening. This would be a big extra added to the first woman player. Jackee told the reporters, "if one word is printed about my visit to the hospital, the next interview with me that the reporter will get, will be right after the first person walks on the sun. You want to write a human interest story about a patient in the hospital, be my guest but leave me out of it."

"You can't dictate to us," one reporter said, "and by league rules you must talk to us."

Jackee just nodded and said, "you all heard what I said." She walked away and got ready for practice. Sunday was an off day from practice as the new arrivals had to get physicals and prepare for tomorrow's opening practice. Jackee and Rona spent the day going over the schedule and some fan mail. She wondered how Roseann was doing and Rona said she was holding her own. Jackee has been given updates from the hospital but Rona had direct communication with the mother. Rona had been asked by Jackee to tell the mother what happened with the reporters and why she hadn't been back. She didn't know that Rona stayed in contact with the mother. The first week of practice, stories went out about Jackee being at practice. Now the world knew that there was a female at the Spring training camp of the Gamblers. When Rona and Jackee went to dinner Sunday night she was hounded by autograph seekers. There will be no sit down dinners for the rest of Spring training, only take out.

The first full practice started with the first talk that coach Wright had given to the pitchers and catchers. As usual there were moans and groans. This was the best training camp Jackee had ever seen. Players were hitting and fielding or doing something all the time. A few were chasing batted balls but everyone else had a purpose. Morning practice flew by and the lunch break was a welcome time off but the afternoon workout was a rude awakening for the new arrivals, especially the one mile run. The coaches were amazed at how many of the people who were trying to make a major league team could come into camp out of shape. They had to be prepared to play baseball for 6 plus months. That meant most every day there would be a game or practice. Maybe during that stretch 10 days off would be a fair estimate. Buddy and Jackee ran with the pitchers and catchers and they finished first in the run. Next day almost all the players who started on Monday were dragging but there was no let up and the words, "you can pack your bags and leave whenever you want" rang in their ears. There were no takers, only more grumbling. Wednesday live pitching was on the schedule. Pitchers were to throw strikes and not try to strike out every batter. Some pitchers were trying to impress but most followed the rules. This practice ran for 10 days and led up to the first scrimmage. Conditioning and practices still were part of the day but full scrimmages were inserted to image game situations. The coaches used the scrimmages to enforce game situation teaching. Jackee and Buddy were now the team leaders by default. Team leaders from the year before had failed to take charge and in fact were worried about even making the cuts.

10 days passed and from those players still alive and kicking a team of 25 players were selected by the coaches. Only two players selected were over 28 years of age. The Gamblers had assembled a team last year that the fans could recognize and it proved to do just what they wanted. Now the coaches were told to assemble a team to be winners in the future. They assembled a team that would have no serious contractual problems for at least 5 years. Baring injuries, this team could be competitive within two years and have championship talent in three.

Coach Wright talking to the team told them right out that they were going to make him coach of the year within two years and everyone on this team would have world series money in their pockets in year three. Not all baseball players are college graduates but all of them understand money in the pocket. Jackee was getting ready for her first game as a major leaguer. Even though it was an exhibition, it was against a major league team. Buddy and Jackee were scheduled to play 6 innings, in the bottom of the fifth Rona brought word that Roseann had joined her heavenly Father an hour ago. Jackee asked Bats to let her finish the game, Bats talked to the head coach and got a positive answer. Jackee had tears in her eyes the rest of the game but Buddy, who also asked to stay in, kept making sure she was ready. In the bottom of the ninth with the score tied and runners on first and second Jackee came to bat and whispered to Roseann, "watch this." A new pitcher was brought in to pitch and Jackee set herself for a fastball down the middle. What pitch came to the plate was a fastball down the middle and Jackee got all of it. Before she reached first the ball had cleared the centerfield fence. While circling the bases she whispered to Roseann, "that one was for you. Please help me the rest of the season like you did now." She came into the dugout and never heard the crowd cheering for her. She never heard the call for a curtain call nor did she even remember shaking the other players hands. She went into her changing room where Rona was waiting. They hugged and Rona held her while she cried and sobbed. The sobbing stopped and Rona brought her something to drink.

Rona told her that the last coherent words that Roseann spoke to her mother was "I hope Jackee does well today".

Jackee told Rona that Roseann was with her going around the bases "and said to me, I knew you could do it. Then I asked her to help me the rest of the season. I can imagine how strange this sounds to you but it is my belief."

Rona said to her, that her people actually talked to God and his Prophets and "I never doubted for a moment that you spoke to Roseann today."

"Let's keep that a secret between us and not let anyone but her mother know. I have to change now and apologize to my teammates." She went into the locker room after changing and checking to make sure everyone was comfortable with her coming in. Immediately after the game Bats told all the other players about the little girl that had just passed away. And how it affected Jackee. So when she came in they mobbed her for the game winning homer and she never had a chance to tell them how sorry she was for not being with them at the end. The reporters however had other ideas and they played the story from every angle. Jackee never reads the paper during the season because it offers no help to her. Whether the story is negative or positive, it has no bearing on her game. Baseball as a game has more negatives than positives. A 30% hitting average, a 60% pitching and team won loss records are considered a success. Most players and teams don't reach that level. Rona, on the other hand, reads all the papers because she must keep in touch with the fast changing world. The funeral for Roseann will be Saturday and they will both be there, because Jackee received permission to attend. There were many more people because of the publicity that was generated by the reporters. Also there was a rumor that the female wonder woman would be there. Jackee attended the church service and followed the cars to the cemetery. She had talked to the mother and told her what happened. The mother told Jackee, that was all Roseann talked about. "She wanted so bad to see you be successful."

Jackee said now she can be with me every step of the way. "I need her faith and the faith of many others to achieve success."

Roseann's mother thanked her for all she did for Roseann while she was alive.

Jackee said, "that's nothing compared to what she will do for me now and in the future." Rona and Jackee went back to the car and headed for the field.

Spring training was coming to an end and it looked like Buddy and Jackee were the starting double play combination and Teddy was the starting catcher. Jackee wore number seven on her uniform and she told her father that it was for him. The family had come to a couple of exhibition games and Rona had a room to go to when Dan visited. William and Dan had the family business going to the point of either stop taking new clients or adding more staff. Jackee had enough offers to last her the next 10 years. Spring training ends next week and the season opener is on Tuesday. Final cuts had to be made before the team breaks camp.

However, cut players would probably go to the Rollers, be offered a trade or be granted their release so they could hookup with another team. All the Rollers who came to camp made the team and most will be starters. Jackee asked Bats what his impressions were and he said he thought that this team could even make the playoffs. Their pitching was good but not great. They did have some depth but the fourth and fifth starters were weak; only one reliever was top of the line. There was a rumor that a trade was very close to being completed and it was for pitching. But in baseball there are rumors all the time usually created by the sportswriters covering the team. The day of the last exhibition game a trade was announced. The gamblers traded Nate Wilson, Roy Ripple and Martin Olsen for two pitchers. One was Jason Nesbit, a top of the line pitcher and Harrison Hastings, a number one pick in the draft two years ago. He is a pitcher who has control problems. Coach Ferris thinks that Hastings had the best pitching qualities of any young pitcher he has seen. "Control is the key to his future success. When he loses control he loses confidence in himself. In his one complete game, he walked only one batter and struck out 13. He also allowed only 2 hits. That proves he has the stuff to be a number one starter. These added pitchers have made the team a better baseball team right now. They will arrive on Monday which is the last day before the season starts on Tuesday."

Nesbit and Hastings did arrive on Monday, just in time to participate in the last team workout before the season opener. Nesbit was penciled in as the number two pitcher. Hastings was being set up to be the number 5 starting pitcher. This would give coach Ferris time to evaluate him since he didn't have the opportunity in Spring training. They seemed to fit right in and before practice was over you could not tell that they had not been here all Spring. Jackee and Buddy introduced themselves and told them how glad they were to have them join the Gamblers. They in turn said how glad they were to be part of this new franchise. Spirits on the team seemed very high and everyone was anxious to get started. Carmela and the family were waiting for Jackee and Rona as they left the clubhouse. Luckily her brother was off from school so most of the family was in attendance. Rose and Sonny came and had Evelyn and the baby with them. Jon could not make it but Rebecca and Rocco did. The organization set up accommodations at the local hotel and the family would see the game from the private booth of the Gamblers. Roseann's family would be guests of the Gamblers and they too would watch the game from the private booth. Reservations were made for all the Gamblers guests at the hotel. Breakfast, lunch and dinner were available and all the guests had to do was sign the check. One drink was allowed with dinner only. Food at the hotel had a five star rating and according to the guests they earned every star. Jackee was thrilled that her family was there but feeling Dan's arms around her made it all perfect. Bats and coach Ferris join the family at dinner. Neither one of them had any family who could be there. As it turns out, both of their wives were pregnant and had other children at home to care for. Coach Ferris asked Jackee if she was nervous about playing her first major league game.

Jackee told him she had been preparing for this game all her life and being nervous about it has long passed. "I'll know when I am introduced if the crowd is with me or not. I suspect that there will be at least 20,000 females helping me during the game. I know many people think this is nothing more than a publicity stunt, but those women came to see me play and I don't intend to disappoint them."

"Bats and I never gave you a failing thought. We were just wondering if you had any doubts, but from what you said I feel sorry for the opposing pitcher tomorrow." Everyone laughed but when all is said and done the only thing that counts is what is done on the field. People started to leave after the meal and Jackee said she had to get some rest, then she took Dan's hand and said good night. When they were getting ready for bed at Jackee's apartment she told Dan that she needed to sleep in his arms all night so she could be ready for tomorrow. He readily agreed and was more than happy to accommodate her.

Tuesday was a perfect day for baseball. It would be 60 degrees by game time and the air was clean and refreshing. Jackee arrived at the stadium at 10am. She had breakfast with Dan and then started preparing for the game. He dropped her off and wished her good luck and sealed it with a kiss. Jackee put on her sweats and worked out for a while. Then she hit in the batting cage for 15 minutes. After hitting she went back to her changing room and put on her new uniform and old but newly cleaned baseball shoes. Coming out she refused all offers of an interview and found her way to the field. Previously, she had asked the manager to make sure she was introduced in her place in the lineup and not at some special moment. Coach Wright agreed and made sure that her wish was followed. Jackee ran about 1 mile and then did her stretching. Buddy came by and she started playing catch. They took some ground balls and then batted. It was now the opposing team's turn to use the field. Once the field was free the ground crew came out to fix it for the game.

Sammy Tuffs the PA announcer introduced the visiting team and all the players and coaches. Next he raised his voice and introduced the home team and their coaches. The starting line up was introduced first and Jackee was the third home team player mentioned. With the stands filled to capacity the roar of the crowd was deafening. Bats looked at Ferris and said she was right again. Stepping out of line and tipping her hat Jackee acknowledged the cheering. When introductions were complete, the Anthem was sung and the home plate umpire shouted play ball. The home team ran out to take their positions and after the warmups a batter stepped up to the plate. Pitching dominated the game and the score was tied at 1 in the eighth inning. Visiting team had runners on first and third with two outs when the batter broke his bat and hit a short pop fly to right center field. Jackee with her back to home plate raced to where she thought the ball would drop. She peeked over her shoulder and saw the ball coming down in front of her and she.dove head first and fully extended, caught the ball in the webbing of her glove. She hit the ground and immediately rolled over holding the ball up in her glove hand. The second base umpire signaled out and the half inning was over. Buddy raced to her side and helped her up. The cheering was getting louder but Jackee never heard a thing. All she could think of was the pain in her chest. As they walked toward the dugout she began to control her breathing. She was not due to bat so there was time for her to shake off the pain. Bats came over and asked if she wanted to come out of the game. Jackee just looked at him and he knew that was not going to happen. She played the top of the ninth inning and did field a ground ball. The bottom of the ninth found Jackee batting with runners on first and second and two outs. Jackee needed a pitch she could handle without too much upper body use. She decided to concentrate on hitting the ball up the middle. All she needed was a single to win the game. She saw a hanging curve and lined a ball that was headed to right center. The second baseman sees the ball leave the bat and jumps for it as it is passing over his head.